LORD O

Guy Gavriel Kay is the award-winning author of seven previous novels. *The Summer Tree*, *The Wandering Fire* and *The Darkest Road* (which comprise *The Fionavar Tapestry*) were followed by *Tigana*, *A Song for Arbonne* and *The Lions of Al-Rassan*, all of which were national bestsellers. *Sailing to Sarantium*, the first volume of *The Sarantine Mosaic*, was published to international critical acclaim and was a national bestseller. Guy Gavriel Kay's work has been translated into fifteen languages. He lives in Toronto.

LORD OF EMPERORS

BOOK II OF THE
SARANTINE MOSAIC

GUY GAVRIEL KAY

PENGUIN BOOKS

PENGUIN BOOKS

Published by the Penguin Group

Penguin Books Canada Ltd, 10 Alcorn Avenue, Toronto, Ontario, Canada M4V 3B2

Penguin Books Ltd, 27 Wrights Lane, London W8 5TZ, England

Penguin Putnam Inc., 375 Hudson Street, New York, New York 10014, U.S.A.

Penguin Books Australia Ltd, Ringwood, Victoria, Australia

Penguin Books (NZ) Ltd, cnr Rosedale and Airborne Roads, Albany,
Auckland 1310, New Zealand

Penguin Books Ltd, Registered Offices: Harmondsworth, Middlesex, England

First published in Viking by Penguin Books Canada Limited, 2000
Published in Penguin Books, 2001

1 3 5 7 9 10 8 6 4 2

Copyright © Guy Gavriel Kay, 2000

Cover design and illustration by Cathy MacLean

Manufactured in Canada

CANADIAN CATALOGUING IN PUBLICATION DATA

Kay, Guy Gavriel
The Sarantine mosaic
Contents: bk. 2. Lord of Emperors

ISBN 0-14-027563-0

1. Ayasofya Muzesi – Fiction. 2. Byzantine Empire – History – Justinian I, 527-565
– Fiction. I. Title. II. Title: Sailing to Sarantium. III. Title: Lord of Emperors

PS8571.A935S3 1999   C813'.54   C98-930800-6
PR9199.3.K39S3 1999

Visit Penguin Canada's website at **www.penguin.ca**

For Sam and Matthew,
'the singing-masters of my soul.'

This belongs to them, beginning and end.

ACKNOWLEDGEMENTS

The Sarantine Mosaic is animated by and in part built around a tension in the late classical world between walls and wilderness. For my own introduction to this dialectic (and how it shifts), I am indebted to Simon Schama's magisterial *Landscape and Memory*. This is also the work that introduced me to the Lithuanian bison and the symbolism surrounding it, giving rise to my own *zubir*.

The general and particular works cited in *Sailing to Sarantium* have anchored this second volume as well, and Yeats remains a presiding spirit, in the epigraph and elsewhere.

I should now add Guido Majno's quite wonderful *The Helping Hand: Man and Wound in the Ancient World*. On Persia and its culture, books by Richard N. Frye and Prudence Oliver Harper were immensely useful. For table matters and manners I was aided by the Wilkins and Hill text and commentary on Archistratus, along with works by Andrew Dalby and Maguelonne Toussaint-Samat. Attitudes to the supernatural are explored in books by Gager, Kieckhefer, and Flint, and in a collection of essays edited by Henry Maguire for the Dumbarton Oaks research facility in

Washington, D.C. Dumbarton Oaks also provided translations of Byzantine military treatises, papers presented at various symposia, and some evocative artifacts in their permanent collection.

On a more personal level, I have been greatly the beneficiary of the skills, friendship, and commitment of John Jarrold, John Douglas, and Scott Sellers, and I am indebted to the careful and sympathetic eye of my copy editor for both volumes of this work, Catherine Marjoribanks. Jennifer Barclay at Westwood Creative Artists has brought intelligence and a necessary sense of irony to increasingly complex foreign language negotiations. Rex Kay, as always, offered early and lucid commentary, especially (but not only) on medical issues.

I also want to record here my appreciation for the encouragement and sustained interest offered by Leonard and Alice Cohen for fifteen years now. Andy Patton has been a source of ideas and support for even longer, and in this case I am particularly indebted to him for discussions about Ravenna and light, and the various doorways (and traps) that must be negotiated when a novelist deals with the visual arts.

There are two others who continue to be at the centre of my world, and so of my work. The usual suspects, one might say, but that flippancy would mask the depth of what I hope to convey. Accordingly, I'll simply conclude here by naming Sybil and Laura, my mother and my wife.

Turning and turning in a widening gyre . . .

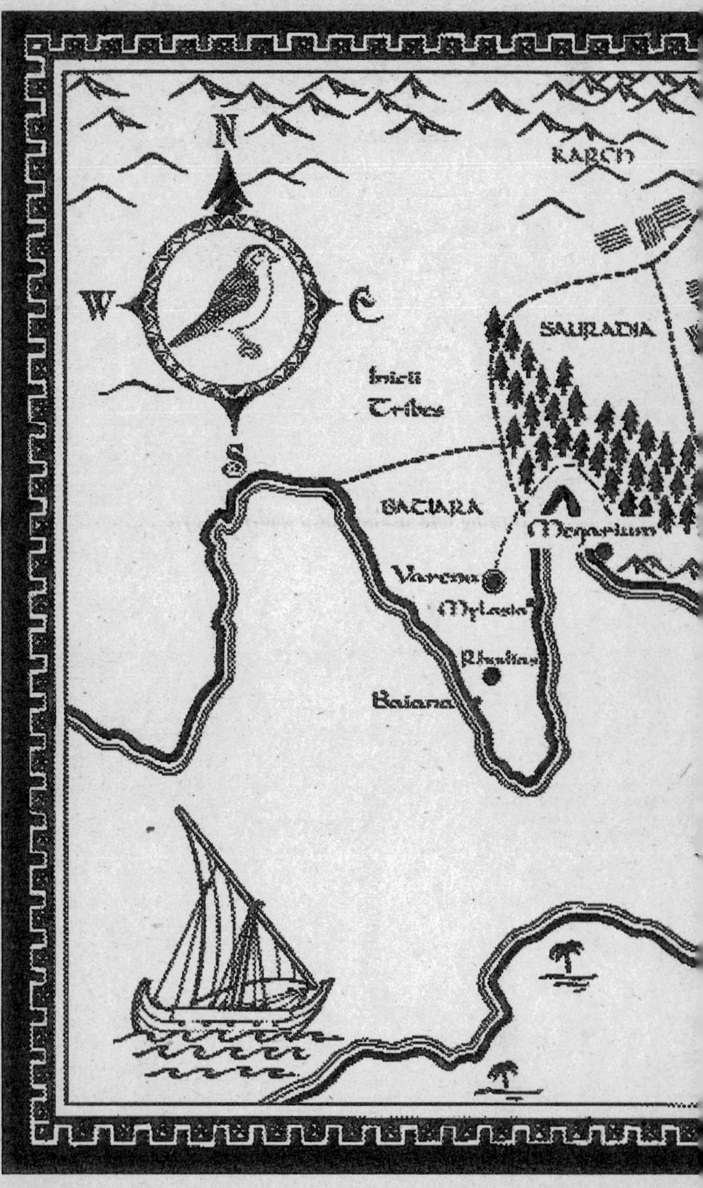
N
W
E
S
KARCH
SAURADIA
Inici
Tribes
BATIARA
Megarium
Varena
Mylasia
Rhodias
Baiana

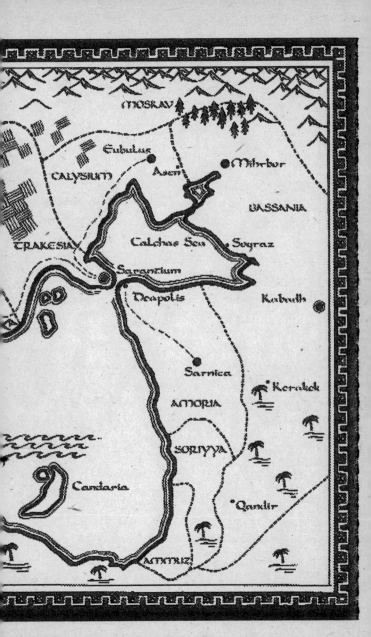

PART I

KINGDOMS OF LIGHT AND DARK

CHAPTER I

Amid the first hard winds of winter, the King of Kings of Bassania, Shirvan the Great, Brother to the Sun and Moons, Sword of Perun, Scourge of Black Azal, left his walled city of Kabadh and journeyed south and west with much of his court to examine the state of his fortifications in that part of the lands he ruled, to sacrifice at the ancient Holy Fire of the priestly caste, and to hunt lions in the desert. On the first morning of the first hunt he was shot just below the collarbone.

The arrow lodged deep and no man there among the sands dared try to pull it out. The King of Kings was taken by litter to the nearby fortress of Kerakek. It was feared that he would die.

Hunting accidents were common. The Bassanid court had its share of those enthusiastic and erratic with their bows. This truth made the possibility of undetected assassination high. Shirvan would not be the first king to have been murdered in the tumult of a royal hunt.

As a precaution, Mazendar, who was vizier to Shirvan,

ordered the king's three eldest sons, who had journeyed south with him, to be placed under observation. A useful phrase masking the truth: they were detained under guard in Kerakek. At the same time the vizier sent riders back to Kabadh to order the similar detention of their mothers in the palace. Great Shirvan had ruled Bassania for twenty-seven years that winter. His eagle's gaze was clear, his plaited beard still black, no hint of grey age descending upon him. Impatience among grown sons was to be expected, as were lethal intrigues among the royal wives.

Ordinary men might look to find joy among their children, sustenance and comfort in their households. The existence of the King of Kings was not as that of other mortals. His were the burdens of godhood and lordship— and Azal the Enemy was never far away and always at work.

In Kerakek, the three royal physicians who had made the journey south with the court were summoned to the room where men had laid the Great King down upon his bed. One by one each of them examined the wound and the arrow. They touched the skin around the wound, tried to wiggle the embedded shaft. They paled at what they found. The arrows used to hunt lions were the heaviest known. If the feathers were now to be broken off and the shaft pushed down through the chest and out, the internal damage would be prodigious, deadly. And the arrow could not be pulled back, so deeply had it penetrated, so broad was the iron flange of the arrowhead. Whoever tried to pull it would rip through the king's flesh, tearing the mortal life from him with his blood.

Had any other patient been shown to them in this state, the physicians would all have spoken the words of formal withdrawal: *With this affliction I will not contend.* No blame for ensuing death could attach to them when they did so.

It was not, of course, permitted to say this when the afflicted person was the king.

With the Brother to the Sun and Moons the physicians were compelled to accept the duty of treatment, to do battle with whatever they found and set about healing the injury or illness. If an accepted patient died, blame fell to the doctor's name, as was proper. In the case of an ordinary man or woman, fines were administered as compensation to the family.

Burning of the physicians alive on the Great King's funeral pyre could be anticipated in this case.

Those who were offered a medical position at the court, with the wealth and renown that came with it, knew this very well. Had the king died in the desert, his physicians—the three in this room and those who had remained in Kabadh—would have been numbered among the honoured mourners of the priestly caste at his rites before the Holy Fire. Now it was otherwise.

There ensued a whispered colloquy among the doctors by the window. They had all been taught by their own masters—long ago, in each case—the importance of an unruffled mien in the presence of the patient. This calm demeanour was, in the current circumstances, imperfectly observed. When one's own life lies embedded—like a bloodied arrow shaft—in the flux of the moment, gravity and poise become difficult to attain.

One by one, in order of seniority, the three of them approached the man on the bed a second time. One by one they abased themselves, rose, touched the black arrow again, the king's wrist, his forehead, looked into his eyes, which were open and enraged. One by one, tremulously, they said, as they had to say, 'With this affliction I will contend.'

When the third physician had spoken these words, and then stepped back, uncertainly, there was a silence in the room, though ten men were gathered amid the lamps and the guttering flame of the fire. Outside, the wind had begun to blow.

In that stillness the deep voice of Shirvan himself was heard, low but distinct, godlike. The King of Kings said, 'They can do nothing. It is in their faces. Their mouths are dry as sand with fear, their thoughts are as blown sand. They have no idea what to do. Take the three of them away from us and kill them. They are unworthy. Do this. Find our son Damnazes and have him staked out in the desert to be devoured by beasts. His mother is to be given to the palace slaves in Kabadh for their pleasure. Do this. Then go to our son Murash and have him brought here to us.' Shirvan paused to draw breath, to push away the humiliating weakness of pain. 'Bring also to us a priest with an ember of the Holy Flame. It seems we are to die in Kerakek. All that happens is by the divine will of Perun. Anahita waits for all of us. It has been written and it is being written. Do these things, Mazendar.'

'No physician at all, my great lord?' said the small, plump vizier, dry-voiced, dry-eyed.

'In Kerakek?' said the King of Kings, his voice bitter, enraged. 'In this desert? Think where we are.' There was blood welling as he spoke, from where the arrow lay in him, the shaft smeared black, fletched with black feathers. The king's beard was stained with his own dark blood.

The vizier bowed his head. Men moved to usher the three condemned physicians from the room. They offered no protest, no resistance. The sun was past its highest point by then, beginning to set, on a winter's day in Bassania in a remote fortress near the sands. Time was moving; what was to be had long ago been written.

Men find courage sometimes, unexpectedly, surprising themselves, changing the course of their own lives and times. The man who sank to his knees by the bed, pressing his head to the carpeted floor, was the military commander of the fortress of Kerakek. Wisdom, discretion, self-preservation all demanded he keep silent among the sleek, dangerous men of the court that day. Afterwards he could not have said why he did speak. He would tremble as with a fever, remembering, and drink an excess of wine, even on a day of abstinence.

'My king,' he said in the firelit chamber, 'we have a much-travelled physician here, in the village below the fortress. We might summon him?'

The Great King's gaze seemed already to be in another place, with Perun and the Lady, beyond the confines and small concerns of mortal life. He said, 'Why kill another man?'

It was told of Shirvan, written on parchment and engraved on tablets of stone, that no man more merciful and compassionate, more imbued with the spirit of the goddess Anahita, had ever sat the throne in Kabadh holding the sceptre and the flower. But Anahita the Lady was also called the Gatherer, who summoned men to their ending.

Softly, the vizier murmured, 'Why not do so? How can it matter, lord? May I send?'

The King of Kings lay still another moment, then he motioned assent, the gesture brief, indifferent. His rage seemed spent. His gaze, heavy-lidded, went to the fire and lingered there. Someone went out, at a sign from the vizier.

Time passed. In the desert beyond the fortress and the village below it a north wind rose. It swept across the sands, blowing and shifting them, erasing dunes, shaping others, and the lions, unhunted, took refuge in their caves among the rocks, waiting for night.

The blue moon, Anahita's, rose in the late afternoon, balancing the low sun. Within the fortress of Kerakek, men went forth into that dry wind to kill three physicians, to kill a son of the king, to summon a son of the king, to bear messages to Kabadh, to summon a priest with Holy Fire to the King of Kings in his room.

And to find and bring one other man.

Rustem of Kerakek, son of Zorah, sat cross-legged on the woven Ispahani mat he used for teaching. He was reading, occasionally glancing up to observe his four students as they carefully copied from one of his precious texts. Merovius on cataracts was the current matter; each student had a different page to transcribe. They would exchange them day by day until all of them had a copy of the treatise. Rustem was of the view that the ancient Trakesian's western approach was to be preferred in treatment of most—though not all—issues relating to the eye.

Through the window that overlooked the dusty roadway a breeze entered the room. It was mild as yet, not unpleasant, but Rustem could feel a storm in it. The sands would be blowing. In the village of Kerakek, below the fortress, the sand got into everything when the wind came from the desert. They were used to it, the taste in their food, the gritty feel in their clothing and bedsheets, in their own intimate places.

From behind the students, in the arched interior doorway that led to the family quarters, Rustem heard a slight rustling sound; he glimpsed a shadow on the floor. Shaski had arrived at his usual post beyond the beaded curtain, and would be waiting for the more interesting part of the afternoon lessons to begin. His son, at seven years of age, showed both patience and a fierce determination. A little less than a year ago he'd begun dragging a small mat of his own from his bedroom to a position just outside the teaching room. He would sit cross-legged upon it, spending as much of the afternoon as he was allowed listening through the curtain as his father gave instruction. If taken away by his mothers or the household servants he would find his way back to the corridor as soon as he could escape.

Rustem's two wives were both of the view that it was inappropriate for a small child to listen to explicit details of bloody wounds and bodily fluxes, but the physician found the boy's interest amusing and had negotiated with his wives to allow Shaski to linger outside the door if his own lessons and duties had been fulfilled. The students seemed to enjoy the boy's unseen presence in the hallway as well, and once or twice they'd invited him to voice an answer to his father's questions.

There was something endearing, even to a careful, reserved man, in a seven-year-old proclaiming, as was required, 'With this affliction I will contend,' and then detailing his proposed treatment of an inflamed, painful toe or a cough with blood and loose matter in it. The interesting thing, Rustem thought, idly stroking his neat, pointed beard, was that Shaski's answers were very often to the point. He'd even had the boy answer a question once to embarrass a student caught unprepared after a night's drinking, though later that evening he'd regretted doing so. Young men were entitled to visit taverns now and again. It taught them about the lives and pleasures of common men, kept them from aging too soon. A physician needed to be aware of the nature of people and their weaknesses and not be harsh in his judgement of ordinary folly. Judgement was for Perun and Anahita.

The feel of his own beard reminded him of a thought he'd had the night before: it was time to dye it again. He wondered if it was still necessary to be streaking the light brown with grey. When he'd returned from Ispahani and the Ajbar Islands four years ago, settling in his home town and opening a physician's practice and a school, he'd considered it prudent to gain a measure of credibility by making himself look older. In the east, the Ispahani physician-priests would lean on walking sticks they didn't need, gain weight deliberately, dole out words in measured cadences or with eyes focused on inward visions, all to present the desired image of dignity and success.

There had been some real presumption in a man of twenty-seven putting himself forward as a teacher of medicine at an age when many were just beginning their studies. Indeed, two of his pupils that first year had been older than he was. He wondered if they'd known it.

After a certain point, though, didn't your practice and your teaching speak for themselves? In Kerakek, here on the edge of the southern deserts, Rustem was respected and even revered by the villagers, and he had been summoned often to the fortress to deal with injuries and ailments among the soldiers, to the anger and chagrin of a succession of military doctors. Students who wrote to him and then came this far for his teaching—some of them even Sarantine Jad-worshippers, crossing the border from Amoria—were unlikely to turn around and go away when they discovered that Rustem of Kerakek was no ancient sage but a young husband and father who happened to have a gift for medicine and to have read and travelled more widely than most.

Perhaps. Students, or potential students, could be unpredictable in various ways, and the income Rustem made from teaching was necessary for a man with two wives now and two children—especially with both women wanting another baby in the crowded house. Few of the villagers of Kerakek were able to pay proper physician's fees, and there was another practitioner—for whom Rustem had an only marginally disguised contempt—in the town to divide what meagre income was to be gleaned here. On the whole, it might be best not to disturb what seemed to be succeeding. If streaks of grey in his beard reassured even one or two possible pupils or military officials up in the castle (where they did tend to pay), then using the dye was worth it, he supposed.

Rustem looked out the window again. The sky was darker now beyond his small herb garden. If a real storm came, the distraction and loss of light would undermine his lessons and make afternoon surgery difficult. He cleared his throat. The four students, used to the routine, put down their writing implements and looked up. Rustem nodded and the one nearest the outer door crossed to open it and admit the first patient from the covered portico where they had been waiting.

He tended to treat patients in the morning and teach after the midday rest, but those villagers least able to pay would often consent to be seen by Rustem and his students together in the afternoons as part of the teaching process. Many were flattered by the attention, some made uncomfortable, but it was known in Kerakek that this was a way of gaining access to the young physician who had studied in the mystical east and returned with secrets of the hidden world.

The woman who entered now, standing hesitantly by the wall where Rustem hung his herbs and shelved the small pots and linen bags of medicines, had a cataract growth in her right eye. Rustem knew it; he had seen her before and made the assessment. He prepared in advance, and whenever the ailments of the villagers allowed, offered his students practical experience and observations to go with the treatises they memorized and copied. It was of little use, he was fond of saying, to learn what al-Hizari said about amputation if you didn't know how to use a saw.

He himself had spent six weeks with his eastern teacher on a failed Ispahani campaign against the insurgents on their north-eastern reaches. He had learned how to use a saw.

He had also seen enough of violent death and desperate, squalid pain that summer to decide to return home to his wife and the small child he had scarcely seen before leaving for the east. This house and garden at the edge of the village, and then another wife and a girl-child, had followed upon his return. The small boy he'd left behind was now seven years old and sitting on a mat outside the door of the medical chambers, listening to his father's lectures.

And Rustem the physician still dreamt in the blackness of some nights of a battlefield in the east, remembering himself cutting through the limbs of screaming men beneath the smoky, uncertain light of torches in wind as the sun went down on a massacre. He remembered black fountains of blood, being drenched, saturated in the hot gout and spray of it, clothing, face, hair, arms, chest . . . becoming a creature of dripping horror himself, hands so slippery he could scarcely grip his implements to saw and cut and cauterize, the wounded coming and coming to them endlessly, without surcease, even when night fell.

There were worse things than a village practice in Bassania, he had decided the next morning, and he had not wavered since, though ambition would sometimes rise up within him and speak otherwise, seductive and dangerous as a Kabadh courtesan. Rustem had spent much of his adult life trying to appear older than he was. He wasn't old, though. Not yet. Had wondered, more than once, in the twilight hours when such thoughts tended to arrive, what he would do if opportunity and risk came knocking.

Looking back, afterwards, he couldn't remember if there *was* a knock that day. The whirlwind speed of what ensued had been very great, and he might have missed it. It seemed to him, however, that the outside door had simply banged open, without warning, nearly striking the patient waiting by the wall, as booted soldiers came striding in, filling the quiet room to bursting with the chaos of the world.

Rustem knew one of them, the leader: he had been stationed in Kerakek a long time. The man's face was distorted now, eyes dilated, fevered-looking. His voice, when he spoke, rasped like a woodcutter's saw. He said, 'You are to come! Immediately! To the fortress!'

'There has been an accident?' Rustem asked from his mat, keeping his own voice modulated, ignoring the peremptory tone of the man, trying to reestablish calm with his own tranquillity. This was part of a physician's training, and he wanted his students to see him doing it. Those coming to them were often agitated; a doctor could not be. He took note that the soldier had been facing east when he spoke his first words. A neutral omen. The man was of the warrior caste, of course, which would be either good or bad, depending on the caste of the afflicted person. The wind was north: not good, but no birds could be seen or heard through the window, which counterbalanced that, somewhat.

'An accident! Yes!' cried the soldier, no calm in him at all. 'Come! It is the King of Kings! An arrow!'

Poise deserted Rustem like conscripted soldiers facing Sarantine cavalry. One of his students gasped in shock. The woman with the afflicted eye collapsed to the floor in an untidy, wailing heap. Rustem stood up quickly, trying to order his racing thoughts. Four men had entered. An unlucky number. The woman made five. Could she be counted, to adjust the omens?

Even as he swiftly calculated auspices, he strode to the large table by the door and snatched his small linen bag. He hurriedly placed several of his herbs and pots inside and took his leather case of surgical implements. Normally he would have sent a student or a servant ahead with the bag, to reassure those in the fortress and to avoid being seen rushing out-of-doors himself, but this was not a circumstance that allowed for ordinary conduct. *It is the King of Kings!*

Rustem became aware that his heart was pounding. He struggled to control his breathing. He felt giddy, light-headed. Afraid, in fact. For many reasons. It was important not to show this. Claiming his walking stick, he slowed deliberately and put a hat on his head. He turned to the soldier. Carefully facing north, he said, 'I am ready. We can go.'

The four soldiers rushed through the doorway ahead of him. Pausing, Rustem made an effort to preserve some order in the room he was leaving. Bharai, his best student, was looking at him.

'You may practise with the surgical tools on vegetables, and then on pieces of wood, using the probes,' Rustem said. 'Take turns evaluating each other. Send the patients home. Close the shutters if the wind rises. You have permission to build up the fire and use oil for sufficient light.'

'Master,' said Bharai, bowing.

Rustem followed the soldiers out the door.

He paused in the garden and, facing north again, feet together, he plucked three shoots of bamboo. He might need them for probes. The soldiers were waiting impatiently in the roadway, agitated and terrified. The air pulsed with anxiety. Rustem straightened, murmured his prayer to Perun and the Lady and turned to follow them. As he did, he observed Katyun and Jarita at the front door of the house. There was fear in their eyes: Jarita's were enormous, even seen at a distance. She stared at him silently, leaning against Katyun for support, holding the baby. One of the soldiers must have told the women what was happening.

He gave them both a reassuring nod and saw Katyun nod calmly back as she put her arm around Jarita's shoulders. They would be all right. If he came back.

He went through the small gate into the road, taking his first step with his right foot, glancing up for any signs among the birds. None to be seen: they had all taken shelter from the rising wind. No omens there. He wished there hadn't been four soldiers sent. Someone ought to have known better. Little to be done about that now, however. He would burn incense at the fortress, in propitiation. Rustem gripped his stick and struggled to present an appearance of equanimity. He didn't think he was succeeding. The King of Kings. An arrow.

He stopped abruptly in the dusty road.

And in the moment he did so, cursing himself for a fool, preparing to go back to the treatment rooms, knowing how very bad an omen that would be, he heard someone speak from behind him.

'Papa,' said a small voice.

Rustem turned, and saw what his son was holding in both hands. His heart stopped for a moment then, or it felt as though it did. He swallowed, with sudden difficulty. Forced himself to take another deep breath, standing very still now just outside the gate.

'Yes, Shaski,' he said quietly. He looked at the small boy in the garden and a strange calm descended upon him. His students and the patients watched in a knotted cluster from the portico, the soldiers from the roadway, the women from the other doorway. The wind blew.

'The man said . . . he said an arrow, Papa.'

And Shaski extended his two small hands, offering his father the implement he'd carried out into the yard.

'He did say that, didn't he?' said Rustem, gravely. 'I should take that with me then, shouldn't I?'

Shaski nodded his head. His small form straight, dark brown eyes serious as a priest's with an offering. *He is seven years old*, Rustem thought. *Anahita guard him.*

He went back through the wooden gate, and he bent and took the slender instrument in its leather sheath from the boy. He had brought it back from Ispahani, a parting gift from his teacher there.

The soldier had indeed said there was an arrow. Rustem felt a sudden, quite unexpected desire to lay a hand upon the head of his son, on the dark brown, curling hair, to feel the warmth, and the smallness. It had to do, of course, with the fact that he might not come back from the fortress. This might be a farewell. One could not decline to treat the King of Kings, and depending on where the arrow had lodged . . .

Shaski's expression was so intense, it was as if he actually had some preternatural apprehension of this. He couldn't, of course, but the boy had just saved him from the terrible auspice of having to re-enter the treatment room after walking out and taking his bamboo reeds, or sending someone back in for him.

Rustem found that he was unable to speak. He looked down at Shaski for another moment, then glanced over at his wives. There was no time to say anything to them, either. The world had entered through his doorway, after all. What was to be had long ago been written.

Rustem turned and went quickly back out through the gate and then with the soldiers up the steep road in the north wind that was blowing. He didn't look back, knowing the omen attached to that, but he was certain that Shaski was still standing there and watching him, alone in the garden now, straight as a spear, small as a reed by a riverbank.

—✦—

Vinaszh, son of Vinaszh, the military commander of the southern fortress of Kerakek, had been born even farther to the south, in a tiny oasis of palms east of Qandir, a sparse, spring-fed island of greenery with desert all around. It was a market village, of course. Goods and services exchanged with the dark, grim peoples of the sands as they came riding in on their camels and went back out again, receding and then disappearing on the shimmering horizon.

Growing up as a merchant's son, Vinaszh came to know the nomadic tribes quite well, both in times of trade and peace and during those seasons when the Great King sent armies south in yet another fruitless attempt to force access to the western sea beyond the sands. The desert, at least as much as the wild tribesmen who shifted across its face, had made this impossible, again and again. Neither the sands nor those who dwelled there were inclined to be subdued.

But his childhood in the south had made Vinaszh—who had chosen the army over a merchant's life—an excellent, obvious choice to take control of one of the desert fortresses. It represented a rare measure of clear thinking on the part of officials in Kabadh that he was, in fact, appointed to govern Kerakek when he attained sufficient rank, rather than being given command of, say, soldiers guarding a fishing port in the north, dealing with fur-clad traders and raiders from Moskav. Sometimes the military succeeded in doing things properly, almost in spite of itself. Vinaszh knew the desert, was properly respectful of it and those who dwelled there. He could manage some of the dialects of the nomads, spoke a little of the Kindath tongue, and was unruffled by sand in his bed or clothing or folds of skin.

Still, there was nothing at all in the background of the man to suggest that the soldier son of Vinaszh the trader might have had the rashness to speak up among the mightiest figures of Bassania and offer the uninvited suggestion that a small-town physician—one not even of the priestly caste—be summoned to the King of Kings where he was dying.

Among other things, the words put the commander's own life at risk. He was a dead man if someone afterwards were to decide that the country doctor's treatment had hastened or caused the death of the king—even though Great Shirvan had already turned his face to the fire as if looking in the flames for Perun of the Thunder, or the dark figure of the Lady.

The arrow was in him, very deep. Blood continued to seep slowly from it, darkening the sheets of the bed and the linens that had been bunched around the wound. It seemed a wonder, in fact, that the king still breathed, still remained among them, fixedly watching the dance of the flames while a wind from the desert rose outside. The sky had darkened.

Shirvan seemed disinclined to offer his courtiers any last words of guidance or to formally name an heir, though he'd made a gesture that implied his choice. Kneeling beside the bed, the king's third son, Murash, who had covered his own head and shoulders with hot ashes from the hearth, was rocking back and forth, praying. None of the other royal sons was present. Murash's voice, rising and falling in rapid incantation, was the only human sound in the room other than the laboured rhythm of the Great King's breathing.

In that stillness, and even with the keening of the wind, the sound of booted feet was clearly heard when it finally came from the corridor. Vinaszh drew a breath and briefly closed his eyes, invoking Perun, ritually cursing Azal the Eternal Enemy. Then he turned and saw the door open to admit the physician who had cured him of an embarrassing rash he'd contracted during an autumn reconnaissance towards the Sarantine border towns and forts.

The doctor, trailed by Vinaszh's obviously terrified captain of the guard, entered a few steps and then paused, leaning on his staff, surveying the room, before looking over at the figure on the bed. He had no servant with him—he would have left in great haste, the captain's instructions from Vinaszh had been unambiguous—and so carried his own bag. Without looking back, he extended the linen bag and his walking stick and some sheathed implement, and Vinaszh's captain moved with alacrity to take them. The doctor—his name was Rustem—had a reserved, humourless manner that Vinaszh didn't really like, but the man had studied in Ispahani and he didn't seem to kill people and he *had* cured the rash.

The physician smoothed his greying beard with one hand and then knelt and abased himself, showing unexpectedly adroit manners. At a word from the vizier he rose. The king hadn't turned his gaze from the fire; the young prince had not ceased his praying. The doctor bowed to the vizier, then turned carefully—facing due west, Vinaszh noted—and said briskly, 'With this affliction I will contend.'

He hadn't even approached—let alone examined—the patient, but he had no real choice here. He had to do what he could. *Why kill another man?* the king had asked. Vinaszh had almost certainly done just that by suggesting the physician be brought here.

The doctor turned to look at Vinaszh. 'If the commander of the garrison will remain to assist me I would be grateful. I might have need of a soldier's experience. It is necessary for all the rest of you, my revered and gracious lords, to leave the room now, please.'

Without rising from his knees, the prince said fiercely, 'I will not leave my father's side.'

This man was almost certainly about to become the King of Kings, the Sword of Perun, when the breathing of the man on the bed stopped.

'An understandable desire, my lord prince,' said the doctor calmly. 'But if you care for your beloved father, as I can see you do, and wish to aid him now, you will honour me by waiting outside. Surgical treatment cannot take place in a crowd of men.'

'There will be no . . . crowd,' said the vizier. Mazendar's lip curled at the word. 'Prince Murash will remain, and I myself. You are not of the priestly caste, of course, and neither is the commander. We must stay here, accordingly. All others will depart, as requested.'

The physician simply shook his head. 'No, my lord. Kill me now, if you wish. But I was taught, and believe, that members of the family and dear friends must not be present when a doctor treats an afflicted man. One must be of the priestly caste to be a royal physician, I know. But I have no such position . . . I am merely attending upon the Great King, at request. If I am to contend with this affliction, I must do so in the manner of my training. Otherwise I can avail the King of Kings not at all, and my own life becomes a burden to me if that is so.'

The fellow was a stuffy prig, greying before his time, Vinaszh thought, but he had courage. He saw Prince Murash look up, black eyes blazing. Before the prince could speak, however, a faint, cold voice from the bed murmured, 'You heard the physician. He is brought here for his skills. Why is there wrangling in my presence? Get out. All of you.'

There was silence.

'Of course, my gracious lord,' said Mazendar the vizier, as the prince, mouth opening and closing, stood up uncertainly. The king had still not taken his eyes from the flames. His voice sounded to Vinaszh as if it already came from somewhere beyond the realms of living men. He would die, the doctor would die, Vinaszh, very probably, would die. He was a fool and a fool, near the end of his days.

Men began moving nervously out into the corridor, where torches had now been lit in the wall brackets. The wind whistled, an otherworldly, lonely sound. Vinaszh saw his captain of the guard set down the doctor's things before quickly walking out. The young prince stopped directly in front of the slim physician, who stood very still, waiting for them to leave. Murash lifted his hands and murmured, fierce and low, 'Save him, or these fingers end your life. I swear it by Perun's thunder.'

The physician said nothing, merely nodded, calmly eyeing the hands of the overwrought prince as they opened and closed and then twisted before his face in a sudden gesture of strangulation. Murash hesitated another moment, then looked back at his father—it might be for the last time, Vinaszh thought, and had a swift, sharp memory of his own father's deathbed in the south. Then the prince strode from the room as others made way for him. They heard his voice rising in prayer again, from the hallway.

Mazendar was last to leave. He paused near the bed, glanced at Vinaszh and the physician, looking uncertain for the first time, and then murmured, 'Have you instructions for me, dear my lord?'

'I gave them,' said the man on the bed quietly. 'You saw who was here. Serve him loyally if he allows. He might not.

The Lord of Thunder and the Lady guard your soul if that is so.'

The vizier swallowed. 'And yours, my great lord, if we meet not again.'

The king made no reply. Mazendar went out. Someone closed the door from out in the corridor.

Immediately, moving briskly, the physician opened his linen bag and extracted a small sachet. He strode to the fire and tossed the contents onto it.

The flames turned blue, and a scent of wildflowers suddenly filled the room like an eastern springtime. Vinaszh blinked. The figure on the bed stirred.

'Ispahani?' said the King of Kings.

The physician looked surprised. 'Yes, my gracious lord. I would not have imagined you—'

'I had a physician from the Ajbar Islands once. He was very skilled. Unfortunately he courted a woman he would have done better not to have touched. He used this scent, I recall.'

Rustem crossed to the bedside. 'It is taught that the nature of the treatment room can affect the nature of the treatment. We are influenced by such things, my lord.'

'Arrows are not,' said the king. But he had shifted a little to look at the physician, Vinaszh saw.

'Perhaps that is so,' said the doctor, noncommittally. He came to the bedside and, for the first time, bent to examine the shaft and the wound. Vinaszh saw him suddenly check his motion. A strange expression crossed the bearded features. He lowered his hands.

Then he looked over at Vinaszh. 'Commander, it is necessary for you to find gloves for me. The best leather ones in the fortress, as quickly as possible.'

Vinaszh asked no questions. He was likely to die if the king died. He went, closing the door behind him, and hurried along the corridor, past those waiting there, and down the stairwell to find his own riding gloves.

Rustem had been terrified when he entered, overwhelmed, summoning all his reserves of composure so as not to show it. He'd almost dropped his implements, feared someone would see his trembling hands, but the captain of the guard had moved quickly to take them. He'd used the formal movements of genuflection to speak a calming invocation in his mind.

After rising, he'd been more blunt than he ought to have been, asking the courtiers—and the vizier and a prince!—to leave the room. But he always used a manner of crisp efficiency to suggest authority beyond his years, and this was no time or place to deviate from his customary methods. If he was to die, it hardly mattered what they thought of him, did it? He asked the commander to stay. A soldier would be unfazed by bloodshed and screaming, and someone might have to hold the afflicted person down.

The afflicted person. The King of Kings. Sword of Perun. Brother to the Sun and Moons.

Rustem forced himself to stop thinking in that way. This was a patient. An injured man. That was what mattered. The courtiers left. The prince—Rustem didn't know which of the king's sons this was—paused in front of him and made vivid with twisting hands the threat of death that had been with Rustem from the moment he'd left his garden.

It could not be allowed to matter. All would be as had been written.

He'd cast the Ajbar powder into the fire to bring the room in tune with more harmonious presences and spirits, then crossed to the bed to examine the arrow and the wound.

And he had smelled *kaaba* there.

His mind reeling with shock, he'd realized that the smell had jogged a hovering awareness, and then a second one had emerged and left him very much afraid. He'd sent the commander hurrying for gloves. He needed them.

If he touched that arrow shaft he would die.

Alone in the room with the King of Kings, Rustem discovered that his fears were those of a physician and not a lowly subject now. He wondered how to say what was in his mind.

The king's eyes were on his face now, dark and cold. Rustem saw rage in them. 'There is a poison on the shaft,' Shirvan said.

Rustem bowed his head. 'Yes, my lord. *Kaaba*. From the *fijana* plant.' He took a breath and asked, 'Did your own physicians touch the arrow?'

The king nodded his head very slightly. No hint of anger diminishing. He would be in very great pain but wasn't showing it. 'All three of them. Amusing. I ordered them to be executed for their incompetence, but they would each have died soon, wouldn't they? None of them noted the poison.'

'It is rare here,' said Rustem, struggling to order his thoughts.

'Not so rare. I have been taking small amounts for twenty-five years,' said the king. '*Kaaba*, other evil substances. Anahita will summon us to herself when she wills, but men may still be prudent in their lives, and kings must be.'

Rustem swallowed. He now had the explanation for his patient's survival to this point. Twenty-five years? An image came into his mind: a young king touching—fearfully, surely—a trace amount of the deadly powder: the sickness that would have ensued . . . doing the same thing again later, and then again, and then beginning to taste it, in larger and larger amounts. He shook his head.

'The king has endured much for his people,' he said. He was thinking of the court physicians. *Kaaba* closed the throat before it reached the heart. One died in agony, of self-strangulation. He had seen it in the east. A method of formal execution. *Amusing,* the king had said.

He was thinking of something else now, as well. He pushed that away for the moment, as best he could.

'It makes no difference,' said the king. His voice was much as Rustem had imagined it might be: cold, uninflected, grave. 'This is a lion arrow. Protection from poison doesn't help if the arrow cannot come out.'

There was a tapping at the door. It opened and Vinaszh the garrison commander returned, breathing as if he'd been running, carrying dark brown leather riding gloves. They were too thick for easy use, Rustem saw, but he had no choice. He put them on. Unlaced the thong of the case that held a long thin metal implement. The one his son had brought out to the garden for him. *He said an arrow, Papa.*

'There are sometimes ways of removing even these,' Rustem said, trying not to think about Shaski. He turned to the west, closed his eyes and began to pray, mentally tabulating the afternoon's omens, good and bad, as he did so, and counting the days since the last lunar eclipse. When he had done the calculations he set out the indicated talismans and wardings. He proposed a sense-dulling herb for the pain of what was to come. The king refused it. Rustem called the garrison commander to the bedside and told him what he had to do to keep the patient steady. He didn't say 'the king' now. This was an afflicted man. Rustem was a doctor with an assistant and an arrow to remove, if he could. He was at war now, with Azal the Enemy, who could blot out the moons and sun and end a life.

In the event, the commander was not needed, nor was the herb. Rustem first broke off the blackened shaft as close to the entry wound as he could, then used a sequence of probes and a knife to widen the wound itself, a procedure he knew to be excruciatingly painful. Some men could not endure it, even dulled by medication. They would thrash and scream, or lose consciousness. Shirvan of Bassania never closed his eyes and never moved, though his breathing became shallow and rapid. There were beads of sweat on his brow and the muscles of his jaw were clenched beneath the plaited beard. When he judged the opening wide enough, Rustem oiled the long, slender, metal Spoon of Enyati and slid it in towards the embedded arrowhead.

It was difficult to be precise with the thick gloves, already blood-soaked, but he had a view of the alignment of the flange now and knew which way to angle the cupping part of Enyati's device. The shallow cup slid up to the flange through the flesh of the king—who had caught his breath now, but moved not at all where he lay. Rustem twisted a little and felt the spoon slip around the widest part of the head, pressing against it. He pushed a little further, not breathing himself in this most delicate moment of all, invoking the Lady in her guise as Healer, and then he twisted it again and pulled gently back a very little.

The king gasped then and half lifted one arm as if in protest, but Rustem felt the catch as the arrowhead was gathered and shielded in the cup. He had done it in one pass. He knew a man, a teacher in the far east, who would have been gravely, judiciously pleased. Now only the smooth, oiled sides of the spoon itself would be exposed to the wounded flesh, the barbed flange safely nestled within.

Rustem blinked. He went to brush the sweat from his forehead with the back of one bloody glove and remembered—barely in time—that he would die if he did so. His heart thudded.

'We are almost home, almost done,' he murmured. 'Are you ready, dear my lord?' The vizier had used that phrase. In this moment, watching the man on the bed deal silently with appalling pain, Rustem meant it too. Vinaszh, the commander, surprised him by coming forward a little at the head of the bed and leaning sideways to place his hand on the king's forehead above the wound and the blood: more a caress than a restraining hold.

'Who is ever ready for this?' grunted Shirvan the Great, and in the words Rustem caught—astonishingly—the ghost of a sardonic amusement. Hearing it, he set his feet to the west, spoke the Ispahani word engraved on the implement and, gripping with both gloved hands, pulled it straight back out from the mortal flesh of the King of Kings.

'I am to live, I take it?'

They were alone in the room. Time had run; it was full dark now outside. The wind was still blowing. On the king's instructions, Vinaszh had stepped out to report only that treatment was continuing and Shirvan yet lived. No more than that. The soldier had asked no questions, neither had Rustem.

The first danger was always excessive bleeding. He had packed the expanded wound opening with lint and a clean sponge. He left the wound unclosed. Closing wounds too soon was the most common error doctors made, and patients died of it. Later, if all went well, he would draw the wound together with his smallest skewers as sutures, taking care to leave space for drainage. But not yet. For now he bandaged the packed wound with clean linen going under the armpit and across the chest, then up and around both sides of the neck in the triangle pattern prescribed. He finished the bandage at the top and arranged the knot to point downwards, as was proper, towards the heart. He wanted fresh bedding and linen now, clean gloves for himself, hot water. He threw the commander's bloodied gloves on the fire. They could not be touched.

The king's voice, asking the question, was faint but clear. A good sign. He'd accepted a sedating herb this time from Rustem's bag. The dark eyes were calm and focused, not unduly dilated. Rustem was guardedly pleased. The second danger now, as always, was the green pus, though arrow wounds tended to heal better than those made by a sword. He would change the packing later, wash the wound, and change the salve and dressing before the end of the night: a variant of his own devising. Most physicians left the first bandage for two or three days.

'My king, I believe you are. The arrow is gone, and the wound will heal if Perun wills and I am careful with it to avoid the noxious exudations.' He hesitated. 'And you have your own . . . protection against the poison that was in it.'

'I wish to speak with you about that.'

Rustem swallowed hard. 'My lord?'

'You detected the *fijana's* poison by the smell of it? Even with your own scented herbs on the fire?'

Rustem had feared this question. He was a good dissembler—most physicians were—but this was his king, mortal kin to the sun and moons.

'I have encountered it before,' he said. 'I was trained in Ispahani, my lord, where the plant grows.'

'I know where it grows,' said the King of Kings. 'What else do you have to tell me, physician?'

Nowhere to hide, it seemed. Rustem took a deep breath.

'I also smelled it elsewhere in this room, great lord. Before I put the herbal scent to the fire.'

There was a silence.

'I thought that might be so.' Shirvan the Great looked coldly up at him. 'Where?' One word only, hard as a smith's hammer.

Rustem swallowed again. Tasted something bitter: the awareness of his own mortality. But what choice did he now have? He said, 'On the hands of the prince, great king. When he bade me save your life, at risk of my own.'

Shirvan of Bassania closed his eyes briefly. When he opened them, Rustem saw a black rage in their depths again, despite the drug he had been given. 'This . . . distresses me,' said the King of Kings very softly. What Rustem heard was not distress, however. It suddenly occurred to him to wonder if the king had also detected *kaaba* on the arrowhead and shaft. He had been ingesting it for twenty-five years. If he had known the poison, he had allowed three physicians to handle it today without warning them, and had been about to let Rustem do the same. A test of competence? When he was on the brink of dying? What sort of man . . . ? Rustem shivered, could not help himself.

'It seems,' said Great Shirvan, 'that someone besides myself has been protecting himself against poisons by building up a resistance. Clever. I have to say it was clever.' He was silent a long time, then: 'Murash. He would have made a good king, in fact.'

He turned away and looked out the window; there was nothing to see in the darkness. They could hear the sound of the wind, blowing from the desert. 'I appear,' the king said, 'to have ordered the death of the wrong son and his mother.' There was another, briefer silence. 'This distresses me,' he said for a second time.

'May these orders not be rescinded, great lord?' Rustem asked hesitantly.

'Of course not,' said the King of Kings.

The finality in the quiet voice was, Rustem would later decide, as frightening as anything else that day.

'Summon the vizier,' said Shirvan of Bassania, looking out upon night. 'And my son.'

Rustem the physician, son of Zorah, wished ardently in that moment to be home in his small house, shuttered against the wind and dark, with Katyun and Jarita, two small children peacefully asleep, a late cup of herbed wine at his elbow and a fire on the hearth, with the knocking of the world at his door something that had never taken place.

Instead, he bowed to the man lying on the bed and walked to the doorway of the room.

'Physician,' said the King of Kings.

Rustem turned back. He felt afraid, terribly out of his depth.

'I am still your patient. You continue to be accountable for my well-being. Act accordingly.' The tone was flat, the cold rage still there.

It did not take immense subtlety to understand what this might mean.

Only this afternoon, in the hour when a wind had arisen in the desert, he had been in his own modest treatment room, preparing to instruct four pupils on couching simple cataracts according to the learned devisings of Merovius of Trakesia.

He opened the door. In the torchlight of the corridor he saw a dozen tired-looking courtiers. Servants or soldiers had brought benches; some of the waiting men were sitting, slumped against the stone walls. Some were asleep. Others saw him and stood up. Rustem nodded at Mazendar, the vizier, and then at the young prince, standing a little apart from the others, his face to a dark, narrow window-slit, praying.

Vinaszh the garrison commander—the only man there that Rustem knew—raised his eyebrows in silent inquiry and took a step forward. Rustem shook his head and then changed his mind. *You continue to be accountable*, the King of Kings had said. *Act accordingly*.

Rustem stepped aside to allow the vizier and the prince to walk into the room. Then he motioned for the commander to enter as well. He said nothing at all, but locked eyes with Vinaszh for a moment as the other man went in. Rustem followed and closed the door.

'*Father!*' cried the prince.

'What is to be has long ago been written,' murmured Shirvan of Bassania calmly. He was propped up on pillows, his bare chest wrapped in the linen bandages. 'By the grace of Perun and the Lady, the designs of Black Azal have been blighted for a time. The physician has removed the arrow.'

The vizier, noticeably moved, passed a hand before his face and knelt, touching the floor with his forehead. Prince Murash, eyes wide as he looked at his father, turned quickly to Rustem. 'Perun be exalted!' he cried, and, striding across the floor, he reached forward and seized both of Rustem's hands in his own. 'You shall be requited, physician!' exclaimed the prince.

It was with a supreme act of self-control and a desperate faith in his own learning that Rustem did not violently recoil. His heart was pounding furiously. 'Perun be exalted!' Prince Murash repeated, turning back to the bed and kneeling as the vizier had done.

'Always,' agreed the king quietly. 'My son, the assassin's arrow rests there on the chest beneath the window. There was poison on it. *Kaaba*. Throw it in the fire for me.'

Rustem caught his breath. He looked swiftly at Vinaszh, meeting the soldier's eyes again, then back to the prince.

Murash rose to his feet. 'Joyfully will I do so, my father and king. But poison?' he said. 'How can this be?' He crossed to the window and reached carefully for a swath of linen that lay beside Rustem's implements.

'Take it in your hands, my son,' said Shirvan of Bassania, King of Kings, Sword of Perun. 'Take it in your bare hands again.'

Very slowly the prince turned to the bed. The vizier had risen now and was watching him closely.

'I do not understand. You believe I handled this arrow?' Prince Murash said.

'The smell remains on your hands, my son,' said Shirvan gravely. Rustem cautiously took a step towards the king.

The prince turned—outwardly perplexed, no more than that—and looked at his hands and then at Rustem. 'But then I will have poisoned the doctor, too,' he said.

Shirvan moved his head to look at Rustem. Dark beard above pale linen bandages, the eyes black and cold. *Act accordingly*, he had said. Rustem cleared his throat. 'You will have tried,' he said. His heart was pounding. 'If you handled the arrow when you shot the king then the *kaaba* has passed through your skin and is within you by now. There is no menace to your touch, Prince Murash. Not any more.'

He believed this was true. He had been *taught* that this was so. He had never seen it put to the test. He felt oddly light-headed, as though the room were rocking slightly, like a child's cradle.

He saw the prince's eyes go black then—much like his father's, in fact. Murash reached to his belt, whipped out a knife, turned towards the bed.

The vizier cried out. Rustem stumbled forward, unarmed.

Vinaszh, commander of the garrison at Kerakek, killed Prince Murash, third of the nine sons of Shirvan the Great, with his own dagger, flung from near the doorway.

The prince, a blade in his throat, dropped his weapon from lifeless fingers and slowly toppled across the bed, his face to his father's knees, his blood staining the pale sheets red.

Shirvan did not move. Neither did anyone else.

After a long, frozen moment the king turned from gazing down at his dead son to look over at Vinaszh and then at Rustem. He nodded his head slowly, to each of them.

'Physician, your father's name was . . . ?' A tone of detached, mildly curious interrogation.

Rustem blinked. 'Zorah, great lord.'

'A warrior-caste name.'

'Yes, lord. He was a soldier.'

'You chose a different life?'

The conversation was so implausible it was eerie. Rustem felt dizzied by it. There was a dead man—a son—sprawled across the body of the man with whom he was speaking thus. 'I war against disease and wounds, my lord.' What he always said.

The king nodded again, thoughtfully, as if satisfied by something. 'You know one must be of the priestly caste to become a royal physician, of course.'

Of course. The world knocking at his door, after all.

Rustem lowered his head. Said nothing.

'It will be arranged at the next Accession Ritual before the Sacred Flame in midsummer.'

Rustem swallowed hard. He seemed to have been doing so all night. He cleared his throat. 'One of my wives is of the commoners' caste, Great King.'

'She will be generously dealt with. Is there a child?'

'A girl, yes, my lord.'

The king shrugged. 'A kindly husband will be found. Mazendar, see it is done.'

Jarita. Whose name meant *desert pool*. Black eyes, black hair, light step entering a room, leaving it, as if loath to trouble the air within. Lightest touch in the world. And Inissa, the baby they called Issa. Rustem closed his eyes.

'Your other wife is of the warrior caste?'

Rustem nodded. 'Yes, my lord. And my son.'

'They may be elevated with you in the ceremony. And come to Kabadh. If you desire a second wife there it shall be arranged.'

Again Rustem closed his eyes.

The world, hammering and hammering at his door, after all, entering like the wind.

'This cannot take place until midsummer, of course. I wish to make use of you before that. You appear a competent man. There are never enough of them. You will treat me here, physician. Then you will undertake a winter journey for me. You are observant, it seems. Can serve your king even before you rise in caste. You will leave as soon as I am well enough to go back to Kabadh, in your own judgement.'

Rustem opened his eyes then. Looked up slowly. 'Where am I to go, great lord?'

'Sarantium,' said Shirvan of Bassania.

He went home briefly when the King of Kings fell asleep, to change his bloodied clothes, replenish his herbs and medicines. It was cold in the windy darkness. The vizier gave him an escort of soldiers. It seemed he had become an important man. Not surprising, really, except that everything was surprising now.

Both women were awake, though it was very late. They had oil lamps burning in the front room: a waste. He'd have chastised Katyun for it on a normal night. He walked in. They both rose quickly to see him. Jarita's eyes filled with tears.

'Perun be praised,' said Katyun. Rustem looked from one to the other.

'Papa,' someone said sleepily.

Rustem looked over and saw a little, rumpled figure stand up from the carpet before the fire. Shaski rubbed at his eyes. He'd been asleep but waiting here with his mothers.

'Papa,' he said again, hesitantly. Katyun moved over and laid a hand across his thin shoulders, as if afraid Rustem would reprimand the boy for being here and awake so late.

Rustem felt an odd constriction in his throat. Not the *kaaba*. Something else. He said, carefully, 'It is all right, Shaski. I am home now.'

'The arrow?' said his son. 'The arrow they said?'

It was curiously difficult to speak. Jarita was crying.

'The arrow is safely removed. I used the Spoon of Enyati. The one you brought out for me. You did very well, Shaski.'

The boy smiled then, shyly, sleepily, his head against his mother's waist. Katyun's hand brushed his hair, tender as moonlight. Her eyes sought Rustem's, too many questions in them.

The answers too large.

'Go to sleep now, Shaski. I will speak with your mothers and then go back to my patient. I will see you tomorrow. Everything is well.'

It was, and it wasn't. Being elevated to the priestly caste was a stunning, miraculous thing. The castes of Bassania were immovable as mountains—except when the King of Kings wished them to move. A physician's position at court meant wealth, security, access to libraries and scholars, no more anxieties about buying a larger house for a family or burning oil lamps at night. Shaski's own future had suddenly expanded beyond all possible hope.

But what could one say to a wife who was to be cast off by order of the King of Kings and given to another man? And the little one? Issa, asleep in her cradle now. The little one would be gone from him.

'Everything is well,' Rustem said again, trying to make himself believe it.

The door had opened to reveal the world on his threshold. Good and evil walked hand in hand, not to be separated. Perun was opposed, always, by Azal. The two gods had entered into Time together; one could not exist without the other. So the priests taught before the Holy Flame in every temple in Bassania.

The two women took the child to his room together. Shaski reached up and held each of their hands, walking through the door, claiming them both. They indulged him too much, Rustem thought. But this was not a night to dwell upon that.

He stood alone in the front room of his own small house amid the burning of lamps and the firelight and he thought about fate and the chance moments that shaped a man's life, and about Sarantium.

CHAPTER II

Pardos had never liked his hands. The fingers were too short, stubby, broad. They didn't *look* like a mosaicist's hands, though they showed the same network of cuts and scratches all the others' did.

He'd had a great deal of time to think about this and other things on the long road in wind and rain as autumn steadily turned to winter. Martinian's fingers, or Crispin's, or Pardos's best friend Couvry's—*those* were the right shape. They were large and long, appearing deft and capable. Pardos thought his own hands were like a farmhand's, a labourer's, someone in a trade where dexterity hardly mattered. It bothered him, sometimes.

But he *was* a mosaicist, wasn't he? Had finished his apprenticeship with two celebrated masters of the craft and had been formally admitted to the guild in Varena. He had his papers in his purse now, his name was entered on the rolls back home. So appearance wasn't really important, after all. His short, thick fingers were nimble enough to do what needed to be done. The eye and the mind mattered,

Crispin used to say before he went away; the hands could learn to do what they were told.

It seemed to be true. They *were* doing what needed to be done here, though Pardos would never have dreamt that his first labours as a fully-fledged mosaicist would be expended in the remote, bitterly cold wilderness of Sauradia.

He would never have even dreamt, in fact, of *being* this far away from home, and on his own. He had not been the sort of young man who imagined adventures in distant places. He was pious, careful, prone to worry, not at all impulsive.

But he *had* left Varena—his home, all he knew of Jad's created world—almost immediately after the murders in the sanctuary, and that was about as impulsive an action as could be imagined.

It hadn't felt as though he was being reckless, it seemed rather as if there was no real choice in the matter, and Pardos had wondered why the others couldn't understand that. When pressed by his friends, and by Martinian and his concerned, kind-hearted wife, Pardos had only said, over and over, that he could not stay in a place where such things were done. When they told him, in tones of cynicism or sadness, that such things happened everywhere, Pardos replied—very simply—that he hadn't *seen* them everywhere, only in the sanctuary expanded to house the bones of King Hildric outside Varena.

The consecration of that sanctuary had been the most wonderful day of his life, at first. He and the other former apprentices, newly elevated to the guild, had been sitting with Martinian and his wife and with Crispin's white-haired mother in places of honour for the ceremony. All the mighty of the Antae kingdom were there, and many of the most illustrious Rhodians, including representatives of the High Patriarch himself, had come to Varena along the muddy roads from Rhodias. Queen Gisel, veiled and clad in the pure white of mourning, had been sitting so near that Pardos could almost have spoken to her.

Except that it hadn't been the queen. It had been a woman pretending to be her, a lady-in-waiting. That woman had died in the sanctuary, and so had the queen's giant, silent guard, chopped down by a sword that should never have been in a holy place. Then the swordsman— Agila, Master of Horse—had himself been slain where he stood by the altar, arrows whipping down from overhead. Other men had died the same way, while people screamed and trampled each other in a rush for the doors and blood spattered the sun disk beneath the mosaics Crispin and Martinian and Pardos and Radulph and Couvry and the others had laboured to craft in honour of the god.

Violence, ugly and profane, in a chapel of worship, a desecration of the place and of Jad. Pardos had felt unclean and ashamed—bitterly aware that he was Antae and shared the blood, and even the tribe, as it happened, of the foul-tongued man who had stood up with his forbidden sword, smeared the young queen with ugly, vicious words, and then died there with those he'd killed.

Pardos had walked out the double doors into the sanctuary yard even as the services—under the orders of the sleek chancellor, Eudric Goldenhair—had resumed. He had gone past the outdoor ovens where he'd spent a summer and fall attending to the setting lime, out through the gate and then along the road back to the city. Before he'd even reached the walls he had decided he was leaving Varena. And almost immediately after that he'd realized how far he intended to go, though he'd never been away from home in his life and winter was coming.

They'd tried to dissuade him later, but Pardos was a stubborn young man and not easily swayed when his mind and heart were set. He needed to put a distance between himself and what had happened in that sanctuary—what had been done by his own tribe and blood. None of his colleagues and friends were Antae, they were all Rhodian-born. Perhaps that was why they didn't feel the shame as fiercely as he did.

Winter roads to the east might have their dangers, but as far as Pardos was concerned, they could not be worse than what was about to happen here among his people with the queen gone and swords drawn in holy places.

He wanted to see Crispin again, and to work with him, far away from the tribal wars that were coming. Coming again. They had been down this dark path before, the Antae. Pardos would go a different direction this time.

They'd had no word from Martinian's younger, more intense partner since a single relayed message sent from a military camp in Sauradia. That letter hadn't even been addressed to them, it had been delivered to an alchemist, a friend of Martinian's. The man—Zoticus was his name—had passed on word that Crispin was all right, at least to that point in his journey. Why he'd written the old man and not his own partner or mother was not explained, or at least not to Pardos.

Since then, nothing, though Crispin would probably have reached Sarantium by now—if he'd reached it at all. Pardos, with his own decision to leave now firm in his mind, latched onto an image of his former teacher and announced an intention to follow him to the Imperial City.

When they realized he wasn't to be dissuaded, Martinian and his wife Carissa turned their considerable energies to making sure Pardos was properly prepared for the journey. Martinian lamented the recent—and very sudden—departure of his alchemical friend, a man who apparently knew a great deal about the roads east, but he succeeded in canvassing opinions and suggestions from various well-travelled merchants who were former clients. Pardos, who was proud to say he knew his letters, was provided with carefully written-out lists of places to stay and to avoid. His options were limited, of course, since he couldn't afford to bribe his way into the Imperial Inns en route, but it was still useful to learn of those taverns and cauponae where a traveller stood a higher-than-usual chance of being robbed or killed.

One morning, after the sunrise invocations in the small, ancient chapel near the room he shared with Couvry and Radulph, Pardos went—somewhat embarrassed—to visit a cheiromancer.

The man's chambers were towards the palace quarter. Some of the other apprentices and craftsmen working on the sanctuary had been inclined to consult him, seeking advice in gambling and love, but that didn't make Pardos feel easier about what he was doing.

Cheiromancy was a condemned heresy, of course, but the clergy of Jad walked carefully here in Batiara among the Antae, and the conquerors had never entirely abandoned some aspects of their past beliefs. The door had been openly marked with a signboard showing a pentagram. A bell rang when it opened, but no one appeared. Pardos went into a small, dark front room and, after waiting for a time, rapped on an unsteady counter there. The seer came out from behind a beaded curtain and led him, unspeaking, into a windowless back room warmed only by a small brazier and lit with candles. He waited, still silent, until Pardos had placed three copper folles on the table and spoken his question.

The cheiromancer gestured to a bench. Pardos sat down carefully; the bench was very old.

The man, who was rail-thin, dressed in black and missing the little finger of his left hand, took Pardos's short, broad hand and bent his head over it, studying the palm for a long time by the light of the candles and the smoky brazier. He coughed, at intervals. Pardos experienced an odd mixture of fear and anger and self-contempt as he endured the close scrutiny. Then the man—he still had not spoken—had Pardos toss some dried-out chicken bones from his fist down onto the greasy table. He examined these for another long while and then declared in a high, wheezing voice that Pardos would not die on the journey east and that he was expected on the road.

That last made no sense at all and Pardos asked about it. The cheiromancer shook his head, coughing. He put a stained cloth to his mouth. He said, when the coughing subsided, that it was difficult to discern further details. He was asking for more money, Pardos knew, but he refused to offer more than he'd already paid and he walked out into the morning sunshine. He wondered if the man was as poor as he seemed to be, or if the shabbiness of his attire and chambers was a device to avoid drawing attention to himself. Certainly cheiromancers were not short of trade in Varena. The cough and rheumy voice had sounded real, but the wealthy could fall ill almost as easily as the poor.

Still embarrassed by what he'd done, and aware of how the cleric who presided over services in his chapel would feel about his visiting a seer, Pardos made a point of reporting the visit to Couvry. 'If I do get killed,' he said, 'go get those three folles back, all right?' Couvry had agreed, without any of his usual joking.

The night before Pardos left, Couvry and Radulph took him drinking at their favourite wine shop. Radulph was also going away soon, but only south to Baiana near Rhodias where his family lived, and where he expected to find steady work decorating homes and summer retreats by the sea. That hope might be affected if civil war broke out, or an invasion came from the east, but they decided not to talk about that on their last night together. During the course of a liquid farewell, Radulph and Couvry both expressed wistfully intense regret that they weren't coming with Pardos. Now that they were reconciled to his sudden departure, they had begun to see it as a grand adventure.

Pardos didn't view it that way at all, but he wasn't about to disappoint his friends by saying so. He was deeply touched when Couvry opened a parcel he'd brought and they presented Pardos with a new pair of boots for the road. They'd traced his sandals one night while he slept, Radulph explained, to get the size right.

The tavern closed early, by order of Eudric Goldenhair, once the chancellor, who had proclaimed himself regent in the absence of the queen. There had been some unrest in the wake of that proclamation. A number of people had died in street fighting the last few days. The drinking places were under a curfew. Tensions were high and would be rising.

Among other things, no one seemed to have any idea where the queen had gone, clearly a matter of some agitation among those now occupying the palace.

Pardos simply hoped she was all right, wherever she was, and that she would come back. The Antae didn't favour women rulers, but Pardos thought Hildric's daughter would be better, by far, than any of those likely to take her place.

He left home the next morning, immediately after the sunrise invocation, taking the road east towards Sauradia.

In the event, dogs were his biggest problem. They tended to avoid larger parties, but there were two or three dawns and twilights when Pardos was walking on his own, and on one particularly bad night he found himself caught between inns. On these occasions, wild dogs came after him. He laid about with his staff, surprising himself with the violence of his own blows and his profane language, but he took his share of bites. None of the animals appeared to be sick—which was a good thing or he'd have been dying or dead by now and Couvry would have had to go get the money back from the fortune-teller.

The inns tended to be filthy and cold, with food of indeterminate origin, but Pardos's room at home was no city palace and he was hardly a stranger to small biting things sharing his pallet. He observed his share of unsavoury figures drinking too much bad wine on damp nights, but it must have been obvious that the quiet young man had nothing in the way of wealth or goods to steal and they left him pretty much alone. He did take the precaution of smearing and staining his new boots, to make them look older.

He liked the boots. Didn't mind the cold or the walking at all. Found the great black forest to the north—the Aldwood—to be oddly exciting. He enjoyed trying to detect and define shadings of dark green and grey and muddy brown and black as the shifting light caused changes at the edge of the forest. It occurred to him that his grandfathers and their fathers might have lived in these woods; perhaps that was why he was drawn to them. The Antae long had made their home in Sauradia, among the Inicii and Vrachae and other warring tribes, before setting out on their great migration south and west into Batiara, where an empire had been crumbling and ready to fall. Perhaps the trees stretching alongside the Imperial road were speaking to something ancient in his blood. The cheiromancer had said he was expected on the road. He hadn't said *what* was expecting him.

He sought out others to travel with, as instructed by Martinian, but after the first few days he didn't greatly worry if he found no one. He was as faithful as he could be about the morning invocations and the sunset rites, trying to find roadside chapels for his prayers, so he often fell behind less pious companions even when he did link up with them.

One smooth-shaven wine merchant from Megarium had offered to pay Pardos to share his bed—at an Imperial Inn, even—and had needed a rap with a staff on the back of his knees to dissuade him from a grab at Pardos's privates as a masking twilight overtook their party on the road. Pardos had worried that the man's friends might react to his cry of pain and make trouble, but in fact they seemed to be familiar with their colleague's nature and gave Pardos no difficulty. One of them had even apologized, which was unexpected. Their group had stopped at the Imperial Inn when it loomed out of darkness—large and torchlit and welcoming—and Pardos had kept going, alone. That was the night he ended up huddled on the southern side of a stone wall in the knifing cold, dealing with wild dogs in the white moonlight. The wall ought to have kept out the dogs, but it was broken down in too many places. Pardos knew what that meant. Plague had been here as well in the years just past. When men died in such numbers there were never enough hands for what needed to be done.

That one night was very hard and he did wonder, shivering and struggling to stay awake, if he would die here in Sauradia, having lived a brief, utterly inconsequential life. He thought about what he was doing so far away from everything he knew, without the means to make a fire, staring into the black for the lean, slavering apparitions that could kill him if he missed their approach. He heard other sounds, as well, from the forest on the far side of the wall and the road: deep, repeated grunting, and a howling, and once the tread of something very large. He didn't stand up to see what it might be, but after that time the dogs went away, thanks be to Jad. Pardos sat huddled in his cloak, leaning against his pack and the rough shelter of the wall, and looked up at the far stars and the one white moon and thought about where he was in Jad's creation. Where the small, breathing, unimportant thing that was Pardos of the Antae was passing this cold night in the world. The stars were hard and bright as diamonds in the dark.

Later, he was to decide that that long night had given him a new appreciation of the god, if that wasn't a thought too laden with presumption, for how *dare* a man such as he speak of appreciating the god? But the thought remained with him: didn't Jad do something infinitely more difficult each and every night, battling alone against enemies and evil in the bitter cold and dark? And—a further truth— didn't the god do it for the benefit of *others*, for his mortal children, and not for himself at all? Pardos had simply been fighting for his own life, not for anything else that lived.

He'd thought, at one point in the darkness after the white moon set, of the Sleepless Ones, those holy clerics who kept a night-long vigil to mark their awareness of what the god did in the night. Then he'd fallen into a fitful, dreamless sleep.

And the very next day, chilled, painfully stiff and very tired, he came to a chapel of those same Sleepless Ones, set back a little from the road, and he entered, gratefully, wanting to pray and give thanks, perhaps find some warmth on a cold, windy morning, and then he saw what was overhead.

One of the clerics was awake and came forward to greet Pardos kindly, and they spoke the sunrise invocation together before the disk and beneath the awesome figure of the dark, bearded god on the dome above. Afterwards, Pardos hesitantly told the cleric that he was from Varena, and a mosaicist, and that the work on the dome was—truly— the most overwhelming he had ever seen.

The white-robed holy man hesitated, in turn, and asked Pardos if he was acquainted with another western mosaicist, a man named Martinian, who had passed this way earlier in the autumn. And Pardos remembered, just in time, that Crispin had travelled east using his partner's name, and he said yes, he did know Martinian, had done his apprenticeship with him and was journeying east to join him now, in Sarantium.

At that, the thin-faced cleric hesitated a second time and then asked Pardos to wait for him a few moments. He went through a small door at one side of the chapel and returned with another man, older, grey-bearded, and this man explained, awkwardly, that the other artisan, Martinian, had suggested to them that the image of Jad overhead might need a certain measure of . . . attention, if it were to endure as it should.

And Pardos, looking up again, more carefully now, saw what Crispin had seen and nodded his head and said that this was, indeed, so. Then they asked him if he might be willing to assist them in this. Pardos blinked, overawed, and stammered something about the need for a great many tesserae to match those used above for this exacting, almost impossible task. He would require a mosaicist's equipment and tools, and scaffolding . . .

The two holy men had exchanged a glance and then led Pardos through the chapel to one of the outbuildings behind, and then down some creaking stairs to a cellar. And there, by torchlight, Pardos saw the disassembled parts of scaffolding and the tools of his own trade. There were a dozen chests along the stone walls and the clerics opened these, one by one, and Pardos saw tesserae of such brilliance and quality that he had to struggle not to weep, remembering the muddy, inadequate glass Crispin and Martinian had been forced to use all the time in Varena. These were the tesserae used to make that image of Jad overhead: the clerics had kept them down here, all these hundreds of years.

The two holy men had looked at him, waiting, saying nothing at all, until at length Pardos simply nodded his head. 'Yes,' he'd said. 'Yes.' And, 'I will need some of you to help me.'

'You must teach us what we need to do,' the older man had said, holding up a torch, looking down at the shining glass in the ancient chests as it reflected and caught the light.

Pardos ended up staying in that place, working among those holy men, living with them, through almost the whole of the winter. It seemed he had been, in the strangest way, expected there.

There came a time when he reached the limits of what he felt capable of doing without guidance or greater experience, putting his own hands to a work of such holy magnificence, and he told the clerics as much. They respected him by then, acknowledged his piety and care, and he even thought they liked him. No one demurred. Wearing a white robe they offered him, Pardos stayed awake with the Sleepless Ones on the last night and, shivering, heard his own name chanted by holy men in their rituals as someone virtuous and deserving, for whom the god's grace was besought. They gave him gifts—a new cloak, a sun disk—when he set out again with his staff and pack on a bright morning, with birdsong hinting at spring, continuing towards Sarantium.

In all honesty, Rustem had to admit that his vanity had been offended. With the passage of a little more time, he decided, this wounded, unsettled, choleric feeling would probably pass and he might begin to find his wives' reactions and his own response to be amusing and instructive, but an adequate interval had not yet gone by.

It seemed he had indulged himself in some domestic illusions. He wasn't the first man to do so. Slender, fragile Jarita, who was being discarded, cast off by the desire of the King of Kings to raise Rustem of Kerakek to the priestly caste, had appeared entirely content when informed of this development—as soon as she was told of the promise that she was to be given an appropriate, kindly husband. Her only request was that this happen in Kabadh.

It seemed that his second, delicate wife, had a greater dis-like for desert sand and heat than she had ever revealed, and an equally strong interest in seeing and dwelling within the bustle and excitement of the royal city. Rustem, nonplussed, had indicated that it was likely she could be accommodated in this wish. Jarita had kissed him happily, even passionately, and gone off to see her baby in the nursery.

Katyun, his first wife—calm, composed Katyun, who was being honoured, as was her son, by elevation to the highest of the three castes, with the prospect of unimag-ined wealth and opportunity—had erupted in a storm of grief upon hearing these same tidings. She had refused to be consoled, wailing and distraught.

Katyun did *not* have any liking for the great cities of the world, never having seen—or having felt any desire to see—any of them. Sand in clothing or hair was a trivial affliction; the heat of the desert sun could be dealt with if one knew the proper ways to live; small, remote Kerakek was an entirely pleasant place in which to dwell if one were the wife of a respected physician and had the status that came therewith.

Kabadh, the court, the famous water gardens, the *churka* grounds, the flower-laden, crimson-pillared hall of dance ... these were places where women would be painted and perfumed and garbed in exquisite silks and in the manners and malice of long practice and familiarity. A woman from the desert provinces among such ... ?

Katyun had wept in her bed, squeezing her eyes tightly shut, refusing even to look at him, as Rustem strove to comfort her with talk of what opportunities this royal munificence offered for Shaski—and any other children they might now have.

That last had been an impulsive, unplanned comment, but it did produce an ebbing of tears. Katyun wanted another baby and Rustem knew it. With a move to Kabadh, in the lofty role of royal physician, there would be no further arguments about living space or resources that could be applied against the idea of another child.

Inwardly, he had still been wounded, however. Jarita had been *much* too matter-of-fact about being set aside with her daughter; Katyun gave *no* evidence of realizing how astonishing this change in their fortunes was, no sign of pride in him, of excitement in their shared new fate.

The suggestion about a second child did calm her. She dried her eyes, sat up in the bed, looked at him thoughtfully and then managed a brief smile. Rustem spent what was left of the night with her. Katyun, less delicately pretty than Jarita, was also less shy than his second wife and rather more skilled in arousing him by diverse means. Before dawn he had been induced, still half-asleep, to make a first assay at engendering the promised offspring. Katyun's touch and her whispering voice at his ear were balm to his pride.

At sunrise he'd returned to the fortress to determine the status of his royal patient. All was well. Shirvan healed swiftly, signs of an iron constitution and the benign alignment of auspices. Rustem took no credit for the former, was at pains to monitor and adjust for the latter.

In between visits with the king, he found himself closeted with the vizier, Mazendar, others joining them at intervals. Rustem received an education, at speed, in certain aspects of the world as they knew it that winter, with particular emphasis on the nature and the possible intentions of Valerius II of Sarantium, whom some named the Night's Emperor.

If he was going there, and was to do so to some purpose, there were things he needed to know.

When he finally did depart—having made hasty arrangements for his students to continue with a physician he knew in Qandir, even farther to the south—the winter was well advanced.

The most difficult parting—and this was entirely unexpected—was with Shaski. The women were reconciled to what was happening, could understand it; the baby was too young to know. His son, too soft by far, Rustem thought, was visibly struggling not to cry as Rustem finished tightening the drawstrings on his pack one morning and turned to bid a last farewell to all of them.

Shaski had come forward a few steps down the walk. He rubbed at his eyes with bunched fists. He was *trying*, Rustem had to acknowledge. He was attempting not to cry. But what little boy grew so absurdly attached to his father? It was a weakness. Shaski was still of an age when the world he ought to know and need was that of the women. A father was to provide food and shelter and moral guidance and ensure discipline in the home. Perhaps Rustem had made a mistake, after all, in allowing the child to listen to his lessons from the hallway. Shaski had no business reacting this way. There were even soldiers watching; an escort from the fortress would go with him the first part of the way, as a sign of favour.

Rustem opened his mouth to admonish the boy and discovered that—shamefully—he had an awkward lump in his own throat and a constriction of feeling in his chest that made it difficult to speak. He coughed.

'Listen to your mothers,' he said, more huskily than he'd expected.

Shaski nodded his head. 'I will,' he whispered. He still wasn't crying, Rustem saw. His small fists were clenched at his sides. 'When will you come home, Papa?'

'When I have done what I have to do.'

Shaski took another two steps towards the gate where Rustem stood. They were alone, halfway between the women by the door and the military escort a little down the road. He could have touched the boy if he'd reached out. One bird was singing in the bright, crisp winter morning.

His son took a deep breath, visibly summoning courage. 'I don't want you to go, you know,' said Shaski.

Rustem strove for outrage. Children were *not* to speak this way. Not to their fathers. Then he saw that the boy knew this, and had lowered his eyes and hunched his shoulders, as if awaiting a reprimand.

Rustem looked at him and swallowed, then turned away, saying nothing after all. He carried the pack a few steps until one of the soliders jumped down from his mount and took it from him, fastening it efficiently to the back of a mule. Rustem watched him. The leader of the soldiers looked at him and raised an eyebrow in inquiry, gesturing at the horse they'd given him.

Rustem nodded, inexplicably irritated. He took a step towards the horse, then suddenly turned around, to look back at the gate. Shaski was still there. He lifted his hand to wave to the boy, and smiled a little, awkwardly, that the child might know his father wasn't angry about what he'd said, even though he should have been. Shaski's eyes were on Rustem's face. He still wasn't crying. He still looked as though he might. Rustem looked at him another moment, drinking in the sight of that small form, then he nodded his head, turned briskly and accepted a hand up onto his horse and they rode off. The uncomfortable feeling in his chest lingered for a time and then it went away.

The escort rode with him to the border but Rustem continued west into Sarantine lands—for the first time in his life—alone save for a dark-eyed, bearded manservant named Nishik. He left the horse with the soldiers and continued on a mule, now; it was more suited to his role.

The manservant was another deception. Just as Rustem was not, for the moment, simply a teaching physician in search of manuscripts and learned discussions with western colleagues, so was his servant not really a servant. Nishik was a veteran soldier, experienced in combat and survival. In the fortress it had been impressed upon Rustem that such skills might be important on his journey, and perhaps even more so when he reached his destination. He was, after all, a spy.

They stopped in Sarnica, making no secret of their arrival or Rustem's role in saving the life of the King of Kings and his forthcoming status. It had been too dramatic an event: the tidings of the assassination attempt had already run before them across the border, even in winter.

The governor of Amoria requested that Rustem attend upon him and seemed appropriately horrified to learn further details of deadly perfidy within the royal family of Bassania. After the formal audience, the governor dismissed his attendants and confided privately to Rustem that he had been encountering some difficulties in fulfilling his obligations to both his wife and his favourite mistress. He admitted, somewhat shamefacedly, that he'd gone so far as to consult a cheiromancer, without success. Prayer had also failed to be of use.

Rustem refrained from comment on either of these solutions and, after examining the man's tongue and taking his pulse, advised the governor to make a meal of the well-cooked liver of a sheep or cow on those evenings when he wished to have relations with either of his women. Noting the governor's extremely florid complexion, he also suggested refraining from the consumption of wine with that important meal. He expressed great confidence that this would prove helpful. Confidence, of course, was half the treatment. The governor was profuse in his thanks and gave instructions that Rustem was to be assisted in all his affairs while in Sarnica. Two days later he sent a silk robe and an elaborate Jaddite sun disk to Rustem's inn as gifts. The disk, though beautiful, was hardly an appropriate offering to a Bassanid, but Rustem concluded that his suggestions had met with some nocturnal success.

While in Sarnica, Rustem visited with one of his former pupils and met two doctors with whom he'd exchanged correspondence. He purchased a text of Cadestes on skin ulcers and paid to have another manuscript copied and sent to him in Kabadh. He told those physicians he met exactly what had happened in Kerakek, and how, as a consequence of saving the king's life, he was soon to become a royal physician. In the interval, he explained, he had requested and received permission to conduct a journey of acquisition, obtaining further knowledge for himself and written sources from the west.

He gave a morning lecture, pleasingly well attended, on the Ispahani treatment of difficult childbirths, and another on the amputation of limbs when inflammation and noxious exudations followed upon a wound. He left after a stay of almost a month and a gracious farewell dinner hosted by the physicians' guild. He was given the names of several doctors in the Imperial City upon whom he was urged to call, and the address of a respectable inn where members of the healing profession were inclined to stay when in Sarantium.

The food on the road north was wretched and the accommodations worse, but—given that it was the end of winter, not yet spring, when any remotely intelligent people avoided travel entirely—the trip proved largely uneventful. Their arrival in Sarantium was rather less so. Rustem had *not* expected to encounter both death and a wedding on his first day.

It had been years since Pappio, Director of the Imperial Glassworks, had actually done any actual glassblowing or design work himself. His duties now were administrative and diplomatic, involving the coordination of supplies and production and the distribution of tesserae and flat sheets of glass to craftsmen requesting them, in the City and beyond. Determining priorities and placating outraged artisans comprised the most delicate part of his office. Artisans, in Pappio's experience, tended to incline towards outrage.

He had his system worked out. Imperial projects came first, and amongst those Pappio made assessments of how important a given mosaic might be in the scheme of things. This required delicate inquiries in the Imperial Precinct at times, but he *did* have a staff for that, and he had acquired a sufficient polish to his own manners to make it feasible for him to attend upon some of the higher civil service functionaries when necessary. His wasn't the most important of the guilds—the silk guild had that distinction, of course—but it wasn't anywhere near the least significant, either, and under this particular Emperor, with his elaborate building projects, it could be said that Pappio was an important man. He was treated respectfully, in any case.

Private commissions came behind the Imperial ones, but there *was* a complication: the artisans engaged on projects for the Emperor received their supplies free of charge, while those doing mosaic or other glass work for citizens had to buy their tesserae or sheets of glass. The Imperial Glassworks was expected to pay for itself now, in the modern scheme of things devised by thrice-exalted Valerius II and his advisers. Pappio was not, therefore, at liberty to entirely ignore the entreaties of those mosaicists clamouring for tesserae for private ceilings, walls, or floors. Nor, frankly, would it make sense for him to refuse *all* the quiet offers of sums for his own purse. A man had a duty to his family, didn't he?

Over and above these nuanced issues, Pappio had a powerful inclination to favour those craftsmen—or patrons—who had a demonstrated affinity for the Greens.

The Splendid Greens of Great and Glorious Achievement were his own beloved faction, and one of the extreme pleasures attendant upon his rise to this lofty status in his guild was that he was now in a position to subsidize the faction somewhat, and be honoured and recognized accordingly in their banquet hall and at the Hippodrome. He was no longer just another humble supporter. He was a dignitary, present at the feasts, prominently seated at the theatre, among those in the preferred places for the chariot races themselves. Long past were the days when he'd line up before dawn outside the Hippodrome gates to get a standing place to watch the horses run.

He couldn't be *too* obvious in his favouritism—the Emperor's people were present and observing, everywhere—but Pappio did make sure that, all other things being remotely balanced, a Green mosaicist did not go away empty-handed if competing for hard-to-find colours or semi-precious stones with a known follower of the accursed Blues or even someone without declared allegiance.

This was only as it should be. Pappio owed his appointment to his Green partisanship. His predecessor as head of the guild and Glassworks Director—an equally fervent Green—had selected him in large part for that reason. Pappio knew that when he chose to retire he was expected to pass on the position to another Green. It happened all the time, in every guild except the silk, which was a special case and closely scrutinized by the Imperial Precinct. One faction or the other controlled most of the guilds, and it was rare for that control to be wrested away. One had to be blatantly corrupt for the Emperor's people to interfere.

Pappio had no intention of being blatant about anything, or even corrupt, if it came to that. He was a careful man.

And it was that instinctive caution, in part, that had made him a little uneasy about the surprising request he'd received, and the extremely substantial payment that had accompanied it—before he'd even done a preliminary sketch of the glass bowl requested!

He understood that it was his stature that was being bought. That the gift would acquire greatly enhanced value because it had been fashioned by the head of the guild himself, who never did such things any more. He also knew that the man buying this from him—as a wedding gift, he understood—could afford to do so. One didn't need to make inquiries to know that the principal secretary to the

Supreme Strategos, an historian who also happened to be chronicling the Emperor's building projects, had sufficient resources to buy an elaborate bowl. This was a man who, more and more, seemed to require a certain deference. Pappio didn't like the sallow, unsmiling, lean-faced secretary, but what did liking have to do with anything?

What was harder to sort out was *why* Pertennius of Eubulus was buying this gift. Some discreet questions had to be asked elsewhere before Pappio thought he had the answer. It turned out to be simple enough, in the end—one of the oldest stories of all—and it had nothing to do with the bride and groom.

It was someone else that Pertennius was trying to impress. And since that person happened to be dear to Pappio's own heart, he had to overcome a certain indignation— visualizing a woman sleek and splendid as a falcon in the thin arms of the dour secretary—to concentrate on his unaccustomed craft again. He forced himself to do so, however, as best he could.

After all, he wouldn't want the Principal Dancer for his beloved Greens to think him less than an exemplary artisan. Perhaps, he daydreamed, she might even ask for further work on her own behalf after seeing his bowl. Pappio imagined meetings, consultations, two heads bent close over a series of drawings, her notorious perfume—worn by only two women in all of Sarantium—enveloping him, a trusting hand laid on his arm . . .

Pappio was not a young man, was stout and bald and married with three grown children, but it was a truth of the world that certain women carried a magic about them, on the stage and off, and dreams followed where they went. You didn't stop dreaming just because you weren't young any more. If Pertennius could attempt to win admiration with a showy gift given to people he couldn't possibly care about, might not Pappio try to let the exquisite Shirin see what the Director of the Imperial Glassworks could do when he put his hands and mind—and a part of his heart—to his earliest craft?

She would see the bowl when it was delivered to her house. It seemed the bride was living with her.

After some thought, and a morning's sketching, Pappio decided to make the bowl green, with inset pieces of bright yellow glass like meadow flowers in the spring that was coming at last.

His heart quickened as he began to work, but it wasn't the labour or the craft that was exciting him, or even the image of a woman now. It was something else entirely. If spring was nearly upon them, Pappio was thinking, humming a processional march to himself, then so were the chariots, so were the chariots, so were the chariots again.

───※───

Every morning, during the sunrise invocations in the elegant chapel she had elected to frequent, the young queen of the Antae went through an exercise of tabulating, as on a secretary's slate in her mind, the things for which she ought to be grateful. Seen in a certain light, there were many of them.

She had escaped an attempt on her life, survived a late-season sailing to Sarantium, and then the first stages of settling in this city—a process more overwhelming than she wanted to admit. It had taken much from her to preserve an appropriately haughty manner when they had first come within sight of the harbour and walls. Even though she had known Sarantium could overawe, and had been preparing for it, Gisel learned, when the sun rose that morning behind the Imperial City, that sometimes there was no real way to prepare oneself.

She was grateful for her father's training and the self-discipline her life had demanded: she didn't think anyone had seen how daunted she was.

And there was more for which thanks ought to be given, to holy Jad or whatever pagan deities one chose to remember from the Antae forests. She had entirely respectable housing in a small palace near the triple walls, courtesy of the Emperor and Empress. She'd acted quickly enough on arrival to secure adequate funds of her own, by demanding loans to the crown from Batiaran merchants trading here in the east. Despite the irregularity of her sudden arrival, unannounced, on an Imperial ship, with only a small cadre of her guards and women, none of the Batiarans had dared gainsay their queen's regal, matter-of-fact request. If she'd waited, Gisel knew, it might have been different. Once those back in Varena—those doubtless claiming or battling for her throne by now—learned where she was, they would send their own instructions east. Money might be harder to come by. More importantly, she expected they'd try to kill her then.

She was too experienced in these affairs—of royalty and survival—to have been foolish enough to wait. Once she'd acquired her funds, she'd hired a dozen Karchite mercenaries as personal guards and dressed them in crimson and white, the colours of her grandfather's war banner.

Her father had always liked Karchites for guards. If you kept them sober when on duty and allowed them to disappear into cauponae when not, they tended to be fiercely loyal. She'd also accepted the Empress Alixana's offer of three more ladies-in-waiting and a chef and steward from the Imperial Precinct. She was setting up a household; amenities and a reasonable staff were necessary. Gisel knew perfectly well that there would be spies among these, but that, too, was something with which she was familiar. There were ways of avoiding them, or misleading them.

She'd been received at court not long after arriving and welcomed with entirely proper courtesy and respect. She had seen and exchanged formal greetings with the grey-eyed, round-faced Emperor and the small, exquisite, childless dancer who had become his Empress. They had all been precisely and appropriately polite, though no private encounters or exchanges with either Valerius or Alixana had followed. She hadn't been sure whether to expect these or not. It depended on the Emperor's larger plans. Once, affairs had waited on *her* plans. Not any more.

She *had* received, in her own small city palace, a regular stream of dignitaries and courtiers from the Imperial Precinct in that first interval of time. Some came out of sheer curiosity, Gisel knew: she was a novelty, a diversion in winter. A barbarian queen in flight from her people. They might have been disappointed to be received with style and grace by a reserved, silk-clad young woman who showed no sign at all of using bear grease in her yellow hair.

A smaller number made the long trip through the crowded city for more thoughtful reasons, assessing her and what role she might play in the shifting alignments of a complex court. The aged, clear-eyed Chancellor Gesius had had himself carried through the streets to her bearing gifts in his litter: silk for a garment and an ivory comb. They spoke of her father, with whom Gesius had evidently corresponded for years, and then of theatre—he urged her to attend—and finally of the regrettable effect of the damp weather on his fingers and knee joints. Gisel almost allowed herself to like him, but was too experienced to permit herself such a response.

The Master of Offices, a younger, stiff-faced man named Faustinus, arrived the next morning, apparently in response to Gesius's visit, as though the two men tracked each other's doings. They probably did. The court of Valerius II would not be different in this regard from Gisel's father's or her own. Faustinus drank an herbal tea and asked a number of self-evidently harmless questions about how her court had been administered. He was a functionary, these things occupied his attention. He was also ambitious, she judged, but only in the way that officious men are who fear losing the patterns of their established lives. Nothing burned in him.

In the woman who came a few days after, there *was* something burning beneath a chilly, patrician manner, and Gisel felt both the heat and the cold. It was an unsettling encounter. She had heard of the Daleinoi, of course: wealthiest family in the Empire. With a father and brother dead, another brother said to be hideously maimed and hidden away somewhere, and a third keeping cautiously distant from the City, Styliane Daleina, wife now to the Supreme Strategos, was the visible presence of her aristocratic family in Sarantium, and there was nothing harmless about her, Gisel decided very early in their conversation.

They were almost of an age, she judged, and life had taken away both their childhoods very early. Styliane's manner was unrevealing, her bearing and manner perfect, a veneer of exquisite politeness, betraying nothing of what might be her thoughts.

Until she chose to do so. Over dried figs and a small glass of warmed, sweetened wine, a desultory exchange about clothing styles in the west had turned into a sudden, very direct question about Gisel's throne and her flight and what she hoped to achieve by accepting the Emperor's invitation to come east.

'I am alive,' Gisel had said mildly, meeting the appraising blue gaze of the other woman. 'You will have heard of what happened in the sanctuary on the day of its consecration.'

'It was unpleasant, I understand,' had said Styliane Daleina casually, speaking of murder and treason. She gestured dismissively. 'Is this, then, pleasant? This pretty cage?'

'My visitors are a source of very great consolation,' Gisel had murmured, controlling anger ruthlessly. 'Tell me, I have been urged to attend the theatre one night. Have you a suggestion?' She smiled, bland and young, manifestly thoughtless. A barbarian princess, barely two generations removed from the forests where the women painted their naked breasts with dyes.

More than one person, Gisel had thought, leaning forward to carefully select a fig, could preserve her privacy behind empty talk.

Styliane Daleina left soon after, with an observation at the door that people at court seemed to think the principal dancer and actress for the Green faction was the preeminent performer of the day. Gisel had thanked her, and promised to repay her courtesy with a visit one day. She actually thought she might: there was a certain kind of bitter pleasure in this sort of sparring. She wondered if it were possible to find bear grease in Sarantium.

There were other visitors. The Eastern Patriarch sent his principal secretary, an officious, sour-smelling cleric who asked prepared questions about western faith and then lectured her on Heladikos until he realized she wasn't listening. Some members of the small Batiaran community here—mostly merchants, mercenary soldiers, a few craftsmen—made a point of attending upon her until, at some point in the winter, they stopped coming, and Gisel concluded that Eudric or Kerdas, back home, had sent word, or even instructions. Agila was dead; they had learned that by now. He'd died in her father's resting place the morning of the consecration. With Pharos and Anissa, the only two people left in the world who might have been said to love her. She'd heard the tidings, dry-eyed, and hired another half a dozen mercenaries.

The visitors from the court continued for a time. A few of the men gave indications of wishing to seduce her: a triumph for them, doubtless.

She remained a virgin, regretting it occasionally. Boredom was one of the central problems of this new life. It wasn't even really a life. It was a waiting to see if life could continue, or begin again.

And this, unfortunately, was where the dutiful attempt to summon proper gratitude each morning in the chapel usually faltered as the invocations to holy Jad ended. She'd had an existence of real—if precarious—power back home. Reigning queen of a conquering people in the homeland of an empire. The High Patriarch in Rhodias deferred to her, as he had to her father. Here in Sarantium she was subjected to lectures from a lesser cleric. She was no more than a glittering object, a jewel of sorts for the Emperor and his court, without function or access to any role. She was, in the simplest reading of things, a possible excuse for an invasion of Batiara, and little more than that.

Those subtle people from the court who rode or were carried in curtained litters across the city to see her seemed to have gradually come to that same conclusion. It was a long way from the Imperial Precinct to her palace near the triple walls. Midway through the winter, the visits from the court had also begun to grow less frequent. It was not a surprise. At times it saddened her how little ever surprised her.

One of the would-be lovers—more determined than the others—continued to visit after the others had ceased to appear. Gisel allowed him, once, to kiss her palm, not her hand. The sensation had been mildly diverting, but after reflection she'd elected to be engaged the next time he came, and then the next. There hadn't been a third visit.

She'd had little choice, really. Her youth, beauty, whatever desire men might have for her, these were among the few remaining tools she had, having left a throne behind.

She wondered when Eudric or Kerdas would attempt to have her murdered. If Valerius would really try to stop it. On balance, she thought, she was of more use to the Emperor alive, but there were arguments the other way, and there was the Empress to consider.

Every such calculation she had to make by herself. She'd no one she trusted to advise her here. Not that she'd really had that back home, either. At times she found herself feeling furious and bereft when she thought of the grey-haired alchemist who had helped her in this flight but had then abandoned her to pursue his own affairs, whatever they might have been. She had last seen him on the wharf in Megarium, standing in the rain as her ship sailed away.

Gisel, having returned from the chapel to her home, was sitting in the pretty solarium over the quiet street. She noted that the rising sun was now over the roofs across the way. She rang a small bell by her chair and one of the very well trained women the Empress had sent to her appeared in the doorway. It was time to begin preparing to go out. It was wrong, in truth, to say that nothing ever surprised her. There *had* been unexpected developments.

In the wake of one of them, involving a dancer who happened to be the daughter of that same grey-haired man who had left her in Megarium, she'd accepted an invitation for this afternoon.

And that reminded her of the other man she had enlisted to her service back home, the red-haired mosaicist. Caius Crispus would be present today as well.

She had ascertained that he was in Sarantium shortly after her own arrival. She'd needed to know; he raised considerations of his own. She had entrusted him with a dangerously private message, and had no idea if he'd delivered it, or even tried. She'd remembered him to be bitter, saturnine, unexpectedly clever. She'd needed to speak with him.

She hadn't invited him to visit—as far as the world knew, he had never met her, after all. Six men had died to preserve that illusion. She'd gone, instead, to observe the progress being made on the Emperor's new Sanctuary of Jad's Holy Wisdom. The Sanctuary wasn't yet open to the general public, but a visit was an entirely appropriate—even a pious—outing for a visiting monarch. No one could have possibly queried it. Once she'd entered, she'd decided, entirely on impulse, on an unusual approach to this matter.

Thinking back to the events of that morning in early winter, as her women now began preparing her bath, Gisel found herself smiling privately. Jad knew, she wasn't inclined to give way to impulse, and few enough things ever gave her occasion to be amused, but she hadn't conducted herself in that stupefying place with what might be considered decorous piety, and she had to admit she'd enjoyed herself.

The tale had run around Sarantium by now. She'd intended it to.

A man on a scaffold under a dome with glass in his hands, trying to make a god. More than one, in truth, though that particular truth was not one he proposed to reveal. Crispin was, that day—early winter in Jad's holy city of Sarantium—happy to be alive and not anxious to be burned for heresy. The irony was that he hadn't yet realized or acknowledged his own happiness. It had been a long time since he'd known the feeling; he was a stranger now to such a mood, would have glowered in vexation and snapped off a brittle insult to someone who'd dared make the observation that he seemed content with his lot.

Brow unconsciously furrowed, mouth a line of concentration, he was attempting to finally confirm the colours of his own image of Jad above the emerging skyline of Sarantium on the dome. Other artisans were creating the City for him under his supervision; he himself was rendering the figures, and he was beginning with Jad, that an image of the god might look down upon all who entered here while the dome and semidomes and walls were being achieved. He wanted the god he made to echo, in a tacit homage, the one he'd seen in a small chapel in Sauradia, but not slavishly or too obviously. He was working on a different scale, his Jad a ruling element of a larger scene, not the entirety of the dome, and there were matters of balance and proportion to be worked through.

At the moment, he was thinking about eyes and the lines in the skin above and below them, remembering the wounded, haggard vision of Jad in that chapel he'd seen on the Day of the Dead. He'd fallen down. Had literally collapsed beneath that gaunt, overpowering figure.

His memory for colours was very good. It was flawless, in fact, and he knew this without false humility. He'd worked closely with the head of the Imperial Glassworks to find those hues that most precisely matched the ones he remembered from Sauradia. It helped that he was now in charge of the mosaic decoration for the most important, by far, of all Valerius II's building projects. The previous mosaicist—one Siroes—had been dismissed in disgrace, and had somehow broken the fingers of both hands that same night in an unexplained accident. Crispin, as it happened, did know something about that. He wished he didn't. He remembered a tall, fair-haired woman in his bedroom at dawn, murmuring, *I can attest that Siroes was not in a position to hire assassins tonight.* And she'd added, very calmly, *Trust me in this.*

He did. In that, if in nothing else. It was the Emperor, however, not the yellow-haired woman, who had shown Crispin this dome and offered it to him. What Crispin asked for now he tended to receive, at least insofar as tesserae were concerned.

In the other spheres of his life, down among the men and women of the City, he hadn't yet decided what it was he even wanted. He only knew that he had a life below this scaffolding, as well, with friends, enemies—attempts on his life within days of his arrival—and complexities that could, if allowed, distract him dangerously from what he needed to do up here on this dome that an Emperor and an architect of genius had given to him.

He ran a hand through his thick red hair, rendering it even more haphazard than usual, and decided that the eyes of his god would be dark brown and obsidian like those of the figure in Sauradia, but that he would not evoke the pallor of the other Jad with grey hues in the skin of the face. He would pick up the two shades again when he did the long, thin hands, but would not make them ruined, as the other's had been. An echoing of elements, not a copying. It was pretty much what he'd thought before coming back up here—first instincts tended to hold for him.

Having decided as much, Crispin took a deep breath and felt himself relax. He could begin tomorrow, then. With the thought he detected a slight stirring of the scaffold, a swaying movement, which meant someone was climbing.

This was forbidden. It was utterly and absolutely forbidden to the apprentices and artisans. To everyone, in fact, including Artibasos, who had built this Sanctuary. A rule: when Crispin was up here, no one climbed his scaffolding. He had threatened mutilation, dismemberment, death. Vargos, who was proving to be as competent an assistant here as on the road, had been scrupulous in preserving Crispin's sanctity aloft.

Crispin looked down, more stunned by the breach than anything else, and saw that it was a woman—she had discarded a cloak for easier movement—who was ascending the scaffold rungs towards him. He saw Vargos among those far below on the marble tiles. His Inici friend spread his hands, helplessly. Crispin looked at the climber again. Then he blinked and caught his breath, gripping the low railing tightly with both hands.

Once before he had looked down from this great height, just after arriving, when he'd been using his fingers like a blind man to map this dome where he intended to make the world, and had seen a woman far below, feeling her very presence as an irresistible pull: the force and draw of the world where men and women went about their lives.

That time it had been an Empress.

He had gone down to her. Not a woman to be resisted, even if she simply stood below, waiting. Had gone down to speak of dolphins and of other things, to rejoin and be reclaimed by the living world from the place where love lost to death had taken him.

This time, staring in mute stupefaction at the climber's steady, quite competent progress, Crispin tried to deal with who this was. Too astonished to call out or even know how to react, he simply waited, heart pounding, as his own queen came to him, high above the world, but in plain sight of all below.

She reached the last rung, then the scaffold itself and—ignoring his hastily extended hand—stepped onto it, a little flushed, breathless, but visibly pleased with herself, bright-eyed and unafraid, to stand in this place of absolutely private speech on a precarious platform just under Artibasos's dome. However many listening ears there might be in dangerous Sarantium, there were none here.

Crispin knelt and lowered his head. He had last seen this young, beleaguered woman in her own palace, in his own city far to the west. Had kissed her foot in farewell and felt her hand brush his hair. Then he had left, having somehow promised to try to deliver a message to an Emperor. And he'd learned the morning after that she'd had six of her own guards killed—simply to preserve the secret of their encounter.

On the scaffolding below the dome, Gisel of the Antae brushed his hair again with a light, slow hand. Kneeling, he trembled.

'No flour this time,' his queen murmured. 'An improvement, artisan. But I prefer the beard, I think. Has the east claimed you so soon? Are you lost to us? You may stand, Caius Crispus, and tell what you have to tell.'

'Your Majesty,' Crispin stammered, rising, feeling himself flushing, terribly unsettled. The world, coming up to him, even here. 'This is . . . this is *not* a safe place for you, at all!'

Gisel smiled. 'Are you so dangerous, artisan?'

He wasn't. *She* was. He wanted to say that. Her hair was golden, her gaze a deep, remembered blue—she had the same colouring, in fact, as another of the very dangerous women he knew here. But where Styliane Daleina was ice with an edge of malice, Gisel, the daughter of Hildric the Great, showed something wilder and sadder, both.

He'd known she was here, of course. Everyone had heard of the arrival of the Antae queen. He'd wondered if she'd send for him. She hadn't. She'd climbed up to find him, instead, graceful and assured as an experienced mosaicist. This was Hildric's daughter. An Antae. Could hunt, shoot, ride, probably kill with a dagger secreted somewhere on her person. No delicate, sheltered court lady, this.

She said, 'We are waiting, artisan. We have come a long way to see you, after all.'

He bowed his head. And told her, unvarnished and with nothing that mattered held back, of his conversation with Valerius and Alixana, when the small, brilliant figure that was the Empress of Sarantium had turned in a doorway to her inner chamber and asked—with seeming casualness—about the marriage proposal he undoubtedly carried from Varena.

Gisel was disturbed, he realized. Was trying to hide that and might have done so from a less observant man. When he finished, she was silent awhile.

'Did she sort it through or did he?' she asked.

Crispin thought about it. 'Both of them, I believe. Together, or each on their own.' He hesitated. 'She is . . . an exceptional woman, Majesty.'

Gisel's blue gaze met his briefly, then flicked away. She was so young, he thought.

'I wonder what would have happened,' she murmured, 'had I not had the guardsmen killed.'

They'd be alive, Crispin wanted to say, but did not. He might have, a season ago, but was not quite the same angry, bitter man he'd been at the beginning of autumn. He'd had a journey, since.

Another silence. She said, 'You know why I am here? In Sarantium?'

He nodded. It was all over the city. 'You avoided an attempt on your life. In the sanctuary. I am horrified, Majesty.'

'Of course you are,' said his queen, and smiled, almost absently. For all the terrible nuances of what they were discussing and what had happened to her, an odd mood seemed to be playing about her, in the dance and drift of sunlight through the high windows all around the dome.

He tried to fathom how she must feel, having fled from her throne and people, living here on sufferance, devoid of her own power. He couldn't even imagine it.

'I like it up here,' the queen said suddenly. She went to the low railing and looked down, seemingly unfazed by how high they were. Crispin had known people to faint or collapse, clutching at the planks of the scaffold up here.

There were other platforms, around the eastern perimeter of the dome, where men had begun setting tesserae on Crispin's sketched pattern, to make a cityscape and the deep blue and green of the sea, but no one else was aloft just now. Gisel of the Antae looked at her own hands on the rail, then turned and held them up to him. 'Could I be a mosaicist, do you think?' She laughed. He listened for desperation, fear, but heard only genuine amusement.

He said, 'It is a craft only, unworthy of you, Majesty.'

She looked around for a time without answering him. 'No. This isn't,' she said finally. She gestured at Artibasos's dome, at the beginnings of Crispin's own vast mosaic upon it. 'This isn't unworthy of anyone. Are you pleased you came now, Caius Crispus? You didn't want to, I recall.'

And in response to the direct question, Crispin nodded his head, admitting it for the first time. 'I didn't want to, but this dome is a life's gift for such as I.'

She nodded. Her mood had changed, swiftly. 'Good. We also are pleased you are here. We have few we may trust in this city. Are you one such?'

She had been direct the first time, too. Crispin cleared his throat. She was so alone in Sarantium. The court would use her as a tool, and hard men back home would want her dead. He said, 'In whatever ways I may help you, my lady, I shall.'

'Good,' she repeated. He saw her colour had heightened. Her eyes were bright. 'I wonder. How shall we do this? Shall I order you to come now and kiss me, so that those below can see?'

Crispin blinked, swallowed, ran a hand reflexively through his hair.

'You do not improve your appearance when you do that, you know,' the queen said. 'Think, artisan. There has to be a reason for my coming up here to you. Will it help you with the women of this city to be known as a queen's lover, or will it mark you as . . . untouchable?' And she smiled.

'I . . . I don't have . . . My lady, I . . . '.

'You don't want to kiss me?' she asked. A mood so bright it was a danger in itself. She stood very still, waiting for him.

He was entirely unnerved. He took a deep breath, then a step forward.

And she laughed. 'On further thought, it isn't necessary, is it? My hand will do, artisan. You may kiss my hand.'

She lifted it to him. He took it in his own and raised it to his lips, and just as he did so she turned her hand in his and it was her palm, soft and warm, that he kissed.

'I wonder,' said the queen of the Antae, 'if anyone could see me do that.' And she smiled again.

Crispin was breathing hard. He straightened. She remained very near and, bringing up both her hands, she smoothed his disordered hair.

'We will leave you,' she said, astonishingly composed, the too-bright manner gone as swiftly as it had come, though her colour remained high. 'You may call upon us now, of course. Everyone will assume they know why. As it happens, we wish to go to the theatre.'

'Majesty,' Crispin said, struggling to regain a measure of calm. 'You are the queen of the Antae, of Batiara, an honoured guest of the Emperor . . . an artisan cannot *possibly* escort you to the theatre. You will have to sit in the Imperial Box. Must be seen there. There are protocols . . .'

She frowned, as if struck only now by the thought. 'Do you know, I believe you are correct. I shall have to send a note to the Chancellor then. But in that case, I may have come up here to no purpose, Caius Crispus.' She looked up at him. 'You must take care to provide us with a reason.' And she turned away.

He was so deeply shaken that she was five rungs down the ladder before he even moved, offering her no assistance at all.

It didn't matter. She went down to the marble floor as easily as she'd come up. It occurred to him, watching her descend towards a score of unabashedly curious people staring up, that if he was marked now as her lover, or even her confidant, then his mother and his friends might be endangered back home when word of this went west. Gisel had escaped a determined assassination attempt. There were men who wanted her throne, which meant ensuring she did not take it back. Those linked to her in any way would be suspect. Of what, it hardly mattered.

The Antae were not fastidious about such things.

And that truth, Crispin decided, staring down, applied as much to the woman nearing the ground now. She might be young, and terribly vulnerable here, but she'd survived a year on her throne among men who wished her dead or subjected to their will, and had managed to elude them when they did try to kill her. And she was her father's daughter. Gisel of the Antae would do whatever she had to do, he thought, to achieve her purposes, until and unless someone did end her life. Consequences for others wouldn't even cross her mind.

He thought of the Emperor Valerius, moving mortal lives this way and that like pieces on a gameboard. Did power shape this way of thinking, or was it only those who already thought this way who could achieve earthly power?

It came to Crispin, watching the queen reach the marble floor to accept bows and her cloak, that he'd been offered intimacy by three women in this city, and each occasion had been an act of contrivance and dissembling. Not one of them had touched him with any tenderness or care, or even a true desire.

Or, perhaps, that last wasn't entirely so. When he returned home later in the day to the house the Chancellor's people had by now arranged for him, Crispin found a note waiting. Tidings took little time to travel in this city—or certain kinds of tidings did. The note, when unfolded, was not signed, and he'd never seen the round, smooth handwriting before, but the paper was astonishingly fine, luxurious. Reading the words, he realized no signature was needed, or possible.

You told me, Styliane Daleina had written, *that you were a stranger to the private rooms of royalty.*

Nothing more. No added reproach, no direct suggestion that he'd deceived her, no irony or provocation. The stated fact. And the fact that she'd stated it.

Crispin, who'd intended to have a midday meal at home and then return to the Sanctuary, had taken himself off instead to his preferred tavern and then to the baths. In each of these places he'd had more wine than was really good for him.

His friend Carullus, tribune of the Fourth Sauradian, had found him later in the evening, back at The Spina. The burly soldier had seated himself opposite Crispin, signalled for a cup of wine for himself and grinned. Crispin had refused to smile back.

'Two pieces of news, my inexplicably drunken friend,' Carullus had said breezily. He held up a finger. 'One, I have met with the Supreme Strategos. I have met with him, and Leontes has promised half the arrears for the western army will be sent before midwinter and the rest by spring. A personal promise. Crispin, I've done it!'

Crispin looked at him, trying to share in his friend's delight and failing utterly. This *was* hugely important news, though—everyone knew about the army unrest and the arrears of pay. It was the reason Carullus had come to the City, if one excepted a desire to see chariots in the Hippodrome.

'No, you haven't done it,' he said morosely. 'It just means there's a war coming. Valerius is sending Leontes to Batiara, after all. You don't invade with unpaid troops.'

Carullus only smiled. 'I know that, you sodden dolt. But who gets the *credit*, man? Who writes his governor in the morning that he has succeeded in getting the payment released when everyone else has failed?'

Crispin nodded and reached for his wine again. 'Pleased for you,' he said. 'Truly. Forgive, if I'm not as pleased to hear that my friends and my mother are now to be invaded.'

Carullus shrugged. 'Warn them. Tell them to leave Varena.'

'Get fucked,' Crispin had said, uncharitably. Whatever was happening was *not* Carullus's fault, and his advice might be good—even more so in the light of what had happened that morning on the scaffolding.

'That activity on your mind? I heard about your visitor this morning. Do you keep pillows up on that scaffold of yours? I'll let you sober up but I'll expect a *very* detailed explanation in the morning, my friend.' Carullus licked his lips.

Crispin swore again. 'It was play-acting. Theatre. She wanted to talk to me and needed to give people something to think.'

'I'm sure,' said Carullus, his eyebrows arched high. '*Talk* to you? You rogue. They say she's magnificent, you know. Talk? Hah. Maybe you'll make me believe that in the morning. In, ah, the meantime,' he added after an unexpected pause, 'that, er, reminds me of my second bit of news. I suppose I'm, ah, out of that sort of game now, myself. Actually.'

Crispin had looked muzzily up from his wine cup. 'What?'

'I'm, well, as it happens, I'm getting married,' Carullus of the Fourth said.

'*What?*' Crispin repeated, cogently.

'I know, I know,' the tribune went on, 'Unexpected, surprising, amusing, all that. A good laugh for all. Happens, though, doesn't it?' His colour heightened. 'Ah, well, it *does*, you know.'

Crispin nodded his head in bemusement, refraining only with some effort from saying, 'What?' for a third time.

'And, um, well, do you, er, mind if Kasia leaves your house now? It won't look right, of course, not after we have it proclaimed in chapel.'

'What?' Crispin said, helplessly.

'Wedding'll be in the spring,' Carullus went on, eyes bright. 'I promised my mother back when I first left home that if I ever married I'd do it properly. There'll be a season's worth of proclaiming by the clerics, so someone can object if they want to, and then a real wedding celebration.'

'Kasia?' Crispin said, finally getting a word in. '*Kasia?*'

And as his brain belatedly began to function, to put itself tentatively around this astonishing information, Crispin shook his head again, as if to clear it, and said, 'Let me be certain I understand this, you bloated bag of wind. Kasia has agreed to marry you? I don't believe it! By Jad's bones and balls! You bastard! You didn't ask my permission and you don't fucking *deserve* her, you military lout.'

He was grinning widely by then, and he reached a hand across the table and gripped the other man's shoulder hard.

'Of *course* I deserve her,' Carullus said. 'I'm a man with a brilliant future.' But he, too, had been smiling, with unconcealed pleasure.

The woman in question was of the northern Inicii, sold by her mother into slavery a little more than a year before, rescued from that—and a pagan death—by Crispin on the road. She was too thin and too intelligent, and too strong-willed, though uneasy in the City. On the occasion of their first encounter she had spat in the face of the soldier who was now grinning with delight as he announced that she'd agreed to marry him.

Both men, in fact, knew what she was worth.

And so, on a bright, windy day at the beginning of spring, a number of people were preparing themselves to proceed to the home of the principal female dancer of the Green faction where a wedding was to commence with the usual procession to the chosen chapel and then be celebrated with festivity afterwards.

Neither bride nor groom was in any way from a good family—though the soldier showed signs of possibly becoming an important person—but Shirin of the Greens had a glittering circle of acquaintances and admirers and had chosen to make this wedding the excuse for an elaborate affair. She'd had a very good winter season in the theatre.

In addition, the groom's close friend (and evidently the bride's, it was whispered by some, with a meaningful arch of eyebrows) was the new Imperial Mosaicist, the Rhodian who was executing the elaborate decorations in the Sanctuary of Jad's Holy Wisdom—a fellow perhaps worthy of cultivation. There were rumours that other significant personages might attend—if not the actual ceremony, then the celebration in Shirin's home afterwards.

It had also been widely reported that the food was being prepared in the dancer's kitchen by the Master Chef of the Blue faction. There were those in the City who would follow Strumosus into the desert if he took his pots and pans and sauces.

It was a curious, in many ways a unique event, this celebration orchestrated by Greens and Blues together. And all for a middle-ranking soldier and a yellow-haired barbarian girl from Sauradia just arrived in the city with a completely unknown background. She was pretty enough, it was reported by those who'd seen her with Shirin, but not in the usual way of those girls who made a surprising marriage for themselves. On the other hand, it wasn't as if she was wedding a *really* significant fellow, was it?

Then another rumour started that Pappio, the increasingly well-known Director of the Imperial Glassworks, had personally made a bowl commissioned as a gift for the happy couple. It seemed he hadn't done any actual crafts-manship himself for years and years. No one could under-stand that, either. Sarantium was talking. With the chariot races not beginning again for some few days, the event was well timed: the City liked having things to talk about.

'I'm not happy,' said a small, nondescript artificial bird in an inward, patrician voice heard only by the hostess of the day's affair. The woman was staring critically at her own image in a round, silver-edged mirror held up by a servant.

'Oh, *Danis, neither am I!'* Shirin murmured in silent reply. *'Every woman from the Precinct and the theatre will be dressed and adorned to dazzle and I look like I haven't slept in days.'*

'That isn't what I meant.'

'Of course it isn't. You never think of the important things. Tell me, do you think he'll notice me?'

The bird's tone became waspish. *'Which one? The chariot-racer or the mosaicist?'*

Shirin laughed aloud, startling her attendant. *'Either of them,'* she said inwardly. Then her smile became wicked. *'Or perhaps both, tonight? Wouldn't that be something to remember?'*

'Shirin!' The bird sounded genuinely shocked.

'I'm teasing, silly. You know me better than that. Now tell me, why aren't you happy? This is a wedding day, and it's a love match. No one made this union, they chose each other.' Her tone was surprisingly kind now, tolerant.

'I just think something's going to happen.'

The dark-haired woman in front of the small mirror, who did not, in fact, look at all as if she needed sleep or anything else beyond extremes of admiration, nodded her head, and the servant, smiling, set down the mirror and reached for a bottle that contained a perfume of very particular distinctiveness. The bird lay on the tabletop nearby.

'*Danis, really, what sort of party would this be if something didn't happen?*'

The bird said nothing.

There was a sound at the doorway. Shirin turned to look over her shoulder.

A small, rotund, fierce-looking man stood there, clad in a blue tunic and a very large bib-like covering tied at his neck and around his considerable girth. There were a variety of foodstains on the bib and a streak of what was probably saffron on his forehead. He possessed a wooden spoon, a heavy knife stuck into the tied belt of the bib, and an aggrieved expression.

'Strumosus!' said the dancer happily.

'There is no sea salt,' said the chef in a voice that suggested the absence amounted to a heresy equivalent to banned Heladikian beliefs or arrant paganism.

'No salt? Really?' said the dancer, rising gracefully from her seat.

'No *sea* salt!' the chef repeated. 'How can a civilized household lack sea salt?'

'A *dreadful* omission,' Shirin agreed with a placating gesture. 'I feel simply terrible.'

'I request permission to make use of your servants and send one back to the Blues compound immediately. I need my undercooks to remain here. Are you aware of how little time we have?'

'You may use my servants in any way you see fit today,' Shirin said, 'short of broiling them.'

The chef's expression conveyed the suggestion that matters might come to that pass.

'This is a completely odious man,' the bird said silently. 'At least I might assume you don't desire this one.'

Shirin gave a silent laugh. 'He is a genius, Danis. Everyone says so. Genius needs to be indulged. Now, be happy and tell me I look beautiful.'

There was another sound in the hallway beyond Strumosus. The chef turned, and then lowered his wooden spoon. His expression changed, grew very nearly benign. One might even have exaggerated slightly and said that he smiled. He stepped farther into the room and out of the way as a pale, fair-haired woman appeared hesitantly in the doorway.

Shirin did smile, and laid a hand to her cheek. 'Oh, Kasia,' she said. 'You look beautiful.'

CHAPTER III

 Earlier that same morning, very early in fact, the Emperor Valerius II of Sarantium, nephew to an Emperor, son of a grain farmer from Trakesia, could have been seen intoning the last of the antiphonal responses to the sunrise invocation in the Imperial Chapel of the Traversite Palace where he and the Empress had their private rooms.

The Emperor's service is one of the first in the City, beginning in darkness, ending with the rising of the reborn sun at dawn when the chapel and sanctuary bells elsewhere in Sarantium are just beginning to toll. The Empress is not with him at this hour. The Empress is asleep. The Empress has her own cleric attached to her own suite of rooms, a man known for a relaxed attitude to the hour of morning prayer and equally lenient, if less well-publicized, views regarding the heresies of Heladikos, the mortal (or half-mortal, or divine) son of Jad. These things are not spoken of in the Imperial Precinct, of course. Or, they are not spoken of freely.

The Emperor is, as it happens, meticulous in his

observations of the rituals of faith. His long engagement with both the High and the Eastern Patriarchs in an attempt to resolve the myriad sources of schism in the doctrines of the sun god is as much begotten by piety as it is by intellectual engagement. Valerius is a man of contradictions and enigmas, and he does little to resolve or clarify any of these for his court or his people, finding mystery an asset.

It amuses him that he is called by some the Night's Emperor and said to hold converse with forbidden spirits of the half-world in the lamplit chambers and moonlit corridors of the palaces. It amuses him because this is entirely untrue and because he is here—as at every dawn—awake before most of his people, performing the rituals of sanctioned faith. He is, in truth, the Morning's Emperor as much as he is anything else.

Sleep bores him, frightens him a little of late, fills him with a sense—in dream or near to dream—of a headlong rushing of time. He is not an old man by any means, but he is sufficiently advanced in years to hear horses and chariots in the night: the distant harbingers of an end to mortal tenure. There is much he wishes to do before he hears—as all true and holy Emperors are said to hear—the voice of the god, or the god's emissary, saying, *Uncrown, the Lord of Emperors awaits you now.*

His Empress, he knows, would speak of dolphins tearing the sea's surface, not onrushing horses in the dark, but only to him, since dolphins—the ancient bearers of souls—are a banned Heladikian symbol.

His Empress is asleep. Will rise some time after the sun, take a first meal abed, receive her holy adviser and then her bath attendants and her secretary, prepare herself at leisure for the day. She was an actress in her youth, a dancer named Aliana, tuned to the rhythms of late nights and late risings.

He shares the late nights with her, but knows better, after their years together, than to intrude upon her at this hour. He has much to do, in any case.

The service ends. He speaks the last of the responses. Some light is leaking through the high windows. A chilly morning outside, at this grey hour. He dislikes the cold, of late. Valerius leaves the chapel, bowing to the disk and altar, lifting a brief hand to his cleric. In the hallway he takes a stairway down, walking quickly, as he tends to. His secretaries hurry another way, going outdoors, taking the paths across the gardens—cold and damp, he knows—to the Attenine Palace, where the day's business will begin. Only the Emperor and his appointed guards among the Excubitors are allowed to use the tunnel constructed between the two palaces, a security measure introduced a long time ago.

There are torches at intervals in the tunnel, lit and supervised by the guards. It is well ventilated, comfortably warm even in winter or, as now, on the cusp of spring. Quickening season, season of war. Valerius nods to the two guards and passes through the doorway alone. He enjoys this short walk, in fact. He is a man in a life that allows of no privacy at all. Even in his sleeping chamber there is always a secretary on a cot and a drowsy messenger by the door, waiting for the possibility of dictation or a summons or instructions to be run through the mysteries and spirits of a dark city.

And many nights, still, he spends with Alixana in her own intricate tangle of chambers. Comfort and intimacy there, and something else deeper and rarer than either—but he is not alone. He is never alone. Privacy, silence, solitude are limited to this tunnel walk underground, ushered into the corridor by one set of guards, received at the other end by another pair of the Excubitors.

When he raps and the doorway is opened at the Attenine Palace end, a number of men are waiting, as they always are. They include the aged Chancellor Gesius; Leontes, the golden Strategos; Faustinus, Master of Offices; and the Quaestor of Imperial Revenue, a man named Vertigus, with whom the Emperor cannot say he is well pleased. Valerius nods to them all and ascends the stairs quickly as they rise from obeisance and fall into place behind him. Gesius needs assistance now, at times, especially when the weather is damp, but there has been no sign of any similar impairment of the Chancellor's thinking, and Valerius will trust no one in his retinue half so much.

It is Vertigus he briskly quizzes and unsettles this morning when they come to the Audience Chamber. The man is hardly a fool—he'd have been dismissed long ago if he were—but he cannot be called ingenious, and almost everything the Emperor wishes to achieve, in the City, the Empire, and beyond, turns upon finances. Competence is not, unfortunately, sufficient these days. Valerius is paying a great deal for buildings, a very great deal to the Bassanids, and he has just yielded (as planned) to entreaties from several sources and released the final arrears of last year's payment for the western army.

There is never enough money, and the last time measures were enacted to try to generate a sufficiency Sarantium burned in a riot that almost cost him his throne and his life and every plan he'd ever shaped. It had required some thirty thousand deaths to avoid those consequences. Valerius is of the hope that his unprecedented, almost-completed Great Sanctuary of Jad's Holy Wisdom will serve as his expiation before the god for those deaths—and certain other things—when the day for such a reckoning comes, as it always does. Given this, the Sanctuary serves more than one purpose in his designs.

Most things do.

※

It was difficult. She was aware that Carullus loved her and that an astonishing number of people were treating their wedding as an occasion for celebration, as if the marriage of an Inici girl and a Trakesian soldier were an event of significance. She was being wed at an exquisite, patrician chapel near Shirin's house—the Master of the Senate and his family were among the regular attendees there. The banquet would take place back here in the home of the Greens' Principal Dancer. And the round, fierce man acclaimed by everyone as the finest chef in all the Empire was preparing Kasia's wedding feast.

It was hard to believe. Mostly, she *didn't* believe it, moving through events as in a dream, as though expecting to wake up in Morax's inn in a chill fog with the Day of the Dead still to come.

Kasia, who had been seen as the clever one by her mother, and unmarriageable, the daughter sold to the slavers, was aware that all of this extravagance had to do with the people they knew: Crispin and his friends Scortius the chariot-racer and Shirin, into whose house Kasia had moved when the betrothal was announced early in the winter. Carullus had actually met—twice now—with the Supreme Strategos himself and had achieved a success regarding the arrears of soldiers' pay. There was a rumour that Leontes might even make an appearance at the tribune's wedding party. At *her* wedding party.

The other part of this exaggerated attention had to do, she'd come to understand, with the fact that for all their vaunted cynicism (or perhaps because of it) the Sarantines were almost unfailingly intense and emotional by nature, as if living here at the centre of the world heightened and added significance to every event. The notion that she and Carullus were marrying for love, having chosen each other freely, held extravagant appeal for those surrounding them. Shirin, witty and ironic as she was, could go misty-eyed at the very thought.

Such marriages tended not to happen.

And it wasn't happening here, whatever people were thinking, though Kasia was the only one who knew that. She hoped.

The man she desired—and loved, though something in her fought the word—was the one who would stand with them today in the chapel holding a symbolic crown over his friend's head. It wasn't a truth she liked, but it didn't seem to be something she could *do* anything about.

Shirin would stand behind Kasia with another crown, and an elegant gathering of white-clad people from theatre and court and a number of rather more bluff military men would smile and murmur in approval and then they would all come back here to eat and drink: fish and oysters and winter game and wine from Candaria and Megarium.

What woman, really, married purely by choice? What sort of world would it be if that could happen? Not even aristocrats or royalty had such a luxury, so how could it descend to a barbarian girl who had been a slave in Sauradia for a bitter year that would linger in the soul for who knew how long?

She was marrying because a decent man wanted her and had asked. Because he offered the promise of shelter and support and some real kindness was in his nature, and because, failing this union, what life was there for her? Dependent on others all her days? Servant to a dancer until the dancer made her own prudent choice of husband? Joining one of the sects—the Daughters of Jad—who took eternal vows to a god in which Kasia didn't really believe?

How could she believe, having been offered as a sacrifice to Ludan, having seen a *zubir*, creature of her tribe's long faith, in the depths of the Aldwood?

'You look beautiful,' Shirin said, turning from a conversation with the chef to look at Kasia in the doorway.

Kasia smiled warily. She didn't really believe it, but it might even be true. Shirin's house was efficiently run by her servants; Kasia had been living with her through the winter more as a guest and friend than anything else and she'd eaten better food and slept in a softer bed than ever in her life. Shirin was quick, amusing, observant, always planning something, very much aware of her position in Sarantium: both the implications of renown and the transitory nature of it.

She was also more than any of these things, because none of them spoke to what she was on the stage.

Kasia had seen her dance. After that first visit to the theatre, early in the winter season, she had understood the other woman's fame. Seeing the masses of flowers thrown down onto the stage after a dance, hearing the wild, shouted acclamations—both the ritual ones of Shirin's Green faction and the spontaneous cries of those who were simply enraptured with what they'd seen—she had felt awed by Shirin, a little frightened by the change that took place when the dancer entered this world, and even more by what happened when she stepped between the torches and the music began for her.

She could never have exposed herself willingly the way Shirin did each time she performed, clad in streaming silks that hid next to nothing of her lithe form, doing comical, almost obscene things for the raucous delight of those in the less expensive, distant seats. But nor could she ever in her life have moved the way the Greens' dancer did, as Shirin leaped and spun, or paused with arms extended like a sea-bird, and then gravely stepped forward, bare feet arched like a hunter's bow, in the older, more formal dances that made men weep. Those same silks could lift like wings behind her or be gathered into a shawl when she knelt to mourn a loss, or into a shroud when she died and the theatre grew silent as a graveyard in a winter dark.

Shirin changed when she danced, and changed those who saw her.

Then she changed back, at home. There she liked to talk about Crispin. She had accepted Kasia as a houseguest as a favour to the Rhodian. He knew her father, she'd told Kasia. But there was more to it than that. It was obvious that he was often on the dancer's mind, even with all the men—young and less young, many of them married, from court and aristocratic houses and military officers' quarters—who regularly attended upon her. After those visits Shirin would talk to Kasia, revealing detailed knowledge of their positions and ranks and prospects: her finely nuanced social favours were part of the delicate dance she had to perform in this life of a dancer in Sarantium. Kasia had the sense that however their relationship had begun, Shirin was genuinely pleased to have her in the house, that friendship and trust had not before been elements in the dancer's life. Not that they ever had been in her own, if it came to that.

During the winter Carullus had come by almost every day when he was in the City. He'd been absent a month amid the rains, leaving to escort—triumphantly—the first shipment of the western army's arrears to his camp in Sauradia. He was thoughtful when he came back, told Kasia there seemed to be very strong indicators that a war was coming in the west. It was not precisely surprising, but there was a difference between rumours and onrushing reality. It had occurred to her, listening, that if he were to go there with Leontes he could die. She'd taken his hand as he talked. He liked it when she held his hand.

They'd seen little enough of Crispin during the winter. He had apparently chosen his team of mosaicists as quickly as possible and was up on his scaffolding all the time, working as soon as the morning prayers were done and into the night, by torchlight aloft. He slept on a cot in the Sanctuary some nights, Vargos reported, not even returning to the home the Chancellor's eunuchs had found and furnished for him.

Vargos was working in the Sanctuary as well, and was their source for the best stories, including the one about an apprentice chased by Crispin—the Rhodian roaring imprecations and waving a knife—all around the Sanctuary of Jad's Holy Wisdom, for having let something called the quicklime be spoiled one morning. Vargos had started to explain about the quicklime, but Shirin had pretended to scream with boredom and had thrown olives at him until he'd stopped.

Vargos came by regularly to take Kasia to chapel in the morning if she'd go with him. Often she did. She was working to accustom herself to the noise and crowds, and these morning walks with Vargos were a part of that. He was another kind man, Vargos. She'd met three of them in Sauradia, it seemed, and one of them had offered marriage to her. She didn't deserve such fortune.

Sometimes Shirin came with them. It was useful to make an appearance, she explained to Kasia. The clerics of Jad disapproved of the theatre even more than they disliked the chariots and the violent passions and pagan magic they inspired. It was prudent for Shirin to be seen kneeling in sober garb, without evident adornment, her hair pinned back and covered, as she chanted the morning responses before the sun disk and the altar.

Sometimes Shirin would take them to a rather more elegant chapel than Vargos's, nearer to the house. After services there one morning, she had submissively accepted the blessing of the cleric and introduced Kasia to two of the other people attending—who happened to be the Master of the Senate and his much younger wife. The Senator, Plautus Bonosus by name, was a wry-looking, slightly dissipated man; the wife seemed reserved and watchful. Shirin had invited them to the wedding ceremony and the celebration after. She'd mentioned some of the other guests attending and then added, casually, that Strumosus of Amoria was preparing the feast.

The Master of the Senate had blinked at this, and then quickly accepted the invitation. He looked like a man who enjoyed his luxuries. Later that morning, over spiced wine at home, Shirin had told Kasia some of the scandals associated with Bonosus. They did offer some explanation, Kasia had thought, for the young, second wife's very cool, self-contained manner. She had realized that it was something of a coup for Shirin to have so many distinguished people coming to a dancer's home, a defining and asserting of her preeminence. It was good for Carullus too, of course—and so for Kasia. She'd understood all of this. There had still been an aura of unreality to what was happening.

She had just been saluted by the Master of the Sarantine Senate in a chapel filled with aristocrats. He was coming to her wedding ceremony. She had been a slave when autumn began, thrown down on a mattress by farmers and soldiers and couriers with a few coins to spend.

The wedding morning was well advanced. They would be going to the chapel soon. The musicians would be their signal, Carullus arriving with them to escort his bride. Kasia, standing for inspection before a dancer and a chef on her marriage day, wore white—as all the wedding party and guests would—but with a bride's red silk about her waist. Shirin had given that to her last night, showed her how to knot it. Had made a sly joke, doing so. There would be more jests and bawdy songs later, Kasia knew. That much was exactly the same here in the City of Cities as it was at home in her village. Some things didn't change no matter where you went in the world, it seemed. The red was for her maidenhead, to be lost tonight.

It had been lost, in fact, to a Karchite slaver in a northern field some time ago. Nor was the man she was to wed today a stranger to her body, though that had happened only once, the morning after Carullus had almost died defending Crispin and Scortius the charioteer from assassins in the dark.

Life did strange things to you, didn't it?

She had been going to Crispin's room that morning, unsure of what she wanted to say—or do—but had heard a woman's voice within, and paused and turned away without knocking. And had learned on the stairway from two of the soldiers about the attack in the night just ended, their comrades dead, Carullus wounded. Impulse, concern, extreme confusion, destiny—her mother would have said the last, and shaped a warding sign—had made Kasia turn after the soldiers had gone and walk back down the long upstairs hallway to knock on the tribune's door.

Carullus had opened, visibly weary, half-undressed already. She had seen the bloodstained bandage wrapped around one shoulder and across his chest, and then she'd seen and suddenly understood—she *was* the clever one, wasn't she?—the look in his eyes as he saw that it was she.

He wasn't the man who had saved her from Morax's inn and then from death in the forest, who had offered her a glimpse one dark night of what men might be like when they hadn't bought you, but he could be—she had thought, lying beside Carullus, after, in his bed—the one who saved her from the life that *followed* being saved. The old stories never talked about that part, did they?

She'd thought, as she watched the sun rise higher that morning, and heard his breathing settle as he fell into needed sleep beside her like a child, that she might become his mistress. There were worse things in the world.

But only a little while after, even before winter began, with the midnight Ceremony of Unconquered Jad, he'd asked her to marry him.

When she'd accepted, smiling through tears he could not have properly understood, Carullus had vowed with an uplifted hand, swearing by the sexual organs of the god, that he wouldn't touch her again until their wedding night.

A promise he'd made long ago, he explained. He'd told her (more than once) about his mother and father, his childhood in Trakesia in a place not so different from her own village; he'd told of Karchite raids, his older brother's death, his own journey south to join the army of the Emperor. He talked, Carullus, quite a lot, but amusingly, and she knew now that the unexpected kindness she'd sensed in this burly, profane soldier was real. Kasia thought of her own mother, how she'd have wept to learn that her child was alive and entering into a protected life so unimaginably far away, in every respect, from their village and farm.

There was no way to send a message. The Imperial Post of Valerius II did not include farms near Karch on its customary routes. For all her mother knew, Kasia was dead by now.

For all Kasia knew, her mother and sister were.

Her new life was here, or wherever Carullus, as a tribune of the Fourth Sauradian, was posted, and Kasia—in white, with a bride's crimson girdling her waist on her wedding day—knew that she owed lifelong thanks to all the gods she could ever name for this.

'Thank you,' she said to Shirin, who had just told her she looked beautiful, and was still gazing at her and smiling. The chef, an intense little man, seemed to be trying *not* to smile. His mouth kept twitching up-wards. He had sauce on his forehead. On impulse, Kasia used her fingers to wipe it away. He did smile then and extended his apron. She dried her fingers on it. She wondered if Crispin would be with Carullus when her husband-to-be came to bring her to the chapel, and what he might say, and what she would say, and how strange people were, that even the fairest day should not be without its sorrow.

Rustem hadn't been paying attention to where they were going, or who was around them, and he would blame himself for that later, even though it hadn't been his responsibility to look to their safety. That was why Nishik, querulous and dour, had been assigned to a travelling physician, after all.

But as they'd crossed the choppy strait from straggling Deapolis on the southeastern coast towards the huge, roiling port of Sarantium on the other side, negotiating past a small, densely wooded island and then bobbing ships and the trailing nets of fishing boats, with the City's domes and towers piled up and up behind and hearth-smoke rising from innumerable houses and inns and shops all the way to the walls beyond, Rustem had found himself more overwhelmed than he'd expected to be, and then distracted by thoughts of his family.

He was a traveller, had been farther east, for example, than anyone he knew, but Sarantium, even after two devastating plagues, was the largest, wealthiest city in the world: a truth known but never fully apprehended before this day. Jarita would have been thrilled and perhaps even aroused, he mused, standing on the ferry, watching the golden domes come nearer. If his newfound understanding of her was correct, Katyun would have been terrified.

He had shown his papers and Nishik's false ones and dealt with the Imperial Customs Office on the wharf in Deapolis before boarding. Getting to the wharf had been a process in itself: there were an extraordinary number of soldiers quartered there and the sounds of ship construction were everywhere. They couldn't have hidden anything if they'd wanted to.

The customs transaction had been costly but not unpleasant: it was a time of peace, and Sarantium's wealth was largely derived from trade and travel. The customs agents of the Emperor knew that perfectly well. A discreet, reasonable sum to assuage the rigours of their painstaking labour was all that proved necessary to expedite the entry of a Bassanid physician and his manservant and mule—which had proved on examination not to be carrying silk or spice or any other tariffed or illicit goods.

As they disembarked in Valerius's city, Rustem took care to ensure that no birds were aloft on his left side and to set his right foot down first on the dock, just as he had boarded the ferry with his left boot first. It was noisy here, too. More soldiers, more ships and hammering and shouts. They asked directions of the ferryman and made their way along a wooden quay, Nishik leading the mule, both men wrapped in cloaks against a sharp spring breeze. They crossed a broad street, waiting for carts to rumble past, and came into a narrower lane, passing an unsavoury assortment of the usual waterfront sailors and whores and beggars and soldiers on leave.

Rustem had been vaguely aware of all this as they went, and of how ports seemed to be the same from here to Ispahani, but he had mostly been thinking about his son as they'd moved away from the docks, leaving the noises behind them. Shaski would have been wide-eyed and open-mouthed, taking all this in the way parched ground absorbs rain. The boy had that sort of quality, he decided—he'd been thinking of him more than a man ought to dwell on his small child at home—an ability to *take things in* and then try to make them his own, to know when and how to use them.

How else explain the uncanny moment when a seven-year-old boy had come after his father into a garden carrying the implement that ended up saving the life of the King of Kings? And making the fortune of their family? Rustem shook his head, remembering it on a morning in Sarantium, walking with his soldier-servant towards the forum they'd been directed to and the inn beside it where they would stay if there were rooms to be had.

He was under instructions not to establish any direct link with the Bassanid envoy here, only the expected, routine note sent to report his arrival. Rustem was a physician searching for medical treatises and knowledge. That was all. He would seek out other physicians—he'd been given names in Sarnica and had set out with some of his own. He would make his contacts, attend lectures, give some perhaps. Buy manuscripts or pay scribes to copy them. Stay until summer. Observe what he could.

Observe *all* he could, in fact, and not just about the healing profession and its treatises. There were things they wished to know, in Kabadh.

Rustem of Kerakek was a man who ought not to attract any attention at all in a time of harmony between the Emperor and the King of Kings (a peace bought expensively by Valerius) with only the occasional border or trade incident to mar a smooth surface.

That *ought* to have been so, at any rate.

The outrageously clothed and barbered young man who wove his way unsteadily towards Rustem from a tavern doorway as he and Nishik ascended a steep, unfortunately quiet laneway, heading for the Mezaros Forum, seemed oblivious to such carefully thought out considerations.

This seemed equally true of the three friends similarly dressed and adorned who followed behind him. All four were dressed in Bassanid-style robes for some reason, but with crudely designed golden jewellery in their ears and about their necks and with their hair worn untidily long down their backs.

Rustem stopped, having little option. The four youths barred their way and the laneway was narrow. The leader swayed a little to one side then straightened himself with an effort. 'Green or Blue?' he rasped, wine fumes on his breath. 'Answer or be beaten like a dry whore!'

This question had something to do with horses. Rustem knew that much, but had no idea what answer would be best. 'I beg your indulgence,' he murmured in what he knew by now to be perfectly adequate Sarantine. 'We are strangers here and don't understand such things. You are blocking our way.'

'We are, aren't we? Fucking observant, you are. Bassanid butt-fucker,' said the young man, switching away from the Blue-or-Green business readily enough. Rustem's origin and Nishik's was obvious from their clothing; they hadn't made any effort to hide it. The vulgarity was disconcerting and the sour smell of wine on the young man's breath so early of a morning sickened Rustem a little. The fellow was doing damage to his health. Not even the rawest recruits off duty in the fortress drank this early.

'Mind your foul tongue!' Nishik exclaimed loudly, playing the loyal servant, but with a little too much edge in his voice. 'This is Rustem of Kerakek, a respected physician. Make way!'

'A doctor? Bassanid? Saves the fucking lives of slime who kill our soldiers? The *fuck* I'll make way, you goat-faced castrate slave!' Saying which, the young man proceeded to alter the nature of an already unfortunate encounter by drawing a short, quite elegant sword.

Rustem, taking a quick breath, noticed that the other youths looked alarmed at this. *Not as drunk*, he thought. *There's a hope here.*

There was, until Nishik snarled an oath of his own and, unwisely, turned to the mule that had stolidly accompanied them all this way, grappling for his own blade strapped to the animal's side. Rustem was sure he knew what was in Nishik's mind: the soldier, outraged by insults and impediment from a civilian, and a Jaddite at that, would be determined to disarm him in a swift lesson. A well-deserved tutoring, undoubtedly. But it was *not* the way to enter Sarantium quietly.

Nor, in fact, was it wise for other reasons entirely. The man with the already-drawn sword happened to know how to use it, having had instruction in the blade from a very early age at his father's city home and country estate. He was also, as Rustem had already noted, well past the point of prudently evaluating his own conduct or that of others.

The young man with the stylish blade took a single step forward and stabbed Nishik between the third and fourth ribs as the Bassanid soldier was pulling his own weapon free of the ropes about the mule.

A chance encounter, purest accident, a wrong laneway taken at a wrong moment in a city full of lanes and streets and paths. Had they missed the ferry, been detained by customs, stopped to eat, taken another route, things would have been entirely otherwise at this moment. But the world—guarded by Perun and Anahita and menaced always by Black Azal—had somehow reached this point: Nishik was down, his blood was red on the street, and a drawn sword was pointed unsteadily at Rustem. He tried to think back to which omen he'd missed that all should have gone this terribly awry.

But even as he pondered this, struggling to deal with the sudden randomness of death, Rustem felt a rare, cold fury rising, and he lifted his walking staff. As the young swordsman looked down in either drunken confusion or satisfaction at the fallen man, Rustem dealt him a quick, sharp, punishing blow across the forearm with the staff. He listened for the sound of a bone cracking and was actually distressed not to hear it, though the vicious youngster let out a scream and his sword fell clattering.

All three of the others, unfortunately, promptly drew their own blades. There was a disconcerting absence of people in the morning lane.

'Help!' Rustem shouted, not optimistically, 'Assassins!' He looked quickly down. Nishik had not moved. Things had gone appallingly wrong here, a catastrophe swirling up out of nothing at all. Rustem's heart was pounding.

He looked back up, holding his staff before him. The man he'd injured and disarmed was clutching at his elbow, screaming at his friends, his face distorted by pain and a childish outrage. The friends moved forward. Two daggers had been drawn, one short sword. Rustem understood that he had to flee. Men could die in the city streets like this, without purpose or meaning. He turned to run—and caught a flashing blur of movement from the corner of his eye.

He spun back swiftly, raising his staff again. But he wasn't the target of the figure he'd glimpsed.

A man had burst out from a tiny, flat-roofed chapel up the lane and, without breaking stride, now barrelled from behind into three armed men, wielding only a traveller's staff almost identical to Rustem's own. He used it briskly, clubbing the sword-wielder hard across the back of the knees. As the man cried out and pitched forward, the new figure stopped, wheeled, and whipped his staff back the other way, clipping a second assailant across the head. The young man let out an aggrieved sound—more a boy's cry than anything else—and fell, dropping his knife, clutching at his scalp with both hands. Rustem saw blood welling between his fingers.

The third one—the only one left armed now—looked at this compact, bristling new arrival, then over at Rustem, and finally down to where Nishik lay motionless on the street. 'Holy fucking Jad!' he said, and bolted past Rustem, tearing wildly around the corner and out of sight.

'You'd be advised to do the same,' Rustem said to the pair felled by the man who'd intervened. 'But not you!' He pointed a shaking finger at the one who had stabbed Nishik. 'You stay where you are. If my man is dead I want you brought before the law for murder.'

'Fuck that, pig,' said the youth, still clutching at his elbow. 'Get my sword, Tykos. Let's go.'

The one called Tykos made as if to claim the blade but the man who'd saved Rustem stepped forward quickly and stamped a booted foot down upon it. Tykos looked sidelong at him, frozen in the act of bending, then straightened and sidled away. The leader snarled another foul-mouthed oath and the three youths followed their vanished friend swiftly down the lane.

Rustem let them go. He was too stunned to do anything else. Heard his own heart pounding and fought for control, breathing deeply. But before turning the corner, their assailant stopped and looked back up, pushing his long hair from his eyes, then gesturing obscenely with his good arm. 'Don't think this is over, Bassanid. I'm coming for you!'

Rustem blinked, then snapped, *entirely* uncharacteristically, 'Fuck yourself,' as the young man disappeared.

Rustem stared after him a moment, then knelt quickly, set down his staff, and laid two fingers against Nishik's throat. After a moment he closed his eyes and withdrew his hand.

'Anahita guide him, Perun guard him, Azal never learn his name,' he said softly, in his own tongue. Words he had spoken so often. He had been at war, seen so many people die. This was different. This was a city street in morning light. They had simply been walking. A life was done.

He looked up and around, and realized that there had, in fact, been watchers from the recessed doorways and small windows of the shops and taverns and the apartments stacked above them along the lane.

An amusement, he thought bitterly. It would make a tale.

He heard a sound. The short, stocky young man who'd intervened had reclaimed a pack he must have dropped. Now he was slipping the first assailant's sword into the ropes on the mule, beside Nishik's.

'Distinctive,' he said tersely. 'Look at the hilt. It may identify him.' His accent, speaking Sarantine, was heavy. He was dressed for travel, in a nondescript brown tunic and cloak, belted high, with muddy boots and the heavy pack now on his back.

'He's dead,' Rustem said, unnecessarily. 'They killed him.'

'I see that,' said the other man. 'Come on. They may be back. They're drunken and out of control.'

'I can't leave him in the street,' Rustem protested.

The young man glanced back over his shoulder. 'Over there,' he said, and knelt to slip his hands under Nishik's shoulders. He smeared blood on his tunic, didn't seem to notice. Rustem bent to pick up Nishik by the legs. Together they carried him—no one helping, no one even coming into the lane—up to the small chapel.

When they reached the doorway, a cleric in a stained yellow robe stepped out hastily, his hand outthrust. 'We don't want him!' he exclaimed.

The young man simply ignored him, moving straight past the holy man, who scurried after them, still protesting. They took Nishik into the dim, chill space and set him down near the door. Rustem saw a small sun disk and an altar in the gloom. A waterfront chapel. Whores and sailors meeting each other here, he thought. More a place of venal commerce and shared disease than prayer, most likely.

'What are we supposed to *do* with this?' the cleric protested in an irate whisper, following them in. There were a handful of people inside.

'Pray for his soul,' the young man said. 'Light candles. Someone will come for him.' He glanced meaningfully at Rustem, who reached for his purse and took out a few copper folles.

'For the candles,' he said, extending them to the cleric. 'I'll have someone get him.'

The cleric made the coins disappear—more smoothly than a holy man ought, Rustem thought sourly—and nodded briefly. 'This morning,' he said. 'By midday he's tossed into the street. This is a Bassanid, after all.'

He *had* been listening, earlier. Had done nothing at all. Rustem gave him his coldest look. 'He was a living soul. He is dead. Show respect, for your own office and your god if for nothing else.'

The cleric's mouth fell open. The young man laid a hand on Rustem's arm and drew him outside.

They went back and Rustem took the mule's halter. He saw the blood on the stones where Nishik had lain, and he cleared his throat. 'I owe you a great debt,' he said.

Before the other man could reply, there came a clatter-ing sound. They both spun to look.

Fully a dozen long-haired youths careened around the corner and skidded to a halt.

'There!' cried their first assailant savagely, pointing in triumph.

'*Run!*' snapped the young man at Rustem's side.

Rustem grabbed his own pack from the mule, the one with his papers from home and the manuscripts he'd bought in Sarnica, and he sprinted uphill, leaving behind the mule, his clothing, his staff, two swords, and all shreds of the dignity he'd imagined himself bearing as he entered the city of cities that was Sarantium.

───※───

At this same hour, in the Traversite Palace of the Imper-ial Precinct, the Empress of Sarantium is lying in a scented bath in a warm, tiled room through which wisps of steam are drifting, while her secretary—sitting on a bench, his back carefully turned to the exposed, reclining form of the Empress—reads aloud to her a letter in which the leader of the largest of the dissident tribes in Moskav pro-poses that she induce the Emperor to fund his long-planned revolt.

The letter also, with little subtlety, intimates that the writer is prepared to personally attend to the Empress's physical delight and rapture at some time in the future, should this persuasion of Valerius take place. The document concludes with an expression of well-phrased sympathy that a woman of the Empress's manifest mag-nificence should still be enduring the attentions of an

Emperor so helplessly unable to conduct his own affairs of state.

Alixana stretches her arms out of the water and above her head and allows herself a smile. She looks down at the curves of her own breasts. The fashion in dancers has changed since her day. Many of the girls now are much as the male dancers are: small breasts, straight hips, a boyish look. This would not be a way to describe the woman in her bath. She has seen and lived through more than thirty quite remarkably varied years now and can still stop a conversation or double a heartbeat with her entrance into a room.

She knows this, of course. It is useful, always has been. At the moment, however, she is remembering a girl, about eight years of age, taking her first proper bath. She had been fetched from a laneway south of the Hippodrome where she'd been wrestling and tumbling with three other children in the dust and offal. It had been a Daughter of Jad, she remembers, a square-jawed, stern-faced woman, grey and unsmiling, who had separated the brawling off-spring of the Hippodrome workers and then taken Aliana off with her, leaving the others watching, open-mouthed.

In the forbidding, windowless, stone-walled house where that sect of holy women resided, she had taken the now silent, overawed girl to a small, private room, ordered hot water brought, and towels, and had stripped and then bathed her there in a bronze tub, alone. She had not touched Aliana, or not intimately. She'd washed her filthy hair and scrubbed her grimy fingers and nails, but the woman's expression had not changed as she did so, or when she leaned back after, sitting on a three-legged wooden stool, and simply looked at the girl in the bath for a long time.

Thinking back, the Empress is very much aware of what must have been the underlying complexities of a holy woman's actions that afternoon, the hidden and denied impulses stirring as she cleansed and then gazed at the undeveloped, naked form of the girl in the bath. But at the time she had only been aware of apprehension slowly giving way to a remarkable sensation of luxury: the hot water and the warm room, the hands of someone else tending to her.

Five years later she was an official dancer for the Blues, growing in recognition, the child-mistress of one of the more notorious of the faction's aristocratic patrons. And she was already known for her love of bathing. Twice a day at the bathhouse when she could, amid languorous perfumes and warmth and the drifting of steam, which meant shelter and comfort to her in a life that had known neither.

Nor has this changed, though she now knows the most extreme comforts in the world. And to her the most remarkable thing, really, about all of this is how vividly, how *intensely*, she can still remember being the girl in that small bath.

The next letter, read while the Empress is being powdered, dried, painted, and dressed by her ladies, is from a nomadic religious leader in the desert south of Soriyya. A certain number of these desert wanderers are now Jaddite in their beliefs, having abandoned their incomprehensible heritage built around wind spirits and sets of holy lines, invisible to sight, mapping and crisscrossing the sands, marking sacred places and correspondences.

All the desert tribes embracing Jad have also adopted a belief in the god's son. This often happens among those converting to the faith of the sun god: Heladikos is the way to his father. Officially, the Emperor and Patriarchs have forbidden such beliefs. The Empress, usefully thought to be sympathetic to such out-of-favour doctrines, tends to conduct the exchange of letters and gifts with the tribesmen. They can be significant, often are. Even with the expensively bought peace with the Bassanids in place, in the unstable regions of the south allies are impermanent and important, valuable for hired warriors, and for gold and *silphium*—that extravagantly expensive spice—and for offering caravan routes for eastern goods coming around Bassania.

This letter ends without any promise of physical delight. The Empress refrains from expressing disappointment. Her current secretary has no sense of humour and her attendants become distracted when amused. The desert leader does offer a prayer for light to attend upon her soul.

Alixana, dressed now, sipping at a cup of honeyed wine, dictates replies to both communications. She has just finished the second when the door opens, without a knock. She looks up.

'Too late,' she murmurs. 'My lovers have fled and I am, as you see, entirely respectable.'

'I shall destroy forests and cities searching for them,' the thrice-exalted Emperor, Jad's holy regent upon earth, says as he takes a cushioned bench and accepts a cup of the wine (without honey) from one of the women. 'I shall grind their bones into powder. May I please proclaim that I found Vertigus importuning you and have him torn apart between horses?'

The Empress laughs and then gestures, briefly. The room empties of secretary and attendants. 'Money, again? I could sell my jewels,' she says, when they are alone.

He smiles. His first smile of the day, which for him has gone on for some time by now. She rises, brings a plate of cheese, fresh bread, cold meats to him. It is a custom, they do this every morning when demands allow. She kisses his forehead as she sets down the plate. He touches her wrist, breathing in her scent. In a way, he thinks, a new part of his day begins when he first does so. Each morning.

'I'd make more selling you,' he says.

'How exciting. Gunarch of Moskav would pay.'

'He can't afford you.' Valerius looks around the bathing room, red and white marble and ivory and gold, jewelled chalices and drinking cups and alabaster caskets on the tables. Two fires are lit; oil lamps hang from the ceiling in silver-wire baskets. 'You are a very expensive woman.'

'Of course I am. Which reminds me. I still want my dolphins.' She gestures towards the upper part of the wall on the far side of the room. 'When are you done with the Rhodian? I want him to start here.'

Valerius looks at her repressively, says nothing.

She smiles, all innocence, wide-eyed. 'Gunarch of Moskav writes that he could offer me delights such as I have only dreamt of in the dark.'

Valerius nods absently. 'I'm sure.'

'Speaking of dreams . . .' his Empress says. The Emperor catches the shift in tone—she is skilled at such changes, of course—and looks at her as she returns to her own seat.

'I suppose we were,' he says. There is a silence. 'Better than talking of illicit dolphins. What is it now, love?'

She shrugs, delicately. 'Clever you. The dream *was* about dolphins.'

The Emperor's expression is wry. 'Clever me. I have just been steered like a boat where you wanted to go.'

She smiles, but not with her eyes. 'Not really. It was a sad dream.'

Valerius looks at her. 'You really do want them for these walls?'

He is deliberately misunderstanding, and she knows it. They have been here before. He doesn't like talking about her dreams. She believes in them, he does not, or says he does not.

'I want them *only* on the walls,' she says. 'Or in the sea far from us for a long time yet.'

He sips his wine. Takes a bite of cheese with the bread. Country food, his preference at this hour. His name was Petrus, in Trakesia.

'None of us knows where our souls travel,' he says, at length, 'in life, or after.' He waits until she looks up and meets his eyes. His face is round, smooth, innocuous. No one is deceived by this, not any more. 'But I believe I am unshakeable on this war in the west, love, proof against dreams and argument.'

After a time, she nods. Not a new conversation, or a new conclusion. The dream in the night was real, though. She has always had dreams that stay with her.

They talk of affairs of state: taxation, the two Patriarchs, the opening ceremonies for the Hippodrome, a few days off. She tells him of an amusing wedding taking place today, with a surprisingly fashionable guest list.

'There are rumours,' she murmurs, pouring more wine for him, 'that Lysippus has been seen in the city.' Her expression is suddenly mischievous.

His looks rueful, as if caught out.

She laughs aloud. 'I knew it! You've been planting them?'

He nods. 'I *should* sell you somewhere, far away. I have no secrets. Yes, I'm . . . testing things.'

'You would really bring him back?'

Lysippus the Calysian, gross of body and of appetite, was nonetheless the most efficient and incorruptible Quaestor of Imperial Revenue Valerius has ever had. His association with the Emperor is said to go back a very long way and involve some details that are unlikely to ever be made known. The Empress has never even asked, in fact; not really wanting to know. She has her own memories—and dreams, sometimes—of men screaming in the street one morning below rooms he'd rented for her in an expensive district, in the days when they were young and Apius was Emperor. She is not overly delicate about such things, cannot be after that childhood in the Hippodrome and the theatre, but this memory—with the smell of charred flesh—has lingered and will not leave.

The Calysian has been exiled nearly three years now, in the wake of the Victory Riot.

'I'd bring him back,' the Emperor says. 'If they let me. I'd need the Patriarch to absolve him and the accursed factions to be calm about it. Best during the racing season, when they have other things to scream about.'

She smiles a little. He doesn't like the racing, it is an ill-guarded secret. 'Where is he now, really?'

Valerius shrugs. 'North still, I assume. He writes from an estate near Eubulus. Has resources enough to do whatever he likes. Is probably bored. Terrifying the countryside. Stealing children by dark of moon.'

She makes a face, at that. 'Not a pleasant man.'

He nods. 'Not in the least. Ugly habits. But I need money, love, and Vertigus is next to useless.'

'Oh, I agree,' she murmurs. 'You can't *imagine* how useless.' She runs a tongue across her lips. 'I think Gunarch of

Moskav will please me *much* more.' She is hiding something, though. A feeling, distant intuition. Dolphins and dreams and souls.

He laughs, has to laugh, eventually takes leave after finishing his quick meal. There are reports from the military and provincial governors to be read and responded to back in the Attenine Palace. She is receiving a delegation of clerics and holy women from Amoria in her own reception rooms, will sail in the harbour after, if the winds are light. She enjoys going out to the islands in the strait or the inner sea, and with winter ending she can do so again on a mild day. There is no formal banquet tonight. They are to dine together with a small number of courtiers, listening to a musician from Candaria.

In the event, they will do this, enjoying the elusive, plangent instrumentation, but they will be joined for wine afterwards—some might think unexpectedly—by the Supreme Strategos Leontes and his tall, fair wife, and a third person, also a woman, and royal.

Pardos sprinted for all he was worth, cursing himself all the while. He had spent his entire life in the rougher quarters of Varena, a city known for drunken Antae soldiers and for brawling apprentices. He knew he was an idiot for having intervened here, but a drawn sword and a man slain in broad daylight had taken the laneway encounter past the point of the usual bruises and bangings. He'd charged in, not stopping to think, administered some blows of his own—and now found himself pelting headlong beside a greying Bassanid through a city he didn't know at all, with a shouting band of young aristocrats in flat-out pursuit. He didn't even have his staff.

He'd been known for a cautious young man at home, but being careful didn't always keep you out of trouble. He knew what they had to do, prayed only that the doctor's older legs were equal to the pace.

Pardos whipped out of the laneway, skidding left into a wider street, and knocked over the first cart—a fishmonger's—that he saw. Couvry had done that once under similar circumstances. A shriek of outrage followed him; he didn't look back. Crowds and chaos were what they needed, to screen their flight and to provide some deterrent to fatal violence if they were caught—though he was uncertain how easily deterred their pursuers might be.

Best not to test that.

Beside him the doctor seemed to be keeping up—he even reached over as they careened around another corner and pulled down the awning over the portico of an icon shop. Not the wisest choice for a Bassanid, perhaps, but he did succeed in spilling a table full of Blessed Victims into the muddy street, scattering the beggars gathered around it, creating further disruption behind them. Pardos glanced over; the doctor was grim-faced, his legs pumping hard.

As they ran, Pardos kept looking for one of the Urban Prefect guards—surely they would be about, in this rough neighbourhood? Weren't swords supposed to be illegal in the City? The young patricians pursuing them appeared not to believe so, or to care. He abruptly decided to make for a chapel, a larger one than the nondescript little hole in which he'd been chanting the morning invocation after arriving in the city at sunrise and weaving his way down from the triple walls. He'd been planning to take an inexpensive room near the harbour—always the cheapest part of a city—and then head for an encounter he'd been thinking about since leaving home.

The room would have to wait.

There were heavy morning crowds now, and they had to twist and dodge as best they could, earning curses and a tardy blow aimed at Pardos from one off-duty soldier. But this meant that those chasing them would surely be stringing out by now, and might even lose sight of them if Pardos and the doctor—he really was moving quite well for a greybeard—managed to take a sufficiently erratic path.

Glancing up constantly to get his bearings, Pardos glimpsed—through a break in the multi-storied buildings— a golden dome larger than any he'd ever seen before, and he abruptly changed his thinking, even as they ran.

'That way!' he gasped, pointing.

'Why are we running?' the Bassanid burst out. 'There are *people* here! They won't dare—'

'They will! They'll kill us and pay a fine! Come on!'

The doctor said no more, saving his breath. He followed as Pardos cut sharply off the street they were on and angled across a wide square. They hurtled past a bedraggled Holy Fool and his small crowd, hit by a whiff of the man's foul, unwashed odour. Pardos heard a sharp cry from behind— some of the pursuers still had them in sight. A stone whizzed past his head. He looked back.

One pursuer. Only one. That changed things.

Pardos stopped, and turned.

The doctor did the same. A fierce-looking but extremely young man in green robes, eastern-styled, with earrings and a golden necklace and long, unkempt hair— not one of the original group—slowed uncertainly, then fumbled at his belt and pulled out a short sword. Pardos looked around, swore, and then darted up to the Holy Fool. Braving the maggoty, fetid stench of the man, he seized his oak staff, snapping an apology over his shoulder. He ran directly at their young pursuer.

'You idiot!' he screamed, waving the staff wildly. 'You're alone! There's *two* of us!'

The young man—belatedly apprehending this significant truth—looked quickly over his shoulder, saw no immediately arriving reinforcements, appeared suddenly less fierce.

'*Run!*' screamed the doctor at Pardos's side, brandishing a knife.

The young man looked at the two of them and elected to follow the advice. He ran.

Pardos hurled the borrowed staff back towards the Holy Fool on his small platform. 'Come on!' he rasped at the doctor. 'Head for the Sanctuary!' He pointed. They turned together, crossed the square, and raced up another laneway on the far side

It wasn't far now, as the lane—blessedly level now—gave suddenly onto an enormous forum with arched porticoes and shops all around it. Pardos swept past two boys playing with a hoop and a man selling roasted nuts at a brazier. He saw the looming bulk of the Hippodrome on his left and a pair of huge bronze gates in a wall that had to be the one guarding the Imperial Precinct. There was an enormous equestrian statue in front of the gates. He ignored these splendours for now, running for all he was worth diagonally across the forum towards a long, wide, covered porch with two more huge doors behind it and a dome rising above and behind that would have taken away his breath if he'd had any breath left to lose.

He and the Bassanid leaped and dodged among masons and masonry carts and brick piles and—familiar sight!—an outdoor oven for quicklime near the portico. As they reached the steps, Pardos heard the pursuing cry behind him again. He and the doctor took the steps side by side and stumbled to a stop, breathing hard, before the doors.

'No one allowed!' snapped a guard—there were two of them. 'They are at work inside!'

'Mosaicist,' gasped Pardos. 'Here from Batiara! Those youths are after us!' He pointed back across the forum. 'They killed someone already! With swords!'

The guards glanced over. Half a dozen of the young pursuers had now made it this far, running in a tight cluster. They had weapons drawn—in daylight, in the forum. Impossible to credit, or so wealthy they didn't even care. Pardos seized one of the heavy door handles, pulled it open, pushed the doctor quickly inside. Heard the piercing, satisfying sound of a guard whistling for support. They would be safe in here for now, he was sure of it. The doctor was bent over, hands on his hips, breathing heavily. He gave Pardos a sidelong glance and a nod, obviously registering the same thing.

Later, much later, Pardos would give some thought to what the morning's sequence of interventions and activities suggested about changes in himself, but for the moment he was only moving and reacting.

He looked up. He reacted, but he didn't move.

In fact, he felt suddenly as though his boots were set into the marble floor like ... tesserae in a setting bed, fixed for centuries to come.

He stood so, rooted, trying to deal first with the sheer size of the space encompassed here, the dim, vast aisles and bays receding into an illusion of endlessness down corridors of pale, filtered light. He saw the massive columns piled upon each other like playthings for the giants of legend from Finabar, the lost, first world of the Antae's pagan faith, where gods walked among men.

Overwhelmed, Pardos looked down at the flawless, polished marble of the floor, and then—taking a deep breath—up again, all the way up, to see, floating, floating, the great dome itself, inconceivably immense. And upon it, taking shape even now, was what Caius Crispus of Varena, his teacher, was devising amid this holiness.

White and gold tesserae on a blue ground—blue such as Pardos had never seen in Batiara and had never expected to see in his life—defined the vault of the heavens. Pardos recognized the hand and style immediately. Whoever had been in charge of these decorations when Crispin arrived from the west was no longer the designer here.

Pardos had been *taught* by the man doing this, master to apprentice.

What he couldn't yet begin to grasp—and he knew he would need to spend a long time looking to even make a start—was the colossal scale of what Crispin was doing on this dome. A design equal to the vastness of the setting.

The doctor, beside him, was leaning against a marble column now, still catching his breath. The marble was the green-blue colour, in the muted light, of the sea on a cloudy morning. The Bassanid was silent, slowly looking about. Above the grey-streaked beard his eyes were wide. Valerius's Sanctuary was the talk and rumour of the known world, and they were standing within it now.

There were labourers at work everywhere, many of them at corners, so distant they were invisible, could only be heard. But even the noise of construction was changed by the huge space, echoing, a hollow resonance of sound. He tried to imagine the liturgy being chanted here, and a lump rose in his throat at the thought.

Dust danced in the slanting beams of sunlight that fell down through the windows set high on the walls and all around the dome. Looking up past suspended oil lamps of bronze and silver, Pardos saw scaffolding everywhere against the marbled walls, where mosaics of interwoven flowers and patterned shapes were being laid. One scaffolding only went all the way up to the dome, towards the northern side of that great curve, opposite the entrance doors. And in the soft, sweet morning light in the Sanctuary of Jad's Holy Wisdom, Pardos saw upon that high scaffolding the small figure of the man he'd followed all the way east, unasked, and unwanted—for Crispin had flatly refused the company of any apprentices when he'd set out on his own journey.

Pardos took another steadying breath and made the sign of the sun disk. This place was not formally consecrated yet—there was no altar, no suspended golden disk behind it—but for him, it was holy ground already, and his journey, or this part of it, was over. He gave thanks to Jad in his heart, remembering blood on an altar in Varena, wild dogs on a bitterly cold night in Sauradia when he had thought he would die. He was alive, and here.

Pardos could hear the guards outside—more of them now. A young man's voice was raised in anger, and was then sharply cut off by a soldier's reply. He looked at the doctor, and allowed himself a crooked smile. Then he remembered that the Bassanid's servant was dead. They had escaped, but it was not a moment for pleasure, not for the other man.

Not far away, two artisans stood together, and Pardos decided that if he could make his feet obey commands, he'd go over and speak to them. Before he could do so, he heard their voices raised in anxious colloquy.

'Where's Vargos? *He* could do it.'

'Gone to get dressed. You *know* that. He was invited too.'

'Holy Jad. Maybe . . . um, one of the mason's apprentices can do it? Or the bricklayer's? They may not . . . know him?'

'Not a chance. They all know the stories. We have to do it, Sosio, right now. It's late! I'll dice you.'

'No! I am *not* going up there. Crispin kills people.'

'He talks about killing people. I don't think he's ever done it.'

'You don't *think* he has. Good. Then you go up.'

'I said I'd dice, Sosio.'

'And I said I won't go. I don't want you to go, either. I don't *have* any other brothers.'

'He'll be *late*. He'll kill us for letting him be late.'

Pardos found that he could move, and that—notwithstanding the events of the morning—he was struggling not to grin. Too many memories were with him, sudden and vivid.

He went forward over marble in the serene light. His booted footsteps echoed softly. The two brothers—they were twins, utterly identical—turned and looked at him. In the distance, someone dropped a hammer or a chisel and the sound rang softly, almost music.

'I gather,' said Pardos gravely, 'this is a question of interrupting Crispin on the scaffold?'

'Caius Crispus, yes,' said the one called Sosio quickly. 'You, er, know him?'

'He has to be at a wedding!' said the other brother.

'Right away! He's in the wedding party.'

'But he doesn't allow anyone to interrupt him!'

'Ever! He *killed* someone for it once!'

'Back in Varena. With a trowel, they say! Inside a holy chapel!' Silano's expression was horrified.

Pardos nodded in sympathy. 'I know, I know. He did do that. In a chapel! In fact, I was the person he killed. It was *terrible*, dying like that! A trowel!' He paused, and winked as their mouths fell open, identically. 'It's all right, I'll get him for you.'

He went forward, before his smile—which he really *couldn't* suppress any longer—completely betrayed him. He passed right under the staggering sweep of the dome. Looking up, he saw Crispin's rendering of Jad in the east above the emerging details of Sarantium seen as if on the horizon, and because he'd just spent an entire winter in a certain chapel in Sauradia, Pardos perceived immediately what his teacher was doing with his own image of the god. Crispin had been there too. The Sleepless Ones had told him that.

He came to the scaffold. Two young apprentices were standing there, bracing it, as they always had to do. Usually those on that task were bored and idle. This pair looked terrified. Pardos found that he really couldn't stop smiling.

'Hold steady for me, will you?' he said.

'You *can't*!' one of the boys gasped in horror. 'He's *up* there!'

'So I understand,' said Pardos. He could remember, so easily, feeling—and probably looking—exactly as this white-faced apprentice did. 'He needs to be given a message, though.'

And he grasped the rungs of the scaffold ladder and started up. He knew that high above, Crispin would soon feel, if he hadn't immediately, the tug and sway. Pardos kept his eyes on his hands, as they were all trained to do, and climbed.

He was halfway up when he heard a well-known voice he'd travelled the world to hear again call down in cold, remembered fury, 'Another step up and I end your wretched existence and powder your bones into the setting bed!'

That's very good, actually, Pardos thought. *A new one.* He looked up. 'You shut up,' he cried. 'Or I'll carve your buttocks with tesserae and feed them to you in segments!'

There was a silence. Then, '*I* say that, rot your eyes! Who the—?'

Pardos continued upward without answering.

Above him, he felt the platform shift as Crispin came to the edge and looked down.

'Who *are* you?' Another silence, followed by: 'Pardos? *Pardos?*'

Pardos didn't speak, kept climbing. His heart was full. He reached the top and stepped over the low rail and onto the platform under the mosaic stars of a dark blue mosaic sky.

To be enveloped in a hard embrace that almost toppled them both.

'Curse you, Pardos! What *took* you so long? I've *needed* you here! They wrote that you left in the fucking autumn! Half a year ago! Do you know how late you are?'

Ignoring for the moment the fact that Crispin, on departing, had explicitly refused accompaniment, Pardos disengaged.

'Do you know how late *you* are?' he asked.

'Me? What?'

'Wedding,' said Pardos happily, and watched.

It gave him even greater pleasure, later, to recollect the

appalled dawning of awareness on Crispin's unexpectedly smooth-shaven features.

'Ah! *Ah!* Holy Jad! They'll *kill* me! I'm a dead man! If Carullus doesn't, bloody Shirin will! Why didn't one of those imbeciles down there *tell* me?'

Without delaying for the extremely obvious answer, Crispin rushed past Pardos, vaulted recklessly over the railing and began hurtling down the ladder, sliding more than stepping, the way the apprentices did when they raced each other. Before following, Pardos glanced over at where Crispin had been working. He saw a bison in an autumn forest, huge, done in black, edged and outlined in white. It would be *very* strong, that way, against the brilliant colours of the leaves around it, a dominant image. That had to be deliberate. Crispin had taken the apprentices once to see a floor mosaic at an estate south of Varena, where black and white had been used against colour in this way. Pardos went back down, feeling suddenly thoughtful.

Crispin was waiting at the bottom, grimacing, dancing from foot to foot in his impatience. 'Hurry, you idiot! We're so late it kills me. It *will* kill me! Come on! Why did you take so poxed long to get here?'

Pardos stepped deliberately down off the ladder. 'I stopped in Sauradia,' he said. 'A chapel by the road there. They said you'd been there too, earlier.'

Crispin's expression changed, very quickly. He looked intently at Pardos. 'I was,' he said after a pause. 'I was there. I told them that they had to . . . Were you . . . Pardos, were you *restoring* it?'

Pardos nodded slowly. 'As much as I felt I could, on my own.'

Crispin's expression changed again, warming him, sun-light on a raw morning. 'I'm pleased,' his teacher said. 'I'm very pleased. We'll speak of this. Meanwhile, come, we'll have to run.'

'I've *been* running. Through the whole of Sarantium, it feels like. There are a group of young men outside, rich enough not to care about the law, who are trying to kill me and this Bassanid doctor.' He gestured at the physician, who had approached with the artisan brothers. The twins' faces were a paired study in confusion. 'They killed his manservant,' Pardos said. 'We can't just walk outside.'

'And my man's body will be thrown into the street by certain of your *most* pious clerics if he is not claimed by midday.' The doctor spoke excellent Sarantine, better than Pardos's. He was still angry.

'Where is he?' Crispin said. 'Sosio and Silano can get him.'

'I have no idea of the name of—'

'Chapel of Blessed Ingacia,' Pardos said quickly. 'Near the port.'

'What?' said the twin named Sosio.

'What were you doing *there*?' said his brother in the same breath. 'It's a terrible place! Thieves and whores.'

'How do *you* know so much about it?' Crispin asked wryly, then appeared to recollect his urgency.

'Get two of the Imperial Guard to go with you. Carul-lus's men will all be at the accursed wedding by now. Tell them it is for me, and why. And you two,' he turned to Par-dos and the doctor. 'Come on! You'll stay with me for the morning, I have guards.' Crispin snapping orders was some-thing Pardos remembered. His moods had always changed like this. 'We'll go out a side door and we have to *move*! You'll need something white to wear, this is a *wedding*! Idiots!' He hurried off; they followed quickly, having little choice.

Which is how the mosaicist Pardos of Varena and the physician Rustem of Kerakek came to attend—wearing white over-tunics borrowed from Crispin's wardrobe—the formal ceremony and then the celebration banquet of a marriage on the day they each arrived in Jad's holy and august city of Sarantium.

The three of them *were* late, but not hopelessly so, in the event.

The musicians were lingering outside. A soldier, waiting anxiously by the doorway, saw their approach and hurried inside to report it. Crispin, murmuring a rapid stream of apologies in all directions, was able to hastily take his place before the altar in time to hold a slender golden crown over the head of the bridegroom for the ceremony. His own hair was considerably disordered, but it almost always was. Pardos noticed that the very attractive woman who was to hold the crown above the bride did fist his teacher hard in the ribs just before the service began. There was a ripple of laughter through the chapel. The presiding cleric looked startled; the groom smiled and nodded approval.

The bride's face Pardos didn't see until afterwards. She was veiled in the chapel as the words of union were spoken by the cleric and then in unison by the couple being wed. Pardos had no idea who they were; Crispin hadn't had time to explain. Pardos didn't even know the name of the Bassanid standing beside him; events had unfolded at an unbelievable speed this morning, and a man was dead.

The chapel was elegant, gorgeous in fact, an extravagance of gold and silver, veined marble pillars, a magnificent altar of jet-black stone. Overhead, on the small dome, Pardos saw—with surprise—the golden figure of Heladikos, carrying his torch of fire, falling in his father's chariot. Belief in the god's son was banned now, images of him deemed a heresy by both Patriarchs. It seemed the users of this patrician chapel had sufficient importance to prevent their mosaic being destroyed thus far. Pardos, who had adopted the god's bright son with the god himself, as had all the Antae in the west, felt a flicker of warmth and welcome. A good omen, he thought. It was unexpected and comforting to find the Charioteer waiting for him here.

Then, partway through the service, the Bassanid touched Pardos on the arm and pointed. Pardos looked over. He blinked. The man who'd killed the doctor's servant had just entered the chapel.

He was quiet and composed, clad in exquisitely draped white silk, with a belt of links of gold and a dark green cloak. His hair was neatly tucked away now under a soft, green, fur-trimmed hat. The gaudy jewellery was gone. He moved discreetly to take his place between an older, handsome man and a much younger woman. He didn't look drunken now. He looked like a young prince, a model for Heladikos in splendour overhead.

There were those of the Imperial Precinct and the higher civil offices who actively courted the racing factions, either or both of them. Plautus Bonosus, Master of the Senate, was not one of these. He took the view that a benign detachment from both Blues and Greens best suited his position. In addition, he was not, by nature, one of those inclined to lay siege to the girl dancers and, accordingly, the charms of the notorious Shirin of the Greens were purely a matter of aesthetics for him and not a source of desire or enticement.

As such, he'd never have attended this wedding, had it not been for two factors. One was his son: Cleander had desperately urged him to attend, and to bring him, and since it was increasingly unusual for his son to show the least interest in civilized gatherings, Bonosus had been reluctant to pass up an opportunity to have the boy appear presentable and functional in society.

The other reason, a little more self-indulgent, had been the information, conveyed smoothly by the dancer with her invitation, that the banquet in her home was to be prepared by Strumosus of Amoria.

Bonosus did have his weaknesses. Charming boys and memorable food would probably lead the list.

They left the two unmarried girls at home, of course. Bonosus and his second wife attended—scrupulously punctual—at the ceremony in their own neighbourhood chapel. Cleander arrived late, but he was clean and appropriately garbed. Looking with some bemusement at his son beside him, Bonosus was almost able to remember the dutiful, clever boy he'd been as recently as two years ago. Cleander's right forearm seemed puffy and discoloured but his father elected not to ask about that. He didn't want to know. They joined the white-clad procession and the musicians (very good ones, in fact, from the theatre) for the short, rather chilly walk to the dancer's home.

He did feel briefly uneasy as the musical parade through the streets ended before a portico with a well done copy of a classical Trakesian bust of a woman. He knew how his wife would feel about entering here. She'd said nothing, of course, but he knew. They made their way into a common dancer's abode, thereby conferring all the symbolic dignity of his office upon the woman and her house.

Jad alone knew what went on in here at night after the theatre. Thenaïs was impeccable, as ever, revealing not the least trace of disapproval. His second wife, significantly younger than he was, was flawlessly well bred and famously reticent. He'd chosen her for both qualities after Aelina had died in a summer of plague three years ago, leaving him with three children and no one to manage the house.

Thenaïs offered a gracious smile and polite murmur as Shirin of the Greens, slender and vivacious, welcomed them at her door. Cleander, between his father and step-mother, blushed crimson as Bonosus presented him, and locked his eyes on the floor as the dancer lightly touched his hand in greeting.

One mystery solved, the Senator thought, eyeing the boy with amusement. Now he knew why Cleander had been so eager to attend. At least he has good taste, Bonosus thought wryly. The Senator's mood was further assuaged as a servant handed him wine (which proved to be a splendid Candarian) and another woman deftly presented a small plate holding delicate morsels of seafood.

Bonosus's view of the world and the day grew positively sunny as he tasted his first sampling of Strumosus's artistry. He let out an audible sigh of pleasure and gazed about with a benign eye: a Green hostess, the Blues' chef in the kitchen, a number of guests from the Imperial Precinct (making him feel less conspicuous, in fact, as he noted their presence and nodded at one), sundry performers from the theatre, including one curly-haired former lover whom he promptly resolved to avoid.

He saw the rotund head of the silk guild (a man who seemed to attend every party in the City), the Supreme Strategos's secretary, Pertennius of Eubulus, surprisingly well turned out, and the Greens' burly, beak-nosed factionarius, whose name he could never remember. Elsewhere, the Emperor's much-favoured Rhodian mosaicist was standing with a stocky, rough-bearded young man and an older, also bearded fellow, distinctly Bassanid. And then the Senator noticed another unexpected, noteworthy guest.

'Scortius is here,' he murmured to his wife, sampling a tiny, pickled sea urchin, in *silphium* and something unidentifiable, an astonishing flavour that tasted of ginger and the east. 'He's with the Green racer from Sarnica, Crescens.'

'An eccentric gathering, yes,' Thenaïs replied, not even bothering to follow his gaze towards where the two chariot-drivers were surrounded by a cluster of admirers. Bonosus smiled a little. He *liked* his wife. He even slept with her on occasion.

'Taste the wine,' he said.

'I have. Candarian. You'll be happy.'

'I *am*,' said Bonosus happily.

And he was, until the Bassanid fellow he'd noticed with the mosaicist came striding over to accuse Cleander of murder, in an eastern voice that was explicit enough—if blessedly low in volume—to eliminate all possibility of avoiding an unpleasantness.

CHAPTER IV

He hadn't known Nishik long at all—only for the duration of their journey here—and he couldn't have said he liked the man. The stocky soldier made a poor manservant and an insufficiently respectful companion. He hadn't troubled himself to disguise the fact that he regarded Rustem as no more than a burdensome civilian: the traditional soldier's attitude. Rustem had made a point in the first days of mentioning his travels a few times, but when that elicited no useful response he stopped, finding the exercise of attempting to impress a common soldier to be undignified.

Having acknowledged this, it remained to note that the casual killing of a companion—whether one was partial to him or not—was hardly something one ought to countenance, and Rustem had no intention of doing so. He was still outraged about the morning's deadly encounter and his own humiliating flight through the Jaddite city.

This information he conveyed to the big, red-haired artisan at the wedding celebration to which he'd been brought. He was holding a cup of excellent wine, but could take no pleasure in the fact or the reality of his arrival—finally—in the Sarantine capital after a hard winter trek. The presence of the murderer at the same gathering undermined any such feelings and gave an edge to his anger. The young man, dressed now like some Sarantine lordling, bore no resemblance at all to the profane, drunken bully who'd accosted them with his cronies in the laneway. He didn't even seem to have recognized Rustem.

Rustem pointed out the fellow at the request of the mosaicist, who seemed a brisk, no-nonsense person, belying a first impression of unhealthy choler and passion. The artisan swore under his breath and promptly fetched the bridegroom to their little group.

'Cleander's fucked up again,' the mosaicist—his name was Crispin—said grimly. He seemed prone to vulgar language.

'Tried to grab Shirin in the hallway?' The soldier bridegroom continued to present an inordinately cheerful visage.

'I wish it were that. No, he killed this man's servant this morning, in the street, with witnesses around. Including my friend Pardos, who just arrived in the City. Then he and a swarm of Greens chased both of them all the way to the Sanctuary, with swords drawn.'

'Oh, fuck,' said the soldier, with feeling. His expression had changed. 'Those stupid little boys.'

'They aren't boys,' said Rustem coldly. 'Boys are ten years old or such. That fellow was drunk at sunrise and killed with a blade.'

The big soldier looked at Rustem carefully for the first time. 'I understand that. He's still very young. Lost his mother at a bad time and left some intelligent friends for a wild group of younger ones in the faction. He's also hopelessly smitten with our hostess here and will have been drinking this morning because he was terrified of coming to her house.'

'Ah,' said Rustem, using a gesture his students knew well. 'That *explains* why Nishik had to die! Of course. Forgive me for mentioning the matter.'

'Don't be a shit, Bassanid,' said the soldier, his eyes briefly hard. 'No one's condoning a killing. We'll try to do something. I'm explaining, not excusing. I should also mention that the boy is the son of Plautus Bonosus. There's a need for some discretion.'

'Who is—?'

'Master of the Senate,' said the mosaicist. 'He's over there, with his wife. Leave this with us, physician. Cleander can use a good scare put into him and I can promise you we'll make it happen.'

'A *scare*?' said Rustem. He felt his temper rising again.

The red-haired fellow had a direct gaze. 'Tell me, doctor, would a member of the court of the King of Kings be more severely punished for killing a servant in a street fight? A Sarantine servant?'

'I have no idea,' said Rustem, although he did, of course.

Pivoting on a heel, he strode past the yellow-haired bride in her white garment and red belt and went right across the room towards the murderer and the older man the artisan had indicated. He was aware that his swift progress through a relaxed gathering would attract attention. A female servant, perhaps sensing a problem, appeared right in front of him, smiling, carrying a tray of small plates. Rustem was forced to stop; there was no room to pass. He drew a breath and, for want of evident alternatives, accepted one of the little plates she offered. The woman— young, full-figured, and dark-haired—lingered in his path.

She balanced her round tray and took his wine cup, freeing his two hands. Her fingers touched his. 'Taste it,' she murmured, still smiling. Her tunic was cut distractingly low—not a fashion that had reached Kerakek.

Rustem did as she suggested. It was rolled fish of some sort, in pastry, a sauce on the plate. As he bit down, a mildly stunning explosion of flavours took place in his mouth and Rustem could not suppress a grunt of astonished pleasure. He looked at the plate in his hand, and then at the girl in front of him. He dipped a finger in the sauce and tasted it again, wonderingly.

The dancer hosting this affair clearly had a cook, he thought. And comely servants. The dark-haired girl was gazing at him with dimpled pleasure. She handed him a small cloth to wipe at his mouth and took the tiny plate from him, still smiling. She gave him back his wine.

Rustem discovered that his surge of anger appeared to have dissipated. But as the servant murmured something and turned to another guest, Rustem looked at the Senator and his son again and was struck by a thought. He stood still a moment longer, stroking his beard, and then moved forward, more slowly now.

He stopped before the slightly florid figure of the Master of the Sarantine Senate, noting the austere, quite handsome woman beside him and—more to the point—the son at his other side. He felt very calm now. He bowed to the man and the woman and introduced himself formally.

As he straightened, Rustem saw the boy finally recognize him and go white. The Senator's son glanced quickly towards the front of the room where their hostess, the dancer, was still greeting late arrivals. *No escape for you,* thought Rustem coldly, and he spoke his accusation to the father in a deliberately low-voiced, cool tone.

The mosaicist had been right, of course: discretion and dignity were critical when people of stature were involved. Rustem had no desire to become embroiled with the law here; he intended to deal with this Senator himself. It had just occurred to him that although a physician might learn much of Sarantine medicine and perhaps hear a little chatter about affairs of state, a man owed a debt by the Master of the Senate might find himself in a different situation— to the greater benefit of the King of Kings in Kabadh, who had things he wished to know about Sarantium just now.

Rustem saw no reason to have poor Nishik, his long-serving, much-loved servant, die in vain.

The Senator cast his son a satisfyingly poisonous glance and murmured, 'Killed? Holy Jad. I am *appalled*, of course. You must allow—'

'He was drawing his own sword!' the boy exclaimed in a low, fierce tone. 'He was—'

'Be silent!' said Plautus Bonosus, a little more loudly than he'd perhaps intended. Two men not far away glanced over. The wife, all reserve and composure, appeared to be gazing idly about the room, ignoring her family. She was listening, however; Rustem could see it.

'As I was saying,' Bonosus continued more softly, turning back to Rustem, his colour even more heightened, 'you must allow me to offer you a cup of wine at our home after this charming celebration. I am grateful that you chose to speak with me directly, of course.'

'Of course,' said Rustem gravely.

'Where would we find your unfortunate servant?' the Senator asked. A practical man.

'The body is being attended to,' Rustem murmured.

'Ah. So there are . . . others who have already learned of this?'

'We were pursued through the streets by sword-wielding youths led by your son,' Rustem said, allowing himself a shade of emphasis. 'I imagine a number of people did observe our passage, yes. We received assistance in the Emperor's new Sanctuary from his mosaicist.'

'Ah,' said Plautus Bonosus again, glancing across the room. 'The Rhodian. He does get about. Well, if that matter is attended to . . . '

'My mule and all my goods,' said Rustem, 'were left behind when we were forced to flee. I have just arrived in Sarantium this morning, you see.'

The wife turned to him then, eyeing him thoughtfully. Rustem met her gaze briefly and turned away. The women here appeared to be rather more . . . present . . . than those in other places he'd been. He wondered if it had to do with the Empress, the power she was said to wield. A common dancer once. It was a remarkable story, really.

The Senator turned to his son. 'Cleander, you will excuse yourself to our hostess and leave now, before the dinner is served. You will ascertain the whereabouts of this man's animal and goods and have them brought to our home. You will then wait there for me to arrive.'

'*Leave?* Leave already?' said the boy, his voice actually breaking. 'But I haven't even . . . '

'Cleander, there is a possibility you might be branded or exiled for this. Get the accursed mule,' said his father.

His wife laid a hand on his arm. 'Shh,' she murmured. 'Look.'

A hush had descended over the large room full of animated, pleasure-seeking Sarantines. Plautus Bonosus looked
past Rustem's shoulder and blinked in surprise.

'Now how do *they* come to be here?' he asked of no one
in particular.

Rustem turned. The silence became a murmurous
rustling as those assembled—fifty or more—bowed or sank
low in acknowledgement of the man and the woman who
stood now in the entrance to the room with the hostess
behind them.

The man was very tall, smooth-shaven, compellingly
handsome. He was bareheaded, which was unusual and
showed his thick golden hair to good effect. He wore a
knee-length, deep-blue tunic slashed to show gold at the
sides, with gold hose and black boots like a soldier and a
dark green panelled dress cloak, pinned at one shoulder
with a blue gem, large as a man's thumbnail. He held a
white flower in one hand, for the wedding.

The woman beside him had her own yellow hair gathered up loosely under a white mesh cap, with artful ringlets
spilling down. Her floor-length garment was crimson and
there were jewels at the hem. She wore gold at her ears and
a necklace of gold with pearls and a golden cloak. She was
nearly as tall as the man. A sallow, lean fellow materialized
at the man's elbow and whispered briefly in his ear as those
attending the celebration rose from homage.

'Leontes,' said the Senator softly to Rustem. 'The Strategos.'

It was a courtesy. Rustem could not have known this
man, though for years he had heard of him—and feared
him, as did everyone in Bassania. There was a glow cast by
renown, Rustem thought, something almost tangible. It was

Leontes the Golden (and the origin of the name became clearer now) who had comprehensively beaten the last fully mustered northern army east of Asen, almost capturing the Bassanid general, forcing a humiliating peace. The general had been invited to kill himself when he returned to Kabadh, and had done so.

It was Leontes who had also won lands (and productive, taxable citizens) for Valerius in the great spaces stretching all the way west and south to the fabled Majriti deserts, who had brutally quelled incursions from Moskav and Karch, who had been honoured—they'd heard of it even in Kerakek—with the most elaborate Triumph an Emperor had ever granted a returning Strategos since Saranios had founded this city.

And who had been given the tall, ice-elegant woman beside him as a further prize. They knew of the Daleinoi in Bassania, as well—even in Kerakek, which was on the southern trade routes, after all. The family's wealth had begun with a spice monopoly, and the eastern spices usually came through Bassania, north or south. Ten or fifteen years ago, Flavius Daleinus had been killed in some appalling fashion at a time of Imperial succession. A fire of some kind, Rustem recalled. His elder sons had been killed or crippled in the same attack, and the daughter was . . . here in this room, brilliant and golden as a prize of war.

The Strategos gestured briefly and the dark-haired serving girl hurried over with wine for him, her cheeks flushed with excitement. His wife also accepted a cup, but stayed behind as her husband stepped forward so that he appeared alone now, as if an actor on a stage. Rustem saw Styliane Daleina glancing around slowly, registering, he was certain, presences and alignments utterly invisible to him. Her expression was as unrevealing as that of the Senator's wife, but the impression given by the two women was in no other way the same. Where the wife of Plautus Bonosus was reserved and detached, the aristocratic spouse of the most powerful soldier in the Empire was cold and brilliant and even a little frightening. Awesome wealth and great power and violent death were in her lineage. Rustem managed to look away from her just as the Strategos began to speak.

'Lysurgos Matanios once said that it is a finer thing to see a friend well wed than to sip from even the rarest wine,' Leontes said, lifting his cup. 'It is a pleasure to enjoy both today,' he added, pausing to drink. There was laughter: well-bred from the courtiers, more obviously excited from the theatre and army people.

'He always uses that line,' murmured Bonosus to Rustem, drily. 'I wish I knew why he was *here*, though.'

As if answering, the Strategos went on. 'It seemed proper to stop and lift a cup in honour of the marriage of the only man in the army who could talk so much and so well and so much and . . . so much, that he extracted the arrears of payment for the soldiers from the Precinct coffers. I do not urge anyone ever to put themselves in the position of being persuaded by the tribune of the Fourth Sauradian to do *anything* . . . unless they have a great deal of time to spare.'

Laughter again. The man was smooth as a courtier but his manner was direct and unassuming, the teasing rough and easy as a soldier's. Rustem watched the military men in the room as they gazed at the speaker. There was adoration written in their features. The wife, motionless as a statue now, seemed vaguely bored.

'And I fear,' Leontes was saying, 'that we do *not* have a great deal of time today, so the Lady Styliane and I are not able to join you in sampling the delights prepared by Strumosus of the Blues in a Green household. I do commend the factions for this rare conjunction and hope it bodes well for a peaceful racing season.' He paused, an eyebrow raised for emphasis: this was an authority figure, after all. 'We came that we might salute the groom and his bride in Jad's most holy name, and to convey a piece of information that may add in some small way to the felicity of the day.'

He paused again, sipped his wine. 'I addressed the bridegroom as tribune of the Fourth Sauradian just now. I was behind the tidings, as it happens. It seems that some Supreme Strategos or other, anxious to put a certain mellifluous voice far away from his overburdened ears, rashly signed papers this morning affirming the promotion of the tribune Carullus of Trakesia to his new rank and appointment . . . as chiliarch of the Second Calysian, such position to be assumed in thirty days . . . which will allow the new chiliarch time here with his bride, and a chance to lose some of his increased pay at the Hippodrome.'

There was a shout of pleasure and laughter, nearly drowning out the last words. The bridegroom came quickly forward, his face flushed, and knelt before the Strategos.

'My lord!' he said, looking up, 'I am . . . I am speechless!'

Which elicited its own burst of laughter from those who knew the man. 'However,' added Carullus, lifting a hand, 'I do have a question I must ask.'

'Speechlessly?' said Styliane Daleina, from behind her husband. Her first comment, softly spoken, but everyone heard it. Some people did not need to raise their voices to be heard.

'I lack that skill, my lady. I must use my tongue, though with far less skill than my betters. I only wish to ask if I may decline the promotion.'

Silence fell. Leontes blinked.

'This is a surprise,' he said. 'I would have thought . . .' He let the sentence trail off.

'My great lord, my commander . . . if you wish to reward an unworthy soldier, it will be by allowing him, at any rank at all, to fight at your side in the next campaign. I do not believe I am saying anything untoward if I suggest that Calysium, with the Everlasting Peace signed in the east, will be no such place. Is there nowhere in . . . in the west where I might serve with you, my Strategos?'

At the reference to Bassania, Rustem heard the Senator beside him shift a little, uneasily, and clear his throat softly. But nothing of note had been said. Yet.

The Strategos smiled a little now, his composure regained. He reached down, and in a gesture almost fatherly, ruffled the hair of the soldier kneeling before him. His men loved him, it was said, the way they loved their god.

Leontes said, 'There is no campaign declared anywhere, chiliarch. Nor is it my practice to send newly married officers to a war front when there are alternatives, as there always are.'

'Then I *can* be attached to you, since there is no war front,' said Carullus, and he smiled innocently. Rustem snorted; the man had audacity.

'*Shut up*, you idiot!' The entire room heard the red-haired mosaicist. The laughter that followed affirmed as much. It had been intended, of course. Rustem was quickly coming to realize how much of what was being said and done was carefully planned or cleverly improvised theatre. Sarantium, he decided, was a stage for performances. No wonder an actress could command so much power here, induce such prominent people to grace her home—or become Empress, if it came to that. Unthinkable in Bassania, of course. Utterly unthinkable.

The Strategos was smiling again, a man at ease, sure of his god—and of himself, Rustem thought. A *righteous* man. Leontes glanced across at the mosaicist and lifted his cup to him.

'It is good advice, soldier,' he said to Carullus, still kneeling before him. 'You will know the pay difference between legate and chiliarch. You have a bride now, and should have strong children to raise soon enough, in Jad's holy service and to honour his name.'

He hesitated. 'If there *is* a campaign this year—and let me make it clear that the Emperor has offered no indications yet—it might be in the name of the poor, wronged queen of the Antae, which means Batiara, and I will *not* have a newly married man beside me there. The east is where I want you for now, soldier, so speak of this no more.' The words were blunt, the manner almost paternal—though he wouldn't be older than the soldier before him, Rustem thought. 'Rise up, rise up, bring us your bride that we may salute her before we go.'

'I can just *see* Styliane doing that,' the Senator beside Rustem murmured under his breath.

'Hush,' said his wife, suddenly. 'And look again.'

Rustem saw it too.

Someone had now come forward, past Styliane Daleina, though pausing gracefully beside her for an instant, so that Rustem was to carry a memory for a long time of the two of them next to each other, golden and golden.

'Might the poor, wronged queen of the Antae have any voice at all in this? In whether war is brought to her own country in her name,' said this new arrival. Her

voice—speaking Sarantine but with a western accent—
was clear as a bell, bright anger in it, and it cut into the
room like a knife through silk.

The Strategos turned, clearly startled, swiftly concealing
it. An instant later he bowed formally and his wife—smiling a little to herself, Rustem saw—sank down with perfect
grace, and then the entire room did so.

The woman paused, waiting for this acknowledgement
to pass. She hadn't been at the wedding ceremony, must
have just this moment arrived. She, too, was clad in white
under a jewelled collar and stole. Her hair was gathered
under a soft hat of a dark green shade and as she shed an
identically hued cloak now for a servant to take, it could
be seen that her long, floor-length garment had a single
vertical stripe down one side, and it was porphyry, the
colour of royalty everywhere in the world.

As the guests rose in a rustle of sound, Rustem saw that
the mosaicist and the younger fellow from Batiara who'd
saved Rustem's life this morning remained where they
were, kneeling on the dancer's floor. The stocky young man
looked up, and Rustem was startled to see tears on his face.

'The Antae queen,' said the Senator in his ear. 'Hildric's
daughter.' Confirmatory, but hardly needed: physicians
draw conclusions from information gathered. They had
spoken of this woman in Sarnica, too, her late-autumn
flight from assassination, sailing into exile in Sarantium. A
hostage for the Emperor, a cause of war if he needed one.

He heard the Senator speak to his son again. Cleander
muttered something fierce and aggrieved behind him but
made his way out of the room, obeying his father's orders.
The boy hardly seemed to matter just now. Rustem was
staring at the Antae queen, alone and far from her home.

She was poised, unexpectedly young, regal in her bearing as she surveyed a glittering crowd of Sarantines. But what the doctor in Rustem—the physician at the core of what he was—saw in the clear blue northern eyes across the room was the masked presence of something else.

'Oh dear,' he murmured, involuntarily, and then became aware that the wife of Plautus Bonosus was looking at him again.

A feast for fifty people was not, Kyros knew, particularly demanding for Strumosus, given that they often served four times that number in the Blues' banquet hall. There was some awkwardness in using a different kitchen, but they'd been over here a few days earlier and Kyros—given larger responsibilities all the time—had done the inventory, allocated locations, and supervised the necessary rearrangements.

He'd somehow overlooked the absence of sea salt and knew Strumosus wouldn't soon forget it. The master chef was not—to put it mildly—tolerant of mistakes. Kyros would have run back to their own compound to fetch it himself, but running was one thing he wasn't at all good for, given the bad foot he dragged about with him. He'd been busy by then with the vegetables for his soup in any case, and the other kitchen boys and undercooks had their own duties. One of the houseservants had gone, instead—the pretty, dark-haired one the others were all talking about when she wasn't nearby.

Kyros seldom engaged in that sort of banter. He kept his passions to himself. As it happened, for the last few days—since their first visit to this house—his own daydreams had been about the dancer who lived here. This might have been disloyal to his own faction, but there was no one among the Blue dancers who moved or sounded or looked like Shirin of the Greens. It made his heartbeat quicken to hear the ripple of her laughter from another room and sent his thoughts at night down corridors of desire.

But she did that for most of the men in the City, and Kyros knew it. Strumosus would have declared this a boring taste, too easy, no subtlety in it. The reigning dancer in Sarantium? What an *original* object of passion! Kyros could almost hear the chef's astringent voice and mocking applause, the back of one hand slapping into the palm of the other.

The banquet was nearly done. The boar, stuffed with thrushes and wood pigeons and quail eggs, served whole on an enormous wooden platter, had occasioned an acclamation they'd heard even in the kitchen. Shirin had earlier sent the black-haired girl to report that her guests were in paroxysms of delight over the sturgeon—king of fish!— served on a bed of flowers, and the rabbit with Soriyyan figs and olives. Their hostess had conveyed her own impression of the soup earlier. The exact words, relayed by the same girl with dimpled mirth, were that the Greens' dancer intended to wed the man who'd made it before the day was done. Strumosus had pointed with his spoon to Kyros and the dark-haired girl had grinned at him, and winked.

Kyros had immediately ducked his head down over the herbs he was chopping as raucous, teasing voices were raised all around, led by his friend Rasic. He had felt the tips of his ears turning red but had refused to look up. Strumosus, walking past, had rapped him lightly on the back of the head with his long-handled spoon: the chef's version of a benign, approving gesture. Strumosus broke a great many wooden spoons in his kitchen. If he hit you gently enough for the spoon to survive you could deduce that he was pleased.

It seemed the sea salt had been forgotten after all, or forgiven.

The dinner had begun on a high-pitched note of distraction and excitement, the guests chattering furiously about the arrival and immediate departure of the Supreme Strategos and his wife with the young western queen. Gisel of the Antae had arrived to join the banquet here. An unanticipated presence, a gift of sorts offered by Shirin to her other guests: the chance to dine with royalty. But the queen had then accepted a suggestion made by the Strategos that she return with him to the Imperial Precinct to discuss the matter of Batiara—her own country, after all—with certain people there.

The implication, not lost on those present, and relayed to a keenly interested Strumosus in the kitchen by the clever dark-haired girl, was that the certain person might be the Emperor himself.

Leontes had expressed distress and surprise, the girl said, that the queen had *not* been consulted or even apprised to this point and vowed to rectify the omission. He was impossibly wonderful, the girl had added.

So, in the event, there was no royalty at the U-shaped table arrangement in the dining room after all, only the memory of royalty among them and royalty's acid, castigating tone directed at the most important soldier in the Empire. Strumosus, learning of the queen's departure, had been predictably disappointed but then unexpectedly thoughtful. Kyros was just sorry not to have seen her. You missed a lot in the kitchen sometimes, attending to the pleasure of others.

The dancer's servants and the ones she'd hired for the day and the boys they'd brought with them from the compound seemed to have finished clearing the tables. Strumosus eyed them carefully as they assembled now, straightening tunics, wiping at spots on cheek or clothing.

One tall, very dark-eyed, well-made fellow—no one Kyros knew—met the chef's glance as Strumosus paused in front of him and murmured, with an odd half-smile, 'Did you know that Lysippus is back?'

It was said softly, but Kyros was standing beside the cook, and though he turned quickly and busied himself with dessert trays he had good ears.

He heard Strumosus, after a pause, say only, 'I won't ask how you came by that knowledge. There's sauce on your forehead. Wipe it off before you go back out.'

Strumosus moved on down the line. Kyros found himself breathing with difficulty. Lysippus the Calysian, Valerius's grossly fat taxation master, had been exiled after the Victory Riot. The Calysian's personal habits had been a cause of fear and revulsion among the lower classes of the City; his had been a name used to threaten wayward children.

He had also been Strumosus's employer before he was exiled.

Kyros glanced furtively over at the chef, who was sorting out the last of the serving boys now. This was just a rumour, Kyros reminded himself, and the tidings might be new to him but not necessarily to Strumosus. In any case, he had no way to sort out what it might mean, and it was none of his affair in any possible way. He was unsettled, though.

Strumosus finished arranging the boys to his satisfaction and sent them parading back out to the diners with ewers of sweetened wine and the great procession of desserts:

sesame cakes, candied fruit, rice pudding in honey, musk melon, pears in water, dates and raisins, almonds and chestnuts, grapes in wine, huge platters of cheeses—mountain and lowland, white and golden, soft and hard—with more honey for dipping, and his own nut bread. A specially baked round loaf was carried up to the bride and groom with two silver rings inside that were the chef's gift to them.

When the last platter and tray and flask and beaker and serving dish had gone out and no sounds of catastrophe emerged from the dining hall, Strumosus finally allowed himself to sit on a stool, a cup of wine at his elbow. He didn't smile, but he did set down his wooden spoon. Watching from the corner of his eye, Kyros sighed. They all knew what the lowered spoon meant. He allowed himself to relax.

'I imagine,' said the chef to the room at large, 'that we have done enough to let the last of the wedding day be mild and merry and the night be what it will.' He was quoting some poet or other. He often did. Meeting Kyros's glance, Strumosus added, softly, 'Rumours of Lysippus bubble up like boiled milk every so often. Until the Emperor revokes his exile, he isn't here.'

Which meant he knew Kyros had overheard. He didn't miss much, Strumosus. The chef looked away and around the crowded kitchen. He lifted his voice, 'A serviceable afternoon's work, all of you. The dancer should be happy out there.'

<hr />

'She says to tell you that if you do not come rescue her immediately she will scream at her own banquet and blame you. You

understand,' added the bird, silently, *'that I don't* like *being made to talk to you this way. It feels unnatural.'*

As if there was anything remotely natural about any of these exchanges, Crispin thought, trying to pay attention to the conversation around him.

He could hear Shirin's bird as clearly as he'd heard Linon—provided he and the dancer were sufficiently close to each other. At a distance, Danis's inward voice faded and then disappeared. No thoughts he sent could be heard by the bird—or by Shirin. In fact, Danis was right. It *was* unnatural.

Most of the guests were back in Shirin's reception room. The Rhodian tradition of lingering at table—or couch in the old-style banquets—was not followed in the east. When the meal was done and people were drinking their last cups of mixed or honey-sweetened wine, Sarantines tended to be on their feet again, sometimes unsteadily.

Crispin glanced across the room and was unable to suppress a grin. He brought a hand up to cover his mouth. Shirin, wearing the bird about her neck, had been cornered against the wall—between a handsome wood-and-bronze trunk and a large decorative urn—by the Principal Secretary of the Supreme Strategos. Pertennius, gesturing in full conversational flight, showed little inclination to register her attempts at shifting to rejoin her guests.

This was an accomplished, sophisticated woman, Crispin decided cheerfully. She could deal with her own suitors, welcome or unwelcome. He turned back to the conversation he'd been following. Scortius and the muscular Green charioteer, Crescens, were discussing alternative dispositions of the horses in a quadriga. Carullus had left his new bride and was hanging on their every syllable. So were a number of others. The racing season was about to start; this exchange was visibly whetting appetites. Holy men and charioteers were the figures most revered by Sarantines. Crispin remembered hearing that even before he'd begun his journey. It was true, he had come to realize—at least as far as the charioteers went.

Kasia, not far away, was in the company of two or three of the younger Green dancers, with Vargos hovering protectively nearby. The dancers were likely to be tormenting her about the night to come; it was part of the wedding tradition. It was also a teasing that would be appallingly inappropriate for this particular bride. It occurred to Crispin that he ought to go over and salute her properly himself.

'*She now says to say she will offer you pleasures you have only imagined if you'll only come over here,*' said the dancer's bird abruptly in his head. Then added, '*I hate when she does this.*'

Crispin laughed aloud, occasioning curious glances from those following the debate beside him. Turning the sound into a cough, he looked across the room again. Shirin's mouth was fixed in a rigid smile. Her eyes met his over the shoulder of the lean, sallow secretary and there was black murder in them: nothing that promised delight at all, of the flesh or the spirit. Crispin realized, belatedly, that Pertennius must be very drunk. That, too, diverted him. Leontes's secretary was normally the most controlled of men.

Even so, Shirin could cope, he decided. This was all very amusing, in fact. He lifted a hand in a wave and smiled affably at the dancer before turning back again to the chariot-racers' conversation.

He and Zoticus's daughter had achieved an understanding, built around his ability to hear the bird and the story he'd told her about Linon. She had asked him, that chilly afternoon in autumn—it seemed a long time ago—if what he'd done with his bird meant that she should release Danis in the same way. He had been unable to answer that. There had ensued a silence, one that Crispin understood, then he had heard the bird murmur, inwardly, *'If I weary of this I will tell you. It is a promise. If that happens, take me back.'*

Crispin had shivered, thinking of the glade where Linon's surrendered soul had saved their lives in the mist of the half-world. Taking one of the alchemist's birds back to the Aldwood was not a simple matter, but he hadn't spoken of that then, or since.

Not even when a letter came from Martinian to Shirin and she sent word to Crispin in the Sanctuary and he came and read it. It seemed that Zoticus had left instructions with his old friend: if he were not home from an unexpected autumn journey by midwinter, or had not sent tidings, Martinian was to act as if he were dead and divide the alchemist's estate according to directions given. The servants were attended to; there were various personal bequests; some named objects and documents were burned.

The house near Varena and all that lay within it undestroyed were left to his daughter Shirin, to use or deal with as she saw best.

'Why did he *do* that? What in Jad's impossible name,' the girl had exclaimed to Crispin in her own sitting room, the bird lying on the chest by the fire, 'am I to do with a house in Batiara?'

She'd been bewildered and upset. She had never met her father in her life, Crispin knew. Nor was she his only child.

'Sell it,' he'd said. 'Martinian will do it for you. He's the most honest man in the world.'

'Why did he leave it to *me*?' she'd asked.

Crispin had shrugged. 'I didn't know him at all, girl.'

'Why do they think he's dead? Where did he go?'

And that answer he thought he did have. It wasn't a difficult puzzle, which didn't make the solution easier to live with. Martinian had written that Zoticus had taken a very sudden, late-season trip to Sauradia. Crispin had earlier written to the alchemist about Linon, a cryptic retelling of what had happened in the glade.

Zoticus would have understood the implications: far more of them than Crispin had. He was quite certain, in fact, where Shirin's father had gone.

And reasonably sure what would have happened when he got there.

He hadn't told this to the girl. Instead, he'd carried some difficult thoughts out into the wintry cold and a slanting rain, and had had a great deal to drink later that night in The Spina and then a quieter tavern, his assigned guards following him about, protecting the Emperor's so-valued mosaic artisan from all possible harm. Worldly harm. There were other kinds. The wine didn't do what he needed it to do. The memory of the *zubir*, the dark, huge presence of it in his life, seemed destined not to leave him.

Shirin herself was a balancing spirit. He'd come to think of her that way as the winter deepened. An image of laughter, movements quick as hummingbirds, with a cleverness equally quick and a generosity one might not have expected in a woman so celebrated. She couldn't even walk out-of-doors in the City without hired guards of her own to fend off admirers.

It appeared—and he hadn't known *this* until today—that the dancer had formed a relationship of sorts with Gisel, the young Antae queen. He had no idea when that had begun. They certainly hadn't told him. The women he knew here were . . . complicated.

There had been a moment earlier this afternoon when Crispin had been excruciatingly aware that there were four women in the room who had entangled him in intimacies recently: a queen, a dancer, a married aristocrat . . . and the one he'd saved from slavery, who was a bride today.

Only Kasia had touched him, he had thought, with what he knew to be tenderness, on a windy, black, dream-haunted night in Sauradia. The memory made him uncomfortable. He could still hear the shutter banging in the wind outside, still see Ilandra in his dream, the *zubir* between them, and then gone. He had been awake and crying out and Kasia had been beside his bed in the cold room, speaking to him.

He looked over at her, newly married to his closest friend here, and then glanced quickly away when he saw that her eyes had been resting on him.

And that, too, was an echo of a different exchange of glances earlier this afternoon, with someone else.

In the moment when Leontes the Golden had been speaking to Carullus, and an assembly of wedding guests had hung upon his words as upon holy text, Crispin had been unable not to look at another recent bride.

His reward, Styliane had called herself last autumn, in the half-light of Crispin's room at an inn. Crispin, listening to Leontes now, had understood something, remembering the Strategos's direct words and manner in the Attenine Palace the night of his own first appearance there. Leontes spoke to the court like a blunt soldier, and to soldiers and citizens with the grace of a courtier, and it worked, it worked very well.

As the unflawed mingling of charm and pious honesty captured and held this mixed gathering like some fortress under siege, Crispin had found Styliane Daleina staring back at him, as if she'd been waiting to gather in his gaze.

She had lifted her shoulders a little, gracefully, as if to say without the need for words, *Do you see now? I live with this perfection, as an ornament.* And Crispin had been able to hold those blue eyes for only a moment and had then turned away.

Gisel, his queen, had not lingered long enough to even notice his presence here, let alone resume the charade of intimacy between them. He had visited her twice during the winter—as bidden—at the small palace they'd given her near the walls, and each time the queen's manner had been regally detached, matter-of-fact. No thoughts or surmises about their country and invasion had been exchanged. She had not yet seen the Emperor in private. Or the Empress. It chafed her, he could see, living here with few tidings from home and no way of doing or achieving anything.

Crispin had tried, and failed, to imagine the shape and tenor of an encounter between the Empress Alixana and the young queen who had sent him here with a secret message in autumn half a year ago.

In Shirin's reception hall, with the world poised on the brink of springtime now, his thoughts turned back to the bride. He could remember his first sight of her in the front hallway of Morax's inn. *They are going to kill me tomorrow. Will you take me away?*

He still felt a sense of responsibility for her: the burden that came with saving someone, extending and utterly changing their life. She used to look at him, in the days when she shared a city home with him and Vargos and the servants the Chancellor's eunuchs had assigned to him, and there had been questions in her eyes that made him deeply uneasy. And then one night Carullus had found him drinking in The Spina and announced he was going to marry her.

A declaration that had brought them all here now, a gathering winding towards its twilit end and the bawdy, age-old songs that would precede the curtained wedding bed, sprinkled with saffron for desire.

He looked over towards Shirin again, by the far wall. Someone else had joined Pertennius now, he saw, grinning. Another smitten suitor, one had to assume. They were legion in the City. You could make up a regiment of those who longed for the Greens' dancer with an aching need that led to bad verse, musicians on her porch in the middle of the night, street fights, tablets of love bought from cheiromancers and tossed over the wall into her courtyard garden. She had shown some of these to Crispin: *Spirits of the newly dead, journeyers, come now to my aid! Send sleep-destroying, soul-ravaging longing into the bed of Shirin, dancer of the Greens, that all her thoughts in the dark be of yearning for me. Let her come forth from her doors in the grey hour before sunrise and make her way boldly, unashamed, with desire, to my house . . .*

One could be afraid and disturbed, reading such things.

Crispin had never touched her, nor had she made overtures to him that went beyond teasing intimations. He couldn't have said *why*, in fact: they were bound to no one and shared a secret of the half-world with no other people alive. But there was still something that kept him from seeing Zoticus's daughter in a certain light.

It might have been the bird, the memory of her father, the dark complexity of what they shared. Or the thought of how weary she must be of men pursuing her: the crowds of would-be lovers in the street, those stone tablets in the garden invoking named and nameless pagan powers, merely to bed her.

Not, Crispin had to admit, that he was above being amused just now, seeing her cornered by suitors in her own house. A third man had joined the other two. He wondered if a fight would start.

'She says she will kill you immediately after she kills these two merchants and the wretched scribe,' said the bird. 'She says for me to scream in your head when I say this.'

'My dear, dear Rhodian!' said a polished, rich voice at that same moment, approaching from the other side. 'I understand you intervened earlier to save this visitor to our city from harm. It was *very* good of you.'

Crispin turned, saw the Master of the Senate with with his wife, the Bassanid beside them. Plautus Bonosus was well known, both for his private weaknesses and his public dignity. The Senate was a purely symbolic body, but Bonosus was said to conduct its affairs with style and order, and he was known for a man of discretion. His handsome second wife was impeccably proper, still young, but modest and dignified before her time. It crossed Crispin's mind briefly to wonder what—if anything—she did to salve herself while her husband was out at night with boys. He couldn't readily imagine her yielding to passions. She smiled politely now at the two chariot-racers nearby, in the midst of their admirers. Both of them bowed to her and to the Senator. A little distracted, Scortius took a moment to resume the thread of his argument.

Crispin saw Pardos detach himself from those around the charioteers and come nearer. There had been changes here in half a year, but these he would sort through when he had time alone with his former apprentice. He did know that his feelings when he'd seen that it was Pardos on the ladder this morning had been those of unalloyed pleasure.

It was rare to find or feel anything unalloyed here amid the mazelike intricacies of Valerius's city. A reason he still preferred to try to live on his scaffolds overhead, with gold and coloured glass and an image of the world to make. A wish, but he knew the City and himself well enough by now to realize it wouldn't happen. Sarantium was not a place in which one found refuge, even in pursuit of a vision. The world claimed you here, caught you up in the swirling. As now.

He nodded respectfully to Bonosus and his wife and murmured, 'I understand you might have a personal reason for wishing to make matters right with this physician. I am happy to leave the affair in your hands, if our eastern friend'—he looked politely at the doctor—'is willing to have it so.'

The Bassanid, a prematurely greying, rather formal man, nodded his head. 'I am content,' he said, his Sarantine really quite good. 'The Senator has been generous enough to offer me a residence while I conduct my researches here. I shall leave it to him and to those more versed than I in the justice of Sarantium to determine what should be done with those who killed my servant.'

Crispin kept his expression innocent as he nodded his head. The Bassanid was being bribed, of course—the house was a first instalment. The boy would be given some penance to perform by his father, the dead servant buried quickly in a grave outside the walls.

Curse-tablets would be thrown there by night. The racing season was starting soon: the cheiromancers and other self-declared traffickers in half-world power were already busy with maledictions against horses and men—and defences against the same. A charlatan could be paid to invoke a broken leg for a celebrated horse, and then be paid to provide protection for that same animal a day later. The burial place of a murdered pagan Bassanid, Crispin thought, would probably be said to contain even greater power than the usual run of graves.

'Justice *will* be done,' said Bonosus soberly.

'I rely upon it,' said the Bassanid. He looked to Pardos. 'We will meet again? I am in your debt and would like to repay your courage.' A stiff man, Crispin thought, but courteous enough, knew the things to say.

'No need for that, but my name is Pardos,' said the young man. 'I'll be easy enough to find in the Sanctuary, if Crispin doesn't kill me for setting tesserae at the wrong angle.'

'Don't set them at the wrong angle,' Crispin said. The Senator's mouth quirked.

'I am Rustem of Kerakek,' said the Bassanid, 'here to meet my western colleagues, share what I know, and obtain what further learning I can, for the better treatment of my own patients.' He hesitated, then allowed himself a smile, for the first time. 'I have travelled in the east. It seemed time to journey west.'

'He will be living in one of my houses,' Plautus Bonosus said. 'The one with the two round windows, in Khardelos Street. We are honoured, of course.'

Crispin felt himself go suddenly very cold. A wind seemed to pass into him: chill, damp air from the half-world, touching the mortal heart.

'Rustem. Khardelos Street,' he repeated, stupidly.

'You know it?' the Senator smiled.

'I . . . have heard the name.' He swallowed.

'Shirin, I will not *say that!'* he heard inwardly, still struggling with a sudden fear. There was a silence, then Danis again: *'You cannot possibly expect me to . . .'*

'It is a pleasant house,' the Senator was saying. 'A little small for a family, but near the walls, which was convenient in the days when I was travelling more.'

Crispin nodded distractedly. Then heard: *'She says to tell you that you are to imagine her hands right now, as you stand before this jaded boychaser and his too-prim wife. Think of her fingers slipping your tunic up from behind and then sliding back down along your skin, inside your undergarments. Think of them now, lightly touching your naked flesh, arousing you. She says to say that . . . Shirin! No!'*

Crispin coughed. He felt himself flushing. The Senator's allegedly too-prim wife eyed him with a mild interest. Crispin cleared his throat.

The Senator, endlessly experienced in meaningless chat, was saying, 'It is quite close, actually, to the Eustabius Palace—the one Saranios built by the walls. You know he loved to hunt, begrudged the long ride across the city from the Imperial Precinct on a good morning.'

'She wants you to think of her touching you right now, just where you are standing with them, her fingers stroking your most private places, down and further down, even as the woman in front of you watches this, unable to turn away, her own lips parting, her eyes growing wide.'

'Indeed!' Crispin managed, in a strangled voice. 'Loved to hunt! Yes!' Pardos glanced at him.

'She . . . she says that you can feel her nipples against your back now. Firm, proof of her own excitement. And that down

below . . . that she is becoming . . . Shirin, I will absolutely not say that!'

'And so Saranios would spend the night there,' Plautus Bonosus was saying. 'Bring favourite companions, a few girls when he was younger, and be outside the walls with bows and spears by sunrise.'

'She says her fingers are now touching your . . . your, ah, sex from . . . beneath . . . ah, stroking you, and . . . er, sliding? She says the Senator's young wife is staring at you, her mouth open, as your firm, hard . . . no!'

The bird's voice became a silent shriek, then blessedly stopped. Crispin, struggling for the scattered shreds of composure, hoped desperately that no one would look down towards his groin. Shirin! Jad-cursed Shirin!

'Are you well?' the Bassanid asked. His manner had changed; he was all solicitous, attentive concern. A physician. He would probably look down soon, Crispin thought despairingly. The Senator's wife was still gazing at him. Her lips, fortunately, had not parted.

'I'm a little . . . warm, yes, er, not serious . . . am sure, greatly hope, we'll meet again,' Crispin said with urgency. He bowed quickly. 'If you'll all excuse me now, ah, there's a . . . wedding matter. Must . . . speak about.'

'What matter?' accursed Carullus said, glancing across from beside Scortius.

Crispin didn't even bother to answer. He was already crossing the room towards where a slender woman was still standing against the far wall, almost hidden behind three men.

'She says to say she is now forever in your debt,' the bird said as he approached. *'That you are a hero like those of yesteryear and that your lower tunic shows signs of disarray.'*

This time he heard amusement even in the tone of Danis: in the singular voice Zoticus the alchemist had given to all his captured souls, including this shy young girl killed—as they all had been—on an autumn morning long ago in a glade in Sauradia.

She was laughing at him.

He might have been amused, himself, even coping with embarrassment, but something else had just happened, and he didn't know how to deal with it. More brusquely than he'd intended, he shouldered his way in between the figure of Pertennius and the paunchy merchant—almost certainly a Green patron—on his left. They glared at him.

'Forgive me, friends. Forgive me. Shirin, we have a small problem, will you come?' He took the dancer by the elbow, not gently, and guided her away from the wall, out of the half-circle of men that had surrounded her.

'A problem?' Shirin said prettily. 'Oh dear. What sort of . . . ?'

As they crossed the room together, Crispin saw people watching and hoped, sincerely, that his tunic was decent by now. Shirin smiled artlessly at her guests.

For want of any better idea, aware that he wasn't thinking clearly, Crispin steered her through the open doors back into the dining room where half a dozen or so people were lingering, and then into the kitchen beyond.

They stopped just inside the doorway: two white-clad figures amid the after-meal disarray and chaos of the kitchen and the stained and weary chefs and servers there. The talk subsided as people became aware of them.

'Greetings!' said Shirin brightly, as Crispin found himself wordless.

'And to you both,' said the small, plump, round-faced

man Crispin had first met in a pre-dawn kitchen somewhat larger than this. Men had died that night. An attempt on Crispin's own life. He remembered Strumosus holding a thick-handled chopping knife, preparing to use it on any intruders into his domain.

The chef was smiling now as he stood up from a stool and approached them. 'Have we given satisfaction, my lady?'

'You know you have,' Shirin said. 'What could I offer you to come live with me?' She, too, smiled.

Strumosus looked wry. 'Indeed, I was about to make you a similar offer.'

Shirin raised her eyebrows.

'It is very crowded here,' the cook said, gesturing at the piled implements and platters and the assortment of people standing around the kitchen. Hostess and guest followed him through to a smaller room where dishes and food were stored. There was another doorway here, giving onto the inner courtyard. It was too cold to go outside. The sun was west, it was growing dark.

Strumosus swung the door to the kitchen shut. It became quiet suddenly. Crispin leaned back against the wall. He closed his eyes briefly, then opened them; wished he'd thought to collect a cup of wine. Two names were reverberating in his head.

Shirin smiled demurely at the little chef. 'Whatever will people say of us? Are you proposing to me even as I try to win you, dear man?'

'For a cause,' the cook said, his expression serious. 'What would the Blues have to offer you to become their Principal Dancer?'

'Ah,' said Shirin. Her smile faded. She looked at Crispin then back to the cook. Then she shook her head.

'It cannot be done,' she murmured.

'At no price? Astorgus is generous.'

'So I understand. I hope he is paying you what you deserve.'

The chef hesitated, then bluntly named a sum. 'I trust the Greens are not offering you less.'

Shirin looked down at the floor, and Crispin saw that she was embarrassed. Not meeting the chef's eyes, she said only, 'They aren't.'

The implication was clear, if unspoken. Strumosus coloured. There was a silence. 'Well,' he said, rallying, 'it only makes sense. A Principal Dancer is more . . . prominent than any cook. More visible. A different level of fame.'

'But not more talented,' Shirin said, looking up. She touched the little man on the arm. 'It isn't a matter of payment for me. It is . . . something else.' She paused, bit her lip, then said, 'The Empress, when she sent me her perfume, made clear I was only to wear it for so long as I was a Green. This was just after Scortius left us.'

There was a silence.

'I see,' said Strumosus softly. 'Balancing the factions? She is . . . they are very clever, aren't they?'

Crispin thought of saying something then, but did not. *Very clever* was not the phrase, though. It didn't go nearly far enough. He was certain this touch would have been Alixana's own. The Emperor had no patience for faction issues; everyone knew it. It had almost cost him his throne during the riots, Scortius had told him. But the Empress, who had been a dancer for the Blues in her youth, would be attuned to such matters like no one else in the Imperial Precinct. And if the Blues were allowed to raid the pre-eminent charioteer of the day, then the Greens would keep the most celebrated dancer. The perfume—no one else in the Empire was allowed to wear it—and the condition attached would have been her way of making sure that Shirin knew this.

'A pity,' the little chef said thoughtfully, 'but I suppose it makes sense. If one looks at all of us from above.'

And *that* was about right, Crispin thought.

Strumosus changed the subject. 'Was there a *reason* you came into the kitchen?'

'To felicitate you, of course,' Shirin said quickly.

The chef looked from one to the other. Crispin was still finding it difficult to focus his thoughts. Strumosus smiled a little. 'I'll leave you alone for a moment. Incidentally, if you *are* looking for a cook, the fellow who made the soup today will be ready to work on his own later this year. His name's Kyros. The one with the bad foot. Young, but a very promising lad, and intelligent.'

'I'll remember that,' Shirin said, and returned the smile.

Strumosus went back to the kitchen. He closed the door behind him.

Shirin looked at Crispin. 'Thank you,' she said. 'You bastard.'

'You had your revenge,' he sighed. 'Half the guests here will have an image of me as some pagan fertility figure, rampant as a pole.'

She laughed. 'It's good for you. Too many people are afraid of you.'

'Not you,' he said absently.

Her expression changed, eyeing him. 'What happened? You don't look well. Did I really—?'

He shook his head. 'Not you. Your father, actually.' He took a breath.

'My father is dead,' Shirin said.

'I know. But half a year ago he gave me two names he said might help me in Sarantium. One was yours.'

She was staring at him now. 'And?'

'And the other was that of a physician, with a house and street where I might find him.'

'Doctors are useful.'

Crispin took another deep breath. 'Shirin, the man he named to me last autumn just arrived in Sarantium this morning, and was offered a residence on the named street only this afternoon, just now, here in your home.'

'Oh,' said the alchemist's daughter.

There was a silence. And in it they both heard a voice: *'But why,'* said Danis, *'is this so unsettling? You must have known he could do such things.'*

It was true, of course. They did know. Danis was her own proof of it. They were hearing the inward voice of a crafted bird that was the soul of a slain woman. What more evidence of power was required? But knowing and *knowing* were different things, at these borders of the half-world, and Crispin was pretty certain he remembered Zoticus denying being able to foretell the future, when asked. Had he lied? Possibly. Why should he have told all the truth to an angry mosaicist he hardly knew?

But why, then, should he have given that same stranger the first bird he'd ever fashioned, dearest to his own heart?

The dead, Crispin thought, stay with you.

He looked at Shirin and her bird and found himself remembering his wife and realizing it had been some days since he'd thought about Ilandra, which never used to happen. He felt sorrow and confusion and the effects of too much wine.

'We had better go back out,' Shirin said. 'It is probably time for the wedding-bed procession.'

Crispin nodded. 'Probably.'

She touched his arm, opened the door to the kitchen. They went through and back out to rejoin the party.

A little later, Crispin found himself in the darkening street among carried torches and music-makers and bawdy songs, with soldiers and theatre people and the usual cluster of hangers-on joining the loud parade as they led Carullus and Kasia to their new home. People banged things, sang, shouted. There was laughter. Noise was good, of course: it frightened away any evil spirits that might blight the marriage bed. Crispin tried to join in the general merriment, but failed. No one seemed to notice; night was falling and the others were more than loud enough. He wondered how Kasia felt about all of this.

He kissed bride and groom, both, at their doorway. Carullus had leased a set of rooms in a good neighbourhood. His friend, now a genuinely high-ranking officer, held him close and Crispin returned the embrace. He realized that neither he nor Carullus was entirely sober. When he bent to salute Kasia he became aware of something new and subtle about her, and then realized with a shock what it was—a scent: one that only an Empress and a dancer were supposed to wear.

Kasia read his expression in the darkness. They were standing very close. 'She said it was a last gift,' she whispered shyly.

He could see it. Shirin was like that. Kasia would be as royalty for this night. A rush of affection for this girl swept over him now. 'Jad love you and your own gods defend you,' he whispered fiercely. 'You were not saved from the grove for sorrow.'

He had no way of knowing if that was true, but he *wanted* it to be. She bit her lip, looking up at him, but said nothing, only nodded her head. Crispin stepped back. Pardos and Vargos were standing by. It had turned cold now.

He stopped by Shirin, eyebrows raised. 'A risky gift?' he asked.

She knew what he meant. 'Not for one night,' she said softly. 'In a bridal chamber. Let her be an Empress. Let him hold one.'

As those who hold you do? he thought suddenly, but did not say. It might have been in his face, though, for Shirin abruptly looked away, nonplussed. He walked over to Pardos. They watched bride and groom pause on their threshold, amid jests and cheering.

'Let's go,' said Crispin.

'Wait!' said the bird.

He looked back. Shirin, hooded and cloaked now in the darkness, stepped forward again and laid a gloved hand on his arm. She said, beseechingly, and to be heard, 'I have a last favour to ask. Will you escort a dear friend home? He's not quite . . . himself, and it isn't fair to take the soldiers from their celebrating now, is it?'

Crispin glanced beyond her. Swaying unsteadily, with a wide, entirely uncharacteristic smile spread across his face and eyes glazed like an enamel icon of some holy figure, was Pertennius of Eubulus.

'But of course,' Crispin said evenly. Shirin smiled. Her composure had returned, very quickly. She was a dancer, an actress, trained.

'She says you are not to take any sexual advantage of the poor man in his disordered state.' Even the accursed bird seemed amused again. Crispin gritted his teeth, said nothing.

Carullus and Kasia disappeared within, to a last lewd chorus from the musicians and the soldiers.

'No, no, no, no!' said the secretary, stepping forward too quickly from behind Shirin. 'Dear woman! I'm well, I'm *entirely* well! In fact I shall . . . escort *you* home myself! Honoured! Honoured to—'

Vargos, who was nearest, managed to catch the man before he toppled in the process of demonstrating the excellence of his state.

Crispin sighed. The fellow did need an escort, and Shirin was right about the soldiers, who were collectively as far gone in drink as the secretary and loudly proclaiming intentions of further celebration in honour of the newest chiliarch in the Sarantine army.

He sent Vargos with Pardos back to his own home and began walking—slowly, of necessity—with the secretary towards Pertennius's chambers, next to the Strategos's city residence. He didn't need directions: in addition to having the use of an entire wing of one of the palaces in the Imperial Precinct, Leontes owned the largest house in Sarantium. It happened to be nowhere close to Crispin's own home and mostly uphill from where they were; Shirin had known that, of course. It occurred to him that she really had bested him in their encounters today. He should probably be more irked by that than he was. He was still touched by her gesture with the perfume, though.

Looking back over his shoulder, carrying his own torch, he saw that the Greens' dancer would not lack for escorts on her own short journey home.

It was cold. He hadn't thought to take a cloak, of course, in that mad rush to change and make the ceremony in time.

'Fucking Jad,' he said under his breath.

Pertennius giggled, almost fell. 'Fucking!' he agreed and then giggled again, as if he'd startled himself. Crispin snorted; controlled men could be amusing when in drink.

He steadied the secretary with a hand on his elbow. They trudged on, close as cousins, as brothers, clad in white under the white moon. At intervals, out of the corner of his eye, Crispin saw tongues of flame flicker and vanish along the streets. You always saw those at night in Sarantium; no one even commented on it after they'd spent any time in the City.

A little later, as they passed behind the Sanctuary and turned up the wide street that would bring them to the secretary's rooms, they saw a sumptuous litter appear in front of them, its curtains closed. They both knew where they were, however, and who, almost certainly, would be inside.

Neither man commented, though Pertennius took a sudden deep breath of the cold night air and straightened his shoulders, walking a few steps alone with an exaggerated gravity, before stumbling again and accepting Crispin's guiding hand. They passed a watchman of the Urban Prefecture and nodded gravely to him: two inebriated men, out later than was safe, but well dressed, suited to this neighbourhood. Ahead, they saw the litter turn into a torchlit courtyard as servants swung open the gates and then closed them quickly.

The blue moon was up now above the houses, a crescent. A faint white line of flame appeared to run right across a laneway where it met the wide street and then it disappeared.

'Must come in!' Pertennius of Eubulus said as they went past the massive stone house and the barred gates where the litter had been admitted and came to his door. 'A chance to converse. Away from the street crowd, the soldiers. Actors. Uneducated rabble.'

'Oh, no,' Crispin demurred. He achieved a smile. There was something sourly amusing about the man taking that tone in his current state. 'We both need sleep, friend.' He was feeling his own wine now, and other things. A restlessness of spring. Night. A wedding. The presence of the past. This wasn't the person he wanted to be with now. He didn't know who was.

'Must!' the secretary insisted. 'Talk to you. My own task. Write about the Emperor's buildings, the Sanctuary. Your work. Questions! Why a bison? Those women? On the dome? Why so much of . . . of *you*, Rhodian?' The gaze, in moonlight, was direct for a disconcerting instant, could almost have been called lucid.

Crispin blinked. More here than he'd expected, from the man, from the moment. After a long hesitation, and with a mental shrug, he went to the door with Leontes's secretary and entered when a servant admitted them. Pertennius stumbled on his own threshold, but then led him heavily up a flight of stairs. Crispin heard the door being closed below.

Behind them in the night streets of the City, flames appeared and disappeared as they always did, seen or unseen, unlit by any taper or spark, unfathomable as the moonlit sea or the desires of men and women between their birth and dying.

CHAPTER V

The first thing Gisel came to understand, as she and the Strategos and his exquisitely haughty wife entered the presence of the Emperor and Empress of Sarantium, was that they were expected.

She was not *supposed* to realize that, she knew. They wanted her to believe that Leontes's impulsive action in inviting her had taken Valerius and Alixana by surprise here. She was to labour under this misapprehension, feel emboldened, make mistakes. But she had lived in a court all her life and whatever these arrogant easterners might believe about the Antae in Batiara, there were as many similarities as there were differences between her own palace complex in Varena and the Imperial Precinct here.

Weighing alternatives quickly as the musician lowered his instrument and the Emperor and a very small gathering of companions turned to her, Gisel elected to offer a full, formal salutation, brushing the floor with her forehead. Valerius—smooth-cheeked, bland, genial of expression—looked at Leontes and then back to Gisel as she rose. His mouth curved in a hesitant welcome. Alixana, in a low-backed ivory chair, dressed in deep red and adorned with jewellery, offered an entirely gracious smile.

And it was the ease of this on both their parts, the effortless deception done together, that made Gisel suddenly afraid, as if the walls of this warm room had given way to reveal the vast, cold sea beyond.

She had sent an artisan here half a year ago with an offer of marriage for this man. The woman, the Empress, knew of it. The artisan had told her about that. They had both anticipated—or deduced it—Caius Crispus said, before he had even spoken with them. She believed him. Seeing them now, the Emperor feigning surprise, Alixana offering the illusion of full welcome, she believed him implicitly.

'Forgive us, thrice-exalted, this unplanned intrusion,' said Leontes briskly. 'It is royalty I bring you, the queen of the Antae. It is past time, in my view, she was here among us. I will accept any fault attached to this.'

His manner was blunt and direct. No trace of the suave, courtly pacing and tone he'd revealed in the dancer's home. But he *had* to know this was no surprise, didn't he? Or was she wrong about that? Gisel stole a quick glance at Styliane Daleina: nothing to be read in those features.

The Emperor gestured in a distracted way, and servants hastened to offer seats to the two women. Styliane smiled a little to herself, holding a private amusement close, as she crossed the room and accepted a cup of wine and a chair.

Gisel also sat down. She was looking at the Empress. Doing so, she felt a faint but very real horror at her own folly of the year before. She had proposed that this woman—old, childless, surely worn out and tiresome by now—might be expendable.

Folly was not, really, an adequate word. Alixana of Sarantium, polished and smooth as a pearl, glittered with light where it reflected from her jewels and found her dark eyes. There was amusement there too, but of a very different sort from what could be seen in the Strategos's wife.

'No intrusion, Leontes,' she murmured now, speaking first. Her voice was low, honeyed, calm. 'You honour us, of course, all three of you. You have come from a wedding, I see. Will you take wine and share some further music here and then tell us about it?'

'Please,' said Valerius II earnestly, Emperor of half the world. 'Regard yourselves as invited and honoured guests!'

They were perfect, the two of them. Gisel made her decision.

Ignoring an offered cup, she rose smoothly from her seat, clasped her hands before her and murmured, 'The Emperor and Empress are far too good. They even allow me the flattering illusion that this visit was unanticipated. As if anything that transpires in great Sarantium could possibly pass unnoticed by their all-seeing eyes. I am deeply grateful for this courtesy.'

She saw the thin, aged Chancellor Gesius look suddenly thoughtful where he sat warming himself near the fire. There were only five other guests here, all superbly dressed and barbered men, and the balding, plump musician. Leontes looked irate suddenly, even though he'd surely have *had* to be the one who'd warned Valerius they were coming. Styliane was smiling again, behind her wine cup and her rings.

Valerius and Alixana laughed aloud. Both of them.

'And so we learn our lesson,' the Emperor said, a hand rubbing at his soft chin. 'Like impish children caught out by their tutor. Rhodias is older than Sarantium, the west came long before the east, and the queen of the Antae, who was daughter to a king before she ruled in her own name, was always likely to be aware of courtly practices.'

'You are clever and beautiful, child,' said Alixana. 'A daughter such as I might wish to have had.'

Gisel drew a breath. There could not possibly be anything sincere in this, but the woman had just casually drawn attention to their ages, her own childlessness, Gisel's appearance.

'Daughters are seldom in demand at a court,' she murmured, thinking as quickly as she could. 'We are only tools for marriage most of the time. A complication in other ways, unless there are also sons to smooth a succession.' If Alixana could be direct, so could she. There was an undeniable ripple of excitement within her: she had been here almost half a year, doing nothing, suspended like an insect in Trakesian amber. What she did now might end in death, but she realized she was prepared to court that.

This time it was Gesius who smiled briefly, she saw. She was conscious of his measuring gaze upon her.

'We are aware, of course, of your difficulties at home,' said Valerius. 'Indeed, we have spent a winter pondering ways of addressing them.'

There was little point, really, in not responding to this, either.

'We have spent a winter,' Gisel murmured, 'doing the same thing. It might have been appropriate to do so together? We did accept an invitation to come here in order to do that.'

'Indeed? Is that so? It is my understanding,' said a man dressed in figured silk of a deep green, 'that our invitation and an Imperial ship were what saved your life, queen of the Antae.' His tone, eastern, patrician, was just barely acceptable in this company. The Master of Offices paused, then added, 'You do have a savage history in your tribe, after all.'

This she would not countenance. East and the fallen west again? The glorious Sarantine heirs of Rhodias, the primitive barbarians from the northern forests? Not still, not here. Gisel turned her gaze to him.

'Somewhat,' she said coldly. 'We are a warlike, conquering people. Of course succession here in Sarantium always proceeds in a more orderly fashion. No deaths *ever* attend upon a change of Emperors, do they?'

She knew what she was saying. There was a little silence. Gisel became aware that glances were being cast—quickly, and then away—towards Styliane Daleina, who had seated herself behind the Empress. She made a point of not looking that way.

The Chancellor gave a dry cough behind his hand. Another of the seated men glanced quickly at him and then gestured briefly. The musician, with alacrity and evident relief, made a hasty obeisance and left the room with his instrument. No one paid him the least attention. Gisel was still glaring at the Master of Offices.

The Emperor said, in a thoughtful voice, 'The queen is correct, of course, Faustinus. Indeed, even my uncle's ascension was accompanied by some violence. Styliane's own dear father was killed.'

So much cleverness here. This was not a man, Gisel thought, to allow a nuance to slip by, if he could make it his own. She understood this, as it happened: her father had been much the same. It gave her some confidence, though her heart was racing. These were dangerous, subtle people, but she was the daughter of one herself. Perhaps she *was* one herself? They could kill her, and they might, but they could not strip her of pride and all legacies. She was aware of a bitter irony, however: she was defending her people against an allegation that they were murderous, barbaric, when she herself had been the intended victim of an assassination—in a holy, consecrated place.

'Times of change are seldom without their casualties,' said the Chancellor softly, his first words. His voice was thin as paper, very clear.

'The same must be said of war,' said Gisel, her tone blunt. She would *not* let this become an evening discussion of philosophers. She had sailed here for a reason, and it was not merely to save her life, whatever anyone might think or say. Leontes was looking at her, his expression betraying surprise.

'Truly so,' said Alixana, nodding her head slowly. 'One man burns and dies or thousands upon thousands do. We make our choices, don't we?'

One man burns and dies. Gisel looked quickly at Styliane this time. Nothing to be seen. She knew the story, everyone did. Sarantine Fire in a morning street.

Valerius was shaking his head. 'Choices, yes, my love, but they are not arbitrary ones if we are honourable. We serve the god, as we understand him.'

'Indeed, my lord,' said Leontes crisply, as if trying to draw a sword through the seductive softness of the Empress's voice. 'A war in the name of holy Jad is *not* as other wars.' He glanced at Gisel again. 'Nor can it be said that the Antae are unfamiliar with invasions.'

Of course they weren't. She'd implied as much herself. Her people had conquered the Batiaran peninsula, sacking Rhodias, burning it. Which made it difficult to argue against the idea of an invading army, or ask for mercy. She wasn't doing that. She was trying to steer this towards a truth she knew: if they invaded—and even if this tall, golden general succeeded in the beginning—they would not hold. They would never hold against the Antae, with the Inicii on the borders and Bassania creating another war front as it grasped the implications of a reunited Empire. No, the reclaiming of Rhodias could happen in only one way. And she, in her youth, in her person, a life that could end with a cup of poisoned wine or a silent, secret blade, was that way.

She had such a narrow, twisting path to try to walk here. Leontes, the handsome, pious soldier gazing at her now, was the one who would bring ruin to her country if the Emperor gave him word. *In the name of holy Jad*, he'd said. Did that make the dead less dead? She could ask them that, but it wasn't the question that mattered now.

'Why have you not spoken with me before?' she said, fighting a sudden, rising panic, looking at Valerius again, the calm, soft-faced man she had invited to marry her. She still had difficulty meeting the gaze of the Empress, though Alixana—of all of them—had been the most welcoming. Nothing here could be taken for what it seemed to be, she kept telling herself. If there was any truth to cling to, it was that.

'We were in negotiation with the usurpers,' Valerius said with brutal frankness. *He uses directness as a tool*, she thought.

'Ah,' she said, hiding discomfiture as best she could. 'Were you? How very . . . prudent.'

Valerius shrugged. 'An obvious course. It was winter. No armies travel, but couriers do. Foolish not to learn as much as we could about them. And they would have known if we had received you formally here, of course. So we didn't. We did have you watched, guarded against assassination all winter. You must be aware of that. They have spies here—just as you did.'

She ignored that last. 'They wouldn't have known if we had met like this,' she said. Her heart was still pounding.

'We assumed,' said the Empress gently, 'that you would refuse to be received in any way but as a visiting queen. Which was—and is—your right.'

Gisel shook her head. 'Should I insist on ceremony when people die?'

'We all do that,' said Valerius. 'It is all we have at such times, isn't it? Ceremony?'

Gisel looked at him. Their eyes met. She thought suddenly of the cheiromancers and the weary clerics and an old alchemist in a graveyard outside the city walls. Rituals and prayers, when they raised the mound of the dead.

'You should know,' the Emperor went on, his voice still mild, 'that Eudric in Varena, who calls himself regent now, by the way, has offered an oath of fealty to us and—something new—to begin paying a formal tribute, twice annually. In addition, he has invited us to place advisers in his court, both religious and military.'

Details, a great many of them. Gisel closed her eyes. *You should know.* She hadn't, of course. She was half a world away from her throne and had spent a winter waiting to be seen here in the palace, to have a role to play, to justify her flight. Eudric had won, then. She had always thought he would.

'His conditions,' the Emperor continued, 'were the predictable ones: that we recognize him as king, and accomplish a single death.'

She opened her eyes and looked at him again, unflinching. This was familiar territory, easier for her than they might guess. There had been wagers back home that she would die before winter. They had tried to kill her in the sanctuary. Two people she loved had been slain there, for her.

She was her father's daughter. Gisel lifted her chin and said hardily, 'Indeed, my lord Emperor? Sarantine Fire? Or just a knife in the night for me? A small price to pay for such resounding glory, isn't it? A fealty oath! Tribute, advisers? Religious *and* military? Great Jad be praised! The poets will sing and the years resound with the splendour of it. How could you refuse such glory?'

A rigid silence followed. Valerius's expression changed, only a little, but watching the grey eyes Gisel understood how people might fear this man. She could hear the crackle of the fire in the stillness.

It was Alixana, predictably, who dared speak. 'You are bested, love,' she said lightly. 'She is too clever for you. *Now* I understand why you won't cast me aside to marry her, or even properly receive her at court.'

Someone made a choking sound. Gisel swallowed, hard.

Valerius turned to his wife.

He said nothing, but his expression changed yet again, became odd now, strangely intimate. And a moment later it was Alixana who coloured a little and then looked down.

'I see,' she said quietly. 'I hadn't actually thought . . . ' She cleared her throat, fingered the necklace she wore. 'That wasn't . . . necessary,' she murmured, still looking down. 'I am not so fragile as that. My lord.'

Gisel had no idea what this meant, suspected no one else did. An intensely private exchange in a public space. She looked from one to the other again and then—quite suddenly—she *did* understand. Was sure of it.

Things were not what she had taken them to be.

She hadn't been invited to the Imperial Precinct before tonight, not because of negotiations with the usurpers in Varena or any rigidities of protocol, but because the Emperor Valerius was shielding his wife from Gisel's youthful presence and what—in purely formal terms—it meant, or could mean.

They all knew there was a way to simplify this reconquest of the Empire's homeland. She wasn't the only one who had seen it, sending an artisan on the long journey here with a private message. The logic, the *sense,* of a marriage was overwhelming. And the husband had been overriding the Emperor. Amazingly.

Which meant, if she was right in this sudden line of thought, that she had been admitted here now, tonight, *only* because . . . because a different decision had now been made.

Spring was coming. Was here, in fact. She took a breath.

'You are invading us, aren't you?' she said flatly.

Valerius of Sarantium turned from his wife to look at Gisel. His expression grave as a cleric's again, thoughtful as an academician, he said simply, 'Yes, in fact, we are. In your name and the god's. I trust you will approve?'

He wasn't really asking, of course. He was telling her. And not just her. Gisel heard, almost *felt* a ripple pass through the small, luxurious room as men shifted where they stood or sat. The Strategos's nostrils actually flared, like a racehorse's hearing the trumpet. He had surmised, anticipated, but had not known. Until now. She understood. This was the moment of telling that Valerius had just chosen, moving with the moment, the mood, her own arrival here. Or perhaps this entire evening of music among intimates on the trembling brink of springtime had been arranged to achieve this instant, with *none* of the others knowing, not even his wife. A man who pulled hidden strings, made others dance for his needs, or die.

She looked at Alixana and found the other woman's steady gaze waiting for hers. Gisel, gazing into those depths, imagining what those dark eyes could do to a man or a certain kind of woman, understood something else, entirely unexpected: improbable as it was, she had an ally here, someone else who also wanted to find a way to guide them all around this invasion and what it portended. Not that it seemed to matter.

'The Emperor is to be congratulated,' a third woman's voice interjected, Styliane's tone cool as the night wind outside. 'It seems his taxation officers have been more diligent than rumour suggests. It is a miracle of the god and his regent upon earth that adequate funds for an invasion are in the treasury after all.'

The ensuing pause was brittle. Styliane, Gisel thought, had to have extraordinary confidence in her situation to speak in this way, in this company. But she would, wouldn't she? By birth and marriage—and disposition.

Valerius turned to look at her and his expression, remarkably, was amused again. 'An Emperor receives the aid he deserves, Saranios once said. I don't know what that suggests about me and my servants, but there are ways of funding a war. We've decided to rescind pay for the eastern army this year. No point bribing Bassania for a peace *and* paying soldiers to keep it.'

Leontes looked startled. He cleared his throat. 'This has been decided, my lord?' He had obviously not been consulted.

'A fiscal matter, Strategos. I do wish to meet with you tomorrow to discuss the possibility of offering the soldiers land in the east to settle. We have discussed this in the past, and the Chancellor has now proposed we do it.'

Leontes was too experienced to further betray his surprise. 'Of course, my lord. I will be here at sunrise. Though I regret that I have been made a liar over something I said this afternoon at the wedding. I promoted the bridegroom and posted him east. Now he loses not only his promised increase in salary but *all* his income.'

Valerius shrugged. 'Re-post him. Take the fellow west with you. A small matter, surely.'

Leontes shook his head. 'I suppose it is. But I never take newly married men to a campaign.'

'Commendable, Leontes,' said the Empress. 'But I'm sure you can make exceptions.'

'Bad for an army, exalted lady.'

'So is obduracy, surely,' said his own wife, from her seat near the Empress. She set down her wine cup. 'My dear, really. You obviously think the fellow is competent. Appoint him to your private staff, pay him yourself as you pay the others, post him east to Eubulus as your observer for a year—or until you think it is all right for him to be called west and killed in war.'

The crisp precision of this in a woman, Gisel thought, looking from face to face to face, must surely be galling to the men assembled. Then she reconsidered, looking at the Empress. They might be accustomed to such things here— unlike her own court, where a woman speaking with authority could be marked for murder.

On the other hand, Gisel had *reigned* in Varena, in her own name. Neither of these women did. It mattered. It *did* represent a difference. And as if to underscore that, Styliane Daleina spoke again. 'Forgive me, my lords, this presumption.

I was ever too inclined to speak my mind.' There was no real contrition in her tone, however.

'A trait of your father's,' the Emperor said quietly. 'It . . . need not be a failing.'

Need not be, Gisel thought. The room seemed laden and layered with intricacies of past and present and what was to come. Nuances coiling and spreading like incense, subtle and insistent.

Styliane rose and made a graceful obeisance. 'Thank you, my lord. I will ask your permission and the Empress's to withdraw. If matters of war and policy are to be discussed, it is proper that I take my leave.'

It was, of course. No one spoke to gainsay her. Gisel wondered if she'd expected someone to do so. Her husband? If so, she would be disappointed. Leontes did escort his wife towards the door but turned back to the room as she went out. He looked at the Emperor, and smiled.

The two men had known each other, Gisel remembered hearing, from before the day when the first Valerius had been placed upon the throne. Leontes would have been very young then.

'My dear lord,' the Strategos said, unable to keep his voice entirely steady, 'may I ask that all those here be cautioned that this information is to go no further yet? I can make use of the advantage of time.'

'Oh, my dear,' said the wife at the Emperor's side, 'they will have been preparing for you since *long* before this child fled her throne. Ask her, if you really need to.'

Gisel ignored that, both the *child* and the *fled*, and saw that Valerius was looking at her, and she realized belatedly that he was actually waiting for an answer to the question he'd asked of her. *I trust you will approve?*

Formality, a courtesy, she thought. Such things mattered to him, it seemed. Worth knowing. He would always be courteous, this man on the Golden Throne. Even as he did exactly what he chose to do and accepted—or courted—any consequences that might fall to others.

'Do I approve?' she repeated. 'My lord, of course I do,' she lied. 'Why else did I sail to Sarantium?'

She sank low in obeisance again, mainly to hide her face now and what was in her eyes. She was seeing the burial mound again, not this elegant, lamplit palace room, was remembering civil war and famine, the festering aftermath of plague, was savagely lamenting the absence of a single living soul she could trust. Wishing, almost, that she had died in Varena, after all, and not lived to hear this question asked of her as she stood utterly alone in a foreign land where her answer—truth or lie—carried no weight or meaning in the world.

'I really do *not* feel well,' said Pertennius of Eubulus, spacing his words with care.

They were in a modest room on the upper floor of the secretary's home. Pertennius lay prostrate on a dark green couch, one hand over his eyes, the other on his stomach. Crispin, at a small window, stood looking down on the empty street. The stars were out, a wind was blowing. There was a fire lit on the hearth. On a desk against the wall between couch and window was an assortment of documents, books, writing implements, papers of different colours and textures.

Scattered among these—Crispin had seen them as soon

as he'd entered the room—were his own early sketches for the dome and wall of the Great Sanctuary.

He had wondered how they came to be here, and then remembered that Leontes's secretary was also the official historian of Valerius's building projects. In an unsettling way, Crispin's work was part of his mandate.

Why a bison? Pertennius had said, standing unsteadily in the street outside his door. *Why so much of* you *on the dome?*

Both, as it happened, shrewd questions. Crispin, no admirer of the dry-as-dust secretary, had come inside and up the stairs. Challenged, intrigued, both? Probably a waste of time, he realized, glancing over at the recumbent secretary. Pertennius looked genuinely ill. If he'd liked the man more, he might have been sympathetic.

'Too much wine of an afternoon can do that to you,' he said mildly. 'Especially if one doesn't normally drink.'

'I don't,' said Pertennius. There was a silence. 'She likes you,' the secretary added. 'More than me.'

Crispin turned away from the window. Pertennius had opened his eyes and was looking at Crispin. His gaze and tone were both quite neutral: a historian noting a fact, not a rival making complaint.

Crispin wasn't deceived. Not about this. He shook his head, leaning back against the wall by the window. 'Shirin? She likes me, yes, as a link to her father. Not as anything more.' He wasn't actually certain that was true, but he thought it was, most of the time. *Think of her fingers slipping your tunic up from behind and then sliding back down along your skin.* Abruptly, Crispin shook his head again, for a different reason this time. He hesitated, then said, 'Shall I tell you what I think?'

Pertennius waited. A listening sort of man, privy to much: in his profession, by his nature. He really didn't look well.

Crispin suddenly wished he hadn't come up here. This wasn't a conversation he wanted to be having. With an inward shrug and a flicker of irritation that he was being placed in this situation—or had placed himself in it—he said, 'I think Shirin is tired of being beset by men every time she steps out-of-doors. It makes for a difficult life, though some women might think they want it.'

Pertennius nodded slowly, his head heavy on his shoulders. He closed his eyes, struggled to open them again.

'Mortals seek fame,' he said sententiously, 'unaware of all it means. She needs a . . . protector. Someone to keep them away.'

There was truth to all of this, of course. Crispin decided not to say that a secretary and historian was unlikely to prove sufficient deterrent as an acknowledged lover to achieve that protection. Instead, he murmured, temporizing, 'You know there are those who have commissioned love spells from the cheiromancers.'

Pertennius made a sour face. 'Foh!' he said. 'Magic. It is unholy.'

'And it doesn't work,' Crispin added.

'You *know* this?' the other man asked. His eyes were briefly clear.

Aware, suddenly, of a need for caution, Crispin said, 'We are taught by the clerics that it doesn't, friend.' Irritated again, he added, 'In any case, have you ever seen Shirin wandering the streets before dawn against her will and desire, her hair unbound, compelled to where some man waits in his open doorway?'

'Oh, Jad!' said Pertennius, with feeling. He groaned. Illness and desire, an unholy mix.

Crispin suppressed a smile. Looked out the partly open window again. The air was cool. The street below was empty and silent. He decided to leave, considered asking for an escort. It was not particularly safe to cross the City at night alone and his own house was a distance away.

He said, 'You'd do well to get some sleep. We can talk another—'

'Do you know that they *worship* bison in Sauradia?' said Pertennius abruptly. 'It is in Metractes's *History of the Rhodian Wars.*'

Again, Crispin felt a flicker of alarm. His regret at being here grew more intense. 'I remember Metractes,' he said casually. 'I was made to memorize him as a child. Dismally dull.'

Pertennius looked offended. 'Hardly so, Rhodian! A fine historian. A model for my own histories.'

'I beg your pardon,' Crispin said quickly. 'He is, ah, voluminous, certainly.'

'Comprehensive,' said Pertennius. He closed his eyes again. The hand came back up to rest over them. 'Will this feeling pass?' he asked plaintively.

'In the morning,' Crispin said. 'With sleep. There is little else to be done for it.'

'Am I going to be sick?'

'It is certainly possible,' Crispin said. 'Do you want to stand by the window?'

'Too far. Tell me about the bison.'

Crispin drew a breath. Pertennius's eyes had opened again, were on him. 'There is nothing to tell. And everything. How does one *explain* these things? If words would do, I wouldn't be a mosaicist. It is as the roebuck and the rabbits and the birds and the fish and the foxes and the grain in the fields. I wanted them all on my dome. You have the sketches here, secretary, you can see the design. Jad created the world of animals as well as mortal man. That world lies between walls and walls, west and east, under the hand and eye of the god.'

All true, not the truth.

Pertennius made a vague sign of the sun disk. He was visibly struggling to stay awake. 'You made it very big.'

'They *are* big,' Crispin said, trying to keep the edge out of his voice.

'Ah? You've seen one? And Rhodias is up there too? *My dome*, you said. Is that pious? Is it . . . proper in a sanctuary?'

Crispin had his back to the window now, leaning against the ledge. He was about to answer, or try, when he realized there was no need any more. The secretary was asleep on the green couch, still in his sandals and the white garb of a wedding guest.

He took a deep breath, felt an undeniable sense of relief, escape. It was time to go, escort or not, before the other man awoke and asked further questions of this disconcertingly sharp nature. *He's harmless*, Shirin had said to Crispin on that first day they met. Crispin had disagreed. He still did. He crossed from the window, making for the door. He would send the servant up, to attend to his master.

If he hadn't seen scribbled handwriting across his own sketch on the table, he would have walked out. The temptation was irresistible, however. He paused, glanced quickly again at the sleeping man. Pertennius's mouth had fallen open. Crispin bent over the sketches.

Pertennius—it had to be him—had written a series of cryptic notes all over Crispin's drawings of the dome and wall decorations. The writing was crabbed, almost illegible. These were his notes for himself—not worth bothering with. There was nothing privileged about sketched proposals.

Crispin straightened to go. And as he did his eye fell across another page half-hidden under one of the sketches, written in the same hand, but more carefully, even elegantly, and this time he could read the words.

It was revealed to me by one of the officials of the Master of Offices (a man who cannot here be named for reasons of his life and security) that the Empress, remaining as corrupt as she was in her youth, is known to have certain of the younger Excubitors brought to her in her baths of a morning by her ladies who are, of course, chosen for their own depraved morals. She greets these men wantonly, naked and shameless as when she coupled with animals on the stage, and has the soldiers' clothing stripped from them.

Crispin found that he was having trouble breathing.

Very carefully, with another glance at the couch, he shifted the paper a little and read on, in disbelief.

She will have congress with these men, insatiably, sometimes two of them at one time using her like a whore in her own bath while the other women fondle themselves and each other and offer lewd, lascivious encouragement. A virtuous girl from Eubulus, the official told me in great secrecy, was poisoned by the Empress for daring to say that this conduct was impious. Her body has never been found. The unspeakable whore who is now our Empress always has her holy men detained outside the baths in the morning until after the soldiers have been dismissed through a hidden inner door. She then greets the clerics, half-naked, the reek of carnality about her, making a mockery of the morning prayers to holy Jad.

Crispin swallowed hard. He felt a pulse throbbing in his temple. He looked over at the sleeping man. Pertennius was snoring now. He looked ill and grey and helpless. Crispin became aware that his hands were shaking. He released the sheet of paper when it began to rattle in his grasp. He felt rage and fear and—beneath them both like a sounding drum—a growing horror. He thought he might be sick.

He ought to go, he knew. He *needed* to go from here. But there was a power to this exquisitely phrased vituperation, this venom, that caused him—almost without volition, as if he'd been rendered subject to a dark spell—to leaf to another page.

When the Trakesian farmer who foully murdered to claim the throne for his illiterate relative was finally seated there in his own right, though not his own peasant name (for he abandoned that as a vain effort to abandon the dung smell of the fields), he began to more openly practise his nighttime rites of daemons and black spirits. Ignoring the desperate words of his holy clerics, and ruthlessly destroying those who would not be silent, Petrus of Trakesia, the Night's Emperor, turned the seven palaces of the Imperial Precinct into unholy places, full of savage rituals and blood at darkfall. Then, in a vicious mockery of piety, he declared an intention to build a vast new Sanctuary to the god. He commissioned evil, godless men—foreigners, many of them—to design and decorate it, knowing they would never gainsay

*his own black purposes. It was truly believed by many in the
City in this time that the Trakesian himself conducted rituals of human sacrifice in the unfinished Sanctuary by night
when none were allowed but his own licensed confederates.
The Empress, besmeared with the blood of innocent victims,
would dance for him, it was said, between candles lit in
mockery of the holiness of Jad. Then, naked, with the
Emperor and others watching, the whore would take an
unlit candle from the altar, as she had done in her youth on
the stage, and she would lie down in sight of all and . . .*

Crispin crammed the papers back together. It was
enough. It was more than enough. He did feel ill now. This
unctuous, watchful, so-discreet secretary of the Strategos,
this official chronicler of the wars of Valerius's reign and his
building projects, with his honoured place in the Imperial
Precinct, had been spewing forth in this room the accu-
mulated filth and bile of hatred.

Crispin wondered if these words were ever meant to be
read. And when? Would people *believe* them? Could they
shape, in years to come, an impression of truth for those
who had never actually known the people of whom these
ugly words were written? Was it possible?

It occurred to him that if he but walked from here with
a randomly chosen sheaf of these papers in his hand
Pertennius of Eubulus would be disgraced, exiled.

Or, very possibly, executed. A death to Crispin's name.
Even so, it stayed in his mind to do it, standing there over
the cluttered table, breathing hard, imagining these pages as
crimson-hued with their hatred, listening to the sleeping
man's snores and the snap of the fire and the faint, distant
sounds of the night city.

He remembered Valerius, that first night, standing under the stupendous dome Artibasos had achieved. The intelligence and the courtesy of the Emperor as he patiently watched Crispin come to terms with the surface he was being given for his own craft.

He remembered Alixana in her rooms. A rose in gold on a table. The terrible impermanence of beauty. Everything transitory. *Make me something that will last,* she had said.

Mosaic: a striving after the eternal. He'd realized that she understood that. And had understood even then, that first night, that this woman would be with him always, in some way. That had been before the man now sleeping gape-mouthed on his couch had knocked and entered, bearing a gift from Styliane Daleina.

Crispin remembered—and now understood in a very different way—the devouring glance Pertennius had cast about Alixana's small, rich, firelit chamber, and the expression in his eyes when he'd seen the Empress with her hair unbound and seemingly alone with Crispin late at night. *The unspeakable whore who is now our Empress.*

Abruptly, Crispin left the room.

He went quickly down the stairs. The servant was dozing on a stool in the hallway under an iron wall sconce. He snapped suddenly awake at the sound of footsteps. Sprang up.

'Your master is asleep in his clothing,' Crispin said brusquely. 'See to him.'

He unlocked the front door and went out to where there was cold air and a darkness that appalled him so much less than what he had just read by firelight. He stopped in the middle of the street, looked up, saw stars: so remote, so detached from mortal life, no one could invoke them. He welcomed the cold, rubbing hard at his face with both hands as if to cleanse it.

He suddenly wanted, very much, to be home. Not in the house he'd been given here, but half a world away. Truly home. Beyond Trakesia, Sauradia, the black forests and empty spaces, in Varena again. He wanted Martinian, his mother, other friends too much neglected these past two years, the comfort of the lifelong-known.

False shelter, that. He knew it, even as he shaped the thought. Varena was a cesspool now, as much or more than Sarantium was, a place of murder and civil violence and black suspicions in the palace: without even the possibility of redemption that lay overhead here on the Sanctuary dome.

There was, really, nowhere to hide from what the world seemed to be, unless one played Holy Fool and fled into a desert somewhere, or climbed a crag. And, really, in the great scale and scheme of things—he took another deep breath of the cold night air—how did a fearful, bitter scribe's malevolence and lecherous dishonesty measure against . . . the death of children? It didn't. It didn't at all.

It occurred to him that sometimes you didn't really arrive at a conclusion about your life, you just discovered that you already had. He wasn't about to flee from all this, let his hair grow wild and his garments stink of unwashed sweat and excrement in the desert while his skin blistered and burned. One lived in the world. Sought what slender grace was to be found, however one defined such things, and accepted that Jad's creation—or Ludan's, the *zubir's*, or that of any other worshipped power—was not a place where mortal men and women were meant to find tranquil ease. There might be other worlds—some taught as much—better than this, where such harmonies were possible, but he didn't live in one and was not ever going to live in one.

And thinking so, Crispin turned and looked down the street a little way and he saw the torchlit wall of the enormous house adjacent to Pertennius's and the gated courtyard into which an elegant litter had been carried a little time ago, and in the starlit dark he saw that the front door of that house now stood open to the night and a servant woman was there, robed against the chill, a candle in her hand, looking at him.

The woman saw that he had noticed her. Wordlessly, she lifted the candle and gestured with her other hand towards the open doorway.

Crispin had actually wheeled around to face the other way before he'd even realized he was doing so, the movement entirely involuntary. His back to the dark invitation of that light, he stood very still again in the street, but all was changed now, changed utterly, by that open door. To his left, above the handsome stone and brick façades of the houses here, the arc of the starlit dome rose, a serene curve above all these jagged, wounding mortal lines and edges, disdainful of them in its purity.

But *made* by a mortal man. A man named Artibasos, one of those who lived down here among all the cutting, human interactions of wife, children, friends, patrons, enemies, the angry, indifferent, bitter, blind, dying.

Crispin felt the wind rise, imagined the slim serving girl shielding her candle in the open doorway behind him. Visualized his own tread approaching her, passing through that door. Became aware that his heart was pounding. *I am not ready for this*, he thought, and knew that in one way it was simply untrue, and in another he would *never* be ready for what lay beyond that door, so the thought was meaningless. But he also understood, alone on a starlit night in Sarantium, that he needed to enter that house.

Need had many guises, and desire was one of them. The jagged edges of mortality. A door his life had brought him to, after all. He turned around.

The girl was still there, waiting. Her task was to wait. He went towards her. No supernatural fires flitted or sparked in the night street now. No human voices came to him, of watchman's cry or night walker's song or faction partisans careening from a distant tavern, heard over the rooftops. There were four torches spaced evenly in iron brackets along the beautifully fashioned stone wall of the great house. The stars were bright above him, the sea behind now, almost as far away. The woman in the doorway was very young, Crispin saw, no more than a girl, fear in her dark eyes as he came up to her.

She held out her candle to him and, without speaking, gestured again inside, towards the stairs which were unlit by any lamps at all. He took a breath, felt the hammering presence of something deep within himself and acknowledged a part, in the heavy current of the moment, of what the intensity of this stirring meant. The fury of mortality. Darkness, some light carried, but not very much.

He took the flame from the girl's cold fingers and went up the winding stair.

There was no illumination but his own, throwing his moving shadow against the wall, until he reached the upper landing and turned and saw a glow—orange, crimson, yellow, rippled gold—through the partly opened door of a room along the corridor. Crispin remained still for a long moment, then he blew out his candle and set it down: a blue-veined marble-topped table, iron feet like lion's paws. He went down the hallway, thinking of stars and the cold wind outside and his wife when she died and before, and then of the night last autumn here when a woman had been waiting for him in his room before dawn, a blade in her hand.

He came to her door now through this dark house, pushed it open, entered, saw lamps, the fire, low and red, a wide bed. He leaned back against the door, closing it with his body, his heart drumming in his chest, his mouth dry. She turned; had been standing by a window over an inner courtyard.

Her long pale golden hair was unpinned and down, all her jewellery removed. She wore a robe of whitest silk, a bride's night raiment. In bitter irony, in need?

His vision actually blurred with apprehension and desire, seeing her, his breath coming ragged and quick. He feared this woman and almost hated her and he felt that he might die if he did not have her.

She met him in the middle of the room. He was unaware of having stepped forward, time moving in spasms, as in a fever dream. Neither of them spoke. He saw the fierce, hard blue of her eyes, but then she suddenly twisted and lowered her head, exposing her neck like a wolf or a dog in submission. And then before he could even react, respond, try to understand, she had lifted her head again, the eyes uncanny, and took his mouth with her own as she had done once, half a year ago.

She bit him this time, hard. Crispin swore, tasted his own blood. She laughed, made to draw back. He cursed again, aroused beyond words, intoxicated, and held her by the curtain of her hair, pulling her back to him. And this time as they kissed he saw her eyes fall shut, her lips part, a pulsing in her throat, and Styliane's face in the flickering firelight of her room was white as her robe, as a flag of surrender.

There was none, however. No surrendering. He had never known lovemaking as a battle before, each kiss, touch, coming together, twisting apart for desperate breath an engagement of forces, the need for the other hopelessly entangled with anger and a fear of never coming back out, never controlling oneself again. She provoked him effortlessly, would approach, touch, withdraw, return, lowered her neck again once in that brief, submissive averting—her throat long and sleek, the skin smooth and scented and young in the night—and he felt a sudden, genuinely shocking tenderness entwine with anger and desire. But then she lifted her head again, the eyes brilliant, mouth wide, and her hands raked his back as they kissed. Then, very swiftly, she lifted his hand and, twisting away, bit him there.

He was a worker in mosaic, in glass and tile and light. His hands were his life. He snarled something incoherent, lifted her off the ground, carried her before him to the high, canopied bed. He stood a moment there, holding her in his arms, and then he laid her down. She looked up at him, light caught in her eyes, changing them. Her robe was torn at one shoulder. He had done that. He saw the shadowed curve of her breast with the firelight upon it.

She said: 'Are you certain?'

He blinked. *'What?'*

He would remember her smile then, all that it meant and said about Styliane. She murmured, ironic, assured, but bitter as the ashes of a long-ago fire, 'Certain it isn't an empress or a queen you want, Rhodian?'

He was speechless a moment, looking down upon her, his breath caught as on a fishhook embedded in his chest. He became aware that his hands were shaking.

'Very certain,' he whispered hoarsely, and pulled his own white tunic over his head. She lay motionless a moment then lifted one hand and traced a long finger lightly, slowly down his body, a single straight movement, illusion of simplicity, of order in the world. He could see that she was struggling hard for her own control, though, and that added to his desire.

Very certain. It was entirely true, and yet hopelessly not so, for where could certainty lie in the world in which they lived? The clean, straight movement of her finger was *not* the movement of their lives. It didn't matter, he told himself. Not tonight.

He let the questions and the losses slip from him. He lowered himself upon her and she guided him hard into her, and then those long slender arms and her long legs were wrapped around his body, hands gripping in his hair and then moving up and down his back, mouth at his ear whispering things, over and again, rapid and needful, until her own breathing grew more ragged and terribly urgent, exactly as his own. He knew he must be hurting her but heard her cry out harshly only as her body curved upwards in its own arc and lifted him with her for that moment, away from all the jagged edges and the broken lines.

He saw tears startle like diamonds on her cheekbones and he knew—*knew*—that even consumed like a burning taper by desire she was raging within against the revealed weakness of that, the dimensions of longing betrayed. She could kill him now, he thought, as easily as kiss him again. Not a haven, this woman, this room, not a shelter of any kind at all, but a destination he'd needed overwhelmingly to reach and could not, by any means, deny: these bitter, furious complexities of human need, down here beneath the perfect dome and the stars.

'You have no dread of high places, I may assume?'

Lying beside each other. Some of her golden hair across his face, tickling a little. One of her hands on his thigh. Her face was averted, he could see only a profile as she stared at the ceiling. There was a mosaic there, he now saw, and abruptly remembered Siroes who had made it, whose hands had been broken by this woman for his failings.

'A fear of heights? It would be an impediment in my work. Why?'

'You'll leave through the window. He may be home soon, with his own servants. Go down the wall and across the courtyard to the far end by the street. There is a tree to climb. It will take you to the top of the outer wall.'

'Am I leaving now?'

She turned her head then. He saw her mouth quirk a little. 'I hope not,' she murmured. 'Though you may have to depart in haste if we delay too long.'

'Would he . . . come in?'

She shook her head. 'Unlikely.'

'People die because of unlikely things.'

She laughed at that. 'True enough. And he *would* feel compelled to kill you, I suppose.'

This surprised him a little. He'd somehow concluded that these two—the Strategos and his aristocratic prize—had their shared understandings in matters of fidelity. That servant with her candle, visible to the street in the open doorway . . .

He was silent.

'Do I frighten you?' She was looking at him now.

Crispin shifted to face her. There seemed no reason to dissemble. He nodded his head. 'But in yourself, not because of your husband.' She held his glance a moment and then, unexpectedly, looked away. He said, after a pause, 'I wish I liked you more.'

'Liking? A trivial feeling,' she said, too quickly. 'It has little to do with this.'

He shook his head. 'Friendship begins with it, if desire doesn't.'

Styliane turned back to him. 'I have been a better friend than you know,' she said. 'From the outset. I did tell you not to become attached to any work on that dome.'

She *had* said that, without explaining it. He opened his mouth but she held up a finger and laid it against his lips. 'No questions. But remember.'

'An impossibility,' he said. 'Not to be attached.'

She shrugged. 'Ah. Well. I am helpless against impossibilities, of course.'

She shivered suddenly, exposed to the cold air, her skin still damp from lovemaking. He glanced across the room. Rose from the bed and tended to the guttering fire, adding logs, shifting them. It took him a few moments, building it up again. When he stood, naked and warmed, he saw that she was propped on one elbow, watching him with a frank, appraising gaze. He felt abruptly self-conscious, saw her smile, seeing that.

He crossed back towards the bed and stood beside it, looking down at her. Without shame or evasion she lay, unclothed and uncovered, and let him track with his gaze the curves and lines of her body, arc of hip, of breast, the fine bones of her face. He felt the stirrings of desire again, irresistible as tides.

Her smile deepened as her glance flicked downwards. Her voice, when she spoke, was husky again. 'I did hope you weren't in haste to find the courtyard and the tree.' And she reached out with one hand and stroked his sex, drawing him to the bed and back to her that way.

And this time, in a slower, more intricate dance, she did eventually show him—as she'd offered half a year ago—how Leontes liked to use a pillow, and he discovered something new about himself, then, and illusions of civility. At one point, later, he found himself doing something to her he'd only ever done for Ilandra, and it came to him, feeling her hands tightening in his hair, hearing her whispering a stream of incoherent words as if unwilling, compelled, that one might feel the sadness of loss, of absence, love and shelter gone, but not be endlessly consumed and destroyed as by an ongoing lightning bolt of tragedy. Living was not, in and of itself, a betrayal.

Some had tried to tell him this before, he knew.

She made a higher sound then, on a taken breath, as if in pain, or fighting something. She drew him up and into her again, her eyes tightly closed, hands pulling him, and then swiftly turned them both together so she rode upon him now, harder and harder, imperative, her body glistening in the firelight. He reached up and touched her breasts, spoke her name, once: resisting that but impelled, exactly as she had been. Then he gripped her hips and let her begin to drive them both, and at length he heard her cry aloud and opened his eyes to see that arcing of her body again, the skin taut across her ribs as she bent back above him like a bow. There were tears on her cheeks, as before, but this time he reached up and drew her slowly down and kissed them, and she allowed him to do so.

And it was then, lying upon him in an aftermath, her body shaking, and his, her hair covering them both, that Styliane whispered without warning, eerily gentle in his memory of the moment after, 'They will invade your country later in the spring. No one knows yet. It was announced to some of us tonight in the palace. Certain events must happen now. I will not say I am sorry. A thing was done once, and all else follows. Remember this room, though, Rhodian. Whatever else. Whatever else I do.'

In his confusion, his mind not yet working properly, the sudden knife's blade of fear, all he could say was, '*Rhodian? Only that? Still?*'

She lay upon him, not moving now. He could feel the beating of her heart. 'Rhodian,' she repeated, after a considering silence. 'I am what I've been made to be. Don't be deceived.'

Then why were you weeping? he wanted to ask, but didn't. He would remember these words, too, all of them, and the straining backwards arcing of her body and those bitter tears at her own exposed need. But in the silence that came after she spoke what they both heard was the front door down below closing heavily, reverberating.

Styliane shifted a little. Somehow he knew she would be smiling, that wry, ironic smile. 'A good husband. He always lets me know when he comes home.'

Crispin stared at her. She looked back, eyes wide, still amused. 'Oh dear. Really. You think Leontes *wants* to spend his nights killing people? There's a knife in here somewhere. You want to fight him for my honour?'

So there *was* an agreement between them. Of some kind. He really wasn't understanding these two at all, was he? Crispin felt heavy-headed and tired now, and afraid: *A thing was done once.* But a door had slammed, down below, leaving no space for sorting matters through. He stumbled from the bed, began to dress. She watched him calmly, smoothing the sheets about her, her hair spread out on the pillows. He saw her drop her torn garment on the floor, not bothering to hide it further.

He adjusted his tunic and belt, knelt and quickly tied his sandals. When he stood again, he looked at her for a moment. The firelight was low again, the candles burnt out. Her naked body was chastely covered by the bed linens. She sat propped on pillows, motionless, receiving and returning his gaze. And Crispin abruptly realized then that there was a kind of defiance in this, as much as anything else, and understood that she was very young, and how easy it was to forget that.

'Don't deceive *yourself*,' he said. 'While trying so hard to control the rest of us. You are more than the sum of your plans.' He wasn't even sure what that meant.

She shook her head impatiently. 'None of that matters. I am an instrument.'

His expression wry, he said, 'A prize, you told me last time. An instrument tonight. What else should I know?' But there was an odd, entirely unexpected ache in him now, looking at her.

She opened her mouth and closed it. He saw that she'd been taken off guard, heard footsteps in the hallway outside.

'Crispin,' she said, pointing to the window. 'Go. Please.'

It was only when he was crossing the courtyard, past the fountain, making for the indicated olive tree at the corner near the street, that he realized she'd spoken his name.

He climbed the tree, crossed to the top of the wall. The white moon was up now, halfway to full. He sat on a stone wall above the dark, empty street, and he was remembering Zoticus, and the boy he'd once been himself, crossing from wall to tree. The boy, and then the man. He thought of Linon, could almost *hear* her commenting on what had just passed. Or perhaps he was wrong: perhaps she would have understood that there were elements here more complex than simple desire.

Then he laughed a little, under his breath, ruefully. For that was wrong, too: there was nothing the least simple about desire. He looked up and saw a figure silhouetted in the window he'd just left. Leontes. The window was pulled shut, the curtains drawn in Styliane's bedroom. Crispin sat motionless, hidden upon a wall.

He looked across the street and saw the dome rising above the houses. Artibasos's dome, the Emperor's, Jad's. Crispin's own? Below—a flicker at the corner of his eye— one of those utterly inexplicable eruptions of flame that defined Sarantium at night appeared in the street and vanished, like dreams or human lives and their memory. What, Crispin wondered, was ever left behind?

They will invade your country later in the spring.

He didn't go home. Home was very far away. He jumped down from the wall, went across the street, cutting up a long dark lane. A prostitute called to him from shadow, her voice a kind of song in the night. He kept going, following an angling of the laneway, and eventually came to where it opened onto the square across from the Imperial Precinct gates, with the front of the Sanctuary on his right. There were guards on the portico, all night long. They knew him as he approached, nodded, opened one of the massive doors. There was light inside. Enough to let him work.

CHAPTER VI

Same hour of night, same wind, four men walking elsewhere in the City, under that risen moon.

It was never entirely safe in Sarantium after nightfall, but a party of four could feel reasonably secure. Two of them carried heavy sticks. They walked briskly enough in the cold, slowed somewhat, as the road sloped downwards and then back up, by wine consumed and the bad foot one of them dragged. The oldest, small and portly, was wrapped in a heavy cloak to his chin but swore whenever the wind gusted and sent debris tumbling down the dark street.

The were women abroad, too, in doorways for shelter, for they wore too little clothing in the nature of their profession. A number of them could be seen lingering with the unhoused beggars by the heat of the bakers' ovens.

One of the younger men showed an inclination to slow down here, but the one in the cloak rasped an oath and they kept moving. A woman—a girl, really—followed them a little way and then stopped, standing alone in the street before retreating to the warmth. As she did, she saw an enormous litter carried by eight bearers—not the usual four or six—come around a corner and then move down the street, following the four men. She knew better than to call out after this aristocrat. If such as these wanted a woman, they made their own choices. If they did call one over to the curtained litter, it wasn't necessarily safe for the girl. The wealthy had their own rules here, as elsewhere.

None of the men walking were sober. They had been given wine at the end of a wedding feast by the hostess, and had only just emerged from a noisy tavern where the oldest one had bought several more flasks for all of them to share.

It was a long walk now, but Kyros didn't mind. Strumosus had been astonishingly genial in the tavern, discoursing volubly upon eel and venison, and the proper marriage of sauce and principal dish as recorded by Aspalius four hundred years ago. Kyros and the others had been aware that their master was pleased with how the day had unfolded.

Or he had been until they'd stepped back outside and realized just how cold it was now, and how late, with a long way yet through the windy streets to the Blues' compound.

Kyros, reasonably immune to the chill, as it happened, was too exhilarated to care: the combination of a successful banquet, too much wine, intense images of their hostess—her scent, smile, words about his own work in the kitchen—and then Strumosus's affable, expansive mood in the tavern. This was one of the *very* good days, Kyros decided. He wished he were a poet, that he could put some of these tumbling-about feelings into words.

There was a clatter of noise ahead. Half a dozen young men spilled from the low door of a tavern. It was too dark to see them clearly: if they were Greens this could be dangerous, with the season soon to start and anticipation rising. If they had to run, Kyros knew he would be the problem. The four men bunched themselves more closely together.

Unnecessarily, as it turned out. The tavern party meandered untidily down the hill towards the waterfront, attempting a marching song of the day. Not Greens. Soldiers on leave in the City. Kyros drew a relieved breath. He glanced back over his shoulder—and so he was the one who saw the litter following behind them in the darkness.

He said nothing, walked on with the others. Laughed dutifully at Rasic's too-loud joke about the inebriated soldiers—one of them had stopped to be sick in a shop doorway. Kyros looked back again as they turned a corner, passing a sandal shop and a yogurt stand, both long since closed for the night: the litter came around the corner, keeping pace with them. It was very large. Eight men carried it. The curtains were drawn on both sides.

Kyros felt a queasy apprehension. Litters at night weren't at all unusual—the well-to-do tended to use them, especially when it was cold. But this one was moving too precisely at their own speed and going exactly where they went. When it followed them diagonally across a square, around the central fountain, and then up the steep street on the opposite side, Kyros cleared his throat and touched Strumosus on the arm.

'I think . . .' he began, as the chef looked at him. He swallowed. 'It is possible we're being followed.'

The other three stopped and looked back. The litter immediately halted, the dark-clad bearers motionless and silent. The street was empty around them. Closed doors, closed shop fronts, four men standing together, a patrician's curtained litter, silence, nothing else.

The white moon hung overhead above a small chapel's copper dome. From a distance there came the flaring sound of sudden, raucous laughter. Another inn, patrons leaving. Then that sound faded away.

In the stillness the three young men heard Strumosus of Amoria let out a long breath, then swear, quietly but with intense feeling.

'Stay where you are,' he told them. And he walked back towards the litter.

'Fuck,' whispered Rasic, for want of anything better to say. Kyros felt it too: a sense of menace, oppression.

They were silent, watching the little chef. Strumosus approached the litter. None of the bearers moved or spoke. The chef stopped by the drawn curtains on one side. He appeared to be speaking, but they couldn't hear him, or any reply from within. Then Kyros saw the curtain lifted and pulled back slightly. He had no idea who was inside, man or woman, or more than one person—the litter was easily large enough for that. He did know that he was afraid now.

'Fuck,' said Rasic again, watching.

'Fuck,' Mergius echoed.

'Shut up,' Kyros said, uncharacteristically. 'Both of you.'

Strumosus appeared to be speaking again, then listening. Then he folded his arms across his chest and said something else. After a moment the curtain fell closed, and a moment later the litter was turned around and began to move the other way, back down towards the square. Strumosus stayed where he was, watching, until it disappeared beyond the fountain. He walked back to the three young men. Kyros could see that he was disturbed, but he didn't dare ask any questions.

'Who in the god's name was that?' Rasic said, not feeling the same compunction.

Strumosus ignored him, as if the young man hadn't even spoken. He started walking; they fell in stride with him. No one said anything more, not even Rasic. They came to the compound without further incident, were known by torchlight and admitted.

'Good night,' Strumosus said to the three of them, at the entrance to the dormitory. Then he walked away without waiting for a response.

Rasic and Mergius went up the steps and in, but Kyros lingered on the porch. He saw that the chef did not go towards his private rooms. Instead, he walked across the courtyard to the kitchens. A moment later Kyros saw lamps being lit there. He wanted to go over but did not. Too much presumption. After another moment, he took a last breath of the cold air and stepped inside after the others. He went to bed. Didn't sleep for a long time. A very good day and night had been, obscurely, changed into something else.

In the kitchen, Strumosus of Amoria moved with precision to build up the fire, light the lamps, pour himself a cup of wine. He watered it judiciously, then took a knife, sharpened it, and rhythmically chopped vegetables. He cracked two eggs, added the vegetables, sea salt, a generous pinch of expensive eastern pepper. He beat the mixture in a small, chipped bowl he'd had for years and used only for himself. Heated a saucepan on a grate placed over the cooking fire, drizzled olive oil into it, and made himself a flat-bottomed egg dish, flipping it intuitively. He set the saucepan down on a stone surface and selected a white-and-blue patterned plate from a shelf. He transferred his swift creation to the plate, decorated the surface with flower petals and mint leaves and then paused briefly to evaluate the effect. *A chef who is careless about how he feeds himself,* he was fond of telling his assistants, *will become careless about feeding others.*

He wasn't hungry at all, but he was disturbed and had needed to cook, and once a dish had been well made it was very much a crime in his interpretation of Jad's created world not to enjoy it. He sat on a high stool at the work island in the centre of the room and ate alone, drinking the wine, refilling his cup, watching the white moon's light falling on the courtyard outside. He'd thought Kyros might come over here and wouldn't entirely have minded company, but the boy lacked—as yet—confidence to go with his perceptiveness.

Strumosus realized that his wine cup was empty again. He hesitated, then refilled it, mixing less water than before. It was rare for him to drink this much, but he didn't often have an encounter like the one in the street just now.

He'd been offered a job and had refused. Two such proposals today, in fact. First from the young dancer, and then in the dark just now. Not a problem, those, in themselves. It happened often. People knew of him, desired his services, some had the money to pay him. He was happy here with the Blues, however. It wasn't an aristocratic kitchen but it was an important one, and he had a chance to play a role in changing perceptions about his own art and passion. It was said that the Greens were now searching for a master chef. Strumosus had been amused and pleased.

But the person who'd made him the offer from inside that sumptuous litter was different. Someone he knew very well, in fact, and memories—including those of his own deferential, complicitous silences on certain matters in times past—were with him now. *The past does not leave us until we die*, Protonias had written long ago, *and then we become someone else's memories, until they die. For most men it is all that endures after them. The gods have made it so.*

The old gods themselves were almost gone now, Strumosus thought, looking at his wine cup. And how many living souls remembered Protonias of Trakesia? How *did* a man leave a name?

He sighed, looking around his familiar kitchen, every corner of it thought out, allocated, an imposing of order in the world. *Something is about to happen*, the little chef thought suddenly, alone in a circle of lamps. He'd thought he knew what it was—hadn't been shy about offering his views. A war in the west: what thinking man could miss the signs?

But sometimes thought and observation were not the keys. Sometimes the locked doors were opened by something within the blood, in the soul, in dream.

He wasn't so sure any more of what it was that was approaching. But he did know that if Lysippus the Calysian was in Sarantium again, and moving about in his litter in the darkness, that blood and dream would be part of it.

Someone else's memories, until they die.

He wasn't afraid for himself, but it did cross his mind to wonder if he should be.

It was time to go to bed. He didn't want to go to bed. He ended up dozing where he sat on his stool, bent forward, the plate and cup pushed away, his head pillowed on his folded arms as the lamps burned slowly down and the dark drew back in.

In the heart of that same night, the wind so keen outside it seemed the god was withholding spring from his world, a man and a woman were drinking spiced wine by a fire on their wedding night.

The woman sat on a backless, cushioned seat, the man on the floor by her feet, his head resting against her thigh. They watched the flames in a silence characteristic of her but unusual for him. It had been a very long day. One of her hands rested lightly on his shoulder. Both of them were remembering other flames, other rooms; a slight awkwardness inhabited the place, an awareness of the other chamber—and the bed—just beyond the beaded arch of a door.

He said, at length, 'You haven't worn that scent before, have you? You don't wear any perfume usually. Do you?'

She shook her head, then realizing he couldn't see her, murmured, 'No.' And, after a hesitation, 'It's Shirin's. She insisted I wear it tonight.'

He turned his head then and looked up at her, his eyes wide. 'Hers? Then . . . it's the Empress's perfume?'

Kasia nodded. 'Shirin said I should feel like royalty tonight.' She managed a smile. 'I think it is safe. Unless you've invited guests.'

Their guests had left them some time ago at the front door, departing with bawdy jests and a ragged soldiers' chorus of one particularly obscene song.

Carullus, newly appointed chiliarch of the Second Calysian Cavalry, chuckled briefly, then fell silent.

'I can't imagine wanting anyone else to be with me,' he said quietly. And then, 'And you don't need Alixana's scent to be royal here.'

Kasia made a wry face, an expression from her past, at home. She seemed to be recovering those aspects of herself, slowly. 'You are a flatterer, soldier. Did that work on the girls in taverns?'

She had been a girl in a tavern.

He shook his head, still serious, intent. 'Never said it. Never had a wife.'

Her expression changed, but he was looking into the fire again and couldn't see it. She looked down at him. At this soldier, this husband. A big man, black hair, broad shoulders, thick hands, a burly chest. And she abruptly realized, wondering at it, that he was afraid of her, of hurting or distressing her.

Something twisted, oddly, within Kasia then as the firelight danced. There had been a pool of water once, far in the north. She would go there to be alone. *Erimitsu*: the clever one. Too sharp, disdainful. Before the plague and then an autumn road with her mother standing among falling leaves watching them lead her away, roped to the other girls.

The gods of the north, those windswept open spaces, or Jad, or the *zubir* of the southern Aldwood—someone or something had led her to this room. There seemed to be shelter here. A fire, walls. A man sitting quietly on the floor at her feet. A place out of the wind, for once.

It was a gift, it was a gift. The twist in her heart tightened as she looked down. A gift. Her hand, in turn, tightened on his shoulder, moved to brush his hair.

'You do now,' she said. 'You have a wife now. Will you not take her to bed?'

'Oh, Jad!' he said, releasing his breath in a rush, as if he'd been holding it for a long time.

She actually laughed. Another gift.

Mardoch of the First Amorian Infantry, summoned north from the borderlands to Deapolis with his company—none of the officers would say for certain why, though everyone had guesses—was half convinced he'd been poisoned by something he'd eaten in one of the cauponae they'd sampled tonight. Wretched luck. His very first leave in the City, after six months in the Emperor's army, and he was sick as a Bassanid dog, with the older men laughing at him.

A few of the others had waited the first two times he'd been forced to stop and heave his guts in a shop doorway, but when his belly churned again and he slowly recovered to stand precariously upright, wiping his wet chin, shivering against a wall in the butt-freezing wind, he discovered that the bastards had gone on without him this time. He listened, heard singing voices somewhere ahead, and pushed off from the wall to follow.

He was far from sober, in addition to the extreme disarray of his internal organs. He soon lost track of the singing and he had no real idea where he was. He decided he'd head back towards the water—they'd been going that way in any case—and find either another caupona or their inn or a girl. The white moon had to be east, which gave him a direction. He didn't feel as sick any more, either, which was a blessing of bright Heladikos, ever the soldier's friend.

It was cold, though, and the downward-sloping way seemed longer and the lanes more twisty than earlier in the evening. It was strangely difficult to keep going in the proper direction. He kept seeing those eerie flames as he went, appearing, disappearing. You weren't supposed to talk about them, but they were unsettling, in the extreme. Made him jump, they did. Mardoch kept walking, cursing under his breath.

When a litter he hadn't seen or heard pulled up beside him and a clipped, aristocratic voice from inside asked if a citizen could assist a brave soldier of the Empire, he was entirely happy to accede.

He achieved a salute, then climbed inside as one of the big bearers pulled the curtain back for him. Mardoch settled himself on plump cushions, aware of his own unsavoury smell, suddenly. The man inside was even bigger than the litter-bearer—stupefyingly so, in fact. He was huge. It was very dark when the curtain fell back, and there was a sweetish scent, some perfume that threatened to churn Mardoch's stomach again.

'You are heading for the waterfront, I assume?' the patrician asked.

''Course I am,' Mardoch snorted. 'Where else'll a soldier find a whore he can afford? Begging your lordship's pardon.'

'Best to be careful of the women there,' the man said. His voice was distinctive, curiously high-pitched, very precise.

'Everyone says that.' Mardoch shrugged. It was warm here, the pillows were astonishingly soft. He could almost sleep. In the dark it was hard to make out the details of the man's face. The bulk of him was what registered.

'Everyone is wise. Will you take wine?'

Two days later, when muster was taken in Deapolis among the First Amorians, Mardoch of Sarnica would be among three men reported missing and routinely declared a deserter. It did happen when the young country soldiers went into the City and were exposed to what it offered in the way of temptation. They were all warned, of course, before being allowed to go on leave. Recaptured men could be blinded or maimed for desertion, depending on their officers. For a first offence and a voluntary return, you would probably just be whipped. But with rumours of war growing and the frenzy of building in the shipyards in Deapolis and on the other side of the strait, past the small forested islands, the soldiers knew that those who didn't return on their own might expect much worse when they were tracked down. Men were killed for deserting in wartime.

Within another day or two some of the rumours would become more specific. The eastern army was losing half its pay, it was said. Then someone heard they'd lose *all* of it. Some business about farmland granted to compensate. Farmland at the edge of the desert? No one found it amusing. Those plans were said to be for those who stayed behind in the east. The rest of them were going to war— in those boats being slapped together much too quickly for an infantryman's comfort. *That* was why they'd been ordered to Deapolis. To sail that long way west, far from home, to Batiara, to fight the Antae or the Inicii—those savage, godless tribes that ate their enemies' cooked flesh and drank their hot blood, or gouged knife slits in bellies and raped soldiers in there before gelding and skinning them and hanging them from oak trees by their hair.

Two of the three missing soldiers would come back to the company on that second day, white-faced and apprehensive, badly the worse for drinking binges. They would take their lashes, be routinely salved by the company physician with wine in the wounds and down their throats. Mardoch of Sarnica didn't return, was never found, in fact. A lucky bastard, some of his companions would decide, looking anxiously at the boats being built.

'Will you take wine?' Mardoch heard the light, clipped voice ask him in the shadowed warmth of the enclosed litter. The movement of the bearers was steady, soothing.

Silly question to ask a soldier. Of course he'd take wine. The cup was heavy, had jewels set into it. The wine was dark and good. The other man watched him as Mardoch drained the cup.

When he held it out for more, the enormous patrician shook his head slowly in the close, scented darkness. 'That will be sufficient, I think,' the man said. Mardoch blinked. He had a blurred, confused sense that a hand was lying on his thigh, and it wasn't his own.

'Fuck off,' he thought he said.

~~~

Rustem was a physician, and had spent too much time in Ispahani to be shocked or startled by iron rings set into bedposts or the other, more delicate devices he found in the room they showed him to in the Senator's small, elegant guest-house near the triple walls.

This was, he concluded, a bedroom wherein Plautus Bonosus was evidently inclined to amuse himself away from the comfort—and the constraints—of his family.

It was hardly unusual: aristocrats all over the world did variants of the same thing if they lived in circumstances that allowed for some privacy. Kerakek had no such houses, of course. Everyone in a village knew what everyone else was doing, from the fortress on down.

Rustem placed the series of thin golden rings—designed, he had belatedly realized, to fit over the shafts of variously sized male sexual organs—back into their leather bag. He pulled the drawstrings closed and replaced the bag beside the silken scarves and lengths of thin cord and a number of more obscure objects in the brass-lined trunk from which he'd taken it. The trunk hadn't been locked, and the room was now his own, as a guest of the Senator. He'd felt no guilt about looking around while arranging his own belongings. He was a spy for the King of Kings. He needed to become skilful at this. Scruples would have to be expunged. Would Great Shirvan and his advisers be interested to learn of the night-time inclinations of the Master of the Sarantine Senate?

Rustem closed the trunk and glanced over at the subsiding fire. He could stoke it himself, of course, but he made a different decision. The objects he had just observed and held had induced unusual feelings, and an awareness of just how far away he was from his own wives. Despite the fatigue attendant upon a long and turbulent day—with a death at the outset—Rustem noted, with professional expertise, the signs of arousal within himself.

He went to the door, opened it, and called down for someone to build up the fire. It was a small house. He heard an immediate reply from below stairs. With some satisfaction he saw the young serving girl—Elita, she'd named herself earlier—enter the room, eyes deferentially lowered, a few moments afterwards. He'd thought it might be the rather officious steward, but that fellow was clearly above such duties and probably asleep already. The hour was late.

Rustem sat in the window seat and watched the woman attend to the flames and sweep the ashes. When she'd done and had risen to her feet, he said mildly, 'I tend to be cold at night, girl. I should prefer you to stay.'

She flushed, but made no demur. He'd known she wouldn't, not in a house of this sort. And he was an honoured guest.

She proved to be soft, agreeably warm, compliant if not truly adept. He preferred that, in a way. If he'd wanted extreme carnal experience he'd have inquired after an expensive prostitute. This was Sarantium. One could get anything here, word was. Anything in the world. He treated the girl kindly, letting her stay in the bed with him after. Her own was certainly going to be no more than a pallet in a cold room below, and they could hear the wind outside.

It did occur to him, as he felt his mind beginning to drift, that the servants might have been instructed to keep a watchful eye on this visiting Bassanid—which would explain the girl's acquiescence as easily as anything else. There was something amusing in that, and something disturbing, too. He was too tired to sort it through. He fell asleep. He dreamed of his daughter, the one he was losing as the King of Kings raised him to glory and the priestly caste.

The girl, Elita, was still with him some time later when the entire house was roused by an urgent pounding and a shouting at the door in the depths of the night.

❧

Moving in a litter through darkness from the Imperial Precinct to her own city home, an unexpected escort riding beside her, Gisel decided, long before they arrived, what she intended to do.

She thought that she might in time be able to reclaim some pride in that fact: it would be her choice, her decision made. That didn't mean that anything she did would necessarily succeed. With so many other plans and schemes now in place—here and back home—the odds were overwhelmingly against her. They always had been, from the time her father died and the Antae had reluctantly crowned his only living child. But at least she could think, act, not bob like a small boat on the great wave of events.

She had known, for example, exactly what she was doing when she sent an angry, bitter artisan halfway across the world with a proposal of marriage to the Emperor of Sarantium. She remembered standing before that man, Caius Crispus, alone at night in her palace, letting him look—demanding that he gaze his fill of her.

You may tell the Emperor you have seen the queen of the Antae very near . . .

She flushed, remembering that. After what she'd encountered in the palace tonight, the measure of her innocence was clear. It was past time to lose some of that innocence. But she couldn't even really say *what* plan tonight's decision—with the unworthy thread of fear still in it—might further. She only knew she was going to do it.

She lifted the curtain a little, could see the horse still keeping pace beside her litter. She recognized a chapel door. They were nearing her house. Gisel took a deep breath, tried to be amused at her fear, this primitive anxiety.

It was simply a question, she told herself, of putting something new into play, something that came from *her*, to see what ripples it might create. In this tumble and rush of huge events, one used whatever came to hand or mind—as always—and she had decided to treat her own body as a piece in the game. In play.

Queens lacked, really, the luxury to think of themselves otherwise. In an elegant room in a palace tonight, the Emperor of Sarantium had taken away from her any lingering illusions about consultation, negotiation, diplomacy, anything that might forestall for Batiara the iron-edged truth of war.

Seeing him in that exquisite small chamber with his Empress, seeing *her*, had also removed certain other illusions. In that astonishing room, with its fabrics and wall hangings and silver candlesticks, amid mahogany and sandalwood, and leather from Soriyya, and incense, with a golden sun disk on the wall above each door and a golden tree wherein sat a score of jewelled birds, Gisel had felt as if the souls in the room were at the very centre of the spinning world. *Here* was the heart of things. Sudden, violent images of the future had seemed to dance and whirl in the firelit air, hurtling past at a dizzying speed along the walls while the room itself remained, somehow, motionless as those birds on the golden branches of the Emperor's tree.

Valerius was going to war in Batiara.

It had been resolved in his mind long ago, Gisel finally understood. He was a man who made his own decisions, and his gaze was on generations yet to be born as much as on those he ruled today. She had met him now, she could see it.

She herself, her presence here, might be of assistance or might not. A tactical tool. It didn't matter, not in the larger scheme. Neither did anyone else's views. Not the Strategos's, the Chancellor's, not even Alixana's.

The Emperor of Sarantium, contemplative and courteous and very sure of himself, had a vision: of Rhodias reclaimed, the sundered Empire remade. Visions on this scale could be dangerous; such ambition carried all before it sometimes. *He wants to leave a name,* Gisel had thought, kneeling before him to hide her face, and then rising again, her composure intact. *He wants to be remembered for this.*

Men were like that. Even the wise ones. Her father no exception. A dread of dying and being forgotten. Lost to the memory of the world as it went mercilessly on without them. Gisel searched within herself and found no such burning need. She didn't want to be hated or scorned when Jad called her to him behind the sun, but she felt no fierce passion to have her name sung down the echoing years or have her face and form preserved in mosaic or marble forever—or for however long stone and glass could endure.

What she liked, she realized wistfully, was the idea of rest at the end, when it came. Her body beside her father's in that modest sanctuary outside Varena's walls, her soul in grace with the god the Antae had adopted. Was such grace allowed? The possibility of it?

Earlier, in the palace, meeting the watchful eyes of the eunuch Chancellor Gesius for a moment, Gisel had thought she'd seen pity and understanding, both. A man who'd survived to serve three Emperors in his day would have some knowledge of the turnings of the world.

But Gisel was still inside these turnings, still young and alive, far from detached serenity or grace. Anger caught in her throat. She hated the very *idea* that someone might pity her. An Antae, a *queen* of the Antae? Hildric's daughter? *Pity?* It was enough to make one kill.

Killing was not, in the circumstances, a possibility tonight. Other things were, including the spill of her own blood. An irony? Of course it was.

The world was full of those.

The litter stopped. She lifted the curtain again, saw the door of her own home, night torches burning in their brackets on the wall to either side. She heard her escort swing down from his horse, saw his face appear beside her. His breath made a puff of smoke in the very cold night air.

'We have arrived, gracious lady. I am sorry for the chill. May I help you alight?'

She smiled at him. Found that she could smile quite easily. 'Come in to warm yourself. I'll have a mulled wine made before you ride back through the cold.' She looked straight into his eyes.

The pause was brief. 'I am greatly honoured,' said golden Leontes, Supreme Strategos of the Sarantine armies. A tone that made one believe him. And why *not* believe him? She was a queen.

He handed her out of the litter. Her steward had already opened the front door. The wind was gusting and swirling. They went in. She had servants build the fires on the ground floor and upstairs and prepare spiced, heated wine. They sat near the larger fire in the reception room and spoke of necessarily trivial things. Chariots and dancers, the day's minor wedding at a dancer's home.

War was coming.

Valerius had told them tonight, changing the world.

They talked of games in the Hippodrome, of how unseasonably windy it was outside with winter due to have ended by now. Leontes, easy and relaxed, told of a Holy Fool who had apparently just installed himself on a rock beside one of the landward gates—and had vowed he would not descend until all pagans and heretics and Kindath had been expelled from the Holy City. A devout man, he said, shaking his head, but one who did not understand the realities of the world.

It was important, she agreed, to understand the realities of the world.

The wine came, a silver tray, silver cups. He saluted her formally, speaking Rhodian. His courtesy was flawless. It would be, she knew, even as he led an army ravaging through her home, even if he burned Varena to the ground, unhousing her father's bones. He would *prefer* not to torch it, of course. Would do so if he had to. In the god's name.

Her heart was pounding but her hands, she saw, were steady, revealing nothing. She dismissed her women and then the steward. A few moments after they left she stood and set down her cup—her decision, her act—and crossed the room. She stopped before his chair, looking down at him. Bit her lower lip, and then smiled. She saw him smile in turn, and pause to drain his wine before he stood up, entirely at ease, accustomed to this. A golden man. She took him by the hand and up the stairs and to her bed.

He hurt her, being unprepared for innocence, but women from the beginning of time had known this particular pain and Gisel made herself welcome it. He was startled and then visibly pleased when he saw her blood on the sheets. Vanity. A royal fortress conquered, she thought.

He spoke generously of the honour, of his astonishment. A courtier, at least as much as a soldier. Silk over the corded muscle, devout faith behind the wielded sword and the fires. She smiled, said nothing at all. Made herself reach for him, that hard, scarred soldier's body, that it might happen again.

Knew what she was doing. Had no idea what it might achieve. Something in play, on the board, her body. Face to a pillow that second time, she cried out in the dark, in the night, for so many reasons.

He'd thought of going to the stables, but it seemed there were some conditions, some states of mind, that not even standing with Servator in the mahogany stall the Blues had made for his horse would address.

There had been a time—long ago, not so long ago—when all he'd wanted was to be among horses, in their world. And now, still a young man by most measures, the finest stallion the world knew was his own and he was the most honoured charioteer on the god's created earth, and yet somehow tonight such dreams made real were not enough to assuage.

An appalling truth.

He had been to a wedding ceremony today, watched a soldier he knew and liked marry a woman clearly worthy of him. He'd had a little too much to drink among convivial people. And he had seen—first at the ceremony and then during the reception afterwards—the woman who troubled his own nights. She had been with her husband, of course.

He hadn't known Plautus Bonosus and his second wife would be among the guests. Almost a full day in her presence. It was ... difficult.

And so it seemed the undeniable good fortune of his life was not sufficient to address what was afflicting him now. Was he hopelessly greedy? Covetous? Was that it? Spoiled like a sulky child, demanding far too much of the god and his son?

He had broken a rule of his own tonight, a rule of very long standing. He had gone to her home in the dark after the wedding party broke up. Had been absolutely certain Bonosus would be elsewhere, that after the raillery of the celebration and the bawdy mood it induced, the Senator's well-known, if discreetly managed, habits would assert themselves and he'd spend the night at the smaller home he maintained for his private use.

Not so. Inexplicably not so. Scortius had seen lights blazing in the iron-barred upper windows over the street at the mansion of Senator Bonosus. A shivering servant relighting wind-snuffed torches in the walls had descended from his ladder and volunteered, for a small sum, the information that the master was indeed home, closeted with his wife and son.

Scortius had kept a shrouding cloak over his face until his footsteps had led him away into the narrow lanes of the City. A woman called from a recessed doorway as he passed: 'Let me warm you, soldier! Come with me! It isn't a night to lie alone.'

It wasn't, Jad knew. He felt old. Partly the wind and cold: his left arm, broken years ago, one of so many injuries, ached when the wind was bitter. The humiliating infirmity of an aged man, he thought, hating it. Like one of those hobbling, crutch-wielding old soldiers allowed a stool by the fire in a military tavern, sitting there all night, boring the unwary with a ten-times-told story of some minor campaign of thirty years before, back when great and glorious Apius was Jad's dearly beloved Emperor and things hadn't descended to the sad state of today and could an old soldier not be given something to wet his throat?

He could become like that, Scortius thought sourly. Toothless and unshaven at a booth in The Spina telling about the magnificent race day once, long ago, during the reign of Valerius II, when he had . . .

He caught himself massaging the arm and stopped, swearing aloud. It ached, though, it really did. They didn't run the chariots in winter, or he'd have had a problem handling a quadriga in the turns. Crescens of the Greens hadn't looked this afternoon as if anything ached in him at all, though he must have had his injuries over the years. Every rider did. The Greens' principal driver was obviously ready for his second season in the Hippodrome. Confident, even arrogant—which was as it should be.

The Greens also had some new horses up from the south, courtesy of a high-ranking military partisan; Astorgus's sources said two or three were exceptional. Scortius knew they *did* have one outstanding new right-sider, a trace horse the Blues had dealt them in a transaction Scortius had encouraged Astorgus to make. You gave up some things to gain something else, in this case a driver. But if he was right about the horse and about Crescens, the Greens' standard-bearer would have quickly claimed the stallion for his own team and be that much more formidable.

Scortius wasn't worried. He even enjoyed the idea of someone thinking he could challenge him. It stirred fires within him, the ones that needed stoking after so many years in ascendancy. A formidable Crescens was *good* for him, good for the Hippodrome. It was easy enough to see that. But he wasn't easy tonight. Nothing to do with horses, or his arm, really.

It isn't a night to lie alone.

Of course it wasn't, but sometimes lovemaking—bought

in a doorway or otherwise—wasn't the real need either. There were notes lying on a table in his home from women who would be exquisitely happy to relieve him of the burden of being by himself tonight, even now, even so late. That wasn't what he wanted, though for a long time it had been.

The woman he'd gone trudging uphill in the cutting wind to see was . . . closeted with her husband, the servant had said. Whatever *that* meant.

He swore again, fiercely. Why wasn't the accursed Master of the Senate off playing his night games with this season's boy? What was *wrong* with Bonosus, in Jad's name?

It was at this point, walking alone (a little reckless, but one didn't normally bring companions when attending upon one's mistress at night, intending to climb her wall), that he'd thought of going to the stables. He wasn't far from the compound. They'd be warm; the smells and night sounds of horses would be those he'd known and loved all his life. He might even find someone awake in the kitchens to offer a last cup of wine and a quiet bite of food.

He didn't *want* wine or food. Or even the presence of his beloved horses now. What he wanted was denied to him, and the degree of frustration he felt was what—perhaps more than anything—was disturbing him. It felt childish. His mouth twitched at the irony. Did he feel old or young or both? Past time to make up one's mind, wasn't it? He considered, decided: he wanted to be a boy again, simple as a boy, or failing that, he wanted to be in a room alone with Thenaïs.

He saw the white moon when it rose. Was passing a chapel of the Sleepless Ones just then, walking east, could hear the chanting inside. Could have gone in, a few moments out of the cold, praying among holy men, but the god and his son at this immediate moment didn't offer any answers either.

Perhaps they would have, had he been a better, more pious man, but he wasn't and they didn't and that was that. He saw a quick blue flicker of flame further down the street—a reminder of the half-world's presence among men, never far away in the City—and he came, in that moment, to a sudden, unexpected decision.

There *was* another wall he could climb.

If he was awake and abroad and this restless perhaps he could put the mood to use. On the thought, not allowing himself time to hesitate, he turned and set off along a lane angled to the street.

He walked briskly, kept to shadows, became motionless in a doorway when he saw a party of drunken, singing soldiers stumble out of a tavern. He remained where he was a moment and watched a massive litter appear from blackness at the other end of the street and then turn down the steep road they took, heading towards the harbour. He considered this for a moment, and then shrugged. There were always stories unfolding in the night. People died, were born, found love or grief.

He went the other way, uphill again, rubbing his arm at intervals, until he came again to the street and then the house where he'd spent much of the afternoon and evening in celebration of a wedding.

The house the Greens provided for their best dancer was handsome and well maintained, in an extremely good neighbourhood. It had a wide portico, and a well-proportioned solarium and balcony overlooking the street. He had been in this home before today, as it happened, and even upstairs—visiting earlier inhabitants.

Sometimes those living here placed their own bedroom at the front, using the solarium as an extension, a place from which to watch the life below. Sometimes the front chamber was a sitting room, with the bedroom at the back, over the courtyard.

Without much to rely upon but instinct, he decided that Shirin of the Greens would not be the sort who placed herself over the street. She spent enough of her days and nights looking out on people from a stage. She'd be sleeping above the courtyard, he decided. Unfortunately the houses were set so closely together here that there was no way to get to the courtyards from the front.

He looked up and down the empty street. Torches burned fitfully on walls; some had been extinguished by the wind. He looked up, and sighed. In silence, having done this sort of thing many times before, he moved to the end of the portico, mounted the stone railing and, reaching above his head with both hands, gripped and then pulled himself straight upwards in one smooth motion onto the porch roof.

One became very strong in the upper body and legs after years of mastering four horses in a chariot.

One also developed injuries. He paused long enough to give vent under his breath to the pain in his arm. He really *was* becoming too old for this sort of thing.

From portico roof to solarium balcony involved a short vertical jump, another hard gripping, and then a steady pull upwards until one knee could get purchase. Life would have been easier if Shirin had chosen to make this her bedchamber, after all. She hadn't, as he'd surmised. A glance inside—darkness, some benches, a fabric hanging on the wall above a sideboard. It was a reception room.

He swore again, and then stepped up on the balcony railing, balancing. The roof above was flat, as they all were in this neighbourhood, no edging at all, to let the rain run off. Made it hard to find a grip. This, too, he remembered from elsewhere. Other houses. He could fall here if his hands slipped. It was a long way down. He imagined some servant or slave finding him in the morning street, neck broken. A sudden hilarity entered into him. He was being indescribably reckless here and he knew it.

Thenaïs ought to have been alone. She hadn't been. He was here, climbing to another woman's roof in the wind.

Footsteps sounded in the street below. He remained motionless, both feet on the railing, a hand on a corner column for balance, until they went away. Then he let go of the column and jumped again. He got both hands flat on the roof—the only way to do this successfully—and, grunting, levered himself up and onto it. A hard movement, not without cost.

He remained lying where he was for a time, on his back, determinedly not rubbing at his arm, looking up at the stars and the white moon. The wind blew. Jad had made men to be foolish creatures, he decided. Women were wiser, on the whole. They slept at night. Or closeted themselves with their husbands. Whatever that meant.

He laughed this time, softly to himself, *at* himself, and stood up. He walked, treading lightly, towards the place where the roof ended at a view of the interior courtyard below. He saw a small fountain, dry still at winter's end, stone benches around it, bare trees. The white moon shone, and the stars. Windy night, brilliantly clear. He realized that he felt happy, suddenly. Very much alive.

He knew exactly where her bedroom would be, could see the narrow balcony below. He took another look at the pale moon. A sister of the god, the Kindath called it. A heresy, but one could—privately—understand it sometimes. He looked over the roof edge. Going down would be easier. He dropped to his stomach, swung his legs over the side, lowered himself as far as he could, hands stretched above him. Then he dropped neatly to the balcony, landing silently, like a lover or a thief. He straightened from a crouch, moved softly forward to peer through the two glass-panelled doors into the woman's room. One door, oddly, was ajar in the cold night. He looked at the bed. No one there.

'There is a bow trained on your heart. Stop where you are. My servant will kill you happily if you do not declare yourself,' said Shirin of the Greens.

It seemed wise to stop where he was.

He had *no* idea how she'd known he was there, how she'd had time to summon a guard. It also occurred to him—very belatedly—to wonder why he'd assumed she would be sleeping alone.

Declare yourself, she'd ordered. He did have his self-respect.

'I am Heladikos, son of Jad,' he said gravely. 'My father's chariot is here. Will you come ride with me?'

There was a silence.

'Oh, my!' Shirin said, her voice changing. '*You?*'

Speaking quickly, in a low tone, she dismissed the guard. After he'd left, she swung open the door to the balcony herself and Scortius, pausing to bow, entered her chamber. There came a light tapping at the inner door. Shirin crossed, opened it only a crack, accepted a lit taper from the servant briefly revealed in the hallway and then closed the door again. She moved about the room lighting candles and lamps herself.

Scortius saw the bedcovers in disarray. She *had* been asleep; was dressed now, however, a dark green robe buttoned high over whatever she wore to bed, if anything. Her dark hair, cut short, just reached her shoulders. A fashion emerging; Shirin of the Greens set fashions for the women of Sarantium. She was barefoot, high-arched, moving dancer-light over her floor. He felt, looking at her, a quick pulse of desire. This was a *very* attractive woman. He loosened his cloak, let it fall to the floor behind him. He began to feel a measure of control returning with the warmth. He knew all about this sort of encounter. She finished with the candles, turned back to him.

'I take it Thenaïs was with her husband?'

Asked it with *such* a wide-eyed, innocent smile.

He swallowed hard. Opened his mouth. Closed it. Watched her sit, still smiling, on a cushioned seat near the banked fire.

'Do sit down, charioteer,' she murmured, her back straight, exquisitely poised. 'One of my women will bring us wine.'

With great confusion and very real relief, he sank into the indicated seat.

The problem was that he was an absurdly attractive man. Shedding his cloak, clad still in white from the wedding, Scortius appeared permanently young, immune to all the aches and doubts and infirmities of lesser mortals.

She'd been lying alone, by choice of course. Jad knew there were enough who would have offered their versions of solace in the dark had she asked or allowed. But Shirin had discovered that the greatest luxury of status, the real privilege it conveyed, was the power to not allow, and to ask only when and where she truly desired.

There would come a time when it would make sense to take a protector, perhaps even an important husband from the army or one of the wealthy merchants or even someone from the Imperial Precinct. There was a living Empress who was proof of such possibilities. But not now. She was young still, at the apex of her fame in the theatre, and had no need—yet—for a guardian.

She *was* guarded, by celebrity, and other things. Among those other things was the fact that she had someone here to warn her when there were those who sought her room after darkfall.

'I understand that he couldn't be killed, but why is the man sitting at his ease with wine to come? Enlighten me, please.'

'Danis, Danis. Isn't he gorgeous?' she asked silently, knowing what the bird would say to that.

'Oh. Wonderful. Wait for him to smile once more, then take him to bed, is that the idea?'

Scortius of Soriyya smiled, uneasily.

'Why, ah, would you think that, I, er . . .'

'Thenaïs?' she finished for him. 'Oh, women know these things, dear man. I saw you looking at her this afternoon. I must say she's exquisite.'

'Um, no! I mean, I'd, ah, say rather that . . . women may see strands of stories, where none are really to be found.' His smile grew more assured. 'Though I must say *you* are exquisite.'

'You see? I knew it!' said Danis. *'You know what this man is like! Stay where you are. Don't smile back!'*

Shirin smiled. Lowered her eyes demurely, hands in her lap. 'You are too kind, charioteer.'

A scratching at the door again. To preserve her guest's identity—and avoid the windstorm of gossip this visit would cause—Shirin rose and took the tray herself from Pharisa, not letting her in. She set it down on the side table and poured for both of them, though Jad knew she didn't need more wine at this hour. There was a tingle of excitement in her that she couldn't deny. The whole of the City—from palace to chapel to wharfside caupona—would be stupefied were it to learn of this encounter between the First of the Blues and the Greens' Principal Dancer. And the man was—

'*More water in yours!*' Danis snapped.

'Quiet, you. *There's plenty of water in it.*'

The bird sniffed. '*I don't know why I bothered to warn you of sounds on the roof. Might as well have let him find you naked in bed. Save him so much bother.*'

'We didn't know who it was,' she said reasonably.

'How did you, ah, realize I was there?' Scortius asked, as she handed him his cup. She watched him take a long drink.

'You sounded like four horses landing on the roof, Heladikos,' she laughed. Untrue, but the truth was not for him, or anyone. The truth was a bird her father had sent her, with a soul, never sleeping, supernaturally alert, a gift of the half-world where spirits dwelled.

'*Don't make jokes,*' Danis complained. '*You'll encourage him! You* know *what they say about this man!*'

'Of course I do,' Shirin murmured inwardly. '*Shall we test it, my dear? He's famously discreet.*'

She wondered how and when he was going to make his overture of seduction. She took her seat again, across the room from him, and smiled, amused and at ease, but feeling an excitement within her, hidden like the soul of the bird. It didn't happen often, this feeling, it really didn't.

'You do know,' said Scortius of the Blues, not moving from his seat, 'that this visit is entirely honourable, if . . . unusual. You are completely safe from my uncontrolled desires.' His smile flashed, he set down his cup with an easy hand. 'I'm only here to make you an offer, Shirin, an agent with a business proposal.'

She swallowed hard, tilted her head thoughtfully. 'You, ah, have control of the uncontrollable?' she murmured. Wit could be a screen.

He laughed, again easily. 'Handle four horses from a bouncing chariot,' he said. 'You learn.'

'What is the man talking about?' Danis expostulated.

'Quiet. I may decide to be insulted.'

'Yes,' she said coolly, sitting up straight, holding her wine carefully. 'I'm sure you do. Go on.' She lowered her voice, changed its timbre. Wondered if he'd notice.

The change in her tone was unmistakable. This was an actress: she could convey a great deal merely with a shift of voice and posture. And she just had. He wondered again why he'd assumed she'd be alone. What that said about her, or his sense of her. An awareness of the woman's pride, at the very least . . . self-contained, making her own choices.

Well, this *would* be her own choice, whatever she did. That was, after all, the point of what he'd come to say, and so he said it, speaking carefully: 'Astorgus, our factionarius, has been wondering aloud and at some length what it would take to induce you to change factions.'

What she did was change position again, rising swiftly, a taut uncoiling. She set down her cup, staring coldly at him.

'And for *this,* you enter my bedchamber in the middle of the night?'

It began, more and more, to seem a bad idea.

He said, defensively, 'Well, this isn't really the sort of proposal one would want to make in a public—'

'A letter? An afternoon visit? A private word exchanged during today's reception?'

He looked up at her, read the cold anger, and was silent, though within him, looking at the fury of her, something else registered and he felt again the stirrings of desire. Being the man he was, he thought he knew the source of her outrage.

She said, glaring down at him, 'As it happens, that last is exactly what Strumosus did today.'

'I didn't know that,' he said.

'Well, obviously,' she said tartly.

'Did you accept?' he asked, a little too brightly.

She wasn't about to let him off so easily. 'Why are you here?'

Scortius became aware, looking at her, that she was wearing nothing at all beneath the silk of her dark green robe. He cleared his throat.

'Why do any of us do what we do?' he asked, in turn. Question for question for question. 'Do we ever really understand?'

He hadn't expected to say that, actually. He saw her expression change. He added, 'I was restless, couldn't sleep. Wasn't ready to go home to bed. It was cold in the streets. I saw drunken soldiers, a prostitute, a dark litter that unsettled me for some reason. When the moon came up I decided to come here . . . thought I might as well try to . . . accomplish something, so long as I was awake.' He looked at her. 'I'm sorry.'

'Accomplish something,' she echoed drily, but he could see her anger slipping away. 'Why did you assume I'd be alone?'

He'd been afraid she'd ask that.

'I don't know,' he admitted. 'I was just asking myself the same question. There is . . . no man's name linked to yours, I suppose, and I have never heard you to be . . . ' He trailed off.

And saw the ghost of a smile at the edge of her mouth. 'Attracted to men?'

He shook his head quickly. 'Not that. Um . . . reckless with your nights?'

She nodded. There was a silence. He needed more wine now but was reluctant to let her see that.

She said, quietly, 'I told Strumosus I couldn't change factions.'

'Couldn't?'

She nodded. 'The Empress has made that clear to me.'

And with that said, it seemed painfully obvious, actually. Something he ought to have known, or Astorgus certainly. Of course the court would want the factions kept in equilibrium. And this dancer wore Alixana's own perfume.

She didn't move, or speak. He looked around, thinking it through, saw the wall hangings, the good furnishings, flowers in an alabaster vase, a small crafted bird on a table, the disturbing disarray of the bed coverings. He looked back up at her, where she stood in front of him.

He stood up as well. 'I feel foolish now, among other things. I ought to have understood this before troubling your night.' He made a small gesture with his hands. 'The

Imperial Precinct won't let us be together, you and I. You have my deepest apologies for the intrusion. I will leave you now.'

Her expression changed again, something amused in it, then something wry, then something else. 'No you won't,' said Shirin of the Greens. 'You owe me for an interrupted sleep.'

Scortius opened his mouth, closed it, then opened it again when she came forward and put her hands behind his head and kissed him.

'There are limits to what the court can decree. And if there are images of others that lie down with us,' she murmured, drawing him to the bed, 'it will not be the first time in the history of men and women.'

His mouth was dry with excitement, unexpectedly. She took his hands and drew them around her body by the bed. She was sleek, and firm, and extremely desirable. He didn't feel old any more. He felt like a young chariot-racer up from the south, new to the glories of the great City, finding a soft welcome in candlelit places where he had not thought to find such a thing at all. His heart was beating very fast.

'Speak for yourself,' he managed to murmur.

'Oh, but I am,' she said softly, cryptically, before letting herself fall back onto the bed and pulling him down with her amid the scent, unmistakable, of a perfume only two women in the world could wear.

'Well, I'm grateful you had the decency to silence me before you—'

'Oh, Danis, please. Please. Be gentle.'

'Hah. Was he?'

Shirin's inward voice was lazy, slow. *'Some of the time.'*

The bird made an indignant sound. *'Indeed.'*

'I wasn't,' said the dancer, after a moment.

'I don't want to know! When you behave—'

'Danis, be gentle. I'm not a maid, and it has been a long time.'

'Look at him, sleeping there. In your bed. No care in the world.'

'He has cares, trust me. Everyone does. But I'm looking. Oh, Danis, isn't he a beautiful man?'

There was a long silence. Then, *'Yes,'* said the bird, silently; the bird that had been a girl slain at dawn one autumn in a grove in Sauradia. *'Yes, he is.'*

Another stillness. They could hear the wind outside in the dark, turning night. The man was, indeed, asleep, on his back, hair tousled.

'Was my father?' asked Shirin abruptly.

'Was he what?'

'Beautiful?'

'Oh.' Another silence, inward, outward, darkness in the room with the candles burnt out. Then, *'Yes,'* said the bird, again. *'Yes, he was, my dear. Shirin, go to sleep. You are dancing tomorrow.'*

'Thank you, Danis.' The woman in the bed sighed softly. The man slept on. *'I know. I will now.'*

The dancer was asleep when he woke, still in the dark of night. He had trained himself to do this: lingering until dawn in a strange bed was dangerous. And although there was no immediate threat here, no lover or husband to fear, it would be awkward in the extreme, painfully public, to be seen leaving the house of Shirin of the Greens in the morning.

He looked over at the woman a moment, smiling a little. Then he rose. Dressed quickly, glancing once more around the silent room. When he looked back at the bed she was awake, and gazing at him. A light sleeper? He wondered what had awakened her. Then wondered, again, how she'd known he was on the roof.

'A thief in the night?' she murmured sleepily. 'Take what you want and go?'

He shook his head. 'A grateful man.'

She smiled. 'Tell Astorgus you did all you possibly could to persuade me.'

He laughed aloud, but softly. 'You assume this is all I can do?'

Her turn to laugh, a low ripple of pleasure. 'Go,' she said, 'before I call you back to test it.'

'Good night,' he said. 'Jad shelter you, dancer.'

'And you. On the sands and off.'

He went out the doors to the balcony, closed them behind him, mounted the balustrade. He leaped up to the roof, swung himself onto it. His shoulder didn't hurt at all now. The cold wind blew but he didn't feel it. The white moon was over towards the west, though much of the night was yet to run before the god finished his battles under the world and dawn could come. The stars were bright overhead, no clouds at all. Standing on Shirin's roof in this elevated quarter of the vast city he could see Sarantium spread below him, domes and mansions and towers, random torches in stone walls, clustered, jumbled wooden houses, shop fronts closed up, squares, statues in them, an orange glow of flame where the glassworks were, or perhaps a bakery, lanes running crazily downward, and beyond them, beyond them all, the harbour and then the sea, vast and dark and deep, roiled by the wind and hinting at forever.

In a mood he could only call exhilarated, one he could remember from long ago but hadn't experienced in some time, Scortius retraced his steps to the front edge of the roof, swung himself down to the upper balcony there, and then, moving lightly, lowered himself to the portico. He stepped down into the street, smiling behind the cloak he drew across his face.

'*Fuck him!*' he heard. 'That bastard! Look! He came from her balcony!'

Exhilaration could be dangerous. It made you careless. He turned swiftly, saw half a dozen shadowy figures, and wheeled to run. He didn't *like* running away, but this wasn't a situation that presented options. He was feeling strong, knew he was fleet of foot, was certain he could outsprint whoever these assailants were.

He very likely would have, in fact, had there not been as many others coming at him from the other side. Twisting away, Scortius saw the glint of daggers, a wooden staff, and then an entirely illegal drawn sword.

They had been planning to sing to her. The idea was to gather in the street below what they assumed to be her bedroom above the front portico and offer music in her glorious name. They even had instruments.

The plan, however, had been Cleander's—he was their leader—and when it emerged that his father had confined him to his quarters for the accidental death of that Bassanid servant, the young Green partisans had found themselves drinking irritably and without purpose in their usual tavern. The talk had been of horses and prostitutes.

But no self-respecting young man of lineage could be expected to submit tamely to confinement on a spring night in the very week the racing was to begin again. When Cleander showed up he seemed a shade uneasy to those who knew him best, but he grinned in the doorway as they shouted their welcome. He'd actually *killed* a man today. It was undeniably impressive. Cleander drank two quick glasses of unmixed wine and offered a definitive opinion about one woman whose rooms were not far from his father's house. She was too expensive for most of them, so no one was in a position to refute his observations.

Then he pointed out that they'd planned to chorus Shirin's undying fame and he saw no reason to allow the late hour to forestall them. She'd be *honoured*, he told the others. It wasn't as if they were intruding upon her, only offering a tribute from the street. He told them what she'd been wearing at her reception that afternoon when she greeted him—personally.

Someone mentioned the dancer's neighbours and the Urban Prefect's watchmen, but most of them knew enough to laugh and shout the craven fellow down.

They made their way out the door. Ten or twelve young men (they lost a few en route) in a stumbling cluster, variously garbed, one with a stringed instrument, two with flutes, moving uphill through a sharp, cold wind. If an officer of the watch was anywhere about he elected—prudently—not to make his presence visible. The partisans of both factions were notoriously unstable in the week the racing began. End of winter, beginning of the Hippodrome season. Springtime did things to the young, everywhere.

It might not feel like spring tonight but it was.

They reached her street and divided themselves, half to each side of her wide portico where they could all see the solarium balcony, should Shirin elect to appear above them like a vision when they sang. The one with the strings was swearing about the numbing cold on his fingers. The others were busily spitting and clearing throats and nervously muttering the verses of Cleander's chosen song when one of them saw a man climbing down from that same balcony to the porch.

It was an obscene, monstrous outrage. A violation of Shirin's purity, her honour. What right did someone *else* have to be descending from her bedroom in the middle of the night?

The contemptible coward turned to run as soon as they cried out.

He had no weapon, didn't get far. Marcellus's staff caught him a heavy blow to the shoulder as he tried to dodge around the group of them to the south. Then quick, wiry Darius knifed him in the side, ripping the blade upwards, and one of the twins got him with a kick in the ribs on the same side while the bastard was flattening Darius with a blow of his fist. Darius moaned. Cleander came running up then, with his sword drawn—the only one of them reckless enough to carry one. He'd already killed today, and he was the one who *knew* Shirin.

The others backed away from the man, who was lying on the ground now, holding his torn side. Darius got to his knees, then moved away. They fell silent, a sense of awe, the power of the moment overtaking them. They were all looking at the sword. There were no torches burning on the walls; the wind had blown them out. No sight or sound of the night watch. Stars, wind, and a white moon westering.

'I am reluctant to kill a man without knowing who he is,' said Cleander with really impressive gravity.

'I am Heladikos, the son of Jad,' said the bastard lying on the road. He appeared—amazingly—to be struggling with hilarity as much as anything else. He was bleeding. They could see dark blood on the road. 'All men must die. Stab away, child. Two in a day? A Bassanid servant and a god's son? Makes you a warrior, almost.' He'd kept the cloak about his face, somehow, even as he fell.

Someone gasped. Cleander made a startled movement.

'How the fuck do you know about—?'

Cleander moved closer, knelt. Sword to the wounded man's breast, he twitched the cloak aside. The man on the ground made no movement at all. Cleander looked at him for one instant—then let the cloak fall from his fingers as if it were burning to the touch. There was no light. The others couldn't see what he saw.

They heard Cleander, though, as the cloak fell once more over the downed man's face.

'Oh, fuck!' said the only son of Plautus Bonosus, Master of the Sarantine Senate. He stood up. 'Oh, no. Oh, fuck. Oh, holy Jad!'

'My great father!' said the wounded man brightly.

This was followed, unsurprisingly, by silence. Someone coughed nervously.

'Does this mean we aren't singing?' Declanus asked plaintively.

'Get out of here. All of you!' Cleander rasped hoarsely over his shoulder. 'Go! Disappear! My father will fucking *kill* me.'

'Who is it?' snapped Marcellus.

'You don't know. You don't *want* to know. This never happened. Get home, go *anywhere*, or we're all dead men! Holy Jad!'

'What the—?'

'*Go!*'

A light appeared in a window overhead. Someone began shouting for the watch—a woman's voice. They went.

Thanks be to Jad, the boy had a brain and wasn't hopelessly drunk. He had quickly covered Scortius's face again after their eyes locked in the darkness. None of the others—he was sure of it—knew who it was they'd attacked.

There was a chance to get out of this.

If he lived. The knife had gone in on his left side, and ripped, and then the kick in the same side had broken ribs. He'd had breaks before. Knew what they felt like.

They felt very bad. It was, putting it mildly, not easy to breathe. He clutched his side and felt blood pouring from the wound through his fingers. The boy with the knife had jerked it upwards after stabbing him.

But they left. Thanks be to Jad, they left. Leaving only one behind. Someone at a window was calling for the watch.

'Holy Jad,' whispered Bonosus's son. 'Scortius. I swear . . . we had no idea . . . '

'Know you didn't. Thought . . . were killing just anyone.' It was irresponsible to be feeling such hilarity, but the absurdity of this was so extreme. To die, like this?

'No. We didn't! I mean . . . '

Not really the time to be ironic, actually.

'Get me upright, before someone comes.'

'Can you . . . can you walk?'

'Of course I can walk.' Probably a lie.

'I'll take you to my father's house,' the boy said. Bravely enough. The charioteer could guess what consequences would await Cleander after he appeared at the door with a wounded man.

Closeted with his wife and son.

Something became clear, suddenly. *That* was why they'd been together tonight. And then something else did, driving amusement entirely away.

'Not *your* house. Holy Jad, no!'

He was *not* going to appear at Thenaïs's door at this hour of night, having been wounded by partisans after descending from the bed chamber of Shirin of the Greens. He winced at the image of her face, hearing this. Not at the outraged expression that would ensue: the *lack* of one. The detached, ironic coldness coming back.

'But you need a physician. There's blood. And my father can keep this—'

'Not your house.'

'Then where? Oh! The Blues' compound! We can—'

A good thought, but . . .

'Won't help. Our doctor was at the wedding today and will be drunk and unconscious. Too many people, too. We *must* keep this quiet. For . . . for the lady. Now be silent and let me—'

'Wait! I know. The Bassanid!' exclaimed Cleander.

It was, in fact, a good thought.

And resulted in the two of them arriving, after a genuinely harrowing progress through the city, at the small house Bonosus kept for his own use near the triple walls. On the way they passed the enormous dark litter again. Scortius saw it stop, was aware of someone watching them from within, making no movement at all to help. Something made him shiver; he couldn't have said what.

He had lost a fair bit of blood by the time they reached their destination. Every step with his left foot seemed to drive the kicked ribs inward, shockingly. He'd refused to allow the boy to get help at any tavern. No one was to know of this. Cleander almost carried him the last part of the way. The lad was terrified, exhausted, but he got them there.

'Thank you, boy,' he managed to say, as the house's steward, in a nightshirt, grey hair disconcertingly upright in the glow of the candle he held, opened the door to their pounding. 'You did well. Tell your father. *No one else!*'

He hoped that was clear enough. Saw the Bassanid coming to stand behind the steward, lifted one hand briefly in apologetic greeting. It occurred to him that if Plautus Bonosus had been in this house tonight instead of the eastern doctor, none of this would have happened. Then he did, in fact, lose consciousness.

She is awake, in her room with the golden rose that was made for her long ago. Knows he will come to her tonight. Is looking at the rose, in fact, and thinking about frailty when she hears the door open, the familiar tread, the voice that is always with her.

'You are angry with me, I know.'

She shakes her head. 'Afraid of what will come, a little. Not angry, my lord.'

She pours his wine, waters it. Crosses to the seat he has taken by the fire. He takes the wine, and her hand, kisses the palm. His manner is quiet, easy, but she knows him better than she knows anyone alive and can read the signs of his excitement.

'It was finally useful,' she says, 'to have the queen watched all this time.'

He nods. 'She's clever, isn't she? Knew we weren't surprised.'

'I saw that. Will she be difficult, do you think?'

He looks up, smiles. 'Probably.'

The implication being, of course, that it doesn't really matter. He knows what he wants to do, and to have others do. None of them will learn all the details, not even his Empress. Certainly not Leontes, who will lead the army of conquest. She wonders, suddenly, how many men her husband will send, and a thought crosses her mind. She dismisses it, then it slips back in: Valerius is, in fact, more than subtle enough to be careful, even with his trusted friends.

She does not tell him that she, too, had a warning that the Strategos was bringing Gisel to the palace today. Alixana believes, privately, that her husband *does* know she's watching Leontes and his wife and has done so for some time, but it is one of the things they do not discuss. One of the ways in which theirs is a partnership.

Most of the time.

The signs have long been present—no one will be able to claim to have been taken entirely by surprise—but without warning or consultation, the Emperor has just declared an intention to go to war this spring. They have been at war for much of his reign, to the east, north, southeast, far off in the Majriti deserts. This is different. This is Batiara. Rhodias. Heartland of the Empire. Sundered, then lost beyond a wide sea.

'You are sure of this?' she asks him.

He shakes his head. 'Sure of the consequences? Of course not. No mortal can claim to know the unknown that might come,' her husband says softly, still holding her hand. 'We live with that uncertainty.' He looks at her. 'You *are* angry with me. For not telling you.'

She shakes her head again. 'How could I be?' she asks, meaning what she says. 'You have always wanted this, I have always said I did not think it could be done. You see it differently, and are wiser than any of us.'

He looks up, the grey eyes mild. 'I make mistakes, love. This might be one. But I need to try, and this is the time to do it, with Bassania bribed to be quiet, and chaos in the west, and the young queen here with us. It makes too much . . . sense.'

His mind works that way. In part.

In part. She draws a breath, and murmurs, 'Would you still need to do this if we had a son?'

Her heart is pounding. That almost never happens any more. She watches him. Sees the startled reaction, then what replaces it: his mind engaging, addressing, not flinching away.

After a long time, he says, 'That is an unexpected question.'

'I know,' she says. 'It came to me while I was waiting here for you.' Not entirely true. It came to her first a long time ago.

He says, 'You think, if we did, that because of the risk . . . ?'

She nods. 'If you had an heir. Someone you were leaving this to.' She does not gesture. There is more than any gesture could compass. *This.* An empire. A legacy of centuries.

He sighs. Has still not released her hand. Says, softly, looking into the fire now, 'Maybe so, love. I don't know.'

An admission. For him to say that much. No sons, no one to come after, to take the throne, light the candles on the anniversary of their deaths. There is an old pain in her.

He says, still quietly, 'There are some things I have always wanted. I'd like to leave behind Rhodias reclaimed, the new

Sanctuary and its dome, and . . . and perhaps some memory of what we were, you and I.'

'Three things,' she says, not able to think, just then, of anything more clever. It occurs to her that she will weep if she does not take care. An Empress ought not to weep.

'Three things,' he echoes. 'Before it ends, as it always ends.'

Uncrown, a voice was said to say when it ended for one of Jad's holy, anointed ones. *The Lord of Emperors awaits you now.*

No one could say if it was true, if those words were truly spoken and heard. The god's world was made in such a way that men and women lived in mist and fog, in a wavering light, never knowing with certainty what would come.

'More wine?' she says.

He looks at her, nods his head, lets go of her hand. She takes his cup, fills it, brings it back. It is silver, worked in gold, rubies set around it.

'I am sorry,' he says. 'I'm sorry, love.'

He isn't even certain why he says this, but a feeling is with him now, something in her face, something hovering in the air of this exquisite room like a bird: not singing, enchanted into invisibility, but present nonetheless in the world.

───※───

Not far away from that palace room where no bird is singing, a man is as high in the air as birds might fly, working from a scaffold under a dome. The exterior of the dome is copper, gleaming under moon and stars. The interior is his.

There is light here in the Sanctuary; there always is, by order of the Emperor. The mosaicist has served tonight as his own apprentice, mixing lime for the setting bed, carrying it up the ladder himself. Not a great amount, he isn't covering a wide area tonight. He isn't doing very much at all. Only the face of his wife, dead now two years, very nearly.

There is no one watching him. There are guards at the entrance, as always, even in the cold, and a small, rumpled architect is asleep somewhere in this vastness of lamplight and shadow, but Crispin works in silence, as alone as a man can be in Sarantium.

If anyone *were* watching him, and knew what it was he was doing, they would need a true understanding of his craft (of all such crafts, really) not to conclude that this was a hard, cold man, indifferent in life to the woman he is so serenely rendering. His eyes are clear, his hands steady, meticulously choosing tesserae from the trays beside him. His expression is detached, austere: addressing technical dilemmas of glass and stone, no more.

No more? The heart cannot say, sometimes, but the hand and eye—if steady enough and clear enough—may shape a window for those who come after. Someone might look up one day, when all those awake or asleep in Sarantium tonight are long dead, and know that this woman was fair, and very greatly loved by the unknown man who placed her overhead, the way the ancient Trakesian gods were said to have set their mortal loves in the sky, as stars.

Eventually, morning came. Morning always comes. There are always losses in the night, a price paid for light.

PART II

THE NINTH DRIVER

CHAPTER VII

Men and women were always dreaming in the dark. Most of the night's images fell away with sunrise, or before if they harried the sleeper awake. Dreams were longings, or warnings, or prophecies. They were gifts or curses, from powers benevolent or malign, for all knew—whatever the faith into which they had been born—that mortal men and women shared the world with forces they didn't understand.

There were many who plied a trade in city or countryside telling those troubled by visions what they might signify. A small number saw certain kinds of dream as actual memories of a world other than the one into which the dreamer and the listener had been born to live and die, but this was treated in most faiths as a black heresy.

As winter turned towards spring that year, a great many people had dreams they were to remember.

A moonless night, late in winter. At a watering place in the far south, where camel routes met in Ammuz, near to where men had decreed a border with Soriyya—as if the shifting, blowing sands knew of such things—a man, a leader of his tribe, a merchant, awoke in his tent and dressed himself and went out into the dark.

He walked past tents where his wives and children and his brothers and their wives and children slept, and he came, still half asleep but strangely disturbed, to the edge of the oasis, a place where the last of the green gave way to the endless sands.

He stood there under the arc of the heavens. Under so many stars it seemed impossible to him, suddenly, to comprehend their number in the sky above men and the world. His heart, for no reason he could understand, was beating rapidly. He had been in a deep sleep moments ago. Was still uncertain how and why he had come to be out here now. A dream. He had had a dream.

He looked up again. It was a mild night, generous, spring coming. Summer to follow: the burning, killing sun, water a longing and a prayer. A trace of a breeze flicked and eddied in the soft darkness, cool and reviving on his face. He heard the camels and the goats behind him, and the horses. His herds were large; he was a fortune-favoured man.

He turned and saw a young boy, one of the camel herders, standing not far away: on watch, for the moonless nights were dangerous. The boy's name was Tarif. It was a name that would be remembered, become known to chroniclers of generations yet unborn because of the exchange of words that followed.

The merchant drew a breath, adjusting the drape of his white robes. Then he gestured for the boy to approach and he instructed him, speaking carefully, to find the merchant's full-brother Musafa in his tent. To wake him, with apologies, and advise him that as of the sun's rising Musafa was to take command of and responsibility for their people. That he was particularly charged, in the name and memory of their father, to be mindful of the well-being of his absent brother's wives and children.

'Where are you going, lord?' Tarif asked, becoming immortal with a handful of words. A hundred thousand children would bear his name in years to come.

'Into the sands,' said the man, whose name was Ashar ibn Ashar. 'I may be some time.'

He touched the boy on the forehead, and then turned his back on him, on the palm trees and night flowers and water, the tents and animals and movable goods of his people, and he walked out alone under the stars.

So many of them, he thought again. How could there be so many? What could it *mean* that there were so many stars? His heart was full as a water gourd with their presence overhead. He felt, in fact, like speaking a prayer, but something stopped him. He made a decision that he would be silent, instead: open to what lay all about him and above, not imposing himself upon it. He took a fold of the garment he wore and drew it deliberately across his mouth as he went.

He was gone a very long time, had been given up for dead by the time he returned to his people. He was greatly changed by then.

So, too, not long after, was the world.

The third time Shaski ran away from home that winter he was found on the road west out of Kerakek, moving slowly but with resolution, carrying a pack much too large for him.

The patrolling soldier from the fortress who brought him back volunteered, amused, to beat the child properly for his mothers, in the obvious absence of a paternal hand.

The two women, anxious and flustered, hastily declined, but did agree that some measure of real chastisement was required. Doing this once was a boy's adventure, three times was something else. They'd attend to it themselves, they promised the soldier, and apologized again for the trouble he'd been caused.

No trouble, the man said, and meant it. It was winter, a bought peace silencing the long border all the way from Ammuz and Soriyya to Moskav in the freezing north. The garrison in Kerakek was bored. Drinking and gambling could only amuse one so much in a place as hopelessly remote as this was. You weren't even allowed to ride out and chase nomads or find a woman or two in one of their camps. The desert people were important to Bassania, it had been made explicitly, endlessly clear. More important, it seemed, than the soldiers themselves. Pay was late, again.

The younger of the two women was dark-eyed, quite pretty, if distraught at the moment. The husband, as noted, was away. It seemed reasonable to contemplate a return visit, just to make sure everything was all right. He could bring a toy for the lad. One learned these tricks with the young mothers.

Shaski, standing between his two mothers just inside the fence around their small front yard, looked up stonily at the man on the horse. Earlier that morning, laughing, the soldier had held him by his ankles upside-down in the road until—blood rushing dizzily to his head—Shaski had named the house where he lived. Told to say thank you now, he did so, his voice flat. The soldier left, though not before smiling at his mother Jarita in a way Shaski didn't like.

When questioned by his mothers in the house after—a catechism that included a vigorous shaking and many tears (from them, not him)—he simply repeated what he'd said the other times: he wanted his father. He was having dreams. His father needed them. They needed to go to where his father was.

'Do you know how *far* that is?' his mother Katyun shrieked, rounding upon him. This was the worst part, actually: she was normally so calm. He didn't like it at all when she was upset. It was also a difficult question. He didn't really know how far away his father was.

'I took clothes,' he said, pointing at his pack on the floor. 'And my second warm vest you made me. And some apples. And my knife in case I met someone bad.'

'Perun defend us!' his mother Jarita exclaimed. She was dabbing at her eyes. 'What are we to do? The boy isn't eight years old!'

Shaski wasn't sure what that had to do with anything.

His mother Katyun knelt down on the carpet before him. She took his hands between her own. 'Shaski, my love, little love, listen to me. It is too far away. We do not have flying creatures to carry us, we have no spells or magic or anything to take us there.'

'We can walk.'

'We *can't*, Shaski, not in this world.' She was still holding his hands. 'He doesn't need us now. He is helping the Kings of Kings in a place in the west. He will meet us in Kabadh in the summer. You will see him then.'

They still didn't understand. It was strange how grown people could fail to understand things, even though adults were supposed to know more than children and kept telling you that.

He said, 'Summer is too long from now, and we mustn't go to Kabadh. That is the thing we have to tell father. And if he is too far to walk, let's get horses. Or mules. My father got a mule. I can ride one. We all can. You can take turns holding the baby when we ride.'

'Holding the baby?' his mother Jarita exclaimed. 'In the Lady's holy name, you want us *all* to do this mad thing?'

Shaski looked at her. 'I said that. Before.'

Really. Mothers. Did they ever listen? Did they think he *wanted* to do this alone? He didn't even have any idea where he was going. Only that his father had gone one way on the road out of town, so he had gone that way himself, and the place he was at was called Sarantum, or nearly that, and it was far. Everyone kept saying that. He had *understood* that he might not be there by nightfall, walking alone, and he didn't like the dark now, when his dreams came.

There was a silence. His mother Jarita slowly dried her eyes. His mother Katyun was looking at him strangely. She had let go of his hands. 'Shaski,' she said finally, 'tell me why we mustn't go to Kabadh.'

She had never asked him that before.

What he learned, as he explained to his mothers about the dreams and how he *felt* certain things, was that other people *didn't*. It confused him, that the pull to go away, and the other feeling—the shape of a black cloud hovering whenever they said the name *Kabadh*—was not something either of his mothers shared, or even understood.

It frightened them, Shaski saw, and that scared him. Looking at their rigid expressions when he finished speaking, he finally began to cry, his face crumpling, knuckles rubbing at his eyes. 'I'm— I'm sorry,' he said. 'For run— running away. I'm sorry.'

It was seeing her son in tears—her son who never cried— that made Katyun realize, finally, that there was something very large at work here, even if it was beyond her grasp. It was possible that the Lady Anahita had come to Kerakek, to this insignificant fortress town at the desert's edge, and had laid her finger on Shaghir, their darling child, Shaski. And the Lady's touch could mark a human being. It was known.

'Perun guard us all,' Jarita murmured. Her face was white. 'May Azal never know this house.'

But he did, if what Shaski had told them was in any way the truth. The Enemy knew Kerakek already. And even Kabadh. A cloud, a shadow, Shaski had said. How should a child know of shadows like that? And Rustem, her husband, needed them in the west. More north than west, actually. Among the infidels in Sarantium, who worshipped a burning god in the sun. Something no one who knew the desert could ever do.

Katyun drew a breath. She knew there was a trap here for her, something seductive and dangerous. She didn't want to go to Kabadh. She had *never* wanted to go there. How could she survive in a court? Among the sort of women who were there? Even the idea kept her up at night, trembling, sick to her stomach, or brought dreams, shadows of her own.

She looked at Jarita, who had been so very brave, hiding the blackness of her grief at the tidings of Rustem's elevation in caste, his summons to the court. The summons that meant they were to find her another husband, another home, another father for Inissa, little Issa.

Jarita had done something Katyun didn't think she herself could have done. She had let Rustem, the husband she loved, go on his journey thinking she accepted this, that it even *pleased* her, so that his heart might not be troubled in the wake of such great tidings as he had received.

In Perun's name, the things that women did.

It *didn't* please her. It was tearing her apart. Katyun knew it. She could hear Jarita in the dark at night, both women awake in the small house. Rustem ought to have seen through the deception, but men—even clever men— tended to miss these things, and he'd been so greatly caught up in healing the king, and then the caste elevation and his mission to the west. He had *wanted* to believe Jarita's deception, and so he had. And in any case, it was not as if a man could refuse the King of Kings.

Katyun looked from Shaski to Jarita. Rustem had told her the night before he left that she would have to do the thinking for the family, that he was relying on her. Even the students were gone, to other masters. She was on her own with this, as with all things now.

The baby cried from the other room, waking from her afternoon sleep, swaddled in her wooden cradle near the fire.

Kerakek. Kabadh. The Shadow of Black Azal. The finger of the Lady touching them. Shaski's . . . *feelings* about these things. An understanding coming, late, of how he had always been . . . different from the other children they knew. She had seen it, actually, had resisted. Perhaps in the same way that Rustem had resisted knowing how Jarita really felt: wanting to believe she was happy, though it might wound his pride. Poor Jarita, so delicate and so beautiful.

Sometimes there could be flowers in the desert, but not in many places and not for very long.

Sarantium. Even larger than Kabadh, they said. Katyun bit her lip.

She hugged Shaski and sent him to the kitchen to ask the cook for something to eat. He hadn't had his breakfast yet, had left the house in the dark while they slept. Jarita, still white-faced as a priestess on a night of the Sacred Flame, went to the baby.

Katyun sat alone, thinking hard. Then she summoned a servant and sent him to the fortress with a request that the garrison commander be so good as to honour them with a visit when time allowed.

Boredom. A sense of injustice. A peace bought with gold. They all came together for Vinaszh, son of Vinaszh, in that winter of bitterness.

He never *used* to find it tedious here in Kerakek. He liked the desert, the south: it was what he knew, the world of his childhood. He enjoyed the visits from the camel-riding nomads, going out to drink palm wine with them in their tents, the slow gestures, silences, words doled out as carefully as water. The people of the sand were important here, buffers against the Sarantines, trading partners bringing spices and gold from the distant, fabled south on the ancient camel routes. And they were advance troops in any war.

Of course some of the desert wanderers were allied with Sarantium and traded there ... which was why it mattered so much to keep those tribes that favoured Bassania happy. The soldiers didn't always understand that, but Vinaszh had grown up in Qandir, even farther south: the nuances of Ammuz and Soriyya and the nomads were no mystery to him. Or less of a mystery than they were to most men: no one could truthfully say they understood the peoples of the sand.

He had never nourished visions of himself in a more prominent place or role. He was a garrison commander in a world he comprehended well enough. It had been, until recently, a life that pleased him.

But this winter the court had come to Kerakek, and a good part of it—with the king himself—had lingered as an arrow wound healed, and the ripples that followed upon the deaths (some deserved, some not) of princes and royal wives subsided.

Vinaszh, who had played no small part in the events of a terrible day, had found himself altered after Shirvan and the court left. The fortress seemed empty to him. Bleak and echoing. The town was what it always had been . . . a dusty, eventless cluster of little homes. And the wind kept blowing from the desert. He had dreams in restless nights.

A disquiet had entered into the soul of Vinaszh the commander. The winter stretched like an uncrossable abyss, day passing, day passing, painfully slow, and then darkfall. The sand, which had never bothered him in his life, he now noticed all the time, everywhere, slipping through cracks in windows and under doors, into clothing, food, folds of skin, one's hair and beard, one's . . . thoughts.

He had begun drinking too much, starting too early in the day. He was intelligent enough to know that this was dangerous.

And it was as a consequence of all of these things that, when the doctor's servant climbed the winding path and steps up from the town and delivered that household's request for a visit when time allowed, time did allow, almost immediately.

Vinaszh hadn't the least idea what they wanted. It was a change, however, something new in the blank, stolid routine of the days. That was enough. The doctor had left a while ago. He'd been planning to spend some days in Sarnica, Vinaszh seemed to remember. Depending on how long he'd lingered there, he might even be in Sarantium by now. The doctor's women were pretty, he recalled, both of them.

He sent the servant back with a coin and word that he'd be down the hill later in the day. As it happened, it was easy to be agreeable when the request came from the household of a man about to be elevated in caste and summoned to the royal court by the King of Kings himself. Honour beyond belief, really.

Not that Vinaszh, son of Vinaszh, had been summoned anywhere, or promoted, or honoured, or . . . anything at all, actually. Not that anyone in the court had paid the least attention while they were here to whose *idea* it had been to intervene in that mighty company and—at considerable personal risk—urge the summoning of a local physician to the king's bedside that dreadful day earlier this winter. And who had then assisted the doctor *and* killed a murderous prince with his own blade.

It had crossed his mind to wonder if he was being—however unfairly—punished for the flung blade that stopped a treacherous son.

It could be. No one had said this, no one had even *spoken* to him, but someone like the round, shrewd vizier might say that his continued existence after such a deed was—or ought to be—seen as gift enough. He had slain royalty. Blood of the Great King's blood. With a dagger drawn and thrown in the presence of the king, the sacred Brother to the Sun and Moons. And yes, yes, he *had* done that, but he had been *ordered* to be on the alert for danger when Murash came back to the room. It had been an act of absolute duty.

Was he to be abandoned, forgotten here in the desert, for having saved the life of his king?

It happened. The world of Perun and Lady could not be said to be a place where just rewards held sway. The presence of Azal the Enemy meant that this would always be so, until Time itself came to an end.

Vinaszh was a soldier. He knew this to be true. The army was rife with injustice and corruption. And civilians—perfumed, sensuous court advisers, sly and unctuous—could choose to block the paths of honest, rough soldiers for their own reasons. It was the way of things. Not that understanding this made it easier to be enduring the process, if that was what was happening.

His father had never wanted him to go into the army. Had he remained a merchant down in Qandir, none of this would ever have come into his life.

He would have sand in his wine cups and bed and wouldn't care.

Men changed, Vinaszh decided, it was as simple—and as complicated—as that. It seemed that he himself had now changed. Things happened, small events or large ones, or perhaps time passed, nothing more than that—and you woke up one morning and were different. There had probably been a time, he thought, when Murash was content to be a prince of Bassania, son of his great father.

Difficult thoughts for a soldier. It would have been better to be in the field with an enemy to face. But there was no one to fight, nothing to do, and the wind kept blowing. There was sand in his cup right now, grit in the wine.

He ought to have been recognized for what he'd done. Truly, he ought to have been.

Some time after midday he went down the hill, riding towards the doctor's house. He was received by the two women in a front room with a fireplace. The younger one was *really* quite lovely, very dark eyes. The older was more poised, did all of the talking, her voice modestly low. What she said, however, took Vinaszh's thoughts abruptly from his own affairs.

Fate, chance, accident? An intercession of Perun? Who would presume to say? But the simple truth was that the soldier son of a merchant from Qandir, who happened at that time to be commander of the garrison at Kerakek, was a man more than a little disposed towards accepting such things as the woman told him that winter afternoon. The nature of the world was far beyond the grasp of men, everyone knew that. And here in the south, near the desert peoples with their inscrutable tribal rites, reports like this were not unknown.

At one point they sent for the boy at his request and Vinaszh asked him some questions, then they sent him back out again. He had answered readily enough, a serious child. He was happiest in his father's empty treatment rooms now, one of the women said, almost apologetically. They allowed him to play there. He was almost eight years old they said, when Vinaszh asked.

He declined their offered wine, accepted a cup of herbal tea instead while he considered what he'd learned. The nomads had tales and names in their own languages for people such as this child might be. Vinaszh had heard such stories, even when young. His nurse had enjoyed telling them. He had seen a Dreamer himself, once, on a desert journey with his father: a glimpse, as a tent flap fell shut too slowly. A large-bodied, soft man among a lean people. No hair on his head at all. Deep, parallel scars on both cheeks, he remembered.

The woman's story, therefore, was not one he was inclined to dismiss out of hand, but aside from finding it interesting, he remained unsure of what, exactly, they expected of him, why he was being told this, and so he asked. And so they told him.

He laughed aloud, in startled dismay, then fell silent, looking from one mother's still, grave face to the other's. They meant it, he realized. They really meant it. He heard a sound: the boy was at the doorway. He hadn't gone to the treatment rooms, after all. A listening sort of child. Vinaszh had been one himself. Shaski came out when they called to him and he stood by the beaded curtain of the door, waiting. Vinaszh stared at him.

Then he looked back at the older of the two mothers, the one who'd done the talking, and said, as gently as he could, that what she asked was simply out of the question.

'Why?' said the younger, pretty one, unexpectedly. 'You take merchant parties west sometimes.'

This was true, as it happened. Vinaszh, an honest man, and confronting two attractive women with earnest, steady gazes, was compelled to agree.

He looked back at the boy. The boy was still waiting, in the doorway. The silence was unsettling, actually. In it, Vinaszh addressed an unexpected question to himself: why, indeed? Why *was* it out of the question to provide them with an escort? There was no law being broken if wives wished to follow their husband on a journey. If the man was angry when they arrived that was, surely, *their* problem, or his. Not the escort's. Vinaszh had to assume that the doctor had left his women with sufficient finances to pay for a journey. And once they all ended up at court in Kabadh, issues of money would become trivial for this family. They might be useful people to have in his debt. No one *else* seemed to feel indebted to Vinaszh, after all. The commander resisted an impulse to scowl. He sipped his tea, made the mistake of looking back at the boy again. The grave, watchful face. Waiting for him. Children. The boy ought to be playing, outside or somewhere, surely.

Under any normal circumstances, Vinaszh considered, there would have been nothing he'd have wanted to do about any of this. But this winter wasn't . . . normal.

And the the too-obvious trust in the boy's eyes arrested his thinking. He contrasted it with his own state of mind of late. He was in danger of drinking away the reputation he'd built up for himself over the years. Bitterness could destroy a man. Or a child? He sipped his tea. The women watched him. The boy watched him.

As commander of the garrison it was within his power to assign soldiers as escorts to private parties. Merchants, usually, crossing the border with their goods in a time of peace. Peacetime didn't mean the roads were safe, of course. Normally the mercantile parties would pay for their military escort, but not invariably. Sometimes a commander had his own reasons for sending soldiers across the border. It gave restless men something to do, tested new soldiers, allowed a separation of those showing the tensions of being too much together for too long. He'd sent Nishik with the doctor, hadn't he?

The garrison commander of Kerakek didn't know—there was no reason for him to know—the arrangements proposed for the younger wife and daughter. If he had, he might not have done what he did.

Instead, he made a decision. Reversed a decision, actually. Swiftly, precise now, befitting his rank. Made a choice that might have been considered by any detached observer to be folly on a grand scale. As he spoke, both women began to cry. The boy did not. The boy went away. They heard him a little later in his father's treatment rooms.

'Perun guard us. He's packing things,' the younger mother said, still weeping.

The folly of Vinaszh, son of Vinaszh, resulted, at the end of that same week, in two women, two children, a garrison commander (that was the *point*, after all, and his second-in-command could use the experience of a period in control), and three chosen soldiers setting off on the dusty, wind-swept road towards the border of Amoria, bound for Sarantium.

As it happened, Rustem the physician, oblivious as all travellers must be to events behind them, was still in Sarnica on the day his family set out after him. He was buying manuscripts, giving lectures, would not leave that city for another week. They weren't, in fact, very far behind him.

The plan was for the four soldiers to escort the women and children and do some inconspicuous observing of their own as they went west and north through Amoria. The physician would have to deal with his family when they reached him. It would be his task to get them all to Kabadh when the time came. And it would be the women's problem to explain their sudden presence to him. It might be amusing to see that first encounter, Vinaszh thought, riding west along the road. It was curious how much better he'd felt the moment he made the decision to leave Kerakek. The doctor's women, the child, this request—they had been a gift of sorts, he decided.

He and his three men would simply go north with this small party and turn around, but the journey, even a winter journey, would be so much better than lingering in the sand and wind and emptiness. A man needed to *do* something when the days darkened early and his thoughts did the same.

He would send a written report to Kabadh when they returned, containing whatever observations they had made. The journey could be couched, described, represented as something routine. Almost. He would decide later whether to mention the boy. There was no hurry with that. For one thing, the fact that such people existed didn't mean this child, Shaghir, son of Rustem, was one of them. Vinaszh had yet to be persuaded of that. Of course, if the child wasn't what his mother thought he was, then they were all making an absurd winter journey simply because a small boy missed his father and was having bad dreams because of it. Best not, for the moment, to think about that, Vinaszh decided.

That proved easy enough. The energy of travel, of the road woke dormant feelings in the commander. Some feared the open spaces, the rigours of travelling. He wasn't one of them. Setting out on a day so mild it seemed a blessing of Perun and the Lady upon the journey, Vinaszh was happy.

Shaski was very happy.

Only as they approached Sarantium, some time later, would his mood change. Never a talkative child, he'd been in the habit of singing sometimes to himself as they went along or to calm his infant sister at night. The singing stopped about a week north of Sarnica. And shortly after that the boy grew entirely silent, looking pale and unwell, though voicing no complaint. A few days later they would finally reach Deapolis on the southern bank of the famous strait and see black smoke across the water, and flames.

In Kabadh, in his glorious palace above the gardens that hung as if by miracle down along the slope to the lowest riverbed, with contrived waterfalls running through and behind the flowers, and trees growing upside-down, Shirvan the Great, King of Kings, Brother to the Sun and Moons, lay with one wife or another that winter or with favoured concubines, and his sleep was disturbed and restless, despite drinks and powders administered to him by his physicians and priestly incantations at head and foot of his bed before he retired for the night.

This had been going on for some time.

Every night, in fact, since his return from the south, where he had almost died. It was said quietly—though never in the presence of the Great King himself—that dark dreams before dawn were not infrequently an aftermath of great peril survived, a lingering awareness of a near visitation from Azal the Enemy, the touch of black wings.

One morning, however, Shirvan awoke and sat straight up in his bed, barechested, the mark of a fresh wound still red at his collarbone. His eyes fixed on something invisible in the air, he spoke two sentences aloud. The young bride beside him sprang from the bed and knelt, trembling, on the richly textured carpet, naked as when she had entered the world of Perun and Azal's undying conflict.

The two men honoured with places in the king's bed-chamber at night, even when he bedded a woman, also knelt, averting their eyes from the shapely nakedness of the girl on the carpet. They'd learned to ignore such sights, and to keep silent about what else they saw and heard. Or, most of what they saw and heard.

The eyes of the King of Kings had been like cold iron that morning, one of them was later to say admiringly: hard and deadly as a sword of judgement. His voice was that of the judge who weighs the lives of men when they die. It was considered acceptable to report this.

The words Shirvan spoke, and was to say again when his hastily summoned advisers met him in the adjacent room, were: 'It is not to be allowed. We will go to war.'

It is often the case that a decision avoided, wrestled with, provoking intense anxiety and disturbed nights, seems obvious once made. One looks back in bemusement and consternation at the long hesitation, wondering what could *possibly* have deferred a resolution so transparent, so evident.

It was so with the King of Kings that morning, though his advisers, not sharing his winter dreams, required matters to be put in language they understood. It was possible, of course, to simply tell them what to do without explaining, but Shirvan had reigned a long time now and knew that most men did better when they grasped certain ideas for themselves.

There were two facts, really, that compelled a war, and a third element that meant they had to do it themselves.

One: the Sarantines were building ships. Many ships. Traders to the west and spies (often the same men) had been reporting this since the beginning of autumn. The shipyards of Sarantium and Deapolis were resounding with the sounds of hammers and saws. Shirvan had heard this hammering in the darkness of his nights.

Two: the queen of the Antae was in Sarantium. A living tool in the hand of Valerius. A different kind of hammer. How the Emperor had achieved *this* (and Perun knew Shirvan respected the other ruler as much as he hated him) no one had been able to say, but she was there.

These things, taken together, spelled out an invasion of the west for any man who knew how to read such signs. Who could now fail to see that the vast sums of gold Valerius had paid—two instalments now—into Bassania's coffers were designed to keep the eastern border quiescent while he sent his army west?

Shirvan had taken the money, of course. Had signed and sealed the Eternal Peace, as they named it. He had his own border problems, north and east, and his own difficulties paying a restive army. What ruler did not?

But the King of Kings needed no dream-reader now to unveil for him the meaning of his nights. The charlatans might have tried to tell him the sounds of hammering, the images of fire and the restlessness flowed from the arrow wound and the poison in his neck. He knew better.

The poison that mattered had not been on his son's arrow, but was lying in wait: the venom lay in how much power Sarantium would have if Batiara fell into its grasp. And it might. It could. For the longest time he had almost *wanted* the Sarantines to go west, believing they would never succeed. He didn't think that any more.

The lost homeland of the Empire was fertile and wealthy—why else had the Antae tribes moved down there in the first place? If the golden Strategos, hated Leontes, could add that richness to Valerius's treasury, give him wealth and security in the west, no troops tied down in Sauradia, then . . .

Then how much more beleaguered would anyone sitting on the throne in Kabadh feel?

It could not be allowed to unfold in that way. There *was* poison in all of this, deadly and absolute.

Some in that room might have hoped, wistfully, that a portion of the Sarantine money, if diverted to Moskav, could pay for a summer of unrest in the north, forcing Valerius to keep a part of his army back, undermining his invasion.

An idle thought, no more than that. The fur-clad barbarians of Moskav could as easily take the offered money and sweep down upon Mihrbor's wooden walls, within Bassania itself. They attacked when they were bored, where they chose, as they smelled weakness. There was no sense of honour, of proper conduct among those savage northerners, so sure of their safety in their wild, vast land. A bribe, an agreement would mean nothing to them.

No, if Valerius were to be impeded, they would have to do it themselves. Shirvan felt no compunction at all. No ruler who truly loved and guarded his country could be expected to be stopped in this resolve by something so trivial as a treaty of Eternal Peace.

Once a decision was made, Shirvan of Bassania was not the sort to waste time pondering such nuances.

An excuse would be created, some concocted incursion along the northern border. A Sarantine border raid from Asen. They could kill a few of their own priestly caste, burn a small temple, say the westerners had done so, breaching the sworn peace. It was the usual thing.

Asen, which had been burned and looted and bartered back and forth half a dozen times, would be the obvious target again. But there was more in Shirvan's thought, there was something new this time.

'Go farther west,' the King of Kings said to his generals, in his deep, cold voice, looking at Robazes first and then the others. 'Asen is nothing. A coin for exchanging. You must *force* Valerius to send an army. And so you will go to Eubulus itself this time, starve and batter it. And bring me back the wealth that lies within those walls.'

There was a silence. There was always silence when the King of Kings was speaking, but this was different. In all their wars with Valerius and his uncle before him and Apius before *him*, Eubulus had never been taken or even besieged. Neither had their own great northern city of Mihrbor. The battles between Sarantium and Bassania had been entirely about gold. Border raids to north and south for plunder, ransom, money for the treasuries on each side, payment for the armies. Conquest, the sack of major cities, had never been an issue.

Shirvan looked from one of his generals to another. He knew he was forcing them to change the way they thought—always a risk with soldiers. He saw Robazes, as expected, grasp the implications first.

He said, 'Remember, if they *are* going to Batiara, Leontes will be in the west. He will not be at Eubulus to face you. And if we draw enough soldiers from his army of invasion because they must go north to meet you instead, he will fail in the west. He may . . . die.' He said that last very slowly, giving it time to register. They needed to understand this.

Leontes would be west. Their scourge. The too-bright image of terror in *their* dreams, golden as the sun the Sarantines worshipped. The military commanders of Bassania looked at each other. Fear and excitement were in the room now, a slow dawning of comprehension, first awareness of possibility.

Awareness also came, after, of certain other things. How this breaking of the peace would put those Bassanids in western lands—merchants, most of them, a handful of others—desperately at risk. But that always happened when a war began, and there weren't so many in any case. Such considerations could not be permitted to alter anything. Merchants always knew there were risks in going west (or east, for that matter, into Ispahani). That was why they charged so much for what they brought back, how they made their fortunes.

As Shirvan gestured his dismissal and the gathering made obeisance and began to break up, one other man did venture to speak: Mazendar the vizier, who was always licensed to do so in the presence of his king. A small, round man, his voice light and dry as the king's was grave and deep, he offered two small suggestions.

The first was about timing. 'Great King, did you propose we attack *before* they sail west?'

Shirvan narrowed his eyes. 'That is one possibility,' he said carefully. And waited.

'Indeed, my dread lord,' Mazendar murmured. 'I see a glimmer of your mighty thoughts. We can do that, or wait until they have set off for the west and *then* cross the border for Eubulus. Leontes will be pursued by fast ships with panic-stricken tidings. He may be ordered to send some of his fleet home. The remainder will feel exposed and disheartened. Or he may press on, always fearing what we do behind him. And Sarantium will feel utterly exposed. Does the King of Kings prefer that, or the other approach? His advisers await the light of his wisdom.'

Mazendar was the only one of them worth listening to. Robazes could fight, and lead an army, but Mazendar had a mind. Shirvan said, gravely, 'It will take us some time to assemble our army north. We will attend upon events in the west and make our decision accordingly.'

'How large an army, my lord?' Robazes asked the soldier's question. He blinked in astonishment when Shirvan gave him a number. They had never sent so many men before.

Shirvan kept his expression grim and hard. People should see the countenance of the King of Kings and remember it and report it. Valerius of Sarantium was not the only ruler who could send large armies into the world. The king looked back at Mazendar. He had spoken of two suggestions.

The second concerned the queen of the Antae, in Sarantium.

Listening, the king nodded his head slowly. Was graciously pleased to agree that this proposal had virtue. Gave his consent.

Men went forth from that room. Events began to move at speed. The first signal fires were lit at darkfall that same day, sending messages of flame from hilltop to fortress tower to hilltop beyond, in all necessary directions.

The King of Kings spent much of the day with Mazendar and Robazes and the lesser generals and his treasury officials, and the afternoon in prayer before the palace's ember of the Holy Fire. At the dinner hour, he felt unwell, feverish. He spoke of this to no one, of course, but reclining upon a couch to dine he suddenly remembered—belatedly—the unexpectedly competent physician who was to be coming to Kabadh in the summer. He'd ordered the man to Sarantium in the interval, until after his necessary elevation in caste. He'd been an observing sort of man; the king had sought a way to utilize him. Kings needed to do that. Useful men had to be put to use.

Shirvan sipped at a bowl of green tea and then shook his head. The movement made him feel dizzy and so he stopped. That doctor would have left for the west already. For Sarantium itself. An unfortunate place to have him now.

It couldn't be helped. A ruler's own health and comfort surely had to give way to the needs of his people. There were burdens that came with royalty, and the King of Kings knew them all. One's personal concerns had to yield at certain times. Besides which, there simply *had* to be more than one effective doctor in Bassania. He resolved to have Mazendar initiate a proper search . . . it was not something he'd ever done, in fact.

But one grew older, good health became less sure. Azal hovered with black wings. Perun and the Lady waited for all men in judgement. One didn't have to . . . rush to them beforetimes, however.

A thought came to him as the dinner ended and he retired to his private quarters. His head was still hurting. Nevertheless, he sent for Mazendar. The vizier appeared almost immediately. It seemed to Shirvan at times that the man lived his life poised on the other side of a door, so swift was he always to appear.

The king recollected to his vizier the thought Mazendar had voiced in the morning, about the Antae queen. Then he reminded him of that physician from the south who was in Sarantium, or would be soon enough. He'd forgotten the man's name. It didn't matter; Mazendar would know it. The vizier, by a very great deal the quickest of those around him, smiled slowly and stroked his small beard

'The king is truly brother to the lords of creation,' he said. 'The king's eyes are as the eagle's eyes and his thoughts are deep as the sea. I shall act upon this, at speed.'

Shirvan nodded, then rubbed at his forehead and finally had his physicians summoned. He didn't trust any of them very much, having had the three deemed best killed in Kerakek for their own failings, but *surely* those here at court were adequate to preparing a concoction of some kind that could ease this pain in his head and help him sleep.

They were, in fact. The King of Kings did not dream that night, for the first time in a long while.

CHAPTER VIII

 In winter in Sarantium, when the enormous bulk of the Hippodrome stood quiet, the faction rivalry shifted to the theatres. The dancers, actors, jugglers, clowns vied in performance and the faction members in their assigned sections would produce acclamations (or loud denunciations) of an increasingly sophisticated nature. The rehearsals involved in achieving these spontaneous demonstrations could be quite demanding. If you knew how to follow directions, were willing to spend much of your free time practising, and had an acceptable voice, you could earn yourself a good spot for performances and privileged admission to the faction banquets and other events. There was no shortage of applicants.

The Blues and Greens were separated in the theatres as they were in the Hippodrome, standing off to the sides of the curved audience space, nowhere near each other. The Urban Prefecture was not deficient in rudimentary good sense, and the Imperial Precinct had made it abundantly clear that an excess of violence could darken the theatres for the whole of a winter. A grim prospect; sufficiently so to ensure a certain level of decorum—most of the time.

The court and visiting dignitaries, along with high-ranking civil servants and military officers, had the only seats, in the centre down front. Behind them was standing space for the non-aligned theatre-goers, prioritized by guild seniority or military rank, and here, too, could be found the couriers of the Imperial Post. Farther up in the middle came ordinary soldiers and sailors and citizens and, in this enlightened reign (rather too much so for the more fiery of the clerics), even the Kindath in their blue robes and silver caps. The occasional Bassanid or pagan traders from Karch or Moskav with a curiosity about what happened here might find a few spots assigned them towards the very back.

The clergy themselves were never at the theatre, of course. Women were very nearly naked there sometimes. They had to be careful with the northerners, actually: the girls could excite them a little too much, a different sort of disruption ensuing.

While the Principal Dancers—Shirin and Tychus for the Greens, Clarus and Elaïna for the Blues—led their colours in performance once or twice a week and the Accredited Musicians coordinated the acclamations and the younger partisans goaded and brawled with each other in various smoky cauponae and taverns, the leaders of the two factions spent the winter aggressively preparing for spring and what *really* mattered in Sarantium.

The chariots were the heart of the City's life and everyone knew it.

There was, in truth, a great deal to be done in a winter. Riders would be recruited from the provinces, dropped or sent away for various reasons, or subjected to additional training. The younger ones, for example, were endlessly drilled in how to fall from a chariot and how to arrange a spill if one was needed. Horses were evaluated, retired, groomed, and exercised; new ones were bought by agents. The faction cheiromancers still cast their attacking and warding spells (with an eye to useful deaths and fresh graves beyond the walls).

Every so often the two faction managers would meet at some neutral tavern or bathhouse and carefully negotiate, over heavily watered wine, a transaction of some kind or other. Usually this involved the lesser colours—the Reds and Whites—for neither leader would want to run the risk of losing such an exchange in an obvious way.

This, in fact, was how it came to pass that young Taras of the Reds, some time after the end of his first season in the City, found himself brusquely informed by the Green factionarius one morning after chapel services that he'd been dealt to the Blues and Whites for a right-side trace horse and two barrels of Sarnican wine, and was expected to clear out his gear and head for the Blues' compound that same morning.

It wasn't said in an unkind way. It was brief, utterly matter-of-fact, and the factionarius had already turned to discuss a new shipment of Arimondan leather with some-one else by the time Taras had fully grasped what he'd been told. Taras stumbled out of the factionarius's very crowded office. No one met his eye.

It was true that he hadn't been with them for long, and had only been riding for the Reds, and he was shy by nature, so Taras was certainly not a well-known figure in the compound. But it still seemed to him—young and not yet accustomed to the hard ways of the City—that his former comrades might have shown a little less enthusiasm when word of the transaction reached the banquet hall and the main barracks. It wasn't pleasant to hear people *cheering* when they heard the tidings.

The horse was said to be a very good one, agreed, but Taras was a man, a charioteer, someone who'd had a bed in the room with them, had dined at the table, done his very best all year in a difficult, dangerous place far from his home. The celebration wounded him, he had to admit it.

The only ones who even bothered to come by to wish him luck as he was packing his things were a couple of the grooms, an undercook he'd gone drinking with on occasion, and one of the other Red riders. In fairness, he had to acknowledge that Crescens, their burly First, did pause in his drinking long enough to note Taras crossing the banquet hall with his things and call a jocular farewell across the crowded room.

He got Taras's name wrong, but he always did that.

It was raining outside. Taras tugged down the brim of his hat and turned up his collar as he went through the yard. He belatedly remembered that he'd forgotten to take his mother's remedy against all possible ailments. He'd probably get sick now, on top of everything else.

A horse. He'd been dealt for a *horse*. There was a bad feeling in the pit of his stomach. He could still remember his family's pride when the Greens' recruiter in Megarium had invited him to the City a year ago. 'Work hard, and who knows what might happen,' the man had said.

At the compound entrance one of the guards stepped out of the hut and unlocked the gates. He waved casually and ducked back in out of the rain. They might not yet know what had happened. Taras didn't tell them. Outside, two young boys in blue tunics were standing in the laneway, getting wet.

'You Taras?' one of them asked, chewing at a stick of skewered lamb.

Taras nodded.

'Let's go, then. Take you there.' The boy flipped the remains of his skewer into the gutter, which was running with rainwater.

An escort. Two street urchins. How flattering, Taras thought.

'I *know* where the Blues' compound is,' he muttered under his breath. He felt flushed, lightheaded. Wanted to be alone. Didn't want to *look* at anyone. How was he going to tell his mother about this? The very thought of dictating such a letter to a scribe made his heart beat painfully.

One of the boys kept pace with him through the puddles; the other disappeared after a while into the misty rain, obviously bored, or just cold. One urchin, then. A triumphant procession for the great charioteer just acquired for a horse and some wine.

At the gates to the Blues' compound—his new home now, hard as it was to think that way—Taras had to give his name twice and then explain, excruciatingly, that he was a charioteer and had been . . . recruited to join them. The guards looked dubious.

The boy beside Taras spat into the street. 'Fucking unlock the gate. It's raining and he's who he says he is.'

In that order, Taras thought glumly, water dripping from his hat and down the back of his neck. The metal gates were reluctantly swung open. No word of welcome, of course. The guards didn't even believe he was a chariot-racer. The compound's courtyard—almost identical to that of the Greens—was muddy and deserted in the wet, cold morning.

'You'll be in that barracks,' the boy said, pointing off to the right. 'Don't know which bed. Astorgus said drop your stuff and see him. He'll be eating. Banquet hall's that way.' He went off through the mud, not looking back.

Taras carried his gear to the indicated building. A long, low sleeping quarters, again much like the one he'd lived in this past year. Some servants were moving about, tidying up, arranging bed linens and discarded clothing. One of them looked over indifferently as Taras appeared in the doorway. Taras was about to ask which bed was his, but suddenly the prospect seemed too humiliating. That could wait. He dropped his wet bags near the door.

'Keep an eye on these for me,' he called out with what he hoped sounded like authority. 'I'll be sleeping in here.'

He shook the rain off his hat, put it back on his head, and went out again. Dodging the worst puddles, he angled across the courtyard a second time, towards the building the boy had indicated. Astorgus, the factionarius, was supposed to be in there.

Taras entered a small but handsomely decorated front room. The double doors leading to the hall itself were closed; it was quiet beyond, at this hour of a grey, wet morning. He looked around. There were mosaics on all four walls here, showing great charioteers—all Blues, of course—from the past. Glorious figures. Taras knew them all. All the young riders did; these were the shining inhabitants of their dreams.

Work hard, and who knows what might happen.

Taras felt unwell. He saw a man, warmed by two fires, sitting on a high stool at a desk near the interior doors that led to the dining hall itself. There was a lamp at his elbow. He looked up from some writing he was doing and arched an eyebrow.

'Wet, aren't you?' he observed.

'Rain tends to be wet,' Taras said shortly. 'I'm Taras of the . . . I'm Taras of Megarium. New rider. For the Whites.'

'Are you?' the man said. 'Heard of you.' At least *someone* had, Taras thought. The man looked Taras up and down, but he didn't snicker or look amused. 'Astorgus is inside. Get rid of that hat and go on in.'

Taras looked for somewhere to put his hat.

'Give it to me.' The secretary—or whatever he was—took it between two fingers as if it were a rancid fish and dropped it on a bench behind his desk. He wiped his fingers on his robe and bent to his work again. Taras sighed, pushed his hair out of his eyes, and opened the heavy oak doors to the banquet hall. Then he froze.

He saw a huge, brightly lit room, packed with people at every table. The morning stillness was shattered by a sudden, vast, thundering roar erupting like a volcano, loud enough to shake the rafters. He realized, as he stopped dead on the threshold, heart in his throat, that they were all leaping to their feet—men and women—cups and flasks uplifted in his direction, and they were shouting his name so loudly he could almost imagine his mother hearing it, half a world away in Megarium.

Stupefied, frozen to the spot, Taras tried desperately to grasp what was happening.

He saw a compact, much-scarred man throw his cup down, bouncing it off the floor, spilling and spattering the lees of his wine, and stride across the room towards him. 'By the beard of the beardless Jad!' cried the celebrated Astorgus, leader of all the Blues, 'I cannot fucking *believe* those idiots let you go! Hah! *Hah!* Welcome, Taras of Megarium, we're proud to have you with us!' He wrapped Taras in a rib-cracking, muscular embrace and stepped back, beaming.

The noise in the room continued unabated. Taras saw Scortius himself—the great Scortius—grinning at him, cup held high. The two urchins who had fetched him were both here now, laughing together in a corner, sticking fingers in their mouths to whistle piercingly. And now the secretary and one of the guards from the gate came in behind Taras, clapping him hard on the back.

Taras realized his mouth was gaping open. He closed it. A young girl, a dancer, came forward and gave him a cup of wine and a kiss on each cheek. Taras swallowed hard. He looked down at his cup, lifted it hesitantly to the room, and then drank it off at a gulp, eliciting an even louder shout of approval and whistling everywhere now. They were still crying his name.

He was afraid, suddenly, that he was going to cry.

He concentrated on Astorgus. Tried to appear calm. He cleared his throat. 'This is . . . this is a generous welcome for a new rider for the Whites,' he said.

'The Whites? The fucking *Whites*? I love my White team as a father loves his youngest child, but you aren't with them, lad. You're a Blue rider now. *Second* of the Blues, behind Scortius. *That's* why we're celebrating!'

Taras, blinking rapidly, abruptly decided he was going to have to get to a chapel very soon. Thanks had to be given somewhere, and Jad was surely the place to start.

Approaching the barrier in his quadriga, controlling the restive horses on the second day of the race season, springtime sunlight pouring down on a screaming Hippodrome crowd, Taras hadn't the least inclination to rescind the thanks and candles he'd offered months ago, but he was still terrified this morning, aware that he was doing something significantly beyond him, and feeling the strain of that every moment.

He understood now exactly what Astorgus and Scortius had been thinking when they had manœuvred to bring him to the Blues. The second driver for the last two years had been a man named Rulanius, from Sarnica (as so many of the drivers were), but he had become a problem. He thought he was better than he was, and he drank too much as a consequence.

The role of the Second driver for a faction that had Scortius wearing the silver helmet was essentially defined by tactical challenges. You didn't *win* races (except lesser ones, when the two leaders weren't running), you attempted to make sure your First driver wasn't stopped from winning them.

That involved blocks (subtle ones), holding lanes against the Greens, forcing them wide on turns, slowing down to slow others, or dropping back hard at a precisely judged moment to open space for your leader to come through. Sometimes you even crashed at opportune times—with the very considerable risks attendant upon that. You needed to be observant, alert, willing to be banged and bruised, attentive to whatever coded instructions Scortius might shout to you on the track, and fundamentally reconciled to being an adjunct to the leader. The cheering would never be for you.

Rulanius, increasingly, had not been reconciled.

It had begun to show more and more as the last season had gone on. He was too experienced to simply be

dismissed, and a factionarius had more than just Sarantium to think about. The decision had been made to send
him north to Eubulus, second city of the Empire, where
he could ride First in a smaller hippodrome. A demotion;
a promotion. However defined, it put him out of the way.
The warning about drinking, however, had been very
specific. The track was no place for men who were not at
their sharpest, all morning, all afternoon. The Ninth
Rider was too near them, always.

But *that* problem solved had left another behind. The
current Third rider for the Blues was an older man, more
than content with his lot in life, running in the minor races,
backing up Rulanius on occasion. He'd been judged by
Astorgus, bluntly, as not equal to the tactical demands and
the frequent spills of facing Crescens of the Greens and his
own aggressive number two on a regular basis.

They could promote or recruit someone else from the
smaller cities, or approach this a different way. They chose
the latter course.

It appeared that Taras had made an impression, a significant one, especially during one memorable race at the very
end of last year. What he himself had seen as a wretched
failure, when his explosive start had been undermined by
Scortius's brilliant slashing run down behind him, had been
regarded by the Blues as a splendid effort, subverted only by
an act of genius. And then Taras had come second in that
same race, a major achievement with horses he didn't know
well, and after burning his team so much as they broke
from the line.

Some discreet enquiries into his background, some internal discussion, and a decision had been made that he'd be
suited to the role of riding Second. He would be thrilled by

the task, not chafing at it. He'd appeal to the crowd because of his youth. This had the potential to become a glorious coup for the Blues, Astorgus had concluded.

He'd negotiated a transaction. The horse, Taras had learned, was a significant one. Crescens had speedily claimed it as his own right-sider. He'd be even more formidable now, and they knew it.

That awareness had placed an additional burden of anxiety on Taras's shoulders, despite the generosity of his welcome and the meticulous tactical training he'd been undergoing with Astorgus—who had been, after all, the most triumphant rider in the world in his own day.

But that anxiety, the steadily growing sense of responsibility he'd felt from the beginning, was as nothing to what he was dealing with now as the chariots paraded back out onto the Hippodrome sands for the afternoon session of the second meeting of the new season.

The winter training had been rendered almost meaningless, all the tactical discussions purely abstract. He wasn't riding Second. He had the magnificent, fabled Servator in the left traces in front of him, and the three other horses of the lead team. He was wearing the silver helmet. He was First Chariot of the Blues.

Scortius had disappeared. Hadn't been seen since the week before the season began.

The opening day had been brutal, overwhelming. Taras had gone from riding Fourth for the lowly Reds to wearing the silver helmet for the mighty Blues, leading the grand procession out, then battling Crescens in front of eighty thousand people who had never even heard of him. He had thrown up violently twice between races. Had washed his face after, listened to Astorgus's fierce words of encouragement, and gone back out again onto the sands that could break your heart.

He'd managed to come second four of six times that first day, and three times again in the four races he'd ridden this morning. Crescens of the Greens, confident, ferociously aggressive, showing off his brilliant new right-sider, had won seven on that opening day and four more this morning. Eleven victories in a session and a half! The Greens were delirious with joy. The notion of unfair advantage didn't even enter the picture when you started a season *this* brilliantly.

No one knew, even now, where Scortius was. Or, if anyone did know, they weren't telling.

Taras was in over his head, trying not to drown.

———

There *were* a certain number of people who knew, in fact, but fewer than one might have supposed. Secrecy had been the first item of discussion with the Master of the Senate, when he'd answered an urgent request that he attend at his own small house. There were, in truth, a variety of ways to play this situation, Bonosus had thought, but the absolute insistence of the injured man had ended the conversation. Accordingly, Astorgus and Bonosus himself were the only significant figures aware of where Scortius was right now. The recently arrived (and blessedly competent) Bassanid physician also knew, of course, and so did the household servants. The latter were famously discreet, and the doctor was unlikely to betray the confidence of a patient.

The Senator did *not* know that his own son was privy to— and instrumental in—these highly unusual circumstances.

Nor did he know that one other person was to receive a brief note:

> *Very obviously you are a dangerous person and your street more perilous than one might have supposed. I appear unlikely to go to the god yet, to complain, and I believe our failed negotiations will remain unreported. It may be necessary to resume them at some point.*

Another note, in the same hand, went by way of Astorgus and one of the Blues' messenger boys to the house of Plautus Bonosus, but not to the Senator. It read,

> *I hope one day to tell you how greatly inconvenienced I have been by your family conference the other night.*

The woman who read this did not smile, doing so. She burned the note in her fireplace.

The Urban Prefecture was quietly advised that the charioteer was alive, had been injured in the course of a tryst he preferred to keep private. It happened often enough. They saw no reason to intervene further. They became very busy keeping order in the streets not long after: the Blue partisans, reeling from the disappearance of their hero and the spectacular opening day of the Greens, were in an ugly mood. More injuries and deaths than customary had ensued after the first race day, but on the whole—with so many soldiers in the City now—the mood of Sarantium was more tense and watchful than actively violent.

The seeds were there, mind you. The most celebrated charioteer in the Empire couldn't simply vanish without serious unrest emerging. The Excubitors were put on notice that their services might yet be required.

All of this had been part of the aftermath. On the night a very badly wounded man had shown up at the door, barely upright, but apologizing politely for his intrusion, the issues in the city house of Plautus Bonosus had been otherwise. Certainly for Rustem of Kerakek they had been.

He had thought he might lose this man, had been secretly grateful he was in Sarantium and not back home: there, having taken on the treatment, he'd have been expensively and perhaps even fatally liable if the chariot-racer had died. This was a very significant figure. There was no parallel in Bassania that came to mind, but it was impossible to ignore the stunned faces of the steward or the Senator's murderous offspring as they helped lay the man named Scortius onto a table that night.

The stab wound was bad, he saw—a deep thrust and then an upward, raking movement. And closing the wound, slowing the heavy bleeding, was severely compromised by the ribs fractured—three or four of them—on the same side. A shortness of breath—that was expected. The lung might well have fallen against the ribs. It might or might not kill. Rustem was astonished to learn that the charioteer had *walked* here through the streets with these injuries. Carefully he observed the man's breathing on the table, desperately shallow, as if he were belatedly acknowledging the pain.

Rustem set to work. A sedative from his travelling bag, towels, hot water, clean linens, vinegar on a sponge to clean out the wound (painfully), kitchen ingredients he instructed the servants to mix and boil for a temporary dressing: once Rustem was engaged, by the light of the lanterns they'd lit for him, he stopped thinking of implications. The charioteer cried out twice, once with the vinegar (Rustem would have used wine which was easier, if less efficacious, but had judged this man could cope with the pain), and then again, beads of sweat pouring down his face, when Rustem attempted to determine the extent and inward penetration of the broken ribs around the wound. After that he was silent, though breathing very rapidly. The sedative might have helped, but he never lost consciousness.

They controlled the bleeding eventually with lint in the wound. Afterwards, Rustem carefully removed all the packing (following Galinus in this much, at least) and inserted a tube for drainage. That, too, would have hurt. A steady flow of blood-coloured liquid ensued. More than he liked. The man didn't even move. Eventually it slowed. Rustem looked at the household skewers and pins they'd brought him—all he had for fibulae to close the wound. He decided to leave it open for now. With that much liquid he might need to drain again. He wanted to watch the lungs, the breathing.

He applied the household's quickly made poultice (adequately done, with good texture, he noted) and wrapped linens loosely as a first bandage. He wanted a better wound dressing, was inclined to use cinnabar—in modest proportions—for a wound of this sort, knowing it to be poisonous if overemployed. He would try to find proper ingredients somewhere in the morning.

He needed more drainage tubes as well. The ribs required a firmer support but the wound needed to be reachable and observed during the first few days. Merovius's famous quartet of danger signs: *redness and swelling with heat and pain*. Among the first things a physician learned, east or west.

They moved the charioteer upstairs on the plank of the table. Some bleeding started again when they did so, but that too was to be expected. Rustem mixed a heavier dose of his usual sedative and sat by the man's bed until he saw him sleep.

Just before he did so, his eyes already closed, the charioteer murmured softly in a flat, distant voice that nonetheless suggested he was trying to explain something, 'She was closeted with her family, you see.'

It was not uncommon for the sedative to cause men to say nonsensical things. Rustem set one of the servants to watch with instructions to summon him immediately if anything at all untoward took place, then he went to bed. Elita was already there—he had told her she should retire to his room. The bed was comfortable, warm with her presence. He fell asleep almost immediately. Physicians needed to know how to do that, among other things.

The girl was no longer with him when he woke in the morning, but the fire was freshly built up and a basin of water lay on the hearth to warm, with linen beside it and his clothing on a rack, also near the flames. Rustem lay still a moment, orienting himself, then made his first gesture with his right arm towards the east, murmuring the name of the Lady.

There came a knocking. Three times. First significant sound. The sound and the number benign omens for the day. The steward entered to his call. The man seemed anxious and disconcerted. Not surprisingly, given the events of the night before.

But there was more to it than that, evidently.

It seemed that Rustem had people attending upon him already. A number of them, and some were distinguished. It had not taken any time at all after the wedding yesterday for word to spread of the arrival in the City of a Bassanid physician and teacher, temporarily residing in a city home of the Master of the Senate. And whereas drunken young Hippodrome partisans might be viciously abusive of all foreigners, those afflicted in body and soul had a differing view of the arcane wisdoms of the east.

Rustem had not given this possibility any thought at all, but it was hardly an unwelcome development. And might prove useful. Sitting up in bed he stroked his beard, thinking quickly, and instructed the steward—whose manner had visibly gained in deference since last night—to have the patients return after midday. He also told him to advise them frankly that Rustem's fees were very high and to be prepared for that. Let them all decide he was no more than a greedy Bassanid, simple in his purposes here.

What he wanted was high-born or wealthy patients. The ones who could pay those fees. The ones who might possibly *know* things that mattered, and might confide them to a doctor. People did that, everywhere, and he was here for a reason, after all. He asked after his patient, and the steward reported that the wounded man was still asleep. He gave instructions to have someone look in on the fellow at intervals and report—discreetly—when he woke. No one was supposed to know that the man was here. It was still a source of some amusement to Rustem, how utterly overwhelmed the very dour, proper steward had been last night by the arrival of a mere athlete, a person from the games.

'Jad of the blessed Sun!' he had cried out when the charioteer had been helped across the threshold. His hand had shaped a religious sign, his tone had suggested he was *seeing* the named deity, not merely invoking him.

*Holy men and charioteers, that is who they honour in Saran-
tium.* An old saying. It appeared to be true. Divertingly.

After washing and dressing himself and taking a light
morning meal downstairs, Rustem had the servants set
about rearranging two of the main-floor rooms into
examination chambers and fetching certain necessary
things. The steward proved to be efficient and composed.
They might be spying on him, but Bonosus's people were
well trained, and by the time the sun was high on what
had become a mild and beneficent day in early spring,
Rustem had rooms and implements sufficient to his needs.
He formally entered the two chambers, left foot first on
each threshold, invoking Perun and the Lady. He bowed to
the four corners, beginning with the east, looked around,
and pronounced himself satisfied.

A little before midday the boy, the Senator's son who had
brought the athlete to them last night, had appeared again,
his face tinged a greyish-white with strain. It seemed unlikely
he'd had any sleep. Rustem had briskly sent him off to buy
linens and certain items for the wound dressing. Tasks were
what the boy needed. It was actually necessary to remind
himself now that this was the person who'd killed Nishik
yesterday morning. Things changed swiftly here, it seemed.

The lad looked grateful and frightened at the same time.
'Um, if you please . . . ? My father won't know I was the
one who . . . brought him here? Please?'

That had been said last night, as well. It appeared the boy
had been abroad without permission. Well, of course: he
had *killed* someone in the morning. Rustem had nodded
then and did so again now. The growing web of secrecy
might also be useful, he had decided. People in his debt.
The day was beginning well.

He would want a student or two eventually, for the proper tone and gravity, but they could come later. For now, he had Elita dress herself in a long, dark green tunic and showed her how to present patients to him in the inner chamber while others waited in the second room. He explained that she was to remain with him if the patient was female. Physicians were vulnerable to wild, inflammatory allegations and a second woman was a necessary precaution if there were no students available.

Just past midday he was informed by the steward that more than twenty people had now gathered—or sent their servants to wait—in the street outside the door. There had already been complaints from the neighbours, the man reported. It was a dignified district.

Rustem told the steward to make immediate apologies along the street and then take names of those waiting and set a limit of six patients for each day. It was necessary, if he was to achieve any of the other tasks he'd set himself while here. Once he had students they could begin a process of selecting among those who had most need of him. It was a waste of his time, really, to treat routine cataracts. After all, it was Merovius of Trakesia whose methods he used, and they *had* to know those techniques here in the west.

Elita, rather appealing in the green tunic and looking somewhat less shy, came hurrying into the room. The fellow upstairs was awake. Rustem went up quickly and entered the room, left foot first.

The man was sitting up, propped by pillows. He was very pale, but his eyes were clear and his breathing seemed less shallow.

'Doctor. I owe you my thanks. I need to be able to race

a chariot in five days,' he said, without preamble. 'Or twelve at the outside. Can you do this?'

'Race a chariot? I certainly can't,' Rustem said pleasantly. He walked over and examined the patient more carefully. For a man who might have died the night before, he seemed alert. The breathing, on closer attention, wasn't as good as he'd like. Not surprising.

The man smiled wryly after a moment. There was a brief silence. 'You are indirectly telling me to slow down, I suspect.'

He had had a deep, ripping stab wound that had barely missed reaching a *maramata* point and ending his life. He had then been kicked in the same ribs the knife had slid between, causing what must have been appalling pain. It was very possible his lung was collapsed, fallen from where it should lodge, against the ribs.

It was something of a wonder to Rustem that this fellow had actually walked to this house. It was unclear how he'd managed to breathe adequately or stay conscious. Athletes would have high tolerance for discomfort, but even so . . .

Rustem picked up the fellow's left wrist and began counting through the various indicia. 'Have you urinated this morning?'

'I haven't left the bed.'

'Nor will you. There is a flask on the table.'

The man made a face. 'Surely I can—'

'Surely you can't, or I withdraw treatment. I understand there are physicians attached to your racing group. I am happy to have someone alert them and have you transferred by litter.' Some people needed this manner. The signals from the pulse were adequate, though there was more agitation than was good.

The man named Scortius blinked. 'You are accustomed to getting your way, aren't you?' He tried to shift a little more upright and gasped, surrendering the attempt.

Rustem shook his head. In his most measured, calming voice now he said, 'Galinus here in the west taught that there are three elements to any sickness. The disease, the patient, the physician. You are stronger than most men, I believe that. But you are only one of three parts here and this is a grave injury. Your entire left side is . . . unstable. I can't bind the ribs properly until I am certain of the stab wound and your breathing. Am I used to having my way? Not in most things. What man is? In treatment a doctor must, however.' He permitted his tone to soften further. 'You do know they can have us fined or even executed in Bassania if an accepted patient dies.' A personal revelation was sometimes effective.

After a moment the charioteer nodded. He was a small-ish, exceptionally handsome man. Rustem had seen the network of scars on his body last night. From his colouring, he was from the south. The same desert spaces Rustem knew. A hard place, making hard men.

'I'd forgotten. You are a long way from your home, aren't you?'

Rustem shrugged. 'Injuries and sickness change little enough.'

'Circumstances do. I do *not* wish to be difficult, but I can't afford to go back to the faction compound and face questions just now, and I *must* race. The Hippodrome is opening in five days, these are . . . complex times here.'

'They may well be so, but I can swear to you by my deities or yours that there is no doctor alive who would agree to that, or could achieve it.' He paused. 'Unless you wish to simply get into a chariot and die on the track from loss of blood, or when your crushed ribs cave inward and stop your breathing? A heroic ending? Is that it?'

The man shook his head, a little too vigorously. He winced at the movement, and put a hand to his side. He then swore, with great feeling, blaspheming both his deity and the controversial son of the Jaddite god.

'The next week then? Second race day?'

'You will remain in a bed for twenty or thirty days, charioteer, then you will begin very careful walking and other movements. This bed or another, I hardly care. It isn't only the ribs. You were stabbed, you know.'

'Well, yes, I do know. It hurt.'

'And must heal cleanly, or you may die of the inflammation's exudation. The dressing must be examined and changed every second day for two weeks, fresh poultices applied and left undisturbed by further bleeding. I have to drain the wound again, in any case—I haven't even stitched it yet and I will not for several days. You are going to be in extreme discomfort for some time.'

The fellow was staring at him intently. With certain men it was best to be honest about this. Rustem paused. 'I am not unaware that the games in your Hippodrome are important, but you will not be part of them until summer and it were best if you made yourself easy with that. Wouldn't it be the same if you'd had a fall of some kind? Broken your leg?'

The charioteer closed his eyes. 'Not quite the same, but yes, I take your point.' He looked at Rustem again. His eyes really were encouragingly clear. 'I am being insufficiently grateful. It was the middle of the night and you had no preparation at all. I seem to be alive.' He grinned wryly.

'Able to be difficult. You have my thanks. Would you be good enough to have someone bring me writing paper and let the steward send a discreet runner to Senator Bonosus letting him know I am here?'

A well-spoken man. Not at all like the wrestlers or acrobats or horseback performers Rustem had known as entertainers back home.

His patient dutifully provided a sample of urine and Rustem determined that the colour was predictably red but not alarmingly so. He mixed another dose of his soporific and the charioteer was quite docile about accepting it. Then he drained the wound again, checking the flow and colour carefully. Nothing unduly alarming yet.

Men such as this one, who had experienced pain on a regular basis, knew the needs of their own bodies, Rustem thought. He changed the dressing, looking closely at the crusted blood around the wound. It was still bleeding, but not heavily. He allowed himself a small flicker of satisfaction. There was a long way to go, however.

He went downstairs. There were patients waiting. The six he had allowed. Today it was simply the first six in line; they'd devise a more precise system as soon as they could. The morning's first omens had proven true, even here among the unbelieving Jaddites. Events were developing in a *very* benign way.

That first afternoon he examined a merchant dying of a tumour that was eating at his stomach. Rustem was unable to offer anything at all, not even his usual mixture for this extreme level of pain, since he hadn't brought that with him and had no connections here with those who mixed physicians' private remedies. Another task for the next few days. He would make the Senator's boy be useful. Employ him like the servant he'd killed. It appealed to his sense of irony.

Looking at the gaunt, wasted figure of the merchant, Rustem spoke the necessary words with regret: 'With this I will not contend.' He explained the Bassanid practice in this. The man was calm, unsurprised. Death was seated in his eyes. One grew accustomed to it, and yet one never did. Black Azal was always at work among the living in the world Perun had made. A physician was a minor soldier in their endless war.

Next, however, came a scented, subtly painted court woman who appeared only to want to see what he looked like. Her servant had held a place in line for her from before sunrise.

This sort of thing happened often enough, especially when a doctor came to a new place. Bored aristocrats, looking for diversion. She giggled and talked through his examination of her, even with Elita present. Bit her lower lip and looked at him through half-lowered eyelashes when he took her perfumed wrist to obtain the counts there. She chattered about a wedding yesterday—the very one Rustem had attended, as it happened. She hadn't been there, appeared piqued about that. Seemed even more displeased when he reported that she seemed to have no ailments that required his intervention, or another visit.

There followed two other woman—one evidently wealthy, the other rather a common sort—complaining of barren wombs. This, too, was normal when physicians arrived in a new place. The endless search for someone who could *help*. He confirmed that the second woman had been able to pay the steward, and with Elita present each time performed his examinations as the Ispahani doctors did (though never those in Bassania, where to see a woman unclothed was forbidden to physicians). Both women were unruffled by this, though Elita flushed red, watching. Settling into routine, Rustem asked his usual questions and came—quickly in each instance—to his conclusions. Neither woman seemed surprised, which was often the case in these matters, though only one of them was in a position to find solace in what he said.

Next he saw and diagnosed two cataracts—as expected— and lanced them with his own implements, charging for the examination, the procedure, and a considerable, deliberately inflated sum for the visits he would make to their homes.

By the middle of the afternoon he had heard a significant amount of gossip and knew much more than he really wanted to know about the Hippodrome season that was starting soon. Blues and Greens, Blues and Greens. Scortius and Crescens. Even the dying man had mentioned the two charioteers. The Sarantines were collectively obsessed, Rustem decided.

At one point Elita slipped out and returned, reporting quietly that the much-discussed fellow upstairs was asleep again. Rustem diverted himself briefly by imagining the reaction if people knew he was here.

Everyone had talked, but they offered only trivial information. That would change, Rustem thought. People confided in their doctors. This exercise held great promise. He went so far as to smile at Elita and offer praise for her demeanour. She flushed again, looking down at the floor. When the last patient left, Rustem went out of the treatment rooms, feeling quite pleased.

Awaiting him was a two-person delegation from the physicians' guild.

His mood changed, very quickly.

Both men were visibly and vocally outraged to find a foreigner having set himself up to practise medicine in Sarantium in a private home without so much as a visit to the guild or a by-your-leave. Given that he was here—ostensibly—to lecture, to learn, to buy manuscripts, share information with western colleagues, this anger was likely to bring consequences.

Rustem, furious with himself for an obvious oversight, took refuge in ignorance and earnest apologies . . . he was from a small town only, had no *idea* of the complexities of things in a great city, had had no intention at all to offend or transgress. Patients had gathered outside without his having put forth any word at all. The steward would confirm that. His oath—just like their own in the tradition of the west's great Galinus—*required* him to try to be of aid. He would be *honoured* to attend upon the guild. Immediately, if permitted. Would cease seeing patients, of course, if they requested it. Was entirely in their hands. And, in passing, might his distinguished visitors wish to join him in dining with the Master of the Senate tonight?

They registered that last remark, more than anything else. Declined the offer, of course, but noted it, along with where he was staying. Whose house it was. Access to corridors of power. The possibility he might be someone not to be offended.

One could be amused, really. Men were the same all over the world.

Rustem escorted the two Sarantine doctors to the door, promised to be at the guild rooms by mid-morning tomorrow. Begged their expert assistance in all matters there. Bowed. Expressed, again, his contrition and the degree to which he was gratified by their visit and looked forward to sharing their knowledge. Bowed again.

The steward, expressionless, closed the door. Rustem, an eccentric mood coming upon him, actually winked at the man.

Then he went up to attend to the streaking of his beard again (it needed regular care) and change for dinner at the Senator's house. Bonosus had been asked by the patient to come here. He probably would. By now Rustem had a pretty good idea of the importance of the wounded man asleep in the next room. *Charioteers and holy men.* He wondered if he'd be able to turn tonight's dinner talk to the possibility of war. Too soon, he decided. He had just arrived, spring was only beginning. Nothing could or would happen at speed, surely. Except the racing, he thought.

Everyone in Sarantium—even the dying—seemed to be thinking about chariots. A frivolous people? He shook his head: too hasty an assessment, likely wrong. But in his new role as an observer of the Sarantines for the King of Kings he would have to attend the Hippodrome, he decided, like a physician visiting a patient.

It came into his mind abruptly to wonder if Shaski liked horses. He realized that he didn't know, and that since he was so far from home he couldn't ask.

It changed the feel of the afternoon, for a time.

When the Senator came, late in the day, his manner was grave and brisk. He noted the changed downstairs rooms without comment, heard Rustem's account of the night before (with, as promised, no mention of the boy), and then entered the room of Scortius and firmly closed the door behind himself.

Rustem had urged him to keep the visit brief and Bonosus did so, coming out a short while later. He said nothing, of course, about the conversation that had taken place within. They were carried by litter to his principal residence. He remained singularly distracted during the dinner that followed.

It was an immensely civilized evening, nonetheless. The guests were served wine as they entered by the Senator's charming daughters: clearly the children of an earlier wife, the one here was much too young to be their mother. The two girls withdrew before the party was led to the dining couches.

Rustem's experience of such things owed more to his time in Ispahani lands than to any encounters at home, of course. Kerakek was not a place where invisible music played softly through the evening and impeccable servants hovered behind each couch, attentive to the least hint of a need. Under the polished guidance of the Senator's wife Rustem was made welcome with the other guests, a Bassanid silk merchant (a courteous touch, that) and two Sarantine patricians and their wives. The Senator's wife and the other two women, all elegant, poised and at ease, were much more conversational than those in Ispahani ever tended to be at such gatherings. They asked him a great many questions about his training, his family, drew him out on the subject of adventures in Ispahani lands. The mysteries of the far east, rumours of magics and fabled creatures, held an obvious fascination here. There was a discreet avoidance of Rustem's dramatic arrival in Sarantium the morning before; the drama, after all, had been occasioned by the Senator's son—who was nowhere to be seen.

It became clear that no one knew about the equally

dramatic late-night events involving the charioteer. Bonosus said nothing. Rustem wasn't about to bring it up.

A physician owed a duty to his patient.

In his best robe and carrying his walking staff, he attended at the guild the next morning, conducted by one of the household servants, bearing a note of introduction offered him by the Senator over the last wine of the evening.

Rustem made all the necessary gestures and remarks, and found himself welcomed with courtesy. It was peacetime, and these *were* members of his own profession. He wasn't about to stay long enough to represent a threat, and he might be useful to them. It was arranged that he would deliver a lecture in two weeks' time here at the guild-hall. They sanctioned his treatment of a handful of patients a day in the rooms he'd set up, and he was given the names of two apothecary and herbalist shops where accurately mixed medicines could be obtained. The matter of students was deferred (a bit too much permanence implied?) but Rustem had already decided that would have to wait in any event, as long as the charioteer was in the house.

And so he set in motion—more easily than he could have expected—a life, a pattern to his days, as springtime flowered in Sarantium. He paid a visit to a public bathhouse with the Bassanid merchant of the night before and established that the man had access to messengers going to Kabadh. Nothing was said explicitly, much exchanged by inference.

A few days after that a message arrived *from* Kabadh, and a great deal was altered.

It came by way of yet another Bassanid. At first, when the steward informed Rustem of the presence of one of his countrymen in the morning line of patients, Rustem had simply assumed that an eastern merchant had chosen to be treated for some ailment by a physician familiar with eastern regimens. The fellow was his third patient of the day.

When the man entered, soberly garbed, neatly barbered, Rustem turned to him with an inquiring glance and asked after his health in their own tongue. The patient said nothing, merely withdrew a parchment from within his clothing and extended it.

There was no formal seal that might have given warning.

Rustem opened the parchment and read. He sat down as he did so, felt himself going pale, was aware that this ostensible patient was watching him closely. When he finished, he looked up at the other man.

It was difficult to speak. He cleared his throat. 'You . . . know what this says?'

The man nodded. 'Burn it now,' he said. His voice was cultured.

There was a brazier in the room; the mornings were still cold. Rustem went over to it and put the parchment in the flame, watching until it was consumed.

He looked back at the man from Kabadh. 'I was . . . I thought I was here as an observer.'

The man shrugged. 'Needs change,' he said. He rose. 'Thank you for your assistance, doctor. I am sure your help will address my . . . difficulty.' He walked out.

Rustem remained where he was for a long time, then remembered that the servants of Plautus Bonosus were almost certainly reporting on him and he forced himself to move, to reassume the movements of normality, though all had changed.

A physician, by his oath, was to strive to heal the sick, to do battle with Azal when the Enemy laid siege to the bodies of mortal men and women.

Instead, his king, the Brother to the Sun and Moons, had just asked him to kill someone.

It was important to conceal the signs of his disquiet. He concentrated on his work. As the morning passed, he persuaded himself that his having any opportunity to do what had been asked of him was so remote that surely he could not be faulted for a failure. He could say as much when he went home.

Or, more correctly, he *almost* persuaded himself of that.

He had seen the King of Kings, in Kerakek. It could not be said that Great Shirvan had conveyed any sense of indulgence towards those who might claim . . . difficulty in executing orders he conveyed to them.

In the small house of Plautus Bonosus he finished with his morning patients and went upstairs. He decided it was time to stitch the charioteer's wound. By now he had proper fibulae with clips for the ends. He performed that procedure. Routine, effortless. Requiring no thought at all, which was good.

He continued to watch for and was relieved not to see the green oozing of pus. After a number of days had passed with the wound healing, he had just about decided it was time to bind the ribs more firmly. The patient had been entirely cooperative, if legitimately restless. Active, physical men took confinement badly, in Rustem's experience, and this man wasn't even able to have regular visitors, given the secrecy surrounding his presence here.

Bonosus had come twice, on the pretence of seeing his

houseguest from Bassania, and once, at night, a cloaked figure appeared who turned out to be a man named Astorgus, evidently of significance in the Blues' group. It appeared that some unhappy results had transpired on the first day of the racing. Rustem didn't ask for details, though he did mix a slightly stronger sedative for his patient that night, noting signs of agitation. He was prepared for such things.

He wasn't prepared, at all, to go along the hall one morning, in the second week after the charioteer had arrived in the dead of night, and find the bedroom empty and the window open.

There was a folded note, set beneath the urine flask. '*Do come to the Hippodrome,*' it read. '*I owe you some amusement.*'

Above the paper, the flask had been dutifully filled. His brow furrowed, Rustem noted with a quick glance that the colour was satisfactory. He walked over to the window, saw a tree quite close to hand, thick branches, not yet hidden by budding leaves. It wouldn't have been hard for a fit man to get out and down. For someone with inadequately wrapped, badly broken ribs and a deep, still-healing stab wound . . .

Glancing at the window ledge Rustem saw blood.

Looking more closely down on the small courtyard he observed a thin trail of it crossing the stones to the wall by the street. Suddenly angered, he looked up at the sky. Perun and the Lady knew, surely, that a physician could only do so much. He shook his head. It was a beautiful morning, he realized.

He decided that after seeing his patients he would attend at the Hippodrome that afternoon for the second day's racing. *I owe you some amusement.* He sent a runner to the Master of the Senate, asking if Bonosus might assist him in obtaining admission.

He was being very naive, of course, though excusably, as a stranger in Sarantium.

Plautus Bonosus was already at the Hippodrome by then, in the kathisma, the Imperial Box, the servant reported when he returned. The Emperor himself was attending the morning's races, would retire at midday to deal with larger affairs in the palace. The Master of the Senate would remain all day, a representative of the state.

Larger affairs. From the harbour the sound of shouts and hammering could be heard, even this far inland towards the walls.

Ships were being made ready to sail. It was said that there were ten thousand foot-soldiers and cavalry assembled here and in Deapolis across the straits. As many were reported to be gathering in Megarium to the west, Rustem had been told by a patient a few days ago. The Empire was clearly on the brink of war, an invasion, something indescribably dramatic and exciting, though nothing, as yet, had been announced.

Somewhere in the City a woman Rustem had been ordered to kill was going about the rhythm of her days.

Eighty thousand Sarantines were in the Hippodrome, watching chariots run. Rustem wondered if she would be there.

CHAPTER IX

Crispin, in a mood he'd have been unwilling to define, was beginning work on the images of his daughters on the dome that same morning when the Empress of Sarantium came and took him away to see dolphins among the islands in the straits.

Looking a long way down from the scaffold when Pardos, working beside him, touched his arm and pointed, he registered the explicit demand of Alixana's presence. He looked back for a moment at Ilandra where he had placed her on the dome—a part of this holy place and its images—and then over at the surface nearby where his girls were awaiting their own incarnation out of memory and love. He would give his daughters form in a different guise, in light and glass, as Zoticus had given souls bodily form in the crafted birds of his alchemy.

What was this but a different kind of alchemy, or the attempt to make it so?

At the rail Pardos was anxiously glancing down and then back at Crispin and then down again. Less than two weeks in the City and his apprentice—his associate now—was obviously aware of what it meant to have an Empress waiting for you on the marble floor below.

Crispin, along with Artibasos the architect, had received invitations to two large banquets in the Attenine Palace over the winter, but had not spoken privately with Alixana since autumn. She had come here once before, had stood very nearly where she was standing now, to see what was being done overhead. He remembered coming down to her, to all of them.

He was unable to deny the quickening beat of his heart now. He cleaned his hands of plaster and lime as best he could, wiped at a cut finger—bleeding slightly—with the cloth tucked in his belt. He discarded the cloth and even allowed Pardos to adjust and brush his tunic, though he swatted the younger man away when he gestured towards Crispin's hair.

On the way down, though, he paused long enough on the ladder to push a hand through the hair himself. Had no idea if that improved anything.

Evidently it didn't. The Empress of Sarantium, richly if soberly garbed in a long blue gold-belted tunic and a porphyry cloak that came to her knees, with only rings and earrings for jewellery, smiled with amusement at him. She reached down as he knelt before her and ordered his much-abused red hair more to her satisfaction.

'Of course the wind in the straits will undo my efforts,' she murmured in the instantly memorable voice.

'What straits?' Crispin asked, rising to her gesture.

And so he learned that the dolphins of which she'd spoken on his first night in the palace half a year ago remained on her mind. She turned and walked serenely past a score of still-kneeling artisans and labourers. Crispin followed, feeling excitement and the presence of danger—as he had from the very beginning with this woman.

Men were waiting outside in the livery of the Imperial Guard. There was even a cloak for him in the litter he entered with the Empress of Sarantium. This was all happening very quickly. Her manner, as they were lifted and began to move, was matter-of-fact, entirely pragmatic: if he was to render dolphins leaping from the sea for her, he ought to see them first. She smiled sweetly from across the curtained litter. Crispin tried and failed to return the smile. Her scent was inescapable in the cushioned warmth.

A short time later Crispin found himself in a long, sleek Imperial craft cutting through the crowded harbour, past a cacophony of construction and the loading and unloading of barrels and crates of goods, out to where the noise receded and a clean wind was there to be caught by the white and purple sails.

On the deck, at the railing, Alixana was looking back at the harbour. Sarantium rose beyond it, brilliant in sunlight, domes and towers and the piled houses of wood and stone. They could hear another sound now: the chariots were in the Hippodrome today. Crispin looked up at the sun. They were probably up to the sixth or seventh race by now, the midday break to come, then the afternoon's running. Scortius of the Blues had still been missing as of last night. The City spoke of that as much as it talked of war.

He stood uncertainly a little behind the Empress. He didn't like boats, but this one was moving easily through the sea, expertly handled, and the wind was not yet strong. They were the only passengers, he realized. He made a concerted effort to bring his mind, his thinking, back from the scaffolding and his daughters, what he had *expected* would be the nature of today's demands upon him.

Without turning her head, Alixana said, 'Have you sent to Varena to advise them what is coming? Your friends, family?'

Today's demands were evidently going to be otherwise.

He remembered this from before: she used directness as a weapon when she chose. He swallowed. What use dissembling? 'I wrote two letters, to my mother and my dearest friend . . . but there isn't much point. They all know there is a threat.'

'Of course they do. That's why the lovely young queen sent you here with a message, and then followed herself. What does *she* have to say about all . . . this?' The Empress gestured at the ships massed behind them in the harbour. Gulls wheeled in the sky, cutting across the line of their own wake in the sea.

'I have no idea,' Crispin said truthfully. 'I would assume you'd know that far better than I, thrice-exalted.'

She looked over her shoulder at him then. Smiled a little. 'You'll see better at the rail, unless it makes you unwell to look down at the waves. I ought to have asked before . . . '

He shook his head and came resolutely forward to stand beside her. White water streamed away from the sides of the ship. The sun was high, glinting ōn the spray, making rainbows as he watched. He heard a snapping sound and looked up to see a sail fill. They picked up speed. Crispin put both hands on the railing.

Alixana murmured, 'You warned them, I assume? In the two letters?'

He said, not fighting the bitterness, 'Why should it matter? Whether I've sent warnings? Empress, what could ordinary people do if an invasion came? These are not people with any power, any ability to influence the world. They are my mother and my dearest friend.'

She looked at him again for a moment, without speaking. She was hooded now, her dark hair bound up in a golden net. The severity of the look accented her features, the high cheekbones, perfect skin, enormous dark eyes. He thought suddenly of the slender, crafted rose he had seen in her room. She had asked him for something more permanent, the golden rose speaking to the fragility of beautiful things, a mosaic hinting at that which might last. A craft that aspired to endure.

He thought of Jad, slowly crumbling on a dome in a Sauradian chapel bordering the Aldwood, tesserae falling in the filtered light.

She said, 'The world can be . . . influenced in unexpected ways, Caius Crispus. The Emperor has been hoping that letters were being sent, actually. That's why I asked. He is of the belief that the native Rhodians might welcome our arrival, given the chaos in Varena. And since we are sailing in the name of your queen, there is some hope that many of the Antae themselves might not fight. He wants them to have time to consider possible . . . interventions.'

It suddenly occurred to him that she was speaking as if he *knew* an invasion had been announced. It hadn't been. Crispin looked at her, his emotions roiling again. 'I see. So even letters home to loved ones are a part of the design?'

Her gaze met his. 'Why should they not be? He thinks in that way. If we are unable to do so, does that make him wrong? The Emperor is trying to change the world as we know it. Is it a transgression to bring all the elements one can to something as large as this?'

Crispin shook his head and looked away, at the sea again. 'I told you half a year ago, Majesty, I am an artisan. I can't even guess at these things.'

'I wasn't asking you to,' she said, mildly enough. Crispin felt himself flush. She hesitated. Looked out at the waves as well. Said, a little stiffly, 'It is to be formally proclaimed this afternoon. In the Hippodrome by the Mandator after the last race of the day. An invasion of Batiara in the name of Queen Gisel, to reclaim Rhodias and remake a sundered Empire. Does it not sound glorious?'

Crispin shivered in the mild sunlight of that day, then felt a burning sensation, as if something had touched him, like a brand. He closed his eyes on a sudden, vivid image: flames ravaging Varena, taking the wooden houses like so much kindling for a summer bonfire.

They had all *known*, but . . .

But there was a tone in the voice of the woman beside him, something to be read in her profile now, even within the dark hood. He swallowed again, and said, 'Glorious? Why do I imagine you don't find it so?'

No visible response, though he was watching for it. She said, 'Because I am allowing you to see that, Caius Crispus. Though, to be entirely truthful, I'm not certain why. I confess that you . . . Look!'

She never finished that thought for him.

Broke off, instead, pointing. He had time to recollect that she was an actress, above all things, and then he looked. Saw dolphins breach the sea, tearing it sharply, their bodies arcing like the perfect curve of a dome, racing the ship through the ruffled water. Half a dozen of them, surfacing in sequences, as if choreographed in a theatre, one, then two, then a pause, then again, the sleek, exultant leap and splash of it.

Playful as . . . children? Exquisite as dancers, as the dancer beside him. Carriers of the souls of the dead, bearers of drowned Heladikos when he fell burning into the sea with the chariot of the sun. The paradox and the mystery of them. Laughter and darkness. Grace and death. She wanted dolphins for her rooms.

They watched for a long time, then there came a point when the dolphins did not leap with them any more and the sea rolled beneath and beside the ship, untorn, hiding things, as it always did.

'They do not like to come too near the island,' said the Empress Alixana, turning her head to look towards the bow.

Crispin turned as well. 'Island?' he said.

He saw land, unexpectedly near, densely forested with evergreen trees. A stony beach, a wooden dock for mooring the boat, two men waiting in Imperial livery. No other signs of human life. Gulls crying all about them in the morning.

'I had another reason for coming out this morning,' said the woman beside him, not smiling now. She had lowered her hood. 'The Emperor doesn't like my doing this. He believes it is . . . wrong. But there is someone I want to see before the army sails. A . . . reassurance. You and the dolphins were my excuse today. I believed you could be trusted, Caius Crispus. Do you mind?'

She didn't wait for an answer, of course, was simply giving him as much as she thought he needed to know. Grains doled out from the guarded storehouse of their knowledge. Valerius and Alixana. He wanted to be angry, but there was something in her manner, and in the mood from which she'd claimed him. She'd thought he could be trusted but hadn't said *why* she wanted to trust him.

He wasn't about to ask. She had turned away in any case, walked across to the other side of the ship, where men were readying them for docking.

He followed, his heart beating too fast again, the inward image of a great burning in Varena cutting against the memories he had awakened this morning intending to try to shape. Two girls in their youth, a part of the world the god had made. Their youth and their dying. He had been going there. And now before him, instead, was this deceptive, mild placidity of blue sea and sky and dark green trees in morning light. *You and the dolphins were my excuse today.*

For what?

The mooring of the craft was flawless, nearly silent. The slap of waves and the calling birds in the sky. A ramp was lowered, a crimson carpet unrolled for the Empress's feet. Formalities: she was what she was. It was never to be forgotten. You were not to think of her as anything else.

They went down the landing ramp. Four soldiers followed at a little distance. They were armed, Crispin saw, looking over his shoulder.

The Empress, not looking back at all, led him from the sea along a path that went from the white, round stones into pine trees that soon hid the sun. Crispin drew his cloak around himself as the day's light failed.

There was no god here, no emblem, symbol, incarnation thereof. There was a single mortal woman, straight-backed, not tall, to be followed over pine needles and amid the scent of pine, and after a little time—it wasn't a large island—there was an ending to the path and the woods and Crispin saw a cluster of buildings. One house, three or four smaller huts, a tiny chapel with a sun disk carved above the door. The Empress stopped a little distance into that open space between the trees and the houses men had made and she turned to him as he came up beside her.

'I dislike speaking in this manner,' she said, 'but I must say that if you tell of what you see here now you will be killed.'

Crispin's hands clenched. Anger again, despite everything. He, too, was what he was, what the god and loss had made of him.

'You contradict yourself, thrice-exalted.'

'How so?' The voice brittle. He could see that there was some strain within her now that they had reached this place. He didn't understand it, or any of this, and he didn't care. Had thought to spend today on a scaffolding alone with his craft and memories of his girls.

'You just said you were of the belief I could be trusted. Obviously this is not so. Why not leave me on the ship? Empress, why am I here, to face such a threat? To *be* such a threat? What am I in this?'

She was silent, looking at him. Her face was very white. The Excubitors had halted, discreetly, some distance behind them at the edge of the trees. There were other soldiers, Crispin now saw, appearing at the doorways of the smaller houses. Four of them, wearing the livery of the Urban Prefecture. No one moved by the largest house. Smoke rose from chimneys, drifted.

'I don't know,' said the Empress Alixana finally. She was staring up at him. 'A fair question, but I do not know the answer. I know that I . . . do not like to come here any more. He frightens me, makes me dream. That's one reason Petrus . . . why the Emperor doesn't want me coming.'

The stillness of the clearing, of that single larger house, had something uncanny about it. Crispin realized all the shutters were closed. There would be no sunlight there.

'In Jad's name, who is here?' he asked, too loudly. His voice seemed an abrasion in the waiting air.

Alixana's dark eyes were enormous. 'Jad has little enough to do with him,' she said. 'Daleinus is here. Styliane's brother. The oldest child.'

Rustem would have preferred to deny it, but both of his wives and all of his teachers had characterized him (sometimes with amusement) as a stubborn, willful man. An idea in his head was unlikely to be readily dislodged.

Accordingly, when the servant of Plautus Bonosus returned to the house near the walls and reported that the Senator was already among the crowd gathered at the Hippodrome and could not be of any assistance, Rustem shrugged his shoulders, turned to attend to a revision of the lecture he was soon to give, and—a short while after—put it aside and impatiently put on boots and a cloak to venture forth with two guards to attend at the house of Bonosus himself.

The streets were deserted, eerily so. Many shops were boarded up, the markets almost silent, taverns and cookshops empty. From a distance as they went Rustem heard a dull, punishing sound, a steady roar, rising at intervals into something more than that. It would be frightening if you didn't know what it was, he thought. In fact, it could be frightening even if you did know.

He wanted to see these races now. To know what his patient was doing. He even saw himself as having some responsibility to be present. And if this Jaddite charioteer was going to kill himself—and past a certain point no physician could do anything about that—Rustem felt a measure of curiosity as to the ways and means. He was in the west, after all, to try to understand these people. Or, that was why he had *come* here, what he had thought his role would be. His more recent task was one he tried to avoid considering. He had some vague hope that circumstances might make the whole thing . . . go away.

It was obviously impossible for a visiting Bassanid to simply walk up to the Hippodrome and gain admission. The physicians' guild might have helped, given notice, but Rustem had had no warning at all that his patient would leave his room via a window, a tree, and the courtyard wall, trailing blood behind him as he went.

In a case of this sort, one needed to invoke more powerful connections of a personal nature. Rustem was looking for Cleander.

He knew from the boy himself that Bonosus had forbidden his son to attend the first five meetings of the race season, as punishment for the incident that had killed Nishik. One might quarrel with equating the death of a man (even a foreigner, even a servant) with five lost days of amusement, but that wasn't Rustem's concern today.

Today he wanted to persuade Cleander's mother to override her husband's dictate. He was well aware, from glosses in the texts of the western physicians, that in ancient Rhodias a man's will was utterly binding, even to death, upon wives and children. A father had once been able to have his son executed by the state for simple disobedience.

There had been a brief time in the old days in the west when this had been seen as demonstrating virtue, the exemplary discipline and rectitude that could forge an empire. Rustem was of the view that in the modern Sarantium of Valerius and the Empress Alixana, women might have a greater degree of authority in the home. He had cause to know that the boy was an intensely partisan follower of the chariots. If someone knew how to get into the Hippodrome—for the afternoon at least, as the morning was well advanced by now—it would be Cleander. But he would need his stepmother's consent.

The Senator's steward was swift to alert his mistress when Rustem presented himself at the door. Thenaïs Sistina, quite unruffled, coolly elegant, greeted him in her morning room with a gracious smile, setting aside pen and paper. Rustem noted that she appeared to be literate.

He apologized, discussed the mild weather, explained that he wished to attend the races.

She did show surprise, the merest flicker and blink of her eyes. 'Really?' she murmured. 'I hadn't expected the games to appeal to you. They don't hold much allure for me, I confess. Noise and dirt, and there is often violence in the stands.'

'None of which would draw me,' Rustem agreed.

'But I suppose there *is* an element of spectacle. Well, I shall be certain to inform my husband that you'd like to accompany him to the next games day . . . it ought to be within a week or two if I understand the process rightly.'

Rustem shook his head. 'I'd really like to attend this afternoon.'

Thenaïs Sistina assumed a distressed expression. 'I don't see any way to get a message to my husband in time. He's with the Imperial party, in the kathisma.'

'I understand as much. I was wondering if Cleander might . . . ? As a courtesy and great favour to me?'

The Senator's wife looked at him for a long moment. 'Why today, so urgently, if I might ask?'

Which compelled an indiscretion. In light of the morning's open window and the fact that this was Bonosus's wife and Bonosus already knew, Rustem felt justified. The man's physician *ought* to be in attendance, in fact. No one else could possibly know the precise nature of his patient's injuries. It could be said he had duties and would be remiss in them did he not make his best effort to be present.

So he told the wife of Plautus Bonosus, in formal confidence, that his patient, Scortius of Soriyya, had violated medical advice and left his bed in the Senator's city home, where he had been recovering from wounds. Given the fact that there was racing today, it was not difficult to deduce why he had done so and where he would be.

The woman showed no reaction to learning this. The whole of Sarantium might be talking of this missing man, but either she'd already known where he was from her husband, or she was truly indifferent to the fate of these athletic sorts. She did, however, summon her stepson.

Cleander appeared sullenly in the doorway a short time later. It had occurred to Rustem that the boy might have breached this parental order already and been gone from the house, but it appeared that Bonosus's son had been sufficiently chastened by two violent incidents in one day and night to obey his father, for now.

His stepmother, with a few impressively precise questions, succeeded in unearthing from the flushed young man the fact that it was Cleander who had conveyed the charioteer to Rustem in the middle of the night, and from where and under what circumstances. Rustem hadn't expected this. She had made an impressive leap of reasoning.

He could not help but note the boy's discomfiture, but he also knew that he himself had betrayed no secret in this regard. He hadn't even *known* that the incident had taken place in front of the dancer's home. He hadn't asked, or cared.

The woman was disconcertingly clever, that was all. It came with her detachment and composure, he decided. Those able to modulate and control their inner passions, to view the world with a cold eye, were best equipped to think things through in this way. Of course that same coldness might also be a reason why the husband had a chest with certain implements and toys in another house in a distant part of town. On the whole, though, Rustem decided he approved of the Senator's wife. He had, in fact, attempted to structure his own professional demeanour in this same fashion.

It was unexpected to see it in a woman, mind you.

Also unexpected was the fact that she seemed to be coming with them to the Hippodrome.

Cleander's extreme discomfort changed—in the overheated manner of youth—to a stunned elation as he understood that his stepmother was undertaking to waive a part of his punishment in favour of the duties owed a guest and Rustem's own professed obligations as a physician. She would accompany them, she said, to ensure Cleander's good behaviour and swift return home, and to assist the doctor if he needed any intervention. The Hippodrome could be a dangerous place for a foreigner, she said.

Cleander would go ahead of them, immediately, taking the steward and using his mother's name for any outlays required, employing whatever unsavoury contacts he undoubtedly had in and around the Hippodrome Forum to secure proper seating after the midday interval—*not* standing places, and most certainly not in any area containing faction partisans or anyone whose conduct might be disagreeable. And he would not, under any circumstances, wear green. Did Cleander understand?

Cleander did.

Would Rustem of Kerakek be pleased to take a modest midday meal with her while Cleander attended to these matters of seating and admission?

Rustem would.

They had ample time to dine, and then she would need more suitable clothing for a public appearance, she said, putting aside her writing and rising from her backless chair. Her manner was impeccably calm, precise, superbly efficient, her posture flawless. She put him in mind of those fabled matrons of Rhodias, in the days before it declined into Imperial decadence and then fell.

He wondered abruptly—startling himself, in fact—if either Katyun or Jarita could have grown into this poise and authority had they been raised in a different world. There were no women like this in Ispahani and certainly none in Bassania. Palace intrigues among the cloistered wives of the King of Kings were something else entirely. He thought, then, of his baby, his girl—and made himself stop doing that. Inissa was being taken from him, was gone, in the wake of his great good fortune.

Perun and Anahita guided the world, Azal needed to be kept constantly at bay. No man could say where his footsteps might lead him. Generosity needed to be embraced, even if there was a price to be paid. Certain gifts were not offered twice. He could not let himself dwell upon Issa, or her mother.

He could think about Shaski and Katyun, for he would see them in Kabadh, soon enough. *If the Lady wills it,* he added hastily in his mind and turned quickly to face east, on the thought. He had been instructed to try to kill someone here. Generosity might now have conditions attached to it.

The wife of Plautus Bonosus was looking at him, eyebrows slightly arched. She was too well bred to say anything, however.

Hesitantly, Rustem murmured, 'In my faith . . . the east . . . I was averting bad fortune. I had a reckless thought.'

'Ah,' said Thenaïs Sistina, nodding her head as if this were entirely clear to her. 'We all have those, from time to time.' She walked out of the room and he followed her.

In the kathisma, a very well-turned-out cluster of court figures was busily performing its assigned task. Gesius had been explicit and had ensured that many of the more decorative members of the Imperial Precinct were on hand this morning, dressed flamboyantly, glittering with jewellery and colour.

They managed—with polished ease—to both enjoy themselves and blur, with their highly visible and audible reactions to events below, the absence of the Empress, the Supreme Strategos, the Chancellor, and the Master of Offices. They also masked the steady, low-voiced dictation of the Emperor to the secretaries crouched against the front railing of the box, invisible to the stands.

Valerius had dropped the white handkerchief to start the program, had acknowledged his people's cheers with the ancient gesture of Emperors, and had taken his cushioned seat and immediately set to work, ignoring the chariots below and the noise all around. Whenever the Mandator, schooled to this, murmured discreetly at his elbow Valerius would stand up and salute whoever was currently doing a victory lap. For much of the morning it had been Crescens of the Greens. The Emperor didn't seem to notice, or care.

The mosaic image on the roof of the kathisma above them was of Saranios, who had founded this city and named it for himself, driving a quadriga and crowned not with gold but with a charioteer's victory laurel. The links in the symbolic chain were immensely powerful: Jad in his chariot, the Emperor as mortal servant and holy symbol of the god, the charioteers on the Hippodrome sands as the most dearly beloved of the people. But, thought Bonosus, this particular successor in the long chain of Emperors was . . . detached from the power of that association.

Or he tried to be. The people brought him back to it. He was here, after all, watching the chariots run, even today. Bonosus had a theory about the attraction of the racing, actually. He was prepared to bore people with it if asked, or even if not. In essence, he'd argue, the Hippodrome stood in perfectly balanced counterpoint to the rituals of the Imperial Precinct. Courtly life was entirely structured around ritual, predictable as anything on earth could be. An ordained practice for everything from the Emperor's first greeting when awakened (and by whom and in what order), to the sequence of lighting the lamps in the Audience Chamber, to the procession for presenting gifts to him on the first of the New Year. Words and gestures, set and recorded, known and rehearsed, never varying.

The Hippodrome, by contrast, Bonosus would say, and shrug . . . as though the rest of the thought ought to be transparently clear to anyone. The Hippodrome was *all* uncertainty. The unknown was . . . the very essence of it, he would say.

Bonosus, chattering and cheering this morning with the others in the Imperial Box, prided himself on detached perspectives of this sort. But jaded as he might be, he was unable to entirely control the excitement he was feeling today, and it had nothing to do with the uncertainty of horses, or even the younger riders down below.

He had never seen Valerius like this.

The Emperor was always intense when engaged by matters of state, and always irritably distracted when forced to attend at the Hippodrome, but this morning the ferocity of his concentration and the endless stream of notes and instructions aimed in a low voice at the secretaries—there were two, alternating, to keep up with him—had a rhythm, a compelling pace, that seemed, in the mind of the Master of the Senate, to be as poundingly urgent as the horses and quadrigas below.

On the sands the Greens were proving wildly triumphant, as they had been a week before. Scortius of the Blues was still absent, and Bonosus was one of the handful of people in the City who knew where he was and that it would be weeks before he reappeared in the Hippodrome. The man had insisted on secrecy and he had more than enough stature in Sarantium to have his wishes obeyed in this.

There was probably a woman involved, the Senator decided—with Scortius, never a difficult surmise. Bonosus didn't at all begrudge the charioteer the use of his own smaller city home while he recovered. He rather enjoyed being privy to cloaked affairs. It wasn't as if being Master of the Senate conferred any *real* significance, after all. His second home wasn't available for his own diversions in any case, with the bone-dry Bassanid physician staying there. That part of the current situation he owed to Cleander, who was a problem that would need attention soon. Barbarian hair-styling and outlandish garb in the cause of faction identity was one thing, murdering people in the street was . . . another.

The factions could become dangerous today, he realized. He wondered if Valerius was aware of it. The Greens in full rapture, the Blues seething with humiliation and anxiety. He decided he was going to have to speak with Scortius after all, this evening perhaps. Secrecy in one's own causes was something that might have to give way to order in the City, especially given what else was awesomely afoot. If both factions knew that the man was all right, would be returning at some named date, some of this tension could be dissipated.

As it was, Bonosus felt sorry for the youngster riding First for the Blues. The boy was clearly a charioteer, had instincts and courage, but he also had three problems that Bonosus could see—and the god knew he *ought* to be able to see things down there on the sands, given the number of years he'd been coming here.

First problem was Crescens of the Greens. The muscular fellow from Sarnica was superbly confident, had had a year to settle in to Sarantium now, and had his new team under perfect control. Nor was he the sort to show any mercy to the disorganized Blues.

That disorganization was the other part of the difficulty. Not only was the youngster—Taras was his name, a Sauradian apparently—unfamiliar with riding First chariot, he didn't even know the horses of the lead team. Magnificent as a stallion such as Servator was, any horse needed a hand on the reins that knew what it could do. And besides, young Taras, wearing the silver helmet for the Blues, wasn't getting any adequate back-up at all, because *he* was the one who'd been training to ride Second and knew *those* horses.

Given all this, the Blues' temporary leader had been doing well to come in second place, three times beating back aggressively coordinated attacks from both Green riders. Jad alone knew what the mood would be if the Greens succeeded in sweeping the board once or twice. Such sweeps of the first and second placings gave rise to the most exultant of faction celebrations—and sullen despair on the other side. It could yet happen before the day was out. The Blues' rider might have the stamina of youth, but they could wear him down. Bonosus thought they would, in the afternoon. On another day he might have considered some wagers.

There was, one might say in a literary mode, a grand slaughter building down below. Being the man he was, Bonosus was inclined to perceive it this way, to see it as an ironic foretaste of the Imperial announcement of war, still to come at the end of the day.

The morning's last race came to an end—as usual, a minor, chaotic endeavour among the Reds and Whites, driving two-horse bigas. The Whites' lead driver emerged triumphant in a typically sloppy affair, but the victory was treated by the Blues and Whites with an enthusiasm (more than slightly forced, to Bonosus's ear) that was almost certainly unique in the experience of the White charioteer. Surprised or not, he appeared to greatly enjoy his victory lap.

The Emperor stopped dictating and rose at the Mandator's murmured hint. He briskly saluted the fellow passing beneath him just then and turned to go. An Excubitor had already unbarred the door at the rear of the kathisma. Valerius would go back down the corridor to the Imperial Precinct for final consultations before the afternoon's proclamation: the Attenine Palace for the Chancellor, the Master of Offices, and the Quaestor of Revenue, then across through the old tunnel under the gardens to the Traversite to meet Leontes and the generals. Everyone knew his routines. Some people—Bonosus among them—believed they had by now discerned the thinking behind this separation of advisers. It was dangerous, however, to assume you understood what this Emperor was thinking. As everyone else rose and stood gracefully aside, Valerius paused by Bonosus.

'Do our honours for the afternoon, Senator. Barring the unforeseen, we shall return with the others before the last race.' He leaned closer and lowered his voice. 'And have the Urban Prefect find out where Scortius is. A bad time for this sort of thing, don't you think? We may have been remiss, ignoring it.'

He didn't miss anything, Bonosus thought.

'I know where he is,' he said quietly, breaking a promise without compunction. This *was* the Emperor.

Valerius didn't even raise an eyebrow. 'Good. Inform the Urban Prefect, and tell us about it after.'

And while eighty thousand of his people were still reacting in a variety of ways to the White rider's last lap, and just beginning to rise and stretch and think about a midday meal and wine, the Emperor left his kathisma and that thronged place where the announcements and events that defined the Empire had so often been witnessed.

Even before he passed through the opened door, Valerius had begun removing the ornate ceremonial garb he had to wear in public.

The servants began spreading a meal on large side tables and smaller round ones beside the seats. Some of those in the kathisma preferred to go back to the palaces to dine, while the younger ones might venture into the City itself, tasting the excitement of the taverns, but it was pleasant to linger here if the weather was fine, and today it was.

Bonosus discovered, to his surprise, that he had both an appetite and a thirst. He stretched his legs—there was room now—and held out his cup for wine.

It occurred to him that the next time he ate a meal he would be a Senator of an empire at war. And not just the usual skirmishing of springtime. This was a reconquest. Rhodias. Valerius's long dream.

No question, it was an exciting thought, stirring up all sorts of . . . feelings. Bonosus wished, suddenly, that he didn't have a Bassanid physician and a recuperating charioteer both staying at his little house near the walls tonight, after all. Guests could be, undeniably, a complication.

'He was allowed to retire to the Daleinus estate at first. He was only brought to this isle—it has been used as a prison for a long time—after trying to have the first Valerius assassinated in his bath.'

Crispin looked at the Empress beside him. They stood alone in the clearing. Her Excubitors were behind them and four guards stood waiting before the doorways of the smaller huts. The larger house was dark, the door barred on the outside, all the windows shuttered against the mild light of the sun. Crispin had an odd difficulty even looking at it.

There was an oppressiveness, a weight, something clinging here. There was little wind now, in the midst of the encircling pines.

He said, 'I thought people were killed for doing that.'

'He should have been,' Alixana said.

He looked back at her. She never took her eyes off the house in front of them.

'Petrus, who was his uncle's adviser then, wouldn't allow it. Said the Daleinoi and their followers needed to be handled carefully. The Emperor listened. He usually did. They brought Lecanus here. Punished but not executed. The youngest one, Tertius, was still a child. He was allowed to stay on the estate and eventually to manage the family affairs. Styliane was permitted to remain in the City, to come to court when she grew older, was even allowed to visit here, though the visits were observed. Lecanus continued plotting, even from this island, kept trying to persuade her. Eventually her visits were stopped.' She paused, looked at him, then back at the cabin. 'I did that, actually. I was the one having them secretly observed. Then I had the Emperor stop her from coming at all, a little before she was married.'

'So no one comes here now?' Crispin saw hearth-smoke rising from the huts and the larger house, straight as the trees, going up then blowing away when it reached the height of the wind.

'I do,' said Alixana. 'After a fashion. You'll see.'

'And I'll be killed if I tell anyone. I know.'

She looked up at him then. He could still see the strain in her. 'I have heard you on that. Leave it be, Crispin. You are trusted. You are with me here.'

The first time she had ever used his name like that.

She went forward without giving him any chance to reply. He couldn't think of any response in any case.

One of the four guards bowed low, then approached the closed door of the house, unlocked it ahead of them. The door swung outward silently. It was almost completely dark inside. The guard went in, and a moment later there was light within as he lit a lamp, and then another. Another man followed the first. He coughed loudly on the threshold.

'Are you dressed, Daleinus? She's here to see you.'

A snuffling sound, almost unintelligible, more an animal noise than speech, came from inside. The guard said nothing, entered the house behind the first one. He push opened the wooden shutters on two iron-barred windows, letting in air and more light. Both guards went out.

The Empress nodded at them. They bowed again and withdrew, back towards the huts. There was no one in hearing distance now, or no one that Crispin could see. Alixana met Crispin's eye briefly, then she straightened her shoulders like a performer going on stage and walked into that house.

Crispin followed, silently, out of the bright sun. There was a constriction in his chest. His heart was hammering. He couldn't have said why. This had so little do with him. But he was thinking of Styliane, the last night he'd seen her, *what* he'd seen in her. And trying to recall what he knew about the death of Flavius Daleinus on the day the first Valerius was acclaimed Emperor in Sarantium.

He stopped just inside the doorway. A fair-sized front room. Two doors opening off it, one at the back to a bed-chamber, one on the right side, he couldn't see to where. A fireplace against the left-hand wall, two chairs, a couch at the back, a bench, a table, a closed and locked chest, nothing on the walls at all, not even a sun disk. The snuffling sound, he realized, was a man, breathing oddly.

Then Crispin's eyes slowly adjusted to the subdued light and he saw a shape move on the couch, sitting up from a reclining position, turning towards them. And so he saw the person who lived—who was imprisoned—within this house, on this island, in his own body, and he *did* remember something, as a sickening, convulsive horror overmastered him. He leaned back against the wall beside the door, a hand going up to shield his face, involuntarily.

Sarantine Fire did bad things to men, even when they survived it.

The father had been killed. A cousin too, Crispin seemed to recall. Lecanus Daleinus had lived. After a fashion. Looking at the blind man before him, at the burned-away ruin of what had been his face, the charred, maimed hands, imagining the burned body beneath the nondescript brown tunic, Crispin wondered, truly, how this man was still alive, and *why*, what purpose, desire, need could possibly have kept him from ending his own life long ago. He didn't think it was piety. There was no least hint of the god here. Of any god at all.

Then he remembered what Alixana had said, and he thought he knew. Hatred could be a purpose, vengeance a need. A deity, almost.

He was working hard not to be physically ill. He closed his eyes.

And in that moment he heard Styliane Daleina, icy-cool, patrician, utterly unmoved by her brother's appearance, murmur from beside him, 'You smell, brother. The room smells. I know they give you water and a basin. Show some respect for yourself and use it.'

Crispin, his jaw dropping, opened his eyes and wheeled to look at her.

He saw the Empress of Sarantium, standing as straight as she could, to be nearer the height of the other woman. And he heard her speak again, the voice and tone and manner terrifyingly precise, unnervingly identical. 'I have told you this before. You are a Daleinus. Even if no one sees or knows, *you* must know it or you shame our blood.'

The hideous, appalling face on the couch moved. It was impossible to decipher what expression that melted ruin was attempting. The eyes were hollow, blackened, gone. The nose was a smear, and made that whistling sound when the man breathed. Crispin kept silent, swallowing hard.

'So . . . sorry . . . sister,' the blind man said. The words were slow, badly garbled, but intelligible. 'I disappoint . . . you dear . . . sister. I will weep.'

'You can't weep. But you can have this place cleaned and aired and I expect you to do so.' If Crispin had closed his eyes he'd have sworn to holy Jad and all the Blessed Victims that Styliane was here, arrogant, contemptuous, fierce in her intelligence and pride. *The actress* she had named Alixana, among other things.

And now he knew why the Empress came here and why there was so much strain in her face.

There is someone I want to see before the army sails.

She was afraid of this man. Was coming only for Valerius, despite her fear, to see what he might be plotting here with the life they'd granted him. But this sightless, noseless figure was alone, isolated, not even his sister coming any more—only this flawless, chilling imitation of Styliane, seeking to draw a revelation from him. Was this a man to be feared in the present day, or just a guilt, a haunting in the soul from long ago?

There came a sound from the couch, from the almost unbearable figure. And a moment later Crispin realized he was hearing laughter. The sound made him think of something slithering over broken glass.

'Come. Sister,' said Lecanus Daleinus, once heir to an extravagantly patrician lineage and an inconceivable fortune. 'No . . . time! Undress! Let me . . . touch! Hurry!'

Crispin closed his eyes again.

'*Good, good!*' came a third voice, shockingly. In his head. '*She hates that. Doesn't know what to believe. There's someone here with her. Red hair. No idea who. You're making him feel ill. You are so hideous! The whore's looking at him now.*'

Crispin felt the world rock and sway like a ship hit hard by a wave. He pressed his hands hard against the wall behind him. Looked around wildly.

Saw the bird, almost immediately, on the window ledge.

'*I don't* know *why she's here today! How can I answer that? Keep calm. She may only be anxious. She may—*'

Alixana laughed aloud. Again the illusion was frightening. It was another woman's laughter, not her own. Crispin remembered Styliane in her own bedchamber, the low, sardonic sound of her amusement, identical to this. 'You are disgusting, by choice,' the Empress said. 'A comic version of yourself, like some cheap pantomime figure. Have you nothing better to offer or ask than a grope in your darkness?'

'What else could I . . . *possibly* . . . offer you, dear sister? Wife of the Supreme Strategos. Did he please . . . you last night? In your dark? Did someone else? Oh, tell me! Tell!' The voice, through the whistling sound, was laboured, broken, as if the sounds were crawling up from some labyrinthine half-blocked tunnel leading down to things below the earth.

'*Good!*' Crispin heard again, in the silence of the half-world. '*I think I'm right. She's just checking on you. The war coming. This is an accident. She's only worried. You'd be pleased—she looks wretched, used by slaves. Old!*'

Fighting nausea, Crispin stayed where he was, his breathing carefully shallow, though there was no actual secret to his presence now. His mind was in a desperate whirl. Out of the chaos, a question spun free and he reached for it: how did this man and his creature know, here, about the war?

There was something ugly at work here. This bird was like none he had yet known or heard. The inner voice wasn't that of Zoticus's creations. This birdsoul spoke in a woman's voice, bitter and hard, from beyond Bassania: Ispahani or Ajbar or lands whose names he did not know. It was dark in hue, small as Linon, but not like Linon at all.

He remembered that the Daleinoi had made their fortune with a monopoly on the spice trade to the east. He looked at the man on the couch, burned so terribly, turned into this horror, and again the thought came to him: how is he alive?

And again the same answer came and he was afraid.

'*I know,*' said the bird abruptly, replying to something. '*I know! I know! I know!*' And what Crispin heard now in the low, harsh voice was exultation, fierce as a blaze.

'I take no delight,' the Empress said, all ice and edge like Styliane, 'in any of this, and see no reason to attend to your pleasures. I prefer my own, brother. I'm here to ask if there's anything you need . . . immediately.' She left an emphasis on the last word. 'You might recall, dear brother, that they leave us alone for only a little while.'

'Of course I . . . recall. That is why you are cruel . . . to be dressed . . . still. Little sister, come closer . . . and tell me. *Tell* me . . . how did he . . . take you, last night?'

Stomach churning, Crispin saw the ruined man's hand, gnarled like a claw, reach under his own tunic to his groin. And he heard the inward laughter of the eastern bird.

'Think of your father,' said Alixana. 'And of your ancestors. If this is all you are now, brother, I shall not return. Consider it, Lecanus. I warned you last time. I'm going to take a walk now and a meal in sunlight on the island. I will come back before I sail. When I do, if this is what you are, still, I will have no more time for this journey and will not return.'

'Oh! Oh!' wheezed the man on the couch. 'I am desolate! I have . . . shamed my dear sister. Our innocent . . . fair child.'

Crispin saw Alixana bite her lip, staring at the figure before her as if her gaze could probe his depths. She couldn't know, Crispin thought. She couldn't know why her immaculate, brilliant deception was being so effortlessly defeated. But she sensed it *was* being foiled, somehow, that Lecanus was playing with her, and perhaps that was why she feared this room so much. And why she still came.

She said nothing more, walked from the room and the house, head high, shoulders straight, as before. An actress, an Empress, proud as some goddess of the ancient pantheon, betraying nothing, unless you looked very, very closely.

Crispin followed, the laughter of the bird drilling in his head. Just as he came into the sunshine, closing his eyes, temporarily blind, he heard, *'I want to be there! Lecanus, I want us to be there!'*

He didn't hear the reply, of course.

*　　*　　*

'Styliane never pleasured him, in the event you were wondering. She's corrupt in her own ways, but she never did that.'

Crispin was wondering how much was known about a certain recent night, and then decided not to think about it. They were on the southern side of the island, facing Deapolis across the water. Her Excubitors had accompanied them through the trees, past a second clearing with another set of huts and houses. These were empty. There had been other prisoners here once, evidently. Not now. Lecanus Daleinus had the isle to himself, with his handful of guards.

It was past midday now, by the sun. They would be racing again in the Hippodrome soon, if they hadn't started already, the day turning steadily towards an announcement of war. Crispin understood that the Empress was simply allowing an interval to pass before she went back to that house in the clearing to see if anything had changed.

It wouldn't have, he knew. What he didn't know was whether to say anything about it. There were so many betrayals embedded here: of Zoticus, of Shirin and her bird, and of his own privacy, his gift, his secret. Linon. At the same time, those last silent words of the eastern creature were still with him, with the undeniable signal of danger in them.

He had little appetite when they sat down to their meal, picked in a desultory fashion at the fish-cakes and the olives. Drank his wine. Had asked for it to be well watered. The Empress was largely silent, had been from the time they'd left the clearing. She had walked off by herself, in fact, when they'd first reached this strand, becoming a small, purple-cloaked dot in the distance along the stony beachfront here, two of her soldiers following at a distance. Crispin had sat down on a grassy place between trees and stones, watching the changing light on the sea. Green, blue, blue-green, grey.

Eventually she had come back, gestured for him not to rise, and had taken her place, gracefully, on a square of silk unfolded for her. The food had been spread on another cloth in this quiet place that ought to have been soothing in its beauty, a benign embodiment of the quickening spring.

Crispin said, after a time, 'You watched them together, I gather. Styliane and . . . her brother.'

The Empress wasn't eating either. She nodded. 'Of course. I had to. How else would I have learned how and what to say, playing her?' She looked at him.

So obvious, seen in that way. An actress, learning her part. Crispin looked back out to sea. Deapolis showed clearly across the water. He could see more ships in the harbour there. A fleet for an army, sailing west, to his home. He had warned his mother, and Martinian and Carissa. It meant nothing. What could they do? There was a dull fear within him; the memory of the bird in that dark cabin a part of that now.

He said, 'And you do this . . . you come here, because . . . '

'Because Valerius won't let him be killed. I thought of doing it, despite that. Killing him. But it matters a great deal to the Emperor. The visible hand of mercy, since the family . . . suffered so much when those . . . unknown people burned Flavius. So I come here, and do this . . . performance, and learn nothing. If I am to believe him, Lecanus is broken and vile and purposeless.' She paused. 'I can't stop coming.'

'Why won't he kill him? There has to be so much hatred. I *know* they think the Emperor . . . ordered it. The burning.' Not a question he'd ever imagined himself asking anyone, let alone the Empress of Sarantium. And not with this terrible inward sense that perhaps the killing of this man *ought* to have been done by now. Perhaps even in mercy. He thought, wistfully, of a scaffold in the air, shining pieces of glass and stone, memory, his girls.

Sorrow was easier than this. The thought came to him suddenly. A hard truth.

Alixana was silent for a long time. He waited. Caught the drift of her scent. That gave him pause for a moment, then he decided that Lecanus couldn't have known about the personal nature of that perfume. He'd been here too long. And then he realized that that wasn't it either: the man's nose was gone. The Empress would have realized that. Crispin shuddered. She saw it. Looked away.

She said, 'You can have no idea what it was like here in the time when Apius was dying.'

'I'm certain of that,' Crispin said.

'He had his own nephews blinded and imprisoned here.' Her voice was flat, lifeless. He had never heard her like this. 'There was no heir. Flavius Daleinus was behaving, for *months* before Apius died, as an Emperor-in-waiting. Receiving courtiers at his estate and even his city home, on a chair in a receiving room on a crimson carpet. Some of them knelt before him.'

Crispin said nothing.

'Petrus . . . believed Daleinus would be entirely, danger-ously wrong as Emperor. For many reasons.' She looked at him, the dark eyes searching his. And he understood what was unsettling him so: he had *no* idea how to react when she spoke, or looked, as a woman, a person, and not as an Imperial power beyond comprehension.

He said, 'So he helped put his uncle on the throne instead. I know this. Everyone does.'

She refused to look away. 'Everyone does. And Flavius Daleinus died in Sarantine Fire on the street outside his house. He was . . . wearing porphyry. He was on his way to the Senate, Crispin.'

The clothing had all burned away, Carullus had told him, but there had been rumours of the purple trim. Crispin, sitting on an island strand these long years after, had no doubt of the truth of what the Empress was saying.

He took a breath and said, 'I am lost here, my lady. I don't understand what I am doing here, why I am hearing this. I am supposed to call you thrice-exalted, kneel in obeisance.'

She smiled a little then, for the first time. 'Indeed, artisan. I had almost forgotten. You haven't done either in a while, have you?'

'I have no idea how to . . . act here.'

She shrugged, her expression still amused, something else in her voice, however. 'Why should you know? I am being capricious and unfair, telling hidden things, enforcing the illusion of intimacy. But I can have you killed and buried here if I say but a word to the soldiers. Why should you assume you might know how to conduct yourself?'

She reached over and chose a pitted olive. 'You can't know this, either, of course, but that ruined figure we just saw was the best of them all. Clever and brave, a splendid, handsome man. He went east himself, many times, with the spice caravans, past Bassania, to learn whatever he could. I regret what the fire did to him more than what happened to his father. He should have died, not lived to become—this thing.'

Crispin swallowed again. 'Why the fire? Why that way?'

Alixana's gaze was steady. His awareness was of her courage . . . and simultaneously of the fact that she might be *showing* him courage, leading him to see it in her, for her own purposes. He was adrift and afraid, continuously aware of how many layers and contours of meaning there were with this woman. He shivered. Even before she answered, he was sorry he'd asked.

She said, 'Empires need symbols. New Emperors need powerful ones. A moment when all changes, when the god speaks with a clear voice. On the day Valerius I was acclaimed in the Hippodrome, Flavius Daleinus wore purple in the street, walked out to claim the Golden Throne as if by right. He died appallingly, as if by a bolt from Jad, a striking down from above for such presumption, never to be forgotten.' Her eyes never left his own. 'It would not have been the same had he been stabbed by some soldier in an alleyway.'

Crispin found that he could not look away from her. The exact, worldly intelligence within her beauty. He opened his mouth, found he could not speak. And seeing that, she smiled. 'You are about to say again,' said the Empress Alixana, 'that you are only an artisan, that you want nothing to do with any of this. Am I right, Caius Crispus?'

He closed his mouth. Took a deep, unsteady breath. She could be wrong, and she was, this time. His heart pounding, an odd, roaring sound in his ears, Crispin heard himself say, 'You cannot deceive the man in that house, my lady, even though he is blind. He has an unnatural creature with him that can see, and speaks to him silently. Something from the half-world. He knows it is you and not his sister, Empress.'

She went white. He would always remember it. White as a shroud. As the winding sheet in which the dead were wrapped for burial. She stood up, too quickly, almost fell, the only graceless movement he had ever seen her make.

He scrambled to his feet as well, the roaring in his head like a surf or a storm. He said, 'He was asking the bird—it is a bird—why you were here, today . . . of all days. They decided it was accident. That you were only worried. Then the bird said that . . . that it wanted to be present when . . . something happened.'

'Oh, dearest Jad,' said the Empress of Sarantium, and her flawless voice cracked like a plate on stone. And then, 'Oh, my love.'

She turned and began to move, almost running, back through the trees on the path. Crispin followed. The Excubitors, alert and attentive as soon as she had stood up, followed them both. One of them sprinted ahead, to guard the path.

No one spoke. They came back to the clearing. It was silent, as before. The smoke was still rising, as before. No movement could be seen.

But the door to the prison house of Lecanus Daleinus was unbarred and open and there were two dead guards lying on the ground.

Alixana stood frozen, rooted to the spot, like one of the pines in the windless air. Her face was riven with anguish, like a tree by a lightning bolt. There were legends, from long ago, of women, wood spirits, changed into trees. Crispin thought of them, seeing her now. There was an appalling, choking sensation in his own chest and the roaring sound had not stopped.

One of the Excubitors swore furiously, shattering the stillness. All four of them dashed across the open space, drawing their blades, to kneel in pairs by the two slain men.

It was Crispin who walked over—he saw that each man had been cut down by a sword, from behind—and re-entered the silent, open house.

The lamps were gone. The front room was empty. He strode quickly to the back and to the kitchen room at the side. No one there. He came back to the main room, looked at the ledge of the window by the door. The bird, too, was gone.

Crispin walked out again, into the gentle, deceiving sunshine. The Empress stood, alone, still rooted to the earth, near the encircling trees. *Dangerous*, he had time to think, before one of the two Excubitors beside the nearest of the dead men stood up and moved behind his fellow soldier. His sword was still drawn. The other man was kneeling, examining the body of the guard. The drawn sword went up, a glinting of metal in the light.

'*No!*' Crispin screamed.

They were the Excubitors, the Imperial Guards, best soldiers in the Empire. The kneeling soldier didn't look up or back. He'd have died, had he done so. Instead, he hurtled straight to one side from his kneeling position, rolling hard as he did, over the flat of his own sword. The blade that had been sweeping down to take him from behind bit, instead, into the body of the already-slain guard. The attacker swore savagely, ripped his blade free, turned to face the other soldier—the leader of this quartet—who was up now, his own sword levelled.

There was still no one near the Empress, Crispin saw.

The two Excubitors faced each other in the sunlight, feet wide for balance, circling slowly. The other two soldiers were on their feet now, halfway across the clearing, but frozen as if in shock.

There was death here now. There was more than that.

Caius Crispus of Varena, in the world, of the world, said a quick silent prayer to the god of his fathers and took three hard running steps, hammering his shoulder with all the force he could command into the small of the back of the traitorous soldier in front of him. Crispin wasn't a fighter, but he was a big man. The man's breath was expelled with a rush, his head snapped back, his arms splayed helplessly out and wide with the impact, the sword spinning from nerveless fingers.

Crispin fell to the ground with him, on top of him, rolled quickly away. He pushed himself up. In time to see the man whose life he'd saved plunge his blade, without ceremony, straight into the back of the other soldier where he lay on the ground, killing him.

The Excubitor threw Crispin one swift, searching look, then wheeled and sprinted towards the Empress, bloodied sword in hand. Struggling up from his knees, heart in his throat, Crispin watched him go. Alixana stood motionless, a sacrifice in a glade, accepting her fate.

The soldier stopped in front of her and spun around to defend his Empress.

Crispin heard a strange sound in his own throat. There were two dead men next to him in this clearing. He ran, stumbling, over to Alixana himself. Her face, he saw, was still chalk white.

The other two Excubitors came quickly over now, their own blades out, horror written in both faces. The leader, standing in front the Empress, waited for them, his head and eyes darting about, scanning the clearing and the shadows of the pines.

'Sheathe!' he snapped. 'Formation. Now.'

They did, drew themselves up side by side. He stood before them, his gaze ferocious. Looked at one, and then the other.

Then he plunged his bloodied sword into the belly of the second man.

Crispin gasped, his fists clenched at his side.

The leader of the Excubitors watched his victim fall, then he turned again and looked at the Empress.

Alixana had not moved. She said, her voice entirely without inflection, almost inhuman, 'He was bought as well, Mariscus?'

The man said, 'My lady, I could not be sure. Of Nerius I am sure.' He gestured with his head at the remaining soldier. He looked at Crispin searchingly. 'You trust the Rhodian?' he asked.

'I trust the Rhodian,' said Alixana of Sarantium. There was no life in her tone, in her face. 'I believe he saved you.'

The soldier showed no response to that. He said, 'I do not understand what has happened here. But it is not safe for you, my lady.'

Alixana laughed. Crispin would remember that sound, too.

'Oh, I know,' she said. 'I know. It is not safe for me. But it is too late now.' She closed her eyes. Crispin saw that her hands were at her sides. His own were twisting and clenching, windows to the roiling he felt within. 'It is so obvious now, much too late. Today will have been a day when they changed the Urban Prefect's guards here, I'll wager. I imagine they were already here, watching, when we sailed in at the end of the morning, waiting until we left this clearing.'

Crispin and the two soldiers looked at her.

'Two dead here,' said Alixana. 'So two of the Prefect's men were bought. And the four new ones arriving on their little boat will have been, of course, or there'd have been no point. And you think two of the Excubitors, too.' A spasm crossed her features, was gone. The mask reasserted itself. 'He will have left as soon as we went away. They'll have reached the City by now. Some time ago, I imagine.'

None of the three men with her said a word. Crispin's heart ached. These were *not* his people, Sarantium was not his place on Jad's earth, but he understood what she was saying. The world was changing. Might have already changed.

Alixana opened her eyes then. Looked straight at him. 'He has something that allows him to . . . see things?' No reproach in her tone. *Nothing* in her tone. Had he told her right away . . .

He nodded. The two soldiers looked uncomprehending. They didn't matter. She did. She mattered very much, he realized, gazing at her. She turned past him, towards the two dead men near the prison house.

And then turned completely away, from the men standing with her, from the dead in the clearing. Faced north, her shoulders straight as always, head lifted a little, as if to see beyond the tall pines, beyond the strait with its dolphins and ships and white-capped waves, beyond harbour, city walls, bronze gates, the present and the past, the world and the half-world.

'I believe,' said Alixana of Sarantium, 'it may even be over by now.'

She turned back to look at them. Her eyes were dry.

'I have placed you in mortal danger, Rhodian. I am sorry for it. You will have to go back on the Imperial ship alone. You may expect to be asked hard questions, perhaps as soon as you land. More likely later, tonight. It will be known you were with me today, before I disappeared.'

'My lady?' he said. 'You don't *know* what has happened.' He paused, swallowed hard. 'He is cleverer than any man alive.' And then her last word penetrated, and he said, 'Disappeared?'

She looked at him. 'I do not know for certain, you are correct. But if things have fallen out in a certain way, the Empire as we have known it is ended and they will be coming for me. I would not care, but . . . ' She closed her eyes again. 'But I do have . . . one or perhaps two things to do. I cannot let myself be found before that. Mariscus will take me back—there will be small craft on this island—and I will disappear.'

She stopped, drew a breath. 'I knew he should have been killed,' she said. And then, 'Crispin, Caius Crispus, if I am right, Gesius will be no help to you now.' Her mouth twitched. A fool might have called it a smile. 'You will need Styliane. She is the one who might guard you. She feels something for you, I believe.'

He didn't know how she might know that. He was far past caring about such things. He said, 'And you, my lady?'

A distant trace of amusement. 'What do I feel for you, Rhodian?'

He bit his lip hard. 'No, no. My lady, what are you to do? May I . . . may we not help?'

She shook her head. 'Not your role. Not anyone's. If I am correct about what has happened, I have a task to do before I die, and then it can end.' She looked at Crispin, standing very near him and yet in another place, another world, almost. 'Tell me, when your wife died . . . how did you go on living?'

He opened his mouth, and closed it without answering. She turned away. They went back through the forest to the sea. On the stony strand of the isle, he was still unable to speak. He watched as she unclipped and let fall her purple cloak, and then dropped the brooch that had pinned it and turned and went away along the white stones. The man named Mariscus followed her out of sight.

How did you go on living?

No answers came to him on the ship when he and the remaining Excubitor came to it and the mariners weighed anchor at the soldier's harsh order and they sailed back to Sarantium.

The Imperial cloak and the golden brooch were left behind on the isle, were still lying there when the stars came out that night, and the moons.

CHAPTER X

Cleander had done well by them, it appeared. They were not among the enormous block of Green partisans—his mother had expressly forbidden that—but it seemed the boy had sufficient contacts by now among the Hippodrome crowd to have obtained excellent seats low down and near the starting line. Some of the morning attendees among the wealthier classes were inclined to miss the afternoon, it seemed. Cleander had found three seats that way. They had a clear, close view of the cumbersome looking start apparatus and the jumble of monuments along the spina, and could even see into the roofed interior space where the performers and charioteers were even now awaiting the signal to come out for the afternoon procession. Beyond that, Cleander had pointed out another entrance to and from the vast spaces under the stands. He called it the Death Gate, with evident relish.

The boy, dressed with perfect sobriety in brown and gold with a wide leather belt and his long, barbarian-style hair brushed back, was urgently pointing out all that took place to his stepmother and the physician whose servant he'd killed two weeks before. He seemed wildly happy and very young, Rustem thought, aware of ironies.

Thenaïs had already been saluted by at least half a dozen men and women sitting nearby and had introduced Rustem with flawless formality to them. No one asked why she wasn't in the kathisma with her husband. This was a well-bred, well-dressed section of the Hippodrome. There might be shouting and jostling above them in the standing places but not down here.

Or perhaps, Rustem thought, not until the horses began running again. He acknowledged, with professional interest, an excitement within himself, undermining detachment. The mood of the crowd—he had never in his life been among so many people—was communicating itself, undeniably.

A trumpet sounded. 'Here they come,' said Cleander, on the far side of his mother. 'The Greens have the most *wonderful* juggler, you'll see him right after the Hippodrome Prefect's horse.'

'No faction talk,' said Thenaïs quietly, eyes on the gateway to the sands, where a horseman had indeed appeared.

'I'm *not*,' said the boy. 'Mother, I'm just . . . telling you things.'

It became difficult to tell—or hear—things just about then, as the crowd erupted into full-throated salutation, like a beast with one voice.

Behind the single horseman came a dazzling, multi-coloured array of performers. The juggler Cleander had mentioned was tossing sticks set on fire. Beside and behind him capered dancers dressed in blue and green, and then red and white, doing backflips and wheel-like movements.

One walked on her hands, shoulders twisted into a position that made Rustem wince. She'd be unable to lift a cup without pain by the time she was forty, the doctor thought. Another entertainer, ducking his head to clear the tunnel roof, came striding out on high sticks that elevated him to giant size, and he managed, somehow, to dance on the sticks from that great height. Clearly a favourite, his appearance led to an even louder roar of approval. There came musicians with drums and flutes and cymbals. Then more dancers sprinted past, criss-crossing each other, long streamers of coloured fabric in their hands, drifting in the breeze and with the speed of their running. Their clothing was lifting, too, and there wasn't over-much of it. The women would have been stoned in Bassania for appearing in public so nearly naked, Rustem thought.

Then there came, just after them, the chariots.

'That's Crescens! Glory of the Greens!' shouted Cleander, ignoring his mother's injunction, pointing at a man in a silver helmet. He paused. 'And beside him, that's the young one. Taras. For the Blues. He's riding first chariot again.' He quickly looked across at Rustem. 'Scortius isn't here.'

'What?' said a florid, ginger-haired man behind Thenaïs, leaning forward, brushing her. Cleander's mother shifted to one side, avoiding the contact, her face impassive as she watched the chariots emerge from the wide tunnel to the left of them. 'You expected him? No one has any *idea* where he is, boy.'

Cleander said nothing to that, which was a blessing. The boy didn't entirely lack sense. Behind the two lead chariots, the others came rolling quickly out as the performers ahead of them danced and tumbled down the long straight towards the kathisma at the far end. It was impossible to make out who was sitting there, but Rustem knew that Plautus Bonosus was among the elite in that roofed box. The boy had told him earlier, with an unexpected note of pride, that his father sometimes dropped the white cloth to start the games if the Emperor was absent.

The last chariots, riders clad in white and red over their leather, rolled out of the tunnel. The single horseman and lead dancers were on the far side now, beyond the monuments, would exit through a second gate over there after leading the parade past those seats and stands.

'I believe,' said Thenaïs Sistina, 'that I require a moment out of the sun. Are there refreshments of any kind through that gate?' She gestured at the space through which the horses had come.

'Well, yes,' said Cleander. 'There are all sorts of food stands inside. But you go back up and then down the stairs to get under. You can't go through the Procession Gate, there's a guard there.'

'Indeed there is,' said his mother. 'I see him. I imagine he'll let me through, spare a woman the long walk around.'

'You can't. And you certainly can't just go alone, mother. This is the Hippodrome.'

'Thank you, Cleander, I appreciate your concern that there might be ... unruly people here.' Her expression was unreadable, but the boy flushed crimson. 'I have no intention of stepping where all those horses have gone, and I wouldn't dream of going alone. Doctor, will you be so good ... ?'

More reluctantly than he'd have wanted to admit, Rustem stood up, holding his walking stick. He might miss the start of this now. 'But of course, my lady,' he murmured. 'Do you feel unwell?'

'A moment in the shade and something cool to drink will be enough,' the woman said. 'Cleander, remain here and conduct yourself with dignity. We will be back, of course.' She rose and moved past Rustem in the aisle to walk down two more steps and then along the narrow space between the first row of seats and the barrier to the sands. As she went, she put up her hood, hiding her face within it.

Rustem followed, stick in hand. No one paid them any attention. He saw people moving about all over the Hippodrome, taking their places or heading for refreshments or the latrines. All eyes were on the noisy procession below. Stopping a discreet distance behind the Senator's wife, he saw her address the guard at the low, gated barrier where the walkway ended, just beside the grand Procession Gates a few steps below.

The guard's initial expression of brusque indifference melted quite swiftly as Thenaïs said whatever it was she said. He looked quickly around to be sure there was no one nearby, and then unbarred the low portal at the end of the walkway and let her through into the covered space beneath the stands. Rustem followed, pausing to give the man a coin.

It was only when he walked into the vaulted tunnel, watching carefully to avoid the evidence that horses had just passed, that Rustem saw a man standing alone in the muted light of this atrium, clad in the leather of a charioteer, and a blue tunic.

The woman had stopped just inside, was waiting for Rustem. She said quietly, from within her sheltering hood, 'You were correct, doctor. It seems your patient, our unexpected houseguest, is here after all. Do give me a moment with him, will you?'

And without waiting for a reply, she walked towards the man standing alone in the tunnel. There were two yellow-clad track attendants by the wide, high gates, not far from the small one where Rustem stood. They had clearly been about to swing them shut. Equally clearly, from the way they were looking at Scortius, they were not about to do so now.

He hadn't yet been noticed by anyone else. Must have remained hidden in the shadows here until the chariots rolled out. There were three main tunnels and half a dozen smaller ones branching from this large atrium. The Hippodrome's interior space was vast, cavernous, could hold more people than dwelled in Kerakek, Rustem realized. People lived their lives here, he knew, in apartments down those corridors. There would be stables, shops, food stalls and drinking places, doctors, whores, cheiromancers, chapels. A city within the City. And this open, high-roofed atrium would normally be a bustling, thronged gathering place, echoing with sounds. It would be again in a few moments, Rustem guessed, when the parade performers returned down tunnels from the far side.

At the moment, it was nearly empty, dim and dusty after the bright light outside. He saw the Senator's wife walk towards the charioteer. She pushed back her hood. He saw Scortius turn his head—rather late—and notice her, and so Rustem registered the sudden change in his posture and manner, and some things came clear with that.

He was, after all, an observant man. A good doctor had to be. Indeed, the King of Kings had sent him to Sarantium because of it.

He had anticipated a number of things, including the distinct possibility that he might collapse before getting to the

Hippodrome, but having Thenäis appear in the empty, echoing space of the Processional Atrium had not been one of them.

The two attendants at the gates had seen him as soon as he came out from one of the residential tunnels, after the last of the chariots had gone. A finger to his lips had ensured their immediate, slack-jawed complicity. They would be drinking until all hours on this tale tonight, he knew. And for many nights to come.

He was waiting for the right moment to go forward. Knew that he had—at best—only one race in him today, and a message had to be given with maximum impact, to sustain the Blues, quiet the roiling of unrest, serve notice to Crescens and the others.

And assuage his own pride. He *needed* to race again, remind them all that whatever the Greens might do during this opening of the season, Scortius was among them yet and was still what he had always been.

If it was true.

He might have made a mistake. It had become necessary to acknowledge that. The slow, long walk from Bonosus's house by the walls had been amazingly difficult, and the wound had opened up at some point. He hadn't even noticed, until he'd seen blood on his tunic. He was very short of breath, felt pain whenever he tried to draw in more air. He ought to have hired a litter, or arranged to have Astorgus send one, but he hadn't even told the factionarius he was doing this. Stubbornness had always had a price—why should it be different now? This arrival for the afternoon's first race, this entrance on foot across the sands to the starting line, was entirely his own statement. No one in Sarantium knew he was coming.

Or so he had thought. Then he saw Thenaïs approaching in the diffused light, and his heart thumped hard within his broken ribs. She *never* came to the Hippodrome. If she was here, it was because she'd come looking for him, and he had no idea how—

He saw the Bassanid then, behind her, grey-bearded, slender, holding that stick he affected for the dignity of it. And silently in that moment, Scortius of Soriyya swore, with intense feeling.

He could see it now. The accursed physician would have felt some wretched sort of professional duty. Would have found him gone, deduced it was a race day, sought a way to attend, and—

This time when he swore it was aloud, like a soldier in a caupona, though under his breath.

The man would have gone to Bonosus's house, of course. To Cleander. Who was banned by his father from attending the races this spring—he had told them so. Which meant they'd have had to talk to Thenaïs. Which meant—

She stopped directly in front of him. Her remembered scent was with him again. He looked at her, met that clear gaze, felt a constriction in his throat. She seemed cool, poised—and he could feel the force of her rage like a blast from an oven.

'All of Sarantium,' she murmured, 'will rejoice to see you well again, charioteer.'

They were alone in a vast space. For a little time. The parade would be ending, the others coming noisily back through the tunnels.

'I am honoured that you are the first to say as much,' he said. 'My lady, I hope you received my note.'

'It was *so* thoughtful of you to write,' she said. The brittle formality was its own message. 'I do apologize, of course, that I was with my family for a short while that night when you felt such an . . . urgent need for my company.' She paused. 'Or for that of any woman who might offer her body to a celebrated charioteer.'

'Thenaïs,' he said.

And stopped. She had, he belatedly saw, a knife in her right hand. And so he finally understood what this encounter really was. He closed his eyes. There had always been this possibility, in the life he'd lived.

'Yes?' she said, the tone as detached, as composed as ever. 'I thought I heard someone say my name.'

He looked at her. He could not have named or even numbered the women who had shared his nights over the years. All the years. Not one had found a way to unsettle him as this one had, and still did. He felt old suddenly, and tired. His wound hurt. He remembered the same feeling, the night he'd gone looking for her. His shoulder aching in the night wind.

'It was me,' he said quietly. 'I said your name. I say it most nights, Thenaïs.'

'Really? How diverting that must be for the woman lying with you at the time,' she said.

The two gatekeepers were watching them. One still had his mouth agape. It could have been amusing. The wretched physician remained a precise, polite distance away. It was probable that none of them had seen the dagger in the soft light.

Scortius said, 'I went to the house of Shirin of the Greens to present her with an offer from Astorgus.'

'Ah. *He* wanted to bed her?'

'You are being unkind.'

He winced at what flashed in her eyes then, realized anew just how enraged she was.

The lifelong mask of control, of absolute, flawless poise: what happened to such a person when something broke right through. He drew a too-deep breath, felt the shock of pain in his ribs, said, 'He wanted to invite her, discreetly, to join the Blues. I had promised to add my voice to the proposal.'

'Your voice,' she said. There was a glitter in her eyes. He had never seen it before. 'Just your voice? In the middle of the night. Climbing up to her bedroom. How ... persuasive.'

'It is the truth,' he said.

'Indeed. And did you bed her?'

She had no right to ask. To answer was a betrayal of another woman who had offered him wit and kindness and shared pleasure.

It never occurred to him not to answer, or to lie. 'Yes,' he said. 'Unexpectedly.'

'Ah. Unexpectedly.' The knife was very still in her hand. 'Where did they hurt you?' she asked.

There were noises now from one of the tunnels. The first dancers had left the sands. Beyond her, through the Processional Gates, he could see the eight chariots of the first race wheeling back around and up towards the slant of the start line.

And suddenly it seemed to him that it might actually be enough, what he had done with his life thus far. That the look in this woman's eyes spoke to a level of pain he'd caused—an unfair burden, perhaps, but how did fairness enter into life?—and he could die here, after all, accepting it from her, in this place. He had never expected to grow old.

He said, 'Left side. A stab wound, broken ribs around it.'

All he had wanted to do once, long ago, was race horses.

She nodded, biting at her lower lip thoughtfully, a single line across her brow. 'How unfortunate. I have a knife.'

'I did see that.'

'If I wished to hurt you very, very much before you died . . . ?'

'You would stab me here,' he said, and showed her. There was blood, in any case. It could be seen welling through the blue tunic.

She looked at him. 'You wish to die?'

He considered it then. 'Not really, no. But I would not want to live if it caused you so much grief.'

She drew a breath then. Courage and pain and a kind of . . . madness. That fierce, never-before-seen glinting in her eye. 'You can't imagine I'd be long behind you.'

He closed his eyes again, opened them. 'Thenaïs, there is . . . so *much* wrong in that. But I am prepared for whatever you desire.'

The knife still did not move. 'You should have lied to me, just now. When I asked.'

So small he had been, that first time his father let him sit astride a stallion. They'd had to lift him up, his legs sticking out almost straight when he was seated on the big horse. Laughter at that. Then a sudden silence from the men around them, when the animal grew still under the touch of the child on its back. In Soriyya. Far away. Long ago.

A lifetime. He shook his head. 'You shouldn't have asked,' he said. It was truth, he would not lie.

She drew back the blade then. He was looking straight into her eyes, at what was—so terribly—revealed there when another lifetime's composure fell entirely away.

And because he was doing so, almost falling into her gaze, entangled in her and in memory, oblivious even to the hard upward movement of the small hand that held the knife, he didn't see the swift-striding man come from behind her then and seize her by the wrist, screening the gesture with his own body.

He twisted. The knife fell.

She made no sound, after the first sharp whimper of shock.

'My lady,' said Crescens of the Greens, 'forgive me.'

She looked at him. Scortius looked at him. The three of them stood alone in a huge, dim space. Crescens said, 'No man who ever lived is worth what this would mean to you. Put up your hood, please, my lady. There will be people here very soon. If he has offended, there are so many of us who will deal with that.'

It was uncanny—and the memory was to stay with Scortius—how swiftly her face changed, how the conduit to a kind of fever in her soul slammed shut to the world as Thenaïs looked at the Greens' charioteer. She didn't even give any sign that her wrist was paining her, though it had to be. He had moved very fast, twisted hard.

'You misunderstand,' she murmured. And even smiled. A perfect court smile, detached and meaningless. The iron bars of control crashing down again. Scortius actually shivered, seeing it, hearing her voice change. He was aware of the rapid thread of his pulse. A moment ago he had actually expected . . .

She put up her hood. Said: 'It seems my wayward stepson played a role in our mutual friend's injury. He has told my husband a version of the tale. It is not believed. Before we punish the boy—the Senator is furious, of course—I wanted to ascertain from Scortius himself just what took place. It involved a knife, you see, and an allegation of a stabbing.'

It was nonsense. Words spoken to have words spoken. A tale that could not possibly hold, unless one wished to *allow* it to hold. Crescens of the Greens might be a brawling, hard man on the track and in the taverns and the in Green compound, and he'd only been a single year in Sarantium, but he was First of the Greens, had been invited to court by now, spent a winter in the aristocratic circles the leading racers came to know. He'd have seen his share of bedrooms, too, Scortius thought.

The man knew what this was, how to conduct himself.

His apology was passionate, immediate—and brief, for there were loud sounds now in the southern tunnels. 'You must allow me,' said Crescens, 'to call upon you, I beg, to more fully express my contrition. I appear to have blundered like an untutored provincial. My lady, I am ashamed.' He looked over. 'And I must return to the sands, while you should—if I may urge you—allow your escort to take you from this space, which will be no place at all for a lady in a moment.'

They could hear rolling wheels and boisterous laughter around the dark curve of the largest tunnel. Scortius had said nothing, had not even moved. The knife lay on the ground. He bent now, carefully, and picked it up with his right hand. Gave it back to Thenaïs. Their fingers touched.

She smiled, a smile thin as river ice in the north when the winter's freezing has not yet made it safe. 'Thank you,' she said. 'Thank you both.' She looked over her shoulder. The Bassanid doctor had stayed where he was through all of this. Now he came forward, impeccably grave.

He looked at Scortius first. His own charge. 'You understand your coming here . . . alters things?'

'I do,' Scortius said. 'I am very sorry.'

His physician nodded. 'With this,' said the Bassanid, 'I will not contend.' There was a blunt finality to his tone.

'I understand,' said Scortius. 'I am grateful for all you have done until now.'

The doctor turned away. 'May I escort you, my lady? You mentioned a cooling drink?'

'I did,' she said. 'Thank you, yes.' She looked at the Bassanid thoughtfully for a moment as if considering new information, and then turned back to Scortius. 'I expect you to win this race,' she murmured. 'From what my son tells me, our dear Crescens has won sufficiently in your absence.'

And with that, she turned and went away with the physician, towards the stairs and the concession booths and stalls on the level above them.

The two charioteers stood alone, looked at each other.

'What was he talking about?' Crescens jerked his chin towards the receding figure of the physician.

'Disclaiming responsibility if I kill myself.'

'Ah.'

'They do that in Bassania. You needed a piss?'

The Green rider nodded. 'Always do, after lunch.'

'I know.'

'Saw you. Came to say hello. Saw the knife. You're bleeding.'

'I know.'

'Are you . . . back for good?'

Scortius hesitated. 'Probably not yet. I recover quickly, mind you. Or I used to.'

Crescens smiled sourly. 'We all used to.' His turn to hesitate. People would be emerging any moment now. They both knew it. 'She couldn't possibly have hurt you unless you let her.'

'Yes, well, that's . . . Tell me, how's your new trace horse?'

Crescens looked at him a moment, then nodded his head in acceptance. 'I like him. Your young driver . . .'

'Taras.'

'Taras. Bastard has the makings of a racer. I didn't see it last year.' He grinned, wolfishly. 'I'm planning to break his heart this spring.'

'Of course you are.'

The Green rider's smile deepened. 'You wanted a lovely appearance all by yourself, didn't you? Returning hero, walking across the sand alone? By Heladikos, what an entrance!'

Scortius's expression was wry. 'I'd thought of it.'

But he was really thinking about the woman, images interwoven with memories of his childhood, amazingly, and the feeling he'd had looking into her eyes just before the knife moved. *You should have lied to me.* He had been about to let her stab him. Crescens was right. An otherworldly mood, a state of being she had shaped, with those glittering eyes, in the dusty half-light. It seemed a dream already, only moments after. He didn't think the dream was going to go away.

Crescens said, 'I don't believe I can allow you that entrance. I'm sorry. Saving your fucking life's one thing. Trivial. But giving you that kind of a return's another. Very bad for Green morale.'

One had to smile. One was back in the Hippodrome. The world it made within the world. 'I can see that. Let's go together, then.'

They went together, just as the first dancers began emerging from the darkness of the tunnel to their left.

'Thank you, by the way,' Scortius added, as they approached the two yellow-clad guards at the doors.

I expect you to win this race, she had said. After the doctor had formally disclaimed responsibility if he killed himself. She had come under the stands with a knife. She had come to the Hippodrome with one. She knew what she was saying. *You can't imagine I'd be long behind you.* He had long thought, before ever really knowing her, that there was something extraordinary beneath her celebrated reserve. Then he'd thought, arrogantly, that he'd found it, defined it. He'd been wrong. There was so much more. Should he have known?

'Thank you? Not at all,' said Crescens. 'Too boring here without you, winning against children. Mind you, I do want to keep winning.'

And as they passed the two guards, just before they walked out on the bright sands together, into the sight of eighty thousand people, he hammered an elbow entirely without warning into the injured man's left side.

Scortius gasped, staggered. The world reeled, went red in his sight.

'Oh! Sorry!' the other man exclaimed. 'Are you all right?'

Scortius had doubled over, clutching his side. They were in the entrance now. Would be seen in a stride or two. With a shuddering, racking effort he forced himself to straighten, started moving again, an act of will more than anything else. Was still desperately fighting for breath. Heard, as in a fever, the first roars of the crowd nearest to them.

It began. The volume of noise growing, and growing, rolling along the first straightway like a wave, the sound of his name. Crescens was beside him but it was a mistake on his part, really, for only one name was heard, over and again. A screaming. He struggled to breathe without passing out, to keep moving, not to double over again, not put a hand to his wound.

'I'm a terrible man,' said Crescens cheerfully beside him, waving to the crowd as if he'd personally fetched the other rider back from the dead like some hero of the ancient tales. 'By Heladikos, I really am.'

He wanted to kill, and to laugh at the same time. Laughing would probably kill him. He was back in the Hippodrome. The world of it. Out on the sands. Saw the horses up ahead. Wondered how one walked so far.

Knew he was going to do it, somehow.

And in that same moment, seeing the drivers ahead of them swivelling to look back and stare, looking at the teams and their positions, and at one in particular, he had his idea, swift as horses, a gift. He actually smiled, baring his teeth, though breathing was very difficult. There was more than one wolf here, he thought. By Heladikos, there was.

'Watch me,' he said then, to the other charioteer, to himself, to the boy he'd been once on that stallion in Soriyya, to all of them, the god and his son and the world. He saw Crescens look quickly over at him. Was aware, triumphantly, through the red, stabbing pain, of sudden anxiety in the other man's features.

He was Scortius. He was still Scortius. The Hippodrome *belonged* to him. They built *monuments* to him in this place. Whatever might happen elsewhere, in darkness, with the sun below the world.

'Watch me,' he said again.

West of them, not all that far, as the two charioteers are leaving their tunnel, the Emperor of Sarantium is heading towards his own, to pass under the Imperial Precinct gardens from one palace to another where he is about to make the final dispositions for a war he has thought about from the time he placed his uncle on the Golden Throne.

The Empire had been whole once, and then sundered, and then half of it had been lost, like a child might be lost. Or, better put, a father. He has no children. His father died when he was very young. Did these things matter? Had they ever? Did they now? Now that he was an adult, growing old, shaping nations under holy Jad?

Aliana thinks so, or wonders about it. She'd put it to him directly one night not long ago. Was he risking so much, seeking to leave so bright and fierce a mark on the world, because he had no heir for whom to guard what they already had?

He didn't know. He didn't *think* this was so. He'd been dreaming of Rhodias for so long—a dream of something made whole again. And made so by him. He knew too much about the past, perhaps. There had been three Emperors once for a short, savage time, and then two, here and in Rhodias, for a long, divisive span of years, then only one, here in the City Saranios made, with the west lost and fallen.

It felt wrong to him. Surely it would to any man who knew the glory of what had been.

Though that, he thinks, walking through the lower level of the Attenine Palace with a courtly retinue hurrying to keep pace with him, is a trick of rhetoric. Of course there are those who know the past as well as he and see things differently. And there are those—such as his wife—who see a greater glory here in the east, in the present world, under Jad.

None of them, even Aliana, rules Sarantium. He does. He has guided them all to this point, has strings in his hand and a very clear vision of the elements in play. He expects to succeed. He usually does.

He comes to the tunnel. The two helmed Excubitors stand rigidly at attention. At a nod, one swiftly unlocks and opens the door. Behind Valerius, the Chancellor and the Master of Offices and the wretchedly inadequate Quaestor of Imperial Revenue all bow. He has dealt with them here in the Attenine over a rapid midday meal. Given orders, heard reports.

Has been awaiting one particular dispatch, from the northeast, but it hasn't yet come. He is, in fact, disappointed in the King of Kings.

He has been expecting Shirvan of Bassania to attack in Calysium by now, to set in motion the *other* part of this vast undertaking. The part no one knows about, unless Aliana has divined it, or perhaps Gesius, whose subtlety is extreme.

But there has come no word yet of an incursion across the border. It's not as if he hasn't given them enough signals as to his intentions, or even his timing. Shirvan *ought* to have sent an army over the border by now, breaching the bought peace in an attempt to undermine a western campaign.

He will have to deal with Leontes and the generals differently, as a consequence. Not an insurmountable problem, but he'd have preferred the elegance of things had there been a Bassanid attack already launched, appearing to force his hand and divert troops before the fleet sailed.

He is, after all, pursuing more than one goal here.

It is, one might say, a character flaw. He *always* has more than one goal, entwines so many threads and designs into everything he does. Even this long-awaited war of reconquest in the west is not a thing that stands entirely alone.

Aliana would understand, even be amused. But she doesn't want this campaign, and he has made things easier for both of them—or so he judges—by not discussing it. He suspects that she is aware of what he is doing. He also knows her unease, and the sources of it. A regret, for him.

He can say, with uncomplicated truth, that he loves her more than his god and needs her at least as much.

He pauses a moment at the open door to the tunnel. Sees the torches flicker ahead of him as the air ripples through. Shirvan has not yet attacked. A pity. He will have to deal with the soldiers now, at the other end. He knows what he will say. Leontes's pride as a military man is his greatest asset, and his core weakness and there is a lesson, the Emperor has judged, that the younger man must learn before various next steps can properly be taken. A staying of reckless pride first, and then a moderating of religious zeal.

He has given thought to these matters, as well. Of course he has. He has no child, and succession is an issue.

He turns briefly, acknowledges the genuflections of his advisers, and then enters the tunnel alone, as he always does. They are already turning to leave as the door closes; he has given them a great deal to do this afternoon before they reconvene in the kathisma at the end of the racing to tell the Hippodrome and the world that Sarantium is sailing to Rhodias. He hears the door close and lock behind him.

He walks over mosaic floor tiles, in the footsteps of Emperors long dead, communing with them, imagining silent dialogues, luxuriating in that silence, the achingly rare privacy of this long, winding corridor between palaces and people. The lighting is steady, the air and ventilation carefully devised. The solitude is a joy for him. He is the mortal servant and exemplar of Jad, lives his life in the bright eye of the world, is never alone save here. Even at night there are guards in his chambers, or women in the rooms of the Empress when he is there with her. He would linger now in the tunnel, but there is much to do at the other end as well, and time is running. This is a day awaited since . . . since he came south from Trakesia at his soldier uncle's command?

An exaggeration, with truth in it.

His pace is brisk, as always. He is some distance down the tunnel, under the evenly spaced torches set in iron brackets in the stone walls, when he hears, in that rich silence, the turning of a heavy key behind him and then a door and then the sound of other footsteps, not hurrying.

And so the world changes.

It changes in every moment, of course, but there are . . . degrees of change.

Half a hundred thoughts—or so it feels—run through his mind between one step and the next. The first thought and the last are of Aliana. In between these he has already grasped what is happening. Has always been known—and feared—for this quickness, has taken an unworthy measure of pride in that, all his life. But subtlety, swiftness, may have just become irrelevant. He continues walking, only a little faster than before.

The tunnel, twisting slightly in the shape of an S for Saranios—a conceit of the builders—is far below the gardens and the light. Meaningless to shout here, and he'll not get close enough to either door to be heard in the lower corridors of either palace. He has understood there is no point running, because those behind him are not: which means, of course, that there is someone ahead of him.

They will have entered before the soldiers meeting him in the other palace arrived outside the door, will have been waiting underground, perhaps for some time. Or perhaps . . . they might have entered through the same door he did and gone towards the other end to wait? Simpler that way? Only two guards to suborn. He thinks back and yes, he does remember the faces of the two Excubitors at the door behind him. Not strangers. His own men. Which means something . . . unfortunate. The Emperor feels anger, curiosity, a surprisingly sharp grief.

The sense of relief that Taras felt when he heard the rolling, rapidly growing explosion of sound and looked back was as nothing he'd ever felt in all his life.

He was saved, reprieved, divested of the massive burden that had been crushing him like a weight too heavy to shoulder and too vital to disclaim.

Amid the noise, which was stunning even for the Hippodrome, Scortius came walking up to him, and he was smiling.

Out of the corner of his eye Taras saw Astorgus hurrying over, his square, bluff features creased with worry. Scortius got there first. As Taras hastily untied himself from the reins of the first chariot and stepped down, lifting off the silver helm, he realized—belatedly—that the other man was not walking or breathing easily, despite the smile. And then he saw the blood.

'Hello there. Have a difficult morning?' Scortius said easily. He didn't reach for the helmet.

Taras cleared his throat. 'I . . . didn't do very well. I can't seem to—'

'He did just fine!' said Astorgus, coming up. 'What the fuck are you doing here?'

Scortius smiled at him. 'Fair question. No good answer. Listen, both of you. I have one race in me, maybe. We need to make it count. Taras, you are staying in this chariot. I'm riding Second for you. We are going to win this race and stuff Crescens into the wall or the spina or up his own capacious rectum. Understood?'

He wasn't saved, after all. Or, perhaps he was, in a different way.

'I . . . stay First?' Taras mumbled.

'Have to. I may not be able to go seven laps.'

'Fuck that. Your doctor knows you are here?' Astorgus asked.

'As it happens, he does.'

'What? He . . . allowed this?'

'Hardly. He's disowned me. Said he takes no responsibility if I die out here.'

'Oh, *good*,' said Astorgus. 'Should I?'

Scortius laughed, or tried to. He put a hand to his side, involuntarily. Taras saw the track steward coming over. Normally this sort of delay for an on-track colloquy would be prohibited, but the steward was a veteran and knew he was dealing with something unusual. People were still screaming. They would have to quiet a bit before the race could start in any case.

'Welcome back, charioteer,' he said briskly. 'Are you riding this race?'

'I am,' said Scortius. 'How's your wife, Darvos?'

The steward smiled. 'Better, thank you. The boy sits out?'

'The boy rides First chariot,' said Scortius. 'I'll take Second. Isanthus sits. Astorgus, will you tell him? And have them redo the reins on the trace horses the way I like them?'

The steward nodded his head and turned away to report to the starter. Astorgus was still staring at Scortius. He hadn't moved.

'You are sure?' he said. 'Is this worth it? One race?'

'Important race,' the injured man said. 'For a few reasons. Some that you won't know.' He smiled thinly, but not with his eyes this time. Astorgus hesitated a heartbeat longer, then nodded slowly and walked away towards the second Blue chariot. Scortius turned back to Taras.

'All right. Here we go. Two things,' the Glory of the Blues said quietly. 'One, Servator is the best trace horse in the Empire, but only if you ask him to be. He's conceited and lazy, otherwise. Likes to slow down and look at our statues. Scream at him.' He smiled. 'Took me a long time to realize what I could make him do. You can go faster in the turns with him holding the inside than you will ever believe you can—until you've done it the first few times. Stay wide awake at the start. Remember how he can make the other three cut with him?'

Taras did remember. It had been done to him, last fall. He nodded, concentrating. This was business, their profession. 'When do I whip him?'

'When you come up to a turn. Hit on the right side. And keep yelling his name. He listens. Concentrate on Servator—he'll handle the other three for you.'

Taras nodded.

'Listen for me during the race.' Scortius put a hand to his side again and swore, breathing carefully. 'You're from Megarium? You speak Inici at all?'

'Some. Everyone does.'

'Good. If I need to I'll shout at you in that tongue.'

'How'd you learn . . . ?'

The older man's expression was suddenly wry. 'A woman. How else do we learn all the important lessons in life?'

Taras tried to laugh. His mouth was dry. The crowd noise was amazing, really. People were still on their feet, all over the Hippodrome. 'You said . . . there were two things?'

'I did. Listen carefully. We wanted you in the Blues because I knew you were going to be as good as anyone here, or better. You've been thrown into something hideous and unfair, never even handled this team before, having to face Crescens and his Second here. You are a fucking idiot if you think you've been doing badly. I'd whack you on the head but it'll hurt me too much. You've been astonishing, and any man with half a brain would know it, you Sauradian lout.'

There was a feeling hot mulled wine could give you, sipped in a tavern on a damp winter day. These words felt like that, actually. With all the self-possession he could command, Taras said to him, 'I *know* I've been astonishing. It's about time you came back to help.'

Scortius let out a bark of laughter, winced in pain. 'Good lad,' he said. 'You're fifth in the lanes, I'm second?' Taras nodded. 'Good. When you get to the line there will be room for you to cut. Watch me, trust Servator, and leave me to deal with Crescens.' He grinned, a thin smile, without any amusement in it.

Taras looked over to where the muscular First of the Greens was wrapping his own reins around himself, in the sixth lane.

'Of course I will. That's your job,' Taras said. 'Make sure you do it.'

Scortius grinned again, and then took the silver processional helmet Taras was still holding and gave it to the groom beside them, taking the battered race helmet in exchange. He put it on Taras himself, like a stable boy. The pandemonium grew even wilder. They were being watched, of course, every movement they made studied the way cheiromancers examined entrails or stars.

Taras thought he was going to cry. '*Are* you all right?' he asked. Blood was visible through the other man's tunic.

'We'll all be just fine,' said Scortius. 'Unless I get arrested for what I'm about to do to Crescens.'

He walked up, rubbed the head of Servator for a moment and whispered something in the horse's ear, then he turned and went down the diagonal line to the second Blue chariot, where Isanthus had already stepped down—his face showing as much relief as Taras's had a moment ago—and where the handlers were furiously adjusting the reins to suit Scortius's well-known preferences.

Scortius didn't get into the chariot yet. He stopped by the four horses, touching each of them, whispering, his mouth close to their heads. There was a change of drivers taking place, they needed to know it. Taras, watching, saw that he presented only his right side and right hand to the stallions, shielding the presence of blood.

Taras stepped back up into his own chariot. Began wrapping the reins around his body again. The boy beside Taras gave the silver helmet to another groom and hurried to help, his face shining with excitement. The horses were restless. They had seen their usual driver but he wasn't with them now. Taras picked up his whip. Set it in its sheath beside him for the moment. He took a deep breath.

'Listen you stupid, fat ploughhorses,' he said to the most

celebrated racing team in the world, speaking in the gentle, soothing tone he always used with horses, 'you don't fucking run for me this time, I'll take you to the tanners myself, you hear me?'

It felt wonderful to be saying that. To feel he could.

The race that followed was remembered for a very long time. Even with the events that ensued that day and immediately after, the first afternoon race of the second Hippodrome session that year was to become legendary. An emissary from Moskav, who had accompanied the Grand Prince's entourage and remained behind through the winter in slow negotiations over tariffs, was in attendance and would chronicle the race in his diary—a record that would be preserved, miraculously, through three fires in three cities, a hundred and fifty years apart.

There were those in the Hippodrome that day for whom the racing held more importance than mighty events of war and succession and holy faith. It is always so. The apprentice, decades after, might recall an announcement of war as having taken place the day the chambermaid finally went up to the loft with him. The long-awaited birth of a healthy child will resonate more for parents than the report of an invading army on the border or the consecrating of a sanctuary. The need to finish the harvest before frost overwhelms any response to the death of kings. A flux in the bowels obliterates the weightiest Pronouncements of holy Patriarchs. The great events of an age appear, to those living through them, as backdrops only to the vastly more compelling dramas of their own lives, and how could it be otherwise?

In this same way, many of the men and women there in the Hippodrome (and some who were not, but later claimed to have been) would cling to one private image or another of what transpired. They might be entirely different things, varying moments, for each of us has strings within the soul, and we are played upon in different ways, like instruments, and how could it be otherwise?

Carullus the soldier, once of the Fourth Sauradian, very briefly a chiliarch of the Second Calysian cavalry, had been most recently reassigned—without ever having reported north, and for reasons he didn't understand as yet—to the personal guard of the Supreme Strategos Leontes, receiving his (quite handsome) pay from the Strategos's own accounts.

He was therefore still in the City and sitting with his wife in the military officers' section of the Hippodrome, having accepted that his current position and rank made it inappropriate for him to stand or sit among the Green partisans any more. There was a palpable undercurrent of tension among the officers in attendance around them, and it had little to do with the racing. It had been made clear that an important announcement would be made here today. It wasn't hard to guess what that might be. Leontes wasn't in the kathisma yet, nor was the Emperor here this afternoon, but the afternoon had a long way to run.

Carullus looked at his wife. Kasia was attending her first racing, was still visibly uneasy in crowds. The unaligned officers' section of the stands was certain to be less unruly than the Greens' standing area, but he was still worrying about her. He wanted her to enjoy this, and be present for what was likely to be a memorable moment at the end of the day. He'd been here by himself in the morning and had collected her at home during the midday recess: an entire day at the Hippodrome would have been rather too much to ask of Kasia.

Notwithstanding his hopes, he was aware that she was here only as an indulgence to him and his passion for the chariots.

It was wondrous, actually, that a woman would do that.

Officers, especially those attached to the Strategos, were well treated in the City. They had splendid seats, not quite halfway along the opening straight, and low down. Most of the crowd was behind and above them, so Kasia could concentrate on the horses and drivers below. He'd thought that would be good.

Being so near, and with the staggered start line that put the outside quadrigas farther along the track, they were quite close to the last three teams. Crescens of the Greens was starting sixth. Carullus pointed him out to his wife, reminded her that the racer had been among those at their wedding, and then made a quick jest when the Greens' First Charioteer withdrew under the stands just before the race was to begin, leaving his team to the handlers. Kasia smiled a little; one of the other officers laughed.

With a real attempt at self-control—though he was very excited and extremely happy—Carullus tried not to point out *everything* going on to his bride. She did know that Scortius was missing. Every soul in Sarantium knew that. He was aware by now that his voice soothed her as much as his protective presence, however, so he did tell her briefly (as brief as he ever was) about the transaction that had led to the right-side horse in Crescens' quadriga being exchanged for the young rider currently wearing the silver helmet for the Blues in the fifth lane. He'd explained about right-side horses, too. And that meant talking about left-siders, of course, which in turn meant . . .

She had been interested in some of it, though not in the way he'd expected. She asked him more about how the boy could be sold from one team to another, whether he liked it or not. Carullus had pointed out that no one was *making* him race, or even remain in Sarantium, but he didn't, somehow, think that her underlying question had been answered. He'd changed the subject, pointing out the various monuments in the spina across the track.

Then a roaring had begun, and he'd turned quickly towards the tunnel, and his jaw had dropped as Scortius and Crescens walked out onto the sands together.

People see different things, remember different things, though all might be looking in the same direction. Carullus was a soldier, had been all his adult life. He saw how Scortius was walking and drew some immediate conclusions, even before they came nearer and he noted blood on the man's left side. It affected everything else he saw and felt when the race began, and everything he would recall afterwards: a shading of crimson to the afternoon, right when it began, before anything was known.

Kasia didn't notice any of this. She was watching the other man—quite close to them actually—the one in Green who now mounted up again in the chariot he'd left before. She remembered him at her wedding: burly, confident, centre of a circle, making others laugh in the way that people laughed when the jests were offered by someone important, whether or not they were truly amusing.

Crescens of the Greens was at the very peak of this profession, Carullus had told her (among the very many things he'd told her), had won every important race last week and this morning, with Scortius missing. The Greens were exultant, in glory, the man was spectacularly triumphant.

For Kasia, that made it genuinely interesting how readily she could read the apprehension in him.

He stood just below them in his chariot, methodically wrapping the long reins about his body. Carullus had explained about that, too. But the Green rider kept casting glances back and to his left where the other man, Scortius, was now entering a chariot, nearer the place where all the statues were. Kasia wondered if others could see this anxiety, or if it was simply that, after a year at Morax's, she was attuned to such things now. She wondered if she always would be.

'Holy Jad in the sun, he's riding Second chariot!' Carullus breathed, as one might speak a prayer. His tone was rapt; his face, when she glanced over at him, was transfixed, almost in pain.

She was intrigued enough to ask. He explained this to her, as well. Did it quickly, mind you, because as soon as all the various reins were tied where they appeared to belong and the handlers had withdrawn to the inside or outside of the track and the yellow-garbed officials had done the same, a white handkerchief was dropped by the Master of the Senate in the kathisma, as a single trumpet blew a single note and a silver seahorse dived from overhead, and the race began.

There was quite a lot of dust then.

Cleander Bonosus ceased to be a Green that day. He didn't switch allegiance, but rather—as he would often tell the tale afterwards, including one memorable oration at a murder trial—he felt as if he had somehow been lifted *above* faction alliances during the first race of the afternoon on the second Hippodrome day of that spring.

Or just before the race, perhaps, when he'd seen the man his friends had stabbed and kicked in a dark street, the man he'd heard ordered to remain at rest until summer, come walking out on the sands to claim the *Second* team of the Blues. Not the silver helmet which was his by right.

Or even before *that*, it could be said. For Cleander, looking for his mother and the Bassanid doctor, had been peering into the tunnel, not admiring the charioteers taking their positions on the sand. He'd been low down and close enough and so he—perhaps alone of eighty thousand—had actually seen Crescens of the Greens hammer an elbow into someone's side just as they came into the light, and then he'd seen who that someone was.

He would always remember that. His heart had begun pounding then, and it went on hammering in his chest all the way to the start of the race, which came just as his mother and the doctor reclaimed their seats. Both of them—at a glance—seemed unexpectedly strained, but Cleander had no time to consider that. There was a race on and Scortius was back.

The seahorse dived. Eight quadrigas burst from the staggered starting line, heading towards the white marking down the track where they could leave their lanes and the wild manoeuvring would begin.

By instinct, habit, force, Cleander's gaze went to Crescens, as the First of the Greens whipped his team off from the sixth position. Not a good start post, but the boy leading the Blues was only in fifth, so it didn't much matter. Scortius was much lower down the track in the second lane, but with a lesser team. Cleander didn't understand how and why that had happened. The Greens' second driver had the rail and would try to keep it until Crescens worked his way down.

Or so it usually unfolded in this sort of alignment.

But Crescens was going to have a slow route down this time, it seemed. Taras of the Blues had his own team out at least as fast. Crescens couldn't cut him off at the chalk without fouling or spilling his own chariot. The two first teams would descend together, and then the Greens would work on the Blue rider in tandem as they had all morning. It was a long race, seven laps. Plenty of time.

Except that everyone knew the starts mattered enormously. A race could end before the first lap was done. And Scortius was in this one.

Cleander turned to see what was happening with the Blues' second team, and then he never looked away. Scortius had brilliantly anticipated the handkerchief and trumpet, had a superb start, was lashing his horses furiously already. He had *burst* from the line, had opened a gap between himself and the Greens on the rail. He might even be able to get down, take the inside lane away as soon as they hit the white chalk. It would be close.

'Which one is he?' his stepmother said beside him.

'Second lane,' he rasped, pointing, never turning away from the track. It only occurred to him later that there had been no need to speak the name. 'He's riding Second chariot, not First! Watch him try for the rail.'

The horses hit the chalk. He didn't try for the rail.

Instead, he went *up* the track, slicing sharply right, well ahead of the slower White and Red quadrigas in the third and fourth lanes. Both of them seized the entirely unexpected opening and went down and left behind him, sacrificing a moment of speed for the vital inner lanes.

Later, Cleander would understand how that must have been part of it. They went to the left, had to slow to do it, and so space was created. It was all about space. Cleander felt, in retrospect, as if all these thundering, bunched chariots at the start, spinning wheels, thirty-two flying horses, lashing, straining men, were all like small wooden toys, the sort a boy played with, imagining a Hippodrome on his bedroom floor, and Scortius was moving them the way that boy might move his toys, godlike.

'*Watch out!*' someone shouted, just behind them. And with cause. The two Blue quadrigas were on a collision course, the boy in the First chariot heading down as expected with Crescens right beside him, Scortius angling straight towards them both, going entirely the wrong way, *away* from the rail. Scortius's mouth was wide open, Cleander saw, and he was screaming something in that chaos of dust and speed and incoherence.

Then it wasn't incoherent at all, for something exquisite took place, clear as anything in the fury and mire of human life could be, if you understood enough to see it.

And being careful in his recollections, tracking back along the arc of his feelings, Cleander would finally decide that *this* was the true moment when allegiance and partisanship gave way to something else in him: a desire that never left him, all his life, to see that level of skill and grace and courage again, garbed in whatever colours they might choose to wear for a moment's bright, sunlit glory on the sands.

In a way, his childhood ended when Scortius went up the track and not down.

His stepmother saw only the same initial confusion of dust and fury that Kasia observed from her similar vantage point farther along. There was a roiling tumult inside her, making it quite impossible for her to sort out the chaos below from the chaos within. She felt unwell, thought she might be physically sick, a humiliation in this public place. She was aware of the Bassanid physician on her other side, was half inclined to curse him for being the agent of her presence here, and for seeing what he ... might have seen in the dim light under the stands.

If he spoke a single word, Thenaïs decided, if he but asked after her health, she would ... she didn't *know* what she would do.

And that was such appalling, unknown terrain for her— not being sure of exactly what to do. He didn't speak. A blessing. Stick at his side—that ridiculous affectation, as bad as the dyed beard—he seemed intent on the chariots with all the others. It was why they were all here, wasn't it? Well, it was, for everyone but her, perhaps.

I expect you to win this race, she had said. In that strange, filtered half-light. After trying to kill him. Had no idea why she'd said that, it had just come out, from the tumult inside her. She *never* did things like that.

It was declared and taught in the holy chapels of Jad that daemons of the half-world hovered, always, intimately close to mortal men and women, and they could enter into you, making you other than what you were, had always been. The knife was in her cloak again. He had given it back to her. She shivered in the sunlight.

The doctor looked over then. Said nothing. Blessedly. Turned back to the track.

'Which one is he?' she asked Cleander. He answered, pointing, never taking his eyes from the impossible confusion below. 'He's riding Second chariot, not First!' he shouted.

That obviously meant something, but she hadn't the

least notion what. Or that it was partly directed at her, and what she had said about winning the race.

Rustem found and began watching his patient from the very start, as soon as he'd sat down again, just as a trumpet sounded. Saw him controlling four racing horses with his left hand, his injured side, while whipping with his right and leaning absurdly far forward on the precarious, bouncing platform on which the racers stood. Then he saw Scortius tilt his body hard to the right, and it seemed to Rustem as if the charioteer was *pulling* his team that way, with his own damaged body above the flashing, spinning wheels.

He felt suddenly and inexplicably moved. The knife he'd seen flash and fall under the stands had been, in fact, quite unnecessary, he now judged.

The man intended to kill himself before them all.

He had been, in his own day, as celebrated as any racer who'd ever driven a quadriga in this place.

There were three monuments to him in the spina, and one of them was silver. The first Emperor Valerius—this one's uncle—had been forced to summon him from retirement twice, so impassioned had been the beseechings of the Hippodrome crowd. The third time—the last time—he'd left the track they'd made a procession for him from the Hippodrome Forum to the landward walls, and there had been people lining the streets several bodies deep all the way there. Two hundred thousand souls, or so the Urban Prefecture had reported.

Astorgus of the Blues (once a Green) had no false modesty at all, no diffidence about his own achievements on these sands where he had dueled and won, and won again, against a succession of challengers and the Ninth Driver, always, for two decades.

It was the very last of those young challengers—the one he'd retired from—who was before him now, riding Second chariot, with broken ribs and an open wound and no longer young. And of all those watching in those first moments of the race, it was Astorgus the factionarius—blunt and scarred, immensely knowledgeable and famously undemonstrative—who first grasped what was happening, reading eight quadrigas in a single capacious glance, their speeds and angles and drivers and capacities, and who then offered a savage, swift prayer aloud to banned, blasphemous, necessary Heladikos, son of the god.

He was along the outside wall, standing for the start where he usually did, two-thirds of the way down the straight, past the chalk line, in a safety zone carved out for the track officials between the outer railing and the first row of seats, which were set back here. As a consequence, he had the illusion that Scortius was driving straight towards him when he took that absurd, unprecedented career towards the outside, not the rail.

He heard the Glory of the Blues (he who had once been the Glory here, himself) screaming over the crashing din, and he was near enough to realize that the words were in Inici, which only a few of them knew. Astorgus was one. The boy, Taras, from Megarium, would be another. Astorgus saw the lad jerk his head swiftly left and immediately, splendidly react, without an instant to think what he was doing. Astorgus stopped breathing, cut off his prayer, watched.

The boy screamed in turn—howling the name of Servator—and went *hard* to his whip on the horse's right side. It happened at a breakneck, utterly insane speed, destructively close to the jammed, crowded start in a madness of thirty-two pounding stallions.

In a precisely simultaneous pulsebeat of time, with no margin at all, none, cut so near there was no space to be seen between the chariot wheels as they crossed each other, Scortius and the boy, Taras, both *hurled* their bodies left, bringing their teams and chariots with them. The sound was deafening, the dust a choking cloud.

And through that dust, right in front of him, as if done for his private, intimate entertainment—dancers hired for a night by an aristocrat—Astorgus saw what happened next and his soul was moved and his spirit shaken and overawed, for he knew that for all he had ever done out there, in a career acclaimed by two hundred thousand souls crying his name, he could not have even *conceived,* in his prime, in his own glory, what Scortius had just implemented.

Taras was angling down, Scortius up. Straight for each other. When the boy pulled violently left, the magnificent Servator pulled the other three horses and the chariot across the track in *exactly* the same manœuvre the Hippodrome crowd would still remember from the last day of autumn, when Scortius had done it *to* him. And that was— oh, it *was*—part of the humbling elegance of this, the perfection. A remembered text being echoed, used again in a new way.

And Scortius threw his team as hard to the left in the exact same needful instant—else the two chariots would have smashed each other to bits of wood, sending screaming horses crashing, riders flying into shattered bones and death. His team slewed, the wheels sliding, then biting *up* the track, straightening out with a terrifying precision *right beside Crescens and his Green team.* In full flight.

Meanwhile, the third and fourth lane teams had been slicing down.

Of course they had. There was room made for them when Scortius bolted from the start and cut up. They'd slowed, seized the startling invitation—and so opened the way, like double doors in a palace, for Taras to make his own violent cut left and straighten back up, and so discover a clean, clear, glorious sweep of open track in front of him near the rail.

He was just behind the Greens' number two, and then— as the boy went to his whip again—he was *beside* him, entering the very first turn under the kathisma, taking the wider route but with the better team, leaning hard left still, crying the name of his magnificent lead horse, letting Servator hold them *tight* to the Greens, and then he was *past* as they came out. And then there was nothing and no one ahead of him on the proving track as they came out into the far side . . . and it had all been done in one single straightway.

Astorgus was crying. Moved as if by something holy in a sanctuary, knowing he had seen a creation as perfect as any artisan had ever made: any vase, gem, poem, mosaic, wall hanging, golden bracelet, jewelled, crafted bird.

And knowing, too, that *this* sort of artistry could not endure past the shaping moment, could only be spoken of after by those who recalled, or misrecalled, who had seen and half seen and not seen at all, distorted by memory and desire and ignorance, the achievement of it written as if on water or on sand.

It mattered, terribly, and just now it didn't matter at all. Or could the fragility, the defining impermanence actually *intensify* the glory? The thing lost as soon as made? In this moment, Astorgus thought, his big hands clenched on the wooden rail before him—for this one flawless, diamond moment offered to time—it was the two charioteers, the young one and the genius guiding him, who were lords of the world on the god's earth, lords of Emperors, of all men and women, fallible and imperfect and one day to fail and die leaving nothing at all behind, lost as soon as made.

Plautus Bonosus stood up in the Imperial Box as the two lead chariots came towards them and pounded into the first turn together. He was unaccountably stirred by what was happening, felt briefly self-conscious until he became aware that half a dozen others among this overbred, jaded cluster of courtiers were also on their feet. He exchanged a fleeting, wordless glance with the Master of the Imperial Horse and turned again to the sands below.

There was a quadriga above their heads on the elegantly arched ceiling of the kathisma: a mosaic of Saranios, crowned with victory's wreath, driving a team. Below, the young boy for the Blues who had been courageous but overmatched last week and all this morning was now screaming like a barbarian at his team and whipping them past the Greens' second chariot while still in the kathisma turn.

It happened sometimes, it could be done, but not easily or often, and never without an awareness—among those who knew the track—of the risk and skill involved. Bonosus watched. The boy, Taras, was no longer overmatched, no longer diffident.

No longer behind the Green team or beside it.

He had started in the fifth lane. He came out of the first turn half a team in front and then a full length, and then, smooth as eastern silk on skin, he let Servator glide to the rail along the back straight.

Bonosus, instinctively, turned back to watch Scortius and Crescens. They came up to the same turn side by side but at the widest part of the track, for Scortius was refusing to let the other man down, and showed not the least desire to do so himself. He was driving the Second team. His task was to ensure a victory for his teammate. Keeping Crescens wide as long as possible was the way to do just that.

'The other Green's coming back to them,' said the Master of Horse in his raspy voice. Bonosus glanced over, saw it was true. The Greens' Second driver, faced with a miserable choice—to chase the Blues' young leader or come back to aid his own First team—had opted for the latter. Among other things, Crescens of Sarnica was reported to have a vicious, whip-wielding temper with lesser drivers who forgot who was First of the Greens.

'They'll try for second and third now,' said Bonosus, to no one in particular.

'He can catch the lad if he's sprung free quickly enough. We haven't even done a lap.' The Master of Horse was excited. It showed. So was Bonosus. Even with all that was yet to come today, a war that would change their world, the drama below was overwhelming.

The Greens' number two was slowing, drifting back, looking over his right shoulder to judge his angle. As the two celebrated drivers came out of the turn, still wide, still right next to each other, the Second Green team floated out towards Scortius. He was ahead of him. Could, with impunity, move right in front of him. It was delicate—he had to arrest the progress of the Blue quadriga while finding a way to get his own leader free to come sharply down to the rail and take flight after the young boy leading the race. This, however, was what Second teams did here, it was what they were trained to achieve.

The three quadrigas began to merge, coming together into one six-wheeled, twelve-horsed figure in the swirling dust and noise.

'I believe,' said Bonosus suddenly, 'that Scortius expected this to happen, too.'

'*What?* Impossible,' said the Master of Horse, just in time to be proven wrong.

He had to be careful, *extremely* careful. If he fouled either of the others now, any Blue victory would be erased. That was always the constraint on those riding Second or carrying the lesser colours. The yellow-garbed officials were all along the track, watching them.

In addition, he was acutely aware that although he might just manage to roll through seven laps and stay upright, he didn't have much left for manœuvres. Every shallow breath was a struggle against pain. The very idea of having to pull the team hard again was enough to make him wish he were already dead.

There was, he knew, a pool of blood, dangerously slippery, about his feet. He didn't look down.

He watched the Greens' Second team, instead, as it came back towards them—as he'd known it would. Crescens frightened his teammates. In doubt, they'd come to his aid. Not a bad practice, on the whole, but there were moments when it might be. He intended to make this one such moment.

He had pictured this from the moment he'd walked onto the track and seen that the new right-side trace horse on Crescens's team in the sixth lane wasn't blinkered.

He knew the horse they'd traded. Knew it very well. Had slotted a bit of information in his mind back in the winter. It obviously hadn't come up in last week's races or this morning: the Greens' lead team would rarely find itself all the way to the outside.

It was about to do so, any moment now.

The Second team came right back to them, staying in front, but not by much, which gave it licence to drift wider, forcing Scortius to do the same. Crescens was also slightly ahead of him to the outside, which raised the risk of foul if he drifted too much and clipped the other team. The Greens were trying to make him rein up. The moment he did so, the Second team in front of him would do exactly the same thing and Crescens would go to his whip and spring free of both of them like a prisoner from an unlocked cell—then he'd cut down. They knew how to do this. It was delicate, precise work, done at speed, but these were veteran drivers who had worked together for a full year.

It didn't matter.

He let his team drift up, just a little. Crescens looked over quickly, snarling an oath. If the other Green team could be said to have pushed Scortius over then no foul would be called. Especially against the returning champion: all three of them knew that was also a part of the game today.

Crescens went a little higher, nearer the rail.

Scortius and the other Greens went with him. They were most of the way down the back straight now. Scortius slid right again, the smallest amount. Had to be *very* cautious: these horses were not his usual team. All three chariots were terrifyingly close now. Had the wheels been spiked as sometimes in the old days, in Rhodias, someone would have been flying from a smashed-up chariot by now.

Crescens roared another oath at his teammate and went a little higher yet. As high as he could go, in fact, racing along the outermost lane, right against the rail and the screaming, on-its-feet, fist-waving, thunderous crowd.

The new right-side trace horse for the Greens didn't like screaming thunderous fist-waving beside him. At all. He was, in fact, a horse that needed a right-side blinker. It hadn't come up. Crescens had never run him so wide, and this was only the second meeting of the year. They hadn't figured that out yet, the Greens.

A mistake.

Scortius held steady, watched for the moment. Crescens had a tight, grim smile on his face as the quadrigas pelted along. Now that he was at the rail, any further movement towards him by Scortius *would* have to be seen as a foul. The other Green chariot, still ahead, could safely slide a bit farther over and slow, and Scortius would have to pull up hard.

Experienced strategy, sound reasoning. Might well have worked, if the right-sider hadn't jerked its head just then, in blind panic right beside the howling crowd, and broken stride, pulling the other three horses hopelessly out of their own pace, *just* as the Greens' number two performed the entirely correct tactical movement of moving a little more right and slowing a shade.

Scortius did pull up, as hard as they'd ever have wanted him to, even a little sooner than they'd expected, as if he was afraid, or weak.

Doing so, he had an exceptionally vivid, close view of the crash. Crescens's quadriga slewed back inwards, pushed by their panicked, undeniably powerful new right-sider, while the other team was still committed to angling out. They met, unfortunately.

Two wheels flew, instantly. One stayed in the air like a discus, spinning halfway to the spina. A horse screamed and stumbled, dragging the others down with it. A chariot skidded sideways, banged the rail, and then came back the other way, and Scortius, pulling sharply left (and crying aloud with the pain of it this time) saw Crescens's knife flash as he cut his reins and leaped desperately free.

He was past them, then, didn't see what happened to the other Green driver, or the horses, but he knew they were down.

He dealt with the turn then looked back. Saw the Reds and Whites toiling behind him now, four of them, closely bunched, labouring. Had a new idea. There was that odd, crimson hue to his vision again, but he suddenly decided it might be within him to bring one last element into this day's aspiring towards immortality.

Ahead of him, the boy, Taras, was slowing for him, looking back. He lifted his whip hand, waved Scortius forward, offering him the lead and the victory.

Not what he wanted, for more than one reason. He shook his head, and as he came up towards the other driver he shouted, in Inici, 'I'll castrate you with a dull knife if you don't win this race. Keep moving!'

The boy grinned. He knew what they had just done. The glory of it. He was a chariot-racer, wasn't he? He kept moving. Crossed the line six laps later to win the first major race of his life.

The first of what would be one thousand, six hundred and forty-five triumphs for the Blues. By the time the boy in that chariot retired eighteen years later only two names in the long history of the Sarantium Hippodrome would have won more races, and no one who followed him would do so. There would be three statues to Taras of Megarium in the spina to be torn down with all the others, seven hundred years after, when the great changes came.

The First of the Whites came second in that race, the Second of the Whites came third. The track record of the day, meticulously kept by the stewards, as ever, would show that Scortius of the Blues came a wretched distance behind during his only race that afternoon.

The records can miss everything, of course. So much depends on what else is preserved, in writing, in art, in memory, false or true or blurred.

The Blues faction, with their White partners, came first and second and third. And fourth. Fourth, in what was, all things considered, very likely the most spectacularly triumphant race of his entire career on the sands, was Scortius of Soriyya, who had shepherded the White teams through and past him while blocking, with precision, the two hapless Red charioteers, who were all that was left on the track running for the Green faction.

He ought to have died when that race was over. In some ways he *should* have died, he was later to think during some long nights, setting a seal of perfection on a racing life.

Those who came running over saw the pool of blood about his soaked sandals when the race ended. The chariot platform was slippery with it. The Ninth Driver had been beside him for those last laps, running very near from the time the fifth seahorse dived, and closer yet down the final backstretch as he kept on swinging back and forth, almost unable to breathe, holding the Reds before pulling away at the end—alone on the track, in fact, his teammates having finished already, a lap ahead, the Red quadrigas slipping back.

Alone, save for that unseen Ninth beside him, brushing wheels, dark as superstition had him, and crimson, too, like the day. But then, unaccountably, he drifted away, let this reckless mortal go on beneath the streaming sunlight, gathered and held in the enormous cauldron of sound that was the Hippodrome.

No one knew it then, no one *could* have known, among eighty thousand and more in that place, but there was richer blood for the claiming in Sarantium that day.

There would be time yet to take a charioteer.

Scortius slowed, just across the finish line, swayed where he stood as the quadriga drifted to an awkward halt. He was unable to even begin unwrapping his reins, which were also soaked through with blood by then. He was alone, motionless, done.

They came to help him, sprinting across the track, leaving the victory lap to the boy and the two White teams. Astorgus and two others cut him free, tenderly, as if he were a babe. He saw, with some surprise, that all three of them were weeping, and others who came up behind them, even the stewards. He tried to say something about that, a jest, but couldn't seem to speak just yet. It was very hard to breathe. He suffered them to help him back under the stands, a redness in the air.

They went past Crescens, in the Greens' space along the spina. He seemed to be all right, and the other Green rider was there as well. There was something odd about their faces, a working of emotion being fought. There really did seem to be a lot of noise. More, even, than usual. They took him—carried him, mostly—back through the Processional

Gates to the dimly lit atrium. It was a little quieter here, but not very much.

The Bassanid was there. Another surprise. There was a pallet next to him.

'Lay him down,' he snapped. 'On his back.'

'I thought . . . you had disowned me,' he managed to say. First words. There was so much pain. They were laying him down.

'So did I,' said the grey-haired physician from the east. He threw aside his stick, angrily. 'Makes two fools here, doesn't it?'

'Oh, at least,' said Scortius, and then he did, finally, by the very great mercy of Heladikos, lose consciousness.

CHAPTER XI

It is true, undeniably, that the central moments of an age occur on the margins of the lives of most people. A celebrated play from the early years of the eastern empire in Sarantium begins with shepherds quarrelling over their entangled flocks when one of them notices a flare of light in the east as something falls from the sky. There is a brief pause in the dispute as the men on the hill slope consider the event; then they return to the matter at hand.

The death of Heladikos in a falling chariot, bearing fire from his father, cannot compete in significance with the theft of a sheep. The drama by Sophenidos (later banned by the clerics as heretical) moves from this beginning to treat matters of faith and power and majesty, and contains the celebrated Messenger's speech about dolphins and Heladikos. But it begins on that hillside, and it ends there, with the sacrifice of the disputed sheep—employing the new gift of fire.

Nonetheless, for all the human truth of Sophenidos's observation that the world's major events might not seem so to those living through a given time, it remains equally true that there *are* moments and places that may properly be seen as lying at the heart of an age.

That day, in the early spring of the year, there were two such places on the earth, far apart. One was in the desert of Soriyya, where a man in a hood, with a cloak drawn over his mouth, preserved a silence among the drifting sands, having remained awake all the night before, fasting, and looking up at the stars.

The other was a tunnel in Sarantium, between palaces.

He stands in a curve of the walls and floor, looking up at torches and a painted ceiling of the night sky, down at a mosaic of hares and pheasants and other creatures in a forest glade: an artisan's illusion of the natural world here underground within city walls. The pagan faiths tell of dark powers in the earth, he knows, and the dead lie underground, when they are not burned.

There are people in wait ahead of him, people who ought not to be here. He has deciphered that from the measured, unhurried footsteps behind. They have no fear that he will flee from them.

The curiosity he feels might be considered a defining trait of the Emperor of Sarantium, whose mind is endlessly engaged by the challenges and enigmas of the world the god has made. The anger he experiences is less characteristic but equally intense just now, and the repeated pulsing of grief, like a heavy heartbeat, is very rare for him.

There were—there *are*—so many things he has intended to do.

What he does do after a moment, rather than continue to wait like one of the hares, frozen in the mosaic glade, is turn and walk back towards those behind him. One may sometimes control the moment and place of one's dying, thinks the man whose mother had named him Petrus, in Trakesia, almost half a century ago, and whose uncle—a soldier—had summoned him to Sarantium in early manhood.

He is not, however, reconciled to his death. Jad waits for every living man and woman, but can wait a little longer for an Emperor, surely. Surely.

He deems himself equal even to this, whatever it turns out to be. Has nothing with which to defend himself, unless one counts a simple, unsharpened blade at his belt used for breaking the seal on correspondence. It is not a weapon. He is not a warrior.

He is fairly certain he knows who is here, is rapidly deploying his thoughts (which *are* weapons) even as he goes back down the tunnel and comes around the curve and sees—with brief, trivial satisfaction—the startled reaction of those coming after him. They stop.

Four of them. Two soldiers, helmed to be unknown but he knows them, and they are the two who were on guard. There is another cloaked man—all these hidden assassins, even with no one to see—and there is one who walks in front, unshielded, eager, almost alight with what Valerius perceives to be desire. He does not see the man he has feared—quite intensely—might be here.

Some relief at that, though he may be among those in wait at the other end of the corridor. Anger, and grief.

'Anxious for an ending?' asks the tall woman, stopping before him. Her surprise was brief, swiftly controlled. Her eyes are blue flames, uncanny. She is dressed in crimson, a gold belt, her hair bound in a net of black. The gold of it shows through in the torchlight.

Valerius smiles. 'Not as anxious as you, I daresay. Why are you doing this, Styliane?'

She blinks, genuinely startled. She had been a child when it all happened. He has always been conscious of that, guided by it, much more so than Aliana.

He thinks of his wife. In his heart, in the pure silence of the heart, he is speaking to her now, wherever she might be under the sun overhead. She had always told him it was a mistake to bring this woman—this girl when the dance began—to court, even to let her live. Her father's daughter. Flavius. In silence the Emperor of Sarantium is telling the dancer he married that she was right and he was wrong and he knows she will know, soon enough, even if his thoughts do not—cannot—travel through walls and space to where she is.

'Why am I *doing* this? Why else am I alive?' the daughter of Flavius Daleinus says.

'To live your life,' he says crisply. A philosopher of the Schools, admonishing a pupil. (He closed the Schools himself. A regret, but the Patriarch needed it done. Too many pagans.) 'Your own life, with the gifts you have, and have been given. Easy enough, Styliane.' He looks past her as fury kindles in her eyes. Deliberately ignores that. Says to the two soldiers, 'You are aware that they will kill you here?'

'I told them you would say that,' Styliane says.

'Did you also tell them it was true?'

She is clever, knows too much of hatred. The rage of the one who survived? He had thought—gambled—the intelligence might win out in the end, saw a genuine need, a place for her. Aliana said it would not, accused him of trying to control too much. A known flaw.

She is *still* so young, the Emperor thinks, looking again at the tall woman who has come to kill him here under the still-cold ground of spring. He doesn't want to die.

'I told them what was—and is—more obviously true: any new court will need Excubitors in the highest ranks who have proven their loyalty.'

'By betraying their oath and Emperor? You expect trained soldiers to believe that?'

'They are here with us.'

'And you will kill them. What does murder say about—'

'Yes,' says the cloaked man, finally speaking, face still hooded, his voice thick with excitement. 'Really. What *does* murder say? Even after years?'

He doesn't remove the hood. It doesn't matter. Valerius shakes his head.

'Tertius Daleinus, you are forbidden the City and know it. Guards, arrest this man. He is banned from Sarantium as a traitor.' His voice crackles with vigour; they all know this tone of command in him.

It is Styliane, of course, who breaks the spell with her laughter. *I'm sorry*, the Emperor is thinking. *My love, you will never know how sorry.*

They hear footsteps approaching from the other end. He turns, apprehensive again. A pain in his heart, a premonition.

Then he sees who has come—and who has not—and that pain slips away. It *matters* to him that someone is not here. Odd, perhaps, but it does matter. And replacing fear, swiftly, is something else.

This time it is the Emperor of Sarantium, surrounded by his enemies and far as his own childhood from the surface world and the mild light of the god, who laughs aloud.

'Jad's blood, you have grown fatter, Lysippus!' he says. 'I'd have wagered it was impossible. You aren't supposed to be in Sarantium yet. I intended to call you back after the fleet had sailed.'

'*What*? Even now you play games? Oh, stop being clever, Petrus,' says the gross, green-eyed man who had been his Quaestor of Revenue, exiled in the smouldering, bloody aftermath of riot two years and more ago.

Histories, thinks the Emperor. We all have our histories and they do not leave us. Only a handful of men and women in the world call him by his birth name. This hulking figure, the familiar, too-sweet scent surrounding him, his fleshy face round as a moon, is one of them. There is another figure behind him, mostly hidden by the spilling shape of Lysippus: it is not the one he feared, though, because this one, too, is hooded.

Leontes would not be.

'You don't believe me?' the Emperor says to the vast, sweating bulk of the Calysian. He is genuinely indignant, no need to pretend. His back is now fully turned to the woman and her cloaked, craven brother and the renegade guards. They will not stab him. He knows that with certainty. Styliane means for this to be theatre, ceremony, not only murder. A lifetime's worth of . . . expiation? For history. There are steps yet to this dance. His dancer is somewhere else, up above, in the light.

They will not let her live.

For that as much as anything he will keep trying here underground, probing, subtle and quick as a salmon, which is holy in the north among the pagans his people once were before Jad came among them. And Heladikos, his son, who fell.

'Believe that you were about to call me back?' Lysippus

shakes his head, jowls quivering. His voice is still distinctive, memorable. Not a man, once met, who can ever be forgotten. His appetites are corrupt, unspeakable, but no man had ever managed the Imperial finances with such honesty or skill. A paradox never fully fathomed. 'Must you, even now, assume all others are fools?'

Valerius gazes at him. He'd actually been a well-formed man once, when first met, handsome, educated, a patrician friend to the young, scholarly nephew of the Count of the Excubitors. Had played a role in the Hippodrome, and elsewhere, on that day when Apius died and the world changed. Rewarded for it with wealth and real power and with eyes averted from what he did in his city palace or in the litter that carried him at night through the streets. Then exiled, of necessity, to the countryside after the riot. Bored there, of a certainty. A man inextricably drawn to the City, to dark things, blood. The reason he is here.

The Emperor knows how to handle him, or did once. He says, 'If they behave as fools, I do. Think, man. Did the country dull you entirely? Why did I have the rumours started that you were back in the City?'

'You start them? I *am* back in the City, Petrus.'

'And were you two months ago? I thought not. Go ask in the faction compounds, friend.' A deliberate word, that last. 'And I will have Gesius give you names. Half a dozen. Ask when word first began to spread that you might be here. I was testing it, Lysippus! On the people and the clerics. Of *course* I want you back. We have a war to win—probably on two fronts.'

A bit of new information dropped there for them. A hint, a tease. To keep the dance going, in any way. Keep holding to life here. They will kill her after him.

He knows Lysippus very well. The torches are bright where they are standing and he sees the registering of a fact, then conjecture at the hint, then the watched-for doubt in the remarkable green eyes.

'Why bother? No need to ask anyone,' says Styliane Daleina behind him, breaking the mood like a glass dropped on stone, shattering into shards.

Her voice, continuing, is a knife now, precise as an executioner's edge. 'This much is perfectly true. A good liar mixes truth in his poison. It was when I first heard those tales and realized what was happening that I saw the chance to invite you back to join us. An elegant solution. If the Trakesian and his whore heard tidings of you they would assume they were their own false rumours.'

Which is what, indeed, has happened. He hears that word *whore*, of course, understands what she so passionately wants from him. He will not give it to her, but is thinking how she is so much more than clever. He turns. The soldiers remain helmed, her brother hooded, Styliane is almost glowing in her intensity. He looks at her, here under the earth where old powers dwell. He thinks that what she would like is to unbind her hair and claw his beating heart from his breast with her fingers and nails like the god-drunk wild women on hills of autumn long ago.

He says, calmly, 'You use a foul tongue for someone of breeding. But it is an elegant solution, indeed. My congratulations on the cleverness. Was it Tertius who thought of it?' His tone is mildly acerbic, giving her nothing of what she wants. 'The loathed, godless Calysian enticed to become a perfect scapegoat for the murder of a holy Emperor. Does he die here with me and these soldiers, or do you hunt him down and produce a confession after you and poor Leontes are crowned?' One of the helmed men behind her shifts uneasily. He is listening.

'Poor Leontes?' She simulates her laughter this time, is not truly amused.

And so he gambles. 'Of course. Leontes knows nothing of this. Is still waiting outside the far doors for me. This is the Daleinoi alone, and you think you'll control him after, don't you? What is the scheme? Tertius as Chancellor?' Her eyes flicker. He laughs aloud. 'How very amusing. Or no, I *must* be wrong. Surely I am. This is all for the greater good of the Empire, of course.'

The craven brother, named twice, opens his mouth within the hood and then closes it. Valerius smiles. 'Or no, no. Wait. Of course! You promised that position to Lysippus to get him here, didn't you? He'll never have it, will he? *Someone* must be named and executed for this.'

Styliane stares at him. 'You imagine everyone treats people as disposable, in the way you do?'

His turn to blink, disconcerted for the first time. 'This, coming from the girl I let live against all advice and brought into my court with honour?'

And it is then that Styliane finally says, with a glacial clarity, the words slow as time, inexorable as the movement of stars across the night sky, an indictment carrying the burden of years (so many nights awake?) behind it: *'You burned my father alive. I was to be bought with a husband and a place on the dais behind a whore?'*

There is a silence then. The Emperor feels the weight of all the earth and stone between them and the sun.

'Who told you *that* absurd story?' Valerius says. His tone is light, but it costs him something this time.

Still, he moves, swiftly, when she swings a palm to strike

him in the face. He catches her hand, holds, though she twists savagely, and he says, in turn, through gritted teeth, 'Your father wore purple in the street on the day an Emperor died. He was on his way to the Senate. He could have been killed by any man in Sarantium with respect for tradition, and burning would have suited so much impiety.'

'He did *not* wear purple,' says Styliane Daleina, as he lets her tear her hand free. Her skin is almost translucent; he sees the marks of his fingers red on her wrist. 'It is a *lie*,' she says.

And now the Emperor smiles. 'In the god's most holy name, you astonish me. I had no idea. None at all. All these years? You honestly believe that?'

The woman is silent, breathing hard.

'*She does . . . believe it.*' Another voice, behind him. A new one. 'She is wrong, but it . . . changes . . . nothing.'

But this mangled, whistling voice changes everything. And it is with a bone-chill now, as if a wind crossing from the half-world has blown into him, bringing death truly into this tunnel where walls and plaster and paint hide the roughness of earth underground, that the Emperor turns again and sees who has spoken, stepping out from behind the obscuring bulk of the Calysian.

There is something this man holds. It is actually tied to his wrists, for his hands are maimed. The tube-like implement, attached to something that rolls on a small cart behind him, is one the Emperor recognizes and remembers, and so it is with a struggle, a real one, that Valerius remains motionless now, betraying nothing.

There is fear in him, however, for the first time since he heard the tunnel door open behind him and understood he was not alone. Histories returning. Sign of a sun disk given to a watching man below a solarium, years and years ago.

Screaming afterwards, in the street. He has reason to know that this is a bad way to die. He looks briefly at Lysippus and from the expression there understands something else: the Calysian, being what he is, would have come here to see this used, if for no other reason at all. The Emperor swallows. Another memory reaches him, from even further back, childhood, tales of the old dark gods who live in the earth and do not forget.

The high, wheezing sound of the new voice is appalling, especially if one recalls—and Valerius does—the resonance of it before. This hood is thrown back now. The man, who is eyeless and whose face is a melted ruin, says, 'If he . . . wore purple to go before . . . the people it was as the . . . proper . . . successor to an Emperor who . . . had named none.'

'He *didn't* wear purple,' Styliane says again, a little desperately.

'Be silent, sister,' says the queer, high whistling voice, the authority in it startling. 'Bring Tertius here . . . if his legs . . . will move him. Come behind me.' The blind, disfigured man wears a trivial, incongruous amulet around his neck, a small bird, it looks like. He shrugs off his cloak now onto the mosaic floor. Those in the tunnel might wish he had not done so, had kept the hood, save for Lysippus. The Emperor sees him regarding the hideous figure of Lecanus Daleinus with the moist, wide, tender eyes one might fix upon an object of yearning or desire.

All three Daleinoi then. The contours of this now terribly clear. Gesius had, discreetly, obliquely, implied they ought to be attended to, at the time the first Valerius took the throne. Had suggested the Daleinoi offspring be regarded as an administrative matter unworthy of the attention of the

Emperor or his nephew. Some things, the Chancellor had murmured, were beneath the proper consideration of rulers taxed with the burden of far greater issues on behalf of their people and the god.

His uncle had left it to him. He left most such things to his nephew. Petrus had declined to kill. Had his reasons, different in each case.

Tertius was a child and then later was manifestly a coward, insignificant, even during the Victory Riot. Styliane he saw from the outset as important, and more so as she grew up through a decade and more. He had plans for her, the marriage to Leontes at the heart of these. He'd thought—arrogantly?—he could use her ferocious intelligence to win her to a larger vision. Had thought he *was* doing so, if slowly, that she grasped the unfolding stages of the game that would have her Empress after all. One day. He and Aliana had no heir. He'd thought she understood all this.

Lecanus, oldest of the three, was something different. Was one of the figures that haunted the Emperor's dreams when he did sleep, seeming to stand like a deformed, dark shadow between him and the promised light of the god. Were faith and piety always born of fear? Was this the secret all clerics knew, foretelling eternal darkness and ice under the world for those who strayed from the light of the god?

Valerius had given orders that Lecanus not be killed, whatever he did, even though he knew that for all real purposes, by any *honest* measure, the eldest child of Flavius Daleinus, a better man than his father had ever been, had died in the street outside their home when the father had. He had just kept on living. Death in life, life in death.

And what he holds now, tied to his wrists to more easily handle it, is one of the siphons that disgorge the same liquid flame, from the canister rolling behind him, that was used on that morning long ago to make a point, an overwhelming assertion, one that every man and woman in the Empire could understand, about the passing of an Emperor and the coming of a new one.

It seems to Valerius as if they have all moved straight from that morning sunlight long ago to this torchlit tunnel, with nothing in between. Time feels strange to the Emperor, the years blurring. He thinks of his god, then, and his unfinished Sanctuary. So many things intended and unfinished. And then again of Aliana up above, somewhere in the day.

He is not ready to die, or to have her die.

He makes the blurring memories stop, thinking quickly. Lecanus has summoned his brother and sister to cross to him. A mistake.

Valerius says, 'Only the two of them, Daleinus? Not these loyal guards who let you in here? Have you told them what happens to those in the line of the flame? Show them the rest of your burns, why don't you? Do they even *know* this is Sarantine Fire?'

He hears a sound from behind him, one of the soldiers.

'Move *now,* sister! Tertius, come.'

Valerius, staring down the nozzle of the black tubing that holds the worst death he knows, laughs again in that moment and turns to the other two siblings. Tertius has taken a tentative step forward, and now Styliane moves. Valerius backs up to stand right beside her. The soldiers have swords. He knows Lysippus will have a blade. The big man is more nimble than one might imagine.

'Hold them both,' the Emperor snaps to the two Excubitors. 'In the god's name, are you fools that wish your own deaths? This is *fire*. They are about to burn you.'

One of the men backs up then, an uncertain step. A fool. The other puts a tentative hand to his sword hilt.

'Do you have the key?' the Emperor snaps. The nearer man shakes his head. 'She took it. My lord.'

My lord. Holiest Jad. He may yet live.

Tertius Daleinus twists suddenly and sidles forward against the tunnel wall to cross to his brother. Valerius lets him go. He is not a soldier, but this is his life now, and Aliana's, and a vision of a world, a legacy, in the shaping. He seizes the woman, Styliane, by the upper arm before she can move past him, and he takes his small knife in his other hand and puts it to her back. It has an edge that can scarcely break skin; they will not know that.

But Styliane, who does not struggle at all, who has not even tried to avoid his grip, looks at him even as he holds her, and the Emperor sees a triumph in her gaze, not far from madness: he thinks again of those women on the hill slopes of myth.

Hears her say with a frightening calm, 'You are mistaken yet again if you believe my brother will refrain from burning you in order to save me. And equally mistaken in thinking that I care, so long as you burn as my father did. Go ahead, brother. End it.'

Valerius is shaken to the core, struck dumb. Knows truth when he hears it; she is not dissembling. *End it.* In a sudden stillness of the soul he hears, then, a faint, far sound like a tolling bell struck once.

He had thought, had always believed, intelligence could overmaster hatred, given time, tutelage. It is not so, he sees now, too late. Aliana was right. Gesius was right. Styliane, brilliant as a diamond, might welcome power, and wield it with Leontes, but it is not her *need*, not the key to the woman. The key, beneath the ice of her, is fire.

The blind man, uncannily precise in where he aims the siphon, moves his gash of a mouth in what Valerius understands to be a smile. He says, 'Such . . . a waste, alas. Such skin. Must I . . . dear sister? Then so be it.'

And the Emperor understands that he *will* do it, sees an unholy, avid hunger in the gross face of the Calysian beside the maimed Daleinus, and with a sudden furious motion— awkward, for he is *not* a man of action—he snatches at the waist purse of the woman and pushes her forward hard so she stumbles and crashes into her blind brother and they both fall. No fire. Yet.

Backing up, he hears the two guards retreating behind him and understands that he has turned them, they are with him. He would pray now, but there is no time. At all. *'Move!'* he snaps. 'Get the siphon!'

Both guards spring past him. Lysippus, never a coward, and having cast his dice with the Daleinoi here, goes for his sword. The Emperor, watching, backing up quickly now, fumbles in the cloth purse, finds a heavy key, knows it. Does pray then, in thanks. Styliane is already up, pulling at Lecanus.

The first Excubitor, upon them, levels his blade. Lysippus steps forward, slashes, is parried. Lecanus is still on his knees, mouthing wild, incoherent words. He reaches for the trigger of the flame.

And it is then, just then, even as he sees this, that the Emperor of Sarantium, Valerius II, Jad's beloved and most holy regent upon earth, thrice-exalted shepherd of his people, feels something white and searing and final plunge into him from behind as he backs towards the door, towards safety and the light. He falls, and falls, his mouth opening, no sound, the key in his hand.

It is not recorded by anyone, for it never is nor ever can be, whether he hears, as he dies, an implacable, vast, infinite voice saying to him and to him alone in that corridor under palaces and gardens and the City and the world, '*Uncrown, the Lord of Emperors awaits you now.*'

Nor is it known if dolphins come for his soul when it leaves, as it does leave then, unhoused, for its long journey. It *is* known, but only by one person in the god's world, that his last thought as a living man is of his wife, her name, and this is so because she hears it. And hearing—somehow hearing him—understands that he is going, going from her, is gone, that it is over, ended, done, after all, the brilliant dance that had begun long ago when he was Petrus and she was Aliana of the Blues and so young, and the afternoon sun is bright above her and all of them, in a cloudless springtime sky over Sarantium.

She cut off most of her hair in the small boat, being rowed back from the isle.

If she was wrong about what Daleinus's departure and the murdered guards meant, shorn hair could be covered, would grow back. She didn't think she was wrong, even then, on the water. There was a blackness in the world, under the bright sun, above the blue waves.

She had only Mariscus's knife with which to cut; it was difficult in the boat. She hacked raggedly, dropped tresses in the sea. Offerings. Her eyes were dry. When the hair was chopped she leaned over the side and used the salt water to scrub the cream and paint and scented oils from her face and blur the scent of her perfume. Her earrings and rings she put in a pocket of her robe (money would be needed). Then she took one of the rings back out and gave it to Mariscus, rowing her.

'You may have a choice to make,' she said to him, 'when we reach the harbour. You are forgiven, whatever you do. This is my thanks to you for this task, and for all that has gone before.'

He swallowed hard. His hand shook as he took it from her. The ring was worth more than he could earn in a lifetime in the Imperial Guard.

She told him to discard his leather armour and Excubitor's over-tunic and sword. He did so. They went overboard. He had not spoken the whole of the way, rowing hard, sweating in the light, fear in his eyes. The ring went into his boot. The boots were expensive for a fisherman, but they would not be together long. She would have to hope no one noticed.

She used his knife again to cut off the lower portion of her robe, did it unevenly, tore it in places. People would see stains and rips, not the fineness of a fabric. She took off her leather sandals, tossed them, too, over the side. Looked at her bare feet: painted toenails. Decided they would be all right. Women of the street painted themselves, not just ladies of the court. She did immerse her hands in the water again, rubbing and roughening them. She pushed off the last of her rings, one she never removed, let it drop down through the sea. There were tales of sea people whose rulers had wed the sea in this way.

She was doing something else.

She spent the last of the journey back to harbour biting and chipping at her fingernails, smeared the torn robe with dirt and salt water from the bottom of the boat, and then her cheeks again. Her hands and complexion, left as they were, would give her away before anything else.

There were other small boats in the water around them by then so she had to be discreet. Fishermen, ferrymen, small craft carrying goods to and from Deapolis in and among the looming shapes of the fleet that was to sail west to war. The announcement planned for today, though none out here knew that. The Emperor in the Hippodrome kathisma after the last race, with all the great ones of the realm. She had timed her morning's outing on the water to be there in time, of course.

Not now. Now what she sensed ahead of her was an aura of death, an ending. She had said in the palace two years ago, when Sarantium was burning in the Victory Riot, that she would rather die in the vestments of Empire than flee and live any lesser life.

It had been true then. Now, something different was true. An even colder, harder truth. If they killed Petrus today, if the Daleinoi did this, she would live long enough herself to see them dead, somehow. After? After would take care of itself, as was needful. There were endings and there were endings.

She could not have known, even self-conscious and aware of her own appearance as she had always been, how she appeared in that moment to the soldier in the boat with her, rowing to Sarantium.

They approached a mooring, far down the slip, manœuvring among the other jostling small boats. Obscenities and jests rang back and forth across the water. Mariscus was only just adequate to navigating his way in. They were loudly cursed, she swore back, crudely, in a voice she hadn't used for fifteen years, and made a caupona jest. Mariscus, sweating, looked quickly up at her and then bent back to his task. Someone in the other boat laughed aloud, back-oared and made way for them, then asked what she'd do in return.

Her reply made them whoop with laughter.

They docked. Mariscus leaped out, tied the boat. Aliana moved quickly, stepping out herself before he could offer a hand. She said, quickly and low, 'If all is well you have earned more than you can dream of, and my thanks for a lifetime. If it is not well, I ask nothing more of you than what you have now done. Jad guard you, soldier.'

He was blinking rapidly. She realized—with surprise—that he was fighting back tears. 'They will learn nothing from me, my lady. But is there nothing more . . . ?'

'Nothing more,' she said briskly, and went away.

He meant what he said, and was a brave man, but of *course* they would learn what he knew if they were shrewd enough to find him and ask. Men had, sometimes, a touching belief in their ability to withstand professional questioning.

She walked up the long slip alone, barefoot, her adornments gone or hidden, her long robe torn into a short, stained tunic (still too fine for her station now, she would need another soon). One man stopped and stared at her and her heart lurched. Then he made a loud offer, and she relaxed.

'Not enough money and not enough man,' said the Empress of Sarantium, looking the sailor up and down. She tossed her shorn, ragged hair, and turned away dismissively. 'Find a donkey to hump for that price.' His outraged protest was drowned in laughter.

She walked on through the thronged, noisy harbour, a silence within her so deep it echoed. She trudged up a narrow street. She didn't know it. So much had changed in fifteen years. Her feet hurt already. She hadn't walked barefoot in a long time.

She saw a small chapel and stopped. Was about to go in to try to order her thoughts, to pray, when—in that moment—she heard from within a known voice speaking her name.

She remained where she was, didn't look around. This was a voice from nowhere and everywhere, someone who was hers alone. Had been hers alone.

She felt an emptiness invade her like an army. She stood very still in that small, steep city street and amid the crowds and bustle, with no privacy at all, she bade a last farewell, by birth name not Imperial one, to the loved soul that was leaving, that was already gone from her and from the world.

She had wanted forbidden dolphins for her room. Had taken the mosaicist, Crispin, to see them this morning. Only this same morning. Petrus had . . . found them first. Or been found by them, and not as a mosaic on a wall. Was perhaps being carried, his soul, to wherever they carried souls on the way to Jad. She hoped they were kind, that the way was easy, that there had not been too much pain.

No one saw her weep. There were no tears to see. She was a whore in the City, with people to kill before they found and killed her.

She had no idea where to go.

———&———

In the tunnel, the two guards made the remarkably foolish mistake of looking back over their shoulders when the

Emperor fell. This entire circumstance, the horror of it, had undermined all their training, unmoored them like ships torn from their anchors in a storm. They burned for the error. Died screaming, as the blind man found and pulled the trigger on the nozzle that released the liquid fire. Lecanus Daleinus was cursing, crying, high-pitched and incomprehensible, wailing as if demented in his own mortal agony, but he aimed the nozzle with uncanny accuracy past his sister and brother straight at the soldiers.

They were underground, far from life and the world. No one heard them screaming or the bubble and sizzle of melting flesh save for the three Daleinoi and the gross, avid man beside them, and the other one, standing behind the dead Emperor, sufficiently far away that he felt a wet surge of heat come down the tunnel and a bowel-gripping fear but was not even singed by that fire from long ago.

He became aware, as the heat died away and the screams and the wet moaning stopped, that they were looking at him. The Daleinoi, and the fat man he remembered very well and had not known was in the City. It . . . pained him that that could have happened without his knowing.

But there were greater sources of distress just now.

He cleared his throat, looked at the bloodied, sticky dagger in his hand. There had never been blood on it before, ever. He wore a blade for display, no more. He looked down at the dead man at his feet.

And Pertennius of Eubulus said then, feelingly, 'This is terrible. So terrible. Everyone *agrees* it is wrong for an historian to intervene in the events he chronicles. He loses so much authority, you understand.'

They stared at him. No one said anything at all. It was possible they were overwhelmed by the truth of what he'd said.

The blind one, Lecanus, was crying, making strangled, ugly sounds in his throat. He was still on his knees. There was a smell of meat in the tunnel. The soldiers. Pertennius was afraid he would be ill.

'How did you get in here?' It was Lysippus.

Styliane was looking at the Emperor. The dead man at Pertennius's feet. She had a hand on her weeping brother's shoulder, but she released him now, stepped past the two burned men and stopped, a little way down the tunnel, staring at her husband's secretary.

Pertennius wasn't at all sure he owed any answers to an exiled monster like the Calysian, but this did not seem the right context in which to explore that thought. He said, looking at the woman, his employer's wife, 'The Strategos sent me to discover what was detaining the . . . the Emperor. There have come . . . have just come, tidings . . . ' He *never* stammered like this. He took a breath. 'Tidings had just come that he thought the Emperor should know.'

The Emperor was dead.

'How did you get in?' Styliane this time, same question. Her expression was odd. Unfocused. Looking at him, but not really. She didn't like him. Pertennius knew that. She didn't like anyone, though, so it hadn't much mattered.

He cleared his throat again, smoothed the front of his tunic. 'I have, happen to have some keys? That . . . open locks.'

'Of course you do,' said Styliane quietly. He knew her irony well, the bite of it, but there was something bloodless, perfunctory about her tone this time. She was looking down again, at the dead man. Untidily sprawled. Blood on the mosaic stones.

'There were no guards,' explained Pertennius, though they hadn't asked. 'No one in the corridor outside. There . . . should have been. I thought . . . '

'You thought something might be happening and you wanted to see it.' Lysippus. The distinctive, clipped tones. He smiled, the folds of his face shifting. 'Well, you did see, didn't you? What now, historian?'

Historian. There was blood on his blade. Mockery in the Calysian's tone. Smell of meat. The woman looked at him again, waiting.

And Pertennius of Eubulus, gazing back at her, not at Lysippus, did the simplest thing. He knelt, very near the body of the anointed Emperor he'd loathed and had killed, and, setting his dagger down, he said softly, 'My lady, what is it you wish me to tell the Strategos?'

She let out a breath. To the secretary, watching her narrowly, she seemed to have become hollowed out, a figure without force or intensity. It . . . interested him.

She didn't even answer. Her brother did, lifting his hideous face. 'I killed him,' Lecanus Daleinus said. 'By myself. My younger brother and sister . . . came and . . . killed me for it. So virtuous! Report it so . . . secretary. Record it.' The whistle in his voice became more pronounced than ever. 'Record it . . . during the reign . . . of the Emperor Leontes and his glorious Empress . . . and of the Daleinus . . . children . . . who will follow!'

A moment passed, another. And then Pertennius smiled. He understood, and it was all as it *should* be. At last. The Trakesian peasant was dead. The whore was or would be. The Empire was turning back—finally—to a proper place.

'I shall,' he said. 'Believe me, I shall.'

'Lecanus?' It was Lysippus again. 'You promised! You did

promise me.' There was desire in his voice, unmistakable, the tone raw with need.

'The Trakesian first, then me,' said Lecanus Daleinus.

'Of course,' said Lysippus, eagerly. 'Of course, Lecanus.' He was bowing and jerking, Pertennius saw, the gross body moving with urgency, hunger, like spasms of faith or desire.

'Holy Jad! I'm leaving,' said Tertius, hastily. His sister moved aside as the youngest Daleinus went hurriedly back along the tunnel, almost running. She didn't follow, turning instead to look at her ruined brother, and at the Calysian, who was breathing rapidly, his mouth open. She bent down and said something then, softly, to Lecanus. Pertennius didn't hear what it was. He hated that. The brother made no reply.

Pertennius lingered long enough to see the blind man extend the nozzle and trigger and observe how the Calysian trembled as he untied Daleinus's maimed hands from them. Then he felt a sickness coming. He reclaimed and sheathed his knife and then he, too, went quickly back towards the door he had unlocked. He didn't look back.

He wasn't going to record this, anyhow. It had never *happened*, wasn't a part of history, he didn't need to watch, he told himself. Only the things written down mattered.

Somewhere men were racing horses, ploughing fields, children were playing, or crying, or labouring at hard tasks in the world. Ships were sailing. It was raining, snowing, sand blew in a desert, food and drink were being taken, jests made, oaths uttered, in piety or rage. Money changed hands. A woman cried a name behind shutters. Prayers were spoken in chapels and forests and before sacred, guarded flames. A dolphin leaped in the blue sea. A man laid tesserae upon a wall. A pitcher broke on a well rim, a servant knew she would be beaten for it. Men were losing and winning at dice, at love, at war. Cheiromancers prepared tablets that besought yearning or fertility or extravagant wealth. Or death for someone desperately hated for longer than one could ever say.

Pertennius of Eubulus, leaving the tunnel, felt another rush of wet, distant heat, but heard no scream this time.

He came out into the lower part of the Attenine Palace again, below ground. A wide staircase led up, the corridor ran both ways to other hallways, other stairs. No guards. No one at all. Tertius Daleinus had already run upstairs. Somewhere. A trivial, meaningless man, Pertennius thought. Not a thought to be written now, of course, or not in any . . . public document.

He took a breath, smoothed his tunic, and prepared to go up, outside, and back across the gardens, and then down in the other palace to tell Leontes what had happened.

It proved unnecessary, that walk.

He heard a clatter of sound from above and looked up, just as, from behind him in the tunnel, there came a muffled, distant cry, and a last blast of heat came down, all the way to the hallway where he stood alone.

He didn't look back. He looked up. Leontes descended the stairs, moving briskly as he always did, soldiers behind him, as there always were.

'Pertennius! What in the god's holy name is keeping you, man? Where's the Emperor? Why is the door . . . *where are the guards*?'

Pertennius swallowed hard. Smoothed his tunic. 'My lord,' he said, 'something terrible has happened.'

'What? In there?' The Strategos stopped.

'My lord, do not go in. It is . . . terrible.' Which was nothing but truth.

And generated the predictable response. Leontes glanced at his guards. 'Wait here.' The golden-haired leader of the Sarantine armies went into the tunnel.

So, of course, Pertennius had to go back in. This might never be recorded, either, but it was impossible for a chronicler not to be present for what would happen now. He closed the door carefully behind him.

Leontes moved quickly. By the time Pertennius had retraced his steps down the tunnel and come to the curve again, the Strategos was on his knees beside the blackened body of his Emperor.

There was a span of time wherein no one moved. Then Leontes reached to the clasp at his throat, undid it, swept off his dark blue cloak and laid it gently over the body of the dead man. He looked up.

Pertennius was behind him, couldn't see his expression. The smell of burnt flesh was very bad. Ahead of them, motionless, stood the other two living people in this place. Pertennius stayed where he was, at the curve of the tunnel, half hidden against the wall.

He saw the Strategos stand. Saw Styliane facing him, her head high. Beside her, Lysippus the Calysian seemed to become aware that he was still holding the nozzle of the fire device. He let it fall. His face was strange now, too. There were three dead bodies beside him, all charred and black. The two guards. And Lecanus Daleinus, who had first burned all those years ago, with his father.

Leontes said nothing. Very slowly he moved forward. Stood before his wife and the Calysian.

'What are you doing here?' he said. To Lysippus.

Styliane was as ice, as marble. Pertennius saw the Calysian looking at the Strategos as though unsure where he'd come from. 'What does it look like?' he said. A memorable voice. 'I'm admiring the floor mosaics.'

Leontes, commander of the armies of Sarantium, was a different sort of man than the dead Emperor behind him. He drew his sword. A gesture repeated more times than could ever be numbered. Without speaking again he drove the blade through flesh and into the heart of the man standing beside his wife.

Lysippus never even moved, had no chance to defend himself. Pertennius, coming forward a step, unable to hold back, saw the astonishment in the Calysian's eyes before the blade was pulled out, hard, and he fell, thunderously.

The echoes of that took time to die away. Amid a stench of meat and the bodies of five dead men now, a husband and a wife faced each other underground and Pertennius shivered, watching them.

'Why did you do that?' said Styliane Daleina.

The slap took her across the face, a soldier's blow. Her head snapped to one side.

'Be brief, and precise,' said her husband. 'Who did this?'

Styliane didn't even bring a hand up to touch her cheek. She looked at her husband. She had been ready to be burned alive, the secretary remembered, only moments ago. There was no fear in her, not the least hint of it.

'My brother,' she said. 'Lecanus. He has taken his revenge for our father. He sent word to me this morning that he was coming here. Had obviously bribed his guards on the island, and through them the Excubitors at the doors here.'

'And you came?'

'Of course I came. Too late to stop it. The Emperor was dead, and the two soldiers. And the Calysian had already killed Lecanus.'

The lies, so effortless, so necessary. The words that might make this work, for all of them.

She said, 'My brother is dead.'

'Rot his evil soul,' said her husband flatly. 'What was the Calysian doing here?'

'A good question to ask him,' Styliane said. The left side of her face was red where he'd hit her. 'We might have an answer had someone not blundered in waving a sword.'

'Careful, wife. I still have the sword. You are a Daleinus, and by your own statement your family has just murdered our holy Emperor.'

'Yes, husband,' she said. 'They have. Will you kill me now, my dear?'

Leontes was silent. Looked back, for the first time. Saw Pertennius watching. His expression did not change. He turned to his wife again. 'We are on the very eve of war. Today. It was to be announced today. And now there are tidings that the Bassanids are across the border in the north, breaking the peace. And the Emperor is dead. We have no Emperor, Styliane.'

Styliane Daleina smiled then. Pertennius saw it. A woman so beautiful it could stop your breath. 'We will,' she said. 'We will very soon. My lord.'

And she knelt, exquisite and golden among the blackened bodies of the dead, before her husband.

Pertennius stepped away from the wall and went forward a few steps and did the same, falling to both knees, lowering his head to the floor. There was a long silence in the tunnel.

'Pertennius,' said Leontes, at length, 'there is much to be done. The Senate will have to be called into session. Go to the kathisma in the Hippodrome. Immediately. Tell Bonosus to come back here with you. Do *not* tell him why but make it clear he must come.'

'Yes, my lord.'

Styliane looked at him. She was still on her knees. 'Do you understand? Tell no one what has happened here, or about the Bassanid attack. We *must* have order in the City tonight, to control this.'

'Yes, my lady.'

Leontes looked at her. 'The army is here. It will not be the same as . . . the last time there was no heir.'

His wife looked back at him, and then at her brother, beside her on the ground.

'No,' she said. 'Not the same.' And then she said it again, 'Not the same.'

Pertennius saw the Strategos reach out then and help her to rise. His hand went to her bruised cheek, gently this time. She did not move, but her eyes were on his. They were so golden, the two of them, Pertennius thought, so tall. His heart was swelling.

He stood and turned and went. He had orders to obey.

He entirely forgot there was blood on his dagger, neglected to clean it all that day, but no one paid any attention to him so it didn't matter.

He was so seldom noticed; an historian, a recorder of events, hovering and grey, present everywhere, but not ever someone who ever played any kind of *role* in events.

Going up the stairs swiftly, then hurrying through the palace towards an upper staircase and the enclosed walkway that led to the rear of the kathisma, he was already casting his mind after phrasings, a way to begin. The proper tone of detachment and reflection at the outset of a chronicle was so important. *Even the most perfunctory study of past events teaches that Jad's just retribution for the godless and evil may be long in coming but . . .*

He stopped abruptly, forcing one of the eunuchs in a corridor to sidestep him quickly. He was wondering where the whore was. She was unlikely—surely—to be in the kathisma, though *that* would have been something to observe. Was she still in her bath in the other palace, naked and slippery with a soldier? He smoothed his tunic. Styliane would deal with her, he thought.

We must have order in the City tonight, she had said.

He knew what she meant. How could he not? The last death of an Emperor without a named heir had been Apius's, and in the violence that followed that—in the Hippodrome and the streets and even the Imperial Senate chamber—an ignorant Trakesian peasant had been lifted on a shield, acclaimed by the rabble, robed in porphyry. Order was hugely important now, and calm among the eighty thousand in the Hippodrome.

It crossed his mind that if all went as it should, by the end of this day his own status might rise a great deal. He thought of another woman, then, and smoothed his tunic again.

He was very happy, a rare, almost an unprecedented state for him, as he carried enormous, world-shaking tidings to the kathisma, with blood on the blade in his belt.

The sun was high above the City, past its peak, going down, but that day—and night—had a long way yet to go in Sarantium.

In the tunnel, among the dead, two golden figures stood looking at each other in silence, and then walked slowly out and up the wide stairs, not touching, but side by side.

On the stones behind them, on the mosaic stones under a blue cloak, lay Valerius of Sarantium, the second of that name. His body. What was left of it. His soul was gone, to dolphins, to the god, to wherever souls go.

Somewhere in the world, just then, a longed-for child was born and somewhere a labourer died, leaving a farm grievously undermanned with the spring fields still to be ploughed and the crops all to be planted. A calamity beyond words.

CHAPTER XII

The Imperial boat tacked across the straits—no dolphins to be seen this time—and was docked with flawless expertise by a worried crew. Crispin was not the only one watching the port anxiously during their approach.

Men had been killed on the isle. At least two of the Excubitors' own number were traitors. Daleinus had escaped. The Empress had left them to row back with one man only. Danger was in the brightness of the air.

No one new was waiting for them, however. No enemies, no friends, no one at all. They came into the slip and the dock crew moored them with the ropes and then stood by, waiting for the Empress to descend.

Whatever the shape of the plot unfolding today, Crispin thought, on the isle, in the Imperial Precinct, it had not been so precisely devised as to include the possibility that the Empress might be taking a pleasure cruise with a visiting artisan, to look at dolphins—and visit a prisoner on an island.

Alixana, he thought, could have stayed with them after all to sail home. But then what? Have herself carried in the litter back to the Attenine Palace or the Traversite to inquire if her husband had been attacked or killed yet by Lecanus Daleinus and the suborned Excubitors, and did they have any immediate plans for her?

It was the Excubitors in the plot, he realized, that had made her certain there was a large scheme unfolding here. If the Imperial Guard were being turned, any of them, something deadly and immediate was at work. This was not simply an escape by a prisoner, a flight to freedom.

No, he knew why she'd left her robe on the strand to make her way back in secrecy. He wondered if he'd ever see her again. Or the Emperor. And then he wondered—for he had to—what would happen to him when it was learned, as it surely would be, that he'd made this morning's journey with the Empress across the water. They would ask him what he knew. He didn't know what he would say. He didn't know, yet, who would be asking.

He thought about Styliane then. Remembering what she'd said to him before he'd left her in the night, through a window into the courtyard. *Some events must happen now. I will not say I am sorry. Remember this room, though, Rhodian. Whatever else I do.*

He was not so innocent as to believe that the ruined brother on the isle, even with his bird-soul, had shaped his escape alone. Crispin wondered where his anger was: it had defined him for two years. Anger, he thought, was a luxury of sorts. It offered simplicity. There was nothing simple here. *A thing was done once,* she had said, *and all else follows upon it.*

All else. An empire, a world, all who lived within that world. The shape of the past defining the shape of the present. *I will not say I am sorry.*

He remembered going up the dark stairs, desire running in him like a river. The bitter complexity of her. Remembered it as he would always now remember Alixana, too. Images begetting images. The Empress on the stony beach. *The whore*, Pertennius had called her in his secret papers. Vile things, such hatred. Anger was easier, Crispin thought.

He looked down. The crew on the dock were standing in order, still expecting the Empress to descend. The Excubitors and sailors aboard looked uncertainly at each other and then—it might have been amusing had there been any space for laughter in the world—at Crispin, for guidance. Their leader had gone with the Empress.

Crispin shook his head. 'I have no idea,' he said. 'Go to your posts. Report, I suppose. Whatever you do when . . . this sort of thing happens.' *This sort of thing*. He felt like an idiot. Linon would have told him as much.

Carullus would have known what to say to them. But Crispin was not a soldier. Nor had his father been. Though that hadn't stopped Horius Crispus from dying in battle, had it? Styliane's father had burned. That abomination on the isle had been handsome once, and proud. Crispin thought of the god's image on the dome in Sauradia, his face grey, his fingers broken in the struggle against evil.

And he was falling, piece by piece.

They lowered the wide plank to the dock. They didn't unroll the carpet. The Empress was not here. Crispin went down and away from all of them amid the bustle of a harbour preparing for war, and no one stopped him, no one even noted his passing.

In the distance as he walked from the sea he could hear a roaring sound. The Hippodrome. Men and women watching horses run for their delight. There was a sickness within him, a black foreboding in the day. *Some events must happen now.*

He had no idea where to go, what to do. The taverns would be quiet, with so many at the Hippodrome, but he didn't want to sit somewhere and get drunk. Yet. With the chariots running, Carullus wouldn't be at home, he thought, nor would Shirin. Artibasos would be in the Sanctuary, and so would Pardos and Vargos, almost certainly. He could go to work. He could always do that. He *had* been working this morning when she'd come for him. He'd been trying to summon the distance and the clarity to render his daughters on the dome, that they might be there for as near to forever as an artisan could dream of achieving.

He didn't have any of it now. Not the girls, or distance or clarity. Not even the simplicity of anger any more. For the first time Crispin could remember, the thought of going up and absorbing himself in craft repelled him. He had seen men die this morning, had struck a blow himself. Going up the ladder now would be . . . a coward's retreat. And he would badly mar whatever work he tried to do today.

Another huge roar from the Hippodrome. He was walking that way. Entered into the Hippodrome Forum, saw the vast bulk of the building, the Sanctuary across the way, the statue of the first Valerius and the Bronze Gates beyond it, leading into the Imperial Precinct.

Events were happening there now, or had already happened. He looked at those gates, standing very still in a huge space. Imagined walking up and seeking admittance. An urgent need to speak to the Emperor. About some aspect of his dome, colour choices, the angle of tesserae. Could he be announced and presented?

Crispin became aware that his mouth was very dry and his heart was hammering painfully. He was a Rhodian, from a fallen, conquered land, one that Valerius was proposing to visit again with devastating war. He'd sent messages home, to his mother, his friends, knowing they would mean nothing, could achieve nothing.

He ought to hate the man who was readying this fleet, these soldiers. Instead, he was remembering Valerius one night in the Sanctuary, running his hand through the hair of a rumpled architect, like a mother, telling him—ordering him—to go home and sleep.

Were the Antae *better* than what Sarantium might bring to the peninsula? Especially the Antae as they would be now, civil war savagely portended. There were more deaths coming, whether Valerius's army sailed or not.

And assassination attempts were not confined to barbarians like the Antae, Crispin thought, looking at the proud glory of those bronze gates. He wondered if Valerius was dead; thought again of Alixana. On the beach just now, the surf-washed stones: *When your wife died . . . how did you go on living?*

How had she known to ask that?

He ought not to care so much. He ought to still be a stranger here, detached from these glittering, deadly figures and whatever was happening today. These people—women and men—were so far beyond him they moved through an entirely different space in Jad's creation. He was an artisan. A layer of glass and stone. Whoever ruled, he had told Martinian once, in his anger, there would be work for mosaicists, why should they be concerned with what intrigues happened in palaces?

He was marginal, incidental . . . and burdened with

images. He looked at the Bronze Gates, still hesitating, still imagining an approach, but then he turned away.

He went to a chapel. Randomly chosen, the first one he came to along a lane running down and east. Not a street he knew. The chapel was small, quiet, nearly empty, a handful of women, mostly older, shapes in shadow, murmuring, no cleric at this hour. The chariots taking the people away. An old, old battle. Here the sunlight almost disappeared into a pallid half-light filtering through too-small windows ringing a low dome. No decorations. Mosaics were expensive, so were frescoes. It was obvious no wealthy people attended here, salving their souls with gifts to the clerics. There were lamps suspended from overhead in a single line from altar to doors, a handful of others at the side altars, but only a few of them were lit: they would be frugal with oil, at winter's end.

Crispin stood for a time facing the altar and the disk, and then he knelt—no cushions here—on the hard floor and closed his eyes. Among women at prayer he thought of his mother: small and brave and exquisite, scent of lavender always about her, alone for so long, since his father died. He felt very far away.

Someone rose, signed the disk, and walked out. An old woman, bent with her years. Crispin heard the door open and swing shut behind him. It was very quiet. And then, in that stillness, he heard someone begin to sing.

He looked up. No one else seemed to stir. The voice, delicate and plaintive, was off to his left. He seemed to see a shadowy figure there, at one of the side altars where the lamp was not burning. There were a handful of candles lit by the altar but he couldn't even tell if the singer was a girl or an older woman, the light was so subdued.

He did realize, after a moment, collecting his meander-
ing thoughts, that the voice was singing in Trakesian, which
was entirely strange. The liturgy here was always chanted in
Sarantine.

His command of Trakesian—the old tongue of those
who had ruled much of the world before Rhodias—was
precarious, but as he listened it came to Crispin that what
he was hearing was a lament.

No one else moved. No one entered. He knelt among
praying women in a dim, holy place and listened to a voice
sing of sorrow in a ancient tongue, and it occurred to him
that music was one of the things that had not been in his
life since Ilandra died. Her night songs for the girls had
been for him, as well, listening in the house.

Who knows love?
Who says he knows love?

This singer, a shape and barely that, a voice without a
body, was not singing a Kindath lullaby. She was offering—
Crispin finally understood—an entirely pagan sorrow: the
corn maiden and the antlered god, the Sacrifice and the
Hunted One. In a chapel of Jad. Images that had already
been ancient when Trakesia was great.

Crispin shivered, kneeling on stone. Looked again to his
left, eyes straining to pierce the gloom. Only a shadow.
Candles. Only a voice. No one moved.

And it came to him then, feeling unseen spirits hovering in the dimness, that Valerius the Emperor had been
Petrus of Trakesia before he came south to his uncle from
the northern fields, and that he would have known this
song.

And with that, there came another thought and Crispin closed his eyes again and named himself a fool. For if this were true—and of course it was—then Valerius would also have known *exactly* what the bison in Crispin's sketches for the Sanctuary was. He was from northern Trakesia, the forests and grainlands, places where pagan roots had been in the soil for centuries.

Valerius would have recognized the *zubir* as soon as he'd seen it in the drawings.

And he had said nothing. Had given the sketches to the Eastern Patriarch, had approved them for the dome of his own legacy, his Sanctuary of Jad's Holy Wisdom. Awareness entered Crispin like a wind. Overwhelmed, he pushed his hands through his hair.

What man dared try to reconcile so many things in the span of a single life, he thought. East and west brought together again, north coming down to south, a faction dancer becoming an Empress. The daughter of one's enemy and . . . victim, married to one's own friend and Strategos. The *zubir* of the Aldwood, huge and wild—the *essence* of the wild—on a dome consecrated to Jad in the heart of the triple-walled City.

Valerius. Valerius had tried. There was . . . a pattern here. Crispin felt he could nearly see it, almost understand. He was a maker of patterns himself, working in tesserae and light. The Emperor had worked with human souls and the world.

There was a voice here, mourning.

Shall the maiden never walk the bright fields again,
Her hair as yellow as the grain?
The horns of the god can hold the blue moon.
When the Huntress shoots him he dies.

How can we, the children of time, ever live
If these two must die?
How can we, the children of loss, ever learn
What we may leave behind?

When the sound of roaring is heard in the wood
The children of earth will cry.
When the beast that was roaring comes into the fields
The children of blood must die.

He struggled to understand the Trakesian words, and yet he understood so much, bypassing thought: the way he'd looked up in that chapel in Sauradia on the Day of the Dead and grasped a truth about Jad and the world on the dome. His heart was full, aching. Mysteries swept through him. He felt small, mortal, and alone, pierced by a song as by a sword.

After a time he became aware that the solitary voice had ended. He looked over again. No sign of the singer. No one there. At all. He turned quickly to the doors. No one was walking out. No movement anywhere in the chapel, no footsteps. None of the others in the dim, filtered light had even stirred, during the song or now. As if they hadn't even heard it.

Crispin shivered again, uncontrollably, a feeling of something unseen brushing against him, against his life. His hands were shaking. He stared at them as if they belonged to someone else. Who was it who had sung that lament? What was being mourned with pagan words in a chapel of Jad? He thought of Linon, in grey mist on the cold grass. *Remember me.* Did the half-world linger forever, once you entered it? He didn't know. He didn't know.

He clasped his hands together, staring at them—scratches, cuts, old scars—until they grew steady again. He spoke the Invocation to Jad into shadow and silence and he made the sign of the sun disk and then he asked the god for mercy and for light, for the dead and the living he knew, here and far away. And then he rose and went back out into the day, walking home along streets and lanes, through squares, under covered colonnades, hearing the noise from the Hippodrome behind him as he went—very loud now, something happening. He saw men running, appearing from all directions, carrying sticks and knives. He saw a sword. His heart was still hammering like a drum, painful in his breast.

It was beginning. Or, seen another way, it was ending. He ought not to care so much. He did, though, more than words could tell. It was a truth, not to be denied. But there was no role left for him to play.

He was wrong, in the event.

Shirin was waiting when he arrived at his home. She had Danis about her neck.

———

The riot boiled up with unbelievable speed. One moment the Blues were running their Victory Lap, the next, the screaming had changed, turned ugly, and there was savage violence in the Hippodrome.

Cleander, in the tunnel where Scortius lay, looked back out through the Processional Gates and saw men battling with fists and then knives as the factions fought through the neutral stands to get at each other. People were being trampled in their efforts to get out of the way. He saw someone lifted bodily and thrown through the air, landing on heads several rows below. As he watched, a woman, twisting to get out of the way of a cluster of antagonists, fell to her knees and Cleander imagined—even at this distance and with the uproar all around—that he could hear her screams as they trampled her. People were milling desperately towards the exits in a brutal crush of bodies.

He looked at his stepmother, then at the kathisma at the far end of the long straight. His father was up there, too far away to be of any help to them at all. He didn't even know they'd come today. Cleander drew a deep breath. He took a last quick look at the doctors labouring over the prone body of Scortius and then he left. He took his stepmother gently by the elbow and led her further into the tunnel. She came obediently, saying nothing at all. He knew this place extremely well. They came at length to a small, locked door. Cleander picked the lock (it wasn't difficult, and he'd done it before) and then unhooked the latch and they emerged at the very eastern end of the Hippodrome.

Thenaïs was compliant, eerily detached, seemingly oblivious to the panic all around them. Cleander looked around the corner for her litter, back near the main gates through which they'd entered, but immediately realized there was no point trying to get to it: the fighting had already spilled out of the Hippodrome. The factions were brawling in the forum now. Men were coming, at a run. The noise from inside was huge, ugly. He took his stepmother's elbow again and they started the other way, as quickly as he could make her go.

He had an image in his mind, couldn't shake it: the expression on Astorgus's face when the yellow-clad gate attendant had stepped forward and reported what Cleander himself had seen but had determined not to tell. Astorgus had gone rigid, his face a mask. After a frozen moment, the Blues' factionarius had turned on his heel without a word and gone back out onto the sands.

On the track, the Blues had still been celebrating, the young rider who'd won the race doing victory laps with the two White riders. Scortius had been unconscious in the tunnel. His Bassanid physician, assisted by the Blues' own doctor, desperately trying to stanch the flow of blood and keep him breathing, among the living. They were covered with blood themselves by then.

A few moments later those in the tunnel had heard the cheering in the stands turn to something else, a deep, terrifying sound, and then the fighting had begun. At that point they didn't know why, or what Astorgus had done.

Cleander hurried his stepmother up onto a colonnade, letting a swarm of young men sprint past in the street, shouting, waving cudgels and knives. He saw someone with a sword. Two weeks ago he could have *been* that man, racing towards bloodshed with a weapon in his hand. Now he saw all of them as threats, wild-eyed and uncontrolled. Something had happened to him. He kept a hand on his stepmother's arm.

He heard himself hailed by name. Turned swiftly to the loud voice and felt a surge of relief. It was the soldier, Carullus: the one he'd met in The Spina last autumn, the one whose wedding feast Shirin had just hosted. Carullus had his left arm around his wife and a knife in his right hand. They came quickly up the steps to the colonnade.

'In stride with me, lad,' he said, his manner brisk but entirely calm. 'We'll get the women home so they can have a quiet cup of something warm on a pleasant day in spring. *Isn't* it a beautiful day? I love this time of year.'

Cleander was unspeakably grateful. Carullus was a big, intimidating man, and he moved like a soldier. No one disturbed them as they went, though they saw one man crack a staff over the head of another right beside them in the street. The staff broke; the struck man fell, awkwardly.

Carullus winced. 'Broken neck,' he said matter-of-factly, looking back, keeping them moving. 'He won't get up.'

They came down into the road again at the end of the colonnade. Someone hurled a cookpot from a window overhead, narrowly missing them. Carullus stooped and picked it up. 'A wedding gift! How unexpected! Is this better than the one we have, love?' he asked his wife, grinning.

The woman shook her head, managed a smile. Her eyes were terrified. Carullus tossed the pot over his shoulder. Cleander glanced at his stepmother. No terror there. *Nothing* there. It was as if she hadn't even heard or seen any of this: the arrival of companions, the man struck down—killed—right beside them. She seemed in another world entirely.

They continued without further incident, though the streets were crowded with running, shouting figures and Cleander saw shopkeepers hastily closing their shop fronts and doors, boarding up. They reached their house. The servants were watching for them. Well trained, they had already set about barricading the courtyard gates, and those waiting at the door were holding heavy sticks. This was hardly the first riot in memory.

Cleander's mother entered the house without speaking. She hadn't spoken since they'd left the Hippodrome. Since the race had begun, he suddenly realized. It fell to him to offer thanks to the soldier. He stammered his gratitude, invited them in. Carullus declined with a smile. 'I'd best report to the Strategos, soon as I get my wife home. A small word of advice: stay indoors tonight, lad. The Excubitors will be out, for certain, and not choosing with any great care where they strike in the dark.'

'I will,' said Cleander. He thought about his father, but decided that wasn't a cause of concern: from the kathisma they could get back into the Imperial Precinct. His father could wait there or get a soldiers' escort home. His own duty was to his mother and his sisters here. Keeping them safe.

Dictating his celebrated *Reflections* forty years afterwards, Cleander Bonosus would describe the day the Emperor Valerius II was assassinated by the Daleinoi, the day his own stepmother killed herself in her bath—opening her wrists with a small blade no one knew she had—as the day he became a man. Schoolboys would learn and copy the well-known phrases, or memorize them for recitation: *Just as it is adversity that hardens the spirit of a people, so can adversity strengthen the soul of a man. What we master becomes ours to use.*

─────◆─────

Sorting through complex and sometimes distant events to determine the causes of a riot is not an easy task, but it fell squarely within the responsibilities of the Urban Prefect, under the direction of the Master of Offices, and he was not unfamiliar with the process.

He also had, of course, access to some acknowledged professionals—and their tools—when it came time to ask significant questions.

As it happened, the more rigorous methods were not required (to the disappointment of some) in the case of the riot that occurred on the day the Emperor Valerius II was murdered.

The disturbance in the Hippodrome began *before* anyone knew of that death. This much was certain. It was an attack on a charioteer that started it, and this time the Blues and Greens were not united as they had been two years before in the Victory Riot. Rather the contrary, in fact.

The inquiry established that it was one of the Hippodrome staff who'd revealed that the Blues' champion, Scortius, had been viciously struck by Crescens of the Greens just before the first race of the afternoon. Crescens, apparently, had been the first to note the reappearance of his rival.

The attendant, on duty at the Processional Gates, later swore on oath to what he'd seen. Corroboration was provided, reluctantly, by the young son of Senator Plautus Bonosus. The lad, to his credit, had kept quiet at the time, though he confirmed afterwards that he'd seen Crescens elbow the other driver in what he personally knew to be already broken ribs. He explained his silence at the time by saying that he had a sense of what the consequences of pointing out the incident might be.

The lad was given a formal commendation in the official report. It was regrettable that the Hippodrome staffer had not had as much good sense, but he couldn't actually be *punished* for what he'd done. The race-track staff were supposed to be resolutely neutral, but that was fiction, not reality. The gatekeeper, it emerged, was a partisan of the Blues. Neutrality was not a Sarantine trait in the Hippodrome.

It was established, accordingly, to the Urban Prefect's satisfaction—and so recorded in his report to the Master of Offices—that Crescens of the Greens had delivered what he'd intended to be an unseen assault on the other driver, a wounded man. Clearly, he had been trying to undermine the impact of Scortius's dramatic return.

This afforded a measure of explanation, though hardly a complete mitigation, for what had apparently happened next. Astorgus, the Blues' factionarius, a man of experience and probity, a man who *ought* to have known better, had walked across the sands to the spina, where Crescens was still standing after suffering an unfortunate fall in his last race, and had struck him in the face and body, breaking his nose and dislocating the rider's shoulder in full view of eighty thousand highly excited people.

He'd had provocation, undeniably—was later to say that he believed that Scortius was about to die—but it was still an irresponsible act. If you wanted to have someone beaten, you did it at night, if you had any sense at all.

Crescens wouldn't race again for almost two months, but didn't die. Neither did Scortius.

About three thousand people did go to the god, however, in the Hippodrome and the streets that day and night. Precise numbers were always demanded by the Master of Offices, always difficult to produce. The toll was a significant but not an outrageous number for a riot that included burning and looting after darkfall. Compared to the last major conflagration, where thirty thousand had been slain, this one was a much more trivial event. Some Kindath homes were set afire in their quarter, as usual, and a few foreigners—Bassanid merchants for the most part— were killed, but this latter development was to be expected, given the perfidious breaching of the Eternal Peace that had, by twilight, been reported in the City, along with the death of the Emperor. Frightened people did unpleasant things.

Most of the killings came after dark, when the Excubitors, carrying torches and swords, marched out of the Imperial Precinct to quiet the streets. By then the soldiers were all aware that they had a new Emperor, and that Sarantine territory had been attacked in the northeast. It was undoubtedly an excess of zeal occasioned by these facts that led to some of the civilian fatalities and a few of the Bassanid deaths.

It was hardly worth noting, really. One couldn't expect the army to be patient with brawling civilians. No blame at all was attached to them. Indeed, another commendation was offered to the Count of the Excubitors, for the swift quelling of the night's violence.

Much later, Astorgus and Crescens would both be tried by the judiciary for their assaults: the first prominent trials conducted under the new Imperial regime. Both men behaved themselves with dignity, declaring extreme remorse for their actions. Both would receive reprimands and fines: identical ones, of course. The matter would then be closed. They were important men in the scheme of things. Sarantium needed them both alive and well and at the Hippodrome, keeping the citizens happy.

The last time an Emperor died without an heir, Plautus Bonosus was thinking, there had been a mob smashing on the doors of the Senate Chamber, battering its way in. This time there was a *real* riot outside, and the people in the streets didn't even *know* the Emperor had died. An aphorism in there somewhere, Bonosus thought ironically, a paradox worth recording.

Paradoxes have layers, irony can be double-edged. He didn't yet know of his wife's death.

In the Senate Chambers they were waiting for others of their number to arrive through the unruly streets. The Excubitors were out and about, collecting Senators, escorting them as quickly as possible. Not surprising, that speed. Most of the City was unaware of the Emperor's death, so far. That ignorance wouldn't last long, not in Sarantium, even in the midst of a riot. Perhaps especially, Bonosus thought, reclining in his seat, in the midst of a riot.

Many levels of memory were competing in his mind and he was also trying—unsuccessfully—to come to terms with the fact that Valerius was dead. An Emperor murdered. It hadn't happened in a very long time. Bonosus had known better than to ask questions.

The soldiers had reason to want the Senate assembled expeditiously. Whatever the story of the death of Valerius turned out to be—the exiled Lysippus had been declared to be back in the City, and involved, as was the banished and imprisoned Lecanus Daleinus—there was no real question as to who should succeed the slain Emperor.

Or, putting it a little differently, thought Bonosus, there were reasons for Leontes to proceed swiftly, *before* such questions might arise.

The Supreme Strategos was, after all, married to a Daleinus, and there might be those who took a reflective view of assassinating one's predecessor on the Golden Throne. Especially when the murdered man had been one's own mentor and friend. And when the deed was done on the eve of war. It could be called—by someone *much* more reckless than Plautus Bonosus—a vile and contemptible act of treachery.

Bonosus's thoughts kept whirling about. Too many shocks in one day. The return of Scortius, that astonishing race that had turned from glory into riot in a heartbeat. And then, just as the fighting began, there had been the voice of Leontes's grey secretary in his ear: *'Your presence is immediately requested in the palace.'*

He hadn't said by whom. It didn't matter. Senators did what they were told. Bonosus had risen to go just as he realized something had happened in the spina—he would learn the details afterwards—and he heard a deep-throated roar as the Hippodrome erupted.

He suspected, looking back, that Leontes (or his wife?) had wanted him to come to them alone, as Master of the Senate, to learn the tidings before anyone else did. That would give them time to quietly summon the Senate, control the release of the terrible news.

It didn't work out that way.

As the stands exploded into fury and a rush for the exits, the inhabitants of the Imperial Box rose to their feet and made a collective rush of their own for the doors leading back to the Attenine Palace. Bonosus remembered the expression on the pallid secretary's face: startled and displeased, and afraid.

When Bonosus and Pertennius did make it back through the long walkway to the palace's audience chamber, it was crowded with noisy, frightened courtiers who'd fled the kathisma ahead of them. Others were arriving. In the centre of the room—near the thrones and the silver tree—stood Leontes and Styliane.

The Strategos lifted a hand for silence. Not the Master of Offices, not the Chancellor. Gesius had just entered the room, in fact, through the small door behind the two thrones. He stopped there, brow furrowed in perplexity. In the stillness his gesture shaped it was Leontes, blunt and grave, who said, 'I am sorry, but this must be told. We have lost our father today. Jad's most holy Emperor is dead.'

There was a babble of disbelief. A woman cried out. Someone near Bonosus made the sign of the sun disk, then others did. Someone knelt, then all of them did, the sound like a murmuring of the sea. All of them except Styliane and Leontes. And Gesius, Bonosus saw. The Chancellor didn't looked perplexed now. His expression was otherwise. He put out a hand to steady himself on a table and said, from directly behind those tall, golden figures and the thrones, 'How? How did this happen? And how is it that you know?'

The thin, precise voice cut hard through the room. This was Sarantium. The Imperial Precinct. Not a place where certain things could be easily controlled. Not with so many competing interests and clever men.

And women. It was Styliane who turned to face the Chancellor, Styliane who said, her voice oddly without force—as if she'd just been bled by a physician, Bonosus thought—'He was murdered in the tunnel between palaces. He was burned, by Sarantine Fire.'

Bonosus remembered closing his eyes at that. Past and present coming together so powerfully he felt dizzied. He opened his eyes. Pertennius, kneeling next to him, was white-faced, he saw.

'By whom?' Gesius released the table and took a step forward. He stood alone, a little apart from everyone else. A man who had served three Emperors, survived two successions.

Was unlikely to last through a third, asking these questions in this way. It occurred to the Senator that the aged Chancellor might not care.

Leontes looked at his wife, and again it was Styliane who replied. 'My brother Lecanus. And the exiled Calysian, Lysippus. They seem to have suborned the guards at the tunnel door. And obviously my brother's guards on the isle.'

Another murmuring. Lecanus Daleinus and fire. The past here with them in the room, Bonosus thought.

'I see,' said Gesius, his papery voice so devoid of nuance it was a nuance of its own. 'Just the two of them?'

'So it would seem,' said Leontes, calmly. 'We will need to investigate, of course.'

'Of course,' agreed Gesius, again with nothing to be discerned in his tone. 'So good of you to point that out, Strategos. We might have neglected to think of it. I imagine the Lady Styliane was alerted by her brother of his evil intent and arrived tragically too late to forestall them?'

There was a small silence. Too many people were hearing this, Bonosus thought. It would be all over the City before sunset. And there was already violence in Sarantium. He felt afraid.

The Emperor was dead.

'The Chancellor is, as ever, wisest of us,' said Styliane quietly. 'It is as he says. I beg you to imagine my grief and shame. My brother was also dead, by the time we arrived. And the Strategos killed Lysippus when we saw him there, standing over the bodies.'

'Killed him,' Gesius murmured. He smiled thinly, a man infinitely versed in the ways of a court. 'Indeed. And the soldiers you mentioned?'

'Were already burned,' Leontes said.

Gesius said nothing this time, only smiled again, allowing silence to speak for him. Someone was weeping in the crowded chamber.

'We must take action. There is rioting in the Hippo-drome,' Faustinus said. The Master of Offices finally assert-ing himself. He was rigid with tension, Bonosus saw. 'And what about the announcement of the war?'

'There will be no announcement now,' said Leontes flatly. Calm, assured. A leader of men. 'And the rioting is not a cause for concern.'

'It isn't? Why not?' Faustinus eyed him.

'Because the army is here,' Leontes murmured, and looked slowly around the chamber at the assembled court.

It was in that moment, Bonosus thought afterwards, that he himself had begun to see this differently. The Daleinoi might have planned an assassination for their own reasons. He didn't believe for a moment that Styliane had arrived too late at that tunnel, that her blind, maimed brother had been able to plan and execute this from his island. Sarantine Fire spoke to vengeance, more than anything else. But if the Daleinus children had also assumed that Styliane's sol-dier husband would be a useful figure on the throne, a gateway for their own ambition . . . Bonosus decided they might have been wrong.

He watched Styliane turn to the tall man she'd married on Valerius's orders. He was an observant man, Plautus Bonosus, had spent years reading small signals, especially at court. She was arriving, he decided, at the same conclusion he was.

The army is here. Four words, with a world of meaning. An army could quell a civilian riot. Obvious. But there was more. The armies had been two weeks away and divided among leaders when Apius died without an heir. They were right here now, massed in and all about the City, preparing to sail west.

And the man speaking of them, the man standing golden before the Golden Throne, was their dearly beloved Strategos. The army was here, and his, and the army would decide.

'I will attend to the Emperor's body,' said Gesius very softly. Heads turned back to him. 'Someone should,' he added, and went out.

Before nightfall that day the Senate of Sarantium had been called into imperative session in its handsome, domed chamber. They accepted formal tidings from the Urban Prefect, clad in black, speaking nervously, of the untimely death of Jad's most dearly beloved, Valerius II. A show-of-palms vote led to a resolution that the Urban Prefect, in conjunction with the Master of Offices, would conduct a full investigation into the circumstances of what appeared to be a foul assassination.

The Urban Prefect bowed his acceptance and left.

Amid noises of clashing weapons and shouting in the street outside, Plautus Bonosus spoke the formal words that convened the Senate to use its collective wisdom in choosing a successor for the Golden Throne.

Three submissions were made to them from the mosaic star on the floor in the midst of their circle of seats. The Quaestor of the Sacred Palace spoke, then the principal adviser to the Eastern Patriarch, and finally Auxilius, Count of the Excubitors, a small, dark, intense man: he had broken the Victory Riot two years ago, with Leontes. All three speakers urged the Senate, with varying degrees of eloquence, to choose the same man.

After they were done, Bonosus asked for further submissions from guests. There were none. He then invited his colleagues to make their own speeches and remarks. No one did. One Senator proposed that an immediate vote be taken. They heard a renewed sound of fighting just beyond their doors.

With no one displaying any sign of disagreement to this proposition, a vote was, accordingly, proposed by Bonosus. The pebbles were distributed in pairs to all present: white meaning agreement with the only name put forward, black indicating a desire for further deliberation and other candidates to be considered.

The motion passed, forty-nine Senators approving, one electing to demur. Auxilius, who had lingered in the visitors' gallery, hastily left the chamber.

As a consequence of this formal vote, Plautus Bonosus instructed the senatorial clerks to draw up a document under seal indicating that the august body of the Sarantine Senate was of the view that the successor to the lamented Valerius II, Jad's Holy Emperor, regent of the god upon earth, ought to be Leontes, currently serving with honour as Supreme Strategos of the Sarantine army. The clerks were instructed to express the collective and fervent hope of the Senate that his would be a reign blessed by the god with glory and good fortune.

The Senate adjourned.

That same night, in the Imperial Chapel inside the walls of the Precinct, Leontes, often called 'the Golden,' was anointed Emperor by the Eastern Patriarch. Saranios had built that chapel. His bones lay within.

It was decided that if the City grew quiet overnight there would be a public ceremony in the Hippodrome the next afternoon, to crown both the Emperor and his Empress. There always was. The people needed to see.

Plautus Bonosus, escorted home that night by a contingent of Excubitors, fingered the unused white pebble in his pocket. On reflection, he cast it away into the darkness.

The streets were indeed much calmer by then. The fires had been put out. Contingents of the army had been sent up from the harbour at sundown and from the temporary barracks outside the walls. The presence of heavily armed soldiers, marching in order, had ended the violence very smoothly. It had *all* gone smoothly today, Bonosus thought. Not like the last time there had been no heir. He was trying to understand why he felt so much bitterness. It wasn't as if there was anyone else more suited to the porphyry robes of Empire than Leontes. That wasn't the point though. Or was it?

The soldiers were still moving through the streets in tightly banded, efficient clusters. He couldn't remember ever seeing the army making itself so obvious within the City. Walking with his escort (he had declined a litter) he saw that the patrols were knocking on doors, entering houses.

He knew why. There was a heavy feeling in the pit of his stomach. He'd been trying to suppress certain thoughts, but not very successfully. He understood too well what was taking place. This happened, it *had* to happen, whenever a violent change of this sort occurred. Valerius, unlike Apius before him, or his own uncle, had not passed to the god in peace, in old age, to lie serenely in state in the Porphyry Room robed for his passage. He had been murdered. Certain things—certain other deaths, if Bonosus was honest with himself—would have to follow upon that.

One, in particular.

And so, these soldiers, spreading through the City with their torches, combing the the lanes and alleys near the harbour, porticoes of the wealthy, warrens within the Hippodrome, chapels, taverns, cauponae (even though those were closed by order tonight), inns and guildhouses and workshops, bakeries and brothels, probably even down into the cisterns . . . and entering citizens' homes in the night. The heavy knock on the door in the dark.

Someone had disappeared, needed to be found.

Nearing his own doorway, Bonosus saw that the house was properly barricaded against a riot. The leader of his escort knocked, politely in this case, and declared their identity.

Locks were unbolted. The door was opened. Bonosus saw his son. Cleander was weeping, his eyes swollen and red. Bonosus, with no premonition at all, asked him why, and Cleander told him.

Bonosus went into his house. Cleander thanked the guards and they went away. He closed the door. Bonosus sat down heavily on a bench in the hallway. His whirling thoughts were stilled. He had no thoughts at all. An emptiness.

Emperors died, before their time. So did others. So did others. The world was what it was.

'There's a riot in the Hippodrome. And there was another bird in the City today!' Shirin said urgently, as soon as Crispin entered his house and saw her waiting in the front room, pacing before the fire. She was agitated: had spoken the words with a servant still in the hallway.

'Another bird!' Danis echoed, silently, almost as upset. *Mice and blood*, Linon would have said. And called him an imbecile for walking the streets alone just now.

Crispin took a deep breath. The half-world. Did you ever leave it, once you entered? Did it ever leave you?

'I know about the fighting,' he said. 'It is in the streets now.' He turned and dismissed the servant. Then registered something. 'You said a bird *was* here. Not any more?'

'I don't feel it now,' Danis said in his mind. *'It was here, and then it was . . . gone.'*

'Gone away? From the City?'

He could see the anxiety in the woman, feel it coming from the bird.

'More than that, I think. I think it is . . . gone. It didn't fade. It was just there and then, not there?'

Crispin needed wine. He saw Shirin looking at him closely. The clever, observant gaze. All flash and play removed from her now.

'You know about this,' she said. Not a question. Zoticus's daughter. 'You don't seem . . . surprised.'

He nodded. 'I know something. Not very much.'

She looked pale and cold, even near the fire. She said, hugging herself with her hands, 'I had two separate messages, two of my . . . informants. They both say the Senate is being summoned. They also say . . . they say that the Emperor may be dead.' He wasn't sure, but he thought she might have been crying. It was Danis he heard next, in silence:

'They said he was murdered.'

Crispin took a breath. He could feel his heart beating, still too fast. He looked at Shirin, slender, graceful, afraid. He said, 'I suspect . . . that might be true.'

When the Huntress shoots him he dies.

There was more sorrow in him than he would ever have expected.

She bit her lip. 'The bird? That Danis felt? She said it was . . . a bad presence.'

No reason, really, not to say this much. Not to her. She was here with him, in the half-world. Her father had drawn them both into it. 'It belonged to Lecanus Daleinus. Who escaped his prison today and came here.'

Shirin sat down suddenly, on the nearest bench. Still hugging herself. She was very white. 'The blind one? The burned . . . ? He left the isle?'

'Had help, obviously.'

'From?'

Crispin drew another breath. 'Shirin. My dear. If your tidings are true and Valerius is dead, there are going to be questions asked of me. Because of where I was this morning. You are . . . better off not knowing. Can say you *don't* know. That I refused to tell.'

Her expression changed. '*You* were on that island? Oh, Jad! Crispin, they will . . . you aren't going to be stupid are you?'

He managed a faint smile. 'For a change, you mean?'

She shook her head fiercely. 'No jesting. At all! If the Daleinoi have killed Valerius, they will be . . . ' He saw something else occur to her. 'Where is Alixana? If they killed Valerius . . . '

She let the thought hang in the air and fade away. Men and women lived, died. Faded away. He didn't know what to say. What he could say. A robe discarded on a stony strand. They would find it. Might even have done so by now. *Shall the maiden never walk the bright fields again?*

'You had better stay here tonight,' he said, finally. 'The streets will be dangerous. You shouldn't have come out, you know.'

She nodded. 'I know.' And then, after a moment, 'Have you any wine?'

A blessedly clever woman. He gave an order to the servant, for wine and water and for food. The eunuchs had staffed this house for him. His people were very good. In the late-afternoon streets outside there was fighting. Soldiers were assembling Senators, escorting them to the Senate Chamber and then returning to the streets to achieve order in a dangerous time.

Not long after darkfall they had done so, and had set about their other task.

When the hard knocking came at his door Crispin was waiting for it. He had left Shirin for long enough to wash and change his clothing: he had still been wearing the nondescript tunic he'd donned for work, the one he'd been wearing on the isle. He put on his best tunic and trousers now, with a leather belt, not at all certain why he was doing so. He went to answer the knocking himself, nodding for the servant to stand back. He swung the door open, was briefly blinded by torches.

'Shall I hit you with my helmet?' Carullus asked, on the threshold.

Memory. Relief. And then swift sorrow: loyalties so hopelessly entangled here. He couldn't even sort out his own. He knew that Carullus must have specifically asked to lead this detail to his door. He wondered who had granted that approval. Where Styliane was, just now.

'Your wife,' he said calmly, 'would probably be upset if you did. She was the last time, remember?'

'Believe me, I remember.' Carullus stepped inside. Spoke a word to his men and they waited on the threshold. 'We're doing a search of the entire city. Every house, not just yours.'

'Oh. Why would mine have been singled out?'

'Because you were with the Emp . . . with Alixana this morning.'

Crispin looked at his friend. Saw worry in the big man's eyes, but also something else: an undeniable excitement. Dramatic times, the most dramatic imaginable, and he was one of Leontes's own guard now.

'I was with the Empress.' Crispin emphasized the word, aware he was being perverse. 'She took me to see dolphins, and then to the prison isle. We saw Lecanus Daleinus in the morning and when we came back, after a meal elsewhere, he was gone. Two of the guards on duty were dead. The Empress went away with one soldier alone. Didn't come back on the ship. They will know all that in the palace by now. What has happened, Carullus?'

'Dolphins?' said other man, as if nothing else had registered.

'Dolphins. For a mosaic.'

'They're heresy. Forbidden.'

'Will she be burned for it?' Crispin asked coldly. Couldn't help but ask.

He saw his friend's eyes flicker.

'Don't be an idiot. What has happened?' Crispin said. 'Tell me.'

Carullus stepped past him into the front room, saw Shirin there, by the fire. He blinked.

'Good evening, soldier,' she murmured. 'I haven't seen you since your wedding. Are you well? And Kasia?'

'I . . . yes, um, yes, we are. Thank you.' Carullus stammered, for once at a loss for words.

'I have been told that the Emperor was killed today,' she said, giving him no respite. 'Is it true? Tell me it isn't.'

Carullus hesitated, then he shook his head. 'I wish I could. He was burned in a tunnel between palaces. By Lecanus Daleinus, who did indeed escape the isle today. And by Lysippus, the Calysian, who was exiled, as you know, but slipped secretly back into the city.'

'No one else?'

'Two . . . Excubitors were also there.' Carullus looked uncomfortable.

'A vast plot, then. Those four?' Shirin's expression was guileless. 'Are we safe now? I heard the Senate was sitting.'

'You are well informed, my lady. They were.'

'And?' Crispin asked.

'They have adjourned for the night. Leontes was named by them and is being anointed Emperor tonight. It will be announced tomorrow morning, with his coronation and that of the new Empress in the kathisma.'

That note again, an excitement the man could not suppress. Carullus loved Leontes, and Crispin knew it. The Strategos had even come to his wedding, promoted him there in person, and had then appointed him to his personal guard.

'Meanwhile,' said Crispin, not fighting the bitterness, 'all the soldiers in Sarantium are hunting for the old Empress.'

Carullus looked at him. 'Please tell me you don't know where she is, my friend.'

There was something painful lodged in Crispin's breast, like a stone.

'I don't know where she is, my friend.'

They stared at each other in silence.

'She says to be careful. And to be fair.'

Crispin wanted to snarl an oath. He did not. Danis was right, or Shirin was. He gestured with one hand. 'Search the house, have them search.'

Carullus cleared his throat and nodded. Crispin looked at him, then added, 'And thank you for doing this yourself. Do you need me to come somewhere for questioning?'

'*Not that fair!*' Danis exclaimed sharply.

Carullus hesitated another moment, then shook his head. He returned to the hallway and opened the outside door. They heard him giving orders. Six men came in. Two went upstairs, the others went towards the back, on the ground floor.

Carullus came back into the front room. 'You might be questioned later. I have no orders about that now. You went to the isle with her, saw Lecanus, then he was gone, and then she left. How?'

'I told you. With one Excubitor. I don't know his name. I don't even know that she left. She may still be on the isle, Carullus. They will kill her when they find her, won't they?'

His friend swallowed. Looked quite miserable.

'I have no idea,' he said.

'Of course you do,' Shirin snapped. 'It just isn't your *fault*, you want to say. Or Leontes's, of course. Nothing's his fault.'

'I don't . . . I truly don't think he had anything to do with this,' the big soldier said.

Crispin looked at the other man. His closest friend here. Kasia's husband. As honest and decent a person as he knew. 'No, I don't think he knew anything about it.'

'Poor helpless man. It must have been Styliane, then,' said Shirin, still furious. 'She *is* the Daleinoi in our day. One brother blind and imprisoned, the other a complete fool.'

Crispin looked at her. So did Carullus. The two men exchanged glances. Crispin said, 'My dear, please leave that thought in this room. You told me not to be stupid, earlier. Let me say the same to you.'

'He's right,' Carullus said soberly.

Jad rot you both! Danis said in silence, and Crispin heard the pain in the bird that could not be spoken by the woman.

'We are all unhappy tonight,' Carullus added. 'These are not easy times.'

'Unhappy? I could laugh! The man is in his glory!' Danis said, with a savagery unknown for her.

It wasn't true, or not entirely true, but Crispin had no way to say so aloud. He looked at Shirin, and belatedly, in the lamplight, he realized that she was weeping.

'You will hunt her down like some beast,' she said bitterly. 'All of you. An army of soldiers after one woman whose husband has just been killed, whose life died with him. And then what? Send her back to a hovel in the Hippodrome? Make her dance naked for their amusement? Or are you to quietly kill her when you find her? Spare poor, virtuous Leontes the details?'

It was a woman speaking, and a performer, Crispin understood finally. Fear and this unexpected depth of rage, thinking of the other dancer who had defined, for all of them, the City and the world.

But even here there were layers, because if Leontes was oblivious to what had happened, Styliane was not. It wasn't just about men pursuing a helpless woman. It was also about two women at war, and only one of them could live now.

'I don't *know* what they will do,' said Carullus, and even Shirin, lifting her face, not hiding her tears, had to have heard the distress in his voice.

There were footsteps. A soldier at the arched entrance to the room. He reported no one hiding in the house or the courtyard within. The others filed past him and outside again.

Carullus looked at Crispin. Seemed about to say something more but did not. He turned to Shirin. 'May we escort you home, my lady?'

'No,' she said.

He swallowed. 'There are orders, everyone to remain inside. There are many soldiers in the streets . . . some of them . . . unused to the city. It will be safer if—'

'No,' she said.

Carullus stopped. After another moment he bowed to her and left the room.

Crispin walked him to the door. Carullus stopped there. 'They are . . . anxious to find her tonight, as you say. There will be some unpleasantness, I suspect, as they search.'

Crispin nodded. *Unpleasantness.* A courtier's masking word. Changes were taking place, even as the night passed, the moons rose. But none of this was Carullus's fault. 'I . . . understand. I am grateful that it was you at my door. Jad guard you.'

'And you, my friend. Stay inside.'

'I will.'

He had truly intended to. Who can know what will come, however, overtaking a life?

Last autumn, at home, it had been an Imperial Courier bearing a summons to Sarantium. Tonight it was something else, but still a summons, for there came another knocking, a quieter one, not long after the soldiers left.

Crispin answered it himself again. No flaring of torches this time, no sight of armed men. This was someone cloaked and hooded, and alone. A woman, breathless with running and fear. She asked his name. He gave it, without thinking, stepped aside, she entered, hurriedly, a glance over her shoulder into the night. He closed the door. In the entrance to his home, she wordlessly extended a written note, and then fumbled in her cloak and produced a ring.

He took both. Her hands were trembling. He recognized the ring, and felt his heart thump once, very hard.

He had forgotten someone.

The sealed note, when torn open, contained a command, not a request, and from someone whom—as he stood there, and felt his heart begin to beat properly again—Crispin realized he did have a duty to obey, however bitter the confusions and torn loyalties shaping a terrible day and night.

It also meant going out into the streets again.

Shirin appeared in the arched doorway.

'What is it?'

He told her. He wasn't sure why, but he told her.

'I'm taking you,' she said.

He tried to say no. A waste of time.

She had a litter and guards, she pointed out. Was known, had the protection that came with that. Could plausibly be heading home with a friend, even with the streets forbidden. He didn't have the force to refuse her. What was she going to do? Stay in his house while he went out?

Shirin had a two-person litter. Crispin ordered the messenger to be attended to, given food, a bed for the night if she wanted. The woman's eyes betrayed her relief: she'd clearly been terrified she'd have to go back out. Crispin put on his own cloak and then, Shirin beside him, opened the door, waiting for a moment when the street was quiet before they stepped out. The darkness was laden with aura and menace, clear as the stars, heavy as the weight of earth on the dead. Valerius had died in a tunnel, Carullus had said.

Her litter-bearers came for them from the shadows at the end of the portico. Shirin gave them instructions to take her home. They started down the street. Peering through the drawn curtains as they moved, they both saw the strange, small flames flitting at corners, unlit by any visible source, darting and vanishing. Souls, spirits, echoes of Heladikos's fire, inexplicable.

But one always saw those flames in Sarantium at night.

What was new were the noises, and the torches everywhere, smoking, casting orange, erratic light. From all around came the sound of booted feet. Running, not marching. A sense of speed, urgency, the night spinning with it. A banging upon doors, shouted commands to open. Searchers. For one woman. They heard two horses gallop past, orders barked, curses. It occurred to Crispin suddenly that most of these soldiers wouldn't have the least idea what Alixana looked like. He thought again of the Imperial robe, discarded on the island. She wasn't about to be adorned and garbed like an Empress. It wouldn't be so easy to find her: unless she was betrayed. That, of course, was a possibility.

They made no attempt at concealment as they went, were stopped twice. The Urban Prefect's men both times, which was fortunate, for these troops knew the Principal Dancer of the Greens immediately, and they were allowed to continue on their way to her house.

They didn't go to her house. As they neared her street, Shirin leaned out and changed her orders, instructing her bearers to continue east, towards the walls. From here on the danger grew, was real, for she couldn't claim to be going home now, but they were not stopped again. The search hadn't come this far yet, it seemed; it was fanning out from the Imperial Precinct and up from the harbour, house to house, street to street in the dark.

In time, they came to a dwelling, not far from the triple walls. Shirin ordered the bearers to stop. In the litter there was a silence.

'Thank you,' Crispin said, at length. She stared at him. Danis was silent, on the chain about her throat.

He got out. Looked at the closed doorway in front of him, and then up at the night stars. Then he turned back to her. She still hadn't spoken. He leaned into the litter and kissed her gently on the lips. He remembered the first day they'd met, that passionate embrace in the doorway, Danis protesting urgently, Pertennius of Eubulus appearing behind her.

There was a man who would be happy tonight, Crispin thought suddenly, with bitterness.

Then he turned away and knocked—one more knocking in Sarantium that night—on the door of the person who had summoned him. A servant opened instantly; had been waiting, he realized. He went in.

The servant gestured nervously. Crispin stepped forward.

The queen of the Antae was waiting in the first room on the right, branching off the hallway.

He saw her standing before the fire, glittering, jewellery at ears and throat and on her fingers and in her hair, garbed in a silken robe of porphyry and gold. Purple, for royalty tonight. Tall and fair and . . . entirely, dazzlingly regal. There was a fierce brilliance to her, a kind of shining like the jewels she wore. It caught at your breath to look at her. Crispin bowed, and then, a little bit overwhelmed, he knelt on the wooden floor.

'No flour sack this time, artisan. I'm using gentler methods, you see.'

'I am grateful, my lady.' He could think of nothing else to say. She had seemed able to read his thoughts back then, too.

'They say the Emperor is dead.' Direct, as always. Antae, not Sarantine. A different world. West for east, forest and field by origin, not these triple walls and gates of bronze and golden trees in the palaces. 'Is it true? Valerius is dead?'

This was his own queen asking. 'I believe he is,' he said, clearing his throat. 'I have no actual—'

'Murdered?'

Crispin swallowed. Nodded.

'The Daleinoi?'

He nodded again. Kneeling, looking at her where she stood before the fire, he thought he had never seen her like this. Had never seen *anyone* look as Gisel did just now. A creature almost alight, like the flames behind her, not entirely human.

She gazed at him, the famously wide-set blue eyes. Crispin's mouth was dry. She said, 'In that case, Caius Crispus, you must get us into the Imperial Precinct. Tonight.'

'Me?' said Crispin, eloquently.

Gisel smiled thinly. 'There is no one else I could think of,' she said. 'Or trust. I am a helpless woman and alone, far from my home.'

He swallowed again, painfully, could find nothing to say. He was thinking suddenly that he might die tonight, and that he had erred, earlier, seeing this terrible day and night as a clash of two women. He'd been wrong. Saw it now. There were three, not two.

In fact, they had all forgotten about her. The sort of over-looking that could matter greatly, change many things about the world—although perhaps not in any immediate, obvious way for some, such as the family on its farm in the northern grainlands, the one whose best labourer had just died, suddenly and too young, with the seeds all to be sown.

CHAPTER XIII

 There was a level of fear in the Blues' compound that Kyros had never known before. It was as if they were all horses, not yet broken, sweating with apprehension, trembling with it. Scortius wasn't the only wounded man. Members of the faction had been coming into the compound with injuries ranging from minor to hideously mortal all afternoon. There was considerable chaos. The wounded were receiving attention from Ampliarus, the new, pale-featured physician of the faction, and from Columella, who was properly their horse doctor but inspired more confidence in most of them than Ampliarus did. There was also a grey-bearded Bassanid doctor no one knew, but who had apparently been treating Scortius somewhere during the time of his absence. A mystery, but no time to consider it.

Beyond the gates at sunset there still came the sounds of running and shouting men, the tread of marching soldiers, clash of metal, horses' hooves, screaming sometimes. Those inside were under ferociously strict orders not to go out.

Adding to the anxiety was the fact that even so late in the day—the sky crimson now in the west above a line of clouds—Astorgus had not returned.

He'd been seized by the Urban Prefect's men as the rioting began, borne off by them for questioning. And they all knew what could happen to men interrogated in that windowless building on the far side of the Hippodrome.

In the absence of the factionarius, control of the compound normally fell to Columella, but he was entirely engaged in treating the wounded. Instead it was the small, rotund cook, Strumosus, who asserted himself, giving calm, brisk instructions, arranging for a steady supply of clean linen and bedding for the injured, assigning anyone healthy—grooms, servants, jugglers, dancers, stableboys—to give assistance to the three doctors, posting additional guards at the compound gates. He was listened to. There was real need for a sense of control.

Strumosus had his own people—the undercooks and kitchen boys and servers—furiously busy preparing soups and grilled meats and cooked vegetables, carrying well-watered wine to the injured and the frantic. Men and women needed food at such a time, the cook told them in the kitchen, astonishingly composed for a man notoriously volatile. Both the nourishment and the illusion of ordinariness had roles to play, he'd observed, as if delivering a lecture on a quiet afternoon.

That last was true, Kyros thought. The act of preparing food had a calming effect. He felt his own fear receding in the mundane, unthinking routine of selecting and chopping and dicing vegetables for his soup, adding spices and salt, tasting and adjusting, aware of the others at their own tasks all around him in the kitchen.

One might almost imagine it was a banquet day, all of them caught up in the usual bustle of preparation.

Almost, but not quite. They could hear men crying in anger and pain as they were helped into the courtyard from the frenzied streets beyond the gates. Kyros had already heard the names of a dozen men he knew who had died today in the Hippodrome or the fighting outside it.

Rasic, at his station beside Kyros, was swearing steadily, chopping with barely controlled fury, treating onions and potatoes as if they were members of the Greens or the military. He'd been at the races in the morning but not when violence exploded in the afternoon: the kitchen workers who drew the lucky straws and were allowed to go to the first races were under standing orders to return before the last morning running, to help prepare the mid-day meal.

Kyros tried to ignore his friend. His own heart was heavy and fearful, not angry. There was great violence outside. People were being badly hurt, killed. He was worried about his mother and father, about Scortius, Astorgus.

And the Emperor was dead.

The Emperor was dead. Kyros had been a child when Apius died, barely more than that when the first Valerius went to the god. And both of them had passed from the world in their beds, in peace. The talk today was of black murder, the assassination of Jad's anointed one, the god's regent upon earth.

It was the shadow over everything, Kyros thought, like a ghost half glimpsed out of the edge of one's eye, hovering above a colonnade or chapel dome, changing the fall of sunlight, defining the day, and the night to come.

*　　*　　*

At darkfall the torches and lamps were lit. The compound took on the altered look of a night camp by a battlefield. The barracks were filled by now with the wounded, and Strumosus had ordered the tables of the dining hall to be covered with sheets and used as makeshift beds for those who needed them. He himself was everywhere, moving quickly, concentrating, unruffled.

Passing through the kitchen, he stopped and looked around. He gestured at Kyros and Rasic and two of the others. 'Take a short rest,' he said. 'Eat something yourselves, or lie down, or stretch your legs. Whatever you like.' Kyros wiped perspiration from his forehead. They had been working almost without pause since the midday meal and it was night now, full dark.

He didn't feel like eating or lying down. Neither did Rasic. They went out of the hot kitchen into the chilly, torchlit shadows of the courtyard. Kyros felt the cold, which was unusual for him. He wished he'd put on a cloak over his sweaty tunic. Rasic wanted to go down to the gates, so they went there, Kyros dragging his foot along, trying to keep up with his friend. Stars were visible overhead. Neither moon was up yet. There was a lull, a hushed feeling out here now. No one crying at this moment, no one being carried in or sprinting past on some errand for the doctors in the barracks or the dining hall.

They came to the gates, to the guards there. Kyros saw that these men were armed, swords and spears and chestplates. They wore helmets, like soldiers. Weapons and armour were forbidden to citizens in the streets, but the faction compounds had been given their own laws and they were allowed to defend themselves.

It was quiet here, too. They looked through the iron

gates down the dark lane. There were occasional movements in the street beyond: distant sounds, a single voice calling, a carried torch passing at the head of their laneway. Rasic asked for news. One of the guards said that the Senate had been summoned into session.

'Why?' Rasic snapped. 'Useless fat farts. Voting themselves another ration of wine and Karchite boys?'

'Voting an Emperor,' the guard said. 'If your brain's small, kitchen boy, keep your mouth shut to hide the fact.'

'Fuck you,' Rasic snarled.

'Shut up, Rasic,' Kyros said quickly. 'He's upset,' he explained to the guards.

'We all are,' the man said bluntly. Kyros didn't know him.

They heard footsteps approaching from behind them, turned. By the torches mounted on the walls by the gate Kyros recognized a charioteer.

'Taras!' said another guard, and there was respect in his voice.

They'd heard, in the kitchens: Taras, their newest driver, had won the first afternoon race, working with the miraculously returned Scortius in some dazzling, amazing fashion. They'd come first, second, third and fourth, entirely obliterating the Green triumphs of the last session and the morning.

And then violence had exploded, during the victory laps.

The young driver nodded his head, came up to stand by Kyros before the gates. 'What do we know about the factionarius?' he asked.

'Nothing yet,' a third guard said. He spat somewhere into the dark beyond the lamplight. 'Fuckers in the Urban Prefect's office won't say a thing, even when they come by here.'

'They probably don't know,' Kyros said. A torch flared, showering sparks, and he looked away. It seemed to him he was always the one trying to be reasonable among men who didn't feel troubled by any need to be. He wondered what it would be like to sprint through the streets waving a blade in his hand, screaming in fury. Shook his head. A different person, a different life. Different foot, for that matter.

'How's Scortius?' he asked, looking at the other charioteer. Taras had a cut on his forehead and an ugly bruise on his cheek.

Taras shook his head. 'Sleeping now, they told me. They gave him something to make him sleep. There was a lot of pain, from where his ribs were broken, before.'

'Will he die?' Rasic asked. Kyros quickly made the sign of the sun disk in the darkness, saw two of the guards do the same.

Taras shrugged. 'They don't know, or they won't say. The Bassanid doctor is very angry.'

'Fuck the Bassanid,' Rasic said, predictably. 'Who is he, anyhow?'

There came a sudden clattering sound from beyond the gates and a sharp, rasped command. They turned quickly to peer down the laneway.

'More of ours coming back,' the first guard said. 'Open the gates.'

Kyros saw a group of men—perhaps a dozen—being herded roughly down the laneway by soldiers. One of the men couldn't walk; he was being supported between two others. The soldiers had their swords out, hustling the Blues along. He saw one of them sweep his blade and hit a stumbling man with the flat of it, swearing in a northern accent.

The gates swung open. Torches and lamps flickered with the movement. The man who'd been hit tripped and fell on the cobbled laneway. The soldier cursed again and prodded him hard with the point of his blade. 'Get up, you lump of horsedung!'

The man pushed himself awkwardly to one knee as the others hurried through the gates. Kyros, without stopping to think, limped out and knelt by the fallen man.

He draped the man's right arm over his shoulder. There was a smell of sweat and blood and urine. Kyros staggered to his feet, swayed, supporting the other fellow. He'd no idea who it was, in the dark, but it was a Blue, they all were, and he was hurt.

'Move, clubfoot! Unless you want a sword up your butt,' the soldier said. Someone laughed. *They're under orders*, Kyros told himself. *There's been rioting. The Emperor's dead. They are afraid, too.*

It seemed a long way, those ten steps back to the gates of the compound. He saw Rasic come running out to help him. Rasic went to lift the injured man's other arm to put it around his own shoulders, but the man between them cried out in agony at the movement, and they realized he had a sword wound in that arm.

'You fuckers!' Rasic snarled, turning on the soldiers in a rage. 'He has no weapon! You goat-fuckers! You didn't have to—'

The nearest soldier, the one who had laughed, turned to Rasic and—expressionlessly, this time—lifted his sword. A mechanical, precise motion, like something not human.

'No!' Kyros shouted, and twisting violently, still supporting the wounded man, he grabbed for Rasic with his free hand. He stumbled sideways with the weight and the too-quick movement, tried to keep his balance.

And it was in that moment, some time after darkfall on the day the Emperor Valerius II died, that Kyros of the

Blues, born in the Hippodrome, who had certainly never thought of himself as one of Jad's beloved and had never even seen from close the god's most holy regent upon earth, the thrice-exalted shepherd of his people, also felt something white and searing plunge into him from behind. He fell then, as Valerius had, and he, too, had a flashing thought of so many things yet desired and not yet done.

This may be shared, if nothing else is shared at all.

Taras, cursing himself as befuddled and hopelessly too slow, sprang through the gates past the guards, who would have been cut down if they'd gone into the lane with weapons.

The man called Rasic stood frozen as a statue, his mouth open as he stared down at his fallen friend. Taras seized him by the shoulders and almost *threw* him back towards the gates and the guards before he, too, could be chopped down. Then he knelt, lifting his hands in a quick, placating gesture to the soldiers, and picked up the man Kyros had been trying to help. The wounded man cried out again, but Taras gritted his teeth and half dragged, half carried him to the gates. He gave him to the guards and turned around again. He was going to go back, but something made him stop.

Kyros was lying face down on the cobblestones and he was motionless. Blood—black in the shadows—was pouring from the sword wound in his back.

In the laneway the soldier who had stabbed him looked indifferently down at the body, and then over at the gates where the Blues stood clustered in the wavering torchlight. 'Wrong horsedung,' he said lightly. 'Don't matter. Take a lesson. People do *not* speak to soldiers that way. Or someone dies.'

'You . . . come in here, say that . . . butt-fucking . . . goat-boy! *Blues! Blues!*' Rasic was crying helplessly even as he stammered his obscenities, his features blurred and distorted.

The soldier took a heavy step forward.

'No!' snapped another of them, the same thick accent, authority in the word. 'Orders. Not inside. Let's go.'

Rasic was still weeping, calling for aid, screaming a foul-mouthed tirade of impotent fury. Taras felt like doing the same, actually. As the soldiers turned to leave, one of them stepping right over the prone body of the slain undercook, he heard footsteps. More torches appeared behind them in the compound.

'What is it? What happened here?' It was Strumosus, with the Bassanid doctor, a number of other men with lights attending them.

'Another dozen of ours brought back,' one of the guards said. 'At least two badly injured, probably by the soldiers. And they just—'

'It's *Kyros!*' Rasic cried, clutching at the cook's sleeve. 'Strumosus, look! It's Kyros they've killed now!'

'*What?*' Taras saw the small man's expression change. '*You! Hold!*' he shouted, and the soldiers—astonishingly—turned in the laneway. 'Bring light!' Strumosus snapped over his shoulder, and he went right out through the gates. Taras hesitated a moment, and then followed, stopping a little behind.

'You foul, misbegotten offal! I want the name and rank of your leader!' the little chef said, barely controlled rage in his voice. 'Immediately! *Tell me!*'

'Who are you to give orders to—?'

'I speak for the accredited Blues faction and you are in our laneway at the gates of our compound, you scabrous vermin. There are regulations about this and there have been for a hundred years and more. I want your name—if you are the pustulent leader of these drunken louts who disgrace our army.'

'Fat little man,' said the soldier, 'you talk too much.' And he laughed and turned and walked away, not looking back.

'Rasic, Taras, you will recognize them?' Strumosus was rigid, his fists clenched.

'I think so,' said Taras. He had a memory of kneeling to claim the wounded man, looking straight up into the face of the one who'd stabbed Kyros.

'Then they will answer for this. They killed a prodigy here tonight, the foul, ignorant brutes.'

Taras saw the doctor step forward. 'That is worse than killing an ordinary man? Or a hundred of them?' The Bassanid's accented voice was almost a whisper, betraying the depths of his weariness. 'Why a prodigy?'

'He was becoming a cook. A real one,' said Strumosus. 'A master.'

'Ah,' said the doctor. 'A master? Young for that.' He looked down at Kyros where he lay.

'You've never seen brilliance, a gift, show itself young? Aren't *you* young—for all the false dyeing of your hair, and that ridiculous stick?'

Taras saw the doctor look up then, and in the light of the carried torches and lanterns, he registered the presence of something—a memory?—in the Bassanid's face.

The man said nothing, though. There was blood all over his clothing, a smear of it on one cheek. He didn't look young, just now.

'This boy was my legacy,' Strumosus went on. 'I have no sons, no heirs. He would have . . . outdone me in his day. Would have been *remembered*.'

Again the doctor hesitated. He looked down again at the body. After a moment, he sighed. 'He may yet be,' he murmured. 'Who decided he was dead? He won't survive if left here on the stones, but Columella should be able to clean the wound and pack it—he saw how I do it. And he knows how to stitch. After that . . . '

'He's alive!' Rasic cried and rushed forward, dropping beside Kyros.

'Careful!' the doctor snapped. 'Get a board and lift him on it. And whatever you do, *don't* let that idiot Ampliarus bleed him. If he suggests it throw him out of the room. Give him to Columella. Now where,' he said, turning to Strumosus, 'is my escort? I am ready to go home. I am . . . extremely tired.' He leaned upon the stick he carried.

The chef looked at him. 'One more patient. This one. Please? I told you, I have no sons. I believe he . . . I believe . . . Do you not have children? Do you *understand* what I am saying?'

'There are doctors here. *None* of these people today were my patients. I shouldn't have even come for the racer. If people insist on being fools—'

'Then they are only being as the god has made them, or as Perun and the Lady have. Doctor, if this boy dies it will be a triumph for Azal. Stay. Honour your profession.'

'Columella—'

'—is a doctor to our horses. Please.'

The Bassanid stared at him a long moment, then shook his head. 'I was promised an escort. This is not the medicine I practise, not the way I conduct my life.'

'None of us conducts his life this way by choice,' said Strumosus, in a voice no one there had ever heard him use. 'Who *chooses* violence in the dark?'

There was a silence. The Bassanid's face was expression-less. Strumosus looked at him a long time. When he spoke again it was almost in a whisper.

'If you are decided, we will not hold you, of course. I regret my unkind words before. The Blues of Sarantium thank you for your aid here, today and tonight. You will not go unrequited.' He glanced back over his shoulder. 'Two of you go down to the street with torches. Don't leave the laneway. Call for the Urban Prefect's men. They won't be far. They'll take the doctor home. Rasic, run back in and bring four men and a table plank. Tell Columella to get ready for us.'

The frieze broke as men moved to his bidding. The doctor turned his back on them all and stood, gazing out at the street. Taras could tell from the way he stood how utterly exhausted he was. The stick didn't look like an affectation; it looked like something he needed. Taras knew the feeling: end of a day's racing, when the simple act of walking off the sands and down the tunnel to the changing rooms seemed to demand more strength than he had.

He looked past the Bassanid to the street as well. And in that instant he saw a sumptuous litter go by at the head of their laneway: an apparition, an astonishing evocation of gilded grace and beauty in an ugly night. The two torch-bearers had neared the end of the lane; the litter was illu-minated with a brief, golden glow and then it moved on, was gone, heading towards the Hippodrome, the Imperial Precinct, the Great Sanctuary, an unreal image, swift as dreaming, an object from some other world. Taras blinked, and swallowed hard.

The two messengers began calling for men of the Urban

Prefect. They were all over the streets tonight. He looked at the eastern physician again and suddenly—incongruously—had an image of his mother, a memory from his own childhood. A vision of her standing in that same way before the cooking fire, having just refused him permission to go out again and back to the stables or hippodrome at home (to watch a foal being birthed or the breaking of a stallion to the harness and chariot, or *anything* to do with horses)—and then taking a deep breath and, out of love, indulgence, some understanding that he himself was only just beginning to realize, turning to her son and changing her mind, saying, '*All right. But take some of the elixir first, it is cold now, and wear your heavy cloak . . .* '

The Bassanid took a deep breath. He turned. In the darkness Taras thought of his mother, far away, long ago. The doctor looked at Strumosus.

'All right,' he said quietly. 'One more patient. Because I am a fool as well. Be sure they lift him onto the board face down, and with his left side first.'

Taras's heart was pounding hard. He saw Strumosus staring back at the doctor. The torchlight was erratic, flickering. There were noises in the night now, ahead of them and coming from behind as Rasic brought aid. A cold wind blew torch smoke between the two men.

'You do have a son, don't you?' Strumosus of Amoria said, so softly Taras barely heard it.

After a moment, the Bassanid said, 'I do.'

The carriers came out then, hurrying behind Rasic, bearing a plank from the dining hall. They lifted Kyros onto it, carefully and as instructed, and then they all went back in. The Bassanid paused at the gates, crossing the threshold with his left foot first.

Taras followed, the last to go in, still thinking of his mother, who also had a son.

———✦———

She had a sense that much of her life here in the city they called the centre of the world was spent at windows, in one room or another over the streets, looking out, observing, not actually *doing* anything. It wasn't necessarily bad, Kasia thought—the things she'd done at the posting inn, the tasks she'd had to perform back home (especially after the men had died) weren't in any way *desirable*, but there was still this odd feeling, at times, that here at the heart of where the world was supposed to be unfolding she was merely a spectator, as if the whole of Sarantium was a kind of theatre or hippodrome and she was in her seat, looking down.

On the other hand, what sort of active role *was* there for a woman to play here? And it certainly couldn't be said that she had any least desire to be in the streets now. There was so much movement in the city, so little calm, so many people one didn't know at all. No wonder people became agitated: what was there to make them feel safe, or sure? If an Emperor was their father, in some complex way, why shouldn't they become dangerously uncontrolled when he died? At her window Kasia decided that it would be good to have a child, a household full of them, and soon. A family, they might be something to defend you—as you defended them—from the world.

It was dark now, the stars overhead between houses, torches below, soldiers marching, calling out. The white moon would be up behind the house: even in the city Kasia knew the phases of the moons. The violence of the day had mostly passed. The taverns had been closed, the whores ordered off the streets. She wondered where the beggars and the homeless would go. And she wondered when Carullus would be home. She watched; had lit no lamps in this room, could not be seen from below.

She was less fearful than she'd thought she might be. Time passing did that. One could adjust to many things, it seemed, given enough time: crowds, soldiers, the smells and noises, chaos of the city, the utter absence of anything green and quiet, unless one counted the silence in the chapels during the day sometimes, and she didn't like the chapels of Jad.

It still amazed her that people here could see the fireballs that appeared at night, tumbling and flickering along the streets—the signifiers of powers entirely outside the ambit of the Jaddite god—and ignore them entirely. As if something that couldn't be explained wasn't to be acknowledged. It didn't exist. People spoke freely of ghosts, spirits, and she knew that many used pagan magics to invoke spells, whatever the clerics might say—but no one *ever* talked about the flames in the street at night.

At her window Kasia watched them, counted them. There seemed to be more than usual. She listened to the soldiers below. She had seen them entering houses along the street earlier, heard the banging on doors in the night. Change in the air, a change in the shape of the world. Carullus had been excited. He loved Leontes, and Leontes was going to be the new Emperor. It meant good things for them, he'd said, when he'd stopped at home for a moment near sundown. She'd smiled at him. He'd kissed her and gone out again. They were looking for someone. She knew who it was.

That had been some time ago. Now, at her window in darkness, she waited, watched—and saw something entirely unexpected. Passing along their quiet, little-trafficked street Kasia saw, like Taras of the Blues a few moments before, a golden litter appear out of the dark. A kind of vision, like the fireballs, something entirely out of tune with the rest of the night.

She had no idea, of course, who might be inside, but she knew they weren't supposed to be out there—and that they knew it, too. There were no runners with torches, as there surely ought to have been: whoever this was, they were trying to pass unseen. Kasia watched it until the bearers reached the end of the street and turned and went out of sight.

In the morning, she thought she might have fallen asleep at the window, dreamt what she saw, something golden, passing below her in a dark of booted soldiers and oaths and hammering at doors, for how could she have known it was gold, without light?

⁂

The august and illuminated, the blessed and revered Eastern Patriarch of most holy Jad of the Sun, Zakarios, had also been awake, and in some distress of body and spirit, in his chamber in the Patriarchal Palace at that same late-night hour.

The patriarchal residence was outside the Imperial Precinct, just behind the site of the Great Sanctuary—both the old one that had burned and the much larger one now risen in its place. Saranios the Great, who had founded this city, had deemed it a useful thing for the clerics and the palace officers to be seen to be separate.

There had been those who had disagreed in later years, wishing they had the Patriarchs more securely under their thumbs, but Valerius II had not been one of these, and Zakarios, who had just come from observing the Emperor's body where it lay in state in the Porphyry Room of the Attenine Palace, was thinking about that, and about the man. He was grieving, in fact.

The truth was, he hadn't actually observed the body. It seemed that only some Excubitors had, and the Chancellor, and then Gesius had made the decision that Valerius's body be covered—entirely wrapped in a purple mantle—and not seen.

He had been burned. Sarantine Fire.

Zakarios found it painful to contemplate. No amount of faith or political worldliness or combination of the two could help him deal easily with an image of Valerius as blackened, melted flesh. It was very bad. His stomach was giving him trouble, even thinking about it.

He had gone—as was necessary and proper—from speaking the holy Words of Passage in the Porphyry Room to the great silver doors of the Reception Chamber in the same palace. And there he had performed the equally holy Ceremony of Anointing for Leontes, now created Emperor in Sarantium by the express will of the Senate, earlier that day.

Leontes, as deeply pious a man as any Patriarch could ask for on the Golden Throne, had knelt and spoken the responses without prompting and with deep emotion in his voice. The wife, Styliane, had stood a little distance away, expressionless. All of the major officials of the court had been present, though Zakarios did note that Gesius, the aged Chancellor (*even older than I am,* the Patriarch thought) had also stood apart, by the doors. The Patriarch had been in his own office long enough to know that there would be swift changes in power within the Imperial Precinct in the days to come, even as the Rites of Mourning were observed.

There was to be a public crowning of husband and wife in the Hippodrome tomorrow, the new Emperor advised his Patriarch when the anointing was done. Zakarios was earnestly entreated to be present in the kathisma to participate. In times such as this, Leontes murmured, it was especially important to show the people that the holy sanctuaries and the court were as one. It was phrased as a request, but it wasn't, really. He was on the throne as he spoke, sitting there for the first time, tall and golden and grave. The Patriarch had inclined his head and indicated his acceptance and agreement. Styliane Daleina, soon to be Empress of Sarantium, had favoured him with a brief smile, her first of the night. She looked like her dead father. He had always thought that.

Zakarios understood, from his privy adviser, the cleric Maximius, that it was the brother, exiled Lecanus, who had been behind this profane and evil deed, along with the equally banished Lysippus—a man the clerics of the City had reason to loathe and fear.

Both of these men were dead, Maximius had reported. Leontes had himself slain the gross Calysian, like the mighty warrior he was. Maximius was very happy tonight, Zakarios thought, hadn't even troubled to hide it. His adviser was still with him now, though the hour was late. Maximius stood on the balcony overlooking the City. Across the way, the dome of the new Great Sanctuary rose. Valerius's Sanctuary. His vast, ambitious dream. One of them.

Leontes had said that the Emperor would be buried

there: fittingly, the first man to be so laid to rest. His regret had seemed genuine; Zakarios knew that his piety was. The new Emperor had views on certain controversial matters of holy faith. Zakarios knew that was part of the reason for Maximius's pleasure now, and that he, too, ought to be pleased. He wasn't. A man he had greatly respected was dead, and Zakarios felt too old for the kind of fight that might now begin in the sanctuaries and chapels, even with the Imperial Precinct supporting them.

The Patriarch felt a griping in his belly and winced. He rose and walked out on the balcony, adjusting the ear flaps on his cap. Maximius looked over at him and smiled. 'The streets are quiet now, Holiness, Jad be praised. Only soldiers and the Urban Prefect's guards, that I have seen. We must be eternally grateful to the god that in this time of danger he has seen fit to look after us.'

'I wish he'd attend to my stomach,' Zakarios said, ungratefully.

Maximius assumed an expression of sympathy. 'Would a bowl of the herbal—'

'Yes,' said Zakarios. 'It might.'

He was unreasonably angered by his adviser tonight. Maximius was too cheerful. An Emperor was *dead*, murdered. Maximius had been put in his place more than once by Valerius over the years, something Zakarios ought to have done more often himself.

The cleric betrayed nothing with his expression now, no response to the Patriarch's bluntness—he was good at that. He was good at a number of things. Zakarios often wished he didn't need the man quite so much. Now Maximius bowed, and went back into the room to summon a servant and have the drink prepared.

Zakarios stood alone at the stone rail of the high balcony. He shivered a little, for the night was cool and he was susceptible to chills now, but at the same time the air was reviving, bracing. A reminder (he suddenly thought) that if others were dead, he himself, by the grace of Jad's mercy, was not. He was still here to serve, to feel the wind in his face, see the glory of the dome in front of him with the stars and—just now—the white moon to the east.

He looked down. And saw something else.

In the dark street where there were no soldiers passing now, a litter appeared from a narrow lane. Moving quickly, unlit by any runners, it was carried up to one of the small rear doors to the Sanctuary. These were always locked, of course. The builders were not yet finished, nor were the decorations complete. Inside was scaffolding, equipment, decorative materials, some of it dangerous, some of it expensive. No one was allowed in without cause, and certainly not at night.

Zakarios, feeling an odd, unexpected sensation, watched as the curtain of the litter was pulled back. Two people emerged. There were no lights, the Patriarch couldn't make out anything about them at all; both were cloaked against the night, dark figures in darkness.

One of them went to the locked door.

A moment later it opened. A key? Zakarios couldn't see. The two of them went inside. The door was closed. The bearers did not linger, carried the exquisite litter away, back the way they had come, and an instant later the street was empty again. As if nothing had ever been there, the whole brief, puzzling episode a fantasy of some kind beneath the starlit, moonlit dome.

'The infusion is being prepared, Holiness,' Maximius

said briskly, reappearing on the balcony. 'I pray that it will bring you ease.'

Zakarios, looking down thoughtfully from beneath his hat and ear flaps, made no reply.

'What is it?' Maximius said, coming forward.

'Nothing,' said the Eastern Patriarch. 'There's nothing there.' He wasn't sure why he said that, but it was the truth, wasn't it?

He saw one of the small, fleeting fires appear just then, at the same street corner where the litter had gone. It, too, vanished a moment later. They always did.

⁂

She entered the Sanctuary ahead of him after he'd turned the two keys in the two locks and swung the small oak door open and stood aside for her. He followed, closed the door quickly, locked it. Habit, routine, the things done each and every ordinary day. Turning a key, opening or locking a door, walking into a place where one has been working, looking around, looking up.

His hands were shaking. They had made it this far.

He hadn't believed they would. Not with the City as it was tonight.

Ahead of him, in a small ambulatory under one of the semi-domes behind the enormous one that was Artibasos's offering to the world, Gisel of the Antae cast back the hood of her cloak.

'No!' Crispin said sharply. 'Keep it up!'

Golden hair, dressed with jewels. The blue eyes bright as jewels, alight in the always-lit Sanctuary. Lamps everywhere here, in walls, suspended on chains from the ceiling and all the domes, candles burning at the side altars, even though Valerius's rebuilt Sanctuary had not yet been opened, or sanctified.

She looked at him a moment but then, surprisingly, obeyed. He was aware that he had spoken peremptorily. It was fear, not presumption, though. He wondered what had become of his anger; he seemed to have misplaced it today, tonight, dropping it the way Alixana had dropped her cloak on the isle.

The sides of the hood came forward, shadowing Gisel's features again, hiding the almost frightening brilliance of her tonight, as if the woman here with him was another light in this place.

In the litter, he had been made aware of desire, forbidden and impossible as mortal flight, or fire before Heladikos's gift: a stirring, utterly irrational, equally unmistakable. Riding with her, aware of her body, her presence, he remembered how Gisel had come to him shortly after she'd arrived here, climbing up to the scaffold where he'd stood alone, and had had him kiss her palm in full view of all those watching, agape, from below. Creating a reason, false as alloyed coins, for him to visit her: a woman alone, without advisers or allies or anyone to trust, and tangled in a game of countries where the stakes were as high as they ever became.

Her reputation was not, he had come to see, what Gisel of the Antae was trying to protect. He could honour her for it, even while aware he was being used, toyed with. He remembered a hand lingering in his hair the very first night in her own palace. She was a queen, deploying resources. He was a tool for her, a subject to be given precise orders when he was needed.

He was needed now, it seemed.

You must get us into the Imperial Precinct. Tonight.

A night when the streets rang with the tread of soldiers looking for a missing Empress. A night after a day when flaming riot and murder defined Sarantium. When the Imperial Precinct would be in a fever and frenzy of tension: an Emperor dead, another to be proclaimed. An invasion from the north, on the day when war was to be proclaimed in Batiara.

He had heard Gisel's words almost without hearing them, so improbable did they seem. But he hadn't said to her, as he'd said so many times before to himself, to others, *I am an artisan, no more.*

It would have been a lie, after what had happened this morning. He was irrevocably down from the scaffolding, had been brought down some time ago. And on this night of death and change, the queen of the Antae, as forgotten here by everyone as a trivial guest might be at a banquet, had asked to be taken to the palaces.

A journey through most of the City, and in the dark, in a litter that turned out to be gilded, sumptuously pillowed, scented with perfume, where two people could recline at opposite ends, bodies unsettlingly near to each other, one of them alight with purpose, the other aware of the degree of his own fear, but remembering—with a wryness that spoke to his nature—that less than a year ago he had had no desire for life at all, had been more than half inclined to seek his death.

Easy enough to find tonight, he'd thought in the litter. He'd dictated to the bearers the route to take and forbidden any torches at all. They had listened to him, the way his apprentices did. It wasn't the same, though: that was his craft, upon walls or domes or ceilings, something touching the world but apart from it. This was not.

They were borne swiftly, almost silently, through the streets, keeping to shadows, stopping when boots were heard or torches seen, crossing squares the long way, through the covered, shadowed colonnades. Once, they'd stopped in the doorway of a chapel as four armed horsemen galloped across the Mezaros Forum. Crispin had drawn back the curtain of the litter to watch, and did so again at intervals, looking out at stars and barred doors and shop fronts as they passed through the night city. He saw the strange fires of Sarantium flare and disappear as they went: a journey as much through a starlit half-world as it was through the world, a feeling that they were travelling endlessly, that Sarantium itself had somehow been carried out of time. He'd wondered if anyone could even see them in the dark, if they were really here.

Gisel had been silent, nearly motionless throughout, adding to the sense of strangeness, never looking out when he pulled the curtains. Intense, coiled, waiting. The perfume in the litter was of sandalwood and something else he didn't recognize. It made him think of ivory, in the way that all things reminded him of colours. One of her ankles lay against his thigh. Unaware: he was almost certain she was unaware of that.

Then they had come, finally, to the door behind the Great Sanctuary and Crispin had put into motion—a movement into time again, as they left the enclosed world of the litter—the next part of what he supposed would have to be called a plan, though it was hardly that, in truth.

Some puzzles, even for one engaged by them, were intractible. Some could destroy you if you tried to solve them, like those intricate boxes the Ispahani were said to devise, where turning them the wrong way caused blades to spring out, killing or maiming the unwary.

Gisel of the Antae had handed him one of those. Or, seen another way, shifting the box a little differently in his hands, she *was* one of those tonight.

Crispin took a long breath, and realized that they weren't together any more. Gisel had stopped, was behind him, looking up. He turned back and followed her gaze to the dome that Artibasos had made, that Valerius had given to him—to Caius Crispus, widower, only son of Horius Crispus the mason, from Varena.

The lamps were burning, suspended from their silver and bronze chains and set into the brackets that ran with the windows all around. The light of the white moon, rising, was coming in from the east like a blessing of illumination upon the work he had achieved here in this place, in Sarantium after his sailing.

He would remember, he would always remember, that on the night when she herself was burning with directed intent like a beam of sunlight focused by glass onto one spot, the queen of the Antae had stopped beneath his mosaics upon a dome and looked up at them by lamplight and moonlight.

At length she said, 'You complained to me, I remember, about deficient materials in my father's chapel. Now I understand.'

He said nothing. Inclined his head. She looked up again, at his image of Jad over this City, at his forests and fields (green with spring in one place, red and gold and brown as autumn in another), at his *zubir* at the edge of a dark wood, his seas and sailing ships, his people (Ilandra there now, and he had been about to begin the girls this morning, filtering memory and love through craft and art), his flying and swimming creatures and running beasts and watchful ones, with a place (not yet done, not yet) where the western sunset flaming over ruined Rhodias would be the forbidden torch of falling Heladikos: his life, all lives under the god and in the world, as much as he could render, being mortal himself, entangled in his limitations.

Much of it done now, some yet to do, with the labour of others—Pardos, Silano and Sosio, the apprentices, Vargos working among them now—taking form under his direction on walls and semi-domes. But the *shape* of it, the overarching design, was here to be seen now, and Gisel paused, and looked.

As her gaze came to him again, he saw that she seemed about to say something else, but did not. There was an entirely unexpected expression on her face, and long afterwards he thought he understood it, what she had almost said.

'*Crispin!* Holy Jad, you are all right! We feared—'

He held up a hand, imperious as an Emperor in this place, urgent with apprehension. Pardos, rushing up, stopped in his tracks, fell silent. Vargos stood behind him. Crispin felt a flicker of relief himself: they had obviously elected to remain in here all day and night, were safe. He was sure Artibasos was somewhere about as well.

'You haven't seen me,' he murmured. 'You are asleep. Go now. Be asleep. Tell Artibasos the same if he's wandering here. No one saw me.' They were both looking at the hooded figure beside him. 'Or anyone else,' he added. She was unrecognizable, he devoutly hoped.

Pardos opened his mouth and closed it.

'Go,' said Crispin. 'If I have a chance to explain after, I will.'

Vargos had come quietly up beside Pardos: burly, capable, reassuring, a man with whom he had seen a *zubir*. Who had led them out of the Aldwood on the Day of the Dead. He said, quietly, 'Is there no help we can offer? Whatever you are doing?'

He wished there were, Crispin realized. But he shook his head. 'Not tonight. I am glad to see you safe.' He hesitated. 'Pray for me.' He'd never said anything like that before. He grinned a little. 'Even though you haven't seen me.'

Neither man smiled. Vargos moved first, taking Pardos by the elbow, leading him away into the shadows of the Sanctuary.

Gisel looked at him. Did not speak. He led her across the marble floor and the vast space under the dome into an ambulatory on the other side, and then to a low door set in the far wall. There he drew a deep breath and knocked—four times quickly, twice slowly—and then a moment later he did it again, remembering, remembering.

There was a stillness, a waiting time, as long as a night. He looked at the massed bank of candles at the altar to their right, thought of praying. Gisel stood motionless beside him. If this failed, he had nothing in reserve.

Then he heard the lock being turned on the other side. And the low door of the only plan he'd been able to devise swung open before them. He saw the white-robed cleric who had opened it, one of the Sleepless Ones, in the short stone tunnel behind the altar at the very back of the small chapel built into the wall of the Imperial Precinct, and he knew the man and gave thanks—with his whole heart—to the god, and he was remembering the first time he'd passed through this same door, with Valerius, who was dead.

The cleric knew him as well. The knock had been the Emperor's, taught to Artibasos and then to Crispin. Working by lamplight, they had opened for Valerius on more than one night through the winter as he came at the end of his own day's labours to look upon theirs. Much later than this, many times. He'd been named the Night's Emperor; it was said he never slept.

The cleric seemed blessedly unperturbed, only raised his eyebrows, without speaking. Crispin said, 'I have come with one who wishes to join me in paying a last tribute to the Emperor. We would speak our prayers by his body and then here again, with you.'

'He is in the Porphyry Room,' the cleric said. 'It is a terrible time.'

'It is,' said Crispin, feelingly.

The cleric had not moved aside. 'Why is your companion hooded?' he asked.

'That the common folk not see her,' Crispin murmured. 'It would be unseemly.'

'Why so?'

Which meant there was no help for it. Even as Crispin turned to her, Gisel had pushed back her hood. The cleric held a lantern. Light fell upon her face, her golden hair.

'I am the queen of the Antae,' she murmured. She was taut as a bowstring. Crispin had a sense she would vibrate like one if touched. 'Good cleric, would you have a woman parade through the streets tonight?'

The man, visibly overawed—and looking at the queen, Crispin could understand why—shook his head and stammered, 'No, of course . . . no, no! Dangerous. A terrible time!'

'The Emperor Valerius brought me here. Saved my life. Purposed to restore my throne to me, as you may know. Is it not seemly in the eyes of Jad that I bid him farewell? I would not rest easy if I did not so.'

The small cleric in his white robe backed up before her, and then he bowed and he shifted to one side. He said, with great dignity, 'It is seemly, my lady. Jad send Light to you, and to him.'

'To all of us,' said Gisel, and walked forward, ahead of Crispin now, ducking at the arch of the low stone tunnel, and then through the small chapel and into the Imperial Precinct.

They were there.

When Crispin had been younger, learning his craft, Martinian had often lectured about the virtues of directness, avoiding the overly subtle. Crispin, over the years, had made the same point many times to their various apprentices. 'If a military hero comes to a sculptor and asks for a statue in his own honour, it would be foolish beyond words *not* to do the obvious. Put the man on a horse, give him a helmet and a sword.' Martinian used to pause, after saying this. So would Crispin, before going on: 'It may feel tired, overdone, but what is the *reason* for this commission, you must ask yourself. Has anything been achieved if the patron doesn't feel honoured by a work designed to honour him?'

Subtle concepts, brilliant innovation came with risks ... sometimes the exercise of the moment would be entirely defeated by them. That was the point.

Crispin led the queen out of the chapel and back into the night, and he didn't ask her to draw up her hood again. They made no attempt to hide at all. They walked along tended paths, gravel crunching underfoot, past sculptures of

Emperors and soldiers (suitably rendered) in the starlit, moonlit gardens, and they saw no one and were disturbed by no one as they went.

Such dangers as might be feared tonight by those who lived here were thought to be outside the Bronze Gates, in the labyrinths of the City.

They went past a fountain, not flowing yet so early in the spring, and then the long portico of the silk guild, and then, with the sound of the sea in his ears, Crispin led his queen up to the entrance of the Attenine Palace, which was alight with lamps tonight. There were guards here, but the double doors stood wide open. He walked straight up the steps to them, and there he saw a man standing just inside, beyond the guards, in the green and brown colours of the Chancellor's eunuchs.

He stopped in front of the guards, the queen beside him. They eyed him warily. He ignored them, pointed at the eunuch. 'You!' he snapped. 'We need an escort for the queen of the Antae.'

The eunuch turned, his training immaculate, betraying no surprise at all, and he stepped out onto the portico. The guards looked from Crispin to the queen. The Chancellor's man bowed to Gisel, and then, a moment later, so did they. Crispin drew a breath.

'Rhodian!' said the eunuch as he straightened. He was smiling. 'You need another shave.' And it was with a sense of being blessed, guarded, granted aid, that Crispin recognized the man who had barbered his beard the first time he'd come to this palace.

'Probably,' Crispin admitted. 'But at the moment the queen wishes to see the Chancellor and to pay her last respects to Valerius.'

'She can do both at once, then. I am at your service, Majesty. The Chancellor is in the Porphyry Room with the body. Come. I will take you there.' The guards didn't even move as they went through, so regal was Gisel, so obviously confident the man escorting her.

It was not a long way, as it turned out. The Porphyry Room, where Empresses of Sarantium gave birth, where Emperors lay in state when they were summoned to the god, was on this level, halfway down a single straight corridor. There were lamps at intervals, shadows between them, no one at all seemed to be about. It was as if the Imperial Precinct, the palace, the hallway lay under some sort of alchemist's spell, so calm and still was it. Their footsteps echoed as they went. They were alone with their escort, walking to visit the dead.

The man who led them stopped outside a pair of doors. They were silver, bearing a pattern of crowns and swords in gold. Two guards here, as well. They seemed to know Gesius's man. Nodded. The eunuch knocked once, softly, and opened the door himself. He gestured for them to go inside.

Gisel went first again. Crispin paused in the doorway, uncertain now. The room was smaller than he'd expected. There were purple hangings on all the walls, an artificial tree of beaten gold, a canopied bed against the far wall, and a bier in the centre now, with a shrouded body upon it. There were candles burning all around, and one man knelt—on a cushion, Crispin saw—while two clerics softly chanted the Mourning Rites.

The kneeling man looked up. It was Gesius, parchment pale, thin as a scribe's pen, looking very old. Crispin saw him recognize the queen.

'I am very pleased to find you, my lord,' Gisel said. 'I wish to pray for the soul of Valerius who has left us, and to speak with you. Privately.' She crossed to a ewer on a stand, poured water on her hands in the ritual of ablution, dried them on a cloth.

Crispin saw something flicker in the old man's face as he looked at her.

'Of course, Majesty. I am at your service in all things.'

Gisel looked briefly at the clerics. Gesius gestured. They broke off their chanting and went out through a single door on the far side of the room, beside the bed. The door closed, candles flickered with the movement.

'You may go, Caius Crispus.' The queen didn't even turn around. Crispin looked at the eunuch who had escorted them. The man turned, expressionless, and went through the door. Crispin was about to follow, but then he hesitated and turned back.

He went forward, past Gisel, and he poured water for himself, in turn, murmuring the words spoken in the presence of the dead, and he dried his hands. Then he knelt at the side of the bier, beside the body of the dead Emperor. He smelled—over the scent of incense in the room—something charred and burnt, and he closed his eyes.

There were words of prayer suited for this moment. He didn't speak them. His thoughts were empty at first, then he shaped an image in his mind of Valerius. A man of ambition, in more ways than Crispin suspected he would ever grasp. Round-faced, soft-featured, mild of voice and bearing.

Crispin knew—still—that he ought to have hated and feared this man. But if there was a truth to be understood down here among the living at the bottom of the scaffold it was that hatred, fear, love, all of them, were never as simple as one might wish them to be. Without praying in any formal way, he bade farewell in silence to the image shaped in his mind, which was all he felt entitled to do.

He rose and went to the door. As he went out he heard Gisel say softly to the Chancellor—and was ever after to wonder if she spoke when she did to *allow* him to overhear, as a gift of sorts—'The dead are gone from us. We can only speak of what will happen now. I have a thing to say.'

The doors swung shut. Standing in the corridor, Crispin felt suddenly weary beyond words. He closed his eyes. Swayed on his feet. The eunuch was at his side. He said, a voice gentle as rain, 'Come, Rhodian. A bath, a shave, wine.'

Crispin opened his eyes. Shook his head. But heard himself saying, even as he did so, 'All right.' He was spent. He knew it.

The went back down the corridor, turned, turned again. He had no idea where they were. They came to a flight of stairs.

'Rhodian!'

Crispin looked up. A man, lean and grey, striding with brisk, angular efficiency, came up to them. There was no one else in the hallway, or on the stairs above them.

'What are you doing here?' asked Pertennius of Eubulus.

He was really very tired. 'Always turning up, aren't I?'

'Very much so.'

'Paying my respects to the dead,' he said.

Pertennius sniffed, audibly. 'Wiser to pay them to the living,' he said. And smiled then, with his wide, thin mouth. Crispin tried and failed to recall the man ever smiling like that before. 'Any tidings from outside?' Pertennius asked. 'Have they cornered her yet? She can't run for long, of course.'

It was unwise. In the extreme. Crispin knew it, even as he moved. It was, in truth, sheerest, self-destructive folly. But it seemed, in that moment, that he had found his anger after all, and in the finding—in the moment of locating it again—Crispin drew back his fist and sent it forward with all the force he had, smashing the secretary of the newly anointed Emperor full in the face, sending him flying backwards to sprawl on the marble floor, motionless.

There was a rigid, an almost intolerable silence.

'Your poor, poor hand,' said the eunuch mildly. 'Come, come let us tend to it.' And he led the way up the stairs without a backwards glance at the unconscious man. Crispin went where he was taken.

They treated him kindly in the upper-level chambers where the Chancellor and his retinue resided. Many of them remembered with amusement his first evening here, half a year ago. He was bathed, as promised, given wine, was even shaved, though there was no jesting tonight. Someone played a stringed instrument. He realized that these men—all Gesius's—were facing very great changes themselves. If the Chancellor fell, which was almost a certainty, their own future became precarious. He said nothing. What could he say?

Eventually he slept, in a good bed and a quiet room they provided for him. And so spent one night of his life sleeping in the Attenine Palace of Sarantium not far from a living Emperor and a dead one. He dreamt of his wife, who was dead too, but also of another woman running and running, fleeing pursuit down an endless, exposed beach of smooth hard stones in too-bright moonlight with dolphins leaping offshore in a black, shining sea.

*　　*　　*

Behind Crispin and the eunuch, as the doors closed in the room with the draped walls and the golden tree and a blackened body in a shroud, an elderly man who had been expecting to meet his own death tonight, and had determined to greet it with dignity in this same room where he had prayed for three dead Emperors, was listening to a young woman speak—a woman he had forgotten tonight, as had they all. With every word spoken he seemed to feel his will reviving, his mind chasing and shaping contingencies.

By the time she stopped, vivid and fierce, looking at him closely, Gesius was entertaining the possibility of life beyond the sunrise after all.

For himself, if not for others.

And in that precise moment, before he could speak his reply, the small inner door to the Porphyry Room was opened without a knock and—as if drawn hither by something supernatural, preordained, in a night fraught with power and mystery—a tall man, broad-shouldered, golden-haired, came in alone.

Thrice-exalted Leontes, regent upon earth now under Jad of the Sun, newly proclaimed, pious as a cleric, come to pray by candlelight with a sun disk in his hands for his predecessor's soul as it journeyed. He stopped on the threshold and glanced briefly at the eunuch, whose presence was expected, and then more carefully at the woman standing by the bier, who was not expected at all.

Gesius prostrated himself on the floor.

Gisel of the Antae did not, or not immediately.

First, she smiled. And then she said (still standing, her father's daughter, courageous and direct as a blade), 'Great lord, thanks be to Jad you have come. The god is merciful beyond our deserving. I am here to tell you that the west is yours now, lord, and lifelong freedom from the stain of this night's black and godless evil. If you but choose.'

And Leontes, who had not been prepared for anything like this at all, said, after a long moment, 'Explain yourself, my lady.'

She looked back at him, unmoving, tall and fair, brilliant as a diamond. An explanation in herself, really, the Chancellor thought, keeping utterly silent, hardly breathing.

Only then did she kneel, gracefully, and lower her forehead to touch the marble floor in obeisance. And then, straightening, but still kneeling before the Emperor with jewels in her hair and all about her, she did explain.

When she was done, Leontes was silent for a long time.

At length, his magnificent features grave, he looked over at the Chancellor and asked one question: 'You agree? Lecanus Daleinus could not have planned this himself from the isle?'

And Gesius, inwardly declaring to the god that he was unworthy of so much largess, said only, seeming calm and unruffled as dark water on a windless morning, 'No, my great lord. Most surely he could not.'

'And we know that Tertius is a coward and a fool.'

It was not a question, this time. Neither the Chancellor nor the woman said a word. Gesius was finding it difficult to breathe, tried to hide the fact. He had a sense that there were scales hovering in the air of the room, above the burning candles.

Leontes turned to the body under silk on the bier. 'They burned him. Sarantine Fire. We all know what that means.'

They had known. The question had been whether Leontes would ever acknowledge it to himself. The answer, in Gesius's mind, had been negative, until the woman—this *other* tall, fair-haired woman with blue eyes—had come and altered everything. She had invited the Chancellor to speak to the new Emperor, had told him what should be said. He had been about to do so, having nothing to lose at all—and then the new Emperor had arrived, himself. The god was mysterious, unknowable, overwhelming. How could men *not* be humble?

Leontes, muscles rippling under his tunic and robe, crossed to the platform where Valerius II lay covered, toe to head, in purple silk. There was a sun disk under the cloth, held in his crossed hands, the Chancellor knew: he had placed it there, along with the coins on Valerius's eyes.

Leontes stood a moment between the tall candles, looking down, and then, with a swift, violent movement, pulled back the cloth from the dead man's body.

The woman looked quickly away from the horror revealed. So did the Chancellor, though he had seen it already tonight. Only the newly anointed Emperor of Sarantium, soldier of half a hundred battlefields, who had seen death in so many shapes and guises, endured looking down at this. It was as though, Gesius thought, staring grimly at the marble floor, he needed to.

At length, they heard Leontes draw the shroud back up, covering the dead again, in decency.

He stepped back. Drew a breath. A last weight settled, with finality, on the scales in the air.

Leontes said, in a voice that did not admit of the possibility of doubt in the world, of error, 'It is a foul and black abomination in the eyes of Jad. He was the god's anointed, holy and great. Chancellor, you will have men find Tertius Daleinus, wherever he may be, and bind him in chains to be executed. And you will bring here to me now in this chamber the woman who was my wife, that she may look a last time upon this, her work tonight.'

Who was my wife.

Gesius stood up, so quickly he became dizzy for a moment. He hurried out, through the same inner door by which the Emperor had entered. The world had changed, and was changing again. No man, however wise, could ever dare say he knew what the future held.

He closed the door behind himself.

Two people were left alone then, with the dead man and the candles and the golden tree in a room devised for the births and deaths of Emperors.

Gisel, still kneeling, looked up at the man before her. Neither of them spoke. There was something within her so overflowing, so intense, it was extremely near to pain.

He moved first, coming towards her. She rose only when he extended a hand to aid her and she closed her eyes when he kissed her palm.

'I will not kill her,' he murmured.

'Of course not,' she said.

And kept her eyes tightly, tightly closed, that what blazed in them in that moment might not be seen.

There were intricate matters of marriage and Imperial succession and a myriad of other details of law and faith that needed attending to. There were deaths to be achieved, with formal propriety. Steps taken (or not taken) at the outset of a reign could define it for a long time.

The august Chancellor Gesius, affirmed in his position that same night, dealt with all of these things, including the deaths.

It did take some little time to observe the necessary protocols. There was, therefore, no Imperial coronation in the Hippodrome until three days after. On that morning, bright and auspicious, in the kathisma, before the assembled, wildly cheering citizens of Sarantium—eighty thousand of them and more shouting at the top of their lungs—Leontes the Golden took the name Valerius III, in humble, respectful homage, and he crowned his golden Empress, Gisel, who did not change the name her own great father had given her when she was born in Varena, and so was recorded in history that way when the deeds of their reign together came to be chronicled.

In the Porphyry Room on the night this was set in motion, a door was opened and a man and woman kneeling in prayer before a covered body turned to see a second woman enter.

She stopped on the threshold and looked at them. Leontes stood up. Gisel did not, clasping her sun disk, her head cast down in what might have been thought to be humility.

'You asked for me? What is it?' said Styliane Daleina briskly to the man she had today brought to the Golden Throne. 'I have much to do tonight.'

'No, you don't,' said Leontes, blunt and final as a judge. And was watching her as she registered—quickly, always quickly—the import of his tone.

If he had hoped (or feared) to see terror or fury in her eyes then he was disappointed (or relieved). He did see something flicker there. A different man might have known it for irony, a vast, black amusement, but the man who could have read her that way lay dead on the bier.

Gisel stood up. And of the three of them living, she was the one wearing the colours of royalty in this room. Styliane looked at her for a moment, and what might perhaps have been unexpected was the measure of her calm, approaching indifference.

She looked away from the other woman, as if dismissing her. She said to her husband, 'You have discerned a way to claim Batiara. How clever of you. Did you do it all by yourself?' She glanced at Gisel, and the queen of the Antae lowered her eyes to the marble floor again, not in apprehension or intimidation, but so that exultation might be secret a little longer.

Leontes said, 'I have discerned murder and impiety and will not live with them under Jad.'

Styliane laughed.

Even here, even now, she could laugh. He looked at her. How could a soldier, who judged so much of the world in terms of courage, not admire this, whatever else he felt?

She said, 'Ah. You will not live with them? You renounce the throne? The court? Will join an order of clerics? Perch on a rock in the mountains with your beard to your knees? I would *never* have imagined it! Jad's ways are mighty.'

'They are,' said Gisel, speaking for the first time, and the mood was changed, effortlessly. 'They are, indeed.'

Styliane looked at her again, and this time Gisel lifted her eyes and met that gaze. It was simply too difficult, after all, to be secret. She had sailed here utterly alone, fleeing death, without allies of any kind, those who loved her dying in her stead. And now . . .

The man did not speak. He was staring at the aristocratic wife Valerius had given him in great honour, for shining conquests in the field. He had summoned her here intending to pull back the cloth again from the dead man and force her to look upon the hideous ruin of him, but in that moment he understood that such gestures held no meaning, or not any meaning one might expect.

He had never really understood her in any case, the daughter of Flavius Daleinus.

He gestured to Gesius, standing behind her in the doorway. His wife saw his movement and she looked at him, and she smiled. She smiled. And then they took her away. She was blinded before dawn by men whose vocation that was, in an underground room from which no sounds could escape to trouble the world above.

<hr />

Through the moonlit streets of the city, past troops of foot-soldiers and mounted men galloping, boarded-up taverns and cauponae and the unlit fronts of houses, past chapels dark and the banked fires of the bakeries, under scudding clouds and stars hidden and revealed, Rustem of Kerakek, the physician, was escorted late that night by men of the Urban Prefect's guard from the Blues' compound to the house near the walls he'd been given for his use.

They had offered him a bed in the compound, but he had been taught long ago that a physician did better to sleep away from where his patients were. It preserved dignity, detachment, privacy. Even bone-weary as he was (he had done three more procedures after cleaning and closing the wound of the boy stabbed from behind), Rustem followed the habits of training and, after turning to the east and praying in silence to Perun and the Lady that his efforts be found acceptable, had asked for the escort promised earlier that night. They'd walked him to the gates again and called for the guards. He'd promised to return in the morning.

The soldiers in the streets gave them no trouble as they went, though there was clearly an agitation among them and the night was raucous with their cries and hammerings upon doors and the horses passing were like drums on the cobblestones. Rustem, in his exhaustion, paid them no attention, moving in the midst of his escort, placing one foot in front of another, using his stick tonight, not just carrying it for effect, hardly seeing where he was going.

At length they came to his door. The door of Bonosus's small house by the walls. One of the guards knocked for him and it was opened quickly. They were probably expecting the soldiers, Rustem thought. The searchers. The steward was there, his expression concerned, and Rustem saw the girl, Elita, standing behind him, still awake at this hour. He stepped over the threshold, left foot first, mumbled a thanks to those who'd walked him here, nodded briefly to the steward and the girl, and went up the stairs to his room. There seemed to be many stairs tonight. He opened the door and went in, left foot first.

Inside, Alixana of Sarantium was sitting by the open window, looking down at the courtyard below.

CHAPTER XIV

He didn't know it was her, of course. Not until she spoke. In his dazed, stumbling state Rustem hadn't the least idea why this unknown woman was in his bedchamber. His first, incoherent thought was that she might be someone Bonosus knew. But that ought to have been a boy, surely?

Then he did believe he recognized her—as a patient, one of those who had come to see him the very first morning. But that made no sense. What was she doing here now? Did the Sarantines know nothing of proper conduct?

Then she stood up beside the window and she said, 'Good evening, physician. My name is Aliana. It was Alixana this morning.'

Rustem fell back against the door, pushing it shut. His legs felt weak. There was a horror in him. He couldn't even speak. She was ragged, dirty, visibly exhausted, looking like nothing so much as a street beggar, and it never for a moment occurred to him to doubt the truth of what she said. The voice, he thought afterwards. It was the voice.

She said, 'They are looking for me. I have no right to place you at risk, but I am doing so. I must rely on your compassion for someone you have treated as a patient— however briefly—and I must tell you I . . . I have nowhere else to go. I have been avoiding soldiers all night. I was even in the sewers, but they are looking there now.'

Rustem crossed the room. It seemed to take a long time. He sat down on the edge of his bed. Then it crossed his mind that he ought not to sit in the presence of an Empress and he stood up. He put a hand on one of the bedposts for support.

'How did you . . . why are . . . how *here?*'

She smiled at him. There was nothing resembling amusement in her face, however. Rustem had been trained to look at people carefully, and now he did. This woman was at the end of whatever reserves of strength she had. He glanced down. She was unshod; there was blood on one foot, and he thought it might be from a bite. She had mentioned the sewers. Her hair had been cropped off, raggedly. A disguise, he thought, as his brain began to work again. Her garment had also been cut, just above the knees. Her eyes looked hollow, dark, as if one could see into the sockets, into the bone behind.

But she smiled at his fumbling incoherence. 'You were much more articulate the last time, doctor, explaining why I might hope one day to bear a child. Why am I here? Desperation, I confess. Elita is one of my women, one of those I trust. I used her to report on Bonosus. It was useful, in obvious ways, to know what the Master of the Senate was doing that he might prefer . . . not be known.'

'Elita? One of . . . ?'

He was having a good deal of trouble. She nodded. There was a smear of mud across her forehead and on one cheek. This was a hunted woman. Her husband was dead. All those soldiers in the streets tonight, mounted, on foot, pounding at doors, they were there for her. She said, 'She has reported generously of your nature, doctor. And of course I know myself that you refused to follow orders from Kabadh and kill the Antae queen.'

'*What?* I . . . You *know* that I . . .?' He sat down again.

'Doctor, we'd have been remiss if we didn't know such things, wouldn't we? In our own City? The merchant who brought you that message . . . have you seen him since?'

Rustem swallowed hard, shook his head.

'It didn't take long to have him offer the details. Of course you were closely watched from then on. Elita said you were unhappy after that merchant left. You don't like the idea of killing, do you?'

They'd been watching him, all along. And what *had* happened to the man who'd brought him the message? He didn't want to ask.

'Killing? Of course I don't,' Rustem said. 'I am a healer.'

'Will you shield me, then?' asked the woman. 'They will be here soon enough.'

'How can I . . . ?'

'They will not know me. Their weakness tonight is that most of the men searching have no idea what the Empress looks like. Unless I am betrayed, they will only be able to find women who don't appear to belong where they are and take them for questioning. They will not know me. Not as I am now.'

She smiled again. That bleakness. Hollow-eyed.

'You understand,' the woman by the window said quietly, 'that Styliane will have my eyes and tongue put out and my nose slit and then she will give me to any men who still want me, in certain rooms underground, and then she will have me burned alive. There is . . . nothing else that matters to her so much.'

Rustem thought of the aristocratic, fair-haired woman standing beside the Strategos at the wedding he'd attended on his first day here. 'She is Empress now?' he said.

The woman said, 'Tonight, or tomorrow. Until I kill her, and her brother. Then I can die and let the god judge my life and deeds as he will.'

Rustem looked at her a long time. He was remembering more clearly now, rational thought coming back, some small measure of composure. She had indeed come to him that first morning, when he and the household had hastened to arrange the ground floor into treatment rooms. A woman of the common sort, he'd thought, had prudently made certain she could afford his fee before admitting and examining her. Her voice . . . had been different then. Of course it had.

The westerners, like his own people, had a limited understanding of conception and childbirth. Only in Ispahani had Rustem learned certain things: enough to understand that a failure to bear might sometimes arise in the husband, not the wife. Men in the west, in his own country, were disinclined to listen to that, of course.

But Rustem was not uncomfortable explaining this to the women who came to him. What they did with the information was not his burden or responsibility.

That woman of the common sort—who turned out to have been the Empress of Sarantium—had been one of those. And had seemed not at all surprised, after his questions and his examination, when he'd said what he said to her.

Looking closely, the physician in Rustem was shaken anew by what he saw: the absolute, clenched rigidity with which the woman was holding herself together, set against the flat, matter-of-fact way in which she spoke of killing and her own death. She was not far from breaking, he thought.

He said, 'Who knows you are here?'

'Elita. I entered over the courtyard wall, and then up into this room. She found me here when she came to make up your fire. I knew she was sleeping here, of course. Forgive me for that. I had to hope she would do the fire in this room. I'd be captured by now if anyone else had come. They will take me right now if you call out, you understand?'

'You climbed the wall?'

That smile that was not a smile. 'Physician, you don't want to know the things I have done or where I've been today and tonight.'

And then after a moment she said, for the first time, *'Please?'*

Empresses never had to say that, Rustem thought, but in the moment just before she'd spoken it they'd both heard, even up here, a pounding at the front door, and through the window Rustem saw a flaring of torches in the garden and heard voices down below.

─·⊛·─

Ecodes of Soriyya, veteran decurion of the Second Amorian, a career soldier, was keenly aware, even with the turmoil of the night and the two fast cups of wine he'd (unwisely) accepted after searching the home of a fellow southerner, that one conducted oneself with composure in the home of a Senator, and had one's men do the same, even if they were frustrated and in a hurry and there was an enormous reward to be pursued.

The ten of them went about their business briskly and very thoroughly but didn't trouble the woman servants and took some care not to break anything as they flung open trunks and wardrobes and checked every room, above and below stairs. Things *had* been broken during searches earlier after they'd helped clear the faction rabble from the streets and Ecodes expected to hear of complaints in the morning. That didn't worry him unduly. The Second Amorian's tribunes were good officers, on the whole, and they knew the men needed some release at times and that soft citizens were always grumbling about the honest soldiers who protected their homes and lives. What was a broken vase or platter in the scheme of things? How far would one go in protesting that a servant had had her breast squeezed or her tunic lifted by a soldier in passing?

On the other hand, there were houses and there were houses, and it could be bad for one's chances of promotion to offend an actual Senator. Ecodes had been given reason to believe that he might make centurion soon, especially if he had a good war.

If there *was* a war. There was a lot of talk going about tonight as soldiers met and passed each other in the streets of Sarantium. Armies fed on rumour, and the latest was that they wouldn't be going west in any great hurry after all. The war in Batiara had been the grand scheme of the last Emperor, the one who'd been murdered today. The new Emperor was the army's own beloved leader, and though no one could possibly doubt the courage and will of Leontes, it did make sense that a new man on the throne might have things to deal with here before sending his armies sailing off to battle.

That suited Ecodes well enough, in truth, though he would never have said as much to anyone. Fact was, he hated ships and the sea with a fear deep as bones or pagan spells. The thought of entrusting his body and soul to one of those round, slow tubs hulking in the harbour with their drunken captains and crews frightened him infinitely more than had any attack of Bassanids or desert tribes, or even the Karchites, foaming at the mouth with battle rage, on his one tour of duty in the north.

In a battle you could defend yourself, or retreat if you had to. A man with some experience had ways of surviving. On a ship in a storm (Jad forbid!) or simply drifting out of sight of land, there was nothing a soldier could do but heave his guts and pray. And Batiara was a long way off. A very long way.

As far as Ecodes of Soriyya was concerned, if the Strategos—the glorious new Emperor—decided to have himself a good long think about the west for a while, direct his armies north and east, say (there was talk in the dark that the fucking Bassanids had breached the peace, sending a force over the border), this would be altogether a proper, wise thing.

You couldn't be promoted to centurion for a good war if you were drowned on the way, could you?

He accepted a terse report from Priscus that the courtyard and garden were empty. They had the house searches pretty much down to a routine now. They'd been in enough of them tonight. The main floor rooms near the front here had been made into some sort of medical chambers, but they were empty. The steward—a lean-faced, officious type—had obediently assembled the servants downstairs and accounted for the three women by name. Priscus and four of the others went down the hall to check the household staff's rooms and the kitchen. Ecodes, speaking as politely as he could, inquired as to who might be occupying the rooms upstairs. There had been two men until this morning, the steward explained. A recovering patient and the Bassanid doctor who was staying here as a guest of the Senator.

Ecodes refrained (politely) from spitting at the mention of a Bassanid.

'What patient?' he asked.

'Not a woman, a man. And we are under instructions not to say,' the steward murmured blandly. The smooth, superior-sounding bastard had exactly the sort of city manner Ecodes most despised. He was a servant, no more than that, and yet he acted as if he'd been born to olive groves and vineyards.

'Fuck your instructions,' Ecodes said, mildly enough. 'I haven't time tonight. What man?'

The steward grew pale. One of the women brought a hand to her mouth. Ecodes thought (couldn't be sure) she might be hiding a giggle. Probably had to hump the thin-blooded bastard to keep her job. Wouldn't be unhappy to see him caught up a bit, Ecodes would wager.

'It is understood that you have ordered me to tell you?' the steward said. Lump of dung, Ecodes thought. Covering himself here.

'Fucking right it's understood. Tell.'

'The patient was Scortius of Soriyya,' said the steward. 'Rustem of Kerakek had been treating him in secrecy here. Until this morning.'

'Holy Jad!' gasped Ecodes. 'You aren't spinning a tale?'

The steward's expression made it clear, if any doubt had hitherto existed, that he wasn't the tale-spinning sort.

Ecodes licked his lips nervously and tried to absorb this information. It had nothing to do with anything, but these were tidings! Scortius was by a long bowshot the most famous son of Soriyya today. The hero of every boy and man in that desert-bordered land, including Ecodes. Enough soldiers on leave had attended the racing today for the story of the Blues' champion's unexpected reappearance in the Hippodrome—and what had followed—to be known to everyone searching tonight. There were rumours he might die of his wounds: the Emperor and the greatest charioteer on the very same day.

And what would *that* do to the superstitious in the army, on the eve of what was supposed to be the grand war of reconquest?

And here was Ecodes, standing in the very house where Scortius had been recovering, treated in secret by a Bassanid! What a tale it would make! He could hardly wait to get back to the barracks.

For the moment, he simply nodded his head to the steward, his expression gravely sober. 'I can see why this was secret. Be easy—it will never be revealed by us. Anyone else in the house?'

'Only the physician himself.'

'The Bassanid? And right now he is . . . ?'

'Upstairs. In his room.'

Ecodes looked over at Priscus, who had come back along the hallway. 'I'll do that room myself. We don't want complaints here.' He glanced an inquiry at the steward.

'First room on the left from the top of the stairs.' A helpful man, if you let him know the rules of the game.

Ecodes went up. Scortius! Had been here! And the man who'd saved his life . . .

He knocked briskly on the first door but didn't wait for an invitation. This was a search. The man might have done a good turn here, but he was still a fucking Bassanid, wasn't he?

He was, it appeared.

The naked woman riding the man in the bed turned as Ecodes opened the door and let out a muffled shriek and then a torrent of what was obviously foul abuse. Ecodes could only get the gist of it: she was swearing in Bassanid.

She dismounted from the man beneath her, swinging around to face the door, covering her nakedness hastily with a sheet as the man sat upright. He had—not unreasonably under the circumstances—an outraged expression on his face.

'How *dare* you!' he hissed, keeping his voice down. 'Is this Sarantine civility?'

Ecodes actually did feel just a little bit intrusive. The eastern whore—there were always some of them here from all over the known world—was spitting and swearing, as if she'd never shown her naked backside to a soldier before. She had switched to Sarantine now, heavily accented but intelligible, and made a number of pungent, explicit assertions about Ecodes's mother and alleys behind cauponae and his own provenance.

'*Shut up!*' The physician slapped her hard on the side of the head. She shut up, whimpering. Women needed that sometimes, Ecodes thought approvingly . . . obviously a truth in Bassania as much as anywhere else and why shouldn't it be?

'What are you doing here?' The grey-bearded doctor struggled to assume a measure of dignity. Ecodes was privately amused: dignity was not easy when surprised beneath the pumping body of a whore. Bassanids. Not even men enough to get their women under them where they belonged.

'Ecodes, Second Amorian Foot. Orders to search all houses in the City. We're looking for a fugitive woman.'

'Because none of you can *get* a woman! They all *run* from you!' the whore beside the doctor cackled, her mouth wide open at her own wit.

'I heard about the search,' the Bassanid said to Ecodes, keeping his composure. 'In the Blues' compound where I was treating a patient.'

'Scortius?' Ecodes couldn't help but ask.

The doctor hesitated. Then he shrugged. *Not my concern,* the gesture seemed to say. 'Among others. The soldiers were not gentle today, you know.'

'Orders,' said Ecodes. 'Trouble to be stopped. How is . . . the charioteer?' This was *huge* gossip.

Again the doctor hesitated, again he shrugged. 'Ribs broken again, a wound ripped open, loss of blood, maybe a fallen lung. I'll know in the morning.'

The whore was still glaring at Ecodes, though at least she'd shut her foul mouth for the moment. She had a nice, ripe body, what he'd seen, but her hair was a tangled nest, her voice shrill and grating, and she didn't look especially clean. As far as Ecodes of Soriyya was concerned, you got mud and swearing with your soldiers, when you went with a girl you wanted . . . something else.

'This woman is . . . ?'

The doctor cleared his throat. 'Well, ah, you do understand that my family is a long way off. And a man, even at my age . . .'

Ecodes grinned a little. 'I won't go to Bassania to tell your wife, if that's what you mean. Must say, you could have done better here in Sarantium than this, or do you like them talking dirty to you in your own language that much?'

'Fuck yourself, soldier,' the woman snarled in that thick accent. 'Since no one else is likely to.'

'Manners, manners,' Ecodes said. 'This is a Senator's house.'

'It is,' said the doctor. 'And manners are in short supply right now. Be so good as to finish doing what you must and leave. I confess I find neither propriety nor diversion in this encounter.'

I'm sure you don't, Bassanid pig, Ecodes thought.

What he said was, 'I understand, doctor. Following orders, as I'm sure you realize.' He had a promotion to protect. The pig was living here and treating Scortius, which meant he was important.

Ecodes looked around. The usual upstairs room for this neighbourhood. Best room, view of the garden. He crossed to the window over the courtyard. It was dark. They'd already searched down there. He went back to the door, looked over at the bed. The two people there gazed at him, sitting up, side by side, silent now. The woman had the sheet up to cover herself, mostly, but not entirely. She was giving him a glimpse, a tease, even as she swore at him. Whores.

You were supposed to look under the beds, of course—obvious hiding places. But you were also supposed to use your judgement as a decurion (a centurion-to-be?) and not waste time. There were a lot of houses to be searched before dawn. There had been no ambiguity about the orders given: they wanted the woman found before the ceremony in the Hippodrome tomorrow. Ecodes was willing to assert with confidence that the woman who had been Empress of Sarantium this morning was not under the bed on which these two Bassanids had been engaged.

'As you were, doctor,' he said, allowing himself a grin. 'Carry on.' He went out, closing the door behind him. Priscus was coming down the hallway with two of the men. Ecodes looked at him; he shook his head.

'One room that was occupied, but it isn't any more. A patient of some sort.'

'Let's go,' Ecodes said. 'I'll tell you about *that* outside. You won't fucking believe it.'

She'd had a filthy mouth, that Bassanid whore, but a nicely curved rump, he thought, going down the stairs ahead of Priscus, remembering that first startling, arousing vision when he'd opened the door. He wondered idly if there'd be any chance of a girl himself, later tonight. Not likely. Not for honest soldiers doing a job.

In the antechamber by the front door he waited for his men to file out and then nodded to the steward. Politely. Even said a thank you. A Senator's house. He'd given them his name when they came in.

'Oh,' he said, as a last thought struck him. 'When did that Bassanid whore upstairs come here?'

The steward looked genuinely scandalized. 'You foul-mouthed man! What a disgusting thought! The Bassanid is a well-known physician and an . . . an honoured guest of the Senator!' he exclaimed. 'Keep your evil thoughts to yourself!'

Ecodes blinked and then laughed aloud. Well, well. Too sensitive by half! Told him something, didn't it? Boys? He made a mental note to ask someone about this Senator Bonosus later. He was about to explain when he saw the woman behind the steward wink at him, holding a finger to her smiling lips.

Ecodes grinned. She was pretty, this one. And it was obvious that the very proper steward didn't know all that was going on in this house.

'Right,' he said, looking at the woman meaningfully. Maybe he'd have a chance to come back later. Unlikely, but you never knew. The steward looked quickly over his shoulder at the girl, whose expression immediately became entirely proper, her hands clasped submissively at her waist. Ecodes grinned again. Women. Born to deceive, all of them. But this one was clean, the way Ecodes liked, a bit of class to her, not like the eastern shrew upstairs.

'Never mind,' he said to the steward. 'Carry on.'

The night was passing, swift as chariots; they were to find the woman before sunrise. The announced reward was extravagant. Even if divided among ten (with a double share to the decurion, of course) they could all retire to lives of leisure when their service was up. Have their own clean serving girls, or wives—or both for that matter. Little chance of any of that if they lingered or delayed. His men were waiting impatiently in the street. Ecodes turned and went down the steps.

'Right, lads. Next house,' he said briskly. The steward closed the door behind him, hard.

He had been embarrassed by his own arousal under the sheets as she simulated lovemaking, appearing to be riding him as the door opened. She hadn't let him lock the door, and belatedly he had understood: the room *was* going to be searched, the whole *idea* was for the soldiers to find them engaged in the act, outraged at intrusion. Her voice, a low snarl changing swiftly to a nasal whine, speaking Rustem's own tongue with ferociously obscene eloquence, had startled him almost as much as it appeared to disconcert the small soldier in the doorway. Rustem, aware that his life was at risk here, had little trouble assuming a pose of anger and hostility.

Alixana had dismounted from her position upon him, clutching the sheets to herself. She fired another volley of invective at the soldier, and Rustem, inspired by fear as much as anything else, had slapped her face, shocking himself.

Now, as the door closed, he waited an agonizingly long moment, heard conversation outside, then steps on the creaking stairs, and finally murmured, 'I am sorry. That blow. I . . . '

Lying beside him, she didn't even look over. 'No. It was well done.'

He cleared his throat. 'I would lock it now, probably, if this were . . . real.'

'It is real enough,' she whispered.

All force seemed drained from her now. He was aware of her naked form beside his own, but not with desire any more. He felt a deep shame about that, and some other emotion that came unexpectedly close to grief. He rose and quickly drew on his tunic, without undergarments. He went over to the door, locking it. When he turned back, she was sitting up in the bed, the sheets wrapped fully around her.

Rustem hesitated, at sea and unmoored, then crossed and sat on the small bench near the fire. He looked at the flames and put a log on, busying himself with trivial activity. He said, not looking at her, 'When did you learn Bassanid?'

'Did I do all right?'

He nodded. 'I couldn't curse like that.'

'I'm sure you could.' Her voice was leached of nuance. 'I picked up some when I was young, mostly the swearing. Learned more when we dealt with ambassadors, later. Men are flattered when a woman speaks to them in their own tongue.'

'And the . . . voice?' That rancid harridan from some dockside caupona.

'I was an actress, doctor, remember? Much the same as a whore, some say. Was I convincing as one?'

This time he did look at her. Her gaze was vacant, fixed on the door through which the soldier had gone.

Rustem was silent. He felt as if the night had become deep as a stone well, as dark. A day so long it seemed beyond belief. Had started with his patient gone in the morning and his own desire to see the racing in the Hippodrome.

It had started differently for her.

He looked narrowly at the too-still figure on his bed. Shook his head at what he saw. He was a physician, had seen this look before. He said, 'My lady, forgive me, but you must weep. You must allow yourself to do that. I say this . . . professionally.'

She didn't even move. 'Not yet,' she said. 'I can't.'

'Yes, you can,' said Rustem, very deliberately. 'The man you loved is dead. Murdered. He is gone. You can, my lady.'

She turned finally to look at him. The firelight caught her flawless cheekbones, shadowed the cropped hair, the smears of dirt, could not reach the darkness of those eyes. Rustem had an impulse—rare for him as rain in the desert—to cross to the bed and hold her. He refrained.

He murmured, 'We say that when Anahita weeps for her children, pity enters the world, the kingdoms of light and dark.'

'I have no children.'

So clever. Guarding herself so very hard. 'You *are* her child,' he said.

'I will not be pitied.'

'Then let yourself mourn, or I must pity the woman who cannot.'

Again, she shook her head. 'A bad patient, doctor. I am sorry. I owe you obedience if nothing else for what you have just done. But not yet. Not . . . yet. Perhaps when . . . everything else is done.'

'Where will you go?' he said, after a moment.

A quick, reflexive smile, meaningless, born of nothing but the habit of wit, from a world lost. She said, 'Now I am truly wounded. You tire of me in your bed already?'

He shook his head. Stared at her, said nothing. Then he turned deliberately back to the fire and busied himself there with movements old as all hearths, that any man or woman might have done in any age, might be doing even now, somewhere else in the world. He took his time.

And a few moments later he heard a harsh, choking noise, and then another. With a great effort, Rustem continued to gaze into the flames, not looking over at the bed where the Empress of Sarantium was grieving in the night, with broken sounds he had never heard before.

It went on a long time. Rustem never looked away from the fire, leaving her at least the semblance of privacy, as earlier they had simulated lovemaking. At length, as he was adding yet another piece of wood to the flames, he heard her whisper, 'Why is this better, doctor? Tell me why.'

He turned. In the firelight he saw the tears shining on her face. He said, 'My lady, we are mortal. Children of whichever gods or goddesses we worship, but only mortal. The soul must bend to endure.'

She looked away, but not at anything in the room. Said nothing for a time, and then, 'And even Anahita weeps? Or the kingdoms would have no pity?'

He nodded, deeply moved, beyond words. A woman such as he'd never encountered before.

She wiped at her eyes with the backs of both hands, a childlike gesture. Looked at him again. 'If you are right, you have saved me twice tonight, haven't you?'

He could think of nothing to say.

'Do you know the amount of the reward they have offered?'

He nodded. It had been proclaimed by heralds in the streets from late in the day. Had reached the Blues' compound before sundown. Treating the wounded, he had heard of it.

'All you need do,' she said, 'is open the door and call out.'

Rustem looked at her, struggling for words. He stroked his beard. 'I may be tired of you, but not *that* tired,' he said, and saw that her smile this time did touch, very briefly, her dark eyes.

After a moment she said only, 'Thank you for that. You are more than I had any right to pray for, doctor.'

He shook his head, embarrassed again.

She said, her voice a little stronger now, 'But you must know you'll have to say something about this in Kabadh. You'll have to give them *something*.'

He stared at her. 'Something for . . . ?'

'Some results from your being sent here, doctor.'

'I don't see . . . I came to obtain some—'

'—medical knowledge from the west before going to court. I know. The physicians' guild filed a report. I looked at it. But Shirvan never has only one string to a bow and you won't be an exception. He'll have ordered you to keep your eyes open. You will be judged on what you have seen. If you return to his court with nothing, you'll give weapons to your enemies, and you have them there already, doctor. Waiting for you. It isn't hard to arrive at a court with people hating you beforehand.'

Rustem clasped his hands together. 'I know little about such things, my lady.'

She nodded. 'I believe that.' She looked at him, and then, as if making a decision, murmured, 'Did anyone tell you that Bassania has crossed the border in the north, breaching the peace?'

No one had. Who would have told him that, a stranger among the westerners? An enemy. Rustem swallowed, felt a coldness enter him. If a war began, and he was still here . . .

She looked at him. 'There were rumours all afternoon in the City. As it happens, I am quite certain they are true.'

'Why?' he whispered.

'Why am I sure?'

He nodded.

'Because Petrus wanted Shirvan to do this, steered him towards it.'

'Wh—why?'

The woman's expression changed again. There were tears still, on her cheeks. 'Because he never had less than three or four strings to *his* bow. He wanted Batiara, but he also wanted Leontes taught a lesson about limitations, even defeat, along the way, and dividing the army to deal with Bassania was a way to achieve that. And of course the payments east would stop.'

'He wanted to *lose* in the west?'

'Of course not.' The same faint, almost indiscernible smile, shaped of memory. 'But there are ways of winning more than one thing, and *how* you triumph matters very much, sometimes.'

Rustem shook his head slowly. 'And how many people would die in achieving all of this? Is it not vanity? To believe we can act like a god? We aren't. Time claims all of us.'

'The Lord of Emperors?' She looked at him. 'It does, but are there no ways to be remembered, doctor, to leave a mark, on stone, not on water? To have . . . been here?'

'Not for most of us, my lady.' Even as he said that he was remembering the chef in the Blues' compound: *This boy was my legacy.* A cry from the man's heart.

Her hands and body were hidden beneath the sheets. She was still as stone herself. She said, 'I'll grant you a half-truth there. But only that much . . . Have you no children, doctor?'

It was so strange, for the chef had asked him the same thing. Twice in a night, speaking about what one might leave behind. Rustem made a sign against evil, towards the fire. He was aware of how odd this conversation was now, yet sensed that somehow these questions lay towards the heart of what this day and night had become. He said, slowly, 'But to be remembered through others, even our own heirs, is also to be . . . misremembered, is it not? What child knows his father? Who decides *how* we are recorded, or if we are?'

She smiled a little, as if he'd pleased her with cleverness. 'There is that. Perhaps the chroniclers, the painters, sculptors, the historians, perhaps *they* are the real lords of emperors, of all of us, doctor. It is a thought.'

And even as Rustem felt an undeniably warming pleasure to have elicited her approval, he also had a glimpse of what this woman must have been like, jewelled upon her throne, with courtiers vying for that approving tone.

He lowered his gaze, humbled again.

When he looked up, her expression had changed, as if an interlude was over. She said, 'You realize that you must be very careful now? Bassanids will be unpopular when word gets out. Keep close to Bonosus. He will protect a guest. But understand something else: you might also be killed when you go back east to Kabadh.'

Rustem gaped at her. 'Why?'

'Because you didn't follow orders.'

He blinked. 'What? The . . . the Antae queen? They *can't* expect me to have murdered royalty so quickly, so easily?'

She shook her head, implacable. 'No, but they can expect you to have died trying by now, doctor. You were given instructions.'

He said nothing. A night deep as a well. How did one ever climb out? And her voice now was that of someone infinitely versed in these ways of courts and power.

'That letter carried a meaning. It was an explicit indication that your presence as a physician in Kabadh was less important to the King of Kings than your services as an assassin here, successful or otherwise.' She paused. 'Had you not considered that, doctor?'

He hadn't. Not at all. He was a physician from a sand-swept village at the southern desert's edge. He knew healing and childbirth, wounds and cataracts, fluxes of the bowel. Mutely, he shook his head.

Alixana of Sarantium, naked in his bed, wrapped in a sheet as in a shroud, murmured, 'My own small service to you, then. A thought to ponder, when I am gone.'

Gone from the room? She meant more than that. However deep the well of night felt to him, hers went deeper by far. And thinking so, Rustem of Kerakek found a courage and even a grace in himself he hadn't known he had (it had been drawn from him, he was later to think), and he murmured, wryly, 'I have done well so far tonight at being careful, haven't I?'

She smiled again. He would always remember it.

There came a knock then, softly at the door. Four times swiftly, twice slow. Rustem stood up quickly, his eyes darting around the room. There was really nowhere for her to hide.

But Alixana said, 'That will be Elita. It is all right. They'll expect her to come here. She's bedding you, isn't she? I wonder if she'll be upset with me?'

He crossed the room, opened the door. Elita entered hurriedly, closed the door behind her. Took one quick, frightened look at the bed, saw that Alixana was there. She dropped to her knees before Rustem and seized one of his hands in both of hers and kissed it. Then turned towards the bed, still on her knees, looking at the ragged, dirty, crop-haired woman sitting there.

'Oh, my lady,' she whispered. 'What are we to do?'

And she took a dagger from her belt, laying it on the floor. Then she wept.

She had long been one of the most trusted women of the Empress Alixana. Took a pleasure in that fact that was almost certainly reprehensible in the eyes of Jad and his clerics. Mortals, especially women, were not to puff themselves up with the sin of pride.

But there it was.

She had been the last person awake in the house, having offered to tend the downstairs fire and put out the lamps before going up to the doctor's bed. She had sat in the front room alone for a time in the dark, watching white moonlight through the high window. Had heard footsteps in the other ground-floor rooms, heard them cease as the others went to their beds. She had remained where she was for a time, anxiously. She had to wait, but feared to wait too long. Finally, she had walked down the main-floor hallway and opened a bedroom door, silently.

She had prepared an excuse—not a good one—if he was still awake.

The steward who ran this house for Plautus Bonosus was an efficient but not an especially clever man. Still, something had been said when the soldiers left—a misunderstanding that could have been amusing but wasn't, at all, with so desperately much at stake. An exchange that might be fatal, if he put the pieces together.

There was a huge reward on offer, incomprehensibly large, in fact, proclaimed by heralds throughout the City all day. What if the steward woke in the night with a blinding thought? If a daemon or ghost came to him carrying a dream? If he realized under the late moons that the soldier at the door hadn't been calling the grey-bearded doctor a whore but had been referring to a woman upstairs? A woman. The steward might wake, wonder, feel the slow licking of curiosity and greed, rise up in the dark house, go down the hallway with a lamp lit from his fire. Open the front door. Call for a guard of the Urban Prefecture, or a soldier.

It was a risk. It was a risk.

She had walked into his room, silent as a ghost herself, looked down upon him where he lay sleeping on his back. Sought a way to make her heart grow hard.

Loyalty, real loyalty, sometimes required a death. The Empress (she would always call her that) was still in the house. It was not a night to take chances. They might trace the steward's murder to her but sometimes the death required was one's own.

'My lady, I could not kill him. I tried, I went to do it, but . . .'

The girl was weeping. The blade on the floor before her was innocent of blood, Rustem saw. He looked at Alixana.

'I ought to have known better,' Alixana murmured, still wrapped in the bed linens, 'than to make you a soldier in the Excubitors.' And she smiled, faintly.

Elita looked up, biting at her lower lip.

'I don't think we need his death, my dear. If the man somehow wakes in the night with a vision and goes for the door and a guard . . . you can run them through with a sword.'

'My lady. I don't have . . .'

'I know, child. I am telling you we need not murder to defend against this chance. If he were going to rethink that conversation, he'd have done it by now.'

Rustem, who knew a little of sleep and dreams, was less sure, but said nothing.

Alixana looked at him. 'Doctor, will you let two women share your bed? I fear it will be less exciting than the words suggest.'

Rustem cleared his throat. 'You must sleep, my lady. Lie in the bed. I will take a chair, and Elita can have a pillow by the fire.'

'You need rest as well, physician. People's lives will depend on you in the morning.'

'And I will do what I can do. I have spent nights in chairs before.'

It was true. Chairs, worse places. Stony ground with an army in Ispahani. He was bone-weary. Saw that she was, as well.

'I am taking your bed from you,' she murmured, lying down. 'I ought not to do that.'

She was asleep when she finished the sentence.

Rustem looked at the servant who had been on the edge of murdering for her. Neither of them spoke. He gestured at one of the pillows and she took it and went to the hearth and lay down. He looked at the bed, and crossed there and covered the sleeping woman with one blanket, then took another and carried it to the girl by the fire. She looked up at him. He draped it over her.

He went back to the window. Looked out, saw the trees in the garden below made silver by the white moon. He closed the window, drew the curtains. The breeze was strong now, the night colder. He sank down in the chair.

It came to him, with finality, that he was going to have to change his life again, what he had thought was to be his life.

He slept. When he woke, both women were gone.

A greyness was filtering palely through the curtains. He drew them back and looked out. It was almost day, but not quite, the hovering hour before dawn. There was a knocking at the door. He realized that was what had awakened him. He looked over, saw that the door was unlocked, as was usual.

He was about to call for whoever it was to come in when he remembered where he was.

He rose quickly. Elita had replaced her pillow and blanket on the bed. Rustem crossed there. Climbed in and under the sheets. There was a scent, faint as a dream receding, of the woman who was gone.

'Yes?' he called. He had no idea where she was, or if he ever would know.

Bonosus's steward opened the door, impeccably dressed already, composed and calm as ever, dry in his manner as a bone. Rustem had seen a knife in this room last night, meant for this man's heart while he slept. He had been that close to dying. So had Rustem, a different way—if a deception had failed.

The steward paused deferentially on the threshold, hands clasped before him. There was an odd look in his eye, however. 'My deepest apologies, but some people are at the door, doctor.' His voice was practised, murmurous. 'They say they are your family.'

He broke stride only long enough to throw on a robe. Dishevelled, unshaven, still bleary-eyed, he bolted past the startled man and tore down the hallway and then the stairs in a manner worlds removed from anything resembling dignity.

He saw them from the first landing, where the stairway doubled back, and he stopped, looking down.

They were all in the front hallway. Katyun and Jarita, one visibly anxious, the other hiding the same apprehension. Issa in her mother's arms. Shaski was a little ahead of the others.

He was gazing up fixedly, eyes wide, an intent, frightening expression on his features that only changed, only melted away—Rustem saw it—when his father appeared on the stairs. And Rustem knew, in that moment he knew as surely as he knew anything on earth, that Shaski was the reason, the *only* reason, the four of them were here and the knowledge hit him in the heart like nothing ever had.

He went the rest of the way down to the ground floor and stood gravely before the boy, hands clasped in front of himself, very like the steward, in fact.

Shaski looked up at him, his face white as a flag of surrender, the small, thin body taut as a bowstring. (*We must bend, my little one, we must learn to bend or we break.*) He said, his voice quivering, 'Hello, Papa. Papa, we can't go home.'

'I know,' said Rustem softly.

Shaski bit his lip. Stared at him. Huge eyes. Hadn't expected this. Had expected punishment, very likely. (*We must learn to be easier, little one.*) 'Or . . . or to Kabadh? We can't go there.'

'I know,' said Rustem again.

He did know. He also understood, after what he'd learned in the night, that Perun and the Lady had intervened here beyond any possible measure of his worthiness. There was something constricting in his chest, a pressure needing release. He knelt down on the floor and he opened his arms.

'Come to me,' he said. 'It is all right, child. It will be all right.'

Shaski made a sound—a wail, a heart's cry—and ran to his father then, a small bundle of spent force, to be gathered and held. He began to weep, desperately, like the child he still was, despite everything else he was and would be.

Clutching the boy to him, lifting him, not letting go, Rustem stood up and went forward and drew both his wives into that embrace and his infant daughter, as the morning came.

It seemed they had inquired of Bassanid mercantile agents on the other bank, and one of them had known where Rustem the physician was staying. Their escorts, the two soldiers who had crossed with them from Deapolis on a fishing boat before daylight (two others remaining behind), were waiting outside in front of the house.

Rustem had them admitted. Given what he now knew, it was not a time for Bassanids to be on the streets of Sarantium. One of them, he saw with astonishment (he had thought himself to have reached a place beyond surprise now), was Vinaszh, the garrison commander of Kerakek.

'Commander? How does this come to be?' It was strange to be speaking his own tongue again.

Vinaszh, wearing Sarantine trousers and a belted tunic and not a uniform, thank the Lady, smiled a little before answering: the weary but satisfied expression of a man who has achieved a difficult task.

'Your son,' he said, 'is a persuasive child.'

Rustem was still holding Shaski. The boy's arms were around his neck, his head on his father's shoulder. He had stopped crying. Rustem looked over at the steward and said, in Sarantine, 'Is it possible to offer a morning meal to my family, and to these men who have escorted them?'

'Of course it is,' said Elita, before the steward could answer. She was smiling at Issa. 'I will arrange it.'

The steward looked briefly irritated by the woman's presumption. Rustem had a sudden, vivid image of Elita standing over the man's body in the night, a blade in her hand.

'I would also like a message taken to the Senator, as soon as possible. Conveying my respects and requesting an opportunity to attend upon him later this morning.'

The steward's expression became grave. 'There is a difficulty,' he murmured.

'How so?'

'The Senator and his family will not be receiving visitors today, or for the next few days. They are in mourning. The lady Thenaïs is dead.'

'*What?* I was with her yesterday!'

'I know that, doctor. It seems she went to the god in the afternoon, at home.'

'How?' Rustem was genuinely shocked. He felt Shaski stiffen.

The steward hesitated. 'I am given to understand there was . . . a self-inflicted injury.'

Images again. From the day that yesterday had been. A shadowy, high-ceilinged interior space within the Hippodrome, motes of dust drifting where light fell, a woman more rigid than even he himself was, confronting a chariot-racer. Another drawn blade.

We must learn to bend, or we break.

Rustem took a deep breath. He was thinking very hard. Bonosus could not be intruded upon, but the need for protection was real. Either the steward would have to make arrangements here himself for guards, or else . . .

It was an answer. It was an obvious answer.

He looked back at the man. 'I am deeply saddened to hear of this. She was a woman of dignity and grace. I will need a different message sent now. Please have someone inform the acting leader of the Blue faction that I and my family and our two companions request admission into the compound. We will need an escort, of course.'

'You are leaving us, doctor?'

The man's expression was impeccable. He had been very nearly killed in his sleep last night. He'd never have awakened. Someone might have been knocking at the steward's bedroom door, finding his body even now, raising a terrible cry.

The world was a place beyond man's capacity to ever fully grasp. It had been made that way.

'I believe we must leave,' he said. 'It appears our countries might be at war again. Sarantium will be dangerous for Bassanids, however innocent we might be. If the Blues are willing, we might be better defended within the compound.' He looked at the man. 'We pose a danger here to all of you now, of course.'

The steward—not a subtle thinker—had not considered that. It showed in his face.

'I will have your message sent.'

'Tell them,' added Rustem, setting Shaski down beside him, a hand across the boy's shoulders, 'that I will, of course, offer my professional assistance for the duration of any stay.'

He looked over at Vinaszh, the man who had set all of this in motion one afternoon in winter when the wind had been blowing from the desert. The commander spoke Sarantine, it appeared: he had followed this. 'I left two men on the other shore,' he murmured.

'It might be unsafe for you to go back to them. Wait and see. I have asked for you to be admitted with us. This place is a guarded compound, and they have reason to be well disposed towards me.'

'I heard. I understand.'

'But I have no right to act for you, it occurs to me. You have brought me my family, unlooked for. For many reasons I want them with me now. I owe you more than I can ever repay, but I do not know your wishes. Will you return home? Does duty demand as much? Did you . . . I don't know if you have heard about a possible war in the north.'

'There were rumours on the other bank last night. We obtained civilian clothing, as you see.' Vinaszh hesitated. He removed his rough cloth cap and scratched his head. 'I . . . I told you your son was very persuasive.'

The steward, hearing them speak in Bassanid, turned politely away and crooked a finger at one of the younger servants: a messenger.

Rustem stared at the commander. 'He is an unusual child.'

He was still holding the boy, not letting go. Katyun watched them, her head turning from one man to the other. Jarita had dried her tears, was making the baby be silent.

Vinaszh was still grappling with something. He cleared his throat, then did it again. 'He said . . . Shaski said . . . told us that an ending was coming. To Kerakek. Even . . . Kabadh.'

'We can't go home, Papa.' Shaski's voice was calm now, a certainty in it that could chill you if you thought about it at all. *Perun defend you, Anahita guard us all. Azal never know your name.*

Rustem looked at his son. 'What kind of ending?'

'I don't know.' The admission bothered the boy, it was obvious. 'From . . . the desert.'

From the desert. Rustem looked at Katyun. She shrugged, a small gesture, one he knew so well.

'Children have dreams,' he said, but then he shook his head. That was dishonest. An evasion. They were only here with him because of Shaski's dreams, and last night Rustem had been told—quite explicitly and by someone who would know—that he was probably a dead man if he went to Kabadh now.

He had declined to try to assassinate someone. And the orders had come from the king.

Vinaszh, son of Vinaszh, the garrison commander of Kerakek, said, softly, 'If your intention is to stay here, or go elsewhere, I humbly ask permission to journey with you for a time. Our paths may part later, but we will offer our assistance now. I believe . . . I accept what the child sees. It happens, in the desert, that some people have this . . . knowing.'

Rustem swallowed. 'We? You speak for the other three?'

'They share my thought about the boy. We have journeyed with him. Things may be seen.'

As simple as that.

Rustem still had his hand across Shaski's too-thin shoulders. 'You are deserting the army.' Harsh word. Needed to be used, brought into the open here.

Vinaszh winced. Then straightened, his gaze direct. 'I have promised to properly discharge my men, which is in my power as their commander. The formal letters will be sent back.'

'And for yourself?'

There was no one who could write such a letter for the commander. The other man drew a breath. 'I will not go back.' He looked down at Shaski, and he smiled a little. Said nothing more.

A life changed, changed utterly.

Rustem looked around the room, at his wives, his infant daughter, the man who had just thrown in his lot with them, and in that very moment—he would say as much long afterwards, telling the tale—the thought came to him where they would go.

He had already been in the distant east, he'd tell guests, over wine in another land, why not journey as far to the west?

Beyond Batiara, well beyond it, was a country still taking shape, defining itself, a frontier, open spaces, the sea on three sides, it was said. A place where they might begin anew, have a chance to see what Shaski was, among other things.

They would need physicians in Esperana, wouldn't they?

They were escorted down through the city, the streets quiet, unnaturally so, to the Blues' compound just before midday. On orders from the factionarius Astorgus—released only that morning from the Urban Prefecture—half a dozen men were sent across the straits with a note from Vinaszh to fetch his other two men from their inn in Deapolis.

On his arrival in the compound, after they were welcomed (respectfully) and given rooms, and just before he went to see his patients, Rustem learned from the small chef who had been in charge last night that the search for the missing Empress had been called off just before dawn.

It seemed that there had been further changes in the Imperial Precinct during the night.

Shaski liked the horses. So did little Issa. A smiling groom with straw in his hair carried her as he rode on one of them and they walked a slow circle around the open yard, the baby's whoops of laughter filling the compound, making people smile as they went about the tasks of a brightening day.

CHAPTER XV

In the morning the eunuchs, almost invariably the first to hear tidings in the palaces, told Crispin what had happened in the night. Their collective mood was entirely different from the subdued apprehension of the evening before. You could have called it exhilarated. A colour of sunrise, unlooked for, if one's mind worked that way. Crispin felt his dreams slipping away in the fierce, hard brightness of what they said, the sudden swirl of activity all around, like cloths unfurling.

He had one of them escort him back to the Porphyry Room. He didn't expect to be able to enter again, but the eunuch simply gestured and the guards opened the doors for them. There were changes here, too. Four of the Excubitors, garbed and helmed for ceremony, were stationed in the four corners of the room, rigidly at attention. Someone had laid flowers about the room, and the traditional plate of food for the dead soul's journey was in place on a side table. The plate was gold, with jewels set around the rim. Torches still burned near the raised bier that held the shrouded body.

It was very early still. No one else was here. The eunuch waited politely by the door. Crispin walked forward and knelt beside Valerius for a second time, making the sign of the sun disk. This time he spoke the Rites, offering a prayer for the journeying soul of the man who'd brought him here. He wished he had more to say, but his own thoughts were still tumbled and chaotic. He rose again and the eunuch took him outside and through the gardens to the Bronze Gates, and he was allowed to exit there into the Hippodrome Forum.

Signs of life here. A normal kind of life. He saw the Holy Fool, standing in his customary place, offering an entirely predictable litany of the follies of earthly wealth and power. Two food stalls were set up already, one selling grilled lamb on sticks, the other roasted chestnuts. People were buying from each of them. As Crispin watched, the yogurt vendor arrived and a juggler set up not far from the Holy Fool.

The beginnings of a new beginning. Slowly, almost hesitantly, as if the dance of the ordinary, the rhythm of it, had been forgotten in the violence of yesterday and needed to be learned again. There were no marching clusters of soldiers now, and Crispin knew that, men and women being what they were, the City would be itself again very soon, past events receding like the memory of a night when one has drunk too much and done things best forgotten.

He took a deep breath. The Bronze Gates were behind him, the equestrian statue of Valerius I rising to his right, the City itself unfurling before him like a banner. Everything possible, as it so often felt in the morning. The air was crisp, the sky bright. He smelled the roasting chestnuts, heard all those here being sternly admonished to forsake the pursuits of the world and turn to the holiness of Jad. Knew it would not happen. Could not. The world was what it was. He saw an apprentice approach two serving girls on their way to the well with pitchers and say something that made them laugh.

The hunt for Alixana had been called off. It was being proclaimed, the eunuchs had said. They still wanted to find her, but for a different reason, now. Leontes wished to honour her and honour the memory of Valerius. Newly anointed, a pious man, wishing to begin a reign in all proper ways. She hadn't reappeared, however. No one knew where she was. Crispin had a sudden memory from the night: that stony moonlit beach in his dream, silver and black the colours.

Gisel of Batiara was to be married to Leontes later today in a ceremony in the Attenine Palace, becoming Empress of Sarantium. The world had changed.

He remembered her in her own palace, back in the autumn with the leaves falling, a young queen sending him east with a message, offering herself to an Emperor far away. There had been wagers throughout Varena that summer and fall on how long she had to live before someone found her with poison or a blade.

She would be presented to the people in the Hippodrome tomorrow or the next day, and she and Leontes would be crowned. There was so much to be done, the eunuchs had told him, hurrying about, an *impossible* number of details to be attended to.

In a real way, he had caused this to happen. Crispin had been the one to bring her into the palace, passing through the streets of the City to the Porphyry Room through the wild night. It might—there was a *chance* it might—mean that Varena, Rhodias, the whole of Batiara would be saved now from assault. Valerius had been about to wage war; the fleet would have sailed any day now, carrying death with it. Leontes, with Gisel beside him, might do things differently. She offered him that chance. This was altogether good.

Styliane had been blinded in the night, they had told him.

She had been put aside by Leontes, their marriage formally renounced for the horror of her crime. You could do these things more quickly, the eunuchs said, if you were an Emperor. Her brother Tertius was dead, they told him, strangled in one of those rooms under the palace no one liked to talk about. His body would be displayed later today, hanging from the triple walls. Gesius was in charge of that, too. No, they'd said, when he asked, Styliane herself had not been reported killed. No one knew where she was.

Crispin looked up at the statue rising before him. A man on a horse, a martial sword, image of power and majesty, a dominant figure. But it was the women, he thought, who had shaped the story here, not the men with their armies and blades. He had no idea what to make of that. He wished he could dispel the heaviness, the tangled, confusing mire of all of this, blood and fury and memory.

The juggler was very good. He had five balls in the air, of different sizes, and a dagger in there with them, spinning and glinting in the light. Most people were ignoring him, hurrying past. It was early in the day, tasks and errands to be done. Morning in Sarantium was not a time for lingering.

Crispin looked over to his left at Valerius's Sanctuary, the dome rising serenely, almost disdainfully above it, above all of this. He gazed at it for a time, taking an almost physical pleasure in the grace of what Artibasos had achieved, and then he went there. He had his own work waiting to be done. A man needed to work.

Others, he was unsurprised to see, were of the same view. Silano and Sosio, the twins, were at work in the small, fenced, temporary yard beside the Sanctuary, tending to the quicklime for the setting bed at the ovens. One of them (he could never tell them apart) waved hesitantly and Crispin nodded back.

Inside, he looked up and saw that Vargos was already overhead on the scaffolding, laying the thinnest, fine layer where Crispin had been about to work the day before. His Inici friend from the Imperial Road had emerged, unexpectedly, as an entirely competent mosaic labourer. Another man who had sailed to Sarantium and changed his life. Vargos never said as much, but Crispin thought that for him— as for Pardos—a good portion of his pleasure in this work came from piety, from working in a place of the god. Neither man would achieve as much satisfaction, Crispin thought, doing private commissions for dining rooms or bedchambers.

Pardos was also overhead, on his own scaffolding, doing the wall design Crispin had assigned him above the double row of arches along the eastern side of the space beneath the dome. Two of the other guild artisans on the team he'd assembled were also here and at work.

Artibasos would be around somewhere as well, though his own labours were essentially done. Valerius's Sanctuary was complete in its execution. It was, in fact, ready for him: to house the ruined body. Only the mosaics and the altars and whatever tomb or memorial they now needed remained to be achieved. Then the clerics would come in and they would hang the sun disks in their proper locations and consecrate this as a holy place.

Crispin gazed at what he had journeyed here to achieve, and it seemed to him as if, in some deep, ultimately inexplicable fashion, just to look was enough to steady him. He felt the images of the day before recede—Lecanus Daleinus in his hut, men dying in that clearing, Alixana dropping her cloak on the beach, the screaming in the streets and the burning fires, Gisel of the Antae in her carried litter, eyes alight as they went through the dark, and then in a purple-draped room where Valerius lay dead—all the whirling visions fell away, leaving him gazing up at what he had made here. The apex of what he could do, being a fallible mortal under Jad.

You had to live, Crispin thought, in order to have anything to *say* about living, but you needed to find a way to withdraw to accomplish that saying. A scaffolding overhead, he thought, was as good a place as any for that and better, perhaps, than most.

He went forward, surrounded and eased by the familiar sounds of work, thinking about his girls now, reclaiming their faces, which he would try to render today, next to Ilandra and not far from where Linon lay on the grass.

But before he reached the ladder, before he began to climb to his place above the world, someone spoke from behind one of the vast pillars.

Crispin turned quickly, knowing the voice. And then he knelt, and lowered his head to touch the perfect marble floor.

One knelt before Emperors in Sarantium.

'Rise, artisan,' said Leontes, in the brisk tone of a soldier. 'We owe you greatly, it seems, for services last night.'

Crispin stood up slowly and looked at the other man. All around the Sanctuary the noises were coming to a halt. The others were watching them, had now seen who was here. Leontes wore boots and a dark green tunic with a leather belt. His cloak was pinned at his shoulder with a golden ornament, but the effect was unassuming. Another man at work. Behind the Emperor, Crispin saw a cleric he vaguely recognized, and a secretary he knew very well. Pertennius had a bruised and swollen jaw. His eyes were icy cold as he looked at Crispin. Not surprisingly.

Crispin didn't care.

He said, 'The Emperor is gracious beyond my deserving. I simply tried to assist my queen in her desire to pay homage to the dead. What came of it has nothing to do with me, my lord. It would be a presumption to claim otherwise.'

Leontes shook his head. 'What came of it would not have happened without you. The presumption is to pretend otherwise. Do you always deny your own role in events?'

'I deny that I *had* any intended role in . . . events. If people make use of me it is a price I pay to have the chance to do my work.' He wasn't sure why he was saying this.

Leontes looked at him. Crispin was remembering another conversation with this man, amid the steam of a bathhouse half a year ago, both of them naked under sheets. *What we build—even the Emperor's Sanctuary—we hold precariously and must defend.* A man had come in to kill Crispin that day.

The Emperor said, 'And was this true yesterday morning, as well? When you went to the isle?'

They knew about that. Of course they did. It was hardly likely to have been kept secret. Alixana had warned him.

Crispin met the other man's blue gaze. 'It is exactly the same, my lord. The Empress Alixana asked me to accompany her.'

'Why?'

He didn't think they would do anything to him now. He wasn't certain (how could one be?), but he didn't think so. He said, 'She wished to show me dolphins in the sea.'

'Why?' Blunt and assured. Crispin remembered that immense self-confidence. A man never defeated in the field, they said.

'I do not know, my lord. Other things happened, it was never explained.'

A lie. To Jad's anointed Emperor. He *would* lie for her, however. Dolphins were a heresy. He would not be the one to betray her. She was gone, had not reappeared. Would have no power at all now even if she did trust them and come from hiding. Valerius was dead, she might never be seen again. But he would not, he would *not* betray her. A small thing, really, but in another way it wasn't. A man lived with his words and actions.

'What other things? What happened on the isle?'

This he could answer, though he didn't know *why* she had wanted him to see Lecanus Daleinus and hear her pretend to be his sister.

'I saw the . . . prisoner there. We were on the isle, elsewhere, when he escaped.'

'And then?'

'As you must know, my lord, there was an attempt on her life. It was . . . repelled by the Excubitors. The Empress left us then and made her own way back to Sarantium.'

'Why so?'

Some men asked questions when they knew the answers. Leontes seemed to be one of those. Crispin said, 'They had tried to kill her, my lord. Daleinus had escaped. She was of the belief that an assassination plot might be unfolding.'

Leontes nodded. 'It was, of course.'

'Yes, my lord,' Crispin said.

'The participants have been punished.'

'Yes, my lord.'

One of the participants, the leader, had been this man's wife, golden as he was. He was Emperor of Sarantium now, because of her plot. Styliane. A child when it had all begun, the burning that had begotten a burning. Crispin had lain with her in a tangled, desperate darkness so little time ago. *Remember this room. Whatever else I do.* The words came to him again. He suspected he could recall every word she'd ever spoken to him, if he tried. She was in a different kind of darkness now, if she was alive. He didn't ask. He didn't dare ask.

There was a silence. Behind the Emperor, the cleric cleared his throat, and Crispin suddenly recollected him: the adviser to the Eastern Patriarch. A fussy, officious man. They had met when Crispin had first submitted the sketches for the dome.

'My secretary . . . has complained of you,' the Emperor said, looking briefly back over his shoulder. A hint of amusement in his voice, almost a smile. A minor disagreement among the troops.

'He has cause,' Crispin said mildly. 'I struck him a blow last night. An unworthy action.'

That much was true. He could say that much.

Leontes made a dismissive movement with one hand. 'I'm sure Pertennius will accept that apology. Everyone was under great strain yesterday. I . . . felt it myself, I must say. A terrible day and night. The Emperor Valerius was like . . . an older brother to me.' He looked Crispin in the eye.

'Yes, my lord.' Crispin lowered his gaze.

There was another brief silence. 'Queen Gisel has requested your presence in the palace this afternoon. She would like one of her countrymen present when we wed, and given your role—denied though it may be—in the events of last night, you are easily the most appropriate witness from Batiara.'

'I am honoured,' Crispin said. He *should* have been, but there was, still, this slow, deep coil of rage within him. He couldn't define it or place it, but it was there. Everything was so brutally entangled here. He said, 'The more so since the thrice-exalted Emperor came to extend the invitation himself.'

A flirting with insolence. His anger had gotten him in trouble before.

Leontes smiled, however. The brilliant, remembered smile. 'I fear I have rather too many affairs to attend to, to have come only for that, artisan. No. No, I wanted to see this Sanctuary and the dome here. I've not been inside before.'

Few people had, and the Supreme Strategos would have been an unlikely man to petition for an early glimpse at architecture or mosaic work. This had been Valerius's dream, and Artibasos's, and it had become Crispin's.

The cleric, behind Leontes, was looking up. The Emperor did the same.

Crispin said, 'I should be honoured to walk you about, my lord, though Artibasos—who will be somewhere in here—is far better able to guide you.'

'Not necessary,' said Leontes. Brisk, businesslike. 'I can observe for myself what is currently done, and Pertennius and Maximius both saw the original drawings, I understand.'

Crispin felt, for the first time, a faint thrill of fear. Tried to master it. Said, 'Then, if my guidance is not needed, and I am requested for later in the day, might I have the Emperor's leave to withdraw to my labours? The setting bed for today's section has just been laid for me up above. It will dry if I delay over-long.'

Leontes returned his gaze from overhead. And Crispin saw a flicker of something that might—just—have been called sympathy in the man's face.

The Emperor said, 'I wouldn't do that. I wouldn't go up, were I you, artisan.'

Simple words, one could even say they had been gently spoken.

It was possible for the world, the sensual evidence of it—sounds, smells, texture, sight—to recede far away, to dwindle down, as if perceived through a keyhole, to one single thing.

All else fell away. The keyhole showed the face of Leontes.

'Why so, my lord?' Crispin said.

He heard his own voice, on the words, crack a little. But he knew. Before the other man replied, he finally understood why these three had come, what was happening, and he cried out then, in silence, within his heart, as at another death.

I have been a better friend than you know. I did tell you not to become attached to any work on that dome.

Styliane. Had said that. The very first time she'd been waiting in his room, and then again, *again*, that night in her own chamber two weeks ago. A warning. Twice. He hadn't heard it, or heeded.

But what *could* he have done? Being what he was?

And so Crispin, standing under Artibasos's dome in the Great Sanctuary, heard Leontes, Emperor of Sarantium, Jad's regent upon earth, the god's beloved, say quietly, 'The Sanctuary is to be holy, truly so, but these decorations are not, Rhodian. It is not proper for the pious to render or worship images of the god or show mortal figures in a holy place.' The voice calm, confident, absolute. 'They will come down, here and elsewhere in the lands we rule.'

The Emperor paused, tall and golden, handsome as a figure from legend. His voice became mild, almost kindly. 'It is difficult to see one's work undone, come to naught. It has happened to me many times. Peace treaties and such. I am sorry if this is unpleasant for you.'

Unpleasant.

An unpleasantness was a cart rumbling through the street below one's bedroom too early in the morning. It was water in one's boots on winter roads, a chest cough on a cold day, a bitter wind finding a chink in walls; it was sour wine, stringy meat, a tedious sermon in chapel, a ceremony running long in summer heat.

Unpleasantness was not the plague and burying children, it was not Sarantine Fire, not the Day of the Dead, or the *zubir* of the Aldwood appearing out of fog with blood dripping from its horns, it was not . . . this. It was not this.

Crispin looked up, away from the men before him. Saw Jad, saw Ilandra, triple-walled Sarantium, fallen Rhodias, the wood, the world as he knew it and could bring it forth. *They will come down.*

This was not an unpleasantness. This was death.

He looked back at those standing before him. He must have looked quite ghastly in that moment, he realized after, for even the cleric seemed alarmed, and Pertennius's newly smug expression altered somewhat. Leontes himself added quickly, 'You understand, Rhodian, that you are accused of no impiety at all. That would be unjust and we will not be unjust. You acted in accord with faith as it was understood . . . before. Understandings may change, but we will not visit consequences on those who proceeded faithfully in . . . good faith . . .'

He trailed off.

It was astonishingly difficult to speak. Crispin tried. He opened his mouth, but before he could even try to shape words another voice was heard.

'Are you barbarians? Are you entirely mad? Do you even know what you are saying? Can someone *be* so ignorant? You lump-witted military imbecile!'

Imbecile. Someone used to use that word. But this time it was not an alchemist's stolen bird-soul addressing Crispin. It was a small, rumpled, barefoot architect, exploding from the shadows, his hair in alarming disarray, his voice high, strident, bristling with rage, carrying through the Sanctuary, and he was addressing the Emperor of Sarantium.

'Artibasos, no! Stop!' Crispin rasped, finding his voice. They would kill the little man for this. Too many people had heard. This was the *Emperor.*

'I will *not* stop. This is an abomination, an act of evil! *Barbarians* do this, not Sarantines! Will you destroy this glory? Leave the Sanctuary naked?'

'There is no fault found with the building itself,' Leontes said. He was exerting real self-restraint, Crispin realized, but the celebrated blue eyes were flinty now.

'How *very* good of you to say so.' Artibasos was out of control, his arms waving like windmills. 'Have you any idea, *can* you have any idea of what this man has achieved? No fault? No *fault*? Shall I tell you how grievous a fault there will be if the dome and walls are stripped?'

The Emperor looked down at him, still controlling himself. 'There is no suggestion of that. Proper doctrine allows them to be decorated . . . with . . . I don't care . . . flowers, fruit, even birds and animals.'

'Ah! *There* is a solution! Of course! The Emperor's wisdom is vast!' The architect was still enraged, wild. 'You will turn a holy place decorated with a vision and grandeur that honours the god and exalts the visitor into a place covered with . . . vegetation and little rabbits? An aviary? A fruit storehouse? By the god! How pious, my lord!'

'Curb your tongue, man!' snapped the cleric.

Leontes himself said nothing for a long moment. And under that silent gaze the little man finally stopped. His furiously waving arms fell to his sides. He did not back down, though. Staring at his Emperor, he drew himself up. Crispin held his breath.

'It would be best,' Leontes murmured, speaking through thin lips, his own colour high, 'if your friends removed you now from us, architect. You have our permission to depart. We do not wish to begin our reign by appearing harsh in our treatment of those who have done service, but this manner before your Imperial lord demands you be branded or executed.'

'Then kill me! I do not wish to live to see—'

'*Stop!*' Crispin cried. Leontes *would* give the order, he knew it.

He looked around frantically and saw, with desperate

relief, that Vargos had come down from the scaffolding. He nodded urgently at the big man and Vargos came quickly forward. He bowed. Then, expressionlessly, without warning, he simply picked up the small architect, threw him over his shoulder, and carried the struggling, loudly protesting Artibasos off into the dimness of the Sanctuary.

Sound carried extremely well in this space—the building had been brilliantly designed. They could hear the architect cursing and shouting for a long time. Then a door was opened and closed, in the shadows of some recess, and there was silence. No one moved. Morning sunlight fell through high windows.

Crispin was remembering the bathhouse again. His first conversation with this man, in the drifting steam. He ought to have known, he thought. Ought to have been prepared for this. He'd been warned by Styliane and even by Leontes himself that afternoon, half a year ago: *I'm interested in your views on images of the god.*

'As I told you, we attach no consequences to those things done before our time.' The Emperor was explaining again. 'But there have been . . . lapses in the true faith, failures of proper observance. Images of the god are *not* to be created. Jad is ineffable and mysterious, entirely beyond our grasp. For a mortal man to dare picture the god behind the sun is a heresy. And to exalt mortal men in a holy place is arrogant presumption. It always has been, but those . . . before us simply did not understand it.'

They will come down, here and elsewhere, in the lands we rule.

'You are . . . changing our faith, my lord.'

It was, barely, possible to shape words.

'An error, artisan. We change nothing. With the wisdom of the Eastern Patriarch and his advisers to guide us—and we expect the Patriarch in Rhodias to agree—we will *restore* a proper understanding. We must worship Jad, not an image of the god. Otherwise we are no better than the pagans before us with their offerings to statues in the temples.'

'No one ... worships this image above us, my lord. They are only made mindful of the power and majesty of the god.'

'You would instruct *us* in matters of faith, Rhodian?' It was the dark-bearded cleric this time. The Patriarch's assistant.

It was all without meaning, these words. One could argue against this as easily as one fought against plague. It was as final. The heart could cry. There was nothing at all to be done.

Or, almost nothing.

Martinian used to say that there was always *some* kind of choice. And here, now, one might yet try to do a single thing. Crispin drew a deep breath, for this would go against everything in his nature: pride and rage, the deep sense of himself as above all such pleading. But there was something too large at stake now.

He swallowed hard and said, ignoring the cleric, looking directly at Leontes, 'My lord Emperor, you were good enough to say you ... owed me greatly, for services?'

Leontes returned his gaze. His heightened colour was receding. 'I did.'

'Then I have a request, my lord.' The heart could cry. He kept his eyes on the man in front of him. If he looked overhead he was afraid he would shame himself and weep.

Leontes's expression was benign. A man accustomed to dealing with requests. He lifted a hand. 'Artisan, do not ask for this to be saved ... it cannot be.'

Crispin nodded. He knew. He knew. He would not look up above.

He shook his head. 'It is ... something else.'

'Then ask,' the Emperor said, with an expansive gesture. 'We are aware of your services to our beloved predecessor, and that you have performed honourably by your own understanding.'

By his own understanding.

Crispin said, speaking slowly, 'There is a chapel of the Sleepless Ones, in Sauradia, on the Imperial Road. Not far from the eastern military camp.' He heard his own voice as if from far away. Carefully, carefully, he did not look overhead.

'I know it,' said the man who had commanded armies there.

Crispin swallowed again. Control. It was necessary to keep one's control. 'It is a small chapel, inhabited by holy men of great piety. There is ...' He took a breath. 'There is a ... decoration there, on the dome, a rendering of Jad done long ago by artisans of a piety as ... as they understood it ... almost unimaginable.'

'I believe I have seen it.' Leontes was frowning.

'It is ... it is falling down, my lord. They were gifted and devout beyond words, but their ... understanding of ... technique was imperfect, so long ago.'

'And so?'

'And so I ... my request of you, thrice-exalted lord, is that this image of the god be allowed to fall down in its own time. That the holy men who live there in peace and offer their night-long prayers for all of us, and travellers on the road, not be forced to see their chapel dome stripped bare.'

The cleric quickly began to speak, but Leontes held up a hand. Pertennius of Eubulus had said nothing the entire time, Crispin realized. He seldom did. An observer, a chronicler of wars and buildings. Crispin knew what else the man chronicled. He wished he'd hit him harder the night before. He wished he'd killed him, in fact.

'It is falling, this . . . rendering?' The Emperor's voice was precise.

'Piece by piece,' Crispin said. 'They know it, the holy ones. It grieves them, but they see it as the will of the god. Perhaps . . . it is, my lord.' He could hate himself for saying that last, but he wanted this to happen. He *needed* it to happen. He did not speak of Pardos and a winter spent in restoration. It was not a lie, any of what he said.

'Perhaps it is,' the Emperor agreed, nodding his head. 'The will of Jad. A sign for all of us of the virtue of what we are doing now.' He looked back at the cleric, who dutifully nodded as well.

Crispin lowered his eyes. Looked at the floor. Waited.

'This is your request of us?'

'It is, my lord.'

'Then it shall be so.' The soldier's voice, crisp with command. 'Pertennius, you will have documents prepared and filed appropriately. One to be delivered above our own seal for the clerics there to keep in their possession. The decoration in that chapel shall be permitted to come down by itself, as a holy sign of the error of all such things. And you will record it as such in your chronicle of our reign.'

Crispin looked up.

He was gazing at the Emperor of Sarantium, golden and magnificent—looking very much the way the god of the sun was rendered in the west, in fact—but he was really seeing the image of Jad in that chapel by the road in the wilderness, the god pale and dark, suffering and maimed in the terrible defence of his children.

'Thank you, my lord,' he said.

He looked upwards then, after all. Despite everything. Couldn't help himself. A death. Another death. She had warned him. Styliane. He looked, but did not weep. He had wept for Ilandra. For the girls.

And thinking so, he realized that there was one last small thing—terribly small, a gesture, no more—that he could still do, after all.

He cleared his throat. 'Have I leave to withdraw, my lord?'

Leontes nodded. 'You have. You do understand we are very well disposed towards you, Caius Crispus?'

Using Crispin's name, even. Crispin nodded. 'I am honoured, my lord.' He bowed formally.

And then he turned and walked to the scaffolding, which was not far away.

'What are you doing?' It was Pertennius, as Crispin reached the ladder and placed a foot upon it.

Crispin didn't turn around.

'I have work to do. Up there.' His daughters. Today's task, memory and craft and light.

'They will only bring it down!' The secretary's voice was uncomprehending.

Crispin did turn then, to look back over his shoulder. They were staring at him, the three of them, so were the others in the Sanctuary.

He said, 'I understand. But they will have to *do* that. Bring it down. I will make what I make, in this civilized, holy place. Others will have to give the orders to destroy. As barbarians destroyed Rhodias . . . since it could not defend itself.'

He was looking at the Emperor, who had spoken to him of exactly this in the wet, drifting steam half a year before.

He could see that Leontes, too, remembered. The Emperor, who was not Valerius, not at all Valerius, but who had his own intelligence, said quietly, 'You will waste your labour?'

And Crispin said, as softly, 'It is not waste,' and turned again and began to climb, as he had so many times, up to the scaffolding and the dome.

On the way up, before he reached the place where the setting bed for the tesserae had been smoothly laid and awaited him, he realized something else.

It wasn't a waste, there was meaning to this, as much as he could bring to bear on any single action in his life, but it *was* an ending.

Another journey lay ahead, home at the end of it.

It was time to leave.

———

Fotius the sandalmaker, in his very best blue tunic, was telling everyone who would listen about the events that had occurred in this same place all those years ago when Apius died and the first Valerius came to the Golden Throne.

There had been a murder then, too, he said sagely, and he, Fotius, had seen a ghost on his way to the Hippodrome that morning, presaging it. Just as he, Fotius, had seen another one three days ago, in broad daylight, crouched on top of a colonnade, on the *very* morning the Emperor had been so foully slain by the Daleinoi.

There was *more*, he added, and he did have listeners, which was always gratifying. They were waiting for the Mandator to appear in the kathisma—the Patriarch would follow, and then the officials of the court and then those who were to be crowned today. It would be impossible to talk then, of course, with the noise of better than eighty thousand people.

In those days, Fotius expounded to some of the younger craftsmen in the Blues' section, there had been a corrupt, evil attempt to subvert the will of the people right here in the Hippodrome—and it had been engineered by the Daleinoi back then, too! And what's more, one of those working to achieve that had been the very same Lysippus the Calysian who had just been part of the murder in the palace!

And it had been Fotius himself, the sandalmaker declared proudly, who had unmasked the slimy Calysian as an imposter when he'd tried to pretend he was a follower of the Blues and incite the faction to acclaim Flavius Daleinus down there on the sands.

He pointed to the exact spot. He remembered it well. Thirteen, fourteen years, and as yesterday. As yesterday.

Everything came around in circles, he said piously, making the sign of the disk. Just as the sun rose and then set and then rose again, so did the patterns and fates of mortal men. Evil would be found out. (He had heard his chapel's cleric say all this, just a week ago.) Flavius Daleinus had paid for his sins in fire that day long ago, and now his children and the Calysian had also paid.

But, someone objected, why did Valerius II die of the same fire, if it was all a matter of justice?

Fotius looked scornfully at the young man, a clothmaker. Would you, he said, seek to understand the ways of the god?

Not really, the clothmaker said. Only those of men here in the City. If the Calysian had been part of the Daleinus conspiracy to claim the throne back then, why did he end up as Quaestor of Revenue for Valerius I and then his nephew? For *both* of them? He wasn't exiled till *we* demanded it, the man said, as others turned to him. Remember? Less than three years ago.

A cheap debating trick, Fotius thought indignantly. It wasn't as if anyone *would* forget. Thirty thousand people had died.

Some people, Fotius retorted airily, had the most limited understanding of affairs in the court. He didn't have enough *time* today to educate the young. There were weighty events unfolding. Didn't the clothmaker know that the Bassanids were across the border in the north?

Well, yes, the man said, everyone knew that. But what did that have to do with Lysippus the—

Trumpets blew.

What followed was performed with rituals of ceremony and precedent laid down in the days of Saranios and revised only marginally in hundreds of years, for what were rituals if they changed?

An Emperor was crowned by a Patriarch, and then an Empress was crowned by the Emperor himself. The two crowns, and the Imperial sceptre and ring, were those of Saranios and his own Empress, brought east from Rhodias and used only on these occasions, guarded in the Attenine Palace at all other times.

The Patriarch blessed the two anointed ones with oil and incense and sea water, and then he gave his blessing to the multitude gathered to bear witness. The principal dignitaries of the court presented themselves—garbed in splendour— before the Emperor and Empress and made the triple obeisance in full view of the people. An aged representative of the Senate presented the new Emperor with the Seal of the City and golden keys to the triple walls. (The Master of the Senate had been graciously excused from appearing today. It seemed there had been a sudden death in his own family, and a burial only the day before.)

There were chants, religious and then secular, for the factions were very much a part of this, and their Accredited Musicians led the Blues and Greens in ritual acclamations, crying the names of Valerius III and the Empress Gisel in that thronged space where the names cried were most often those of horses and the men who rode in chariots behind them. No dancing followed, no racing, no entertainment at all: an Emperor had been assassinated, his body would be laid to rest soon in the Great Sanctuary he'd ordered built after the last one had burned.

There was universal approval of the name Leontes had chosen for his own Imperial title, in homage to his patron and predecessor. A genuine sense of mystery and wonder attached to the fact that his new bride was already a queen. The women in the stands seemed to like that. A romance, and royalty.

Nothing was said (or if something *was* said, it was done very quietly) about the Emperor's put-aside wife or the speed of this remarriage. The Daleinoi had once more proven themselves treacherous beyond description. No Emperor would wish to ascend the Golden Throne of Saranios tainted before Jad and the people by the stain of a murderous spouse.

They said he had let her live.

More justice than she deserved, was the general view in the Hippodrome. Both brothers were dead, however, and the loathed Calysian. One wouldn't ever want to make the mistake of thinking that Leontes—Valerius III—was soft in any way.

The number of armed soldiers present here was evidence of that.

And so, too, was the Mandator's first public announcement after the Investiture Ceremony was done. His words were caught and relayed by official speakers through the vast stands, and their import was clear, and exhilarating.

It seemed their new Emperor would not be lingering long among them. The Bassanid army was in Calysium, had overrun Asen (again) and was said to be marching and riding towards Eubulus even now.

The Emperor, who had been their Supreme Strategos four days before, was disinclined to indulge them in this.

He would lead the assembled armies of Sarantium himself. Not overseas to Rhodias, but north and east. Not over the dangerous, dark waters but up in spring weather along the wide, smoothly paved Imperial Road to deal with the cowardly, truce-breaking soldiers of King Shirvan. An Emperor in the field himself! It had been a very long time. Valerius III, the sword of Sarantium, the sword of holy Jad. There was something awesome and thrilling in just thinking about it.

The easterners had thought to take advantage of Leontes and the army sailing west, had vilely breached the Eternal Peace they'd sworn by their own pagan gods to keep. They would learn the dimensions of their mistake, the Mandator proclaimed, his words picked up and echoed through the Hippodrome.

Eubulus would be defended, the Bassanids driven back across the border. And more. Let the King of Kings defend Mihrbor now, the Mandator cried. Let him *try* to defend it against what Sarantium would bring against him. The time was done when they would pay monies to Kabadh to buy a peace. Let Shirvan sue for mercy. Let him pray to his gods. Leontes the Golden, who was now an Emperor, was coming after him.

The noise that greeted this was loud enough, some thought, to reach the very sky and the god behind the bright sun overhead.

As for Batiara, the Mandator continued, when the shouting subsided enough for his voice to be heard and relayed again, look who was Empress of Sarantium now. Look who might deal with Rhodias and Varena, which were her own! This Empress had a crown of her own and had brought it here to them, was daughter of a king, a queen in her own name. The citizens of Sarantium could believe that Rhodias and the west might be theirs, after all, with no brave soldiers dying on distant western battlefields, or on the trackless seas.

The acclamations that accompanied this were as loud as the ones before, and—the perceptive noted—they were led by the aforementioned soldiers this time.

It was a glittering day, and so most of the histories would describe it. The weather mild, the god's sun shining upon them all. The Emperor magnificent, the new Empress as golden as he, tall for her sex, utterly regal in her bearing and blood.

There were always fears and doubts in a time of change. The half-world might creep closer, ghosts and daemons be seen, when the great of the world died and their souls departed, but who could be *truly* fearful, standing in the Hippodrome in sunshine, looking at these two?

One lamented a dead Emperor, and might wonder about the still-absent figure of his Empress, the one who had been a dancer in her day, born right here in the Hippodrome (not like the new Empress, not like her at all). One might pause to consider the colossal fall of the Daleinoi and the sudden shifting of a theatre of war . . . but in the stands that day there was an undeniable feeling of uplift, of exuberance, something new beginning, and there was nothing compelled or contrived about the approval that resounded.

Then the Mandator declared that the racing season would resume as soon as the period of mourning was over and paused to announce that Scortius of the Blues was healing and well, and that Astorgus, the Blues' factionarius, and Crescens of the Greens had agreed to humbly accept judicial admonishment and had made peace with each other. And as he gestured, those two well-known men stood forward, stepping up upon raised platforms in their factions' sections to be seen. They made the charioteers' open-palmed gesture towards each other and then turned and bowed together towards the kathisma, and eighty thousand people went wild. The holy Patriarch took pains to keep his countenance inscrutable behind his white beard as the crowd celebrated its chariots and horses and the ceremony came to a close.

Nothing at all was said that afternoon, by the Mandator or anyone else, about changes in the doctrines of Jad regarding depictions of the god himself in holy places and elsewhere.

There would be time to present such complex matters to the people, carefully, in the sanctuaries and chapels. The Hippodrome that day was not a place for nuances and subtleties of faith. Timing, as any good general knew, was the essence of a campaign.

Valerius III, wearing the full weight of the garments of Imperial power, stood up easily, as if they were no burden in the least, and saluted his people as they saluted him. Then he turned and extended a hand to his Empress and they walked together from the kathisma through the door at the back and out of sight. The cheering did not stop.

All was well. All would be well, one might truly believe. Fotius accepted a swift, entirely unexpected embrace from the young clothmaker, and returned it, then they both turned to hug others beside them in the stands, all of them shouting the Emperor's name in the clear, bright light.

Over the course of an exhausting ten days in the Blues' compound, Rustem of Kerakek had developed a hypothesis about Sarantines and their physicians. In essence, the instructions of the doctors were accepted or ignored as the patients saw fit.

It was entirely otherwise in Bassania. At home, the doctor was at risk when he took on the care of a patient. By speaking the formal words of acceptance, a physician placed his own worldly goods and even his life at hazard. If the sick person failed to follow precisely the doctor's instructions, this commitment, this hazarding, was negated.

Here, doctors risked nothing but the possibility of a poor reputation, and based on what he'd seen here (in an admittedly short while), Rustem didn't think that constituted much of a concern at all. None of the physicians he'd observed at work seemed to know much more than an inadequately digested muddle of Galinus and Merovius, supplemented by vastly too much letting of blood and their own cobbled-together medications, most of which were noxious in some degree or other.

Given this, it made sense that patients would form their own decisions about whether to heed their physicians or not.

Rustem wasn't used to it, and wasn't inclined to accept it.

As an example, as the *prime* example, from the outset he had firmly instructed the attendants caring for Scortius the charioteer that visitors were limited to one in the morning and one after midday, and only for short periods and with no wine at all to be brought or consumed. He had, as a precaution, relayed these directives to Strumosus (since at least some of the wine came from the casks by the kitchen) and to Astorgus, the factionarius. The latter was soberly attentive and had promised to do his best to enforce compliance. He had, Rustem knew, a profoundly vested interest in the recovery of the invalid charioteer.

They *all* did.

The problem was that the patient didn't see himself as an invalid, or requiring any extremes of care, even after almost dying twice in a short while. A man who would slip from his room out a window and down a tree and over a wall and walk the length of the city to race horses in the Hippodrome with broken ribs and an unhealed wound was unlikely (Rustem had to concede) to take kindly to a limitation on wine or the number of visitors, particularly female, who attended at his bedside.

At least he had stayed in the bed, Astorgus had pointed out wryly, and mostly by himself. There *had* been reports of nighttime activities inconsistent with a healing regimen.

Rustem, still caught up in the bewildering intensity of the past few days and the arrival of his family, found it more difficult than usual to project the proper outrage and authority. He was acutely aware, among other things, that if he or his women or children left this guarded compound they were at grave risk of assault in the streets. Bassanids here, since the news of the border attack, and then the departure of the Sarantine army north, led by the Emperor himself, were in a precarious circumstance, and there had been killings. His own decision not to return home was reinforced by the painful understanding that the King of Kings would have ordered the northern attack while fully aware that this would be a consequence for those of his people in the west. Including the man who had saved his own life.

Rustem owed a great deal to the Blues' faction, and he knew it.

Not that he'd been lax in his recompense. He'd treated the wounded of the riot here on a steady, day-long basis, attending upon them at night, awakened by messengers as needed. He was seriously short of sleep, but knew he could last this way for some time yet.

He took a particular pleasure in the recovery of the young fellow from the kitchen. There had been early and grave signs of infection there, and Rustem had spent one full night awake and very busy by the young man's bedside when the wound changed colour and fever rose. The chef, Strumosus, had come in and out several times, watching in silence, and the other kitchen worker, Rasic, had actually made himself a bed on the floor of the hallway outside. And then, in the midst of the crisis night for the wounded man, Shaski had also appeared. He had gotten out of his bed without either of his mothers knowing and had come, barefoot, to bring his father a drink in the middle of the night, knowing, somehow, exactly where Rustem was. Somehow. Rustem had—unspeaking, at first—accepted the drink and brushed the child's head with a gentle hand and told him to go back to his room, that everything was all right.

Shaski had gone sleepily to bed without saying or doing anything more, as those nearby observed the boy's arrival and departure with expressions that Rustem suspected he and his family would have to grow accustomed to. It was one of the reasons he was taking them all away.

The young man, Kyros, had his fever break towards morning and the wound progressed normally after that. The greatest risk he endured was that the idiot doctor, Ampliarus, might slip into the room unnoticed and pursue his mad fixation with bleeding those already wounded.

Rustem had been present, and undeniably amused (though he'd tried to conceal it, of course), when Kyros regained consciousness just before dawn. Rasic, the friend, had been sitting by the bed then, and when the sick man opened his eyes, the other one let out a cry that brought others hurrying into the room, forcing Rustem to order all of them out in his sternest manner.

Rasic, evidently seeing this order as applying to those other than himself, remained, and went on to tell the patient what Strumosus had said about him outside the gates while Kyros was unconscious, and thought to be dead. Strumosus entered in the midst of this recitation. Paused, briefly, in the doorway.

'He's lying, as usual,' the little chef said peremptorily, coming into the room as Rasic stopped, briefly fearful, then grinning. 'The way he lies about girls. I *wish* you would all keep a firmer grip on the world as Jad made it, not the one in your dreams. Kyros *might* have some excuse, with what ever potions our Bassanid has been pushing down his throat, but Rasic has no justification whatever. A genius? *This* lad? My own legacy? I am insulted by the thought! Does any of that make the *least* sense to you, Kyros?'

The crippled boy, pale, but clearly lucid, shook his head slightly on the pillow, but he was smiling, and then Strumosus was, as well.

'Really!' the little chef said. 'The idea's absurd. If I have a legacy it is almost certainly going to be my fish sauce.'

'Of course it is,' Kyros whispered. He was still smiling. So was Rasic, flashing crooked teeth. So was Strumosus.

'Get some rest, lad,' the chef said. 'We'll all be here when you awake. Come Rasic, you too. Go to bed. You'll work a triple shift tomorrow, or something.'

There were times, Rustem thought, when his profession offered great rewards.

Then there were moments when it felt as if it would be less of a struggle to walk straight into the teeth of a sandstorm.

Scortius could make him feel like that. As now, for example. Rustem walked into the man's sick-room to change his dressing (every third day now) and found *four* chariot-racers sitting and standing about, and not one, not two, but three dancers in further attendance, with one of them—clad in an *entirely* inadequate fashion—offering a performance not at all calculated to assist a recovering patient in keeping a calm, unexcited demeanour.

And there was wine. *And,* Rustem noticed, belatedly, in the crowded room, his son Shaski was there, sitting on the lap of a fourth dancer in the corner, watching it all and laughing.

'Hello, Papa!' his son said, not in the least disconcerted, as Rustem stood in the doorway and glared in an all-inclusive fashion around the room.

'Oh, dear. He's upset. Everyone, out!' Scortius said from the bed. He handed his wine cup to one of the women. 'Take this. Someone take the boy to his mother. Don't forget your clothes, Taleira. The doctor's working very hard for all of us and we don't want him taxed unduly. We want him to stay well, don't we?'

There was laughter and a flurry of movement. The man in the bed grinned. A *wretched* patient, in every possible way. But Rustem had seen what he'd done on the Hippodrome sands at the beginning of the week before, and had known better than anyone else the will that had been required, and it was impossible to deny the admiration he felt. He didn't *want* to deny it, actually.

Besides which, the people were going out.

'Shirin, stay, if you will. I have a question or two. Doctor, is it all right if one friend remains? This is a visit that honours me, and I haven't had a chance to speak to her privately yet. I believe you've met her. This is Shirin of the Greens. Didn't the mosaicists bring you to a wedding feast in her home?'

'My first day, yes,' Rustem said. He bowed to the dark-haired woman, who was remarkably attractive in a small-boned fashion. Her scent was quite distracting. The room emptied, with one of the men carrying Shaski on his back. The dancer rose from her seat to greet him.

She smiled. 'I remember you very well, doctor. You had a servant killed by some of our younger Greens.'

Rustem nodded. 'It is true. With so many deaths since, I'm surprised you remember it.'

She shrugged. 'Bonosus's son was involved. Not a trivial thing.'

Rustem nodded a second time and crossed to his patient. The woman sat down quietly. Scortius had already drawn the bedsheet back, exposing his muscular, bandaged torso. Shirin of the Greens smiled.

'How exciting,' she said, eyes wide.

Rustem snorted, amused in spite of himself. Then he paid attention to what he was doing, unwrapping the layers of dressing to expose the wound beneath. Scortius lay on his right side, facing the woman. She'd have to stand to see the black and purple skin around the twice-over fracture and the deep knife wound.

Rustem set about cleansing the wound again and then applying his salves. No need for any further drainage. The challenge was what it had always been, but more so: to treat broken bones and a stab wound in the same location. He was quietly pleased with what he saw, though he wouldn't have dreamed of letting Scortius see that. A hint that the doctor was content and the man would undoubtedly be out the door and on the race-track, or prowling the night streets to one bedroom or another.

They had told him about this one's nocturnal pursuits.

'You said you had questions,' Shirin murmured. 'Or is the doctor . . . ?'

'My doctor is private as a hermit on a crag. I have no secrets from him.'

'Except when you have plans to depart from your sick-room without leave,' Rustem murmured, bathing the man's skin.

'Well, yes, there was that. But otherwise, you know all. You were . . . even under the stands, I recall, just before the race.'

His tone had changed. Rustem caught it. He remembered that sequence of moments. Thenaïs with her blade, the Green driver coming just in time.

'Oh? What happened under the stands?' Shirin was asking, fluttering her eyelashes at the two of them. 'You *must* tell!'

'Crescens declared his undying love for me and then hammered me half to my grave when I told him I preferred you. Hadn't you heard?'

She laughed. 'No. Come, what happened?'

'Various things.' The chariot-driver hesitated. Rustem could feel the man's heartbeat. He said nothing. 'Tell me,' Scortius murmured, 'Cleander Bonosus, is he still in trouble with his father? Do you know?' Shirin blinked. Clearly not the question she'd expected. 'He did me a great service when I was hurt,' Scortius added. 'Brought me to the doctor.'

The man was being subtle. This wasn't, Rustem surmised, the real question he wanted answered. And because he *had* been under the Hippodrome stands he had an idea what that real question was. Something occurred to him, rather too late.

Scortius was undeniably clever. He was also clearly unaware of something. Rustem had certainly never brought it up, and it seemed evident no one else had. It might be part of the city's talk, or forgotten in a time of uttermost turbulence, but it hadn't penetrated this room.

The Greens' dancer said, 'The boy? I really don't know. I suspect all's changed there, after what happened in their house.'

A heartbeat. Rustem felt it, and winced. He'd been right, after all.

'What happened in their house?' Scortius asked.

She told him.

Thinking back, later, Rustem was impressed, yet again, with the strength of will the wounded man displayed, continuing to speak, expressing conventional, polite sorrow at tidings of a young woman's untimely, self-inflicted death. But Rustem had had his hands on the man's body, and he could feel the impact of the woman's words. Caught breath, then measured, careful breath, a tremor, involuntary, and the pounding heart.

Taking pity, Rustem finished his dressing change more swiftly than usual (he could do it again, later) and reached for the tray of medications by the bed. 'I have to give you something for sleep now, as usual,' he lied. 'You'll be unable to entertain the lady in any proper fashion.'

Shirin of the Greens, by all evidence unaware of anything untoward having just transpired, took her cue like an actress and rose to go. She stopped by the bedside and bent down to kiss the patient on the forehead. 'He never entertains any of us in a proper fashion, doctor.' She straightened and smiled. 'I'll be back, my dear. Rest, to be ready for me.' She turned and went out.

He looked at his patient and, wordlessly, poured two full measures of his preferred sedative.

Scortius stared up at him from his pillow. His eyes were dark, his face quite white now. He accepted the mixture, both doses, without protest.

'Thank you,' he said, after a moment. Rustem nodded.

'I'm sorry,' he said, surprising himself.

Scortius turned his face to the wall.

Rustem reclaimed his walking stick and went out, closing the door behind him, to leave the man his privacy.

He had his speculations but he quelled them. Whatever the man in the bed had said before about his doctor knowing all, it wasn't the truth, ought not to *be* the truth.

It occurred to him, going down the corridor, that they really needed to assert more control over Shaski's movements here. It was not at all proper for a child, the doctor's son, to be part of the disruption in patients' rooms.

He would have to speak with Katyun about it, among other things. It was time for a midday meal, but he paused to look for Shaski in his put-together treatment rooms in the next building. The boy was more often there than anywhere else.

He wasn't now. Someone else was. Rustem recognized the Rhodian artisan—not the young one who'd saved his life in the streets, but the other, more senior fellow who had dressed them in white and taken them all to a wedding feast.

The man—Crispinus was his name, something like that—looked unwell, but not in a fashion likely to elicit Rustem's sympathy. Men who drank themselves into illness, especially this early in the day, had only themselves to blame for the consequences.

'Good day, doctor,' the artisan said, clearly enough. He stood up from the table he'd been sitting upon. No visible unsteadiness. 'Am I intruding?'

'Not at all,' Rustem said. 'How may I . . . ?'

'I came to visit Scortius, thought I'd confirm with his doctor that it was all right.'

Well, wine-smitten or not, at least *this* man knew the protocol in matters of this sort. Rustem nodded briskly. 'I wish there were more like you. There was just a party with dancers in his room, and wine.'

The Rhodian—*Crispin* was the name, actually—smiled faintly. There was a line of strain above his eyes and a degree of unhealthy pallor that suggested that he'd been drinking for longer than this morning. It didn't square with what Rustem remembered of the decisive man he'd encountered that first day here, but this wasn't his patient and he made no comment.

'Who would drink wine this early in the day?' the Rhodian said wryly. He rubbed his forehead. 'Dancers entertaining him? That sounds like Scortius. You threw them out?'

Rustem had to smile. 'Does that sound like me?'

'From what I've heard, yes,' The Rhodian was another clever man, Rustem decided. He kept a hand on the table, supporting himself.

'I gave him a soporific just now, he'll sleep awhile. You'd do better to come back later in the afternoon.'

'I'll do that, then.' The man pushed himself away from the table and swayed. His expression was rueful. 'Sorry. I've been indulging . . . a sorrow.'

'May I help?' Rustem said politely.

'I wish, doctor. No. Actually . . . I'm leaving. Day after next. Sailing west.'

'Oh. Going home? No further employment here for you?'

'You might say that,' the artisan said after a moment.

'Well . . . a safe journey to you.' He really didn't know the man. The Rhodian nodded his head and walked steadily past Rustem and out the door. Rustem turned to follow him. The man stopped in the hallway.

'I was given your name, you know. Before I left home. I'm . . . sorry we never had a chance to meet.'

'Given my name?' Rustem echoed, bemused. 'How?'

'A . . . friend. Too complicated to explain. Oh . . . there's something in there for you, by the way. One of the messenger boys brought it while I was waiting. Apparently left at the gate.' He gestured towards the innermost of the two rooms. An object wrapped in cloth stood on the examining table there.

'Thank you,' Rustem said.

The Rhodian went down the short corridor and out. The sunlight, Rustem thought, was probably an affliction for him just now. *Indulging a sorrow.* Not his patient. They couldn't *all* be his concern.

He was interesting, though. Another stranger, observing the Sarantines. A man he might have liked to know better, actually. Leaving now. It wouldn't happen. Odd, about being given Rustem's name. Rustem walked into his inner room. On the table beside the parcel he saw a note, his name on it.

First, he unwrapped the cloth from the object on the table. And then, entirely overcome, he sat down on a stool and stood staring at it.

There was no one about. He was entirely alone, looking.

Eventually he stood up and took the note. It had a seal, which he broke. He unfolded and read, and then he sat down again.

With gratitude, the brief inscription read, *this exemplar of all things that must bend or they break.*

He sat there for a very long time, becoming aware of how rare it was for him to be alone now, how seldom he had this silence or calm. He stared at the golden rose on the table, long and slim as the living flower might have been, golden petals unfurling, the very last one, at the top, fully opened, rubies in all of them.

He knew then, with that frightening, otherworldly certainty that Shaski seemed to have, that he would never see her again.

He took the rose with him (wrapped and concealed) when he and his family eventually sailed, a very long way west to a land where such objects of uttermost craft and art were, as yet, unknown.

It was a place where competent physicians were urgently needed, and could rise swiftly in a society that was in the process of defining itself. His unusual domestic arrangements were tolerated on that far frontier, but he was advised, early, to change his faith. He did so, adopting the god of the sun in the manner that Jad was worshipped in Esperana. He had responsibilities, after all: two wives, two children (then a third and then a fourth, both boys, not long after they settled), and four former soldiers from the east who had changed their lives to come with them. Two of their new household women from Sarantium had, unexpectedly, also taken ship with his family. And he had an eldest child, a son, who was best made to appear—they all understood this—to fit in, as much as could be, lest he be singled out and danger come to him thereby.

One bent sometimes, thought Rustem, so as not to be broken by the winds of the world, whether of desert or sea or these wide, rolling grasslands in the farthest west.

All of his children and one of his wives turned out to like horses, very much. His longtime soldier friend Vinaszh—who married and had a family of his own but continued to entwine his destiny with theirs—turned out to have an eye for choosing and breeding them. He was a good businessman. So was Rustem, to his own surprise. He ended his days in comfort, a rancher as much as a doctor.

He gave the rose to his daughter when she married.

He kept the note, though, all his life.

CHAPTER XVI

He had known the last days here would be difficult, he hadn't fully grasped just how much so. For one thing, from the time he came down from the dome the second time, late at night, after returning from the Imperial wedding in the palace and working by lantern-light to finish an image of his daughters that would be torn down almost as soon as it had set, Crispin had spent very little time entirely sober.

He wasn't enamoured of the image of himself as someone who drank to blur pain, but he didn't seem able to do much about it, either.

One of the hardest things was the outrage of other people. It enveloped him. For a private man that was difficult. Well-meaning, wildly passionate friends (he had more than he'd realized here, one never really stopped to count), cursing the new Emperor, offering wine in their homes or taverns. Or late at night in the kitchen of the Blues' compound, where Strumosus of Amoria held forth with articulate savagery on barbarism and the presence of it in a civilized place.

Crispin had gone there to see Scortius, but the charioteer

had been asleep, medicated, and he had ended up in the kitchen taking a meal long after dark. He didn't get back to the compound again until just before departing. Scortius was sleeping that time, too. He chatted briefly with the Bassanid physician, the one whose name and address Zoticus had given him before the man was even in Sarantium. He was past the point of trying to sort that through, as well: there were simply things in the world he would never understand, and they didn't all have to do with the doctrines of holy faith.

He finally caught up with Scortius to say goodbye later that same evening. There was a crowd in the man's chambers—a routine circumstance, it appeared. It made that parting casual, which was easier.

He found that too much of the passion of others expended in sympathy for him was both wearying and humiliating. People had *died* here. People were dying all the time. Crispin had had a commission withdrawn, his work found unsatisfactory. It happened.

He tried to make himself see it this way, at any rate, to advise others to perceive it as such. He didn't succeed.

Shirin, when he called on her and said these things, declared him soulless (he made no witty comment about her choice of words, it wasn't the time for that) and an outright liar, and then she stormed out of her own sitting room, tears on her cheeks. Danis, the bird, from around her throat in the hallway as they left, declared silently that he was a fool, unworthy of his own gifts. Of *any* gifts.

Whatever that meant.

She didn't even come back to see him out. One of the household women walked him to the door and closed it behind him.

*   *   *

Artibasos, the next afternoon, serving a good Candarian, well watered, with olives and fresh bread and olive oil, reacted differently.

'Stop!' he cried, as Crispin tried the same explanation about commissions being ended or withdrawn. 'You shame me!'

Crispin fell obediently silent, looking down at the dark wine in his cup.

'You don't believe any of what you say. You are only saying it to make *me* feel better.' The little architect's hair was standing straight up, giving him the unsettling look of a man who'd just been terrified by a daemon.

'Not entirely,' Crispin said. He remembered Valerius smoothing down that hair, the night he'd taken Crispin to see the dome that was his gift.

Unworthy of any gifts.

He took a breath. 'Not just for you. I'm trying to make myself . . . to find a way to . . .'

It wasn't any good. How did you say this aloud, and keep your pride?

For they were profoundly right, all of them. He *was* lying, or trying to. Sometimes you needed a certain kind of dishonesty, even with yourself, to . . . carry on. Of course artisans lost commissions. All the time. Patrons didn't pay to keep a project going, remarried and changed their minds, went abroad. Or even died, and their sons or widows had a different idea of what should be done to the ceiling of the family dining room or the bedroom walls of the country estate.

It was true, everything he'd said about that was true, and it was still a lie, in the heart.

His drinking, starting in the morning, every morning, was its own proof of that, if you thought about it. He didn't *want* to think about it. He looked at the cup Artibasos had poured for him and drained it, held it out for more.

It was a death, what had happened. The heart would cry.

'You will never go back in there, will you?' the little architect had said to him.

Crispin shook his head.

'It is in your mind, isn't it? All of it?'

Crispin had nodded.

'Mine, too,' Artibasos had said.

The Emperor went north to Eubulus with his army, but the fleet, under the Strategos of the Navy, did sail, after all. Leontes, now Valerius III, was hardly a man to let such an assembly go to waste. No good general was. The ships, laden with provisions and siege engines and weapons meant for a war in the west, were sent east instead through the Calchas Sea and then north. All the way through the far straits, to anchor near Mihrbor, firmly in Bassanid territory. Enough soldiers went on board to achieve a landing and defend it.

The army going overland, the troops that had been about to sail for Batiara, would be far larger than any force Shirvan had sent to harry the north. It was an army of invasion, this one, long-planned, and the new Emperor intended to use it that way—but in a different direction.

The Bassanids had breached the peace. A mistake, born of a desire to hamper a western invasion and an understanding—accurate enough—of the desires and designs of Valerius II.

Valerius II was dead.

The consequences of the miscalculation were on the Bassanids' own heads.

The soldier Carullus, once of the Fourth Trakesian, then very briefly of the Second Calysian, more recently a member of the Supreme Strategos's own guard, was not in either force, not those who rode and marched or those who sailed.

He was unhappy about this. In the extreme.

The new Emperor continued to have strong views, amounting almost to an element of his well-known piety, about taking newly married men to a theatre of war if there were options and alternatives. With an army of this size, there were.

Further, there had been dramatic and lethal purges in the ranks of the Excubitors after the role some of them had played in the assassination. Some innocent, highly capable men had undoubtedly been among those executed, but that was a risk to be assumed by those belonging to a small, elite company when absolute truth was hard to come by. At the very least it could be said that they'd failed to detect treachery among their fellows and paid a price for that.

This treachery, of course, had placed the new Emperor on his throne but that—one need hardly say—was not a relevant point.

Carullus, complaining volubly, had had to content himself with yet another shift and promotion—when he was appointed one of the three ranking officers just below the new Count of the Excubitors. It was a very substantial rise this time, a court office, not just a military one.

'You have *any* idea,' he fumed one night, having spent a day in the Imperial Precinct absorbing information, 'how many changes of clothing a man needs in this position? How *often* you change each day? How many ceremonies I'm expected to learn? Want to know what you wear for escorting fucking envoys from the fucking Karchites? I can tell you!'

He did, in detail. It seemed to help him to talk, and it was good, Crispin found, to have someone else's troubles (such as they were) to consider.

They ended up in The Spina every night, Pardos and Vargos accompanying them, various others coming and going at their booth. It was regarded as their booth by then. Carullus was a well-known, well-liked man, and Crispin had achieved, it appeared, a certain notoriety. It had also become known that he was leaving. People kept stopping by.

Pardos had surprised Crispin. He had decided to stay in Sarantium, continue to work at his craft here, despite the changes in matters of faith. With time to reflect, later, Crispin was to understand how he'd misjudged his former apprentice. It appeared that Pardos, now a fully fledged member of the guilds of course, had his own discomfort about working with certain images.

It had begun to change for him, Pardos said, while he was labouring to preserve that vision of Jad in Sauradia. A conflict of piety and craft, he'd said, stumbling, an awareness of his own unworthiness.

'We're *all* unworthy,' Crispin had protested, fist on the table. 'That's part of the *point* of it!'

But he'd let it slide, seeing Pardos's evident distress. What was the profit in making the other man unhappy? When did you ever change someone's views on faith, even a friend's?

Distraught as he obviously was about what was to happen to the work on the dome (spear-butts and hammers pounding, tesserae shattered and falling), Pardos was content to work on a secular scale, to make a life here, doing scenes for the state in administrative buildings, or private commissions for the courtiers and merchants and guilds who could afford mosaics. He could even work for the factions, he said: Hippodrome images for the walls and ceilings within the compounds. The new doctrines prescribed against rendering people only in a holy place. And for the wealthy, a mosaicist could still offer marinescapes, hunting scenes, interwoven patterns for flooring or walls.

'Naked women and their toys for whorehouses?' Carullus had asked, cackling, making the younger man blush and Vargos frown. But the soldier had only been trying to change the mood.

Vargos, for his part, had made an immediate offer to sail west with Crispin. A difficulty, that, one that needed to be addressed.

The next evening, mostly sober, Crispin had gone walking with him through the City. They'd found an inn near the walls, far from anyone they were likely to know, and the two of them talked alone for a time.

In the end, Crispin had dissauded him, not without effort and not without regret. Vargos was well on the way to making himself a life here. He could be more than a simple labourer—could apprentice himself to Pardos, who would be thrilled to have him. Vargos *liked* the City, far more than he'd expected to, and Crispin made him acknowledge that. He wouldn't be the first of the Inicii to force the Imperial City to give him a welcome and a decent life.

Crispin also admitted that he had no idea what he was going to do when he got home. It was hard to see himself doing fish and seaweed and sunken ships on a summerhouse wall in Baiana or Mylasia now. He didn't even know if he would *stay* at home. He couldn't accept the burden of

Vargos's life, of having the other man follow wherever his uncertain path carried him. That wasn't friendship, really. It was something else, and Vargos was a free man here. Had *always* been his own, free man.

Vargos didn't say a great deal, wasn't someone who argued, was certainly not the sort to inflict himself anywhere or on anyone. His expression revealed little as Crispin spoke, but that night was difficult for both of them. Something had happened on the road, and it had made a bond. Bonds could be broken, but there was a price.

It was deeply tempting to invite Vargos to come west. Crispin's uncertainty about his future would be balanced by having this man with him. The big, scarred servant he had hired at the western border of Sauradia to take him along the Imperial Road had become someone whose presence brought a measure of stability to the world.

That could happen, when you went into the Aldwood with someone, and came out. They didn't speak of that day at all, but it underlay everything that *was* said, and the sadness of parting.

Only at the end did Vargos say something that brought it briefly to the surface. 'You're sailing?' he had asked, as they were settling their account in the tavern. 'Not back along the road?'

'I'd be afraid to,' Crispin had said.

'Carullus would give you a guard.'

'Not against what frightens me.'

And Vargos had nodded his head.

'We were . . . *allowed* to leave,' Crispin had murmured, remembering fog on the Day of the Dead, Linon on the dark, wet grass. 'You don't test that by going back.'

And Vargos had nodded again and they had gone back out into the streets.

A few days later they had to pretty much carry Carullus from The Spina. The soldier was caught in such a whirlwind of emotion it was almost comical: his marriage, his meteoric rise, which meant at the same time missing a glorious war, his delight in what had happened to his beloved Leontes set against what that meant to his dear friend, and an awareness, day by passing day, of Crispin's onrushing departure date.

That particular night as they drank he talked even more than usual. The others were almost in awe of his volubility: stories, jests, observations in an endless stream, battlefield experiences, lap-by-lap recollections of races seen years ago. He wept at the end of the night, hugging Crispin hard, kissing both his cheeks. The three others took him home through the streets. Approaching his own door Carullus was singing a victory song of the Greens.

Kasia heard him, evidently. She opened the door herself, in a night robe, holding a candle. The two other men supported Carullus as he saluted his wife and then made his precarious way—still singing—up the stairs.

In the hallway by the door, Crispin stood alone with Kasia. She gestured and they went into the front room. Neither said anything. Crispin knelt and poked at the fire with an iron rod. After a while the other two came down.

'He'll be fine,' Vargos said.

'I know he will,' said Kasia. 'Thank you.'

There was a brief silence. 'We'll wait down the street,' Pardos said.

Crispin heard the door close as they went out. He stood up.

'When do you sail?' Kasia asked. She looked wonderful. Had gained weight, lost the bruised look he remembered in her eyes. *They are going to kill me tomorrow.* First words she'd ever spoken to him.

'Three days,' he said now. 'Someone apparently mentioned I was looking for a ship, word got around, and Senator Bonosus was good enough to send a message that I could have passage on a commercial vessel of his going to Megarium. Kind of him. She, ah, won't be fast, but she'll get me there. Then it's easy to cross the bay from Megarium, this time of year, to Mylasia. Ships go back and forth all the time. Or I could walk, of course. Up the coast, back down. To Varena.'

She smiled a little as he rambled. 'You sound like my husband. Many words to a simple question.'

Crispin laughed. Another silence.

'They'll be waiting for you outside,' she said.

He nodded. There was suddenly a difficulty in his throat. She, too, he'd never see again.

She walked him to the front door. He turned there.

She put her hands to either side of his face and, rising on tiptoe, kissed him on the lips. She was soft and scented and warm.

'Thank you for my life,' she said.

He cleared his throat. Found his head spinning, that no words would come. Too much wine. Amusing: a torrent of words, no words at all. She opened the door. He stumbled onto the threshold, under the stars.

'You are right to leave,' Kasia said softly. She put a hand on his chest and gave him a little push. 'Go home and have children, my dear.'

And then she closed the door before he could say anything at all in reply to something so astonishing.

It *was* astonishing. There were people in the world who could—and would—say such a thing to him.

One person, at least.

'Let's walk for a little,' he said to the other two when he caught up to them, waiting under a wall lamp.

Both were taciturn men, not intrusive at all. They left him to his thoughts, kept their own, as they paced through the streets and squares, offering their presence as security and companionship. The Urban Prefect's guards were about, the taverns and cauponae open again, though the City was still formally in mourning. That meant the theatres were closed and the chariots wouldn't run, but Sarantium was alive now in the springtime dark with smells and sounds and movements into and out of lantern-light.

A pair of women called to the three of them from a doorway. Crispin saw a flame flicker in the lane beyond, one of those he'd had to grow accustomed to, appearing without source, disappearing as soon as seen. The half-world.

He led the others down towards the harbour. The fleet had gone, leaving only the usual naval complement, with the merchant vessels and fishing boats. A rougher neighbourhood, waterfronts always were. The other two, in stride a little behind him, came nearer. Three big men were unlikely to be disturbed, even here.

Crispin felt almost clear-headed now. He made a decision, and he was to keep it: rising the next morning, eating a meal without wine, taking a trip to the baths, having a shave there (a habit by now, he'd break it at sea).

So many farewells, he was thinking, Kasia's words still with him, walking with two friends by the harbour at night. Some goodbyes not yet properly done, some never to be done.

His work not done, never to be done.

It will all come down.

As he walked he found himself continually looking into doorways and down alleys. When the women called to him, offering themselves with promises of delight and forgetting, he turned and looked at them before moving on.

They reached the water. Stopped, listening to the creak of ships and the waves slapping the planks of the piers. Masts moved, the moons appearing to swing from one side of them to another, rocking. There were islands out there, Crispin thought, looking at the sea, with strands of stony beach that would be silver, or blue-tinted in the moonlight beyond the dark.

He turned away. They went on, climbing back up the lanes leading from the water, his companions offering silence as a kind of grace. He was leaving. Sarantium was leaving him.

A pair of women walked by. One stopped and called to them. Crispin stopped as well, looked at her, turned away.

She could change her voice, he knew, sound like anyone at all. Probably *look* like anyone. Artifice of the stage. If she was alive. He had a fantasy, he admitted finally to himself: he was walking in the darkness of the City, thinking that if she was still here, if she saw him, she might call to him, to say farewell.

It was time to go to bed. They walked back. A servant sleepily admitted them. He said goodnight to the others. They went to their rooms. He went up to his. Shirin was waiting there.

Some goodbyes, not yet properly done.

He closed the door behind him. She was sitting on the bed, one leg neatly crossed over the other. Images begetting images. No dagger this time. Not the same woman.

She said, 'It is very late. Are you sober?'

'Tolerably,' he said. 'We took a long walk.'

'Carullus?'

He shook his head. 'We pretty much carried him home to Kasia.'

Shirin smiled a little. 'He doesn't know what to celebrate, what to mourn.'

'That's about right,' he said. 'How did you get in?'

She arched her eyebrows. 'My litter's waiting across the road. Didn't you see it? How did I get in? I knocked at the door. One of your servants opened it. I told them we hadn't yet said goodbye and could I wait for you to return. They let me come up.' She gestured, he saw the glass of wine at her elbow. 'They have been attentive. How do *most* of your visitors get in? What did you think, that I climbed through a window to seduce you in your sleep?'

'I'm not so lucky a man,' he murmured. He took the chair by the window. He felt a need to sit down.

She made a face. 'Men are better awake, most of the time,' she said. 'Though I could make a case the other way, for some of those who send me gifts.'

Crispin managed a smile. Danis was on her thong about Shirin's neck. They'd both come. Difficult. Everything was difficult these last days.

He couldn't really say *why* this encounter was, however, and that was a part of the problem, in itself.

'Pertennius being troublesome again?' he asked.

'No. He's with the army. You should know that.'

'I'm not paying attention to everyone's movements. Do forgive me.' His voice was sharper than he'd meant it to be.

She glared at him.

'*She says she feels like killing you,*' Danis spoke for the first time.

'Say it yourself,' Crispin snapped. 'Don't hide behind the bird.'

'I am *not* hiding. Unlike some people. It isn't . . . polite to say such things aloud.'

He laughed, against his will. Protocols of the half-world. Reluctantly, she smiled as well.

There was a small silence. He breathed her scent in his room. Two women in the world wore this perfume. One now, more likely, the other was dead, or hiding still.

'I don't want you to go,' Shirin said.

He looked at her without speaking. She lifted her small chin. Her features, he had long ago decided, were appealing but not arresting in repose. It was in the expressiveness of her, in laughter, pain, anger, sorrow, fear—any and all of those—that Shirin's face came alive, her beauty compelled attention and awareness and gave birth to desire. That, and when she moved, the dancer's grace, suppleness, unspoken hint that physical needs scarcely admitted could be assuaged. She was a creature never to be fully captured in an art that did not move.

He said, 'Shirin, I cannot stay. Not now. You know what has happened. You called me a liar and an idiot for trying to make . . . less of it, when last we spoke.'

'Danis called you an idiot,' she corrected, and then was silent again. Her turn to gaze at him.

And after a long moment, Crispin said, bringing the thought into words, 'I cannot ask you to come with me, my dear.'

The chin lifted a little more. Not a word spoken. Waiting.

'I . . . have thought of it,' he murmured.

'Good,' said Shirin.

'I don't even know if I'll stay in Varena, what I'll do.'

'Ah. The wanderer's hard life. Nothing a woman could share.'

'Not . . . this woman,' he said. He was entirely sober now. 'You are just about the second empress of Sarantium, my dear. They need you desperately, the new rulers. They'll want continuity, the people diverted. You can expect to be showered with even more than you have now.'

'And ordered to marry the Emperor's secretary?'

He blinked. 'I doubt it,' he said.

'Oh. Do you? You know *all* about the court here, I see.' She glared at him again. 'Why not stay, then? They'll geld you and make you Chancellor when Gesius dies.'

He looked at her. Said, after a moment, 'Shirin, be truthful. Do you honestly fear they'll force you to marry someone—anyone—right now?'

A silence.

'That isn't the point,' Danis said.

Then she shouldn't have mentioned it, he thought, but did not say. Didn't say it, because something was twisting in his own heart as he looked at her. Zoticus's daughter, as brave as her father, in her own way.

He said, 'Did you . . . did Martinian sell your father's farm for you?'

She shook her head. 'I didn't ask him to. Forgot to mention that to you. I asked him to find a tenant, to keep it going. He did. He's written me a few letters. Told me a lot about you, actually.'

Crispin blinked again. 'I see. Another thing you forgot to mention to me?'

'I suppose we simply haven't talked enough.' She smiled.

'So there,' said Danis.

Crispin sighed. 'That feels true, at least.'

'I'm pleased you agree.' She sipped her wine.

He looked at her. 'You are angry. I know. What must I do? Do you want me to take you to bed, my dear?'

'To help with my anger? No thank you.'

'To help with this sorrow,' he said.

She was silent.

'She says to say she wishes you had never come here,' Danis said.

'I'm lying, of course,' Shirin added aloud.

'I know,' Crispin said. 'Do you want me to ask you to come west?'

She looked at him.

'Do you want me to come west?'

'Sometimes I do, yes,' he admitted, to himself as much as to her. It was a relief to say it.

He saw her take a breath. 'Well, that's a start,' she murmured. 'Helps with the anger, too. You might be able to take me to bed for other reasons now.'

He laughed. 'Oh, my dear,' he said. 'Don't you think I—'

'I know. Don't. Don't say it. You couldn't think about . . . any of this when you came, for reasons I know. And now you can't for . . . new reasons, that I also know. What do you want to ask of me, then?'

She wore a soft cap of dark green, a ruby in it. Her cloak lay beside her on the bed. Her gown was silk, green as the cap, with gold. Her earrings were gold and rings flashed on her fingers. He thought, looking at her, claiming this image, that he'd never be gifted enough at his craft to capture how she appeared just then, even sitting still as she was.

Speaking carefully, he said, 'Don't . . . sell the farmhouse yet. Perhaps you'll need to . . . visit your property in the western province. If it becomes a province.'

'It will. The Empress Gisel, I have decided, knows what she wants and how to get it.'

His own thought, actually. He didn't say it. The Empress wasn't the point just now. He discovered that his heart was beating rapidly. He said, 'You might even . . . invest there, depending how events unfold? Martinian's shrewd about such things, if you want advice.'

She smiled at him. 'Depending how events unfold?'

'Gisel's . . . arrangements.'

'Gisel's,' she murmured. And waited again.

He took a breath. A mistake, perhaps; her scent was inescapably present. 'Shirin, there is no way you *should* leave Sarantium and you know it.'

'Yes?' she said, encouragingly.

'But let me go home and find out what I . . . well, let me . . . Ah, well if you *do* marry someone here, by choice, I'd be . . . Jad's blood, woman, what do you *want* me to say?'

She stood up. Smiled. He felt helpless before the layers of meaning in that smile.

'You just did,' she murmured. And bending before he could rise, she kissed him chastely on the cheek. 'Goodbye, Crispin. A safe voyage. I'll expect you to write me soon. About properties, perhaps? That sort of thing.'

That sort of thing.

He stood up. Cleared his throat. A woman desirable as moonlight when the night was dark.

'You, um, you kissed me better the first time we met.'

'I know,' she said sweetly. 'Might have been a mistake.'

And she smiled again and went to the door and opened it herself and went out. He stood rooted to the spot.

'Go to bed,' said Danis. *'We'll have the servants let us out. A good journey, she says to say.'*

'Thank you,' he sent, before remembering they couldn't make out his thoughts. He wished, suddenly, he could make out his own.

He didn't go to bed. There would have been no point. Stayed awake a long time, sitting in a chair by the window. Saw her wineglass and the flask on a tray but didn't take them, didn't drink. He'd made himself a promise about that, earlier tonight, in the street.

He was grateful for clear-headedness in the morning. A message—more than half expected—was waiting for him when he came down the stairs, delivered at sunrise. He ate, went to chapel on impulse, with Vargos and Pardos, then to the baths, had himself shaved, paid some visits in the Blues' compound and elsewhere. Was aware, as the day progressed, of the movement of the sun overhead. This day, this night, one more, then gone.

Some goodbyes not yet done. One more coming at darkfall. In the palace.

'I had considered a flour sack,' said the Empress of Sarantium, 'for memory's sake.'

'I am grateful, my lady, that you left it as a thought.'

Gisel smiled. She had risen from a small desk, where she'd been opening sealed correspondence and reports with a small knife. Leontes was north and east with the army, but the Empire was still to be run, guided through changes. She and Gesius, he thought, would be doing so.

She crossed the room, took another seat. She was still holding the small paper knife. It had an ivory handle, carved in the shape of a face, he saw. She noticed his gaze. Smiled.

'My father gave me this when I was very young. The face is his, actually. It comes off, if you twist.' She did so. Held the ivory in one hand, the suddenly hiltless blade in the other. 'I wore this against my skin when I boarded ship to sail here, had it hidden when we landed.'

He looked at her.

'I didn't know, you see, what they intended to do with me. At the . . . very last, sometimes, we can only control how we end.'

Crispin cleared his throat, looked around the room. They were almost alone, one woman servant with them here in the Traversite Palace, Gisel's rooms, that had been Alixana's. She hadn't had time to change them yet. Other priorities. The rose was gone, he saw.

Alixana had wanted dolphins here. Had taken him to see them in the straits.

Gesius the Chancellor, smiling and benign, had been waiting to escort him to Gisel himself when Crispin presented himself at the Bronze Gates. Had done so, and withdrawn. There was no hidden meaning to this after-dark invitation, Crispin realized: they worked late in the Imperial Precinct, especially in wartime and with a diplomatic campaign already unfolding for Batiara. He'd been invited to see the Empress when she had a moment to grant him in a crowded day. A countryman sailing home, bidding farewell. There was no secrecy now, no abduction in the dark, no private message that could kill him if revealed.

That was past. He had journeyed here, she had journeyed even farther. He was going back. He wondered what he'd find in Varena, in the place where wagers on her life had been drunkenly made in taverns for a year.

Men had won those wagers, lost them. And those of the Antae lords who had sought to murder her and rule in her stead . . . what would become of them now?

'If you'd been a little quicker in your planning,' Gisel said, 'you might have taken an Imperial ship. It left two days ago, with my messages for Eudric and Kerdas.'

He looked at her. Again the eerie sense that this woman could read his thoughts. He wondered if she was like that with everyone. Wondered how any man could have been foolish enough to wager against her. She had glanced away just now, was gesturing to her woman to bring him wine. It was carried across the room on a golden tray inlaid with precious stones around the rim. The riches of Sarantium, the unimaginable wealth here. He poured for himself, added water.

'A careful man, I see,' said the Empress Gisel. She smiled, deliberately.

He remembered these words as well. She'd said the same thing the first time, in Varena. There was such an odd sense to this night encounter. The distance travelled, in half a year.

He shook his head. 'I feel I need my wits about me.'

'Don't you, usually?'

He shrugged. 'I was thinking about the usurpers myself. What is to happen? Or may one ask, Majesty?'

It mattered, of course. He was going back, his mother was there, his house, his friends.

'It depends on them. On Eudric, mostly. I have formally invited him to become Governor of the new Sarantine province of Batiara, in the name of the Emperor Valerius III.'

Crispin stared, then collected himself and looked down. This was an Empress. One didn't gape at her like a fish.

'You would reward the man who . . .'

'Tried to kill me?'

He nodded.

She smiled. 'Which of the Antae nobility did *not* wish me dead last year, Caius Crispus? They all did. Even the Rhodians knew that. What man might I choose if I eliminated all of those? Best to empower the one who won, is it not? An indication of capability. And he will live . . . in some fear, I believe.'

He found himself staring again. Couldn't help himself. She was twenty years old, he guessed, perhaps not even that. As calculating and precise as a . . . as a monarch. Hildric's daughter. They lived, these people, in a different world. Valerius had been like this, he thought suddenly.

He was thinking very quickly, actually. 'And the Patriarch in Rhodias?'

'Good for you,' said the Empress. 'He has messages of his own, arriving on the same ship. The schisms of Jad are to be resolved if he agrees. The Eastern Patriarch will accept his preeminence again.'

'In exchange for . . . ?'

'Pronouncements supporting the reunion of the Empire, Sarantium as the Imperial Seat, and endorsement of a number of specific matters of doctrine, as proposed by the Emperor.'

It was all so neat, unfolding at such speed.

And his anger was hard to check. 'Such matters to include the representation of Jad in chapels and sanctuaries, of course.'

'Of course,' she murmured, unruffled. 'It matters a great deal to the Emperor, that one.'

'I know,' he said.

'I know that you know,' she replied.

There was a silence.

'I expect questions of government to be sorted through more easily than issues of faith. I have told Leontes as much.'

Crispin said nothing.

After a moment she added, 'I was in the Great Sanctuary again this morning. I took that passageway you showed me. I wanted to see the work on the dome again.'

'Before they start scraping it off, you mean?'

'Yes,' she said, undisturbed. 'Before that. I told you when we passed through at night—I have a clearer understanding, now, of matters we discussed at our first meeting.'

He waited.

'You lamented your tools. Remember? I told you they were the best we had. That there had been a plague and a war.'

'I remember.'

Gisel smiled a little. 'What I told you was the truth. What you told me was more true: I have seen what can be done by a master with proper equipment to deploy. Working on my father's chapel, I had you hampered like a strategos on a battlefield with only farmers and labourers to command.'

His father had been like that. Had died like that.

'With deference, my lady, I am uneasy with the comparison.'

'I know,' she said. 'Think about it later, however. I was pleased with it myself, when it came to me this morning.'

She was being entirely gracious, complimenting him, granting a private audience merely to bid him farewell. He had no cause at all to be surly here. Gisel's rise to this throne might save his homeland and hers from destruction.

He nodded. Rubbed at his smooth chin. 'I shall have leisure to do so, I imagine, on board ship, Majesty.'

'Tomorrow?' she asked.

'The next day after.'

He was to realize later (leisure on board ship) that she had known this, had been guiding a conversation.

'Ah. So you are still resolving business affairs.'

'Yes, Majesty. Though I believe I am done.'

'You have been paid all outstanding sums? We would want that properly dealt with.'

'I have, my lady. The Chancellor was good enough to attend to that himself.'

She looked at him. 'He owes you his life. We are . . . also aware of our debt to you, of course.'

He shook his head. 'You were my queen. Are my queen. I did nothing that—'

'You did what was needful for us, at personal risk, twice.' She hesitated. 'I shall not dwell over-long on the other matter—' He was aware she had switched to the personal voice. 'But I am still of the west, and take pride in what we can show them here. It is a regret for me that . . . circumstances have required the undoing of your work here.'

He lowered his eyes. What was there to say? It was a death.

'It has also occurred to me, with what else I have learned these past days, that there is one more person you might desire to see before you sail.'

Crispin looked up.

Gisel of the Antae, Gisel of Sarantium, gazed back at him with those blue eyes.

'She can't see you, however,' she said.

There were dolphins again. He'd wondered if he would see them, and was aware that there was something mortally foolish and vain in that doubting: as if the creatures of the sea would appear or not appear in consequence of whatever men and women did in cities, on the land.

Looked at another way (though it was a heresy), there were a great many souls to be carried these days, in and about Sarantium.

He was on a small, sleek Imperial craft, passage gained merely by showing Gisel's slim dagger with the image of her father in ivory for a handle. A gift, she'd declared it, handing it to him, a way to remember her. Though she'd also said she expected to be in Varena before too many years had passed. If all fell out as it should, there would be ceremonies in Rhodias.

A note had gone before him, alerting the crew that the one bearing the image of the Empress's father could sail to a place otherwise forbidden.

He had been there before.

Styliane was not in the prison cells under the palaces. Someone with a keener sense of irony and punishment—Gesius, most likely, who had lived through so much violence in his days, and survived all of it—had chosen a different place for her to live out the life the new Emperor had granted her, as a mercy to one he had wed and a sign to the people of his benevolence.

And one really didn't have to look further than Leontes on the Golden Throne and Styliane on the isle, Crispin thought, watching the dolphins beside the ship again, to find a sufficiency of ironies.

They docked, were tied, a plank was run out and down for him. The only visitor, only person disembarking here.

Memories and images. He looked, almost against his will, and saw where Alixana had dropped her cloak on the stones and walked away. He'd been dreaming of that place, moonlit.

Two Excubitors met the ship. One of those on board came down the plank and spoke quietly to them. They led him, wordlessly, along the path through the trees. Birds were singing. The sun slanted through the leafy canopy.

They came to the clearing where men had died on the day Valerius was killed. No one spoke. Crispin became aware, try as he might to quell it, that his principal feeling was dread.

He wished he hadn't come. Couldn't have said with any certainty why he had. His escorts stopped, one of them gestured towards the largest of the houses here. He didn't need the indication.

The same house in which her brother had been. Of course.

A difference, however. Windows open on all sides, barred, but unshuttered, to let in the morning light. He wondered. Went forward. There were guards here. Three of them. They looked past him at his escorts and evidently received some signal. Crispin didn't look back to see. The door was unlocked by one of them.

No words, at all. He wondered if they'd been forbidden to talk, to avoid any chance of being seduced, corrupted. He walked in. The door closed behind him. He heard the key turn. They were taking no chances at all. They would know what this prisoner had done.

This prisoner sat quietly in a chair by the far wall, her profile to him, unmoving. No visible response to the arrival of someone. Crispin looked at her, and dread slipped away, to be replaced by a myriad of other things he couldn't even begin to sort out.

She said, 'I told you I am not eating.'

She hadn't turned her head, hadn't seen him.

Couldn't see him. Even from where he stood, across the room, Crispin realized that her eyes were gone, gouged out. Black sockets where the brightness he remembered had been. He pictured, fighting it, an underground room, implements, a burning fire, torches, large men with fat, skilled thumbs approaching her.

One more person you might desire to see, Gisel had said.

'I don't blame you at all,' he said. 'I imagine the food is dreadful.'

She started. There was pity in that, that a woman so flawlessly composed, so impossible to disconcert, should be made to react like this, merely by an unexpected voice.

He tried to imagine being blind. Colour and light gone, shadings, hues, the wealth and play of them. Nothing worse in the world. Death better, he thought.

'Rhodian,' she said. 'Come to see what it is like to bed a blind woman now? Jaded appetites?'

'No,' he said, keeping calm. 'No appetite at all, like you, it seems. Come to say goodbye. I leave for home tomorrow.'

'Finished so soon?' Her tone changed.

She didn't turn her head. They had shorn off almost all her golden hair. With another woman it might have marred her appearance. With Styliane it only revealed the perfection of cheek and bone below the still-bruised and hollowed eye socket. They hadn't marked her, he thought. Only the blinding.

Only the blinding. And this prison on the isle where her brother had lived his days in darkness, burned and burning within, without any light allowed to enter.

And here was, as much as anything, a mark of the nature

of the woman, Crispin thought, of her pride: light flooding the room, useless to her, offered only to whoever might enter. Only the silent guards would come, day by day—but there was no hiding for Styliane Daleina, no shielding herself in darkness. If you dealt with her, you had to accept what there was to see. It had always been so.

'You have finished your work already?' she repeated.

'I haven't,' he said quietly. Not bitter now. Not here, seeing this. 'You warned me, long ago.'

'Ah. That. Already? I didn't think it would be . . .'

'So swift?'

'So swift. He told you it was a heresy, your dome.'

'Yes. Did it himself, I'll grant.'

She turned to him.

And he saw that they *had* marked her, after all. The left side of her face was branded with the symbol of a murderer: a crude blade cut into a circle meant to stand for the god's sun. The wound was crusted with blood, her face inflamed around it. She needed a physician, he thought, doubted they'd made arrangements for one. A cheek scarred into ugliness, with fire.

Again, someone with a dark awareness of irony. Or, perhaps, just a person in a locked and soundproof room under the earth, utterly impervious to such things, only following the duly prescribed protocols of justice in the Imperial Precinct of Sarantium.

He must have made a sound. She smiled, an expression he remembered, wry and knowing. It hurt to see it, here. 'You are heart-struck by my enduring beauty?'

Crispin swallowed hard. Took a deep breath. 'In truth,' he said, 'I am. I could wish it were not so.'

That silenced her a moment.

'That is honest, at least,' she said. 'I recall that you liked him. Both of them.'

'That would have been a presumption for an artisan. I admired him greatly.' He paused. 'Both of them.'

'And Valerius was your patron, of course, surety of all your work. Which will now be lost. Poor Rhodian. Do you hate me?'

'I could wish I did,' he said finally. So much light in the room. The breeze cool, fragrant with wood-smells. Birdsong in the trees, all around the clearing. The green-gold leaves. Born now, green in summer, dying in the fall. *Do you hate me?*

'Is he marching north?' she asked. 'Against Bassania?'

A lifetime in the halls and rooms of power. A mind that could not stop working.

'He is.'

'And . . . Gisel is to negotiate with Varena?'

'She is.'

Gisel, he thought, was exactly the same in this. They did live in a different world, these people. Same sun and moons and stars, but a different world.

Her mouth twisted wryly again. 'I would have done the same, you realize? I told you the night we first spoke that there were those of us who thought the invasion misguided.'

'Alixana was one of them,' he said.

She ignored that, effortlessly.

'He had to be killed before the fleet sailed. If you stop to think, you will see it. Leontes had to be in the City. He wouldn't have turned back, once he'd sailed.'

'How unfortunate. So Valerius had to die, that Leontes—and you—could rule?'

'I . . . thought that was it, yes.'

He opened his mouth, closed it. 'You *thought*?'

Her mouth twisted again. She winced this time, brought a hand up towards her wounded face, then put it down without touching. 'After the tunnel, it didn't seem important any more.'

'I don't . . .'

'I could have killed him years ago. A foolish girl, I was. I thought the thing to do was take power, the way my father ought to have been given power. Leontes ruling, but only needing his soldiers' love and his piety to be content, my brothers and I . . .' She stopped.

I could have killed him years ago.

Crispin looked at her. 'You think Valerius killed your father?'

'Oh, Rhodian. I know he did. What I didn't know was that nothing else mattered. I . . . should have been wiser.'

'And killed sooner?'

'I was eight years old,' she said. And stopped. The birds were loud outside. 'I think my life ended then. In a way. The life I was . . . headed towards.'

The son of Horius Crispus the mason looked at her. 'You think this was *love*, then? What you did?'

'No, I think it was vengeance,' she said. And then added, with no warning at all, 'Will you kill me, please?'

No warning, except that he could see what they had done and were doing to her, in the guise of mercy. Knew how desperately she would want this to end. There weren't even logs here for a fire. Fire could be used to kill oneself. They would probably force food into her, he thought, if she refused to eat. There were ways of doing that. Leontes intended to demonstrate his generous nature by keeping a murderous woman alive for a time, because she had been his wife in the eyes of Jad.

A pious man, everyone knew it. They might even bring her out at times, on display.

Crispin looked at her. Could not speak.

She said, softly, that the guards would not hear, 'You have known me a little, Rhodian. We have ... shared some things, however briefly. Will you leave this room and leave me ... in this life?'

'I am—'

'Just an artisan, I know. But—'

'*No!*' He almost shouted. Then he lowered his own voice. 'That isn't it. I am ... not a man ... who kills.'

His father's head, flying from his shoulders, blood spurting from the toppling body. Men telling the tale in a tavern in Varena. A boy overhearing them.

'Make an exception,' she murmured lightly, but he could hear desperation beneath the cool tone.

He closed his eyes. 'Styliane ... '

She said, 'Or see it another way. I died years ago. I told you. You are just ... signing a deed already executed.'

He looked at her again. She was facing him directly now, eyeless, marred, exquisitely beautiful. 'Or punish me for your lost work. Or for Valerius. Or for *any* reason. But please.' She was whispering. 'No one else will do it, Crispin.'

He looked around. Nothing remotely resembling a weapon in here, guards at all the iron-barred windows and beyond the locked door.

No one else will do it.

And then, belatedly, he remembered how he had gained admission to this isle, and something cried out within him, in his heart, and he wished that he were already gone from here, from Sarantium, for she was wrong. There was someone else who would do it.

He took out the blade and looked at it. At the ivory carving of Hildric of the Antae on the hilt. Fine work, it was.

He didn't know, he really didn't know, if he was being made into an instrument yet again, or was being offered, instead, a dark, particular gift, for services, and with affection, by an Empress who had declared herself in his debt. He didn't know Gisel well enough to judge. It could be either, or both. Or something else entirely.

He did know what the woman before him wanted. Needed. As he looked at her and about this room, he realized that he also knew what was proper, for her soul and his own. Gisel of the Antae, who had carried this blade hidden against her body, sailing here, might also have known, he thought.

Sometimes dying was not the worst thing that could happen. Sometimes it was release, a gift, an offering.

Amid all the turning gyres, all the plots and counterplots and images begetting images, Crispin made them come to a stop, and he accepted the burden of doing so.

He took the ivory handle off the blade, as Gisel had done. He laid the knife down on the table-top, hiltless, so slender it was almost invisible.

Amid the glorious springtime brightness of that room, that day, he said, 'I must go. I am leaving you something.'

'How kind. A small mosaic, to comfort me in the dark? Another gemstone to shine for me, like the first you gave?'

He shook his head again. There was a pain in his chest now.

'No,' he said. 'Not those.' And perhaps something in the difficulty with which he spoke alerted her. Even the newly blind began to learn how to listen. She lifted her head a little.

'Where is it?' Styliane asked, very softly.

'The table,' he said. He closed his eyes briefly. 'Towards me, near the far side. Be careful.'

Be careful.

He watched her rise, come forward, reach her hands towards the table edge to find it, then move both palms haltingly across—still learning how to do this. He saw when she found the blade, which was sharp and sleek as death could sometimes be.

'Ah,' she said. And became very still.

He said nothing.

'You will be blamed for this, of course.'

'I am sailing in the morning.'

'It would be courteous of me to wait until then, wouldn't it?'

He said nothing to this, either.

'I'm not sure,' said Styliane softly, 'if I have the patience, you know. They . . . might search and find it?'

'They might,' he said.

She was silent a long time. Then he saw her smile. She said, 'I suppose this means you did love me, a little.'

He was afraid he would weep.

'I suppose it does,' he said quietly.

'How very unexpected,' said Styliane Daleina.

He fought for control. Said nothing.

'I wish,' she said, 'I'd been able to find her. One thing left unfinished. I shouldn't tell you that, I know. Do you think she's dead?'

The heart could cry. 'If not, I think she will be, most likely, when she learns . . . you are.'

That gave her pause. 'Ah. I can understand that. So this gift you offer kills us both.'

A truth. In the way they seemed to see things here.

'I suppose it might,' Crispin said. He was looking at her, seeing her now, and as she was before, in the palace, in his room, in her own, her mouth finding his. *Whatever else I do . . .*

She had warned him, more than once.

She said, 'Poor man. All you wanted to do here was leave your dead behind and make a mosaic overhead.'

'I was . . . overly ambitious,' he said. And heard her laugh, in delight, for the last time.

'Thank you for that,' she said. For wit. There was a silence. She lifted the sliver of the blade, her fingers as slim, almost as long. 'And thank you for this, and for . . . other things, once.' She stood very straight, unbending, no concessions to . . . anything at all. 'A safe journey home, Rhodian.'

He was being dismissed, and not even by name at the end. He knew suddenly that she was not going to be able to wait. Her need was a hunger.

He looked at her, in the brightness she'd elected to offer here that all might see clearly where she could not, the way a host forbidden drink by his physician might order forth the very best wine he had for his friends.

'And you, my lady,' he said. 'A safe journey home to the light.'

He knocked on the door. They opened it for him and let him out. He left the room, the glade, the woods, the stony, stony beach, the isle.

In the morning he left Sarantium, on the tide at dawn, when hues and shades of colour were just coming back into the world at the end of the god's long voyage through the dark.

The sun rose behind them, filtered by a line of low clouds. As he stood at the stern of the ship upon which Plautus Bonosus, in kindness amid his own sorrow, had offered him passage, Crispin, with the handful of other passengers, looked back upon the City. Eye of the world, they called it. Glory of Jad's creation.

He saw the bustle and brilliance of the deep, sheltered harbour, the iron pillars that held the chains that could be dropped across the entrance in time of war. He watched small boats cut across their wake, ferries to Deapolis, morning fishermen setting out, others coming back from a night's harvesting on the waves, sails of many colours.

He caught a glimpse, far off, of the triple walls themselves, where they curved down to the water. Saranios himself had drawn the line for these when first he came. He saw the glint of this muted early sunlight on rooftops everywhere, watching the City climb up from the sea, chapel and sanctuary domes, patrician homes, guild-house roofs bronzed in ostentatious display. He saw the vast bulk of the Hippodrome where men raced horses.

And then, as they swept from a southwest course more towards the west, clearing the harbour, reaching the swells of the open sea where their own white sails billowed, Crispin saw the Imperial Precinct gardens and playing fields and palaces, and they filled his sight, all of his gaze, as he was carried past them and away.

West they went, on a dawn wind and tide, the mariners calling to each other, orders shouted in the brightening, the zest of something beginning. A long journey. He looked back still, as did the other passengers, all of them caught, held at the stern rail as if in a spell. But at the end, as they drew farther and farther off, Crispin was looking at one thing only, and the very last thing he saw, far distant, almost on the horizon but gleaming above all else, was Artibasos's dome.

Then the rising sun finally burst above those low clouds east, appearing right behind the distant City, dazzlingly bright, and he had to shield his eyes, avert his gaze, and when he looked back again, blinking, Sarantium was gone, it had left him, and there was only the sea.

EPILOGUE

An old man in a chapel doorway, not far from the walls of Varena. Once he would have been engaged in considering the present colour of those walls, somewhere between honey and ochre, pondering ways of using glass and stone and light to accomplish that hue as it appeared in this particular late-spring sunshine. Not any more. Now, he is content to simply enjoy the day, the afternoon. He is aware, in the way that sometimes creeps up on the aged, that there are no assurances of another spring.

He is virtually alone here, only a few other men about, somewhere in the yard or in the unused old chapel adjacent to the expanded sanctuary. The sanctuary is not in use now, either, though a king is buried here. Since an assassination attempt in the autumn, the clerics have refused to conduct services, or even remain in their dormitory, despite substantial pressure from those currently governing in the palace. The man in the doorway has views on this, but for the moment he simply enjoys the quiet as he waits for someone to arrive. He has been coming here for some days now, feeling more impatient than an old man really should, he tells himself, if the lessons of a long life had been properly absorbed.

He tilts the stool on which he sits, leans back against the wood of the doorway (an old habit), and slides forward the remarkably shapeless hat he wears. He is irrationally fond of the hat, enduring all jests and gibes it provokes with perfect equanimity. For one thing, the headgear—absurd even when new—saved his life almost fifteen years ago when an apprentice, fearful in a darkened chapel at evening, thought he was a thief approaching without a light. The blow from a staff that the young fellow (broad-shouldered, even back then) had intended to bring crashing down on an intruder's head was averted at the last instant when the hat was seen and known.

Martinian of Varena, at his ease in the spring light, looks off down the road just before allowing himself to fall asleep.

He saw that same apprentice coming. Or, more accurately, these long years later, he saw his one-time apprentice, now his colleague and partner and awaited friend, Caius Crispus, approaching along the path leading to the wide, low wooden gate that fenced in the sanctuary yard and its graves.

'Rot you, Crispin,' he said mildly. '*Just* as I was about to nap.' Then he considered the fact that he was quite alone, that no one was listening to him, and he allowed himself an honest response, quickly tilting the stool back forward, aware of the sudden hard beating of his heart.

He felt wonder, anticipation, very great happiness.

Watching, shadowed in the doorway, he saw Crispin—hair and beard shorter than when he'd left, but not otherwise discernibly altered—unhook the gate latch and enter the yard. Martinian lifted his voice and called to the other men waiting. They weren't apprentices or artisans: no work was being done here now. Two of those men came striding quickly around the corner of the building. Martinian pointed towards the gate.

'There he is. Finally. I couldn't tell you if he's in a temper, but it is generally safer to assume as much.'

Both men swore, much as he had, though with more genuine feeling, and started forward. They had been in Varena nearly two weeks, waiting with increasing irritation. Martinian was the one who had suggested the odds were good that the traveller, when he did come, would stop at this chapel outside the walls. He is pleased to have been correct, though not happy about what the other man will find here.

In his doorway, he watched two strangers go forward, the first souls to greet a traveller on his return from far away. Both of them are easterners, ironically. One is an Imperial Courier, the other an officer in the army of Sarantium. The army that was supposed to have been invading this spring and wasn't, now.

That being the largest change of all.

Some time later, after the two Sarantines had formally conveyed whatever messages they had lingered to deliver and had gone away, along with the soldiers who had been here on guard with them, Martinian decided that Crispin had been sitting alone by the gate long enough, whatever the tidings had been. He rose slowly and walked forward, nursing the usual ache in his hip.

Crispin had his back to him, seemed immersed in the documents he'd been given. It was not good to surprise a man, Martinian had always felt, so he called the other's name while still a distance away.

'I saw your hat,' Crispin said, not looking up. 'I only came home to burn it, you understand.'

Martinian walked up to him.

Crispin, sitting on the large moss-covered boulder he'd always liked, looked over at him. His eyes were bright, remembered. 'Hello,' he said. 'I didn't think to find you here.'

Martinian had also intended some kind of jest, but found himself incapable of one, just then. Instead, he bent forward, wordlessly, and kissed the younger man on the forehead, in benediction. Crispin stood up, and put his arms around him and they embraced.

'My mother?' the younger man asked, when they stepped back. His voice was gruff.

'Is well. Awaiting you.'

'How did you all . . . ? Oh. The courier. So you knew I was on the way?'

Martinian nodded. 'They arrived some time ago.'

'I had a slower boat. Walked from Mylasia.'

'Still hate horses?'

Crispin hesitated. 'Riding them.' He looked at Martinian. His eyebrows met when he frowned; Martinian remembered that. The older man was trying to sort out what else he was seeing in the traveller's face. Differences, but hard to pin down.

Crispin said, 'They brought the tidings from Sarantium? About the changes?'

Martinian nodded. 'You'll tell me more?'

'What I know.'

'You are . . . all right?' A ridiculous question, but in some ways the only one that mattered.

Crispin hesitated again. 'Mostly. A great deal happened.'

'Of course. Your work . . . it went well?'

Another pause. As if they were fumbling their way back towards easiness. 'It went very well, but . . .' Crispin sat down on the rock again. 'It is coming down. Along with others, everywhere.'

'What?'

'The new Emperor has . . . beliefs about renderings of Jad.'

'Impossible. You must be wrong. That—'

Martinian stopped.

Crispin said, 'I wish I was. Our work will be coming down here, too, I suspect. We'll be subject to Sarantine edicts, if all goes as the Empress intends.'

The Empress. They knew about this. A miracle of the god, some had already named it. Martinian thought there might be more earthly explanations. 'Gisel?'

'Gisel. You heard?'

'Word came from other couriers on the same ship.' Martinian sat down himself now, on the facing rock. So many times, they'd sat here together, or on the tree stumps beyond the gate.

Crispin looked over his shoulder at the sanctuary. 'We're going to lose this. What we did here.'

Martinian cleared his throat. Something needed to be said. 'Some of it has been lost, already.'

'So soon? I didn't think . . .'

'Not for that reason. They . . . scraped down Heladikos in the spring.'

Crispin said nothing. Martinian remembered this expression, too, however.

'Eudric was trying to earn support from the Patriarch in Rhodias, with the invasion looming. Backing away from the heresy of the Antae.'

Heladikos and his torch had been the very last thing Crispin had done before he'd gone away. The younger man sat very still. Martinian was trying to read him, see what had changed, what had not. It felt odd not to understand Crispin intuitively, after so many years. People went away and they changed; hard on those who remained behind.

More sorrow *and* more life, Martinian thought. Both things. The documents from the courier were still clutched between the other man's large hands.

Crispin said, 'Did it work? The . . . backing away?'

Martinian shook his head. 'No. They had shed blood in a chapel, with Patriarchal envoys present and at risk. Eudric has a long way to go to win any kindness there. And he earned a good deal of outrage in Varena when our tesserae came down. The Antae saw it as disrespectful to Hildric. Sacking his chapel, in a way.'

Crispin laughed softly. Martinian tried to remember the last time he'd heard his friend laugh in the year before he'd gone away. 'Poor Eudric. Full circle, that. The Antae protesting destruction in a holy place in Batiara.'

Martinian smiled a little. 'I said that too.' His turn to hesitate. He had expected an angrier reaction. He changed the ground a little. 'It does look as if there will be no attack now. Is that so?'

Crispin nodded. 'Not this year, at least. The army is north and east, against Bassania. We'll become a province of Sarantium, if negotiations hold.'

Martinian shook his head slowly. He took off his hat, looked at it, put it back on his balding head. No attack.

Every man who could walk had been engaged in reinforcing the walls of Varena all winter. They'd been making weapons, drilling with them, storing food and water. There hadn't been much food to store, after a poor harvest.

He was afraid he might cry. 'I didn't think to live so long.'

The other man looked at him. 'How are you?'

An attempt at a shrug. 'Well enough. My hands. My hip, sometimes. Mostly water in my wine, now.'

Crispin made a face. 'Me too. Carissa?'

'Is very well. Anxious to see you. Is probably with your mother now.'

'We should go, then. I was only stopping to see . . . the finished work here. There's little point now.'

'No,' said Martinian. He looked at the papers. 'What . . . what did they bring you?'

Crispin hesitated again. He seemed to measure his words and thoughts more, Martinian thought. Did they teach that in the east?

Without speaking, the other man simply handed over the thick sheaf of documents. Martinian took them and read. He wouldn't have denied a consuming curiosity: some men had waited here a long time to deliver whatever these were.

He saw what these were. Colour left his face as he turned each signed and sealed deed and document of title. He went back and counted. Five of them, six, seven. Then the enumeration of other items and a listing of where they could be found and claimed. He found it difficult to breathe.

'We seem to be wealthy,' Crispin said mildly.

Martinian looked up at him. Crispin was gazing off towards the forest, east. What he'd said was an understatement, prodigiously so. And the 'we' was a great courtesy.

The papers delivered by the Imperial Courier attested, one by one by one, to lands all over Batiara, and moneys and moveable goods, now owned by or belonging to one Caius Crispus, artisan, of Varena.

The last page was a personal note. Martinian glanced up for permission. Crispin, looking back at him now, nodded. It was brief. Written in Sarantine. It read:

> *We did promise certain things if your journey bore fruit for us. Our beloved father taught us to keep royal promises and the god enjoins us to do so. Changes along the way do not change the truth of things. These are not gifts, but earned. There is another item, one we discussed in Varena as you will recall. It is not included among these, remaining yours to consider and choose for yourself—or not. The other conveyance sent herewith is, we trust, further evidence of our appreciation.*

It was signed, 'Gisel, Empress of Sarantium.'

'Jad's blood and eyes and bones, what did you *do* there, Crispin?'

'She thinks I made her Empress,' the other man said.

Martinian could only stare.

Crispin's tone was odd, eerily detached.

Martinian realized, suddenly, that it was going to take a great deal of time to understand what had happened to his friend in the east. There really were changes here. One didn't sail to Sarantium without that happening, he thought. He felt a chill.

'What is the . . . unincluded item she mentions?'

'A wife.' Crispin's voice was flat. A chill, bleak tone, remembered from the year before.

Martinian cleared his throat. 'I see. And the "other conveyance"?'

Crispin looked up. Seemed to make an effort to bestir himself. 'I don't know. There are a lot of keys in here.' He held up a heavy leather purse. 'The soldier said they'd orders to be on guard until I came, then it was my own look-out.'

'Oh. The trunks in the old chapel, then. There are at least twenty of them.'

They went to see.

Treasure, Martinian wondered? Gold coins and precious gems?

It wasn't that. As Crispin turned numbered keys in numbered locks, one after another, and opened trunk lids in the gentle light of the old, little-used chapel adjacent to the expanded sanctuary, Martinian of Varena, who had never travelled to Sarantium or even out of his own beloved peninsula, found himself beginning to weep, ashamed of the weakness of an old man.

But these were tesserae such as he had never seen or ever thought to see in all his days. A lifetime of working with muddied or streaked imitations of the brilliant colours of the mind's imagining had slowly conditioned him to accept the limitations of the possible here in broken Batiara. The deficiencies of the mortal world, the constraints placed upon achievement.

Now, long past a time when he might have fiercely set forth upon some project of a grandeur equal to these dazzling, flawless pieces of glass, they had come.

It was late. It was very, very late.

There was another note, in the first trunk. Crispin looked at it and then gave it to him. Martinian wiped his eyes and read. Same hand, the language changed now, Rhodian, the style personal, not royal.

*I have an undertaking from the Emperor. A promise made
to me. You will not do the god, nor Heladikos. Anything else
you see fit to render in the sanctuary complex housing my
father shall be preserved from edict and pronouncement and
any decreed harm, so far as I may be able to make it so. This,
as small compensation for a mosaic in Sarantium, done with
adequate materials, and taken away.*

The signature was also different: nothing but her name
this time. Martinian laid down the note. Put his hand,
slowly, into that first heavy trunk, into the tesserae—pale
gold in this one, the colour warm and even as honey.

'Careful. They'll be sharp,' Crispin said.

'Puppy,' said Martinian of Varena, 'I was cutting my
hands to pieces on these things before you were born.'

'I know,' said Crispin. 'My point.' He took back the note.
And then he smiled.

Martinian said, 'We can remake the dome in the sanctuary. Not Jad, not Heladikos, she says here. We can find a
new way of doing chapels. Consult with the clerics, maybe?
Here, and in Rhodias? In Sarantium, even?' Martinian's
voice quavered with desire. His heart was racing. He felt an
overwhelming need to keep touching these tesserae, to
bury his hands in them.

It was late, but it wasn't *too* late.

Crispin smiled again, looking around the quiet, dusty
room. They were utterly alone. Two men, twenty enormous,
laden trunks, nothing else. No one came here any more.

They would have to hire guards, Martinian thought
suddenly.

'You will remake it,' Crispin said gently. 'The dome.' His
mouth quirked a little. 'With whomever we have left

working for us, that you haven't driven away with your tyrant nature.'

Martinian ignored that. He was reacting to the gentleness. Something lost for a long time, back again.

'And you?' he asked.

For it occurred to him now that the younger man might not want to work at all. He'd seemed almost indifferent to the news of what had been done to his Heladikos. Martinian thought he understood. How could it even register, after what had happened in the east?.

Crispin had written him a little about that dome in Sarantium, about what he was trying to accomplish there, equal to the setting. And the young woman, Zoticus's daughter, had mentioned it in one of the letters they'd exchanged. A glory of the earth, she'd called it. The dome itself and what his friend was doing upon it.

And the mosaic was coming down. Martinian could picture it happening. Soldiers and labourers. Spear-butt and axe-head and dagger, scraping implements ripping and chopping the surface. Tesserae falling and falling.

How *could* anyone want to work again, after that?

Martinian took his hands from the trunk, the golden glass. He bit his lip. *A glory of the earth*. His friend was still in mourning, he finally realized, and here he was, exulting like a child with a new toy.

But he was wrong. Or, he later realized, not entirely right.

Crispin had walked away from him by then, was gazing absently at the flat, rough walls above the creaking double doors at each end. This little chapel had been built to the oldest floor plan known: two entrances, a central altar under a low, flat dome, curved bays east and west for private prayer and reflection, candle banks at each of these for memorials. Stone floor, stone walls, no benches, no dais. There wasn't even an altar or a sun disk here now. The chapel was at least four hundred years old, dating to the beginnings of the sanctioned worship of Jad in Rhodias. The light entering was soft and mild, falling cool as pale wine on stone.

Martinian, seeing his colleague's gaze move from surface to surface, tracking the fall of sunlight through the smeared and broken windows above (windows could be cleaned, panes replaced), began to look about for himself. And then, after a time, in a silence that aspired to simple happiness, he just watched Crispin as he turned and turned about.

At the last, Crispin was looking from north to south again, at the semicircular arc of the walls directly above each of the doors. He was seeing images not yet in the world, Martinian knew.

He had done it often enough, himself. It was the way you began.

'I'll make something here,' Crispin said.

❧

Varena's very ancient chapel of Jad Without the Walls had not been used for holy purposes since the larger sanctuary beside it had been constructed, about two hundred years afterwards. The complex had been further expanded twice, subsequently, acquiring a dormitory, refectory, kitchen, a bakehouse, a brewery, and a small infirmary with an herbal garden behind, leaving the original chapel to function as a storehouse for a time and then not even as that, lying dusty, untended, home to rodents and other field creatures in winter.

It had a patina of age upon it, an aura of peace even in that untended state, and the stones were very beautiful, taking sunlight with serenity. It was a long time since sufficient lamps had been lit here to judge how the chapel might appear after dark, properly illuminated.

It was an unexpected place for two panels of mosaic art, but the absence of altar or disk could be seen as legitimizing the entirely secular nature of the new work, which was being done—unusually for mosaics—by one man alone.

The works were modestly sized, one above each of the double doors.

Not the god, or Heladikos. Anything else you see fit to render.

He had it as a promise. Her father had taught her to keep promises. It had once been a holy place, but not for centuries. There still clung to the space, to the stones, to the air in the slanting descent of morning or afternoon light, a quiet grace. But it was *not* holy now, so even if there were proscriptions against rendering human figures in such places, this would be exempt, surely, over and above the promise.

He was relying on this, was aware that he ought to have learned by now not to rely on anything, that what a man could make, another man could unmake with sword or fire or decree.

He had it in writing, though, from an Empress. And the light here—never even noticed before—was a different kind of promise. And so it had come to be that he had spent a full year at work here, summer, autumn, through the winter, which had been cold. He'd done everything himself, that being a part of what this labour was, as he had conceived it from the outset, standing with Martinian on the day he'd come home. Everything: cleaning the chapel, sweeping, washing, on his knees, replacing the broken windows, removing the grime from those that had endured. Preparing the quicklime in the exterior ovens, wiping down the surfaces to take the setting bed, even assembling his own two scaffolds and ladders with hammers and nails. They didn't have to be high, could remain fixed in place. He was only working on two walls, not a dome.

Over in the larger sanctuary, Martinian and the employees and apprentices were redoing the dome. In consultation with Sybard of Varena and other clerics here and in Rhodias, they had elected to depict a landscape overhead: the progression from forest to field, farmhouse, harvest . . . an evocation of the progression of the Antae, in fact. No holy figures, no human figures. The Patriarch in Rhodias, as part of complex negotiations still going on with Sarantium and Varena, had agreed to reconsecrate the sanctuary when the work was done.

It was, after all, Hildric's burial place, and his daughter was Empress of Sarantium, which Empire now included Mihrbor and a large part of northern Bassania, subject to whatever the peace treaty—also being negotiated—might stipulate.

Here in Varena, this unused former chapel wasn't a part of any discussions at all. It was an unimportant place. It might even be said that whatever was done here was a foolish labour, unlikely to be seen by many people at all.

That was all right, Crispin thought. Had thought so all through the year, feeling more peace within himself than he could ever remember.

He didn't feel peaceful today, however. He felt a strangeness, at the end of a long, private time. The others had left him almost entirely alone throughout. Martinian would occasionally come by at the end of a day and look quietly for a few moments but he never said anything and Crispin had never asked him to.

This was his own, accountable to no one living. No patron had approved the sketches, no one's dazzling architecture or worldly ambition needed to be matched or understood or harmonized. In a curious way Crispin had had a sense all year that he was speaking to the unborn, not the living, to generations who might or might not come through these doors and find two mosaics, hundreds of years and more from today, and look up, and make of them . . . what they would.

He had been a part, in Sarantium, of something colossal, a shared vision on the largest possible scale, aspiring towards the more-than-human—and it was not to be. His part of that would have been destroyed by now.

Here, his striving was as ambitious (he knew it, Martinian, silent each time he looked, would know it) but it was entirely, profoundly, resolutely mortal in its scale.

And because of that, perhaps, it might last.

He didn't know. (How could a man know?) But here in this soft, kind light Crispin had set stones and glass for a year and a little more (summer again, the leaves dark green outside, bees in the wildflowers and the hedgerows) to leave something behind him when he died. Something that might tell those who came after that a certain Caius Crispus of Varena, son of Horius Crispus the mason, had lived, had *been* here on the god's earth for his allotted time and had known a little of human nature, and of art.

Gathered in this, he had passed a year. And there was nothing left to be done now. He had just finished the last thing, which no one had ever done in a mosaic before.

He was still on the rungs of a ladder beneath the northern wall, the one just done. He tugged at his beard, which was long again, as was his hair, not nearly as orderly as they ought to be for a man of wealth and distinction, but he'd been . . . occupied. He turned, a hand hooked through the ladder for balance, and looked across to the southern doors, at the arc of the wall above them, where he'd done the first of his two panels.

Not Jad. Not Heladikos. Nothing aspiring to holiness or faith. But there, in great and glittering splendour on the wall, in the carefully judged fall of light through the seasons and days (and there were brackets he'd hung himself, for lanterns in the night), were the Emperor of Sarantium, Valerius III, who had been Leontes the Golden, and his Empress, Gisel, who had sent the materials (tesserae like gems) and the promise that had set him free.

They were flanked by their court, but the work was done in such a way that only the two central figures were individually rendered, brought to vivid, golden life (and both of them *were* golden, their hair, their adornments, the gold in their robes). The courtiers, men and women, were hieratic, uniform, done after the old style, individual traits receding, only subtle differences of footwear and garb, stance and hair colour to offer a sense of movement for the eye, which was brought back, always, to the two figures at the centre. Leontes and Gisel, tall and young and magnificent, in the glory of their coronation day (which he had not seen, but that didn't matter, it didn't matter at all), preserved here (given *life* here) until the stones and glass fell or the building burned or the world ended. The lord of Emperors could come, *would* come, and age them, take them both away, but this could still be here.

That panel was done. He had made it first. It was . . . as he had wanted it to be.

He stepped down then, walked across the centre of the small chapel, where the god's altar had stood long ago, to the other side and stepped up on the ladder there, a few steps off the ground, and swung himself around and looked back at the northern wall from exactly the same perspective.

Another Emperor, another Empress, their court. Same colours, almost exactly. And an utterly different work, asserting something (for those who could look, and see) worlds apart, with love.

Valerius II, who had been Petrus of Trakesia in his youth, stood centred here, as Leontes was on the opposite wall, not tall, not golden at all, not young. Round-faced (as he had been), receding hair (as it had been), the wise, amused grey eyes gazing out upon Batiara, where the Empire had begun, the Empire he'd dreamed of reclaiming.

Beside him was his dancer.

And through tricks of line and light and glass and craft the watcher's eye would rest here upon Alixana, even more than upon the Emperor beside her, and find it difficult to leave. *There is beauty*, one might be made to think, *and there is this, which is something more.*

The gaze would move on, however (and come back), because around these two, for ages after to see them and see *into* them, were the men and women of this court, and here Crispin had done it differently.

This time each figure in the panel was unique in his rendering or hers. Stance, gesture, eyes, mouth. A hurried glance upon entering might see the two works as the same. A moment's pause would show them otherwise. Here, the Emperor and Empress were jewels within a crown of others, each of their attendants given their own brightness or shadow. And Crispin—their creator here, their lord—had set their names, in Sarantine, into the drapes and folds of their clothing, that those who came after might know: for naming, and so remembering, was at the heart of this for him.

Gesius, the aged Chancellor, pale as parchment, keen as a knife's edge; Leontes the Strategos (here, too, and so present on each wall); the Eastern Patriarch Zakarios, white of hair and beard, a sun disk in his long fingers. Beside the holy man (not by accident, there were no accidents here), a small, dark, muscular figure with a silver helmet, a brilliant blue tunic, and a whip in one hand. An even smaller figure, startlingly barefoot among the courtiers, had wide-open eyes and brown hair in comical disarray and the name written here was 'Artibasos'.

There was a burly, black-haired, ruddy soldier next to Leontes, not as tall but broader of build, clad not as a courtier but in the colours of the Sauradian cavalry, an iron helmet under one arm. A thin, pale man was beside him (thinner and more pale with the craft of that proximity), sharp of feature, long of nose, watchful. An unsettling face, bitterness in his gaze as he looked towards the pair in the centre. His name was written on a rolled parchment he held.

To the other side were the women.

Nearest to and a little behind the Empress was a lady even taller than Gisel on the opposite wall, as golden, and—it could be said—even more fair, at least as seen by the one who had rendered them both. Arrogant in her stance and tilt of head, a fierce, uncompromising blue in her gaze. A single small ruby worn, oddly, about her throat. A hint of fire in it, but curious for its modesty, given the rest of her jewellery and the dazzle of gold and gems worn by the other ladies on the wall.

One of whom stood next to this golden one, less tall, dark hair showing beneath a green, soft cap, clad in a green robe and a jewelled belt. One could see laughter here, and grace in the way one hand curved up and outward in a gesture of the stage. Another dancer, you might conclude, even before reading the explanation of her name.

To the very edge of the scene, strangely situated on the womens' side of the composition, stood another man, a little detached from the court lady nearest him. He might have been called an afterthought if precision of design had not shown so plainly here. Instead, one might think him . . . out of place. But present. He was there. A big man, this one was, dressed entirely properly, though the silk of his garments draped a little awkwardly on his body. The anger that showed in him might perhaps have been caused by this.

He had red hair and was the only figure there shown with a beard, other than Zakarios, but this was not a holy man.

He was turned inward, looking towards the centre like the scribe, staring at the Emperor or Empress (difficult to tell which). Indeed, it could be observed, upon study of the elements here, that the line of this man's gaze was a balancing one, against that of the lean, thin-faced one on the other side of the panel, and that—perhaps—this was why he was where he was.

This red-haired figure, too, wore an ornament about his throat. (Only he and the tall, fair woman did.) A medallion of gold, with the letter C inscribed within it twice, interlocking. Whatever that might mean.

And this second work, too, was finished save for one small patch near the bottom, below the Emperor, where the smooth, grey-white mixture of the setting bed had received its tesserae just now, drying into place.

Crispin stood, suspended a little above the ground, and he looked at his work for a long time, suspended also, in a different way, in a moment difficult to sort through: the sense that he would be entirely done with this, finished forever, as soon as he stepped down from this ladder. He felt as if he were hovering in a timelessness before that happened and this labour and its achievement moved into the past, or the future, but would never again be *now*.

His heart was full. He thought of centuries of mosaic workers . . . here in Varena, in Sarantium, in Rhodias, or far to the south in lands across the sea, cities on coasts beyond Candaria, or eastward in ancient Trakesia, or in Sauradia (holy men with their gifts, bringing Jad into a chapel there, their names lost to silence) . . . *all* the makers unknown, gone, shrouded in vanished time, dead.

Their works (whatever works survived) a glory of the god's earth and his gift of light, the makers dimmer than shadows.

He looked at that place near the bottom where the tesserae were newly laid, still fixing themselves, and he saw the doubled C of his initials, matching the medallion he wore on the panel. Thinking of them, of all of them, lost or living or yet to come, he had signed his work upon the wall.

He heard a sound as the door opened quietly behind him. End of day, end of last day. Martinian, knowing how near he was to finishing, come to see. He hadn't told his friend, his teacher, about the signing of his name, the initials. It was a kind of gift, perhaps an overwhelming one for an emotional man who would know—better than anyone alive—the thoughts behind those two letters intertwined.

Crispin took a deep breath. It was time to come down again.

He stopped, however, and did not move. For with that taken breath he realized that it wasn't Martinian who had entered to stand behind him on the stone floor. He closed his eyes. Felt a tremor in the hand and arm holding him to the ladder.

A scent. Not ever to be mistaken. Two women in Sarantium had worn it once. No one else allowed. One as her own, the other as a gift, for her art, which was the same as the first's had been, ephemeral as dream, as life. What was the dancer when the dance was done?

Dead. Gone as the artisans' names were gone. Perhaps enduring, for others, after, in the image made here. But not moving and alive on Jad's earth. This was the world of mortal men and women, where certain things did not happen, even with *zubirs*, alchemist's birdsouls, the half-world hovering, love.

And Crispin knew that he would live in this world again, after all, that he could even embrace it in the years left to him before he, too, was called away. There were gifts, graces, compensations, deep and very real. One could even smile, in gratitude.

Without turning, still on the ladder, he said, 'Hello, Shirin, my dear. Did Martinian tell you when to come in?'

And from behind him, then, as the world changes, changes utterly, he hears Alixana say, 'Oh, dear. I am not wanted, after all.'

Not wanted.

One can forget to breathe, can weep, for unworthiness.

And turn, too quickly, almost falling, a cry escaping from the heart's core, and look upon her face again, in life, a thing dreamt of in the long dark, not thought to be possible again.

She is looking up at him, and he sees that she (being what she is) has already read what is in his eyes, his wordless cry, if she hadn't already known it from her image on the opposite wall.

There is a silence as he looks at her and sees her gazing back at him, and then past and across, at what he has made of her above the doors to the north, and then back to where he stands upon the ladder above the ground, and she is alive and here, and he has been wrong, again, about what can happen in the world.

He says, 'I thought you were dead.'

'I know.'

She looks at the wall again where he has placed her at the centre of all eyes, at the heart of light. Looks back at him, says, an unexpected trembling in her voice, 'You made me . . . taller than I am.'

He is looking into her eyes as she says it. Hears, beneath the simple words, what else she is telling him, a year and half a world away from her life.

'No I didn't,' he says. It is difficult to speak. He is still shaking.

She is changed, could never be taken for an Empress now. A way to survive, of course, to cross land or sea. To come here. To where he is. And stand, looking up. Her dark hair is shorter, growing back in. She wears a traveller's robe of good make, dark brown, belted, a wide hood, thrown back. She has not attended (that he can see) to her lips or eyes or cheeks, wears no jewellery at all.

He can only just begin to imagine what this year has been for her.

He swallows hard. 'My lady . . .'

'No,' she says quickly. Lifts a hand. 'I am not that. Here.'

She smiles faintly. 'They believe I'm some disgraceful creature, out there.'

'I'm not surprised,' he manages to say.

'Come to lure you with eastern decadence.'

He says nothing this time. Looks at her.

A year since she laid down her robe on a stony beach, lost a love more swiftly than to plague, laid down a life. There is an uncertainty now, a fragility, as she scans his face. He thinks of the rose in her room.

She murmurs, 'I said on the island ... that I trusted you.'

He nods his head. 'I remember. I didn't know why.'

'I know you didn't. It was the second time I'd come for you.'

'I know. When I first came. Why? Back then?'

She shakes her head. 'I couldn't say. No clear reason. I expected you would finish your work and leave us.'

He makes a wry face. He can do this. Enough time has passed. 'Instead, I finished half my work and left you.'

Her expression is grave. 'It was taken from you. Sometimes half is all we are allowed. Everything we have can be taken away. I always knew that. But sometimes ... people can be followed. Brought back down again?'

He is still trembling. 'Three times? I am unworthy.'

She shakes her head. 'Who is ever worthy?'

'You?'

She smiles a little. Shakes her head again. Says, 'I asked you how you went on living. After.'

On the island, on the beach. In his dreams. 'I couldn't even answer. I didn't know. I still don't. I was only half alive, though. Too bitter. It started to change in Sarantium. But even then I was ... trying to stay away, by myself. Up there.'

She nods this time. 'Lured down by a decadent woman.'

He looks at her. At Alixana. Standing here.

Can see her thinking, teasing out nuances. 'Will I . . . make trouble for you?' she asks. Still that hesitance.

'I have no doubt of it.' He tries to smile.

She is shaking her head again. A worried look. Gestures at the far wall. 'No, I mean, people may know me, from this.'

He takes a breath and lets it out. Understands, finally, that this hesitance is his to take away.

'Then we will go where they will not,' he hears himself say.

She bites her lip. 'You would do that?'

And he says, swept back into the rush and flow of time and the world, 'You will be hard-pressed to think of what I will not do for you.' He grips the ladder tightly. 'Will it . . . be enough?'

Her expression changes. He watches it happen. She bites her lip again, but it means something else now. He knows, has seen that look before.

'Well,' she says, in the voice he has never stopped hearing, 'I still want dolphins.'

He nods his head, as if judiciously. His heart is full of light.

She pauses. 'And a child?'

He draws a breath and steps down off the scaffolding. She smiles.

Aut lux hic nata est, aut capta hic libera regnat.
Light was either born here or, held captive, here reigns free.

—Inscription in Ravenna, among the mosaics

I think that if I could be given a month of Antiquity and leave to spend it where I chose, I would spend it in Byzantium a little before Justinian opened St. Sophia and closed the Academy of Plato. I think I could find in some little wine-shop some philosophical worker in mosaic who could answer all my questions, the supernatural descending nearer to him . . .

W.B. Yeats, *A Vision*